Community Learning & Libraries
Cymuned Ddysgu a Llyfrgelloedd

Newport
CITY COUNCIL
CYNGOR DINAS
Casnewydd

This item should be returned or renewed by the
last date stamped below.

2 1 AUG 2013

1 0 SEP 2013

18/1/20

The Morning Tide

By the same author

THE SKYLARK'S SONG

AUDREY HOWARD

The Morning Tide

C

CENTURY • LONDON

For my Mother, Ada, and Aunty Dolly, the sisters who gave me the idea

First published in 1985 by Century Publishing Co Ltd
Copyright © Audrey Howard 1985

ISBN 0 7126 0479 0

This edition published in 1997 by Century Ltd
Random House, 20 Vauxhall Bridge Road, London, SW1V 2SA

Random House Australia (Pty) Limited
16 Dalmore Drive, Scoresby, Victoria 3179, Australia

Random House New Zealand Limited
18 Poland Road, Glenfield
Auckland 10, New Zealand

Random House South Africa (Pty) Limited
Endulini, 5a Jubilee Road, Parktown 2193, South Africa

A CIP catalogue record for this book is available from the
British Library

Papers used by Random House UK Ltd are natural, recyclable
products made from wood grown in sustainable forests.
The manufacturing processes conform to the environmental
regulations of the country of origin

Printed and bound in the United Kingdom by
Athenaeum Press Ltd, Gateshead, Tyne & Wear

Chapter One

It was exquisitely cold.

Kate could feel it against her face as she lay in the cradle of the large double bed which she had shared with her sister for as long as she could remember. She could feel the cold, and the dark which contained it, so intensely, that the bones beneath her flesh ached with it, and she longed to snuggle down into the straw mattress, and slip back into that warm, drowsy state from which she had just awakened.

Jenny stirred beside her and uttered a tiny sound like the first murmur of a bird at dawn, then was quiet again, as though, even in sleep, she was safe in the certainty that her older sister would do all that was needed to get the house and the family within it started on another day.

The night sounds, vague, unidentified; sounds which are familiar, but have no name in a house, began to intermingle with the noises from the street, those which are born as a city awakens, and its inhabitants begin that slow, purling approach to the day.

A cough hacked the solidarity of the darkness into many pieces, then was gone. The springs of a bed screeched in high-pitched protest as a body thrashed in troubled sleep, and faintly, from the chill step of the back door, a cat's miaow called plaintively as it begged to be allowed to return to its place by the stove after its night's excursion.

From the room next door came the plaint of a woman retching, and Kate sighed with pity for the pain of the sufferer. It was her mother. Each day seemed a little worse than the one just gone, and the harsh gagging groans were commonplace now, and as familiar as the call of the Birkenhead ferry. They were softly apologetic, like the woman herself. It was as if, even in the act of dying, it would not do to awaken the man who lay beside her.

Kate frowned in the thick darkness, bracing herself for the teeth-chattering dash across the icy linoleum to the dresser on which she had flung her clothes the night before in her frantic haste

1

to gain the comparative warmth of the bed. She knew she must make a move soon. Her father would be about in half an hour and would expect to find the fire lit, his clean shirt warming above it, and his breakfast upon the table. It was the start of the pattern which stitched together the pieces of his day, and if it did not immediately fit about him with the ease of a wellmade garment, his anger would be peevishly violent.

Kate turned on her back, pulling the edges of the eiderdown up to the tip of her nose which felt stiff and lumpish with cold. Stretching her legs she thrust her feet to the bottom of the bed. With a gasp she recoiled from the expanse of frozen smoothness which lay there, and drew up her knees, turning back to the warmth of her sister, tucking her toes into the hem of her night-gown in an attempt to warm them. She shivered and pressed her body against the curve of her sister's back, feeling the warmth, comforted by the closeness and familiarity which had been a part of her life since she was a child.

Kate had never slept alone.

First there had been Elly. Eleanor. She could remember the bony shape of her older sister's back, and the warmth she had given off, as they had lain together like two spoons in a case in the nest of the straw mattress. She supposed she must have been removed at some tender age from the protection of her mother's room to the bed she had shared with Elly, but she could not recall it, nor what went before. She only remembered the ease and the companionship, albeit casual, and the welcome presence of someone beside her in the black night.

Then there had been Jenny. She remembered her own surprise at the sudden appearance of the tiny person at their Mam's breast, but with the acceptance of a child, especially that of one brought up within a large family, she had welcomed her new little sister and did not dwell on the mystery of how she came to be there.

After several months in a crib by her mother's bedside, the newcomer had been placed in the centre of the bed which Kate shared with Elly, a bundle of plump flesh and kicking, dimpled feet, sometimes sweet-smelling, but often joyously reeking of the contents of her own soiled napkin. She was always smiling and amiable, even then eager to please. Her golden-brown eyes were warm and placid in her round face and she would grab with fat, starfish hands, laughing and trustful, at Kate's brown ringlets as she leaned over her.

Kate loved her from the first moment, and she slept protectively around her for Mam said she must not be allowed to fall from the

2

high plateau of the mattress which covered the sagging springs of the bed.

Kate had been three years old.

Jenny was the last baby to be born to Henry and Elizabeth Fowler. Kate had five brothers but they all slept in the attic bedroom at the top of the house on an assortment of palliasses spread about the floor and Kate was not allowed to go up there for it was her father's belief that boys and girls must be kept apart for modesty's sake. All her brothers were older than herself except one. Their Robert. She had not questioned the odd fact that they shared a birthday until the day came when she was five years old and they had started school together, and for the first time she was told that she and Robert were something strange called twins. This had come as a surprise to her for she had never heard the word before, so she asked their Elly in the depths of the yielding bed, and Elly, who was ten years older than Kate, had told her all about it, and where she and Robert had come from, and worst of all, how they came to be there.

Kate had been deeply shocked, and half inclined to disbelieve her, but some instinct told her that it was the truth. At breakfast the next day, she had peeped from beneath her lowered lashes at their Mam and Dad, but the pictures which flashed into her child's mind were so beyond her comprehension, and the image of their Dad linked in that way with Mam, so unimaginable, she lost interest and tucked with relish into her fried bread.

Later, as she passed the open door of her parents' room, she had stared curiously at the big bed in which Mam and Dad slept together. It had brass bars at its head and foot, and looked like a prison. Perhaps that was why Mam did it, she thought, because she couldn't escape. At each corner of the bed gleamed a polished brass knob, and the whole thing rattled for ten minutes every Saturday night. The connection with the regular sounds and the act which Elly had described to her so graphically, now became clear to the child, and she averted her eyes as though caught in the act of spying on her parents as they performed their weekly conjugal obligation. For a moment she had lingered, horridly fascinated, then, being a sensible little girl, she had moved on and put it firmly from her mind.

From time to time, as she grew, the memory would return and she would find herself looking with spellbound interest at her mother and father, and she would wonder, aghast at her own temerity, at the thought of her Dad clasping Mam in his meaty arms.

3

Breakfast was the only meal of the day which the family shared, for from then until midnight, each had their allotted tasks, and they rarely sat down together. Mam always stood by the stove, waiting with dumb patience for the commands of her family, the huge brown teapot to hand, and a loaf of bread clasped to her breast. From it she would hack thick slices, always cutting towards herself with the sharp, serrated knife and a swift dexterity which threatened to remove part of her anatomy with each stroke.

Dad never looked at Mam. He told her what he wanted with the minimum of words necessary to convey his needs.

'Fill my cup, Lizzie.'

'I'll 'ave another egg while yer about it,' and she obeyed blindly, resigned, it seemed to Kate, to a life of constant compliance to her husband's demands.

When Kate was seven years old, Elly left home to marry Pat O'Reilly. She had gone to live in Saint Domingo Road, just above the cobblers shop where Pat worked. So Kate and Jenny had the bed to themselves. It was lovely. Two little girls curled together like puppies in a basket, though Kate, mindful of what their Mam had told her, always put Jenny against the wall so that she wouldn't fall out. Jenny was her responsibility, Mam said so.

And thus it grew from that time. The loving dictatorship; the possessive, almost maternal link which was to bond the sisters together for as long as they lived.

Later, Mam began to be poorly a lot, but Dad didn't care. He had two daughters to look after him, didn't he? As long as his children were at home where he could keep an eye on them, and jumped to it when he opened his mouth, he didn't care. As long as his meals were on the table when he was ready; as long as he had a clean shirt and the boys were quiet whilst he dozed before the kitchen fire or read the *Liverpool Echo*, he didn't care. His children kept out of his way as much as they were able, and grew up somehow, bringing each other up, as large families do. His wife's illness, increasingly obvious, even to his indifferent eye, did not discommode him in any way. No one knew of the recently bereaved young widow with five children, all under the age of fourteen, who lived in Agnes Street, or noticed, soon after her husband's death, her suddenly improved appearance, nor the gradual lessening of the gaunt and hungry look from the faces of her children. Certainly not Henry's family, and it is doubtful that, should they have heard of her, they would have connected her with their father's tendency to take a short walk on several evenings each week.

Kate continued to look after Jenny.

In seventeen years they had never spent a night apart. Winter and summer it was always the same. The bed was as much a part of their lives as their parents or brothers. As small girls they had giggled and romped there, when their Dad was out, of course, and sometimes, on a Sunday morning when the shop was closed and Dad gone on some private business of his own, their Bobby and Jimmy would come in and they would have grand games of 'tents' with a sheet and a broom handle as a tent pole.

As they grew, the sisters would sprawl upon it, exchanging girlish confidences. It was a place of comfort when they were indisposed – or allowed to be – a haven from their father's wrath and their brothers' teasing; a meeting place where secrets were traded, a refuge.

Now, as she lay in its familiar, lumpy embrace, Kate could hear the sharp clip-clop of horses' hooves on the cobblestones beneath her bedroom window, and the grate and thud of milk churns grinding together as the milk cart tipped steeply on the gradient of the hill outside the house. It set her teeth on edge. The air was so still, she could hear the 'hrrmmph, hrrmmph' of the animal's breath in its throat as it gathered its strength to pull the heavy cart up the incline of the street.

Breathing in the clean smell of her sister's hair which drifted in clinging wisps across the pillow, Kate drowsed, listening to the sounds of the house stirring.

'Ah-ah' Gertie riddled the fire in the kitchen, scraping the ashpan backwards and forwards to catch the clinkers of dead coal as they fell through the grate. She would use them again to lay on the wood, and twists of newspaper with which she lit the fire. Kate heard the sound of a door opening and the chink of jug on churn as the milk was tipped from the dipper; the quiet murmur of voices; the chink of money as it passed from hand to hand, then, a moment later the resumed sound of Gertie at the coal scuttle. A muted, trembling hum, crept up the stairs as the woman accompanied her own movements with *The Sheikh of Araby*.

Kate smiled in the dark. Poor 'Ah-ah'. Romance on her lips as she skivvied, but let their Dad hear her and she would sing a different tune, scuttling nervously to some corner like a terrified rabbit surprised by the stoat.

Someone yawned, the ululation ending with a snap of jaws and a squeak. That would be their Jimmy. He always yawned like that. It drove their Dad demented.

As though her thoughts had conjured up his presence, she heard Henry Fowler cough in the next room, the phlegm rasping in his chest. The ugly 'splat' as it left his mouth and hit the chamber pot beneath the bed, made her stomach quiver.

'Dirty bugger,' she whispered.

A dog barked, the sound amputated with a swift yelp as though a cuff from a heavy hand had cut off its complaint, and carried on the thin, clear air, as yet untainted by the polluting smoke of a thousand chimneys, came the echoing shriek of a ship's siren, all the way across the rooftops from the river Mersey. A door banged along the street and clogged footsteps rang on the flagstones, closer and closer, then died away as the feet they carried, turned the corner.

Jenny moved again. Kate could see the misty outline of her profile now as the room lightened, and from her parted lips a murmur escaped, the last jumbled words from some night dream in which she dwelled.

Knowing that she could delay no longer, Kate slipped from beneath the covers, gasping as her foot, warm now, touched the icy linoleum. She hastily fumbled her way into her clothes and with a last face-splitting yawn, opened the bedroom door and made her way down the back stairs to the kitchen.

The day had begun.

The Fowlers of West Derby Road were far from wealthy, but by the standards of their neighbours, and the mass of the working class population who made up the citizenry of Liverpool, they were blessed with more than their fair share of this world's goods. They had never gone hungry. Though their clothing was handed down from one member of the family to the next; as one grew the next in line, or size, took over the discarded garment, they were adequately clothed and shod, and the house in which they lived was sparsely comfortable and clean.

Henry Fowler was by trade a bricklayer. He had done his seven years apprenticeship in the building trade and his craft had always kept him and his increasing family in reasonable circumstances. His girls had even had piano lessons, a luxury unheard of in the strata of the class in which they lived, and Kate, striking awe in the hearts of her contemporaries, had learned to play the mandolin. The street marvelled at Henry's superiority.

In 1913, in a timely fashion – Henry was always to be a lucky man – he had fallen from the roof of a two-storey house in Princes Park. He had been laying a beautifully precise row of patterned bricks on the top of a chimney. Stepping back for a second, carried away in admiration for his own handiwork, his foot had caught in a loose tile and he had fallen over thirty feet to the ground. By some miracle he was not seriously hurt, suffering only a broken wrist but by way of compensation for the shoddy workmanship of the man on whose tile he had slipped, Henry was given the sum of fifty pounds, all in gold sovereigns. A princely sum indeed. With it he had bought a fish and chip shop in West Derby Road.

On the first night he opened he took two shillings and sevenpence.

But Henry's luck held out and a year later, in 1914, war was declared. From then on his profits bounded, and it was not unknown for fifty pounds to pass over his counter in one week.

He worked himself and his family from morning till night and by the strictest, and not always honest economies, he continued to become, in a small way, quite a 'warm man'. Long gone, but not forgotten were those hard up days when he had pawned his bag of tools to buy his family a few groceries. He would smile to himself complacently, remembering the tricks to which he'd resorted. Putting bricks in his bag to dupe the pawnbroker – a man could not work without his tools – and the fool, accustomed to the weekly routine, never even looked inside.

Elly was gone by now, of course, but Kate, who was ten years old, served in the shop beside her mother and Ah-ah Gertie. The boys learned to peel potatoes and cut and slice the fish to the wafer-thin proportions Henry gauged a sufficiency, and which were then dipped in batter and fried to a delicious brown crispness.

Henry's thriving business enterprise was further enhanced by the opening of a cigarette factory called Ogdens, on the opposite side of the road to his 'chippie', and with the increased custom brought by the girls who worked there his profits tripled in one week.

He started serving food to be eaten on the premises, and his wife lost her tiny sitting room when he turned it into what he genteelly termed 'a supper room'. Six tables, and around the walls he had mirrors fixed, and on each table, covered by oilcloth which could easily be wiped over, were cruet sets of salt and vinegar bought from Woolworths and looking just like cut glass.

A further room was taken over, Elizabeth's dining room this time, and in 1916, Henry introduced 'the snug', not quite so smart as the supper room, but just as popular, and always packed.

It was an unusual evening when a queue did not form to the corner of Walton Lane, and beyond, the pavement overflowing with eager, hand-blowing, foot-stamping customers, waiting for their turn for one of Henry's fish suppers. A pennyworth of 'mixed' was the serving most requested, especially by those in

7

poorer circumstances, but often it was fish, chips and peas to take out for twopence, and nothing ever wasted. Even the 'scratchings', the fragments of batter which crumbled from the freshly fried fish, were sold for a farthing a bag.

The soldiers came. Wounded veterans who had caught a 'Blighty one', and were brought home from the trenches. They convalesced at Mill Road Hospital, and those who were mobile flocked to Henry's after a pint at the local. Fish and chips served by two pretty girls, for by 1917 Jenny was in the shop, was a satisfying ending to their evening's diversion. How they found their way to Henry's shop was never known, for the working class districts were not a place for sightseeing, but his proximity to Goodison Park may have been a contributing factor. Whether you cheered for Everton or Arsenal or Wolves, a football match was a football match, and what better than a fish and chip supper afterwards, with a pint to follow at the Old Swan.

Fourteen pairs of crutches Henry counted one night, all standing like a row of praetorian guards at the door of his shop, each testifying to the loss of a leg or a foot. But the laughter was loud and the money rolled in, and Henry, sitting behind the till in his white coat, smiled benignly at the 'brave lads back from the Front'.

The chippie suited Henry's expectation of life and his working habits admirably. He would strut about his small domain, thumbs tucked in his braces, issuing orders to his children and the luckless Ah-ah Gertie. He was 'Cock of the North' in his own home and woe betide any offender who strayed from the path set by him. He was not afraid of hard work, though he shared the bigger part amongst the members of his family, and as his daughters became of an age to work fulltime when they left school, he could really take it easy, just keeping an eye on things, and ensuring that each was working with the application he thought necessary.

All his sons followed him into the building trade, but Bobby and Jimmy chose instead to build ships, not houses, working shifts in the dockyard. Seldom were they on the same one and so, one or the other was usually available to work in the shop. The three eldest boys all married at an early age, more to escape their father's domination than from any great passion for the young ladies of their choice.

Henry was a handsome man, strongly built, and proud of his likeness to old King Teddy. He was meticulously clean and though only fifty-five years old, his thick plume of hair and well-trimmed beard were a pure, gleaming white. He always gave the impression that he had just come from the barber, and the smell of Bay Rum with which he applied himself liberally, vied with the aroma of fish and chips which no amount of toileting could remove from his person.

His quick temper and absolute authority in his home had kept the remaining members of his family firmly under his thumb. They feared him, even his sons for the habit of immediate obedience, bred in them from an early age, was hard to break. Their affection went to their mother, Elizabeth, whose gentle nature had been ground to an ox-like humility during her thirty years of marriage to Henry.

She had been a lovely young girl when he had wooed her, her blushing reserve, so completely the opposite to his own extrovert self-assurance, fascinating him to the point where he must have her for his own. But his impatience with the very trait which had won him, had changed her charming shyness into nervous self-distrust, and her sad face and doe-like, stricken eyes, exasperated him beyond control.

If she had once stood up to him, he might have continued to admire her as he had done in the early days of their marriage, but her diffidence and, as he put it 'shilly-shallying', irritated him to abuse. She was the butt of his illhumour and he came to despise her. She received no sympathy from him when she was unwell, for with the intolerance of one who has suffered not a day's illness in his life, he had no time for those who had.

'Get out more, woman. Take a brisk walk,' he admonished her, as she bent her head and kneaded the shrivelling pain in her belly, 'instead of forever lolling about in bed. Look at me. Yer don't find me 'anging about the 'ouse, do yer? That's why I'm so fit,' and he would slap his firm stomach and reach for his grey Homburg and his goldtopped walking stick, ready to stride from the house and make his way towards Agnes Street, and another vigorous encounter with the young widow.

Henry Fowler had come up in the world since he came down off that roof, eight years ago, and he was well suited with his way of life.

9

Chapter Two

Elizabeth Fowler lay in the dark, and listened to the sounds of Henry awakening. First he sighed as he rose slowly through the last layer of sleep to wakefulness. The noise rustled from his chest, disturbing the phlegm which lodged there, and he coughed and hawked, the sputum bubbling up until it reached his mouth, then grumbling wordlessly, he raised his heavy torso to a sitting position, and with unerring accuracy even in the darkness expectorated into a chamber pot. He sank back on his pillow, yawning, and raising his nightgown under the bedclothes, scratched energetically in the region of his groin. His strong fingernails were abrasive as they moved amongst his pubic hair, and he sighed again, this time with sensual pleasure. It was a daily ritual, and one which had led, years ago, to his urgent reaching for her and the quick gratification of his need, but now, as aversion to her age and failing health consumed him, she knew that the very idea would be abhorrent to him, as it had always been to her.

Not once in the thirty years of sharing his bed, had he pleased her with his body, nor could it be said that he had even tried. His ardour had carried him quickly to the peak of his own bodily enjoyment, and even when, in the first flush of his love for her, she had been the object of his passionate desire, he had cared nothing for her pleasure and indeed would have been bewildered and shocked, to find she had needed any.

Now it was over, that humiliating passivity with which she had been forced to bear him. Over and done with. Not for ten years had he touched her. His big body appeared to shrink and strain away from hers in the bed, and he would have slept elsewhere she knew, if there had been another room available in the narrow, three-storeyed house, but there was not, so he was obliged impatiently to endure her nausea and increasing illness.

Elizabeth shuddered delicately and stifled the moan which tried to escape from between her bitten lips. Lord, the pain was bad today. Like barbed wire being drawn through her body, each barb as it snagged her flesh, exploding in agony, making the sweat

10

stand out on her face and neck, soaking her nightdress and bringing the bile to flood her throat. She prayed for strength to hold on until Henry left the room, swallowing and choking on the nauseous mass which filled her mouth. The sound of her vomiting into the large mixing bowl which she kept discreetly hidden beneath the bed, filled him with revulsion, and on the few occasions when she had been unable to control herself, he had been outraged, as though convinced that she had set out deliberately to annoy him.

She clamped her teeth together, like the springs of a trap. Her jaw clenched and stood out from the remains of her once lovely face, and her mouth was a straight gash of pain. In her agony, her mind misted, and roamed from the place where she lay, as it tried to escape, but she pulled it back with the little strength she had left.

Was it the day for the doctor? She became so confused these days. The torment never left her, and her mind was dazed with it. She tried to think. Oh yes, the doctor. She would ask him if he would give her a stronger bottle. Give her some relief. The last few draughts he had left for her did not cut the pain as they once had. She was so tired. She wanted to sleep, to have some ease from the racking which never let her be. Oh, Lord, if she could only sleep. Sleep forever. To go to sleep and fall into that soft bed of eternity and drift away from . . .

A shaft harrowed her and her back arched, then abated, and she relaxed cautiously as the pain passed. She knew it would not be long now. The doctor mouthed platitudes, more for his own comfort than hers, but she knew that the fire in her belly would soon consume her and carry her to a better place than this. Elizabeth waited for that day with the resignation which life, and Henry Fowler, had taught her.

She drowsed a little as the biting teeth of the beast within her loosened their hold. Her mind wandered again, and in the gloom a faint smile touched her lips. It was as though her failing spirit took her back to when life had been pleasing and pain free. For a few moments she was young again and she held a baby in her arms. Her withering flesh felt again the joy of her motherhood, and she looked with loving pride into the golden brown eyes of . . . of . . . who was it? Their Jenny, or was it John. Golden brown eyes like her own. As she gazed fondly, drowning in the depths of pain which tortured her, the brown eyes became blue and it was Kate who smiled serenely. Was it Kate? Her good Kate? Sometimes the features of the eight children she had borne melted like hot wax, ran into each other, and became one in her memory. The blue and

11

brown of their eyes looked out of infant faces, mixed up in time and sweet remembrance, and for an exquisite moment, happiness filled her.

Her babies. The only joy she had known had been in the lives of her children. They had been good to her, as she failed, her sons and daughters. Only Elly had caused her heartache. Brave Elly. Defiant and feckless, fighting to survive. Ah, Elly. What a spirit her eldest child had. If only she, Elizabeth, could have been more like the daughter she had birthed, perhaps things might have been different with Henry. Elly had stood up to him. Oh the rows and screams when Henry strapped her.

But in the end Elizabeth had been glad to see her go. A rare one, their Elly. Should have been a lad . . . should have been a lad . . .

Elizabeth's chin dropped and her lips parted as she dozed, but her half dreaming mind was still with Elly. Always broke, their Elly, always. A soft and tender laugh welled up within the dying woman's heart. If nothing else their Elly's lot should have brains. They ate nothing but the fish and scratchings their mother scrounged when Henry was away from home, and everyone knew fish gave you brains. She was so hard up. Lived between the pawnbroker and the moneylender. Her Pat was a goodhearted lad, but the bare existence he eked out of his cobbling wouldn't keep a flea in socks. They would be in queer street when . . . when . . .

Elizabeth's eyes opened and she looked into the darkness, not just that of her bedroom, but of the black beyond to which she was going. What would become of their Elly . . . and Jenny. The others were survivors and would fash for themselves somehow, but Jenny . . . she was so soft and tenderhearted. Born to be hurt, just like herself.

Kate. Now there was a strong one. Elizabeth's mind became tranquil as she thought of Kate. She would look out for their Jenny. She always had. Right from being a little girl.

Elizabeth sighed and was comforted.

She started up suddenly as the shrillness of voices, young and female, pealed through the window. It was the girls from Ogdens going on the first shift at the factory. The noise contrasted sharply in its youthful vigour, with the fading, silent whispers of the woman in the bed. A hooter brayed, calling the girls to their benches. Laughter surged as the latecomers began to run, and steel-tipped clogs clattered on the cobblestones. Then it was quiet again.

Elizabeth closed her eyes and breathed lightly so as not to disturb the animal which dozed within her. Her mind reached yearningly

12

back again into a time long ago when she had been a young girl herself. How she had admired the strong bull who had courted her. His dominance had thrilled her girlish heart, for she was not to know in her innocence, that under his strength lay nothing. No gentleness, nor understanding. Just the brute determination to have his own way. With her, with his children, with life.

She sighed and shifted her heavy, but stick-like legs. The aimless drifting which takes over as death draws near, moved on again and for an instant, her three older sons stood before her. Their large frames filled the doorway of the room, and she lifted her head and smiled, pleased that they had come to see her. Their feet shuffled awkwardly on the linoleum, and they held their caps in their hands. She knew they wanted to be kind, her boys, but her illness embarrassed them. She tried to reassure them. To say something cheering, comforting so that they would come again, but she felt too weak, too tired.

'How yer feelin', Mam,' they said, and Eddy edged his way towards the door. She remembered then that it was Saturday, and the boys would be on their way to the match. Sadness filled her for she knew that but for the happy circumstance which placed her home on their route to Goodison Park, they would not have been there at all.

But how handsome they were, her boys.

Abruptly her eyes opened and her sons vanished. They had gone and Henry was here beside her, scratching and yawning, and it was not Saturday at all. She could hear Kate's footsteps on the stairs as she went down to the kitchen. She was a good girl, their Kate. The best of the lot, though she said it, as shouldn't. From being a tiny girl she had had within her a great loyal, loving determination that wrapped around those who won her affection. What would she have done without her these last months. Jenny was sweet and lovely, kindhearted and generous, but she lacked the strength of will and stamina which Kate had inherited from her father. It was as though Kate had taken the best from both her parents. Tolerance and understanding, compassion and a loving heart from herself, but the vitality and vigour of Henry, without his cruelty. Now their Jenny, she would need someone to . . .

Without warning, like the swift and agonising thrust from a saw-edged knife, the pain tore her. The knife moved within her, twisting and turning, tearing her flesh to shreds. With a great cry she rose up in the bed and a fountain of vile smelling, souplike fluid spurted in an amorphous torrent from between her lips. She turned desperately towards the basin beneath the bed, but it was

13

too late. The ejection spewed over the bedspread in a wave. On it went, like blood-streaked, yellow and green veined lava, creeping insidiously across the coverlet, dripping and splashing obscenely over the chest of her husband. She tried in her last dying act to stop it, putting out a feeble fluttering hand, soft and paper thin, as though to draw it away from him, and her final words, unheard by the stunned man, were an apology. Her hand moved again, like a white moth, in an effort to cup the bloody mass, to keep it from desecrating the person who had given her not a kind word for twenty years. Her eyes pleaded for forgiveness, for understanding, for . . . something, but she might as well have looked to the bedpost for a sympathetic word. Her eyes turned upwards, the eyelids in spasm, the long lashes fluttering in the final anguish.

She fell back and her head hit the pillow like a fist into a punchbag.

Henry was dozing, his questing hand conjuring up pictures of the widow in Agnes Street. He was in that state of pleasant euphoria which lingers over from sleep, before the necessity arises to leave the warmth of the bed, and he held the widow's buxom form in his arms, and her strong haunches clutched him in a vice-like grip. A sigh of pleasurable remembrance and warm anticipation, rustled from his throat and his fingers closed lovingly about his penis which was becoming turgid with the heat of his thoughts. It was at the very moment when his enflamed imagination had him grasping the heaving buttocks of his partner, that Elizabeth gave her deathcry. The sound of it, the foul stink and the splatter of something warm and wet on to his smiling face, froze him into shock so complete, his penis shrank and almost withdrew itself into his body.

With a roar of wild outrage, he leaped from the bed, crashing to the floor like a felled ox. He rubbed frantically at the stains of blood and vomit which had soaked into his nightgown, and the skin of his face strained across his cheekbones and became a deep and vivid red.

'Wha . . . wha . . . what the bluddy 'ell, woman,' he shouted, incensed by his wife's carelessness. 'Look what yer done over me, yer daft cow. Can't yer reach yer bluddy pot? Can't yer? What's the damn thing there for if yer not gonner use it?'

He hopped from foot to foot as the cold of the linoleum struck his bare soles, and his face crumpled like that of a petulant infant as disgust clutched at his stomach.

'It's bad enough 'avin' ter listen to yer spewin' into it day an'

14

night, wi'out yer do it all over me. All I ask is yer keep it to yerself. Is that too much to ask? Is it?'

His rage was out of control and he glared in the brightening dawn light at the dead woman with a look that would surely have killed her, had not her illness already done so. He waved his arm threateningly in her direction.

'I 'ave ter bluddy sleep in 'ere, but by God, anymore o' this, and I've 'alf a mind to move in wi't lads. Now clean yourself up while I get me breakfast. The stink in 'ere's enough to gas the cat.'

He moved across the room with a heavy tread and threw open the window. Passing beneath his window, an old woman glanced up and seeing the menacing figure above, crossed the road to the safety of the opposite kerb.

Henry continued to address the still figure of his wife as he opened the bedroom door. Prodding the air in her direction with a stiff finger, he thundered, 'Now clean up this mess an' get yerself tidy.'

His bellow could be heard in every corner of the house. The clamour reverberated against ears subconsciously attuned to that one voice, and each member of the household automatically stopped whatever they were doing and froze, minds searching anxiously to recall some misdeed which might innocently have been committed.

Robert and Jimmy, both still in bed, tarrying a moment longer before the inevitable strain of getting up was forced upon them, sprang from the covers like two soldiers snapping to attention at the approach of the Sergeant Major. They stumbled and floundered in a fever of apprehension, tripping over each other in their efforts to regain control of their trembling senses. Had it not been for the wonder that two grown men could be so affected by another, it might have been amusing.

Jenny sat bolt upright in her bed, her eyes wide in the semi-dark of the bedroom, her pleasurable anticipation of the coming Saturday dance and the absorbing question of what she should wear, shattered and scattered to the far corners of the room. When their Dad shouted like that it meant trouble, and it frightened the wits out of her. She clutched the sheet to her chin and waited, trembling, to see in which direction his rage would proceed. Please God, don't let it be me, please God . . . She heard the window crash, and the bedroom door open, and with a sigh of relief the heavy tread of her father's footsteps as he descended the stairs. Another salvo was fired as the door at the bottom was violently slammed. She relaxed and sank back on the pillow and her mind

15

returned to the pleasant problem which had beset it a moment before.

Ah-ah Gertie was day-dreaming in the little recess under the stairs. She was remembering the first day she had seen the shy young girl who had become her mistress, and who was now lying dead upstairs, though Gertie, as yet did not know it. Elizabeth had been a slip of a thing then, clinging to her husband's arm, her face rosy with love and trust. Gertie had adored her from that first moment, for Elizabeth had brought to the maid the first kindness she was ever to know. That first sweet smile in her direction had won Gertie's devotion and despite the fact that she was ten years older than Henry's new wife, she had pretended sometimes that Elizabeth was *her* mother as well. When the kindly young girl had first spoken those words by which Gertie had come to be known, she had meant no harshness, and it had been a small joke between them.

'Ah ah, Gertie, I caught you that time. Not under the carpet, but into the dustpan . . .'

'Ah ah, Gertie, don't forget *behind* the stove as well as the front . . .'

'Ah ah, Gertie, my dear . . .' until everyone was doing it and Gertie's own special link, just between the two of them, was shared, to Gertie's sorrow, by all the family.

She had been known as Ah-ah Gertie, or just plain Ah-ah, from that day onwards.

Now she slipped deeper into her own little den, breathing shakily on the knife she was polishing, and rubbing it with trembling fingers, whilst the fat tabby, kept only to decimate the mice, for Henry would feed no mouth which did not earn its keep, leaped delicately to the floor from the top of the stove. Leaving its toilette to a more fortuitous moment, it disappeared beneath the dresser.

Henry almost fell into the kitchen, the haste with which he had descended the stairs, impelling him forward. His foot caught the last step, and became entangled with the hem of his nightgown, and the sight of her father hopping and floundering, like some elderly soubrette attempting a new step in a dance routine, might have had Kate smiling, but for the blood on his clothes. The muscles of her face were ready for the shaping and forming which were needed to make the smile, but the mind of her was already shrieking a warning of alarm. Something had happened in the few minutes since she had come downstairs, and it told her that this was not the time for laughter. It was not her father's blood, that

16

was certain, for nobody could be as lively as he with wounds from which that scarlet had flowed, so where . . .?

The frying pan she held in a hand gone suddenly limp, dripped its toothsome contents on to the tiled floor, and the cat eased the tip of its twitching nose from beneath the dresser and stared unblinkingly at the tasty pieces of bacon, awaiting the moment when it might safely gather in this manna from heaven.

Henry watched his breakfast hit the floor, hardly able to believe his eyes. – Bluddy 'ell. What was wrong wi' everyone this morning. First Lizzie 'ad to go and puke all over 'im an' now 'ere was their Kate chuckin' good food on the kitchen floor. The household was goin' to pieces. It'd be the lads next, or their Jenny wi' some damn bit o' nonsense . . .

If he could have seen himself from where Kate was standing, the reason for the stupefied expression – loony, he called it – would have been apparent, even to one as heedless as himself.

Elizabeth's bloody vomit stained his nightgown from neck to waist and spots of red-rimmed foam painted his face like that of a child with measles.

'Wha . . . what's the matter, Dad? Where's all that blood come from?' Kate pointed with the dripping pan at her father's nightshirt.

Henry looked down at himself in disgust.

'It's yer Mam. She . . .'

But he got no further. Before his amazed expression could change itself verbally into a command to 'pull 'erself together', Kate dropped the pan and was past him and halfway through the door before the heavy iron utensil hit the floor.

'What the 'ell d'yer think yer doin', yer soft 'apporth,' he shouted to her retreating back. 'It's only yer Mam bein' sick. Where's me breakfast? I've gorrer be in't shop in 'alf an 'our.' He shook his head in rage. – What was up wi't daft cow, fer Christ's sake. Pande-bluddy-monium, just cos Lizzie was throwin' up, and look at 'is breakfast all over't kitchen. He'd have 'er life 'e would, carryin' on like a chicken with it's 'ead cut off, an' all over a bit o' puke.

He glared round the kitchen, and seeing a plate covered by another, keeping warm on the stove, he picked it up with the teacloth, slammed it on the table, sat down and began to eat the eggs and fried bread, already cooked by Kate for her brothers. His lips smacked together and his teeth crunched strongly, and all else was forgotten as he fed his healthy appetite.

The room was warm, glowing and comfortable from the open

17

coal fire. The smell of recently cooked food pleased him after the sour stench of the sick room and Henry smiled with satisfaction. The only offence was his nightgown. It was beginning to annoy him for Henry was clean to the point of mania. An array of freshly washed, ironed, and sweetly fragrant clothes aired above the fire, amongst them his clean nightshirt. Glancing round the quiet kitchen as if expecting to see some lurking figure, he stood up abruptly. With a quick movement, his arms lifted and the offending garment was removed and flung into the corner of the room. For a second his milk white body was naked in the fire glow, then swiftly was covered by the warm, fresh flannelette of his clean nightgown. Sighing with satisfaction, Henry sat down and resumed his breakfast.

Kate ran up the narrow staircase, her feet thumping hollowly in unison with her heart. Mam. Mam. It was Mam. She knew it was. It was *her* blood which spattered her father's nightgown. Primitive instinct told her, though she did not yet acknowledge it, that some disaster had overtaken them. Henry, whose only thought was self, had not the sensitivity to know disaster when it stood up and bit him, but Kate knew. Deep, deep down she knew.

A shadow edged from the first bedroom at the top of the stairs. It was Jenny, pale and virginal in her long white nightdress. Her hand shook as she reached out to Kate, but Kate passed her by as though she did not exist.

'What is it, our Kate?' the girl whispered, faltering nervously behind, one hand holding up her trailing nightdress, but Kate was not even aware that Jenny had spoken. She came to a halt at the wide open door of her parents' room, and despite the window which was flung wide, the smell caught the back of her throat in a savage grasp. She leaned against the doorpost, gagging and pressed a flaccid hand to her lips. Her face was pearly and dewed with sweat, and a groan began deep in her chest. It tore from her in a gasp and behind her Jenny began to mumble in terror.

'Wharris it, Kate? Tell me, please. What's up wi' Dad an' what's he shoutin' for?' She tried to look over Kate's shoulder, and her voice cracked as she spoke to her mother.

'Mam,' she pleaded. 'Mam, what's up wi' Dad. Is he . . . ?'

The light from the landing shone in a clear yellow stream across the bedroom, falling in a shaft of brightness on to the bed, picking out the still figure of Elizabeth Fowler. The open window allowed in a stray, icy breeze, and the net curtains lifted and lightly tapped at the window frame. An early sparrow was lifting a tentative voice to the new day and upstairs Bobby was whistling the cheerful notes

18

of *Chicago*. He began to croon in what he considered a syncopated fashion, '. . . a toddlin' town, de dah de dah dah . . .' and his heavy boots clumped overhead in rhythm with the melody.

In the bedroom the quiet was terrifying and Kate could hear distinctly the rapid acceleration of her own heartbeat.

'Mam,' she said hesitantly.

The woman on the bed made no reply.

'Are yer all right, Mam?' The whisper barely penetrated the distance from the doorway to the bed, and the dreadful, unwelcome knowing forced itself into Kate's shrinking mind.

'Dad said . . .'

She took a cautious step into the bedroom, then another until she looked down into the face of her mother.

Elizabeth's daughter looked timidly for the first time on death.

The ejection which had filled Elizabeth's mouth in her death had magically dispersed itself from her waxen skin, perhaps wiped clean by the movement of the bed sheet which lay beneath her chin, and her face was unsoiled and smooth. Her eyes were open and the illumination from the landing seemed to place a prick of light there, as though she awaited the coming of her daughters before saying a final farewell. Her hair, in a heavy plait which reached her waist when she was upright, was placed tidily across her left shoulder, and had it not been for the state of the bed, and the ghastly reek of vomit, one could have been forgiven for imagining that she lay tranquilly watching for the arrival of a visitor. Her golden brown eyes looked towards the door expectantly.

'Mam.' Kate's voice trembled and she put out her hand to touch her mother's cheek. As she spoke, Elizabeth's head fell to one side, her mouth opened and the last dribble of blood which had been captured within her lips, trickled on to the stained pillow.

Kate jumped backwards, horrified, and Jenny, who still stood nervously in the doorway, moaned low in her throat. She began to whimper, the sound hushed and soft as though she were afraid to disturb the horrid silence of the room. Her face was like putty and her eyes stretched so wide, the iris was completely surrounded by the milky white.

'Mam,' she quavered, 'Mam.' Never in her life had she seen anything so horrendous, or so pitiful as what lay on the bed, and her young mind could not accept it. This was not her Mam. This was not the sweet-faced being . . . this . . . could not be her Mam lying in a pool of . . . Though her eyes recognised her mother's face, her mind would not allow it. The whimper became a choked

19

cry of fear. She could feel her stomach rise up in denial of what she saw and her hand flew to her straining mouth to hold back the bile which rose there, just as her mother had done, only minutes before. Her voice rose in a thin scream, like an animal in a trap, but before she could give rein to the hysteria which was beginning to take hold, Kate turned from the bed and gripped her arm in fingers of steel, bruising the soft white flesh of her underarm, and her breath hissed from between her clenched teeth.

'Be quiet or I'll land yer one.' Thrusting Jenny roughly before her, she turned once more to her mother, and with gentle, loving fingers, softly closed the eyes which stared in death. She stood for a moment, her hand on Elizabeth's brow, as though to impart a benediction for the heart that was now at peace, then followed Jenny on to the landing.

The two girls stood in silence, their pitifully young faces slack with shock. Neither of them moved, for in their distress they did not know in which direction to go. The strength which had held Kate's mind together during the last dreadful moments, deserted her now, and she shook and whimpered like Jenny. Her heart fluttered, where it had hammered, and her stunned brain could repeat only three words. Me Mam's dead. Me Mam's dead. The sisters clung together, frightened and lost, for Elizabeth, pitiful and timid as she was, had been the pivot of their lives; the reason for their remaining in this house, the centre, loving and loyal, of their small world.

The sounds of the kitchen broke suddenly through the shock-induced silence. A pan was placed carelessly on the stove, and the sharp clang echoed up the stairwell. Their father's irritable voice rose sharply in reprimand, then continued in a subdued grumbling, the words of which were unclear, though the meaning was not. One of his sons was 'getting it in the neck'.

At last Kate stirred. Releasing Jenny's shaking figure, she took her hand in her own, drawing her gently across the landing. She hesitated at the top of the stairs.

'Wait here,' she whispered, and stepping back she closed the bedroom door as if afraid she might disturb the poor creature within. Returning to Jenny and placing her sister's hand once more in her own, she began to lead her down the back stairs towards the kitchen.

Henry and his sons were at the table, shovelling the breakfasts which she had cooked so long ago into their mouths as they did every morning. In a remote corner of Kate's mind, she noted that Ah-ah must have fried some more bacon and eggs, for their plates were heaped, and the tea steamed pleasantly in the big mugs from which the men drank. Toast was piled upon the breadboard, and a big dish of Elizabeth Fowler's homemade marmalade, stood in the centre of the table. The scene was so normal and like every other morning, that Kate hesitated for a moment, hardly able to believe the drama which had just taken place in her mother's bedroom. The cat licked her whiskers daintily in the corner, the last drop of bacon fat disappearing on the end of her pink tongue. The fire roared and Gertie scuttled from oven to table to sink in an exact replica of Elizabeth before her illness. It was all so typical of the start to each of Kate's days, she wanted to cry out in resentment at the heartlessness that had them acting so, when Mam lay dead upstairs.

Henry turned as Kate and Jenny edged slowly across the threshold of the room and his face began to crease in a frown, but the sharp words with which he was about to address them were never uttered. One look at their faces was enough.

Without preamble Kate said baldly, 'Mam's dead.' The words fell like plummeting sea birds that dived into a placid sea, making hardly a splash, but they were enough to silence the clattering cutlery, the noise of chomping teeth, and the lipsmacking sounds of a meal being enjoyed. Even the leaping fire seemed to still its cheerful crackle.

The three forks carrying their loads of food to three open mouths were halted in mid-air, and the three faces at the table took on different expressions, varying from disbelief, consternation, derision and slowly as the words took meaning, on the faces of the two young men, the start of grief.

No such emotion touched Henry's heart. He put his fork, dripping with egg yolk into his mouth, and as he chewed his expression became mocking.

'Dead,' he chortled, gulping on his egg, a yellow trickle sliding down through his white beard. 'Don't be daft, girl. I 'eard 'er coughin' norra minute since. Folks don't up an' die over a birrofa cough. It's not the cough what carries yer off, it's the coffin they carry yer off in,' he pantomimed, looking to his sons for their approval of his joke. When none came he turned sulkily to Kate. 'Give over, our Kate. Yer 'avin' us on.'

Kate turned on him, a tiger cub against a tiger, her rage so great she could have slashed his face with her nails.

''Avin' yer on. 'Avin yer on,' she screeched. 'Would I joke about me own Mam's death. Go an' look fer yerself if yer don't believe me.'

She began to cry turning her back on the tableau at the table. Jenny, her icy shock melting with her sister's tears, joined in, her sobs stuttering like those of a child. She turned to Kate and the two young girls put their arms about each other, standing locked in grief, rocking backwards and forwards as women will in the pain of grief.

Speechless, the men at the table remained frozen. Ah-ah Gertie's hands were stilled at the sink, soapy water oozing gently between the red, water-sodden fingers. Her face crumpled and the easy tears of the old dripped down her seamed cheeks into the suds. No one in the room gave her a glance, or even a thought, so wrapped about were they in their own concerns, but she had loved the woman upstairs for the gentle kindness she had given her and she wished with all her heart she had the words to speak of her grief. Gertie was nothing in this house. A skivvy earning ten bob a month. Fourteen hours a day and hardly a sign from the menfolk, but Elizabeth had spared her a thoughtful word and Gertie had loved her.

Now she was gone and life would never be the same. Not for her, nor the family she served. She might be thought daft, but she knew what went on behind *his* back and what his children thought of him. Stuck it for their Mam's sake, they had but not any more! Gertie bent her head and cried.

At the age of forty-nine Elizabeth Fowler was gone and with her went the reason for her children to stay.

Chapter Three

'I'm goin', our Jenny, an' that's final. It was only Mam that kept me
'ere an' I'm not workin' me fingers to't bone fer 'im.'

Kate tossed her head defiantly in the direction of the open back
door which led into the scullery. 'I'm fed up wi' it. Work, work,
work, an' never a word o' thanks. Bloody slaves, that's all we are.
Try to talk about a proper wage, an' 'e goes up in the air. As if 'e was
doin' us a favour. "Yer've gorra bluddy good 'ome 'ere",' she
mimicked, twisting her round face into a sneer, '"a lorrer girls
would give their eye teeth fer what you've got, me girl."' She
snorted. 'Daft bugger. What's 'e take us for? Mugs, that's what.
Nobody'd work 'ere only Ah-ah an' she's not right in the 'ead.'

Kate heaved a sack of potatoes from the ground with a practised
swing, her young body stretching and supple, and in one fluid
movement, she tipped the contents of the sack into the machine
which stood against the wall.

Her face was alive with anger. Her bright eyes snapped at Jenny
indignantly as if it were *she* who had caused that anger, and her
hair stood about her head fiercely, its very strength seeming to
participate in the girl's resentment.

'I've 'ad enough, our Jenny,' she continued. Her voice lowered
on the last sentence, and she looked about her furtively, her head
turning from side to side as she scanned every corner of the small
backyard. It was as though she expected to see the portly figure of
her father lurking behind the privy door, or skulking beside the
pile upon pile of sacks of potatoes, his blue eyes pierced for some
misdemeanour.

The tiny square was crammed with the junk of years, the like of
which Henry could not bear to part with, looking ahead to when
this, or that, might once again be useful. A half-assembled bicycle
their Bobby was repairing, the wheels misplaced, the frame rusted;
a dolly tub and posser; her mam's old mangle, grimed and worn
with age; a delapidated hutch which had once housed a rabbit.
Buckets without handles, tubs in which gaping holes flaked;
brushes and mops, a piece of ragged carpet and a wheelbarrow

23

with only one leg so that it was forced to lean forlornly at a drunken angle. There were sack upon sack of potatoes lurching against stacks of empty crates, waiting to be returned to the market from which they had come full of wet fish that morning. It looked like nothing so much as the city tip, and so heaped about was it, that when nature called, it had become a feat of great skill to manoeuvre oneself from the back door of the house to the privy against the far wall.

Kate's eyes flickered from one hillock of rubbish to the next, then looked sternly into those of her sister. She paused dramatically before saying, 'I'm off, our kid. Yer can come or stay as yer please but I'm off . . .'

Her eyes pleaded with Jenny to come, but her sister continued to eye potatoes as though her life depended upon it.

'. . . but make up yer mind 'cos I'm goin' to town to look fer a job. Lily Donaldson says they're takin' on girls at Wagstaffes. Waitresses, an' I reckon we could do that a treat. It can't be any 'arder than workin' 'ere,' she said bitterly. 'We've 'ad a good groundin', I'll give 'im that.'

She laughed mirthlessly, then went on. '. . . and we'll 'ave to look for somewhere to live.' She paused, and the silence which fell stretched from seconds to minutes.

'Well, are yer on or not?'

Kate and Jenny were in the tiny foot of space by the back door, feeding unpeeled potatoes into the potato machine. Sack after sack was lifted and the contents thrown rhythmically onto the moving belt which fed the potatoes between the rollers of the machine. They looked like revolving cheese graters, rubbing away the dirt encrusted skins, allowing the clean vegetable to drop into the container on the other side. From there it was the girls' job to pick out each potato and with a small pointed utensil, to take out the eyes which the machine had missed. The pristine oval shapes were then thrown with unerring skill, born of years of practice, into a second machine which sliced and chipped the potatoes ready for the fryer. It was an arduous and backbreaking job, hard enough for a man, but the sisters were expected to have a dozen sackfuls ready for the twelve o'clock opening.

Their hands were cracked and raw, and the cold formed clouds of vapour above their bent heads. The sun shone weakly from an ice blue sky, outlining the chimneys which stood in rows like soldiers stiffly to attention. A thin smudge of dirty smoke trailed across the rooftops, to vanish into the general pall which hung over the great city, fed there by a thousand fires. It was a dismal and

24

colourless scene. No warmth from the sun, even in the middle of summer, ever reached this corner of the universe. It was forever in shadow. No flower grew, nor blade of grass attempted to take root, and even the few sparrows which hopped hopefully from wall to wall, were tattered and scrawny, looking as though they had been in a narrowly escaped flight from a pack of alley cats. Two of these were perched eagerly upon the privy roof, attracted by the stink of fish which lay over all.

'I can't stand it, our Jenny,' Kate's voice went on as it became clear that her sister was not going to speak. She rubbed her forearm across her red and dripping nose and sniffed. 'Now that Mam's gone, there doesn't seem any reason to stay. We 'ad to before. Well, we couldn't leave 'er, could we? But now she's . . . gone, well . . .'

It was as though she must justify her actions to her sister, though God knew there was no need, but her voice stumbled on. Perhaps it was herself she needed to convince for the thought of leaving the security of Henry's home and shifting for herself was frightening indeed. Young girls just did not leave home – unless it was to be married – and the sobering thought that their Jenny might not come with her, turned her stomach to lurching jelly.

She watched Jenny's expression anxiously, waiting for some sign, some indication of what was passing in her sister's mind, but the girl's face was veiled by the soft wings of her brown hair, and her eyes were hidden beneath her long, black lashes. She lifted and heaved and bent in relentless rhythm, but she said nothing.

Kate tried again, desperation, despair, making her voice hoarse.

'You know I can't gerron with me Dad. I've 'eld me tongue all these years fer 'er sake, but now there's no need.'

She lifted her head bravely and stood straight.

'I'm off an' 'e can find 'imself another skivvy.'

The silence deepened, broken only by the soft scrape of the potatoes as they passed through the rollers, and the squeak of the handle as Jenny turned it vigorously.

It was two weeks since Elizabeth's funeral and the household was settling back into the routine which had been fragmented by her death. Henry, forced by the simple refusal of his children to work whilst their mother's body lay in the parlour, had closed the shop for three days, but the day after the funeral it was business as usual. Black armbands were worn in deference to his wife's death, and a drape of black crêpe graced the mirror above the fish fryers, but that was as far as Henry was prepared to go, and his family had to be satisfied.

25

But she was missed, that pale ghost of a woman, whose voice had never risen above a gentle murmur. She had spent the last months of her life resting on the sofa in her parlour, and the last weeks, in her bed, but she had always seemed to create a tiny island of calmness wherever she happened to be. When Henry disappeared on one of his nocturnal jaunts, her spirits would become almost gay, and her daughters delighted in the humour she would display. She would talk of her early life in Matlock, for that was where she came from, and the happiness she had known with her parents before Henry had taken her to wife.

Elizabeth had lived a life so different from their own, though her father had been only a step or two above Henry on the social ladder. The Johnsons had enjoyed the life of small town dwellers and Elizabeth, Beth not Lizzie to her parents, had been an only child. She had been petted and loved, and in her innocence had thought to continue that affection with her new husband.

But she spoke of no time *after* her wedding day to her daughters, and her face would close up like a flower at night, when Henry's key was heard in the door.

It had been several years since she had taken an active part in the running of the shop, or in the daily domestic routine of her home, leaving it more and more in the capable hands of her Kate, but somehow, though she had seemed an ephemeral shadow in the wake of her husband's robust constitution, her going was grieved over, and she was looked for in many ways by everyone but Henry.

The absence of the sound of her tearing nausea was a relief to those who had listened to it without let-up for six months, but nevertheless, her gentle loving eyes and frail goodness seemed to haunt them all.

Only Henry delighted in her passing. He had the bed to himself now and could wallow indolently, re-living the last sensual scene between himself and the widow, considering on the matter of how soon he could introduce her to his children as a member of the household. Housekeeper, perhaps, until he had time to weigh up the pros and cons, like. It would be tricky he knew, for the girls had been attached to Lizzie, but give it a few months, he told himself, and they would be taken up with some new fiddle-faddle and their mother's memory would have died. The idea of having continual usage of the energetic body of the widow filled him with pleasure, the only fly in the ointment, as far as he could see, were *her* children. Five she had, but the two eldest could be put to some work and be found lodgings, and the rest, all girls, pushed in a cranny somewhere. They could move in with Kate and Jenny, and no doubt be very useful in the shop.

And so he dreamed his dreams, biding his time, unaware of the seething indignation within his daughter's breast, and of the plans she hatched. He did not miss his wife in any small degree. She had been nothing to him for years. Not companion. Not bedfellow.

Well, now she was gone, and he for one was glad.

But Kate knew the time had come to leave. It was now or never. If she stayed any longer, the dread routine, the safe bars of security, and Henry's will, would have her forever. He could see no view but his own, and would stand for no opinion but the one he expressed from morning till night. She would forfeit her own mind, as her mother had done, bent under his, if she did not go soon. He would manage without her in the shop, she knew that, and anyway, if he didn't, if he fell flat on his face, who was she to care. Serve him right, the old bugger.

If she could only persuade their Jenny . . .

The door to the back kitchen was open wide. Through the scullery and beyond, in the shop, Henry could be seen, laundry fresh in his white coat, directing Bobby in the lighting up of the fish fryers, the laying out of the piles of newspapers in which the servings were wrapped, and the topping up of the vinegar bottles and salt cellars. His voice could be heard censuring their Jimmy, as he mixed up the huge bowl of batter, in which the tiny pieces of cod were coated, before being dropped into the hot fat.

'Not that much, yer daft bugger. 'ow d'yer expect me to make owt if yer stickin' in pieces the size of yer' and. Smaller, smaller, 'alf that size. No, don't throw that piece away. I know it's all skin, but who'll notice when it's battered?'

On and on it went, as his son patiently cut and dipped, his face, so like Henry's in shape and colour, set in a mould of resignation. It spoke, in its stillness, saying, 'Lord, give me the strength to resist the temptation to hit this old sod in the middle of his arrogant face'. One day it would happen. The day would dawn when one or the other of his sons, now as big and as strong as he, and perfectly capable, if their minds could get up the courage, of knocking their father to the floor, would finally be driven to the act of retaliating against the constant humiliation in which Henry placed them.

Ah-ah slipped noiselessly back and forth with piles of gleaming cutlery heaped on a tray, laying the tables up in the snug. When she had finished she would come and sit beside the girls and help to eye the growing mountain of creamy, black specked potatoes, and with that task completed, without rest or pause, she would

27

stand behind the counter in the shop, on her swollen, aching, elderly feet, and serve countless dozens of packets of fish and chips until closing time. Even then she was not finished, for there would be stacks of plates and knives and forks to be seen to, and she must plunge her arms to the elbows in the caustic soda suds, washing the endless piles of greasy dishes which had accumulated during opening time.

Kate watched the scene, her knife idle in her hands. She and Jenny had been in the yard since early morning, and the tubs of chipped potatoes stood in a row beneath the scullery window, ready for the men to carry them into the shop. It was just gone eleven thirty on a Saturday morning, and trade, which began at noon, was expected to be brisk. Everton were playing Aston Villa at home, and already a queue of men and boys, waiting to fill their bellies before moving on to the pub for a couple of bevvies before the match, stretched across the shop front and down towards the corner. They stood, goodhumouredly, in their cloth caps and white mufflers, swopping 'Woodbines' and opinions on the expected quality of the coming match, stamping their steel-tipped boots until the flags rang like an anvil under the hammer.

With a suddenness which made Kate start, Jenny stood up and in a manner completely foreign to her timid nature, flung her knife across the yard, a gesture which seemed to finally denounce, now and forever, the life she now led. It was as though she acclaimed to the world, that from now on she was her own person, and that the knife, symbol of her father's dominance, was of no further use to her.

The cat on the roof, used to alley ways, and the constant danger of being threatened with anything which came readily to hand, jumped, startled, across the privy roof tiles and disappeared over the wall.

Kate watched Jenny's flushed face and abnormally bright eyes and her heart heaved with excitement as she waited for her to speak.

'I'm comin' with yer, our Kate.' Jenny's feet moved like those of a soldier marching on the spot, as though she were eager to be away immediately, but had not the nerve to leave the square foot of safety in which she stood. 'I can't stay 'ere on me own with Dad and the boys. I'd be nowt a pound wi'out you. At 'is beck an' call every hour God sends.' Her face drooped and the brave defiance left it for a moment. 'I don't like leavin' the lads,' she said unhappily, then her face lifted and she looked down into Kate's approving eyes, 'but that can't be helped. I couldn't abide bein' 'ere wi'out you an' Mam, an' they'll have to stand on their own two feet.'

Quick tears stood in her golden brown eyes, and were in danger of starting their journey across the smooth roundness of her cheeks, but she dashed her hand across her face.

'It's on, our Kate. We'll do it.'

It was all Kate could do not to stand up and polka her sister between the piles of junk which surrounded them. It was on! Their Jenny was game and it was on! She felt as if she would burst with excitement, and her face split in a ferocious grin, as if to let out some of the seething steam of emotion within her. She clenched her fists and banged them together, like a child promised a treat, and her eyes glittered in anticipation. She would have gone without their Jenny, she was certain of that, for she loathed the man who was her father, but how much better it would be with Jenny beside her. Together they would win the world; be independent, and taste the freedom which would never be theirs under Henry's domination.

She shivered with delight.

'Eeh, our kid,' she whispered, 'it'll be grand, grand.'

Jenny sat down abruptly and some of the fire left her cheek at the realisation of what they were about to do. That first step to freedom was the hardest to take and now that she was determined upon it, the action necessary to move her forward seemed suddenly to be impossible. She looked at Kate and met the blue steadiness of her eye, the brave, smiling joy, and she knew she *must* do it.

'Where will we stay?' she whispered as though Henry stood a foot away, instead of busy in the shop.

'I don't know yet,' Kate whispered back, 'but we'll find summat, never fear. Our Elly'll give us a bed for a few nights.'

'Will we go soon?'

' 'ow about today?'

'Oh our Kate . . .'

'It's now or never, our kid.'

'But today, it's a bit . . .'

'A bit what?'

'Well, soon.' Jenny hesitated, overwhelmed again by the magnitude of the course on which they were bound. Their Dad would eat them alive when they told him. He'd go daft. His rage was awful to see, and the thought of it falling about her own ears was almost too much to bear.

'D'yer not think we should wait a day or two. Let it settle, like. Give us a bit of time to make some plans. We could . . .'

Kate stood up violently and shook herself, flexing her arms and hands like a boxer about to go into the ring. There was fear in Kate's eyes now, but her round face was stiff with determination.

'No, our Jenny,' she said quietly. 'It's got to be today, at least for me it 'as. You must please yerself.'

As she spoke Jenny began to cry, her stretched nerves tearing what little reserve of calmness she had left. She was Elizabeth's child; gentle, easily hurt, liking nothing better than harmony and peace amongst those she loved and the thought of the coming battle terrified her. But she was even more afraid of being left alone without Kate.

'What's it to be, Jenny?' Kate looked at her inflexibly, her good-humoured face set in serious, almost belligerent lines.

'Me or 'im?'

Jenny sniffed and looked down at her chapped hands. They were so sore, the knuckles cracked where chilblains had split. She must put some vaseline on them tonight, she thought absently, or they'd bleed tomorrow. Tomorrow. Tomorrow, if Kate meant what she said, she'd be out here by herself, with just Ah-ah Gertie for company, which was just as good as saying she'd be all alone. She tried to imagine herself coping with her father's imperious demands, which would be doubled without Kate; his rages, his biting sarcastic humour, and that great empty bed in which she had never slept alone. She would cook and clean and work in the shop, and doubtless, without Kate to accompany her, Henry would no longer allow her to go to the Mecca on a Saturday night. She'd be a virtual prisoner, a drudge. She'd see no one but the family, meet no one. No handsome stranger would come tapping on the chippie counter to carry her away.

She looked up at Kate and knew there was no contest. Her eyes were big and frightened, but Kate's strength brushed her with loving strokes and she nodded her head gently as she answered.

'Yes Kate, I'm coming.'

'Right lass, let's get started.'

Kate took a decisive step away from the stool on which she had so recently squatted, turning to look at Jenny. She straightened and stiffened her back and lifted her head to sit proudly on her shoulders. Her mop of springy hair stood about her skull like the head of a bronze chrysanthemum, and her cheeks were scarlet with fearful excitement. Her eyes snapped and her heart thumped and she felt ready for anything. The fracas with Jenny had set the blood pumping through her veins and she felt able to tackle Goliath himself.

Henry was standing in the centre of the shop, his watch in his hand, unmoved by the line of faces which weaved and bobbed outside his window, mouthing pleas to be allowed inside. It was five to twelve, and the gesticulations, some of them rude, bothered him not at all. He opened his shop door on the dot of twelve and not a moment before. He turned irritably on his daughters as they sidled from the back kitchen into his line of vision.

'Where the 'ell 'ave you two bin,' he demanded, 'can't yer see it's openin' time. Get yer overalls on, do.' He glanced back at the crowd pressed to the shop window and a look of gratification passed across his face. He said absently, more from habit than from any desire to chastise:

'I don't know what you two girls gerrup to out there, I really don't. Lollin' an' gossipin' half the mornin' away when there's work to be done. Come on, come on, don't just stand there gawpin'. There's customers to see to.'

He began to move in a dignified manner towards the door, with the intention of opening it and letting in the restive crowd which thronged outside. A cheer rose and Henry put on his 'the customer is always right' smile.

He never reached the door.

Kate had intended to draw her father as tactfully as she was able into the scullery, and there impart to him the news that at one stroke, he was about to lose two members of his staff. Her brothers worked only when they were able, depending on their shifts at the dockyard, and he would be left with only Ah-ah, until he could find new girls. Telling him would be a fearsome task, and one which filled her with cold dread, but she felt, for her own sake as well as his, that it would be better done out of sight of onlookers. For the sake of her mother's memory she had hoped to leave the house with this fragile link between them still intact.

The implication that she and Jenny had been shirking their duties; had been idling the morning away in the cheerless backyard, made her see red. She could feel the fury rising within her, and the injustice of the accusation made her shake from head to foot, like some machine which has been switched on, then runs out of control.

She lifted her chilblained hands and held them out before her.

'Just a minute,' she shrieked.

Henry tutted, as though to say, what now, but his gaze remained fixed on the crowd beyond the door and his hand reached out to the bolt at the top.

31

'Look at these,' Kate shouted, her voice echoing off the mirrors which lined the room, 'go on, look at them.'

Despite himself, Henry turned and looked obediently.

The crowd was suddenly silent, and the two young men behind the counter froze into stillness. The only sound within the shop was the joyous sizzle of the chips frying and the splutter of fat as it closed around the battered fish.

Kate was beside herself with rage. Her red hands quivered as she held them out at arms length, turning them over and over for her father to see.

'Do they look as though we've bin doin' nowt? Do they? Look at them,' she reiterated, 'Go on. Nice aren't they? The 'ands of a lady, would yer say?'

Henry's face looked as though someone had just placed a left hook in his solar plexus. 'Just bin fer a manicure, me an' Jenny. Go on, our kid. Show 'im yours an' all.'

Kate began to cry harshly, all restraint gone. 'Go an' look in't tubs in't yard,' she sobbed. 'Full a spuds they are, all done by me an' 'er.' She tossed her head in Jenny's direction. She took a step nearer to her father. His amazement was so great at the ferocity of her rage, he actually backed up against the door.

''Ave you ever spent three hours in that bloody yard on a mornin' so cold, it freezes yer bum on the bucket; when yer 'ands are so cold yer can't feel 'em, an' they bleed wi't cracks in 'em. So cold when yer stand up yer fall down again 'cos yer feet 'ave turned to ice. 'Ave yer, 'ave yer? 'Ave yer tried liftin' one o' them sacks o' spuds? The only bloody good yer can say about 'em is, when yer've humped a dozen, it brings yer circulation on a treat.'

She was incensed now, her face drained of the colour which had flooded at her first fury. Her hands flailed in their desire to hit the face before her, a face as red as hers was white, but Henry had recovered from his first incredulous stupor. His face took on the look of a beetroot, and two veins stood out, beating fiercely, one on each side of his temple. The whites of his eyes were suffused with red, as though his rage had pumped the blood from his veins into them, and in the centre, the iris was a startling arctic blue.

His mouth thinned to a dangerous white line.

'Are you quite finished, lady?' he whispered menacingly.

The silence which followed was thick and dangerous, cut by the sound of an anguished moan from the back of the shop where Jenny stood. Henry's sons remained like two effigies, frozen forever in poses of disbelief and horror. Only their eyes moved, darting looks from one enraged face to the other. Jimmy held a

32

piece of cod in his hand from which batter dripped on to the floor in thick creamy blobs, and Ah-ah, whose hands were busy at the cutlery she was arranging on the table in the snug, dropped a fork with a clatter which brought a whimper of fear to her throat.

'No you bloody well 'aven't,' Kate continued, her voice rising, her father's terrible anger ignored as though he had not spoken. 'Why should yer? Yer've gorrus to do it, 'aven't yer? We're the ones who do all the work 'ere.' She looked round wildly, her gaze including Jenny and her brothers. 'Why should you 'ave to do owt when yer've gorrus to skivvy for yer, eh?'

Henry took a step towards her, his left foot placed carefully on the floor, like a cat about to spring. His head sank between his shoulders and he looked at her from beneath lowered brows. The colour congested, then retreated from his cheeks, and his eyes slitted. Never, in the whole of his adult life, had anyone spoken to him as Kate was doing. Only Elly, a voice said in his head, and for a second he was confused. Two of his daughters stood up to him, whilst his sons . . . But he'd soon sort this little lot out, he said to himself, recovering from his momentary doubt, his fury rising like an erupting volcano. If he had had a weapon in his hand, no matter what it might have been, he would have used it against her.

'Well it's finished, d'yer hear, finished. No more. Me an' Jenny's off an' we won't be back.'

Kate faltered for the first time.

'Me Mam . . . well, we 'oped for 'er sake that we could part in a friendly . . .' She did not finish the sentence and her voice strengthened at the remembered insult of a minute ago, and she shouted out the last words, '. . . but by 'ell yer can be damned. We're off for good.'

The roar, like the thunder of a tormented beast, filled the shop and paralysed Jenny who had been just about to move toward the back stair. It turned every head in the queue as one. Jimmy's fingers lost all feeling, and the cod dropped to the tiled floor with a light splat. Bobby started violently and his hand, reaching out involuntarily for a place to support itself, touched the shiny surface of the oven, and a hiss of pain escaped his lips as he twitched it away. Jenny gave a shrill scream, cut off in terror, and turned her face to the wall, her shoulders quivering and jumping beneath the smooth fabric of her blouse.

Only Kate had life in her, and the temper which she had inherited from the man facing her, kept it ablaze. She stood her ground, never even flinching as Henry's voice rose, full-lunged to the ceiling.

33

'What the 'ell are you blatherin' on about, Madam, an' who the 'ell d'yer think yer talkin' to. By God, I've a good mind to strap yer right 'ere in't shop fer all them lot ter see.' He waved his hand in the direction of the shop window, and moved again, taking another ominous step towards his daughter. His voice fell almost to a whisper.

'One more word from you, my lass, an' I'll do it, yer impudent slut. If we weren't just goin' to open shop . . . but just you wait. Yer'll regret the day yer spoke ter me . . . when this shop shuts . . .'

'We won't be 'ere,' shrilled Kate. ''Ave yer gone deaf or summat. We're leavin'. Leavin', d'yer 'ear. We're leavin' this 'ouse and yer can find someone else to knock about.'

'Yer cheeky faggot . . . I'll bluddy kill yer . . . 'Ow dare you backchat me like that . . . I'll . . .'

But it was too late. Nineteen years too late. Kate's voice was low now, her mind white hot with hatred and the tearing violence of rage kept in check too long.

'Don't you raise your voice to me, yer wicked old sod. Yer kept me Mam in fear all 'er life. Drove 'er to 'er grave wi' all yer bullying, and our Elly. She married that . . . that clod just to be shut of you. Well, that's not fer me. I'm off. Yer can get yerself another doormat, 'cos yer've wiped yer feet on me for the last time.'

Henry moved towards her purposefully. He lifted his hand and would have struck her full in the face, but she stepped back quickly, colliding with Jenny who cowered against the wall like a child in a nightmare.

The crowd outside pressed its collective nose to the window, elbowing and shoving to get a better view. Voices could be heard, newcomers questioning those who had been there at the onset of the drama. A woman with the build of a dockie, and a face in which years of being always a loser had painted a belligerent impatience, banged on the door, and mouthed an obscene demand to be let in, pointing a thick finger at the clock on the wall.

The discord, rising as the finger on the clock moved on to five past twelve, suddenly penetrated the savage rage which gripped the man in the white coat. Bewildered, as if caught in an act which he had no knowledge of committing, he turned and looked at the fascinated row of faces. He turned again, a bull baited by a swarm of bees, but into his maddened eyes had come a new look, and into his rage-infused brain, crept the cooling thoughts of reason. He glanced quickly at the clock on the wall, then at his sons, still insensible in the aftermath of shock. Jenny's face remained pressed to the wall, and Kate stood protectively beside her. The indecision which gripped him was as plain to see as had been his rage. Jimmy almost smiled, for he knew what was going on in his father's head. Bluddy, 'ell, it was saying, five past twelve, two dozen people outside the shop fightin' to get in, and their Kate threatenin' to leave an' take their Jenny with 'er. What the 'ell should he do? He couldn't manage with just the lads and Gertie. Busiest time of the day it was, an' busiest day of the week an' this cheeky Madam was talkin' about . . .

For an instant the choler returned to Henry's face, but he pulled it back into a shape which he hoped showed bland tolerance. The effort it cost nearly caused his heart to stop beating, but somehow he did it. But by God, just wait till closing time. He'd show 'er. He'd take the skin off 'er back. He'd lock 'er in 'er room and feed 'er bread and water and just let 'er ask to go dancin' or to see that there Rudolf Valentino and he'd show 'er what for . . . But now, Jesus, it'd cost him, but he'd have to eat humble pie.

'I'll give yer one more chance, our Kate,' he said, almost gently. 'Get back ter work an' I'll forget this, though it'll be 'ard. Fer a daughter o' mine to speak so, after the upbringin' yer've 'ad. Yer mother, God rest 'er soul, would stand up in 'er grave . . .'

Kate spoke quietly, the reference to her dead mother on this old hypocrite's tongue closing the last door on their relationship.

'Go to 'ell,' she said.

She turned from him, and taking Jenny's arm dragged her roughly across the short passageway towards the staircase. Almost carrying her she was up the stairs and into their bedroom, before Henry could even close his mouth on his last word.

But he wasn't finished yet. There was brass standing outside on the flagstones, and he wanted it, and if it meant buttering up their Kate for a couple of hours, he'd do it. But after . . . he could hardly wait. Suppressed rage making him as nimble as a man half his age, he pounded up the echoing, uncarpeted stairs, following his daughters across the landing, pausing at the doorway, just in time to see Kate pull a suitcase from under a pile of boxes which lurched precariously on top of the wardrobe and hurl it on to the bed. Jenny was backed into the angle made by the wardrobe and the wall. She moaned slightly, unaware of what she was doing, her eyes huge and moist with fear.

'Now listen 'ere,' Henry began. Caution was taking him over now, and prudence. The girl meant what she said, he could see that, and where the hell was he to get two efficient, attractive girls, to take their place, especially at what he paid them. He was willing

35

to concede, even now, that his two pretty daughters brought in a lot of trade from the menfolk in the area. Though it tore him to shreds he must wheedle her out of it. Her. Not their Jenny, for Kate was the ringleader. If he had Kate he had Jenny. He would need to step warily.

'I'm not 'avin' any more of this damn nonsense.' He tried to smile winningly, implying the whole thing had been a joke on Kate's part, but his cheek muscle spasmed, and his mouth twitched with the effort. 'Leave 'ome you say. Don't be daft. What the 'ell d'yer think yer'll do. Who'll keep yer?' he blustered. Though he would not admit to it, he had the feeling of a boxer who was down for the count of nine, and his eyes took on the sharp look of discretion as if the thought that he was about to forfeit the two best, unpaid workers a man was likely to have, was only just becoming clear to him.

'Don't be daft, girl,' he continued. 'Yer'll never find a job as good as this.'

Kate laughed incredulously.

He went on. 'This is daft, our Kate.' 'Daft' seemed to be the only word he could conjure up to describe the situation. 'Now come on, let's forget this tomfoolery and I'll give yer another chance. I can't say fairer than that, can I?' He actually managed to smile at last.

'What d'yer say, our kid?'

Kate turned from the wardrobe and jumped down from the chair. She began to open drawers, pulling out underclothes and jumpers, stockings and blouses in an ecstasy of motion, stuffing them haphazardly into the suitcase. She signalled to Jenny to help her, but the girl had eyes for no one but her father, who leaned from one foot to the other, watching Kate, anxiety and rage warring for expression on his face.

Kate looked up and stopped what she was doing. She stared into Henry's ice-blue eyes.

'I'm not sayin' this again, Dad. Me an' Jenny are leavin' this 'ouse now, an' after what's just bin said, I doubt we'll ever be back. Yer've ruled our lives ever since we were born, even the lads, burrif they wanna stay that's their look-out. Me an' our Jenny want a life of our own, yer see, an' this is the only way we'll find it.' Her face hardened. 'Now we're packin' our things an' goin' so gerrout of me way.'

Terrified and appalled at Kate's courage in standing up to their father, Jenny spoke at last, her voice highpitched with nerves at her own audacity.

'P'raps we'd better stay, Kate. If Dad thinks . . .'

36

The man's face took on a sly look as he thought he saw a rift in the concerted wall of defiance which had been erected by his daughters, but he was mistaken. Kate turned on Jenny before the sentence was half out of her sister's mouth, making her shrink further into her corner, her hands outstretched in supplication, palms towards Kate as if warding off a blow.

'I'm goin', our Jenny. Stay or come as yer please, but make it quick cos I shall be out of 'ere in ten minutes. Yer saw what he did to Mam. She was nowt but a skivvy in this 'ouse, an' 'e's gorrus goin' the same way. Well, that's not fer me, so make up yer mind.'

She sounded almost indifferent, as though whether Jenny stayed or not meant nothing to her. She turned to her suitcase and began to move her clothes about in an aimless fashion, almost in tears, the shock of the last thirty minutes beginning to grip her. But for the man staring inflexibly at Jenny, as though hypnotising her to bend to his will, she would have given way and had a good cry, but pride, and something to which she could put no name, stopped her.

For a full minute Henry and Jenny stared at one another. If he could just keep her, he thought, it wouldn't be too bad. She was a good worker and more biddable than Kate, and without Kate behind her she . . .

Jenny came abruptly to life and straightening her shoulders, began to help her sister.

Chapter Four

Kate and Jenny sat with their feet upon the fender, each with a cup of steaming cocoa in her hand. They had removed their shoes and stockings, and their bare toes curled and flexed as the heat from the huge fire curled about them. The leaping flames, orange flowered, yellow centred, spread a delicate colour across the faces of the two young girls, and a faint sheen of perspiration filmed each unclouded brow and upper lip, but they were reluctant to move from the circle of heat, into the goose-pimpling cold at the back of the room. The fan of radiance which spread from the glowing range became diluted the further one got from its warm heart, and to feel its full benefit, one must sit with knees almost up the chimney. Already Kate's legs showed faintly the ugly, red-edged, honeycomb of scorched skin which was the stamp of the working class woman. In kitchens up and down the land they would be found, legs apart, feet planted firmly on their own hearth, comfortably seated to the fireside with the everlasting cup of tea in hand. The bludgeoning heat from the coals wrapped companionably around them, they would sip and stare reflectively, gaining a moment's ease of mind from the one luxury not denied them. Their faces would become rosy and damp, and the skin of their shins take on a monstrous pattern of brown and red which went with them to the grave.

Kate pulled her skirt down from her opened thighs in a half-hearted effort to protect her shins from the heat, but the short waitress uniform was meant to reveal, not conceal, and the attempt was abandoned.

Jenny's eyes were unfocused, enormous brown pools of tranquillity, and her lids lifted and fell in a slow, hypnotic rhythm. The thick, curling lashes were so heavy along their edge, there seemed a distinct possibility that she would be unable to raise them, once they had fallen. A small smile of content lifted the corners of her plump, pink mouth, and her tongue quivered along her lips, licking delicately the creamy cocoa which remained after each sip.

The room was sparsely furnished. Its essence was the range. It

38

was black-leaded and polished, almost mirror-like and bright enough to see one's own reflection in its surface. The brass handles on the oven door were gleaming, brilliant as gold, as was the fender which guarded it, and the heavy poker held in the hearth 'tidy'. A kettle, steam wisping from the spout was embosomed in the nest of glowing embers at the front of the fire, and from a sagging length of twine fastened above, dangled stockings and two freshly ironed aprons. The clean smell of airing clothes, warm and homely, mingled with the sweet fragrance of the cocoa.

A large, round table covered by a red chenille cloth was placed in the middle of the room, the cloth matching the fringed and bobbled pelmet which draped the shelf above the fire.

An enormous, hideously ugly sideboard stood against the back wall. It had thick, carved legs and a mirrored back, and on each side was a cupboard with drawers between.

The chairs in which the girls were sitting were old. Decades of women had rested in the overstuffed armchair which held Kate, from the first genteel lady sipping tea in her drawing room at the manor from where it had originated, to the young girl enjoying her cocoa in the kitchen of a terraced house in a street off Scotland Road. Who knows how many had found peace in its sagging depths in between, or what number of secondhand shops had seen it come and go. The pattern of its fabric had once been bright and pretty, but now it sat in drabness, its beauty gone but built for comfort and still giving it.

The rocking chair in which Jenny dozed had a wicker seat and back, and the patina of the mahogany surrounding it still glowed. Several struts beneath it were broken and had been replaced with handy bits of plywood. There were scars; wounds caused by careless hands and never healed, but the cushions upon it were bright and soft and the rocker moved gently, lulling its occupant into a euphoric trance.

On the sepia coloured, faded wallpaper, hanging from the brown painted picture rail was an oval, gilt framed picture of a Grecian-clad lady collecting shells on a golden beach.

A square of fringed carpet, so threadbare the original pattern and colours were long since gone covered the linoleum and in front of the fire lay a rag rug, brilliant with reds and blues and greens, put together by Elizabeth Fowler years ago, from all the worn out odds and ends of clothing worn by her children. It had been a memory of love and childhood to her, each piece bringing back some re-membrance dear to a mother. Now it warmed the feet of her two daughters, and the fat tabby who drowsed upon it.

There was no window in the room, just a wide opening surrounded by glass panels, which led into the scullery. It was the room's only source of natural light.

The scullery was minuscule. There was a shallow ochre-tinted sink, pitted and chipped from hundreds of clashes with pots and pans, with a draining board to one side, and an old gas oven which was rarely used. In the corner stood a dangerously leaning cupboard full of an assortment of crockery, donated by friends and relatives and not one piece matching another. Most of the furniture had been secured by diligent searching of the local pawnbrokers and secondhand shops.

On several successive Saturday evenings the two girls had walked the length of Great Homer Street, 'Greaty' to the hundreds who crowded its heady stir and bustle, mixing with the multitude who came to find a bargain in the shops which stayed open as long as there was a customer. They bought a frying pan for sixpence, cast iron and made to last a lifetime and saucepans for threepence at 'Duffys' and watched with fascination as the woman in the 'Cowbutter' store shaped and sculpted the creamy mass into designs of rare beauty. The cheese and butter were stored in barrels which hung from the ceiling of the shop, and outside, along the teeming street lurked 'Mary Ellens', shawls tied securely, cloth caps set jauntily upon their ever moving heads. Some pushed wheelbarrows, others handcarts and they stopped only long enough to tempt a passerby with a plate of onions for threepence or oranges for less if the evening was late. Sage, mint and parsley hung in lovely aromatic bunches from their mobile stalls and their cries of 'Sage a mint a parsley, sage a mint a parsley' rang above the noises of the street.

You could buy anything in 'Greaty'.

Their Jimmy and his friend, Charlie Walker, had borrowed from Mick Tully, who was a mate of theirs and worked for the local rag and bone man, a handcart, and had helped the sisters to move their bits and pieces into their new home.

They were completely and rapturously happy.

It was 1922 and women were beginning to enjoy a freedom never before known, especially those who had grown up during the war years. Between 1914 and 1918, many women had, for the first time, been employed in what had previously been considered a man's territory, freeing men for the trenches. They had driven trucks and trams, worked on munitions and in factories and had shown they were more than capable of activities other than those in the home. In 1918, women over the age of thirty were given the vote and attitudes towards the usefulness of women *outside* the kitchen and marital bed, were changing.

Young females talked of independence and careers, of emancipation and equality. They demanded to be allowed to follow the same paths as their brothers, not in ones or twos, as had previously been the case, but in their thousands. It was their right to become doctors, lawyers, or whatever fancy took them, they said. Suffragettes still suffered and died to achieve equal voting rights for their sisters; for universal franchise for women of all ages, but Kate and Jenny, who had no interest in politics, and even less in having the right to vote, were barely aware of this struggle. They knew nothing of such things in their male dominated, working class world. Just to have their freedom from Henry was enough.

They plucked their eyebrows; wore French knickers, and rolled their stockings down to above the knee. They did the tango, and shingled their hair, and combed sugar water through it to keep the finger waves stiff and intact, turning 'spit' curls to lie flat on each cheek. Over this concoction of tortured waves, they wore cloche hats. From the shoulder to the bone of their ankles, their bodies resembled a tube, flat and boy-like, with the waist upon their hips. Busts were flattened and the effect was of a slim boy dressed as a girl. Jenny, who was fine-boned and slender looked superb in the simple lines of the fashion, but Kate, whose robust figure was frankly that of a woman, had more trouble in hiding the lovely curve of her breast and hip.

From throat to knee they hung ropes of cheap beads, which fell in splendid, dangerously swinging abandon, and on each wrist jangled a dozen bracelets.

Amongst a crowd of chattering look-alikes, they went dancing at the Grafton Rooms, and the Mecca Dance Hall in Dale Street. They were dazzled by Gertie Gitana, Shaun Glenville and Dorothy Ward, who appeared at the Pavilion – known locally – and fondly – as the 'Pivvy'. Just to boast that they had been, they even sat through a performance of Shakespeare's *As you like it* at the Olympia, and understood not a word.

They had their photographs taken at Gale's, two roundfaced, darkhaired young girls, their eyes shy and smiling into the camera.

In the smoke-filled excitement of the 'Rialto' they swooned with millions of others around the world, under the flashing eyes and flaring nostrils of Valentino, the restless ebullience of Fairbanks, the flamboyance of Pola Negri, and the sentimental humour and spirit of Mary Pickford.

But it was Saturday night which was the summit of the week on which their eyes were eagerly focused. They lived for it; looked forward to it with an intensity which set their lives, making a pattern of increasing excitement from Sunday morning when it was done, until Saturday when it would begin again. Swarming on to the New Brighton ferry, two small units in a vast machinery which had one function, that of wringing every ounce of enjoyment from this special night. Their faces might have come from the same mould, and their voices peaked with the thrill of it all. The music was enough to shatter the ear drum, clamorous and out of this world, and the dances which were performed to it were lusty, full of vigour, and done with a zest which left the participants wilting and drained, like oranges from which all the juice had been sucked. They snapped their fingers, rotated their hips, and kicked their feet high in the air.

It was the beginning of the Jazz Age.

The sisters had never known the heady thrill of freedom before and in an ecstasy of daring, they declined to sip it, but gulped great draughts, which filled their heads and young hearts with the intoxication which had swept the country in the aftermath of war.

Freedom.

The people had fought for it, and won, and so had Kate and Jenny. They had fought Henry Fowler and beaten him. Their world was their own now, theirs and the other young people with whom they danced and played. Kate and Jenny had scarcely been conscious of the war, but their men had fought in it – their John and Eddy had both been in the trenches in France – and women too, and they believed they had the right to live and be free to think for themselves. They were in love with their way of life, with their world, and the people in it.

They had not seen their father since they had walked out of the shop nearly three months ago. Carrying a suitcase each, and their heads held high, and dressed in the good black costumes bought for them by Henry for their mother's funeral, they had made their way through the throng of well-wishers, whose dinner hour had been made more enjoyable by the spectacle they had just witnessed. The drama had entranced Henry's customers, and their initial annoyance at the late opening was soon dissipated by the entertainment. As good as the Gish sisters any day, they agreed and hands had touched the girls' shoulders as Kate and Jenny passed through the crowd. Faces had smiled encouragingly, and cries of, 'Good luck, Queen', 'Yer done right, Missus' and 'Give the old bastard what for', swirled about them as they left under the hail of goodnatured raillery and appreciative whistles.

42

Their timid hearts had bumped in their breasts as they stood for the last time in the doorway of the chippie, and for a fraction of a second Kate's foot had hesitated as she considered the cold, unnerving fact that from now on she was responsible, not only for herself, but for their Jenny. She had no illusions about that. Whatever she did, she must do also for Jenny. Kate had turned her head at the door, and the admiring face of Bobby, her twin, a man, but still under his father's hand, smiled at her, and he had winked. His teeth shone in his sweat-streaked face, and he had mouthed some words at her.

'Good luck, our kid. See yer at Elly's.'

The small gesture had given her courage.

She could see Ah-ah Gertie quivering like a blade of grass in a wind at the back of the shop, crying in nervous fear as the angry words just spoken rang still in her almost empty head. But Gertie kept on with the constant dip, wash and rinse of the greasy dishes. Kate could see the bewilderment on her face, and the questioning look as if to ask who was to wipe the ever growing pile of clean plates on the draining board by her side.

Kate wondered, too, and a shaft of pity for the old woman almost stopped her. Then Henry was hot on their heels, eager to show the customers his opinion of such ingratitude, and after all he had done. He banged the door shut behind then, rubbing his hands together as if to say, 'Good riddance to bad rubbish', and returned to his stool behind the tall cash register. His manner said plainly that he had done with them.

Kate and Jenny stayed with Elly and Pat. But not for long. The O'Reillys had not had much pleasure out of life, but one of them had been making babies. Not that they clutched each other with that specific purpose in mind, but the end result was the same, nevertheless. In the ten years of their marriage, Elly had given birth ten times. As she said, she had only to sit in a chair which her Pat had just vacated, to become pregnant, but of her ten pregnancies, only five had delivered live children. Even so the tiny house in Saint Domingo Road was filled to the rafters with seven people, five of them noisy, quarrelsome, and cheerfully Irish like their Dad, and when Kate and Jenny turned up, and requested a bed for a few nights, Elly had been hard pushed to be polite.

She was haphazardly fond of her sisters for they had been generous with her. As they grew older they had minded her babies, and were always willing to slip her a few spuds or a piece of cod when Henry's back was turned, but she and the man had just had an 'up and downer', over money as usual, and the sight of her

43

two pretty sisters, smiling hopefully at her front door, had not been a welcome one. On top of that she had just returned from the pawnshop, where she had been forced to pop her wedding ring. Not for the first time, admittedly, but it was a symbol of the days when she and Pat had been full of youthful hope and the expectation of newlyweds, and it grieved her to see it leave her finger. She was not sentimental; she had that knocked from her long since, but some faint memory of the way they had been, filled her with regret. She was sharp with Kate, exasperated, but reluctantly she took them in, moving a couple of children over in the big bed on the top floor, and the few bob slipped her helped to ease the inconvenience.

It was Charlie Walker who found the lodgings. He was their Jimmy's friend, and had been best man at their John's wedding, and it was there that Kate had become friendly with him. Charlie was a merchant seaman, and though he had known her since their schooldays he had scarcely been aware of Kate until their Jimmy had taken him home one Saturday after the match. She had been only fifteen then, but he had liked her bonny, good looks and lively manner, and whilst he ate the fish and chips she cooked for them, his eyes had followed her well-rounded figure, lingering on her swelling bosom and trim ankle. She had caught his glance and he had been the one to blush and look away. Not that she was bold, he told himself. Not Kate. Honest was a word he would have used to describe her. Straightforward. Forthright, but not bold. He had waited patiently for her to grow up and notice him, but so far she had treated him as she would any friend of her brothers.

Over a cup of tea in Elly's kitchen, and glad of the chance to shine in Kate's eyes, he told them about the rooms.

'It's not what yer used to, mind, and probably needs a bit of a scrub, an' p'raps a lick o' paint, but I could help yer there.'

His clear, grey sailor's eyes were bright with admiration and Kate bridled self-consciously. She knew she'd clicked with Charlie, but she wasn't ready for the sort of arrangement he wanted. Not yet. He was nice. Quiet and a bit shy with the lasses. Not the kind of outgoing chap she usually found attractive, but he was . . . nice, and it never hurt to keep a chap in tow. He was pleasant looking. Not flashy, but she wanted a bit of fun before she settled down. Not half. She hadn't even nibbled at the freedom she hungered for, let alone tasted it, but she would keep him in mind, she thought absently.

So the girls moved into thirty-six Seacomb Street.

It was filthy. When the light was turned on, a tide of cockroaches

44

swept back towards the four corners of the scullery, like waves retreating from the beach. It took a week of scrubbing; six bottles of lysol and gallons of water heated laboriously on the roaring fire; three pots of whitewash and two tins of paint before they were satisfied that the three rooms were fit to live in. With Elly eagerly flagging them on, longing to get back to the careless disorder of her life, they were finally ensconced in their new home.

The job was easy. Lily Donaldson helped them there. She was a waitress at Wagstaffe's in Dale Street. She and Kate had been in the same class at Toxteth Street school, and in the chance fashion of friends when school days are done, had met from time to time. At their last encounter, on the corner of West Derby Road and Fedora Street, where Kate had been despatched to fetch a pint of guinness from the Old Swan for her father's dinner, Lily had told her that 'Waggy', as he was known, was looking for staff. Kate had been barely interested at the time for her mother had still been alive, and no thought of working anywhere but the chip shop had ever occurred to her, but the memory of the conversation, had returned to her when the question of employment had become urgent.

Waitresses were required to be reasonably pretty, neat, able to chat politely with customers, work hard for ten hours a day, and to have feet that could bear weight upon them uncomplainingly for twelve.

Mr Wagstaffe – he was to be given his full title to his face – had taken one look at the personable young sisters standing nervously before him, and in his nasal 'scouse' voice, had declared that they would do a treat.

'I'll pay yer twelve bob a week, plus tips, an' yer'll get yer dinner thrown in. Lily'll show yer t'ropes, an' yer can start on Monday.'

It was hard work, but no worse than the chippie, and the delight of answering to no one, of doing exactly as they pleased, of spending their money just as they fancied, was heady stuff. They very quickly got the hang of which 'station' belonged to whom; how to set out the tables assigned to them; to be polite without cheekiness to the lady customers, though many of the male diners were titillated by a bit of cheek, and to run about all day long on feet which gradually swelled and throbbed, so that by the end of the shift, a shoe would leave an imprint in the puffy flesh from which it had just been prised.

They loved it.

Lily was a brick. She was a true Scouser, born in the Pool of Welsh and Irish antecedents, and she had the garrulity of one and the wit of the other. Cheeky and pert, like a brightly feathered sparrow, with flaming red hair and knowing breasts and bottom, she used all her female tricks indiscriminately on every man within a radius of half a mile. They responded to her rougish good humour by making her the recipient of the best tips of all the girls who worked for Waggy. Twopence or threepence was considered fair, but Lily was often in receipt of a tanner from some gentleman who left feeling his dinner hour had been enriched by the sauce he had been given, and not on his plate. Her teeth would gleam between her Clara Bow lips, and her eyebrows, plucked into a look of perpetual astonishment, would lift even higher as her pseudo innocent remarks, leaving no man in doubt of her meaning, tantalised the customers on the top floor. It was here that she shone, the brightest star in the firmament, for lady customers were not allowed beyond the first floor, and Waggy, no slouch where business was concerned, had the sense to keep the impudent minx where she could do most good.

Her goodnatured friendship and willingly given help smoothed the sisters' path in the first few weeks of their new job. She was easygoing and for all her apparent indolence and the time she spent back-chatting the customers, she worked hard.

There were two overlapping shifts. Seven am to five in the afternoon, and two until midnight. The girls learned to lay out the tables with crisp, white tablecloths and sparkling cutlery; to clean the cutlery and the cruet sets, and to skip nimbly from kitchen to table and back again, carrying without apparent effort a tray piled precariously with a dozen plates of steaming hot food straight from the oven, and all with the grace of a ballet dancer, and the strength of a road layer. They learned to smile and dimple at compliments whilst stunned with exhaustion, to chat amiably and to answer the sometimes suggestive remarks directed at them with deft good humour. The trick was to wisecrack in return, but at the same time give the impression that one was a good girl, and not available for any of the hinted propositions put to them.

Kate became adept at this, and with Lily and Josie, another girl whose bantering and lively attractions appealed to the men she served, took over the top floor, making more tips in a day than Jenny made in a week.

But it was not for Jenny. She would blush and stammer and was so taken aback at the laughing invitation to show a customer her wares when she politely asked him what she could do for him, that she burst into tears and handed in her notice. Mr Wagstaffe, realising sensibly that not all girls were capable of the ribaldry that took place on the top floor, moved her downstairs where her sweet

46

shyness and polite civility charmed the morning coffee and afternoon tea ladies, and the old gentlemen who were past the demands of sexuality, and its attendant titivation.

Now it was nearly spring, and the girls were becoming used to their new way of life. Their first timid overtures with budgets and rents, with bills, and wages, had been successfully overcome and they were confident, pleased with themselves and the way in which they managed. With two wages, tips and the main meal of the day to be had at Waggy's, they felt themselves to be quite affluent, and with the thrill of a Vanderbilt or Woolworth investing to make their first million, had even opened a post office savings account into which they each put sixpence a week. They were flushed with the success of it all, and, with the optimism of youth, were convinced that the world was their oyster, and that pearls galore would continue to fall into their lap.

'Is it out again tonight, our kid?'

Kate started as the sleepy, questioning sound of her sister's voice broke the silence of the room. She had been nearly asleep herself in the depths of the elegantly battered armchair, her head nodding, the empty mug resting on the slight mound of her stomach. Her eyes blinked open and she looked across at Jenny. Jenny's were closed now, and her head rested on the back of the chair, but a small smile of satisfaction still wreathed her face. She looked tired though.

'Yer look all in, chuck,' Kate said, not answering Jenny's question. 'Yer want to be away to yer bed.'

Jenny yawned and opened her eyes and the rocking chair creaked and set itself in motion. The cat lifted its head and stared from one girl to the other, then stretched, her legs quivering, her gentle purring rolling in the back of her throat.

'I am wacked,' Jenny replied, 'an' I think I will have an early night. Yer should've seen the crowd of old dears we 'ad in today, an' all at the same time. I must 'ave served tea an' cakes two 'undred times. Must be Easter comin' on, or summat. 'An racin' up and down those stairs trying to keep Waggy's hands off me bum doesn't help.'

Kate laughed. It was not like their Jenny to talk 'cheeky', but she knew what she meant. Waggy was harmless enough, but he did like a bit of a feel now and then and if he caught a girl ahead of him on the stairs she must be nippy on her feet to avoid his friendly hand.

Jenny yawned again, and stretched her feet out before her, her toes moving gently over the soft fur of the droning cat. She was

47

mesmerised by the heat of the fire and the sweet peace of the room. Her eyes half closed again and her face, rosy with a child's glow which comes before sleep, puckered like that of a kitten about to sneeze. She burrowed her back deeper into the floppy cushions and tucking her feet beneath her, she resumed her half-waking, half-dreaming contemplation of the fire.

The doorbell rang sharply, piercing the tranquillity with its clamour.

Kate sat up, taken by surprise.

'Oh, my God, that'll be Charlie.' Flustered, pleased, pretending to be vexed at his promptness, she ran up the narrow hallway to open the door.

Chapter Five

Charlie Walker could remember the exact moment when he had fallen in love with Kate Fowler. She had been a part of his life for as long as he could remember, but she had been the sister of his 'wacker', and hardly to be noticed as she strayed on the edge of his awareness when he went to call for their Jimmy.

He and Jimmy had shared a desk at school. They had grown up together, doing the things that boys do; getting into scrapes and out again; scrumping apples; playing 'footie' in the street; tying door knockers together on opposite sides of the street; fighting; teasing the girls in the school yard, and 'saggin' from school as often as they could manage without the Inspector hauling them to justice. They had stood together in all weathers on the terraces of Goodison Park, cast into the deepest well of despondency when the 'toffeemen' had been beaten, and joyously capering, back slapping and bursting with pride when Everton beat Wolves, or Arsenal, or Manchester United.

As puberty took hold their attentions had suddenly been drawn to the opposite sex. They had stood in milling groups on street corners, smoking, laughing foolishly in voices breaking and squeaking to shrillness over nothing, eyeing the lasses and whistling manfully at anything in a skirt. They made men's jokes in an aside behind boy's hands, and felt themselves to be fine fellows.

But no one made jokes about the Fowler girls. Not with their Jimmy and Charlie amongst them.

When Charlie reached the age of thirteen, he had left school and gone to sea as a galley boy. Charlie had taken to the work and had harboured aspirations to become a cook. He had enjoyed the life. The freedom from his Mam's apron strings, and the places he visited impressed his young mind and broadened the limited outlook his upbringing had imposed upon him.

Soon after Charlie went to sea, a boy hardly older than himself fired a shot which was to set in motion the dread wheels of war. Charlie scarcely noticed the event. It is doubtful that he was even aware of it. His life went on as before.

When he was sixteen he signed for a trip on the *SS Franconia* and in August of that year, his world had almost ended when she was sunk by a submarine. Charlie, along with most of the crew, could not swim, but somehow, clinging to a piece of wreckage which he was never to identify for he was numb with terror, managed to stay afloat and was picked up after two hours in the water.

The experience was to have a great influence on Charlie's young and carefree mind, and he was never quite the same again. When you have stared death in the face, and thought you would never see your Mam again, it takes the boyishness from you with sickening speed. He became quiet and introspective for a while, taking seriously what his peers joked about. He cared more for his mother and sister, and was considerate of their feelings. He still went to see Everton play when he was home, but the cheerful banter of his cronies sometimes made him scornful, though he could not say why. His sense of humour deserted him, and he was considered a bit 'odd' by his pals.

But the inherent strength of his character, passed on to him by his mother; the inevitable healing passage of time which takes the sting from all hurt and dulls the memory of what seemed an unforgettable horror, brought back his sense of perspective. His own fairness – how could those who stay at home know anything of violence and sudden death – made him see the episode with the clarity which comes with maturity, and his appreciation of a bit of a lark returned to him. Once more his whimsical merriment delighted those who knocked about with him.

Nevertheless, under the cheerful exterior, he was to remain a quiet man, and a thoughtful one. It was as though the brush with death had checked his heedless confidence in his own immortality, and had given him a respect for the feelings of others. He was generous to a fault.

For six years he moved about the oceans of the world, his meeting with near extinction not dashing his love of the sea. He went to New York and Montreal; to St Johns in Newfoundland, and to Philadelphia, and even, for a bit of a change, on a luxury cruiser to the West Indies.

He was nineteen when he really saw Kate for the first time. And loved her. Fifteen she had been and as fresh as a newly minted coin. Her young figure was the best it would ever be, for she was later to become plump, but now her waist was tiny; he could have spanned it with his hands, and her hips flowed from it with a youthful sweetness. She had worn a plain striped blouse and an ankle length black skirt. The skirt barely reached her well turned ankle which was encased in a fine black stocking, but it was her lovely thrusting breast which caught his eye. He could see the peak of her nipples through the thin cotton of her camisole and blouse and his breath had become ragged with an emotion which he recognised immediately. He had never loved a lass before, and was never to love another, but he knew it when it came. Charlie believed implicitly in the words, 'He never loved who loved not at first sight' and it was the first time he had really seen Kate, he told himself.

He could scarcely wait for her to grow up.

But she did, and at their John's wedding in 1921, he had held her in his arms for the first time. Eighteen she was then, and already her girlish figure was filling out into the matronly curves, sweet and wholly delightful to Charlie, which were to be hers into middle age and beyond. They had romped through the polka and the Gay Gordons together, their cheeks red, blue and grey eyes sparkling and mouths wide with laughter. Her sweet breath, slightly laced with port, had fanned his cheek and intoxication at her nearness had made him bold. He had kept his hold on her, and in a fumbling, flat-footed sway and dip, for Charlie was no dancer, they had moved around the floor in a slow foxtrot. It was heaven and hell to the young sailor. The proximity and feel of her softness under his hands had made him lusty with longing, but the innocence of her, apparent despite the provocative look she gave him – port induced – made him careful of her. Her father's eye, disapproving, had been upon them, and Charlie had retreated shyly after reluctantly relinquishing the lovely feel of her to another.

From then on, and up until the death of her mother, he had skirted the fringes of her attention, coming and going at the dictates of his seaman's life, sailing each time into Liverpool with his heart thumping in dread for fear that when he saw her again she would be wearing some other chap's ring.

Now her mother was dead and Kate was out on her own. True she had their Jenny with her, but she was away from the protection, – no that wasn't the word he wanted – it sounded as if he was going to take advantage of her defencelessness, but she was no longer hedged about by her family; by her father's constant presence and watched over by his possessive eye. Now Charlie would have the chance to court her openly, let her know his intentions. She would probably play the reluctant miss for a while, still pot valiant with the freedom she had never known before. He knew she would want to get about with her friends, go dancing. Probably see other chaps too. The thought lanced him, but somehow he felt

51

that if he let the halter lie loose in his fingers, did not try to rein her into a sedate walk, she would settle one day to the harness of marriage.

He smiled to himself at his own phraseology. You'd think he'd ridden to hounds with the gentry. All this talk of bridles and reins and halters.

But he wanted to marry her. He wanted to settle down, and more than anything in the world he wanted to tell her so, but something held him back. He sensed that she liked him, more than she knew. He felt that if he could be patient, let her play for a while, she would become aware of the bond which was growing betweeen them. On her own, with no prompting from him. Let her have her head for a few months, he had decided. She had only been away from her father's dominance for a short while; she was enjoying her small measure of independence, making decisions for herself and Jenny, being at no one's beck and call. She wanted to be Kate Fowler, not Henry Fowler's daughter, nor Charlie Walker's wife. So what if she did like a bit of fun with other blokes, there was no more to it than that. Of that he was certain. She wasn't bad, not his Kate. She was a maid now, and would be on her wedding night. But he meant to be the man to alter that. Choose how.

But she did love a good night out and he was away for so long. Who could expect a sweet, lively girl like Kate to sit at home waiting. She was not ready yet, but she soon would be and he meant to be there, in her direct line of vision, when she was.

He'd taken her out a time or two since he had helped her and Jenny to move into their flat. Painted a ceiling for her and put a washer on a leaky tap. Though she was barely conscious of it, he was inching his way, cautiously, into her life. He made himself useful – being there when she needed a shelf knocking up or a night out at the pictures. She'd grown used to the thought of having him around, of . . . He could not pin down the vague drift of his mind or the ideas which filled it but he smiled again. It was like trying to fetter a mettlesome colt, he told himself wryly, and shook his head, amused. There he went again, he who'd never sat a horse in his life, but somehow the words seemed to fit exactly the meaning of the thoughts in his head.

The street was almost empty as he walked along it. A woman with a shawl about her head hurried past, a jug in her hand, her seamed face like a pale walnut in the flickering light from the gas street mantles. She held the thin fabric of her shawl closely about her, and her clogged feet clacked the flagstones as she scuttled in the direction of the boozer on the corner.

52

Two men in cloth caps and mufflers argued passionately the merits of last Saturday's match as they stood in the entrance to the snicket which lay between their homes. One had a bicycle, and he leaned it against the wall of the terraced house to more easily fling his arms about in a point of contradiction.

'. . . an' it shurra bin a bluddy penalty . . .'

Charlie heard the middle of the sentence as he passed and he smiled, for there was nothing a Scouser loved more than to cross swords on the subject of football.

Then he was there, at Kate's door, and his heart beat louder than the rap of his knuckles on the wood.

Kate opened the door to him, and the sight of her, rosy and rumpled from her doze by the fireside, took the breath from his lungs and the words from his lips.

Whipping his cap from his head, he held it in his brown hands, turning it round and round and round. His goodnatured face beamed and his pale grey eyes shone from a network of fine, crinkly lines which radiated outwards to the top of his ears. His skin was tanned from a hundred encounters with hot Pacific suns and freezing Atlantic winds. His teeth were big, even and creamy, slightly prominent, giving his mouth a full generous appearance. He was slim, not tall and his thick wavy hair was the colour of the brown ale which he drank. His expression was one of shy diffidence, combined with admiration for Kate.

'Kate,' he said tenderly, his heart in his eyes.

'Charlie.' Kate's pulses gave a tiny, almost imperceptible quiver under her skin and she was startled.

There was a pause and Charlie's cap whizzed around like a catherine wheel. His feet shuffled, doing a small dance of embarrassment on the gritty surface of the pavement.

'Well, Kate,' he said, and his grin became a trifle strained. Was she going to keep him on t'doorstep all night?

Kate seemed to be in a trance. She could feel her eyes fixed on Charlie's face as though she had not seen it before. Indeed, she could not remember noticing in the past what an unusual shade of grey his eyes were, so pale, as if the bright sunlight in which he sailed had bleached the colour from them. There was a lovely, crystal shine to them, almost silver and the bronzed smoothness of his freshly shaved skin set them off a treat. He really was quite – she was going to say handsome – then changed it in her mind to *agreeable*.

With a startled exclamation, her face flaming, she became aware that Charlie was shuffling about like a cat on hot coals, and no wonder. Here she was gawping like a landed fish, as if Valentino himself was on her front door step, and her with her hair all over the place, and not even washed. It was just that he seemed . . . different all of a sudden. There was something that had changed in him, some indefinable something that she had not seen before.

Blushing, she stepped back and opening the door wide, indicated with her hand for him to step inside.

'Come in,' she said, and her voice quivered.

Charlie stepped eagerly over the doorstep and Kate closed the door on the gathering dusk. The streetlight fell through the fan light above the door, bathing the passage in a half shadowy dusk. For a moment they were close together and Charlie's hands lifted, his cap still clutched in one, as if to clasp her to him, then fell back to his sides. His eyes, gleaming in the pale darkness searched hers questioningly, but at the last moment, she drew back, still not ready for the commitment his were demanding. Confused, she turned and hurried up the narrow hallway and burst into the mellow warmth of the kitchen, with such force that Jenny rose up in her chair alarmed.

'It's Charlie, our Jenny,' Kate said loudly, surprised by her own agitation. What was up with her? She'd known Charlie for years, since she was a kid, and here she was acting like some daft loon from one of those penny romances their Jenny brought home. It was only Charlie. She'd been out with him a few times. Enjoyed it. But there had been nothing else. Not even a kiss.

Jenny was talking to Charlie, giving her time to pull herself together.

'. . . Did yer get back then, Charlie?'

'Came in on't tide this after,' Charlie replied. He liked Jenny. She was a shy little thing, quiet and not a bit like their Kate. But she was so pretty. Delicate like. She and Kate were of the same colouring. Dark hair but there the resemblance ended. Jenny's eyes were brown, Kate's blue. Where Kate was blooming, bountiful, like a showy rose in the centre of a garden, Jenny was fragile, creamy skinned, a snowdrop which might be trodden under foot if care was not taken.

After waiting to see if anything more was to be said, and when it became apparent that it was not, Jenny tried again. She recognised that Charlie was as bashful as herself and this fact helped to boost her own tiny reserve of self confidence.

'How long this time then, Charlie?'

'Four days.'

'Not long.'

54

'No.'

Charlie wished that he could think of some clever thing to say but his brain was blank. Put him amongst the lads on board, or in the pub and his quick wit would keep them laughing all day long, but here, with these pretty judies, he was as tonguetied as a boy.

The sleek tabby leapt like a bird from the armchair where it had settled itself when Kate had gone to answer the door. It entwined its sinuousness between the man's legs and he bent to stroke the smooth fur and pull the twitching ears, glad of the diversion.

For a few seconds there was a thin silence broken only by the rapturous purring of the cat. The sisters looked at each other over Charlie's head. He was away so often, and for so long, it was always difficult to fall back into the easy familiarity which would return just as he was about to leave again.

Jenny made another effort.

'How's yer Mam, Charlie and your Annie?'

Charlie still fiddled with the cat, his face a blaze of colour.

'Fine thanks, Jenny.'

The conversation faltered and stopped completely. Kate moved restlessly from one foot to the other, watching Charlie, feeling that something more should be said, wishing that he would stop messing about with the damn moggy. After all, he'd been away a month or so, and now all he could do was play with the cat as if it was the apple of his eye. He was supposed to be sweet on her, wasn't he? Wasn't that why he was here, after all? He'd hardly looked at her since he came into the room and she felt . . . what the hell did she feel?

Then she knew. It was like a tiny darting bird when it came. A swallow perhaps, or a humming bird. No clap of thunder, or great blaring trumpets like in books. Suddenly, as if in some mysterious way she was standing outside of herself, watching and listening to the thoughts of the *real* Kate; as though her mind, severed from her emotions and therefore unbiased, had told her the truth. She knew.

She loved this man. It was as simple as that.

Out of nowhere the knowledge was there, and she understood in the time it took for Charlie's hand to travel from the cat's head to its twitching tail, why she felt as petulant as a child deprived of a bag of sweeties.

She was jealous.

She was jealous of the bloody cat. She wanted Charlie's attentions turned to her. She wanted his eyes, those cool grey eyes, to be warming in her direction.

She nearly laughed out loud with the joy and the humour and the sheer lunacy of her own foolishness. She was standing watching a man stroke a cat and she was all 'mardy' because he wasn't paying any attention to her.

She wanted to say, 'Look at *me* Charlie, leave the blasted cat alone and look at me. Look at me with those extraordinary eyes of yours and let me feel that melting in the bones of me that I felt when I opened the door to you. Warm me with your regard and touch me with a look of love.'

Instead she said, 'I'll go and get ready then, Charlie.'

He glanced up as she spoke and was surprised by the look on her face. It was an expression he hadn't seen before and he didn't recognise it. Not then.

He stood up and brushed the creases from his trousers, and, not knowing what to do with it, put his cap back on his head. He pushed his hands in his pockets and tried a confident whistle from between dry lips. His eye lit on the picture of the Grecian lady and he moved across the room and began to study it as he might the football fixtures on the back page of the *Echo*.

Kate left the room, smiling now, in the way that women have when they love and know they are loved. There is no smile like it in the world, and no feeling more exquisite. It comes to most, perhaps once, and for a short while – or a lifetime – the world is warm, and lovely and completely perfect.

Kate shivered as the cooler air of the hallway struck her skin, but the serenity of her expression did not falter. She closed the door behind her and entered the tiny bedroom which was just big enough to hold the double bed, an antiquated wardrobe, dark and forbidding with a full length mirror in the central door, and a chest of drawers on which the girls had stuck an assortment of ornaments and knickknacks from the bedroom which they had shared at West Derby Road.

Two weeks previously Bobby had come round to say that the following Saturday Henry would be gone from the house. It was Grand National Day, and though Henry didn't as a rule have much interest in horseracing he did like the 'jumps'. This year he could saunter round openly with the young widow on his arm and he meant to make the most of it. He would be away for the day.

The girls had crept nervously into their old home, glancing over their shoulders, not quite convinced that Henry would not jump out from behind the cellar door, or from the yard, whilst their backs were turned. They tiptoed up the stairs, hesitating for a moment at the door of the room in which their mother had slept and died, and for a tremulous moment they had smelled the lavender she had used, and heard her quiet voice.

Then, hurrying on into the room which had once known all their secrets, and held them securely from early childhood, they gathered the remainder of their clothes and the trinkets and souvenirs which were dear to them, many of them brought by Elizabeth from her home in Matlock. If for no other reason they were treasured.

Now, placed about their new home they gave it an aura of familiarity, of permanence.

Kate whistled softly through her teeth at the same time smiling a lot, the smile of the lover, as she changed from her neat waitress's uniform into a lightweight woollen suit, the colour of ripe plums. The skirt reached her ankles and the loose top pouched over at hip level. She wore high-heeled shoes with long pointed toes, and, after a moment's deliberation and critical examination of her own reflection in the mirror, wrapped a soft, multicoloured headband about her brow, tying it in a fetching knot above one ear. She examined her silk stockings for ladders and adjusted them in a roll above her knee. A dab of face powder, a smear of lipstick, a lick of vaseline on her eyebrows and she was ready.

She smiled at herself in the mirror.

'Not bad, our kid, not bad,' she whispered impishly, and almost ran from the bedroom in her eagerness to bathe once more in Charlie's loving smile.

Charlie could not keep his eyes from straying from the antics of the world's funniest man to the laughing girl at his side. The screen flickered, making a rippling pattern of light and shadow on her face, from which her bright eyes flashed. She was the girl of his youthful dreams, the fantasy of womanliness for which all men long, and his flesh hungered for her. He wanted to touch her. The feeling was so strong that his hand, with a mind apart from the one which usually controlled it, stole across the armrest between them and diffidently rested against hers as it lay on her lap. She gave him a swift look, startled, but not unwilling and allowed him to curl his fingers around hers.

He was enraptured.

He had made the first move and she had not repulsed him. His mind soared and the building rocked and the crowd shouted with laughter, but the silence in Charlie's head was filled with images of himself and Kate. He held her hand as sweetly as though it were a child's, yet the passion, lusty and of the earth, tingled through his fingers to hers, returning a thousandfold, to penetrate every part of his man's body. He wanted her so much, just from that brief touch of their clasped hands, that he felt the warmth in his belly stir and he moved uneasily in his seat. Kate was laughing with the rest of the audience at the celluloid Charlie, as he tripped and stumbled and miraculously recovered to best the 'baddie' as always. The piano at the front of the cinema was rippling the pertinent music for the scene but Charlie Walker was impervious to everything but Kate. He gently pressed her hand in his and she turned again for a second, looking at him, still laughing, her eyes like beacons in the dark.

He loved her absolutely.

They walked away from the cinema in the brisk freshness of the early spring night. The clouds were torn and ragged as they raced across the cerulean darkness, silvered at the edges by the light from the scattering of stars. The streetlamps made bobbing circles of radiance at regular intervals on the pavement as the wind tossed them.

The chattering, chuckling crowd, still transfused by the magic of the clown who had captured the hearts of the world with his brilliance, carried the pair back towards the Pier Head.

Kate was talking, laughing, recalling moments from the film, all inhibitions gone now as they shared the memory of the past few hours. Charlie smiled at her happy face, her radiance infecting him to a certain sureness that he could do anything if he only had Kate by his side. He loved her good humour. Nothing ever seemed to get her down. She was never beaten. She was strong and staunch and trustworthy. She'd had a hard life, working from dawn to dusk under her father's opressive influence. She'd earned, unfairly, many a clout from his heavy fist; she'd nursed her mother with loving patience, and from an early age protected and stood up for their Jenny as if the girl were her own child and not her sister. She had a fierce loyalty towards those she loved, and no matter what, she'd stick to you through thick and thin. He respected her for that. She was his good and bonny lass and he wanted her, and if it meant taking their Jenny and all to get her, he'd do it.

They boarded the tram car at the Pier Head, sitting side by side, stiff with each other again now, constrained as the feeling of oneness, brought out by the spell of Chaplin, shredded away.

They were as all lovers are. Unsure; torn in one moment between confidence in the other's love, and in the next, in the certainty that they were foolish to imagine that they should find favour in the beloved's eyes. Up and down the seesaw went, and with it, the conversation, the familiarity, and the sense of ease which comes only with time.

They walked slowly along Seacomb Street, and as they approached the front door of the small terraced house, identical to all the others in the street, their footsteps slowed even further, echoing against the flat front of the houses.

Trying for careless sophistication, Kate said, 'Will yer come in, Charlie, and I'll make yer a cup of cocoa? It's a long walk 'ome for yer.'

Charlie, elated, needed no second bidding, and was straight in behind her as she opened the front door. Jenny had gone to bed, but the fire was still glowing and the kitchen was warm and cosy after the cool of the night. He sat in the rocker and the cat appeared from nowhere to settle herself in a plethora of newfound friendship on his lap, turning and twisting like a silken eel until she found a position she considered most comfortable.

Charlie felt he was in heaven.

Kate lowered herself into the chair opposite, handing him a mug of fragrant cocoa, the creamy centre still circling from the vigorous stirring it had received. They sat in silence sipping the cocoa, their glances occasionally meeting, their lips smiling shyly, only their eyes speaking.

More than anything in the world Charlie wanted to tell Kate that he loved her; that he wanted her to marry him but something held him back. He sensed that she felt the same way about him; perhaps was not aware of it, but if he could be patient give her time, she would . . .

'What are you thinking about, Charlie?'

Charlie turned his head, looking directly into Kate's eyes. His thoughts had been of her, and, as though those thoughts had touched a response within her, even subconsciously, it was all there for him to see. All at once, everything he wanted to know was shining in her eyes.

He paused before he spoke. His heart surged in his chest and he felt that all he had to do was say the words. But still he held back. He smiled, and Kate felt her bones melt as his mouth lifted in an endearing lopsided grin.

'The future, lass,' he answered, 'but that's a long way ahead, and if I don't let yer get to yer bed, yer'll never get up in the morning.'

They rose from their chairs, and putting their empty mugs on the table, faced each other self-consciously. Charlie put out his hard brown hand and took hers, bringing it up to his lips. He was only a seaman, half-educated, with the rough goodhumoured characteristics of his class, but the gentle, delicate way in which he kissed the pulse in her wrist was worthy of the most experienced lover. Kate felt her knees tremble and her face went hot. She was sexually innocent, unawakened to the delights of fleshly love but the gesture set her blood moving and if Charlie had looked into her eyes at that moment, he would have seen a longing as great as his own. But he didn't.

He tenderly placed her hand back at her side and turned away so that she might not see the expression on his face.

'I'm away then love. I'll meet yer at Waggy's tomorrow,' he said confidently, knowing that something in their relationship had altered that night.

Kate stood for a delicious moment, her heart thumping against her ribs, then she drew a deep shuddering breath and turned to follow him towards the kitchen door.

'Righto, Charlie,' she said submissively. At the front door, he turned towards her and unconsciously she lifted her face for his expected kiss, their first, but she was to be disappointed. Charlie was getting the hang of knowing how to handle Kate and though it cost him much of his newfound composure, he pretended not to see.

'Goodnight love,' was all he said. He placed his cap on his head, tipping it once to her, then setting it at a jaunty angle on his warm brown curls.

'Goodnight Charlie.'

She watched him stride away down the street, disappearing and re-appearing, in and out of the circles of reflected street light. Finally, he was gone and although she waited until he had turned the corner, he didn't look back.

Feeling piqued she closed the door.

Chapter Six

Kate and Jenny quickly settled into their new way of life and the days and weeks sped by like sprinters eager to be first at the winning tape. April came, moving gently with all the time in the world. Trees greened with shy new leaves and grass pushed hesitantly through ground still hard with winter's chill. Colours of butter yellow and misty lilac, of foaming white, apple blossom pink and bluebell, changed the pallor of winter into the delicate tints of spring. May followed quickly and the gentle hues became more brilliant as summer tried to join the race and flaunt her vividness to the winter-tired inhabitants of the city.

But they saw none of this annual unfolding, these denizens of Netherfield and Everton, of Kirkdale and Sandhills. What did they know of daffodils and bluebells? Or even of budding trees? Their world was of tramcars and tracks, high buildings, their antiquity painted with the dirt of centuries; terraced houses and flagged pavements; pawnshops and pubs; horsedrawn drays piled high with barrels, the scream of children, clogs ringing; women in pinnies and shawls, cloth caps and mufflers, chips in newspapers. Cats round dustbins, and dogs barking.

They knew the clean, winking shine of freshly-washed windows and the rich red of newly 'stoned' steps. Not lilac they smelled, but the redolent aroma of freshly baked bread from Lunts. No cuckoos, but the irrepressible laughter of the cheerful men and women who inhabited these dismal, flowerless chasms. The banter, the good humour, was theirs and if one was so inclined and craned a stretching neck, a smear of bright and lovely blue could sometimes be seen, white-streaked between the sloping, slated rooftops of the crowded buildings.

They smelled the sea and the flat muddy stench of the river, and saw its wrinkled pewter greyness part in frothy cream as the ferry boats shuddered by. Seagulls shrieked and dived with their own breathtaking beauty, or hung in the windless grey sky reflected in the water. The Liver Birds grew whiter with their excrement but

61

from the ground they had a certain splendour as they watched over the great sea port.

They loved their city, the Liverpudlians.

The little flat in Seacomb Street quickly became the hub of Kate and Jenny's world, and gradually it took on the look of permanence, of home. Whenever they had a few bob to spare, they would spend hours turning over the contents of the local pawnbroker or secondhand shop, picking up pieces which appealed to them, bringing them home to be cleaned, or painted, or mended by Charlie.

One of these was a cuckoo clock, once the treasured possession of some woman fallen on hard times. The frame and face were in perfect condition, the painting, intricate and delicately lovely, still as bright as the day some craftsman in far off Switzerland had put it there, but the mechanism was rusted and broken. Charlie, who was really getting his feet under the table now, had taken it to pieces, oiled it, found bits to replace the ones missing, and put the whole together again.

He had hung it carefully on the kitchen wall and the three of them had waited anxiously for the hour to strike. At precisely five o'clock with a smooth whirr and a coy chuckling cuckoo, the bird had burst from its nest for the first time in years and triumphantly, as though glad to see the world again, and sounding a might intoxicated with its own resurrection, had informed them of the time of the day. Kate and Charlie, with Jenny between them had capered a jubilant polka around the kitchen table, arms clasped together in the excitement of youth.

Their brothers came, and Elly, and the three rooms would ring with laughter and singing as the family enjoyed itself as it had never done under Henry's roof.

On one of Charlie's trips home he had purchased a table gramophone with a pleated diaphragm which Kate confessed to Jenny with pride, cost £22.10s at Bunnys. 'Could you believe it? Twenty-two pounds ten just for a gramophone,' she said with mock annoyance. He could not resist spending his money on Kate, and with the records to go with it, *Dreamy Melody*, *Whose Baby are You?* and *Please do it again*, the small flat would vibrate to the sound of dancing feet and enthusiastic voices.

Charlie brought his shipmates, hoping that one of them might take a shine to Jenny, or, more importantly, that she would find herself taking a shine to him. It would be heavensent if she could be 'fixed up' and settle down before he married his Kate, but somehow, when he saw the gauche roughness of his mates placed beside the delicate loveliness of Kate's sister, he was forced to admit to himself that he was wasting his time and theirs. It was like putting a carthorse with a thoroughbred and expecting them to pull a plough together. They did their best, those easygoing seamen, only too eager to make up to the pretty girl, but Charlie could see from the corner where he stood, one arm possessively about Kate, that it was hard going, and was not surprised when Bill or Tommy or Fred moved on to the more familiar and racy banter of the animated Lily. Jenny was lovely, with the shy, understated beauty of a wild violet, but these men liked roses and geraniums, something with a bit of colour; someone who could wink, pout and share a joke; someone exactly like Lily.

Elly had transferred her cadging, on her mother's death, from the chip shop to her sisters' home, knowing full well that she would get nothing from her father but the flat of his hand and the edge of his tongue, though their Bob or Jimmy could sometimes be talked into parting with the occasional tanner. She would turn up on the girls' doorstep, her shoulders drooping, her face weary, sometimes sporting a black eye given her by her volatile Irish husband. On one occasion she held a suitcase. She sobbed that she had exchanged one tyrant for another and vowed that she would never return, but after two or three days in the neat, and to her mind, unnaturally tidy flat of her sisters, she would go back to the careless ease and familiar disorder of her own home, usually taking something which did not belong to her.

The last time, it was the girls' good black costumes bought for their mother's funeral. She left a pawn ticket and an apologetic note on the kitchen table.

Kate was wild, but it did no good. No one would ever change their Elly. Kate was aware of the uphill fight Elly had to rear her family of five and of the constant battle that warred with her quick tempered, hard drinking husband, to keep their money from the publican's till.

The days lengthened and thinking that winter was behind them, the city dwellers relaxed in anticipation of the summer to come but with the perversity for which the English weather is famous, it seemed that at the end of May, November had returned. It was cold and wet and windy. Through the damp dismal days of what purported to be summer the girls rose early to catch the tram to the city, hanging like thousands of others to the leather straps which dangled at intervals from the roof along the length of the car. The rattling vehicle would sway and bump its way along Scotland Road travelling with a speed which took everyone from their feet as it turned into Dale Street. The female company aboard laughed and chattered like a swarm of gaily-clothed parakeets as they greeted friends with the enthusiasm of voyagers long lost and returning from their travels though they had only parted the previous evening.

As they entered the cafe, Waggy would be waiting for them, insisting upon his privilege of inspecting each waitress as she took up her station. He enjoyed that, did Waggy. Seams must be straight up the centre of the back of a slim shapely leg; aprons crisp and snowy, tied around a trim waist, the bib fitting snugly over swelling breasts. Frilled caps needed adjustment on softly waved hair, and a girl knew she had passed the test when he patted her bottom, his creased face smiling in approbation, as she waggled her way from the kitchen to the dining room.

On the stroke of seven o'clock they began.

At precisely five o'clock, having been on their feet for ten hours with scarcely a break for a cup of tea, those going off would shrug wearily into their coats convinced that they were able only to crawl home and into their beds. But at the sight of Tom or Dick or Harry – or sometimes Charlie – their vigour would miraculously return, and a few hours later they would be tango-ing around the floor of the Mecca ballroom, or crowded in intimate rows in the company of Mack Sennett, Tom Mix or Clara Bow.

The days moved on, full and overflowing with content. Charlie came and went, always making straight for Seacomb Street as soon as his ship had docked. Kate's welcomes became warmer with every trip and encouraged by her growing accessibility and a certain languishing look in her eye, which he took to be a sign of willingness, he had begun to play the role of serious wooer, and the slow movement of courtship was beginning to take place. He knew the time was fast approaching when his Kate was ripe for plucking and though no words had as yet been spoken, and Kate pretended the line of coy resistance, both knew – and told each other with their eyes – that they were coming to it.

She had begun to sit patiently by her fireside, waiting for her man to return, no longer needing the excitement of other men's company. Hardly aware of the change in herself, the bob or two she used to fritter away on the inconsequential things beloved of young girls now were spent on – the words were never used but their meaning was known – her bottom drawer. A pretty embroidered traycloth, three matching teaspoons, real silver, from the market and a bargain, two pillowslips edged with lace, and a set of Indian cotton sheets, double bed size, which made her shiver deliciously just to hold them to her breast.

Charlie's kisses shy and soft at first, like those of a young and hesitant boy, had become ardent, more demanding, and her responses made him bold. No dancing, he said, looking her straight in the eye, the clear, pale greyness of his fixing her sternly. He wanted strict territorial borders laid down. He considered she was his property now and boundaries must be firmly placed. Pictures with Jenny or Lily, but no dancing. Compliantly she agreed.

Consequently Kate was not with Jenny when she met Nils Jorgensen.

It was a warm evening in September. As if the weather was ashamed of its poor performance during the summer, the last few days had been perfect. Warm and still and cloudless, the city basked in the unexpected gift so late in the year.

Light clothes which had been hardly out of the wardrobe for twelve months were hurriedly extracted from behind woollen coats and warm dresses, and washed in Rinso, ironed and worn with hearts suddenly lighter, as if the golden rays which poured generously from the blue sky, had filled them with its warmth and colour.

Kate was finishing the last of the ironing in the kitchen, humming to herself and spitting periodically on the flat iron to test its heat. As it cooled, she would remove a second from its stand above the glowing coal of the fire, holding the handle with a folded cloth, and putting the first in its place to heat in its turn. Backwards and forwards, spit and hiss, change and change about she worked, sweat staining the underarms of the blouse she wore. A sheen of perspiration dampened her brow and upper lip, testifying to the intense heat of the room, and she continually wiped her face with the edge of her apron as she worked.

A neat pile of freshly ironed blouses and aprons, frilly caps and cuffs, grew on the table beside her. Although windowless, the room was bright with the last rays of the evening sun which poured in a bright brassy stream through the large skylight in the scullery, falling in a dust-filled lambency between the two rooms. The skylight window stood wide open to catch a chance breeze, and the cat was perched on its very edge, drowsing, eyes half-closed, ears pricked to the last quietening chitter of the sparrows.

Kate moved heavily into the scullery and filled a jug with water from the tap. For a moment or two she stood in the cooler air, savouring the feel of it on her flushed face. She looked up, craning

65

her neck to catch a glimpse of the patch of sky which could just be seen over the scabby rooftops. It was the pale, pale blue of a hyacinth, and at its edge, blurring the clear cut line of the rooftops, it faded to lemon and apricot. The sun had almost gone now, but its colour leaked its last rays into the evening sky.

Jenny came into the room, floating on a cloud of 'Evening in Paris', and rose pink chiffon. She wore a simple sheath dress which fitted neatly onto her slim hips from where it fell in handkerchief points, zig-zagging in a charming swirl about her calves. She had made the dress herself, working on the kitchen table, sewing each dainty stitch by hand. Neither she nor a million other young working girls could afford the styles decreed by Paris' Chanel or Patou.

Fashion had always been the prerogative of the well-off, but clothes were beginning to take on a new look as factories mass-produced dresses using the new fabrics, like crêpes, chiffons and georgette. These lovely materials were still beyond the pockets of many of the young and hard-up, but Jenny often found lengths of pretty materials, off-cuts and ends of rolls, at St John's market, and in this way ensured that she, and Kate, were as fashionable as many a lady who shopped at Bunny's or Owen Owen. She could copy it faithfully, cutting confidently without pattern or instructions whilst Kate watched with bated breath, to produce for next to nothing some fetching outfit for herself or her sister.

She looked radiant. Her creamy skin was barely highlighted with a touch of rouge on each high cheekbone and her soft mouth had been outlined with a subdued rosy pink lipstick. Her hair, warm and brown, touched here and there by copper glints, was smooth and gleaming, a neat cap of symmetrically flat waves, dipping into tiny tendrils of curls against her cheek and across her forehead. Her eyes, deep brown in this light but gold-flecked, shone with health and excitement, the lids weighted down with sooty black lashes which softly touched the curve of her cheek.

The dress drifted round her in a slow moving swirl of glowing mist, the skirt so light and soft it seemed to float on the air.

In opposition to the decrees of the day, she wore no jewellery and needed none, for her simple loveliness required no enhancement. She had discarded the binding which flattened the bosoms and made boyish the figures of so many of her contemporaries and her breasts peaked high and round, the bobs of her nipples clearly outlined against the thin material.

Jenny's taste in clothes had altered in the last two months. She had, after the first intoxicating freedom to wear what she pleased, and the consequent rush to garb herself in some of the outlandish styles of the Jazz Age, taken a fancy for the plain and simple as if instinctively knowing what suited her and what did not. No ornaments, beads or bracelets. She had relinquished them all. With one exception.

Charlie with unexpected good taste and as if he too knew what she looked best in had brought her a thin rope of coral, a delicate, almost colourless link of tiny beads. He was like that, Charlie. He never brought Kate a present without something for Jenny, and it was usually some simple but pretty thing. The difference in the sisters was never more apparent than when Charlie's presents were unwrapped. Kate was a good-looking girl; earthy, vibrant, outwardgoing and she liked clothes to match her personality. Charlie would bring her bright, vividly coloured scarves, and bracelets which shook and jangled. Strings of fake pearls, dangling earrings, paste diamond clips and brooches. She had a powder compact with a picture of the Statue of Liberty upon it, and a kimono so strewn about with flowers of every size and colour, it hurt the eyes to look at her.

But for Jenny it would be a tiny leather-bound notebook, a plain silken scarf with her initial discreetly printed in one corner; a silver locket the size of a pea on a thin chain. No one questioned his choice; he surprised himself with it, but her pleasure at his thoughtfulness and her pretty thanks linked them together with a gentle affection a brother might show his sister.

As Jenny stood expectantly waiting with her usual diffidence for her sister's opinion, Kate's mouth opened and she gasped in awe. Her eyes flickered across her sister's face and lingered on the startling beauty which the dress seemed to bring out.

'Eeh, our kid,' she breathed, her genuine pleasure and admiration untinged by jealousy. 'Yer look a picture. That dress suits yerra treat. Eeh, I bet yer made up with it, aren't yer? Turn round, let's 'ave a good look.'

Jenny twirled obligingly and the drifting squares of chiffon lay about her slim legs like rose-coloured smoke. She laughed delightedly and the usual pale porcelain of her skin flushed and her white teeth gleamed between her pink lips.

Kate considered her thoughtfully, her hand to her mouth, whilst Jenny continued to pirouette, carried out of her usual reserve by the feel of the dress and some barely recognised awareness of anticipation.

'It's . . . it's a bit bare,' Kate said. 'It's lovely, don't get me wrong but it just wants summat . . . well summat to give it a lift like.' She continued to study her sister with eyes half-closed, an artist meditating on the possible improvement of a work of art.

'I know, how about that pink silk orchid Charlie brought me? It'd look a treat on your shoulder. I'll get it.'

She banged the iron which was still in her hand onto its stand and made a move to leave the kitchen in search of the bright and hideous artificial flower which had been Charlie's last home-coming gift.

Jenny stopped in mid-twirl, horrified. Dearly as she loved Kate there was just no circumstance in which she could bring herself to wear the gaudy adornment Kate proposed to lend her.

'No, our kid, really, I don't want it.' Kate's face fell and she looked surprised and hurt. 'It's not that I don't like it,' Jenny went on hurriedly, 'but I don't think it's the exact shade . . . and then I might lose it in the Charleston or summat.'

Kate's face cleared.

'Well what about those pearls, those long 'uns. They'd be a lovely match . . .'

'No Kate, honest, ta all the same, but you know me. I can't do with lots of stuff round me neck when I'm dancing . . . anyway I must go. I said I'd meet Lily at eight, and it's five to now.'

Picking up the tiny purse which she had covered in the same material as her dress and twinkling her rose-tinted 'tango' shoes across the scuffed linoleum, she smiled apologetically at Kate and moved towards the door. Abruptly she turned. They weren't ones for fuss, the Fowlers. Demonstrations of affection embarrassed them, but with an unusual show of emotion, Jenny took her sister's arm and smiling diffidently, almost shyly, she kissed her cheek.

'Ta luv, sorry you're not coming, but with Charlie . . .'

She left the sentence unfinished and whirling again, she left the room. The front door banged and for a moment or two Kate could hear her quick light footsteps clicking on the pavement as she hurried up the street. Then there was silence.

Kate sighed and stood for a moment, staring at the half-open door through which Jenny had just gone. She put her hand to her cheek where Jenny's kiss still lingered and her face became pensive. What had she done that for? It wasn't like their Jenny to go in for kissing. Not that the affection wasn't there, it was. They were . . . well, she was . . . she loved Jenny. She'd always minded her, and she knew Jenny felt the same way. They didn't say it, but what were sisters for but to . . .

The clock on the wall ticked, the sound of its beat making her want to tap her feet to the rhythm. With an unexpected hum of machinery and an audible 'clonk', the cuckoo thrust its way from between the miniature painted doors of the clock and merrily announced the hour of eight. Kate jumped, startled out of her reverie, then turned back to the table, bored already with her own company.

Eeh, she'd have loved to have gone with their Jenny, she would an'all. Just to have a bit of a dance, a bit of company; wear a pretty dress. It was over four weeks since Charlie had been home, and sometimes, dearly though she loved him, she wished . . . – Now, now, me girl, she chided herself, none o' that. You an' Charlie have an understanding and it's no good wishing you could get out with your Jenny. She's fancy free and you're not. And you'd have it no other way, would you?

Kate shook her head as if in answer to her own question and she laughed out loud. Charlie'd be home in a day or so and then see. They'd paint the town red, choose how. Not half.

She began to sing in a high, flat soprano and resumed her table thumping attack on the remainder of the ironing.

The contrast between the two pretty girls was sharp.

Lily's hair was blatantly Titian and stood about her perpetually turning head like candyfloss. She had the white skin and freckles which often mate with her colouring, and her body could only be described as lush. She was as generous and openhearted as Mother Earth herself, and could say 'no' to no one, from the request of a loan of a couple of bob, to the winning ways of some smooth-tongued sailor who was willing to spend a few bob on *her*. She gave her easy friendship with the simplicity of a child, and though her womanly curves spoke of maturity, she was artless to the point of foolishness.

She loved dancing, having a good time, men, bright colours, a smutty joke, fish and chips, an outing to Blackpool, French knickers, Valentino, loud music, and inexplicably, Jenny Fowler. Perhaps she was wise in the way some women are wise. In her shrewdness she knew Jenny was no challenge to her own lively good looks, for they attracted a different type of man. Jenny's reserve showed to advantage her own witty repartee, and the kind of man who might see Jenny as his perfect woman, was too quiet, too understated for Lily. No shrinking violet was she, and she wanted no strong and silent men about her. She left those for Jenny.

But she was knowing in the ways of the world. Nothing escaped her flickering glance, from the outfit worn by each female customer in the cafe, to the admiring looks bestowed upon her by every male. Her knowledge of tips given; to which waitress, and the exact amount received each week by every girl in the place, was reckoned to the last farthing. Their lives were an open book to her, due to her skill in extracting disclosures – which they didn't want her to know in the first place – regarding their families' financial state, domestic status, health, love expectations and realities, whose Mam was pregnant again and whose Dad spent more than he should at the pub. She knew who was sweet on whom, and to the last sigh, the depth of their feelings. She had that knack of drawing information from a person with a charm and sympathy which lulled the unwary into divulging the most personal of matters, and all without seeming to pry.

Nevertheless, she had not a mean bone in her body.

Jenny's tranquil loveliness was in no way overshadowed by Lily, rather, as in their personalities, they played foil for one another. The soft pink and cream of Jenny, the amber flush of cheekbone, warm brown of eye, made for a delicate comparison.

Lily did all the talking, as bright and cheerful as a humming bird, and just as colourful. Her face and body were never still. Though she stood in one spot she gave the impression of darting eagerly from one situation to the next, her eyes, dark and flashing, moving constantly from the face of her companion to encompass all of life's parade which passed her by.

There was a small crowd waiting for the tram to town, mostly young people. The Mecca, Dale Street Dance Hall and Dalby Street were the three targets – according to taste and inclination – which drew them like pins to a magnet, particularly on a Saturday night. The men in the group appreciatively eyed the two girls. Jenny stood quietly, demure even, though a small, secret sparkle could be seen in her eyes by anyone quick enough to catch it. She listened to Lily, whose bold glance gave clear signals of her disposition to every male at the tramstop.

The row of terraced houses behind them was rough-surfaced with cracked bricks, from between which the mortar leaked in crumbling showers. Doors stood open and women leaned against them, arms crossed, watching with apathetic envy the city-going youngsters, who, years before might have been themselves. Children sat, barefoot, on doorsteps, dirty faces drooping and tired, waiting for the call to bed. The end house of the row was unoccupied and slogans had been drawn upon the front, mostly concerned with football and the Kaiser.

The tram came and with some good natured pushing and saucy

70

raillery between Lily and a sleek-haired young man who obviously fancied himself with the ladies, the two girls managed to get a seat inside. The forward movement of the tram caused a stiff breeze to whip itself about the heads of those on the upper, outside seats and played havoc with the artfully arranged waves of hairdos which had taken so long to contrive.

The Mecca was lit up like a diamond-hung Christmas tree but the fading evening light diffused the scene as though gauze had been placed across it. A star or two could be seen above the roofs, pale pricks of radiance in the milky blue.

The crowds were thick, all going in one direction, towards the ticket office at the front of the building, and the noise was like that of a thousand chattering starlings as they swooped and swerved, looking for a place to rest. They couldn't wait to get there, these young people and they jostled and shoved, the excitement acting like a drug to the latecomers as though afraid that they might be excluded from paradise.

Saturday night, longed for and looked forward to by the hundreds and thousands who plodded through the seven days between like weary travellers intent only upon the welcoming light of home. From Monday to Saturday the drab routine and rut to which they were tethered, was got through by the sheer necessity of putting food in their mouths. From factory or shop; in office and on building sites and in the case of the great sea port in which they lived, on dockyard or deck of ship.

But Saturday . . . ah, Saturday.

For the men it started with football and the cheerful comradeship of shoulder rubbing shoulder; of nerve tingling silence and trembling anticipation of a goal, of chanting roars and deafening howls of disappointment, and the goodnatured rivalry which existed between supporter and supporter.

The pub was next for an hour or two, for one must have a 'bevvy' to rejoice or sorrow, depending upon the success or failure of one's team, then, when the courage was high, and the spirits higher, it was off to find a 'judy' with whom to finish the day. Wages, paid on a Friday, were wellnigh spent by the end of Saturday, but who cared? Tomorrow was Sunday and they could lie in, indulged by Mam, until dinnertime, and perhaps, if they were lucky and had 'clicked', an evening to look forward to in the company of last night's conquest.

It was magic. It was everything.

'You get the tickets, chuck,' Lily shouted, her voice almost lost in the feverish uproar. ''ere,' she fiddled in her purse, ''ere's mine.'

71

Jenny took the money from Lily's outstretched hand and shuffled slowly forward, surrounded on all sides by young men and women. They were as eager as she to purchase passports to the heaven within the swing doors from between which, as they opened and closed, the sound of lilting music could be heard.

One step forward and stop. One step forward and stop. Lily rattled on at her side as they approached the ticket office. One step forward and stop, one step forward . . . As Jenny braced herself, hemmed in it seemed, like a slim flower in a forest of closely packed trees, the person directly in front of her stepped, not forward, as was expected, but back. A slight disturbance at the box office had caused a shift in the progression, and for a moment, all was sway and confusion. The tall man in front of her leaned back further and the weight of a foot came down upon hers with all the force that six feet and twelve stone of muscle and bone can deliver. She let out a whelp and fell against his back as she lost her balance. The bag and the money in her hand fell to the ground.

In an instant, all was chaos. Voices cried out in sympathy and hands reached to steady her. Lily, no lady when roused – and even when not – raised herself on tiptoe, and oblivious to the laughter which prevailed, gave the offending couple at the head of the queue a piece of her mind.

'Yer daft beggars, why don't yer look where yer goin'. Backing up like that. Yer've damn near crippled my friend 'ere. Yer wanna keep yer eyes on where yer goin', and where's her bag and money?'

In a minute Lily was down on her knees, helped by the willing hands of several young men who were only too pleased to help her find Jenny's bag, and to eye the bewitching sight of her bottom and the swell of her breasts as they almost fell, like two rosy apples, from the front of her lowcut dress.

In the midst of the turmoil and the agony of her crushed toes, Jenny was conscious only of gentle hands on hers and a strong arm supporting her from the crush. A voice deep but soft spoke words she did not understand and she was almost carried to a chair at the side of the foyer. A figure knelt before her and tender hands eased her shoe from her foot. The voice, melodic and lilting begged for forgiveness, the devastation and apology in its timbre, understood, though the language was not.

Tears of pain stood in Jenny's eyes and all she could see as her reeling senses returned was a shape, blurred and misty. The man's hands were about her foot, feeling with delicate and unobtrusive efficiency for signs of damage, and she winced as the

72

probing, gentle fingers touched the spot where recently his heel had ground.

'Ah, there it is. I am so sorry, so sorry. It was my fault but the people . . .' Again the voice and the words became unintelligible, but the hands continued their gentle massage.

'Please use my . . . it is quite clean. The tears . . .'

A crisp white handkerchief was pressed into her hand, and hardly aware of what she was doing, she wiped her brimming eyes, and energetically blew her nose with the carelessness of a child. She sniffed and blinked and looked down into the face of the man who knelt at her feet.

And loved him. In the space of time which exists between one heartbeat and the next she loved him. With the simple ease with which we change from one emotion to another, she loved him.

She stared, transfixed, into the handsomest face she had ever seen. He was beautiful with that beauty so rare in a man, in that it was completely masculine. The lines and planes of his face were moulded by the hand of a sculptor whose skill had not wasted a touch. The colour was painted by a brush so tender each stroke was a masterpiece. The skin of his face and neck were tanned nutbrown by a thousand suns and his eyes, a brilliant sapphire blue were surrounded by a sweep of thick golden lashes tipped with cinnamon. Small lines caused by laughter and squinting against the same sun that had coloured his face, radiated like the spokes of a wheel from the outer corner of each eye. His hair was a cap of golden curls, and as he stood, suddenly diffident as he felt her eyes upon him, she could see he was tall, finely proportioned and slim. His mouth was firm and as he smiled, his teeth gleamed, white and even.

They looked at each other for a shimmering moment, a tick of a second in the passage of time, and he was as mesmerised as she. He saw the dark gold of her eyes first, the black lashes spiked still with her tears. They were soft, startled and her smooth round face was flushed with rose. Her moist pink mouth was opened in a round 'O' of wonder and her small white teeth showed for a second in a smile of delight. He could smell the fragrance of her, and feel still, the softness of her body as she had leaned against him. The touch of the small bones of her feet and the delicate flesh that covered them, tingled yet against his empty fingers.

He was entranced.

They stared at each other, the silence quivering and eloquent, then, with a movement which was a pure, simple reaction to what had come suddenly into their hearts, they clasped hands. To an onlooker it might have seemed that they had just been introduced, though no third person was present, and in a strange way, they had.

They met, smiled, and fell in love all in the space of three minutes.

Chapter Seven

It was a night of enchantment, a night of which dreams are made, a night when young girls are enthralled and young men fulfil their boyish fantasies. Jenny Fowler and Nils Jorgensen were captivated that night by the magic, by the delight, by the dreams, and by each other.

His smile was so sweet and in his eyes was an expression of emotion so honest, it lanced Jenny's heart and for an instant, gone almost before she could grasp its meaning, she was strangely afraid. As he lifted her from her chair his hand under her elbow was warm and firm, and she trembled like a flower in a fall of rain. He kept it there, looking down at her feet, encouraging her to lean on him, speaking in a mixture of English and some language that lilted and rose at the end of each sentence with a melody that sent ripples of pleasure down her spine.

'Do not lean on your foot, hold on to me. There, one step at a time, that's it. That's not so bad, is it?'

Jenny could scarcely breathe for the rush of air in her throat. It seemed to be going down and coming up at the same time, and she felt an intense desire to cry out. He raised his head to look into her face and smiled, and she felt her heart move in her breast in breathless ecstasy. She could feel her hand shaking in his, wanting to withdraw it, so that he wouldn't notice and wonder; yet wanting to leave it there forever.

'Good, good, careful . . . don't stand on it . . . put your weight on me.'

Each phrase was interspersed with words that ran over his tongue like water across stones, strange and rippling.

'So . . . and so . . . does it feel better . . . I'm so sorry. I am clumsy . . . not to see you there.'

'Oh no, it was not your fault, really. I was standing so close and those people at the front . . .' Her voice quavered like someone speaking under water.

'I am unhappy . . . your foot . . .'

'Really . . . it's all right.'

Putting her weight on her good foot, holding the injured one an inch or two above the ground; with his right hand under her elbow and his left holding hers they made a few faltering steps of progress. Their eyes sent tiny messages to each other, then returned their attention to her foot, and each heart pumped and pumped in each cage of ribs, and each throat closed in agony lest something might be said to scatter the delicate sensation which was growing with every second.

Suddenly the words stopped, dried up, as if the polite intercourse which convention demanded was too much for them to bear. As though silence was preferable to idiot words which meant nothing, when there was so much to be said.

Restraint fell about them, the intensity of the emotion which had them in its grip, silencing even the faltering words which are common to two people who have just met. Jenny dropped her gaze shyly, and would not look up at him again, aware suddenly of the curious stares of the milling crowd, and the strange picture they must make. She put out a hand to the back of a chair and leaned against it, slowly drawing away from him. Abashed he reluctantly let her go and his eyes watched her. He put one hand in his pocket and cleared his throat as though searching about in his mind for something which might bring back the glory of a moment ago, but she would not look at him. Her shoe was still in his hand, and not knowing what else to do he held it out to her. She took it, steadying herself against the chair, smiling nervously, wishing suddenly, unaccountably, that he would go away.

With the flamboyance of a firework display and with as much noise, Lily bore down upon them, triumphantly bearing aloft Jenny's purse and the money which had been dropped in the confusion.

'I gorrit kid. Took a birra doin', what with all them clodhoppers trampling all over me, but I found it. Honest, the cheek of some folk. D'ya know what some chap said to me?' She giggled, simpering in pretended dismay. 'Was I scrubbin' t'floors and did I want a hand. Talk about sauce. Any road, I found t' money and yer bag. It's a bit mucky, kid, but I bet yer can purra bit of soap on and it'll come up as good as new.'

Ebullient and exaggeratedly vivacious, like an actress on a stage holding hundreds in the palm of her hand, for she did love to be the centre of everyone's attention, Lily took in with one expert glance the personable young man who stood by Jenny's side. In the blink of an eyelash she noted his good looks, his good suit, the breadth of his shoulders and the slimness of his hips. She noticed his easy

76

way of standing that is common to seamen used to the dip and sway of a deck, and with the speed of an adding machine, determined that he had just docked and must therefore have a pocketful of money. She noted his diffidence and Jenny's seeming lack of interest, and thrilled to the probability of the evening ahead being turned to her own advantage.

With bold glance and explicit movements of her full and bounteous body, she assessed him, found him not wanting and told him – for what man cannot read the signals so blatantly given – that she was available. Her eyes stared directly into his as she continued to talk to Jenny.

'Eeh chuck warra to do. Is yer foot bad then? Will yer be able to dance? Eeh warra a shame.' Without giving Jenny a chance to answer she went on, patting her flaming hair which had sprung about her head in the mêlée on the floor. 'Will yer gerra taxi or what? Can yer manage t'tram?' For the first time, she looked at her friend, then tipping her head seductively and looking under her lashes at the man, she continued, 'P'raps this young chap and me can help yer to t' tram stop.'

She lifted her peaked breasts and stared into the man's eyes. There was absolutely no mistaking her message.

'Give us yer hand and we'll see if you can walk.'

She was the personification of the predatory female and perhaps it was this, who knows, that brought the 'damned if I will' spirit to Jenny's usually placid nature. Lily put out her hand to Jenny, all the while never taking her brazen-eyed glance from the handsome young stranger.

Jenny had been leaning heavily against the wall beside the row of chairs. Her foot was throbbing and her heart jumped like a captured bird. She was bewildered by the emotion set off by this man's glance, and frightened by the strangeness of her own feelings. She wanted to cry, and yet smile at him. She wanted his hand in hers again but the thought terrified her. She longed for him to look at her with those brilliant eyes in which lurked admiration and something else which she could not identify. She knew, she knew without doubt, that if she put her hand in his once more, reserve would be gone and subterfuge impossible. There would be no holding back; she would be committed to . . . to . . . she didn't even know to what. But she'd be damned if she'd be shuffled off home like an unwanted guest at a party. She'd hobble into the ballroom if it killed her.

Jenny stood up straight.

Instantly the man turned to her and again two hands, one slim and white, the other strong and tanned, rose up, and clasped each other. Surprised, it seemed, at the meeting of their flesh, Jenny and the stranger looked at their twined fingers and like clouds racing across an angry sky, disappearing to leave an arch of clear serenity all doubt fell away and they knew, and accepted.

Still unaware, still confident, Lily prattled on, pouting her fine lips, flaunting her figure in the supreme belief that she was still in with a chance. She took Jenny's other hand in the mistaken belief that she was helping her friend to make her crippled way to the tramstop, there to be disposed of before Lily put her whole mind to seducing this lovely chap.

'I think I can manage.'

'I'll give yer a hand chuck, there's a tram in five . . .'

'No, I mean inside.'

'Inside where?'

'The ballroom.'

'Give over, yer can't dance with . . .'

'I can watch, can't I?'

Lily was becoming irritated. Her equable good humour for once was deserting her as the realisation ran through her that for the first time, she and Jenny fancied the same chap. If Jenny stayed and he decided to play the 'gallant' – though this was not the exact term she used – where would that leave her? Up the Swanee wi'out a paddle, that's where. She'd taken a right shine to this sailor, for anyone with half an eye, especially one born and brought up in Liverpool could tell he was of the sea, and she was gonna have him, choose how. Any road up, Jenny couldn't dance and bloke'd want a birrof a cuddle. Didn't they all, and wasn't she equipped to give it him. Jenny was . . . well a bit of a cold fish . . .

The man stood patiently, his warm fingers softly speaking, gentle and strong and pleading in Jenny's.

'Give over, yer can't sit all night doin' nowt,' Lily went on. 'What if I wanna dance, I can't leave yer on yer own . . .'

'Of course yer can, I shan't mind.'

'Oh give over . . .' For once Lily was lost for words. She had never seen Jenny so determined.

'Oh all right then,' she said petulantly. Ungraciously she took Jenny's other hand, almost dragging her towards the swinging doors which led into the ballroom.

The man bought three tickets at the almost deserted ticket office, for by now, all comers were inside and only one or two tardy arrivals still thrust their money towards the girl behind the grill.

With the tenderness of a mother he gently guided Jenny's

hopping progression through the doorway, between the packed tables which surrounded the floor, until he found one which was empty. Solicitously he seated her, fussing like a hen with a chick until he was satisfied she was comfortable.

Mortified by his indifference to her and his concern for Jenny, Lily trailed behind, hindrance more than help, holding Jenny's other hand limply until they reached the table. But she was not one to give up easily.

Dragging the man's attention from Jenny again and again, she teased and flirted and pouted. She prattled prettily and tapped her feet significantly beneath the table, brushing her leg against his. She hummed enticingly and smiled enchantingly. She drank the port and lemon he bought her and went through the complete range of her repertoire – which was considerable – to enslave him, but it was no use. The man had eyes for no one but Jenny. He was courteously polite but it was obvious to the dullest brain that he was waiting only for her to go.

It was no go with this chap, that was plain and if she didn't look lively she'd end up a bloody wallflower, an event which had never yet occurred in her life and she'd no intention of letting it happen now.

Suddenly, admitting defeat she stood up. Her mood changed abruptly and with goodnatured acceptance, telling herself there were more fish in the sea than out, she took herself off.

'Tara then,' she said, 'don't do 'owt I wouldn't do.' She winked suggestively, adjusted her garter, giving the man a last glimpse of what might have been his, and was gone.

For a moment the silence, no longer bolstered by Lily's effervescent presence, overcame them. They each looked with absorbed interest at the gyrating couples on the floor as though afraid that if their eyes met, the magic might have gone, but the moment stretched and the tension became electric and he could stand it no longer. He was the first to move.

Turning to look at her, he held out his hand as though this time they were about to be formally introduced.

He said simply, 'My name is Nils Jorgensen.'

They talked, shyly at first, he stumbling over an odd word or two, with a barely discernible accent. She asked him to speak in his own language and the musical use of the tongue of his birth fell like a song on Jenny's ears and she looked and listened, fascinated to the point of intoxication. He would not tell her what it was he had said, but his eyes were soft and in her heart she knew that it had been

79

words of some emotion of which he could not yet speak. She watched him grope for a word, his beauty almost a blow to the senses, and was nearly overcome with reverence to be in the company of such a creature, a creature from another world, or so he seemed to her with his delightful foreignness. His remarkable eyes glowed with good humour and intelligence, almost disappearing in the mesh of the fine lines about his eyes as he laughed at his own, sometimes amusing, attempts at her language, or were gentle, warm as he listened intently.

And he in his turn, could not look away from her delicate, innocent face, creamy skin aglow with excitement, eyes sparkling with the admiration she was too artless to conceal. Her mouth was like a child's, pink and moist and his gaze constantly returned to it, anticipating how it would feel under his own.

He touched her hand, her wrist, with courtly propriety, never overreaching the standards of respect, careful not to alarm, but unable to resist the need to put his fingers against her soft flesh.

They were entranced with each other.

He was Norwegian, he said, a navigating officer on a merchantman just docked that day from Oslo. His home was in Bergen on the coast of Norway and he had a brother. His father was dead and his mother still lived in the small house to which she had come when she married. He tried in his almost perfect English to make a verbal picture for her of the great fjords and the snowcapped mountains of his home and he spoke about his childhood, and she of hers, and looking deeply into one another's eyes oblivious to the swirl and gaiety about them, they fell deeply and irretrievably in love.

For an hour they talked, then suddenly aware that her foot no longer throbbed, Jenny remembered her shoe which Nils had placed on the chair beside her.

She tried it on, whilst he watched anxiously. She smiled up at him, and his face lit up with that luminous gentle quality that she was beginning to recognise, to know so well. She stood up and immediately he was beside her. His manners were impeccable; she had never known such politeness and again she felt overwhelmed. He saw the uncertainty return to her eyes and though he did not know why, he cast about in his mind, besotted now by the sweet loveliness of her, to find some way to abolish it.

He heard the music, a waltz, and saw the gliding, circling mass of dancers and with a comical expression, for words escaped him, he took her hand, indicated the dance floor and then pointed at her foot.

Jenny laughed, constraint gone. Testing her foot, favouring it slightly, she found she could walk quite easily.

And so they danced. The band played, the sound was sweet, a song of the moment, *My Honey's Lovin' Arms*, and from that moment, it became their song. For the first time he held her in his arms. He felt the smooth lines of her back and her hand was small, soft-boned, in his. His breath touched the wisps of curling hair which lay on her forehead and lifted them, and she looked up into his face. Her eyes melted and told him what he wanted to know and he almost bent his head to kiss her soft lips. They danced every dance together, touching, always touching, as if afraid to lose contact with this incredible feeling. Hand in hand as they moved between the dancers across the floor, shoulder to shoulder as they sat drinking coffee, each flesh seeming to yearn to be always brushing the other, their eyes speaking, brown to blue, blue to brown, saying the words which were not yet ready to be said out loud. All the words of the heart which would soon be uttered, but not yet. Not now. Not here.

Once she saw Lily's face in the crowd, smiling and peering inquisitively over her partner's shoulder, but Jenny made no move to acknowledge her. She didn't care; couldn't seem to make herself care about anything except the warm, strong arms about her, the gentle smiling eyes and the soft almost accentless voice of this man who had so miraculously come into her life.

The National Anthem was playing, and with an outraged sense of shock, Jenny realised that it was over. This mystical, magical evening was over. It couldn't be. Not yet. She wanted to go on for ever being held in these protective arms, to be looked at adoringly, to be the beautiful princess in the fairy story. Now the prince would go away; sail away on his ship and she would return to the prosaic life with which she had been so happy before tonight. The music had stopped, the lights were being turned off, the dancers were streaming towards the exit and she wanted to run after them and tell them to come back. The man who worked the lights must be made to return . . . and the band. Her lovely dream world, her Prince Charming couldn't be allowed to escape.

She almost cried out loud so desperate, so fierce, was her terror. She turned a despairing face towards the man by her side, her hand still clutching his; she looked into his eyes and in the time it takes for the finger of a clock to tick from one second to the next, she was at ease. Comforted. Reassured. It was not going to end. Ever. He was not Prince Charming, but a man, and his candid eyes, serious and wise, told her that her fears were groundless. They told her

81

what she wanted to know and her face relaxed and her eyes smiled into his.

They understood each other at last.

From the crowd she saw Lily coming towards them leading a burly fellow with a smiling Irish face. Irrepressible even now, she ogled Nils, still convinced in her own mind that if it had been she and not Jenny who had first caught his attention, it would be towards her the admiring glances would be heading. Ah well! If she had spoken French she would have sighed deeply, shrugged her shoulders and murmured a Gallic 'C'est la vie', but she did not, so in her broad Liverpool brogue she muttered to herself a few pithy words of regret and took what was available.

'We're off to Waggy's, kid, for a birra supper, me an' Sean,' she said, putting her arm through that of the Irishman's, ''ow about joining us?'

Nils looked pleadingly at Jenny, his reluctance obvious, even to the drunken fellow on Lily's arm. The Irishman's face became truculent at once, and with the volatile excitability of his race, he began to bristle towards the tall seaman. He tried to put up his fists, then changed his mind. If the divil didn't want to come, then the divil take him. He pulled at Lily's arm, falling about his own feet which suddenly seemed to have lost control of themselves. With an apologetic grin, Lily turned, leading the lurching man like a trainer with a shambling bear at her elbow.

Jenny and Nils watched the pair go, then turned to each other and smiled. Restraint had gone between them now, and with the comfortable ease of those who are in perfect accord, they left the ballroom and the Mecca. They began to walk without speaking, hands still clasped, towards the Pier Head. After the warmth of the ballroom, the September air was cool and still without a word, Nils took off his jacket and put it about Jenny's shoulders. It was warm from the heat of his body and smelled faintly in a strange way, of the sea.

Though it was nearly midnight, the streets were filled with people. Laughter and snatches of song drifted about them, and girls walked by in twos, with young men in various stages of foolish inebriation, hanging, arms draped about their shoulders. Groups of sailors, uniformed in the garb of every navy in the world, stood on corners, gabbling, gesticulating, eyeing openly any unaccompanied female who might pass them by, but falling respectfully silent, as Nils passed with Jenny.

Two policemen sauntered side by side, truncheons inches from hands, ready to quell any trouble which might arise in this great sea port for it was the stamping ground of men from every corner of the globe, and the arena for more fights per square yard than any city in the world.

Jenny and Nils passed the imposing bulk of the Cunard building and walked across Georges Pier Head to the water's edge. It was quieter here for there was no excitement to be found where the great ships lay. The water was as flat and shining as a length of satin, stretching across the river to the hazy lights of New Brighton. There was a tiny sickle of a moon, no bigger than a pared fingernail, in the deep black sky, but the light of a billion tiny stars lit the quiet stretches of the river, and outlined the blacker bulk of the ships.

They stopped at an all-night coffee stand, used by the tram drivers whilst they waited for their trams to be turned, the beckoning glow of the lighted stall and the mens' laughter, the redolent aroma of the coffee, luring them irresistibly. They stood in the centre of the goodnatured chaff that circulated amongst the workmen, cupping the thick mugs of steaming brew in their hands, oblivious to the friendly smiles and knowing winks which their appearance had promoted, and once more the magic smote them.

Their eyes could not look away from each other and the joy which they found created an ambience which was almost visible. The men fell silent uneasily, sensing something that was past their understanding, for it comes to few. They turned away from the thralled couple resuming their serious and more easily understood discussion of Everton's play that afternoon, and of the odds against their team's chances in the cup.

Jenny felt that she was in the depths of some exquisite dream from which she never wanted to wake. She could not believe that only a few hours ago she had not known of the existence of the man who now filled her world from horizon to horizon. She felt that she was in a state of shock, marvelling at the sudden depths of her feelings for him and at the response she could plainly see telling her he felt the same.

It was as though some tidal wave had taken her and swept her towards a life so new and wonderful it was beyond her comprehension. For a brief moment the feeling of fear returned, a premonition of approaching disaster, and she was seized with an unaccountable longing for Kate's familiar and comfortable presence. Her eyes misted and dimmed and even in the yellow flickering light that surrounded them, Nils saw the brightness go.

Jenny knew, for she was realist as well as dreamer – as most young girls are – that her nature was to be childlike, trusting. Kate had led her all her life. She had made no decisions, even as a child, happy to follow her outgoing sister, whether it was into trouble or just to which park they should go for a picnic. She was happy with herself. She did not want, in her placid and shy way, to impose her own will on others, for she had none. If others were content, so was she. She had avoided rows and quarrels all her life preferring to give in to a stronger personality than her own, rather than cause discord. There was an innocent, hopeful quality about her, an aura of quiet joyousness that seemed to say that something good was just around the corner, and so far in her life, she had never been disappointed. The scene with her father had distressed her beyond measure, and left to herself she would have given in, turned her back on freedom and probably have done very well, for she did not ask a lot. She was that rare person, one who was at peace with herself.

It was this childlike quality of trust and a belief that all were good about her; that no harm could come to one who did no harm, that and her sweet beauty, which had captivated Nils Jorgensen. He was twenty-eight years old and had travelled the world for over thirteen years. He had known women of all races and colours, and there are no more exquisitely lovely women to be found than in the Orient, but some ingredient of Jenny's nature had called to him; had seemed to compliment his own disposition and to make it whole; some essential part of him that needed what she gave him. He could not put a finger on what it was. A longing perhaps, a fierce masculine yearning for something more than what he had known before. He felt a strong sense of protectiveness towards her. It pleased him. She seemed to him to be the perfect other half of what man and woman should be. Strength and softness, leader and follower. Male and female. She was the perfect woman.

His eyes were upon her face and with that special understanding which had grown so mysteriously between them, he seemed to read her thoughts. He put out his hand and gently ran his finger across her cheek. The touch calmed her, and the feeling of approaching pain left her as quickly as it had come.

They finished their coffee and paid the man behind the counter. They answered politely the cheery 'goodnights' of the men who had now recovered their balance, the familiar subject of football restoring to them the stability and commonsense feeling of everyday things, the stark desire in the eyes of the strange couple soon forgotten.

The man and woman walked slowly away from the sight and sounds and smell of the river, so familiar to them both. She had lived beside it, and he upon the sea for all of their lives, and the

84

melancholy shriek of the tug's hooter in the darkness went unnoticed.

The clock on the tower of St Nicholas church by the Pier Head station which served the overhead railway, struck twelve. The sound of shrieking laughter echoed across the water as the last boat from Woodside ferry to Birkenhead took its cargo of merrymakers back to their own side of the river.

They sat side by side on the tramcar, alone and together in the world which they had entered that evening, conscious only of each other, of the touch of hand, of shoulder, arm and thigh, and it was as though all that had gone before in their lives had been a waiting time in readiness for this day, this moment of beauty.

A pulse started somewhere in Jenny's throat as they neared the stop where they would get off, working its gentle but persistent way to every part of her body. It felt like the wings of a butterfly trapped inside her and she longed for the journey to be over; to be somewhere quiet and alone where she could feel Nils' arms about her. Her thoughts went no further than this. She was not ignorant of the ways of a man and a woman, though she had no experience of it, but her arms seemed to ache strangely with the yearning to fold the man beside her within their loving clasp, and the need to be secure in his.

She stole a look at him from beneath her lashes and was devastated by the answering longing in his.

When they reached the door of number thirty-six, Jenny stopped. Her heart beat like a drum. She was sure Nils would hear it. What should she do now? Should she ask him to come in? Kate would be in bed and asleep and the warm kitchen would be theirs. She turned to him, and her eyelashes fluttered nervously, creating rippling shadows on her rounded cheeks as the light from the street lamp fell about her head. His eyes looked gravely into hers. He was more used to the ways of love, though he had never loved this way before, and he knew with a certainty born of his love that it was too soon to take what was being offered. Jenny's face was like the page of a book, and the print upon it was large and clear. It told him that she was his, now, tomorrow and for always. Her innocence lay about her like a shield, though, and no matter how easily it might be removed, it was not yet time. He could be patient for hadn't they the rest of their lives?

He put a gentle finger under her chin and lifted it. The shadow of the street light shifted and the glow fell on his face. His thoughts were in his eyes, and her heart grew gentle and still with gladness. Nils had interpreted her uncertainty. He had solved it. Without

85

words he had told her he knew of her disquiet and that she must not hurry or panic, or be in fear of her feelings. There was nothing to fear. There was no anxiety that could not be overcome.

His voice was tranquil.

'It is . . . what do you say here? . . . fate that we should have met. I don't know why.' He spoke some words in his own language, the meaning clear even to one who did not speak it. Some destiny had led them to the same spot at the same time. From another country he had come and circumstances had led him to the place where she would be. Even then, in the crush which pervaded the Mecca on a Saturday night it might have been that they would have passed each other by, but an unknown influence had placed them, one behind the other in the queue at the ticket office. So easily they might have missed one another, though with the conviction of lovers the world over, they found this hard to believe.

'So, my sweet Jenny, we met and I am grateful to the god who . . . but now, you are tired, yes?'

Jenny nodded, mesmerised with love.

'You must sleep and tomorrow I will come for you.'

She nodded again.

He took her upturned face between his two brown hands, lean and hard, but so gentle, and bending his head, kissed each corner of her mouth, soft, like the touch of a kitten's ear. He tasted briefly the honey of her lips, and for a fleeting instant the desire to clasp her in his arms, to rain kisses about her face and the sweet hollow of her neck, ran through his body like fire. She was compliant, almost submissive, and he knew that if he said one word, or even none, she would lead him into her house, and . . .

With an effort he withdrew his suddenly trembling hands, but before he knew what she was about she had captured one in hers. She turned it over and with the delicacy and skill of a courtesan, she pressed a loving kiss, soft as the touch of silk, on the calloused palm. He caught a ragged breath, and whispered something with a wealth of love that made even the unintelligible words as clear as a crystal pool.

'Jenny.' It was the barest whisper.

'Nils.'

The names were said with the reverence of worshippers at the altar of God.

Not able to trust another moment in her presence, Nils turned and walked quickly away into the night. Jenny watched him until he turned the corner and disappeared.

Quickly she let herself into the house.

Chapter Eight

In trying to describe Jenny Fowler it would be difficult to avoid using such words as diffident, modest, shy, reserved, timid; all conjuring up a picture of a creature lacking colour, personality, confidence or charm. In short, a dull, lifeless sort of a creature.

This was not so. As has been explained, her nature was to steer clear of any collision which might bring about a quarrel, or the anger of another. Though she would go to great lengths to avoid a clash of will with those who lived within her family or circle of friends, she did this because she wanted simply to make them content. To win their love and to keep the peace. She liked nothing better than to feel the sweet garb of concord envelop the people about her, and to know that each agreed with the other, and to see differences swept away like smoke in a breeze.

Jenny was indubitably the perfect daughter for Henry Fowler, for her submissive obedience fell exactly into line with his idea of how a female should be. On the other hand, her very nature would, in the end, drive him to break her as he had her mother. Jenny was too much like Elizabeth. She wanted to please, to be agreeable, and as a child, with a dull misery which had left her sick and desolate, she had run from the sound of the angry outbursts which her poor mother endured, cringing in her bedroom with her hands over her ears, to shut out the harsh unkindness with which her father punished his wife.

Elizabeth and Jenny did not stand up to Henry. The violence of his nature which forced him to ride roughshod over every opinion but his own had been too much for his wife. With a different man she might have become a different woman. What seemed cringing timidity could have become a gentle charm. Sweetness was driven away by fear and the constant dragging down of her spirit, until she became, to Henry, a creature of contempt. If Elizabeth had married another, one with the understanding of her shyness, her simple longing for harmony and the joy of a peaceful companionable marriage, her nature perhaps would have developed, blossomed into mature womanhood, fulfilled and able to give to her husband and family the substance and security of a happy woman.

Jenny was her mother's daughter, but strangely, what had driven her father to the edge of distraction in her mother, was held to be a virtue in his daughter. As a child and adolescent, he had liked her sweet amenability, her goodhumoured willingness to run to do his bidding, and when she looked at him with her velvety brown eyes full of remorse that she had displeased him, it gratified him to forgive her, to watch the smile of relief slacken the tension about her mouth. She was his pretty little girl and good and obedient. She gave him no trouble. There was no rebellious anger in *her* expression, not like their Kate's, or Elly's, and so she was allowed to grow up – protected and petted by Kate and her brothers for she was the baby – in the relative peace of her father's approval. How long this state of affairs would have continued, no one would ever know, but without Kate's contrasting personality to show hers in a good light, she would have become as her mother had, under Henry's increasing contempt.

But for all her amiability, and the tranquil pool of her mind, she had a sharp streak of practicality that was bred in her by generations of down to earth north countrymen who admired and respected a bit of commonsense, and who inculcated this trait in their children.

As she entered her home that enchanted evening, the last vestige of reason, clinging limpet-like to the edges of her mind, was warring, though it knew it was futile, with all of her awakened emotions. Like most seventeen year olds, she had dreamed, smiling inwardly at her own romanticism, of a handsome prince on a white charger, high stepping down 'Scotty' Road, to swoop her up before him and carry her to his castle, though where that would be, had never crossed her mind. He would be handsome and rich and love her to distraction. She would wear a long white dress and sit behind him, her cheek against his broad back, her arms clasped about his waist . . . With the half of her mind which gazed with dreaming eyes at the celluloid 'sheikh' as he carried the swooning maiden to his tent, she tingled in delicious dread at the prospect, whilst waiting, pragmatically, the appearance of some kind and dependable young man to present himself, offering her a charming semi-detached in Tuebrook and two children, a boy and a girl, of course. Even this, to one born and bred at the back of Scotland Road and its attendant working class terraces, seemed somewhat hopeful, but nevertheless, possible.

Now, this very night with the speed of a hurricane, and with as much force and devastation, she had been swept along like a fragile leaf with no will of its own, helpless to control her own passage, drowning in a tide of emotion which threatened to take her reason, as well as her heart. In a few short hours the foundations on which her life was secured had disappeared, and she felt she walked on a shaking substance from which she was powerless to escape. And would she escape if she were able?

She felt elation. Her heart lifted and throbbed with life and her veins ran with the fire of longing for the touch and presence of another, and yet . . . and yet . . . she was afraid. Her good sense, her inbred streak of no-nonsense practicality which, though buried deeply beneath a young girl's hope of romance, was still there, told her it could not be so. This did not happen . . . this . . . melting, dissolving, hankering for a man who was a perfect stranger. Man and woman did not fall in love with one enraptured glance. Eyes did not meet, and with the impact of an explosion, send messages to brain, of love, of trust, of a oneness that turned the earth and tilted the very ground beneath the feet. It didn't happen like that. Only in books. The heroines of Ruby M. Ayres; of Concordia Merrel – what of *Heart's Journey* – did these things, and had splendid, bosom-heaving romances, but not Jenny Fowler from the 'chippy' in West Derby Road. Mary Pickford and Lilian Gish, yes. They did it all the time. Fell in love at the drop of a hat. But not real people. Not folk who live in Seacomb Street. Not waitresses. Not . . . not . . .

'Not me . . . ,' she breathed into the darkness, but knew it for a lie.

She knew as surely as she knew the familiar sight and smell and feel of her own cosy kitchen, that she loved Nils Jorgensen. She knew and was afraid. In the midst of her joy, she was afraid. But of what, she asked herself.

She walked slowly up the darkened hallway, parting the gloom like a ship in a sea. She felt lit up, luminous, and the greyness about her turned to a silvery earth-shine with the strength of her emotions. Feeling her way like someone suddenly blinded, she slipped through the kitchen doorway and round the periphery of the room holding on to the wall and the familiar sideboard until her hand touched the rocking chair. It moved suddenly, violently, as the tabby sprang from it to the floor but Jenny hardly noticed. Sitting down gently, she took the vibrating animal onto her lap and began to smooth its velvet back with trembling fingers. It was as though she desperately needed contact with some everyday plebeian object from the life she had known five hours since. Her breath came quickly in her throat, quivering, rasping, and the cat, sensing her agitation, was alarmed and jumped to the floor, wanting none of it.

It had come too quickly, Jenny thought. She needed time to encompass, to become familiar with the new and frighteningly exciting thoughts and feelings which invaded her.

She loved. She loved.

She said it to herself over and over again, and the rocking chair squeaked softly against the linoleum. It was a dream, a lovely dream from which awakening would come in the sure, clear light of morning, she told herself. Her floating mind was like smoke, feathering backwards over the evening.

The breathless meeting; that first cataclysmic sight of his beauty; the confusion; the laughter, the gentle sweetness of him, the goodness and honesty in his eyes, and the incontrovertible awareness that, with this night her girlhood, the lighthearted, unthinking oblivion of youth was gone for ever, and a woman had entered the soul of the child she had been.

Back and forth. Back and forth the rocker rocked. Jenny Fowler was unaware of time on that first night of her love. Unaware of what had gone before and unknowing of what was to come. Her mind dwelled in marble halls and her body was as light as swansdown in the chair.

The cuckoo clock spoke once and was silent.

An hour passed, and the cat slumbered on the rag rug before the empty grate, its tail moving in sleep, like a fluffy sinuous snake, as it dreamed its feline dreams.

The cuckoo, as though to remind the bemused girl that time was passing, and the Prince only a man after all, cuckooed twice this time, and as the tiny wooden bird disappeared into its painted home, the kitchen door opened and Kate drifted, eldritch like, on the threshold. Her nightdress dragged the dark floor behind her. Her hair flared about her head like Robertson's golly as she scratched it vigorously, and her mouth was wide in a cavernous yawn.

In the opaque light which filtered feebly from the scullery, Kate Fowler saw her sister in the chair and her ears heard the rhythm of the rocker as it thumped the floor, and for an aching moment, as if she looked into the future, her heart missed a beat and anguish filled her. Her feet faltered; the cascade of her nightdress came to rest about her legs, and the tremor of anticipated fear shot through her.

90

Then she laughed nervously. 'Jenny, warra fright you gave me, sittin' in the dark like that. Why don't yer light the lamp?'

There was no reply.

Kate took a step forward, and the haunted remnants of the past few moments became vague and were dispelled as her earthly self, sensible and standing no nonsense took over again. She shook herself as if to dislodge a light weight which had touched her for an instant then spoke again, loudly, scattering ghosts.

'What yer doin' chuck. Why don't yer light the lamp?'

There was still no answer. It was as though the figure in the chair neither heard, nor was even aware of her presence.

'Jenny,' Kate said sharply. 'What's up with yer?'

Jenny did not so much as turn her head to acknowledge Kate's appearance and a thrill of apprehension trickled across Kate's skin.

''ecky thump, 'ave yer gone deaf or summat?' she exclaimed, exasperation and a nervousness she did not understand making her voice shrill. Irritably she crossed to the sideboard and lit the lamp. As she did so, her eyes strayed automatically to the clock on the wall and she gasped when she saw the time. Her face was stern, like that of a mother about to chide the wrongdoing in a child.

'Look at bloody time our kid. Yer've never bin out till this hour . . .' but the rest of her words went unspoken as she looked fully at her sister for the first time since she had left the house over six hours ago.

The soft light from the lamp fell about the room and on to the still figure by the empty fireplace. Jenny seemed bathed in an unnatural glowing incandescence, whether from within or from the lamp just recently lit, Kate hardly knew, but the strangeness of it and the girl's quiet stiffness, as though she posed for a photograph, frightened her to a breathless palpitation which had nothing to do with physical terror. It was as though a cold finger had run the length of her spine, down and up, and come to rest at the nape of her neck. The hairs there bristled. She could only stand and stare, her customary agile tongue for once silent.

The cat, as if aware even when asleep that tension crackled the air, came awake with the alert instinct of its kind, and leapt, fur standing, to its feet. It skittered sideways towards the relative safety of the scullery and as it streaked, Kate came from her trance.

She took a hesitant step forward, then in a rush of protective anxiety, flew to Jenny and sank to her knees before her chair. ·

'Oh my God,' she whispered, 'what is it?'

Her heart raced in fearful anticipation, and the flesh of her face

91

trembled, ash-coloured, across her high wide cheekbones. She stared wildly up into her sister's face and clasped the hand which lay passively in Jenny's lap.

'What is it chuck. Tell me.' She chafed the limp hands between her own as though to warm them, to bring back the flow of blood, all the while murmuring and repeating Jenny's name. Her gaze searched frantically, seeing the aching sadness in Jenny's eyes, and yet, strangely, the joy which shone there. The two emotions overlapped and ran together, melting in the limpid golden moistness.

'Dear God, our Jenny, tell me, are you . . . has someone hurt you . . . For Christ's sake . . . will you . . . ?'

Kate didn't finish the sentence for the fright in her froze her tongue and lips.

Jenny turned towards her at last. She removed one of her hands from Kate's frantic grip and with a softness born of her new love, gently touched her sister's cheek, tracing the firm apple roundness and smiling, as if the awareness of her sister's distress had suddenly come upon her and must be soothed. Her eyes had the look of wisdom which comes to those who know of the enchantment of love.

Though it had only just come to her, this knowledge, she was like a teacher at whose feet a student sat. In the four hours she had been with Nils Jorgensen she had run the gamut of emotions, many of which will not come in a lifetime. Enchantment, bewilderment, love, joy, awe and lastly, fear. Fear, for could such rapture last? Was it not too delicate to stay forever without becoming shattered?

But she continued to smile.

'No our Kate, not hurt, not hurt.'

'Then what . . . ?'

Jenny stopped her with a finger to Kate's lips.

'Put the kettle on, our kid. Go on, I'm all right really.' She smiled more deeply and a tiny crease, not quite a dimple, indented her left cheek.

'Honest, I'm all right.'

Kate's shoulders sagged with relief and she heaved her nineteen year old frame from the floor as though she were ninety.

'Eeh I could knock yer nose off, our Jenny,' she grumbled, angry now in the way of mothers when a child is safe after a fright. Relief made her sharp.

'You scared the living daylights out of me. P'raps yer'll tell me what yer were doin' sittin' all by yerself in the dark at this hour.

Yer've not just come in, 'ave yer?' she continued suspiciously. 'I'll knock yer block off if yer 'ave.'

Jenny turned her head and stared pensively into the black grate. 'No. I've bin in an hour or so.'

'But why didn't yer come to . . . '

'Put kettle on, our Kate.'

Kate stumped to the scullery, knowing Jenny would say nothing until she was ready. She might be quiet, their kid, but she could be stubborn, and there *was* something. It was more than just the desire to sit alone in the dark which had made Jenny rock quietly by a dead grate.

'What did happen, our kid?' she said quietly as she put a cup of tea in her sister's hand.

Jenny told her.

Kate listened attentively, sipping her tea, watching the play of joy and wonder, of dread and apprehension, of exultation, of bewilderment, chase one another across her younger sister's face. She listened to the lilt of love in her voice as Jenny spoke his name, 'Nils, Nils, Nils'. It was like a sonata, an exquisite piece of music; the song of birds; the harmony of some unearthly choir; the crash of cymbals; the delicate tinkle of bells, all sounding in Jenny Fowler's voice as she spoke of her love. Her eyes brimmed with tears which fell unheeded and her skin was white as a pearl as the depths of her soul was emptied of the fullness of her love.

When she had finished, a hushed quiet fell about the two still figures. Kate felt it enter her heart, and a great dread shouldered its way beside it. Jenny was looking at her expectantly, waiting for her to speak, but what was there to say? It was obvious that some chap had knocked the kid sideways, and the strength of her feelings ill-judged, but genuine, was in no contention, but the whole bloody thing was laughable. After one meeting? Give over! Some sailor had told her a fine tale and she'd fell for it and now fancied herself in love with the bugger. Pull the other one . . .

Kate felt her face stiffen with the effort of keeping it in a mould of impartial interest; she wanted to shout that she had never heard such an incredible piece of nonsense in her whole life, but she knew she must not. Jenny actually believed that she had fallen hopelessly, deeply in love with this . . . this . . . and that he felt the same way about her. Jesus, what some men got up to in their eagerness to find their way into a girl's knickers. It made her sick. But she must say something. Jenny's face was beginning to grow even whiter as the silence continued for too long.

Kate got up quickly, if only to hide the expression in her eyes.

She put her cup on the table, searching desperately for the right words. Jenny's eyes followed her, waiting for her to speak, to marvel with her at the incredible good fortune which had led to her meeting with Nils, to share her ecstasy, to gloat with her over the happiness which she had won. Kate knew her sister. She was a romantic, and every word she had spoken had come from her heart. But this . . . this.

She felt the anger building inside her. The rotten sod – the rotten bastard. He'd taken their Jenny in good and proper and on the strength of one meeting, a couple of kisses and a dance or two, Jenny was innocent enough to believe that they were madly in love and would be fool enough to lie down and let him . . .

Kate turned suddenly, suspicion filtering her mind. Had he . . . ? Was it possible that he had been here . . . that in this very room . . . She glared about her as if to find some evidence that might point to Jenny's guilt, though it wouldn't be her fault, poor kid – but the soft, innocent eyes of the girl by the fireside looked into hers, guileless, without sin, like those of a child waiting to be told that she had done well. Kate relaxed and her breathing calmed.

'Say summat, our kid.' Jenny leaned forward anxiously. Kate sighed and her glance drifted away.

'I . . . dunno what to say, queen. It's a bit . . . well, I never met him did I? You say he . . . he loves yer, but kid, it's only bin a few hours.' She lifted her hands then let them fall to her side. 'Don't yer think yer'd berrer give it a few days, like . . . just let the . . .'

'I 'aven't gorra few days, our Kate. Nils' – she blushed prettily – 'only has four an' he wants me to spend them all with him.'

I berr'e does, the swine. Kate's face was slack and her eyes shifted from side to side. She was afraid to look fully into those of her sister for fear Jenny would see the rage there, and something told her that on no account must she cross their Jenny on this, or she was likely to take off with the bugger. A dirty weekend in a seedy boarding house in Blackpool, no doubt. No. – Say nowt, go along with her, and when the right time comes, nip it in the bud. After all, he'd be away in a few days and Jenny'd soon forget.

'Listen luv, I'm beat, whacked. What d'yer say we get to our beds?' She smiled gaily, the effort of lifting the corners of her mouth like that of trying to up-end a fifty ton locomotive. It didn't reach her eyes. 'I dunno about you, but I always say tomorrow's another day, and we can talk then.'

Her heart felt like a stone in her breast, and she could not ease it, even with her own words. She tried to tell herself as she and Jenny dragged wearily along the hall to the bedroom, that it would all come right in the end, but it seemed to do no good. These bloody sailors, after one thing and one thing only, and she just hoped their kid would see it before it was too late. Four days. A lot could happen in four days, and listen to the way she'd talked. A god! she said. A god!

Kate fell wearily into bed and Jenny beside her, but neither slept until the first tiny sliver of autumn dawn inched its way above the river where it met the sky.

Kate liked him. Who wouldn't? He was everything that Jenny had said he was, and she felt herself, wrapped about in the protective armour of Charlie's love as she was, respond to his charm. It was not just charm though. The word has a shallow ring to it, like that of some sophist who deviously manipulates for his own ends, and she knew instantly that it was not so with Nils. She liked his simple, straightforward manner. There was no 'side' to him. He shook her hand with a tiny bow, and his eyes smiled in a sunny way into hers, lingering only for as long as politeness demanded before returning to rest lovingly upon Jenny. He was tall, taller than Charlie, and as handsome as a film star, and his manners were lovely. If only Charlie could see him helping her into a chair, and springing to his feet when she came to hers. But then Charlie had no need of these things, and perhaps this man did. Who was to say what went on behind that shining smile, and those electric-blue eyes? Still an' all, he did seem to be over the moon about their Jenny. Couldn't keep his eyes off her. She hoped he had better luck with his hands.

But she could feel herself, even in the short space of time he was in the house, warming to him, revising her opinion of the man who brought stars to their Jenny's eyes, and in ten minutes, a flush to her own cheeks.

As Kate watched them walk away, absorbed in each other, laughing, arms entwined, already, though they had known each other only a few hours, as easy in each other's company as are those who are made for each other in heaven, she felt a small pang of envy for their rapture. She and Charlie . . . well . . . their love was strong, basic and down to earth, and in her heart she knew she would have it no other way. It was not of the stars, nor made in heaven, but it would survive. Perhaps it lacked a certain romance, a bewitchment that had struck Jenny and Nils, but it was good. Good, that was the word for it.

'. . . An' yer can't eat cream cakes all the while,' she muttered wisely to herself. 'Yer've gorra 'ave a bit of bread an' butter sometimes.'

Not quite following her own thread of thought, but feeling comforted just the same, she went inside and banged the door.

Chapter Nine

Like four flawless pearls set on a necklace of inconsequential worth, the days of Jenny and Nils were without blemish. They were made up of consummate treasures, the kind one brings out when one is old, fondles lovingly and wraps tenderly away in case of damage, for of such perfection are the most beautiful memories made, and for such memories is the greater price to be paid.

Like two sleepwalkers, oblivious to the world in which they moved and the men and women who peopled it, the couple lived in a fragile bubble of dreams, made by each other, for each other. Every coming together had a symmetry which left them awed and filled with a reverence for the fate which had decreed that they should meet, and every parting was a surgeon's knife, used without opiate, that cut them cruelly apart. Hour followed complete hour; as many as they could pack into twenty-four, filled, overflowing with love, until they were satiated with it, but still it was not enough.

It started, the first one, soft as down, as Nils' hand took Jenny's, flesh touching flesh, coming home, easy, sweet, and their fingers met and held and fitted together like the skin and muscle and bone of one substance. Their steps seemed paired and in rhythm, though those of the man's were longer, and they walked along the mean streets of Liverpool, straight backed, young and beautiful, seeing nothing but each other.

Somehow, though neither could say how it came about, they found themselves upon a tram, but the miles of terraced boxes on either side slipped by unnoticed. Women scrubbed doorsteps, bums in air, wrinkled stocking tops showing white flesh and garters. Men stood against corners, pipes in mouths, hands in pockets, enjoying the mild autumn sunshine and children screamed at one another though they stood not an arm's length apart. Games were played. *'One, two, three, elera, I saw me Aunty Sarah, sittin' on a bambalera, eatin' chocolate biscuits.'*

'The wind, the wind, the wind blows high . . .'

'The good ship sails through the ally-ally o,' and long, twining lines of

hand-holding little girls crept in and out under one another's arms in a pattern that only they could understand.

The sky was high and blue and the wind caught them as Nils and Jenny stood at the Pier Head, and Jenny's hair blew like a silken flowerhead about her small skull and Nils' hand moved, as though it were the most natural thing in the world, to smooth and stroke it back into place. He smiled, and she stood gazing up at him, dark eyes shiningly solemn, and they told him she loved him, but he knew.

They walked with the crowd, for it was Sunday and the customary day for a trip to New Brighton, down the tilting, springy walkway to the docks and for twopence rode the smooth ferry across the Mersey. The water caught the sun and shone like wrinkled grey sateen and over their heads the gulls cried beseechingly and floated on the wind, their beauty breathtaking. Wings like snow, tipped and streaked with palest grey, black heads nodding as if to say they knew and understood. The man and woman stood in the prow of the boat, facing into the sun and wind, and she leaned back in his arms, feeling them, warm and protective about her, and his chin touched the top of her shining head. She turned to look at him and without speaking he placed his lips against her skin. They smiled in perfect understanding.

But when they reached the long stretch of sand which looked out to the Irish Sea, their quiet, inwardlooking absorption with one another was shattered by an upsurge of youthful joy and became a longing to dash and play like children. They ran barefoot, leaving behind the families who sat in deckchairs, dug sandcastles and paddled ankle deep in the muddy water. Hands clasped, Nils pulled Jenny along in a breathless, ecstatic race, feeling her fragile hand strong in his, holding, holding, and her face lit up and was alive and flushed and her eyes were brilliant, sparkling like topaz. Their feet left deep, parallel indentations in the yellow sand. They laughed at nothing and everything. Nils wore Jenny's hat pulled down over his ears, strutting like Chaplin with a piece of wood for his cane, and Jenny, quiet, shy, reserved Jenny, did her impersonation of Zazu Pitts, and they fell in love all over again, for they learned that they shared laughter.

They talked now, sitting side by side at the water's edge, alone and apart, as they watched the ships enter and leave the river's mouth. Of what? Of all the trivial but earth-shattering things which lovers adore. They spoke in awe of the dread chance that had thrown them together, and in horror, that they might have missed each other, but as lovers will they became convinced that given

98

even a different set of circumstances, they would still have met, despite the impossible odds, and gazed into one another's eyes, choked on the thought of the endless, empty days which would have followed should the impossible have happened.

The sun warmed them, bringing a golden glow to Jenny's cheekbones, and the breeze, gentler here away from the river's turbulence, touched them like a lover's kiss. The smells of the water, oily, floating with the debris of a thousand ships, filled their nostrils, but soft upon it came the aroma of warm sand, a fresh salty tang from the sea beyond, and brought from some garden on a vagrant whisper of wind, a faint perfume of honeysuckle.

They walked back along the emptying beach, their hearts over-flowing, the loving warmth escaping, touching the hearts of men and women who responded with smiles, and nods, and memories of their own youth and passion.

On the journey back towards the shore of Liverpool, the deck beneath their feet vibrated with a whispered, 'Good bye, good bye'.

They moved through their four wondrous days together. Every-thing they did was touched with a dazzling fullness, a wholeness that left nothing out, a completeness in which nothing was lacking. There was a balance, a harmony that seemed to crown those days with goodness, with a sure tranquillity which wrapped them both in a cloak of certainty that it would never end. The weather, as if knowing it must be kind to these lovers, was like the gentle hand of heaven upon them. Warm, soft and filled with affectionate sun-shine.

These were the days and innocent love-filled nights.

Inevitably it came.

The last.

Tomorrow he would sail away with the morning tide.

They danced, their final night together in the place where they had met, her head upon his shoulder, his cheek against her hair, and as the time ticked inexorably onwards, their faces took on a strained, pinched appearance, drawn, pale, desperate.

They sat in silence on the tram and the sound of their footsteps was loud and echoing in the mid-week quiet of Seacomb Street as they walked back towards number thirty-six. The night hid the crumbling, poxy-faced houses, the wavering golden-shot street-lights lending an air almost of distinction to the rundown seediness of the area.

Jenny felt drained and empty as if already the being who had been suffused with the joy of loving for four days, had become hollow as that joy drained away. Her hand in Nils' was aching as it clasped his frantically, trying to cling to this moment, to hold back the time of parting. In four days her life had turned upsidedown, and in the centre of it, where once there had been a vacuum, was Nils. Now he was to leave her and how was she to fill that empty space until he returned? She would be like one of those blown-up rubber dolls that she had once seen on the Golden Mile at Blackpool. The right shape and size and colour, but with nothing inside her. Her heart would go with him, and her thoughts and everything that was secret about Jenny Fowler, which only Nils had discovered. How was she to manage? To walk, and talk, and do her job, and go on with the everyday ordinary things of life.

A tremor moved in her chest and made its way to her throat. It ached and ached like her hand. Like the rest of her body. Like her heart. She moaned, a faint whisper of a sound, and not even the man beside her heard it, for he was also crying inside and his own grief at the coming parting made him hurt.

They stopped at the door, hesitant, crushed already by the loneliness they knew would come soon. They looked into each others' eyes, drowning in the love they each saw, and Nils tried to speak, but a catch in his throat at her loveliness stopped the words. He wanted to tell her it would not be for ever. That soon, soon, he would be back again. Four weeks, only four weeks, his mind repeated, but his tongue and lips would not work and he could only look at her imploringly. He wanted to ask her to wait, to be patient. He longed to say a dozen comforting things, to enfold her to his chest, to take from her eyes that look of dread, but it was impossible. Not here. He could not hold her for all the world to see and laugh and whisper at the goings-on at number thirty-six. Not his love, not his sweet Jenny. So they stood and looked and the moment stretched on unendurably.

With a suddenness which made them jump apart in shock the door to the house opened and light spilled out. Someone stood, outlined like a ship's figurehead by the illumination from the passage, the features of the face invisible. But there was no mistaking the breasts and thrusting hips of Lily Donaldson. Her hair flamed around her head, haloed, and she lifted and pointed her nipples in the direction of the man.

Jenny and Nils stood, mouths agape, like two fish just landed on New Brighton jetty.

Lily laughed at their startled faces, and automatically, with a gesture which was entirely her own and belonged to no other, she patted her hair, pouted her lips, then stood, hand to hip, delighted at the sensation she had caused. Though it took only a second or two she seemed to enact a complete performance of *Camille* from smiles to seriousness, from warm welcome to pathos, at the news she was about to impart.

'Eeh, Jenny, 'ere yer are at last. I thought yer'd never gerrere. I've bin waitin' ages.' She simpered and struggled between a desire to give Nils one of her full-blast smiles, and an overwhelming need to hold on to her own self-important role in the current (and serious) drama. The indecision was plain on her face. Should she be gay and charming or softly solicitous? The world was a stage to Lily and for once she was undecided upon her role.

It was Jenny who broke the spell under which the three of them were cast.

'Warrisit Lily?' she exclaimed sharply, her own heartache momentarily pushed aside as fear caught her. She peered over Lily's shoulder and putting a foot on the doorstep, tried to shoulder her aside, looking for Kate.

'Where's our Kate? What are yer doin' 'ere?'

'Nay, it's all right Jenny.' Lily curved her lips and pursed them in the general direction of Nils. 'Your Kate's all right. She asked me to stay and tell yer . . .'

'Tell me what? Where's she gone?'

'Well if yer'd let me finish . . .', Lily's petulance in the face of Jenny's interruptions and Nils' bewilderment, was growing by the minute, and after all she'd done an' all. It wasn't her fault, was it? She was only doin' a good turn . . .

'Will yer tell me what's happened for God's sake?'

With a shrug of annoyance at Jenny for spoiling her big scene, Lily said primly, 'She's gone to Mrs Walker's . . .'

'What for? What's she gone to Mrs Walker's for?'

'Well if yer'd shurrup a minute I'd tell yer.'

'I'm only askin' . . .'

Nils took Jenny's hand and pulled her gently back from the step. His thumb caressed the skin of her palm and instantly she was quiet.

'Let Lily tell you, Jenny. It was good of her to stay and help. She will tell you where Kate is if you let her.'

Lily was diverted, and for a moment she gazed with something like veneration at the handsome face of the seaman. God, he was gorgeous and what a lovely way he had of speaking. It sent shivers up and down her spine like she was a cat being stroked. Her face took on a look of melting humility. She'd do 'owt for a chap like 'im, she would. Jenny Fowler was a lucky beggar.

She pulled her gaze from him with reluctance.

'It's Annie. Charlie's sister. She's bin in an accident. A tram or summat. Any road up, she's in t'infirmary and your Kate's gone to sit with Mrs Walker. I dunno 'ow bad it is, but I said I'd come and get your Kate and of course Kate was worryin' about you, so I'd said I'd stop til yer gorrome.'

Nils stood patiently by Jenny's side. The quick nasal Liverpool twang which the girls spoke was beyond his formal understanding of English.

''Ow long's she bin gone?'

'About an hour, but y'see chuck, she don't know how long she'll be. Maybe all night.'

Her cheeky face assumed a knowing look, sliding from Jenny to Nils and back again. If one of them had happened to look at her she would have winked slyly but neither did. Jenny's mind was like a hive, a seething mass of images, busy, busy, busy, with the thoughts like bees flying in and out, pausing, hovering, swarming, and not one alighting long enough for her to get a grasp of it.

Annie lying bandaged and in pain . . .

Mrs Walker weeping . . .

And poor Charlie . . . she was his little sister . . .

What a cheeky devil that Lily was . . . the way she was eyeing Nils and if she didn't watch out she'd land her one . . .

Kate . . . holding Mrs Walker's hand in that sympathetic way she had . . . a good one to have around was Kate, when there was trouble . . .

And all in the space of time it took to blink an eyelid.

'Well,' chirped Lily brightly, turning back to the door, 'this won't buy the baby a new frock will it, and I've gorra get the tram, or it's shanks' pony for me. I'll just get me coat . . .'

She disappeared and in a moment was back, struggling into her coat and perching a scarlet beret on the top of her puffball hair.

'Tara well. Now don't do 'owt I wouldn't do, an' if yer can't be good be careful.'

Jenny came from her trance, her mind still darting like a firefly, mercifully missing Lily's parting shot, and Nils, still trying to translate Lily's words into something resembling the English he knew, was staring in wonderment at the clash of colour on Lily's head, and the ecstatic bouncing of her bounteous breasts.

'Right, Lil, an' thanks kid. Tell our Kate I'll be all right on me own, will yer, and not to worry.'

'Oh I will, chuck, I will.'

Lily was laughing as she walked away though Jenny was at a loss to see where the joke lay.

Nils stood patiently to one side of the open doorway, waiting for Jenny to notice him again. His natural good manners would not allow him to indicate that they might go inside, though he felt that the eyes which peered from behind curtains across the narrow street must certainly have had their money's worth that night. His brilliant eyes rested on Jenny. They were misted with love and his mouth, though firm, almost stern in its manly beauty, was gently smiling. He had understood scarcely anything that Lily had said, but the troubled look on Jenny's face and the droop at the corners of her vulnerable mouth, filled him with an urgent need to hold her, to smooth away the fine crease between her silky eyebrows.

'I'm afraid your friend talks too quickly,' he said. His eyes were concerned. 'There is something wrong with Kate?'

Jenny turned to him instantly and her smile lifted the corners of *his* mouth. She touched his cheek gently.

'No, not Kate. Her future sister-in-law.' She saw he still did not understand, and her heart turned over for love of him. Turning, she pushed the door open wide and still talking, she stepped inside beckoning him to follow.

'I'll put the kettle on,' she said matter-of-factly, so completely taken out of herself by the events of the past ten minutes, that to invite him into the house – for the first time empty of Kate – seemed the most natural thing in the world. A drama had taken place, something out of the ordinary, and the panacea, the automatic reaction of all women to a crisis was to put on the kettle and make a cup of tea. He followed her into the kitchen, closing the door behind him, aware before she that this was the first time they had been completely alone. Alone in a place shut off and apart from the rest of the world. Jenny was still talking, excitement lifting her voice. She took off her coat, throwing it carelessly across the chair by the fireside. The room was dimly lit with the glow from the fire, for Kate had lit one as the evening turned cool. The walls rippled in gold and rose as the last leaping flames chased away the drabness. The lamp was burning but Lily had turned it down to a thready flicker, as though to set the scene for the lovers, and the gentle delicate tick of the clock upon the wall fell, like a musical benediction into the suddenly electric silence.

Jenny halted halfway to the scullery, the kettle in her hand where she had taken it from the stand before the fire.

Her heart began to thud and a dryness scraped her mouth of every drop of moisture. She wanted more than anything in the world to turn and look at the man she loved, but for some unaccountable reason she found it impossible to move. The kettle was a ton weight in her hand, but she was incapable of loosing her hold upon it. Her breath was torn in her throat and her mind was frozen with only one thought in it. She was alone.

The silence was heartstopping. Pulses beat all over her body, and she felt herself shake with the force of it. She might have stood there till the end of time, for in her innocence, her inexperience, she had not the smallest notion what she should do next. Never had she known such an awareness of another's presence, nor of her own body's responses to it, and she wanted to cry with anguish. She longed for some voice to speak to her, to tell her what she must do, but none came.

With a touch as soft as a leaf come to rest on the autumn ground, she felt Nils' hands on her shoulders. Still she dare not move. If she should turn and see a stranger, a stranger looking from Nils' face, with Nils' eyes, how could she bear it. Might he not be different, now that . . . now that . . .

'Jenny.' His voice was hushed with his love for her and she knew finally, with a frenzied relief, that it was all as it should be. She had nothing to fear. There was no doubt, no mistrust or apprehension in this room, for she was with Nils. She almost laughed aloud with the sheer joy of it; of knowing, at last, that she was safe.

She turned. He took the kettle from her hand and placed it upon the table and her last coherent thought was that their Kate would be livid when she saw the sooty ring the bottom would leave on the red chenille cloth.

His hands cupped her face. He held her, looking into her eyes deeply, strongly, as if to tell her that this was as it should be, would be, world without end, for evermore. Her hands hung limply at her side as she waited to be guided by her love. His mouth came softly upon hers. He moved his lips, and hers opened like petals in the sun and he tasted the moist flesh inside and his tongue gently teased against her teeth. Slowly, slowly, deeper and deeper, soft, soft, then firm, warm, deep. Tongues met and caressed, and at last Jenny knew what she had been born for, what women are made for, what she must do next, and next and next.

Her arms rose and clasped her lover tightly about his neck. Her fingers gripped fiercely the golden curls at the back of his head and she pulled his face down to hers with all the strength she had.

It was their first kiss that was not the gentle, hesitant kiss of the newly met, a farewell brush of mouth upon mouth, the trusting kiss of those who know that their time will come and be all the sweeter for waiting. The man had held back from the first, leashing his own sexuality, for he knew her to be unworldly, and he was conscious only that he must not misuse her purity. For that was how she was to him. Pure, untouched, and in his masculinity he was glad. She was to be his, first and last. His own experience with women had been that of any sailor who roamed the world, finding release in a dozen ports, but never love. He had been 'in love' half a dozen times. Nils Jorgensen attracted women like pretty moths to a candle, and the pleasure he found with them was always freely given. Where other men had to buy, he had their favours almost thrust upon him and, for the most part, they were girls like Jenny. Sweet, soft, appealing to the male in him, enticing him, and he was a man and could not resist. He liked women. He found their company charming and their ways a joy, and what man can say 'no' to an invitation that is implicit in its meaning. He was a man of much experience, but to his credit he only took what was offered willingly. But now he loved. Now his heart was involved and in the ways of love, he was as inexperienced as she. But he knew the ways of the body, and with the wisdom given to him by his feelings for this woman, he combined the two, love and physical rapture, and they entered their new world together for the first time. Jenny and Nils.

Time had no meaning and the cuckoo came and went unheeded. Her breathing quickened and fluttered against his cheek like the wings of a bird. He caressed her ears and neck with gentle fingers and soft warm lips, kissing, always kissing, eyebrow, cheek, closed eyelids, lips, the hollow of her throat. His hands stroked the nape of her neck lifting her hair, smoothing, rumpling, touching, touching. She stood in his arms, shaking with longing for whatever he would do to her, and the moaning began at the back of her throat, his own breathing was hoarse and ragged, and the heat of his loins spread, answered by hers. She felt the hardness of him press against her and his fingers fumbled with the buttons of her dress. She lifted her arms eagerly to help him. With deliberate slowness, for this moment comes only once, the moment when the beloved's flesh is looked upon for the first time, he teased her dress from her shoulders, sliding it down across the silk of her skin, until the rosy, flame-tinted roundness of her breasts was exposed, quivering and pointing with desire. Her nipples were like small, pink pearls, hard and thrusting and his lips went to them, sucking and gently nipping each in turn. Her dress and underslip fell to the floor and kneeling he removed the rest of her garments as she lifted her feet delicately, one, two. She stood proud before him, moaning, sighing, clutching in an ecstasy of wanting him, of wanting his naked body against her own. Deftly, swiftly, he removed his own clothes. Eyes hungered, moving across flesh flushed with longing. Gasping, arms about each other, naked skin against naked skin, they sank, graceful as two seabirds, down, down, through the sea of their love, to the yielding ocean floor of passion. The rug, soft and warm and steeped in memories, made a bed for them before the friendly fire. His hands were gentle on her breasts and belly, brushing with reverent love the dark, silky triangle of her pubic hair. He touched and caressed and kissed, holding back until she cried for him to pierce the core of her, and when he did, it came with the glory they had longed for, unknowingly since the first moment of their meeting. It stilled their ecstatic voices with its clamour and they were spent, drained, floating like driftwood in the tiny ripples that touched the shore after a storm.

For a long while they lay in each other's arms, his head on her shoulder, his hand still at her breast. Their breathing was quiet, and now at last, thirst-quenched, they looked at each other. Jenny sat up, her lovely breasts falling forward. Nils lay on his back, his eyes upon her. Cupping her breast he felt the soft weight fill his hand, and the nipple harden in his palm. Her eyes travelled down his body, lean like that of a sleek young animal, the gentle mound of his penis almost hidden in the brush of his pubic hair. She looked shyly into his eyes, hers round, astonished, as if she would say, 'Where is it, where has it gone, that giver of love and joy?' And he laughed out loud with the wonder of his new love.

Then he sat up abruptly and drew her fiercely into the circle of his arms kissing her brow, her cheeks, her lips passionately with a force almost desperate.

'I love you. I love you, oh, my Jenny . . .' and overcome, his tongue unable to express how he felt in any language but his own, it lilted from him in a torrent.

'You wait, you wait for me . . .' and again he chanted the strange rhythmic cadence of his Norwegian heritage.

She gazed at him adoringly, her head cocked to one side like that of a puppy trying to grasp the meaning of its master's words.

Nils smiled.

'You don't know what I'm saying do you, my love? This is what I said.' His smile deepened. 'In four weeks I shall come back to Liverpool and when I do, we will make the arrangements.' Jenny still looked bewildered. 'Arrangements to marry,' he continued.

Jenny looked down at the hands which held hers, and her heart threatened to tear itself from her with the force of her love. Marry, he had said, marry. She began to sob and the tears gushed and slipped down her cheek and her shoulders shook.

He was aghast.

'No, my Jenny, my sweet Jenny bird. Do not cry. We will marry, say it, say it.'

She was weeping in great gasping gulps now and he wrapped her in his arms in a fury of protective love.

'Why do you cry? Why? We love, we marry. Did you think that after this, the way we feel for each other, that we . . . ?'

He looked down at her, lifting her chin until her tearlogged eyes met his.

'Oh Jenny, say it,' he whispered urgently, 'say that we will marry.'

Jenny looked up at him, worshipping him and her lips formed the words he wanted to hear.

'I love you, Nils . . . and yes, we will marry.' She smiled brilliantly through her tears and her eyes were like stars.

There was a stillness, now, a calmness, and the look which passed between them was steadfast, unchangeable. Each knew the other's body and soul and their love was bound, his to hers, hers to his. They smiled, and a promise as binding as a marriage vow was made, though neither spoke.

He stood up and pulled her to her feet.

'Come, we must dress and talk.' They slowly put on the clothes neither remembered removing, each still drinking the beauty of the other's body. He cupped her breasts and bent his head to put his lips to the soft swell above the nipple, but as she began to respond, he drew back regretfully.

'No, my heart. I must go or the ship will sail without me.'

As he spoke, as if to underline his words the cuckoo came out of his nest and called three times.

'It is three o'clock so I will tell you this and then I must go. First, my little one, this trip is to New York, but in four weeks I will be back in Liverpool. You understand?' He looked into her eyes for confirmation. 'When I return we will be married and I will stay for two or three months. I have money saved, we will find a house. I will sail on another ship. I will soon find one, easy.'

Her eyes were on his face, drinking in every word. The fire clinked as the last ember dropped and died. She jumped, blinking like an owl as she concentrated obediently upon his words.

'Yes Nils,' she breathed, her eyes like a child's at its first sight of a Christmas tree.

'Now while I am away, you look at houses, at where you would

107

like to live, and then . . .' He didn't finish. The look in her eyes caught his breath and he felt the tears start in his own. Pulling her into his arms, he rocked her back and forth, the depth and width of his love endless, wordless. For several minutes they clung together, then putting her from him, he continued.

'October, the first week, my Jenny. Will you remember?' She nodded blindly.

'I will write from New York and give the letter to a seaman coming on a ship to Liverpool. He will post it here. It will tell you where to meet me, what time. If I cannot find anyone to post it, don't worry, I will come.'

They walked slowly to the street door arms about each other, now that the moment had come, their hearts heavy, their faces stiff with the sadness of parting and the need to be brave for the sake of the other. Turning at the door, he held her tenderly and whispered again some words in his own language. His eyes shone in the dim light and the love he had for her was unmistakable. Lifting his hand, he made a tiny sign of the cross on her forehead, and without kissing her again, he opened the door.

Then he was gone.

Chapter Ten

The sound of a key being turned in a lock awakened her, and for the space of a moment, she was disorientated, unaware of who she was, of where she was, or of how she came to be in this strange world completely alone. She was a new person, one who had been born in the ecstasy of last night's loving and who had not yet become familiar with her other self, the one created by Nils. She seemed to hang suspended, in a new dimension; without Kate, without Nils, without even a sense of the identity of Jenny Fowler.

'It's only me,' said a cheerful voice from the hall, and as Kate's familiar voice rang out, Jenny became herself again. Her face flowered in the harsh light of dawn, as sweet memory flooded her first conscious thought, and her eyes became pools of tawny languor, and her limbs stretched and flowed, and her breath quickened. Her lips moved in a half smile, and a happiness so perfect, it was almost more than she could bear, filled her body, from the tip of her toes to the warm brown shining of her hair.

It was true. Last night was real. It had happened and she was a woman now. She was loved. Her body had been touched by a man for the first time and the moment had been like . . . like . . . she moved sensuously beneath the covers which lay in a smooth mound over her body. She must have slept deeply, peacefully for there was scarcely a wrinkle in the bedclothes. She felt refreshed, though she could barely have had more than two or three hours sleep, and a feeling of wellbeing so overwhelming she could not contain it, flowed beneath her skin, making her smooth flesh prickle.

'Nils, Nils,' her pulse and heart's rhythm said, 'Nils, I love you, Nils.'

She snuggled down deeper into the bed and closed her eyes ecstatically. It was like . . . like . . . she tried to compare the incomparable with some happiness she had thought wonderful in the past, but there was nothing boundless enough, nor as flawless, with which to put it against.

Her youthful ingenuousness fancied a thought of Christmas and the brightness and colours of the glittering trinkets on the tree; or spring, when the glory of an orchard of apple blossom she had once seen had hurt the senses with an agony so exquisite it had brought tears of joy. Or perhaps the day when Mam had taken her and Kate to hear the Liverpool Philharmonic. She had not understood the magic which had thrilled her mother so, but her childish heart had soared with the sounds which had filled her head, and she had wept without knowing why. Kate hadn't liked it much, saying it was too 'highbrow' for her; give her a tune you could hum any time and she didn't know what it was all about anyway. But then neither did Jenny. Just the same it had given her goosepimples.

But not one lovely thought she had ever had, not one perfect moment, could match the way she felt at this precise instant, and with its very quality of awesomeness came sadness for poignantly, she felt it would never come again. Though the innocent certainty of love told her that all would be right from now on, she felt that no matter what joy or happiness she and Nils would know in the future, there would never be a moment as complete as this again.

The thought sobered her and in the dim light her bright lovely eyes became serious; took unto themselves a maturity which was foreign to the character of Jenny Fowler. A head filled with daydreams was Jenny, but now, amongst those dreams, was forming a core of good sense, which, if allowed to develop apart from the dependency which unknowingly Kate had thrust upon her over the years, would see the untried young girl become a woman in the true sense of the word.

But at that moment these were not the thoughts of pretty Jenny. Romance filled her. The knight in shining armour *had* come, and in four weeks' time would carry her off to, well not exactly a castle, but a snug home with love in it. How could she not be entranced? Was she not to become a wife? Her body squirmed with delight at the thought. She would run her own home, have children, and in the centre of it all would be Nils.

Flinging her arms above her head, she stretched, staring rapturously at the ceiling and once more her face fell into an expression of beatific bliss.

Nils. Nils.

Footsteps dragged her from her exaltation. She heard Kate go into the kitchen, the sound of running water, the sharp scratching of a match against a box, and the explosive 'pop' of the gas being lit. Footsteps again, and Kate came into the bedroom, attempting to tiptoe now as though suddenly aware that it was scarcely light and her sister probably asleep.

'You awake, our kid?' she whispered.

Jenny smiled. Awake? She had never felt more awake, more alive, more full of gladness in her life and all because of . . . her mind remembered last night, and at the memory she felt her body go hot and the blush of it enveloped her, and in the dimness her face was pink and her eyes shone. Thank God it was dark or their Kate would have known instantly.

'Yes, luv, I'm awake.' Her voice seemed to lilt, but Kate apparently noticed nothing different in it, for she continued to drift about the bedroom as if the day was as ordinary as any other.

'God, warra night,' she moaned, pulling her dress over her head. Guiltily Jenny remembered poor Annie.

'How is she then?'

'She's all right now, but one of her ribs had pierced a lung or summat, and it was a bit nasty. Poor Mrs Walker was nearly out of her mind. I 'ad to stop with 'er. Were you OK on your own, our kid?' The question was asked perfunctorily, needing no answer. 'I could murder a cup of tea,' she continued. 'I've put the kettle on then I'm 'avin an hour in bed and Waggy can jump in t'lake for all I care. Those seats in the waitin' room at the infirmary are bloody hard. Me bum's numb and me back's in two.'

She stretched, her hands to her back, then sat tiredly on the edge of the bed. Jenny jumped out on her side, and padded in the direction of the scullery, her bare feet whispering on the scuffed linoleum.

'I'll make the tea our Kate,' she said solicitously, 'you gerrin bed and I'll bring yer a cup.'

Kate sank back on the pillow and her body melted into the lumpy bed which was a twin to the one she and Jenny had shared at West Derby Road. Her voice droned on saying nothing, just the sound of it ventilating the weariness within her, giving her comfort.

'In fact, I don't think I'm goin' in,' she went on. 'Sod Waggy. After the night I've purrin I'm fit for nowt.'

Realising she still wore her knitted cloche hat, she pulled it from her head, releasing the mass of her thick hair which leapt up like grass after a roller has passed over it. She pushed her hands through it and yawned.

'Eeh, I dunno, you wouldn't think just missin' a couple of hours sleep could knock you out would yer? I suppose it's strain or summat. What d'ya think our kid?' she shouted to Jenny. 'D'ya think it'll be OK me not goin' in?' She giggled, putting her hand to her mouth, 'first you, then me. It's a good job we're hard workers or Waggy'd give us sack. 'Ere give over, you might have the sack

111

any road. Waggy was in a right state yesterday over you not comin' in for the third day runnin'. Eeh, p'raps I'd berrer go in.' A worried look creased her plump face.

She heaved herself wearily up and her eyes wandered round the room, which was nearly light by now. She sighed deeply and Jenny came in and put a cup of tea into her hand. Her eyes for the first time looked fully at her sister and she was startled by the look of . . . by an air of . . . what the 'ell was it? Jenny seemed to glow. Her skin was delicately flushed where usually it was pale, her eyes were brilliant and she seemed to step like one of those horses you see in a circus ring. High and proud and jaunty.

'You look good our kid,' she said, her eyes roaming searchingly over her sister's body as if the answer to her liveliness might be there. Jenny smiled with a serenity which sat strangely on her young face, and for an instant Kate felt a tiny pang of alarm go through her, though she could not have said why.

'Did yer 'ave a good time then?' she said vaguely.

She sipped her tea, losing interest in her sister's appearance and her mind slipped back over the events of the night and she did not really listen to Jenny's answer. She heard her voice from the distance and nodded a time or two, but the content passed her by. The scene which had taken place just a few nights since and the words which Jenny had spoken then, seemed to have slipped from her mind and an enormous weariness overtook her. The dread she had felt appeared to have been wiped away by the more urgent happenings of the past hours. Those words of love felt by Jenny and, according to her, by the man she had met, were unaccountably forgotten for the moment, and her own question had been the automatic politeness spoken to one who had been out on a jaunt.

A silence fell as Jenny finished speaking and with the cup in her hand, Kate began to doze. Jenny took it from her and placed it upon the dresser. She looked down at her sister's face, realising that Kate was engrossed with the drama of Charlie's sister, and for once, her preoccupation with Jenny's well-being was missing. She thanked God for it. It gave her time to put together the words with which she must tell Kate that their life together, as a pair, was nearly over. That in four weeks' time, or thereabouts, they were to part.

Gently she rearranged the eiderdown about Kate's neck and then began to dress.

Kate had slept all day and with her awakening had come, from out of nowhere, the memory of the night – was it only five days ago –

when the outpourings of Jenny's heart had swept like a fast incoming tide, on Kate's reluctant ears. It was as though there had been nothing between them and this moment of awakening. With a sharpness that was as clear as black upon white, every word that had been uttered that evening returned, and she sat up in bed abruptly.

Did their Jenny really believe it? What she had said. Did she really think that this chap – lovely as he was – no doubt of that, and with the manners and ways of a prince – was as genuine as he appeared. Perhaps she had been carried away with the fascination of it all. Perhaps it was just a crush. Had she, Kate, read more into it than Jenny had meant? And hopefully, would their Jenny be resigned to his sailing away and never coming back? Perhaps tonight, she would laugh and chatter in a lighthearted way of the events of the last few days. She would joke and giggle and relegate the whole affair to the level of her other few romances. She had been 'in love' before. 'Sweet' on a fellow, and it had been enjoyable fun whilst it lasted, but long gone and forgotten before the moon had waxed and waned. No real emotional commitments, and no heartaches.

Oh God, she hoped so, but as she climbed slowly from her bed, Kate had the awful feeling that she was clutching at straws, and that this one wouldn't hold her up in half an inch of water. She could see Jenny's face in her mind's eye, and the expression upon it, as it had been that night. She remembered her quiet sureness as she had spoken of her love; that it was a rock which would stand forever, and the firmness in her voice; and the defiance as if daring Kate to disbelieve. A strangeness, one she had never seen before, had come over her, a certainty, as if at the inexorability of her fate, and Kate was troubled as she slipped her feet into her slippers. She could hardly wait for Jenny to come home from work so that she might see her face, and hear her laugh, and know that it was all right.

But when she came, it was as though nothing had happened. The two girls had a meal. They washed the dishes and sat before the fire and Kate waited, her breath light in her throat, but nothing was said. Nothing except general chit-chat about Jenny's day and her tussle with Waggy who had threatened her with the sack if she did it again, and 'where the bloody 'ell was t'other 'un', and so on until Kate thought she would scream.

The warmth of the room and the snuff-coloured glow from the old sepia wallpaper, gave the feeling of being in a cave. As darkness settled, the light from the scullery slowly dissipated and

Kate felt herself drowsing, a heavy relaxing tiredness left over from the night before settling about her. Jenny still said nothing and Kate began to experience a lifting of her spirits. She watched through half-closed lids her sister curled up in the rocking chair, the cat upon her lap, staring with apparent unconcern into the heart of the fire, as she had done on a hundred other occasions. Jenny looked composed, without care or worry, and her hand polished the satin of the animal's fur in a rhythm that spoke of peace and content.

The clock ticked gently and the cat made soft sighing noises as if she too were bone weary. From the street in front of the house the sounds of children screaming in play pierced the calm of the room and footsteps rang clearly as someone ran past, dying away into the distance. The woman next door sang in a cheerful, flat soprano, the words of the song indistinguishable.

Into the tranquillity of the room, Jenny's words tumbled, ragged and shattering.

'I'm goin' to marry Nils, our Kate.'

Kate felt her heart lurch, then begin to race with a speed which frightened her. Her head, which was resting comfortably on the back of the chair, reared, and her eyes flew open. The tiny snore which had been about to escape from between her half opened lips was strangulated in the back of her throat. She jerked forward as if a hand in her back had pushed her and stared at Jenny's face, and there was complete silence, thick and full of disbelief.

Then Jenny smiled gently. The smile beamed and became a laugh and her eyes crinkled. Her mouth opened and her teeth shone against her little pink tongue.

'If you could see your face our Kate!'

Kate slumped back into the enveloping overstuffed chair and a wave of relief hit her. She grinned but the sharpness in her voice spoke of her anxiety, dispersed now, but a grievance nonetheless.

'Give over yer daft'apporth. You really 'ad me believin' yer for a minute. A joke's a joke our Jenny, but you shouldn't do that to me. I nearly 'ad an 'eart attack.' She warmed to what she thought was the funny side of it, relief making her laugh more than was necessary.

'What put that idea in yer 'ead?' she chuckled. 'I bet it wasn't 'im.'

Perhaps it was the need in her to be reassured that Jenny was safe; that she was not to have her heart broken by some heedless, uncaring chap which made her act and speak as she did. Insensitivity was not a part of Kate's nature, particularly where her cherished

114

little sister was concerned, but the load on her mind had been heavy and the smile on Jenny's face gave the impression that it was all over. That it was a matter for fun, for a laugh, and so she made a mistake. A big one.

She slapped her leg in a show of mirth, and laughed loudly, too loudly.

Jenny's face, which had shone with a lovely sweetness; with the knowledge of love given and received, became still and frozen, and her hands clenched as though in sudden anger.

Kate stopped abruptly, the shrill laughter trapped in her throat. At last she understood that this was no joke, that Jenny was no longer smiling; that the words which she had readily taken as a bit of a lark on her sister's part (though why she should, after last Saturday night) had been said in all seriousness. It was her *own* reaction to them which had made Jenny laugh.

But still she persisted.

'Yer don't mean it luv. It is a joke isn't it?' she said hopefully.

Jenny didn't answer, but her eyes did. They were cold now, angry and hurt.

'You do mean it, don't you?' The smile slid from Kate's face like snow melting in June, but she could not stop herself. She was like a mother exasperated beyond control by the confession of her child to a feat greater than its capability.

'Oh give over yer scone 'ead.' It came out half laugh, half grunt. 'Yer've only known him a few days. He's never asked yer 'as he? Go on, be honest. 'As he said in so many words, "will yer marry me", or did he just hint like that if yer . . . well . . . that . . .' She floundered along, lost, knowing she was making it worse but unable to stop. She tried again.

'He's gone now chuck and Lord knows when he'll be back, if ever. Think about it. Go on chuck, think about it sensibly. Yer'll not see 'im again . . .'

But the words stuck in her throat drowned as was the laughter, by the look of contempt in Jenny's eyes. Kate put out her hand beseechingly, but Jenny ignored it and her, as though she had ceased to exist. Her face was *pale*, blanched and her eyes were huge and dark. With a dignity come suddenly from the realisation that Kate thought her, and her love, something to be laughed at, she rose from the chair, crossed the room to the door into the hall, opened it and went through closing it quietly behind her.

Kate put her head into her hands and began to cry. It had happened. What she had feared most had happened. The kid had been taken in by smooth talk and a handsome face. God knows what had occurred in this room last night but by the look on Jenny's face this morning she suspected the worst. Now she, Kate, had put her great bloody foot in her great bloody mouth and Jenny thought she was against her. Poor kid. She was going to need all the support she could get when she realised he wasn't coming back. That he was like all the rest of the fast-talking 'mashers' who abounded in this great port. Sailors, the like the world over, and she was going to marry one.

Kate raised her tear-stained face and stared into the fire. Why should she feel like this about Nils, she thought? Charlie was a seaman and she never thought of him carrying on with a girl in every port. That's because you know him, a voice said. You've known him for years and you know he's dependable and straight and you know nowt about this Nils. And let's face it, you're a bit mished when it comes to your Jenny. Like a mother hen. She smiled to herself. It was true. She clucked after her like she was a baby chick out on its own for the first time in the farmyard.

Kate got to her feet, her face still wet. She rubbed the back of her hand across her nose and sniffed. She'd have to make it up with their Jenny. It was no use going on about this bloke as if he were a monster or something, or Jenny'd never speak to her. She'd have to smooth it over, gain her confidence. Placate her.

She followed Jenny into the bedroom. Jenny was just getting into bed, her eyes frosty.

'I'm sorry, Jenny,' Kate said quietly. 'I'm sorry, luv. I shouldn't have laughed like that but I really thought you were 'avin' me on. I know how much you said you liked . . . loved . . . each other last Saturday, but I never thought it would come . . . well he were that goodlooking and his accent was just lovely an all . . . well I just thought it were a young girl's . . .'

Her voice trailed away and she looked down at the worn bit of carpet on the floor. 'It's just I don't want yer to be upset, yer know, him being a sailor, and yer know what they say about 'em, and yer so young, queen, yer don't know . . . men . . . not that I do,' she added hastily, 'but, well . . . I'm sorry luv, will yer . . . I'm sorry.'

There was silence broken only by the soft wailing of a baby in the house on the other side of the wall. Kate could hear her own breathing harsh in her throat as if she had been running and sweat pricked beneath her armpits. It seemed an hour had passed before Jenny spoke. She did not look up, but picked at a feather which pierced the fabric of the eiderdown covering her. Her voice was quiet, but strong and clear.

'I know it's hard to believe, our Kate, but you might as well get used to the idea. I know what you say about sailors is supposed to be true and he may have had sailors' ways before he met me, but this is different.' She turned her face up to Kate and the flickering light from the candle lit her eyes so that they shone with twin stars. She looked as though she had seen a vision and her face was almost reverent in its loveliness.

'We love each other, don't you understand? There'll never be anyone else for either of us now. We're gonna be married when he gets back. He asked me Kate. He said "we will be married when I come back". He told me to start looking for a house, Kate.'

She smiled tentatively, ready to forgive, already the joy known to lovers when they speak of the beloved working in her, making her forget her previous anger.

'Be pleased for me Kate. Be happy, cos I am. I've never felt like this before. Never.' Her voice became quiet again.

'The only thing to spoil it is the . . . well the quarrel between you and me. Don't let's be like this, our Kate.'

She looked up with her serious brown eyes, a small frown of concentration between her eyebrows.

'You've bin that good to me. All our lives. Even when we were little kids, yer looked after me. I've always turned to yer, even before me Mam died. I don't know why.'

Kate started to speak, but Jenny held up her hand quickly.

'No, let me 'ave me say. You've bin like a mam to me, for all there's only two years between us and I want yer to know I think the world of yer. No, no, let me finish,' as Kate would have spoken again. 'I know yer think that this with me and Nils is a dream, but it's not Kate, please believe me. Something happened between us right from the start. I can't explain it.' Her eyes became unfocused as she looked backwards to the moment when she had first seen Nils, and for a second her heart thrilled at the remembered joy. She looked up into Kate's eyes and her own were shining with unshed tears.

'It wasn't like no thunderclap Kate, like in books, but one minute I was me, Jenny Fowler and the next I was someone else, and that someone else loved Nils and he loved me. And yet, I'm still the same, still Jenny Fowler.' Her face was tranquil and sad and her eyes were bewildered, then they cleared.

'It's all mixed-up Kate, but one thing's not. He's comin' back our Kate, very soon, and when he does, we'll be married. I'm goin' with 'im Kate, wherever he says. I couldn't live without him now.' Her voice was imploring. 'Try to believe in him like I do.'

Kate felt tears prick the back of her eyes again. Jenny's quiet

117

assurance, her confidence in this unknown man's integrity was almost beginning to make *her* hold it for the truth.

'You're so sure of him aren't you?' she said.

Jenny nodded her head emphatically and the rickety old bed shook on its castors. Kate continued, 'You can't blame me for feeling as I do though, our kid. We don't know him, or what he does, or where he comes from. Oh I know he's from Norway, but that tells us nothing. You knew him for four days and I must admit I was . . . taken with him when you brought him 'ere, but you can't judge a parcel by its wrappings luv. Now I'm sayin' no more, not another word except, don't let's go to sleep fightin'.'

In a moment the two sisters were in each other's arms and the tears flowed and they hiccoughed and laughed and swore never to fall out again, but Kate could not shake off the small thread of fear which knotted itself in her stomach.

Though she smiled and listened to Jenny eulogise over Nils, Nils, Nils, her heart was like a lead weight and the effort to keep a look of bright interest, to appear to give approval, where none was felt, was nearly too much for her.

Jenny, Jenny, she wanted to say, he's 'avin yer on, luvly. He just wanted to get between yer legs, can't yer see. Please God he didn't succeed cos I bet he tried. Four days. Things like this don't happen in four days our kid. Only in books or films. Not to the likes of us. He's a seaman. He'll have a girl in every port he visits, all waiting for him to come 'ome, all thinking they're the only one. Oh Jenny, Jenny.

Her heart was breaking for the ecstatic look on her sister's face, and in her bones she felt that look would soon turn to one of sorrow. But she said nothing. She could see that Jenny believed every word she was saying, so she let it be. All the outpourings from her sister's lips shrivelled and fell like cinders into the void of Kate's sad and angry heart and she wished she had him here, just for a moment, the man who was responsible for the radiance on Jenny's face. She'd personally cut 'em off for 'im, with the bloody kitchen knife an' all.

It went on, far into the night. The plans, the joy, the innocent secrets (all but one) the love, who had said what and to whom and when. Kate listened aghast, afraid and bewildered. It was beyond her comprehension and when Jenny finally fell asleep with her lover's name still on her lips, Kate lay, staring into the black night, alone with her thoughts.

It never once occurred to her that all Jenny had told her was true.

118

Across the darkened rooftops, the words of the two young girls soared and drifted, unheard, on the night air. The anger and fear, the love, the hope, the trust, filtered and spiralled like tossing clouds towards the river that wound to the sea, and two seamen lifted their heads for an instant as if their names had been called.

The handsome young sailor who studied a chart on the bridge of a ship, was far off, bound for the shores of America, but it seemed to him that he heard his name sigh over the bow, and linger like a warm hand, about his cheek. He lifted his head and stared through the bridge window, then walked towards it slowly. He looked out into the enormous void of slate grey nothingness that was the sea and the sky, seeing with an inattentive eye, the white tracing of foam which laced each small frill of a wave. The sea was relatively calm at this time of the year and though the sun did not shine it was mild, almost balmy. He knew that the rest of the passage would be uneventful. The weather forecast had promised slight seas, good visibility and the absence of the ferocious winds that could whip the delicate white caps into rollers that were the height of the ship. It was almost the end of his watch, and as he looked, his brilliant eyes caught a glimpse of light several miles off. The sun would be almost below the horizon now and as it sank a sliver of pink and gold tinged the underside of a smoky cloud that drifted towards the land in the same direction as the ship.

A slight smile tilted the corners of Nils Jorgensen's mouth. His eyes, which a moment before had been keen and alert, became soft with some secret thought and his heart tripped a beat as golden brown eyes set in a round, rosy face imprinted themselves on the darkening mirror of the window. He sighed softly, and his lips formed a name, but the crewmen about him did not hear. His arms, which were straight out before him, hands against the bulkhead, flexed and became flaccid as his memory flew back across the silvered waves towards a small, warm room and the white and pliant body of a woman he had held there. Jenny, his mind whispered, and he thrilled to the silent sound of her name in his head.

A voice spoke his name sharply and he turned, reluctant to leave the reverie into which he had fallen, but the seaman who had come to take over his watch laughed and punched his arm and the dream was gone.

A British merchantman steamed slowly up St George's channel towards the port of Liverpool and leaning on the rail, his grey eyes sharp in their attempt to pierce the dark which was all about him, a young sailor who worked in the galley of the ship flicked a glowing cigarette end into the foam which the prow of the ship divided. His white overall gleamed in the dark, and he put up a hand to undo the top button at his neck.

The lights of Birkenhead spangled in the misty darkness on his right, stretched out like a necklace of diamonds on a background of velvet, and the moving glow of a ferryboat passed in ghostly fashion across the bows of his own ship. The North Wall Lighthouse winked cheerily its tempo of welcome. One, bright, two, dark, three, bright, four, dark. Ships towered along the quayside, outlined against the glow of the city of Liverpool, and mens' voices sighed softly across the width of water which carried him homewards. Charlie recognised the familiar berths as the SS *Adriatic* steamed slowly towards her own sanctuary. The 'Canada Basin' leading to 'Canada Lock'. 'Huskisson Dock', and there was the clock tower, Trafalgar Dock, Victoria Dock. The water moved like oil on each side of the ship slipping away to the mouth of the river and the sea, but Charlie's thoughts were on the way ahead.

He bent his head and rested it on his forearms for a moment, then lifted it again and stared with fixed wide eyes towards the shore and the nearing lights which streaked the dockland on either side of the river. Like that other sailor many miles away, Charlie's eyes warmed with love and grew misty.

Tomorrow he would be with his Kate.

Chapter Eleven

During the night the rain had streamed from a black sky onto the roofs of the city, slicking them to a shine like gleaming coal. It cascaded down tiles to gutters, streaming through spouts and across cracked brick walls, sluicing along pavements to be lost in the drains beneath the streets.

It was still raining at dawn as Kate opened the scullery window to admit the angry and bedraggled cat, which in the heat of the melodrama played out the night before, had been let out and then forgotten. It twitched its tail, and flicked its ears as if to say, 'and nobody speak to me today or they'll feel the sharp end of me tongue', as it headed for the rag rug before the coke-piled fire which was just starting to take hold. It turned and turned in a circle before settling down to the time-consuming business of transforming itself to its usual sleek beauty.

Kate fought for a place before the glowing grate as she dressed herself, and she shivered in the chill of the kitchen. Summer was gone with a vengeance, short as it had been, as was autumn, and though it was barely September, it seemed that winter had set about them already.

Jenny drifted into the kitchen, her eyes still cloudy with sleep murmuring, 'It feels like we're up before God this morning'. Her nightdress hung about her slight figure like a shroud and her bare feet cringed from contact with the bare linoleum of the hall. She forced her pace until she reached the rug and the three of them jostled for the warmest spot before the fire. It washed them in an orange, tawny tint, throwing shadows about their shivering forms, painting the nightdresses of the girls from white to a pale apricot and casting the cat with a glint of gold.

The day started badly. The first tram was full, as was the second and the rain poured down straight and sullen. It fell like needles, sharp and pointed, and within minutes both girls were soaked. They stood, dripping and miserable as tram after tram went by, filled to bursting with people who, had the day been fine, would have walked to work to save a penny or two.

121

At last they were able to squeeze on to a number 17 which dropped them off at the top of William Brown Street, with the length of Dale Street still to be walked.

Waggy was waiting for them as they slunk, fifteen minutes late, into the café, and under the amused scrutiny of the first of the breakfast trade, told them in terms varying from sarcastic to explosive, exactly what was his honest opinion of them, and their lackadaisical manner of timekeeping. It seemed he was not running a charitable institution, nor a pleasure palace for the amusement of young ladies, nor yet again a home for the aged and infirm and he would be immensely grateful if they would . . . but the rest was rude and could cause the customers offence and so was spoken in the confines of his office, and unheard by everyone except the two tearful girls. Despite the growing resentment of the two frantically busy waitresses who were covering for Kate and Jenny, he attempted to track down the reason for Kate's absence the day before, returning again and again to Jenny, thrusting aside her parrying, as he did his best to elicit the cause of her non-appearance for three whole days.

But they stuck together these two, and he could find no hole in the fabric of their story of a family crisis.

He let them go reluctantly. They were good girls and had never let him down before, so he decided to give them another chance. He sensed some drama not spoken of, but who was covering for whom he was at a loss to explain. He believed the tale of the girl and the accident with the tram which Jenny had told him about yesterday, but that did not explain the mystery of her own truancy. The old man was consumed with curiosity.

Percival Wagstaffe was one of life's enigmas. Showing one face to the world, he kept his real self hidden, and the girls who worked for him would have laughed at anyone who declared that he had a heart. They knew him for a tyrant who demanded every ounce of effort they could put into their jobs. They knew him for a pedant who would put up with nothing short of perfection; in their appearance, personal hygiene, the set of the cloths on their tables, the sparkle of the cutlery at their station, and the welcoming smile and cheerful words they must allow to flow over every customer. They knew him for a joker who would lock them in the dark cafe at night, and pretend to go home, whilst splitting his sides on the corner of the street as he imagined their terrified shrieks to be let out. There were rats in the cellar at Waggy's despite a cat who was supposed to dispose of them. They knew him for a lecher who couldn't keep his fat, dirty old man's hands off their bums if they

122

should be unlucky enough to walk up the stairs in front of him, and the sound of his bellowing, often impolite voice, was enough to send a girl running as if the hobs of hell were on her heels.

At heart, he was as soft as 'clarts'. He couldn't stand to hear of anyone in trouble, though he went to enormous lengths to conceal the fact, covering his tracks like a hunted animal in his efforts to keep from them the real source of his largesse.

'You wanna get the doc to that Mam of yours,' he would thunder to some worry-racked youngster who confided her anxiety to a workmate and mysteriously the doctor would turn up at the sufferer's door, talking of free treatment and medicine that needed no payment. An extra bob or two would find its way into a pay packet at the whisper of a brother out of work, some excuse being made about a mistake in hours worked for last week, or an error from a month or two back.

One bitter winter's day a pile of warm woolly coats was found, thrown carelessly in the back of the waitresses' cupboard. Waggy did confess absently to a jumble sale and his Mam (an ancient crone of ninety or so) picking them up for sixpence each, but scarcely seemed aware of their existence, let alone value, and that night half a dozen young waitresses who had arrived in clothes more suitable to a walk down Blackpool's promenade on a hot summery day, went home with more warmth about them than they, or any member of their family, had known before or since. The coats probably rested now on coathangers in the pawnshop but Waggy could do nothing about that.

His girls ate as well as any of his customers, and though they worked hard they were fairly paid, and treated. And had they known it, should any of them have responded to Waggy's leers, or winks, or suggestive remarks the old man would have run down Dale Street like a greyhound. Only his mother knew him for what he was and he loved her with a steadfast devotion.

She had been a cook to a big house in her younger days. She was good – one of those women who have a magic in their fingers which does not come from measuring or recipes, or rules of thumb as to the heat of the oven, or the birthplace of the flesh, fish or fowl. She could make horsemeat taste like the sweetest lamb, and her way with a meringue, or a sauce was nothing short of witchcraft. She could find her way around the most exacting menu, and with a little dash of imagination, and a teaspoonful of some secret this or that, her meals were fit to be eaten by royalty and had been, for·was not a certain Prince of the Realm, well known for his appetites, a frequent guest at the big house, and had he not particularly sent

123

down his compliments to her on the occasion of his eating one of the best soufflés she had ever made.

But all that came to an end, when at the age of twenty-five she fell under the spell, only once, but that was enough, of a smooth-talking valet of a guest of her master. Percival was the result. She had to go of course, but one man's loss is another's gain and 'Mrs' Wagstaffe knew only how to do one thing well. Cook.

She and Percy were close, loving and fiercely protective of one another from the day the boy was able to understand that his mother was no ordinary woman. She was tough, hard-headed and had an eye to business seldom seen in this world of men in which she moved. Her little café thrived. She worked hard and so did Percy. He had not much schooling; a month or two here and there when his Mam could spare him, but he got his education just the same, by being with and working beside, his mother.

Now she lived in a big house herself. In Aigburth. It was full of heavy old pieces of furniture and rich drab carpets, trinkets and gee-gaws and hideous ornaments which Percival bought her, and they pottered about together like two maiden aunts, and in his worst nightmare, Percy tried to imagine how he would live without her. From her he got his business head and passion for hard work. Unbeknownst to himself he had inherited a heart as soft as marshmallow from his father.

Now it worried and nagged him all day long, as he watched the two pretty Fowler girls.

During the next ten hours they were up and down the stairs, taking orders, polishing cutlery, setting tables, shaking out cloths, laugh and chat, chat and laugh, carrying this tray up and that tray down the steep flights from the kitchen and back again. Their feet and ankles swelled and their young backs ached and their shoulders became stiff and set from carrying a tray on one upraised hand, but they were used to it and life was good and tomorrow was coming and would be wonderful, for were they not young and was not the world a breathtaking place. Charlie was coming, and so was Nils, and they were in love.

At five o'clock Kate and Jenny finally clattered down the stairs with the rest of the girls who were going off their shift. They were so tired and numb it was almost a surprise to see Charlie, cap in hand, standing among the crowd which streamed in both directions along Dale Street.

The rain had stopped, but the pavements were still wet and shiny, and in the gutters, huge puddles had formed. Lights from shop windows reflected and moved in the water, and sprays of diamond droplets scattered the giggling girls, as trams swished by. It was like no other place on earth. This great sea port. Every language known to man could be heard, clicking and lilting, hissing and grunting, as French, Italian, German, Swedish, Chinese and the sound of every nation which boasted a navy filled the wet air. Sailors of every colour and nationality passed by calling to girls, pushing each other in goodnatured rivalry, for it was still early evening. It would be later that tempers would shorten as bellies filled with drink, and Fritz would take exception to Antoine, or Olaf to Mario.

Charlie did not see the girls for a moment. He was warding off the friendly, and scarcely intelligible enquiries of two sailors who were seeking more erotic pleasures than those to be found with these simple working girls. Their rapid French, or was it Italian, flowed into one ear and out of the other, and his goodnatured face was losing its look of smiling tolerance as he tried to loose their grip on his arm when he caught sight of Kate. He almost slipped on the slick pavement in his hurry to get to her and her heart swelled with fondness for him.

His arms went out to her, then fell abruptly to his sides. The girls about them were giggling at nothing, as young girls will, and his eyes, searching her face earnestly in an effort to determine whether her feelings for him might have altered in four weeks, fell abashed to the cap in his hands. Jenny hung back, her heart soft with happiness for her sister, and her whole being longed for the moment when it would be Nils in Charlie's place and herself where Kate stood now.

Charlie spoke first.

'Hello, Kate.'

Kate bobbed her head and her cheeks flamed.

'Charlie.'

'How are yer then?'

'I'm fine, fine. How's yerself?'

'I'm fine thanks, Kate.'

'Good, good.'

The stilted conversation dried up and Jenny smiled to herself. Why was it, she thought, that just lately every time Kate and Charlie met they were like two strangers recently introduced? So polite, so correct, saying nothing, but she failed to see the eyes of Kate and Charlie melt, and speak, and say all that their words did not. Warm and tender, like loving friends. Not for them the exquisite rapture of Nils and Jenny, but the steady, strong, undemonstrative tried love of two people who knew what they wanted

125

and were prepared to wait patiently for that solid relationship to be cemented in marriage. Not for them 'moons in June', or night-ingales singing, but affection, trust, loyalty and a devotion to one another that would last a lifetime.

Charlie turned to Jenny. He and Kate would say all the things that had been left unsaid later.

'Hello, Jenny.'

'Hello, Charlie' – and so it went for five minutes.

A tram clattered and whined its way up Dale Street from the direction of the Pier Head, its wheels clicking over the points on the track. A fine spray lifted on each side of it as it ran through the water which had collected on the road. People jumped and laughed. The nights were drawing in and the dismal, low-hanging clouds helped to make the evening dark. Shop windows glowed and from behind them, creeping from the entrance to Waggy's place, came the most tantalising smell of food. Jenny's mouth watered and her stomach growled and she thought of the two cornish pasties in her bag which, unaccountably the old man had slipped into her hand. Suddenly she longed to be at home, alone, beside the glowing fire. She would eat her pastries and have a mug of strong sweet tea and curl up in the rocker and dream and dream. She began to run towards the approaching tram. Turning her head she shouted over her shoulder. 'Tara, you two, 'ave a good time,' and in the next moment was leaping onto the platform, with half a dozen others. She waved and grinned, then disappeared up the stairs onto the top deck.

The couple watched her board the tram, then turned to each other once more.

'Kate.'

'Charlie.'

They might have met that moment instead of ten minutes before. With a laugh, pleased with the instant understanding which was growing between them, Kate tucked her hand in Charlie's arm and they began to walk along Dale Street. They stepped out in perfect unison for they were of exactly the same height. They talked as they went along, avoiding the crowds who scattered the pave-ments and jumping the puddles which formed at every gutter.

After a supper of fish and chips, they were going to the Mecca. She and Jenny had worked many evenings bending over the red chenille-covered table, sewing on a cherry red wool dress for Kate to wear for Charlie's homecoming. She wore black, shiny patent leather pointed toe, high heeled shoes and flesh coloured silk stockings, and her hair, following its own dictates, framed her bonny apple-cheeked face. Jenny had waved it for her the night before, attempting to persuade it into the head-hugging style that was popular, but the damp weather and its own inclination made it stand up in a dark spindrift. Her eyes were blue as cornflowers and the dress which was the perfect colour for her outgoing bright good nature, showed off the strong curves of her plump figure.

Charlie was transported. He had never seen Kate quite so lovely and so pleased to see him. She seemed to be exhilarated and her manner was teasing and warm, even tantalising. He was crowned with bliss.

As had Jenny and Nils, Charlie and Kate danced and talked the night away, but the haunting and ethereal relationship of Jenny and the sailor was not for Kate and Charlie. They did not dream into each other's eyes, nor sigh and tremble. They did not speak of poetry, nor music, nor worry at the thought that they might never have met. They laughed and eyed each other appreciatively and felt about them though they were scarcely aware of it, the steady secure strength, the taken-for-granted depths of their love for one another. It was there, now, and they did not question it, nor ask from whence it had come. They had it, and each other and it was enough for them.

It was mid-week but still the ballroom was crowded. The couples swayed and dipped, the rhythm of the music, the click of heel and toe on wood, the rustle of conversation and the bright flow of colourful dresses made a kaleidoscope of patterns which mesmerised. For an hour they danced every dance, eager only to have their arms about each other. Kate's bright eyes laughed into Charlie's and now and again, as the lights dimmed, they stole a hurried kiss.

They made their way upstairs to the tea room and settled themselves, one on each side of the table in a small secluded nook. Kate's cheeks were flushed and not just with dancing and Charlie was unmanned by his love and need for the girl who sat opposite him. He took her hand across the table and squeezed it gently. The room was noisy with the hubbub of young people enjoying themselves, passing to and fro among the tables, and the clattering of crockery as the waitresses collected empty cups and saucers. The music, a lilting melody, soft and misty enough to bring stars to the eyes of the shop and factory girls who dreamed their dreams in the arms of sailors and dock workers, drifted up from the dance floor and under the sweet mosaic of sound, encouraged by her shining eyes and warm loving glances, Charlie said softly,

127

'Have you made up your mind yet, my lovely girl?'

Kate looked up at him and her eyes were melting for him. Her answer was there but he wanted to hear the words.

'I've thought of nowt else, Kate, ever since yer were a lass. You know how I feel about yer, don't yer?'

She nodded. Oh yes, she knew. Though he had said nothing, she had known. He continued, rubbing her hand with his thumb.

'What do you say luv, shall we . . . ?' He ducked his head shyly. His feelings were deep and hidden and were difficult to bring to the surface, especially the telling of them.

'Will you marry me, Kate?'

She looked down at their hands clasped on the table top and her hesitation was plain.

His heart dropped and rose again sickeningly. 'There's . . . there's no one else, is there?'

She looked up quickly and shook her head.

'Oh no, Charlie, no. There's no one but you.'

His face split into a wide grin.

'Well then . . .'

'Oh, Charlie, it's not that easy.'

'Why, our Kate?'

Unnoticed he had applied the possessive before her name.

She hesitated, still looking down at the table. He lifted her chin with his finger and looked into her bright blue eyes.

'Why, our Kate?' he repeated.

'It's Jenny, you see she . . .'

He laughed out loud with relief. 'Eeh luv, she'll come with yer. Did yer think we'd leave 'er on 'er own? I know she's nowt without you, but there'll always be a home for 'er with us, lass. Any road, it'll not be long before some chap'll come along and . . .'

She interrupted him. 'That's just it Charlie, he's already come.'

His face was bewildered and he stared uncomprehendingly.

'Wha . . . what d'ya mean? There was nobody when I was home last. She can't have met someone and got . . .'

'Oh yes, she 'as Charlie, and I'm worried sick about 'er.'

'Why – what's up wi'im?'

'He's a sailor.'

'So what?'

'Norwegian.'

'Well – what's wrong with that?'

'You should see 'im. 'E's got Valentino knocked into a cocked 'at and talk about charm. 'E's just got 'er where 'e wants 'er. Says 'e wants to marry 'er and she's over the bloody moon. She says they're gettin' married when 'e comes back in October.'

Charlie was silent and for the life of him he couldn't see what all the fuss was about. Talk about luck, someone to take on Jenny. That meant he could have Kate all to himself. What if she had just met him? If they were keen on each other . . .

Kate cut in on his quiet elation.

'Charlie, I just don't know what to do. Yer know what they say about sailors, a girl in every port an' all that.' Charlie grinned. 'Now don't you smile at me, Charlie Walker. It's different with us, we're goin' steady, but this with Jenny and Nils – *Nils*, I ask you.' She raised her shoulders in dismay. 'Well, I don't know what to make of it. He might even have a wife in Norway for all we know.'

Charlie watched her worried face, feeling a certain amount of resentment towards Jenny and her unknown sailor. Here he was home after four weeks, feeling all romantic, proposing marriage to his love and all she could do was go on about their Jenny.

'Oh come on, Kate. Don't make more of it than what it is. Just a young girl's fancy, I'll bet. He's likely said summat about a weddin' joking like, and she thinks he wants to marry 'er. Next time 'e comes 'ome she'll 'ave someone else in tow. She's a goodlooking girl and only seventeen. There'll be a few more before she settles, you'll see.'

– And more's the pity, he thought privately. He had nothing against Kate's sister, in fact he was resigned to the idea that where Kate went, Jenny came too, at least for a few years. He was fond of her in a brotherly way and really had no objection to her living with them for a while. She'd be company for Kate whilst he was away, until the babies came, but if she was going to get married, all the better.

'I don't mind if she does settle, Charlie,' Kate continued. 'It's not that I'm worried about. Wharrif 'e lets 'er down? You 'aven't heard 'er. She thinks the sun shines out of his . . . well, you know.'

'Now look, luv,' Charlie said firmly, trying to put Jenny and her love life behind them for the rest of the evening. 'I'm sorry 'an all about your Jenny but I think you're crossing your bridges before you come to 'em. Likely it will be as right as rain. Now come on, Kate, let's go an' 'ave another dance and you can concentrate on me, not Jenny.'

Kate looked up at him as he stood, an angry expression clouding her face, then it faded as she realised he was right. Jenny's problems, if she had any, were not for tonight.

They returned to the dance floor, her arm in his. Charlie put his arms around her and with her cheek next to his she forgot all about Jenny.

Two hours later, in the cosy privacy of the kitchen a very flushed and dishevelled Kate sat up on Charlie's knee and with a sparkle in her eye said,

'Well, Charlie Walker, I reckon after that you an' me will 'ave to be wed.'

Chapter Twelve

Jenny lay in the warmth of the feather bed listening to the sounds of Kate and Charlie creeping up the hall, past the bedroom door and into the kitchen. She heard the door shut and then there was silence.

Charlie had been home for over a week now. His ship, the SS *Adriatic* had sailed three days ago on a West Indies cruise, but Charlie throbbing with love and reluctant to leave his Kate for so long had signed on a new ship the SS *Aurania* and would be leaving for Philadelphia in two days' time.

It was eleven days since Nils had gone, and Jenny's thoughts as they always did when she was alone, drifted back to the four days she had spent with him, days which seemed filled with a dreamlike quality, as if viewed through chiffon. Pictures painted themselves upon her closed eyelids, and she studied each one carefully as if committing it to memory. Like a film run at half-speed, she and Nils floated, light as air, across the warm sands of New Brighton beach, watched by the large, round, laughing faces of the passers-by, balloon-like and distorted. Only she and Nils were clear and perfect. In the midst of the slow parade of gossamer memories, one stood out from the rest.

The feel of the ship's vibration under their feet as they had leaned on the rail, the wind and spray in their faces. A seagull, a grey and white blur as it dived against the harebell sky; the warm hardness of Nils' hand in hers, and his golden face, eyes alight with shining love. In her mind she outlined the firm smiling mouth with her fingertips, before capturing it with her own, and back now, in her own bed, she moved uncomfortably as her body remembered other times, other moments. She felt her nipples thrill and peak, and her hand moved of its own accord across her belly. She felt warm with a heavy longing, and her breath moved roughly in her throat.

Oh Nils, just a few short weeks, less than three now but a lifetime, a lifetime. Her eyelashes fluttered against her cheek. She began to drowse. To dream. Her head was on Nils' shoulder and his arms were strong about her. She was safe, sheltered, loved.

She slept.

Three thousand miles away on the other side of the Atlantic, a cargo vessel of 8,000 tons berthen and eleven days out of Liverpool, was slowly edging its way across New York harbour.

Tugboats pushed and pulled, coaxing the larger ship between the teaming lanes of sea traffic, and the lines which held it fast tautened and slackened spasmodically. Though hooters cried and mens' voices carried across the decks of ships, the wash and suck of the filthy, pewter grey water could be heard distinctly about the vessels.

Seagulls screamed above, flying in wheeling circles against the hazed sky, pale blurs of white, like ghosts of themselves, the beat of their wings and their raucous angry voices mingling with the rest of the noises of the great harbour. Their flashing feathers brushed the oil-slicked water, lifting just in time to soar up and over the grey stream of smoke from the ship's funnel.

Debris clung to the crusted hull of the ship. Orange peel, spent matches, scraps of paper and empty cigarette packets. Dirty brown, frothy scum floated and heaved, rising up and down on the ship's side as it inched its way towards its berth.

The sky was a solid grey, untouched by any other colour, pallid in the dawn light. The hard black outline of tall buildings was etched against the bleakness, and the insubstantial shapes of men and machines could just be made out in the growing light, as they moved about the wharf.

It was the third week in September and the damp chill of the autumn morning could be felt by the seamen on the deck of the cargo vessel. They shuffled their feet and hugged their navy duffle jackets closer around them. They blew on their hands, and their breath hung tonelessly about their tanned faces, only to be wisped away in quick gasps as they began to move in preparation for the vigorous routine of docking.

A tall young seaman stood on the fo'c's'le watching as the squat black tug on the port side guided them towards the dock. His brilliantly blue eyes were intent on the busy scene before him. The tug puffed a tiny mushroom of dark smoke into the air and hooted peevishly as if impatient with the job in hand, eager to be away to the next, and the towline to which it was attached slapped its wet length for an instant above the water line.

In the lightening greyness which hung directly above the man's

132

head, a cloud parted and for an instant the sun gleamed palely, a yellow shaft struggling to find its way through the murk. It laid a tender hand upon the man's short cap of golden curls, before vanishing as quickly as it had come.

The tug strained away; the cargo vessel shuddered and the cable which connected the two became rigid again, rising from the water, straight as a tramline, scraps of the obscene contents of the foul water, hanging like washing along its length.

The whole sweep and movement of the harbour; the busy ships, the bossy tugs; gulls, sailors, clouds, machinery; even the very water which slithered its way along the ship's side, seemed to falter and come to a halt for a split second as, with a harsh, rending sound, strident and metallic, the line parted and whipped through the air, a foot or so from the watchful figure of the man.

Before the horrified eyes of the seaman, petrified by the suddenness of what was happening, the line snaked about him, taking him from his feet. Blood flew around him in a fine spray as the sharp cable sliced into his flesh, even through the thickness of his coat. As his face spasmed in agonised terror, the line threw him high into the air, like a gigantic and playful child with a whip and top, dropping him with hardly a splash into the vile muck of the harbour.

The men on the ship's deck stood frozen, appalled. The tugboat, released at its bow from its hold on the cargo vessel veered sharply, the man at the wheel as stunned as the crew of the larger ship.

They all came to life at the same moment.

A hoarse cry from the wheelhouse was more piercing than those made by the seabirds, and the harbour pilot's face shone a pasty sweating white from the window. A frantic uniformed man of about fifty almost fell down the steps to the deck. With the rest of the crew who now swarmed to the rail, he stared at the widening circles of rubbish where the man had disappeared.

Again the seamen were motionless as they stared at the black water. It was as though the incident had paralysed their limbs, fixing the figures in sculpted stone. Then, as his numbed mind, the first to do so, became alive again, the officer moved. Throwing off his thick coat in one deft movement, his fingers scarcely seemed to touch the buttons, the sailor flung himself over the rail, hurtling twenty feet into the heaving nauseous water below. Where the first sailor had disappeared, the towline floated, the broken end coming gently to the surface, and the officer struck out towards it guided by the shouts of the watching deck crew, all now fully recovered and eager to help. Another man jumped into the filthy water and began to make his way, arms flailing, legs striving, through the mass of debris towards the first.

The two men arrived at the spot together, treading water, reluctant to go beneath the surface to search the unsavoury depths for the missing man. Their faces were slimed and debris clung to their hair. They spat out grey spittle as they gasped for breath and their eyes were desperate.

A shout from the deck which loomed above them like the side of a mountain made them both look up. A hand was lifting and a finger pointed and clear in the muck and rubbish, only yards from where they wallowed, was a gleam of yellow and the outline of a still, grey face. Furiously the two men floundered towards the point where the head bobbed and as it sank slowly beneath the water a hand grasped the short golden curls, clinging, clinging, and with a great heave pulled the body of the injured man to the surface. Four arms grasped him. Ropes and lifebelts were thrown and a boat was lowered.

Twenty minutes later, the blanket-wrapped figure of the golden haired man, lying completely still upon a stretcher, was carried gently from a small boat, up steps that were slippery and green with seaweed and placed for a moment on the stone sets of the quayside. The man's face was drained of colour, his lips so pale it was difficult to see their outline. His eyes were closed and the fan of his thick lashes lay in a shadow of cinnamon on his high cheek-bone. His hair was clotted with blood and clung to his head.

The men who carried the stretcher grouped anxiously about their charge, talking in low voices, the language they spoke lilting, each sentence lifting at its end. One knelt and touched the dirty white face of the injured man, then looked impatiently towards the end of the dock.

The wail of a siren could be heard in the distance, drawing nearer and nearer, and several men who were working in the area, stopped what they were doing, and edged closer to the stretcher, ready to be thrilled in that strangely vicarious way of onlookers at the scene of an accident.

The ambulance screamed its way along the dockside and drew to a convulsive stop, scattering the small knot of workmen who had gathered. White-coated men jumped from the vehicle. One gave the man on the stretcher a cursory examination, lifting his eyelids, feeling his pulse. Words were spoken abruptly and in the space of two minutes the injured man and his attendants were in the ambulance.

With the siren wailing an eerie warning, the vehicle screamed away into the early morning mist. The men on the quayside, hands in pockets, murmured together for a moment or two, reluctant to return to work, then, with only the seagulls to strut and shriek, the dock resumed its previous quiet.

Jenny hadn't seen a lot of Kate during the past week. They smiled and exchanged a word or two at the café, but apart from the journey to work each morning when they sat side by side on the slatted wooden seats of the tram, Jenny dreaming, Kate dozing after her late night out with Charlie, they went their separate ways. Charlie met Kate from work each afternoon, and Jenny caught the tram home to the empty house, happy to sit alone before the fire, the purring cat at her feet. She worked each evening on her sewing, making a soft woollen dress for Nils' homecoming. It was a shade of pale violet, straight, simple with a sash of the same material which girdled her hips, and loose, hanging side panels. Round the neck was a tiny lace collar, creamy and delicate. She sewed the almost invisible cross stitches which would finish the hem, and her fingers smoothed the fabric with the tenderness of a lover's touch on the loved one's cheek.

On the night before Charlie was due to sail on the *SS Aurania*, she was startled when he and Kate returned home early. It was barely eight o'clock. Following a deal of fidgeting on Kate's part, and several embarrassed clearings of the throat from Charlie, she suddenly understood that they would be glad if she would take herself off somewhere.

With an elaborate display of stretching and yawning, she declared herself bored with sewing and announced her intention of paying a visit to Elly. It was only a step to Saint Domingo Road so the fancy did not seem unusual.

Smiling at the look of gratitude on Charlie's face, she put down her sewing and left the pair of them gazing into each other's eyes. As she opened the kitchen door their arms were already reaching for one another. Jenny's glance dropped to the rag rug on which they stood. She felt her skin flush, and her knees trembled as she backed through the doorway into the passage. Would they . . . would Kate and Charlie . . . ? She hardly dared allow the thoughts into her mind. She couldn't blame them for wanting to be alone, but her senses recoiled at the idea that Kate and Charlie might, on this same rug, lie in love together, as had she and Nils. The memory of those hours was as clear as though they had happened only moments before. Her flesh remembered and her breath tugged at her throat. Then she was ashamed. Why shouldn't Kate

135

and Charlie know the delights Nils had shown her? Because she had lain on that same rug with her love, was she to deny her sister . . . but still . . . it seemed . . .

Charlie's eyes were hot and melting, his mouth swelling to meet Kate's, and Jenny hastily shut the door on the sight, feeling as though she had been caught spying on their act of love.

Almost running down the passage, she clutched her old coat and beret from the hook on the wall, and shouting a farewell to which there was no reply, she banged the front door behind her.

It was eight-thirty and the light had almost left the sky. It had been a clear, sunny day, cold, but of the sort which put a spring in the step and a whistle on the lips, and in the west the pale blush of apricot was almost gone as the blue black of night pressed the sun below the horizon. The streetlights came on as Jenny strolled towards the tramstop, casting a shadow which walked behind her, caught up and passed her, before going ahead. The lamp's reflection caught at her face and lit her pensive eyes with a lambent look of tenderness. Her feet were soft on the pavement, as though she walked in fields of daisies and she dawdled, ensnared in her own alluring world.

The air smelled of all the aromas which are generated in a city by the sea; smoke from erupting chimneys, the heavy smell of wet flagstones, fish and chips, a delicious fragrance which lifted over the roofs and came from the biscuit factory in Aigburth Road; a sharp pungency that spoke of the river and the mud that showed at lowtide; unwashed bodies, blocked privies; pigeons, and the unmistakable odour which is the hallmark of any sea port in the world, the smell of ships.

Jenny had no intention of going to see their Elly who would only try to borrow money from her, and besides now that she was out of the house, she had a notion to sit by the river which would bring Nils back to her.

A tram came by and she got on it. Her happiness shone in her eyes and tinted her creamy skin to a pretty flush. The tram conductor winked at her as she handed him her penny, and his teeth shone in his wrinkled face as his mouth lifted in an appreciative smile. Shyly she smiled back, well pleased, even with this small show of esteem, and with a sigh of pleasure for her unexpected outing, she sat back and looked from the window.

Figures hurried and scurried, intent on the business of life, love, pleasure or pain, hastening along the pavements. No one seemed to have the time to saunter, to look up at the last glimpse of pastel blush in the sky, or to listen to the final murmur of the drowsing birds. Jenny could feel the tranquil beat of her own heart. It felt as if it might overflow with the love and joy it held. On the dark window she could see her own reflection, and beside it, another face appeared, its beauty perfect and still. She smiled, and her own reflection smiled back, and so did the pale image by its side and she knew for a certainty that it was Nils calling to her from across the sea. She saw no absurdity in the idea for she had come to believe that two people who were joined in love as were she and Nils, could not be separated by distance. She felt as close to him now as she had when he was with her.

Jenny left the tram at the Cunard building and slowly walked across Georges Pier Head and the floating bridge, coming to the landing stage as the ferry was about to leave. She watched the boat heave backwards, the water churning around it, as it turned its prow towards the far bank of the river. People flowed about her, making their way towards the sloping bridgeways, and the pigeons, disturbed by the confusion and noise, settled once more on ledges and beams, heads under wings, little beady eyes drooping in sleep.

The landing stage was deserted now, between the departure of the last boat and the arrival of the next, and the silence was hardly broken by the slap, slap of the water against the pilings. Jenny wandered, hands in pockets, in the direction of the river mouth, past quiet warehouses until she came to the end of the dock. Two cargo boats were tied up in Princes Dock, huge and black like rusty, leprous whales caught on the beach. Lights shone on decks and in portholes and mens' voices could be heard. A deep baritone sang of Wales from down in the ship's bowels and a clatter told of pans on a stove and a meal preparing.

Jenny sat on a neat coil of thick rope and gazed across the river to the lights of Wallasey. She tried to pierce the darkness of the night, living the moment when she would see Nils' ship steaming in the grey waters towards its berth. Her mind ran on and she imagined his tall figure running down the gangplank, across the landing and into her arms. So clear was the image in her head she turned and looked at the high deck of the nearest vessel and scanned the empty gangplank, half expecting to see him spring upon it and run down its length. He felt so near it was as if he were here in the darkness with her, his earthly body still bound fast to the deck of his ship as he sailed towards her, but his thoughts and his love racing across time and space to wrap around her.

It must be the nearness of the sea, and the ships, and the environment in which he works, she thought as her mind dreamed

137

on. Perhaps the smells of the river, and the sky stretching out until it touched the water, or was it the sad cry of the ship's siren which she remembered from their first meeting. All evoked a picture of the man she loved and she whispered, 'I must come again.' The hushed tranquillity entered and filled her quiet heart.

Charlie sailed the next morning and Kate and Jenny resumed the pattern of their lives which had been disrupted almost three weeks since on the night Jenny had met Nils Jorgensen.

Resumed with one exception.

They no longer went dancing. Lily couldn't understand it.

'It's norras if yer'd gorra ring to show for it,' she announced plaintively, for in her mind no man owned you until he'd put a gold band on your finger, and why Kate and Jenny should sit at home on their bums was beyond her. Lily liked the fragile loveliness of Jenny beside her, for it showed off a treat her own buxom charms, and Kate was a laugh a minute and made for a real good night out. Her arguments were clear and pithy, and to her simple and direct mind perfectly logical. When a chap wed you he had a right to you, hook line and sinker. You didn't go out looking for other blokes or know the excitement of meeting one. You didn't dress up and head for town and wink and smile and feel the thrill of clicking. When you were wed, and not before, you stayed at home and had kids and washed and cleaned and cooked, and life must not be worth living, she privately thought. But not until! Charlie Walker hadn't even given Kate a bloomin' ring, and as for their Jenny, mooning over a sailor who would probably never be seen again, well it was beyond her, it really was.

That night, as Kate and Jenny were preparing for bed, Kate was not surprised when Jenny took her hand, leading her to the chair before the dying fire. She looked up at her younger sister, her face still, waiting for the words which she knew would concern that chap. Jenny's face had taken on the look that she was getting to know so well, and when it did, it always meant she was going to speak of Nils.

'He'll be here tomorrow, Kate,' Jenny spoke softly. 'I know I haven't heard from him but he did say he might not be able to find someone who was turning round and could post a letter from the Pier Head, and it wouldn't be worth 'im posting one from New York. It'd be 'ere the same time as 'im.' Jenny smiled nervously, 'But he said it'd be the sixth, and that's tomorrow.'

'I know luv.'

'I just want yer to know that . . . after . . . when I'm in me own place . . . and you're with Charlie . . . well, you an' me we'll be the same won't we? I . . . think the world of you, our Kate.' Jenny's head ducked and Kate stared at the sharp white parting in her brown hair. 'Yer'll like 'im Kate, really yer will, when yer get to know 'im.' She looked up and her eyes misted with tears, 'It's just that I'm so 'appy Kate. I couldn't bear it if you didn't approve. I want yer to love 'im like I do.' She laughed through her tears '. . . well not like I do, but yer know what I mean.'

The expression in her eyes was filled with joy and shining with happiness and anticipation.

Kate's heart missed a beat. She stood up and pulling Jenny to her, hugged her. If he hurts her I'll kill him, she thought, as Jenny babbled on, her face flushed, her hands moving in an ecstasy of motion.

In Kate's head two words kept repeating themselves over and over again.

Please God . . . Please God . . . Please God, though she got no further for she did not know what she wanted to say, but God knew.

Chapter Thirteen

The day was bright and clear. The last faint star was still to be seen, pricking the pale silvery blue of the dawn sky, and already in the east a flush of washed rose proclaimed the rising of the sun below the horizon.

It was going to be a perfect day.

Jenny stood in the kitchen looking upwards through the half open window, the fat round ball of the cat held gently in her arms. She rested her cheek against the silk of its fur, and her body was still and quiet, with a soft glowing happiness that touched her face with the serenity of a madonna.

At last it had come. The day for which she had waited with all the patience her youth and her longing would allow. The day she had conjured up as a vision, a goal to be attained; the weeks between to be got through as rapidly as time could move. How slowly it had crept and yet it seemed a mere hour since Nils had left her, and as she created in her mind's eye the last picture she had of him bending to touch her lips in farewell, a new image appeared, and she saw his face as it smiled a greeting.

In an instant the tranquillity was gone and a wave of incredible excitement swept through her body, stopping her breath; racing the blood through her veins and setting her life's pulse beating at the base of her creamy throat.

Nils was coming and soon, soon, in a few hours, she would have his arms about her. He would fold her to his breast and his eyes would shine into hers. Oh God, it was almost too much for her to bear. She must be about and doing some task or the sheer joyousness would carry her away and her brain would addle, and she had so much to do. What if he should come and find her not ready? The prospect was appalling, and with a whirl, she spun round like a child in a delirium of gladness, swinging the tabby until its tail lashed and its yellow eyes blurred with the force of its journey.

'Oh Kitty, Kitty, it's here. The day is here and today I shall see him.'

She tucked the dizzy animal under her chin where it rested

140

amiably for a moment, then, collecting its dignity, it leaped from her arms and skittered, kitten-like, across the kitchen to its favourite corner by the fireplace.

Jenny had worked hard since Nils' departure. She had laboured extra hours, doing a shift and a half when one of Waggy's girls fell ill, fifteen hours in all. Twice she had managed it, until Waggy refused her, saying she was fit for nowt if she were goin' to fall asleep on her feet, but he did give her a few extra hours on two consecutive Saturdays, and with a couple of days thrown in, which would come off her week's holiday, she had accumulated four days to spend with Nils. She didn't know how long he would be in port, it might be longer than four days, but if they were to be married soon – her breath caught and she shivered with delight at the very thought – she would be handing in her notice anyway.

With her arms held as though she had an imaginary partner against her, she foxtrotted about the table, tossing her head as she looked up into mythical eyes. She smiled and spoke in a falsely genteel voice and her voice was high and charged with excitement.

'Do you come here often Miss Farquharson?' – she had read the name in an Ethel M. Dell – 'Only when the grouse are in season, Mr Ponsonby.'

Her happiness exploded and she stopped and held her hands to her brilliant cheeks, then looked about her and giggled as though someone had joined in her merriment.

'They'll be comin' to take you away soon, our kid,' she laughed, but her own madness filled her with enchantment.

She began to make her preparations. She had washed her hair the night before, and although she had lain awake for most of the night in a fever of impatience for it to be over – how could she possibly sleep – she looked fresh and lovely. There would be no need for rouge or lipstick today, for the euphoria of love coloured her face and made brilliant her eyes so that she had never before looked more exquisite. The gloss of polished mahogany was in her hair and it fell about her head in a soft smooth cap, turning under at its ends, swinging against her cheek as she moved. She had abandoned the teasing spit curls and her forehead was almost covered by a curving fringe.

Kate had left her only minutes before, rushing as always to catch the tram and avoid Waggy's displeasure, but for a moment or two, she had watched as Jenny stood simply breathing in the day, and she had realised, perhaps for the first time, the depths of her sister's feelings for this man who was virtually a stranger to them both. Jenny's rejoicing heart was shining for all to see, and Kate felt

141

strangely humbled and ashamed at her own disbelief. She had taken a faltering step or two in Jenny's direction and smiled, her eyes warm with affection.

''Ave a luvly day, our kid, an' let on to Nils for me, won't yer?' and then was gone, grumbling about the earliness of the day, the unfairness of having to work on it, and the inconsistency of the tram which was sure to be early, making her miss it, as though to cover her own creeping feelings of fear.

Jenny sang as she stoked the range to heat the water for her bath.

Ma, he's making eyes at me,
Ma, he's awful nice to me . . .

and the fire roared halfway up the chimney. The cat hotched up to the heat and blissfully turned itself a couple of times to make sure it was done on all sides, before finding a place on the rug which was to her liking. The flames seemed in danger of leaping from the grate, and the coal roared as it was consumed. The shadows licked the walls, dancing with orange and red reflections and the content of both young animals was as tangible as the solid four square sideboard against the wall.

Lifting the old tin bath from its hook on the scullery wall, Jenny carried it through to the kitchen, and nudging aside the protesting cat with her foot, placed it on the rug. She paused for a moment once more, holding this moment of sheer happiness to her breast, then sped again on wings that seemed to have just come to her feet, to collect a towel from the bedroom.

The gentle flutter of the butterfly was beginning to quiver within her.

She poured the first panful of hot water into the bath.

Her new dress lay across the bed, waiting for a shape to be placed within it before it could be given life and form. The pale violet of it was lovely against the white counterpane, and placed beside it were the shockingly extravagant, but exquisitely lacy underwear of almost the same shade as her dress. Her only ornament would be a tiny gold locket on a thin chain given to her by her mother on her fifteenth birthday.

It took her an hour to have her bath, empty it, dress, brush her hair until it gleamed, touch a dab of pale pink lipstick to her mouth, cream her hands, buff her nails; a spray of scent, just enough, no more, and it was done.

At exactly eight o'clock she was ready.

Jenny stood before the spotted mirror in the wardrobe door and knew she was beautiful.

Walking slowly from the bedroom and through the kitchen to the scullery, she opened wider the window, to allow some of the heat from the slowly dying fire to escape. Turning back she sat down at the table and began her patient vigil. Tranquilly she picked up the buffer which she had left on the table and began to re-polish her nails. A slight irregularity in the contour of one offended her, and she rose gracefully, and going quickly into the bedroom, as though Nils was to arrive at any moment, as well he might, she re-filed the nail until it was shaped to her satisfaction. She replaced the file carefully in the drawer and returning to the kitchen sat once more at the table.

Her glance wandered about the room, checking it for imperfections. There were none. Everything was placed tidily, dusted carefully, polished thoroughly, even the cat sitting in the exact centre of the rug, like an ornament on a doyley.

Jenny sighed. There was nothing to do but wait.

Vaguely the sounds from the street filtered into her consciousness. She had not been aware of them before as she had busied herself, but now she heard the sound of iron-rimmed wheels on the cobblestones and the clatter of horses' hooves; the hoarse shout of a driver's voice as he cleared some obstruction from his cart's path, and the answering cheeky tinkle of a bicycle bell. From over the backyard wall, a baby screamed desperately, and was rewarded with a hearty slap from some exasperated hand.

Jenny felt a thrill run through her nerves, and she yawned. Dear God, she couldn't just sit here doin' nowt. That yawn was a sign that she was getting the jitters. She wasn't bored, or tired, was she? Well then! It must be her nerves beginning to play up a bit. Couldn't blame them, poor things. Expected to sit about and behave themselves on a day like this. It was more than a body, or its nerves could stand. She picked at the chenille tablecloth with suddenly twitching fingers, glancing continually at the clock on the wall.

At nine o'clock the cuckoo shot out, making her jump and she counted the chimes carefully as though she did not believe the evidence of her own eyes. She let out her breath, which unknowingly, she had been holding, and in a small explosion of laughter and with a rueful catch in her voice, announced to the heat mesmerised cat that, '. . . If I don't find summat to do I'll be barmy by the time Nils arrives. I should have stayed in bed,' knowing as she spoke that nothing on earth could have kept her in her bed another minute.

Springing to her feet, determined to calm herself and find some means with which to pass the moments until Nils arrived, she searched in the dresser drawer and found an old Berta Ruck novel which she had read once and had enjoyed so much, she had put away to read again.

Sinking into the rocker, careful not to crease her dress she began to read. She was on page ten before she realised that not a word of the prose had entered her darting excited brain. What was the romance between *its* pages compared with her own?

Throwing the book onto the table, she walked from the kitchen and into the bedroom, stepping out of her new high-heeled shoes on the way. She would put them on again the minute she heard Nils' knock at the door. There was no use starting the day off with aching feet. They'd be bad enough at the end, when she and Nils . . .

She peered through the window into the street. It was empty save for a woman on her knees industriously red-leading her doorstep, and a horse drawn coal cart. Jenny watched the woman, fascinated by the sway and dip of her buttocks as she moved her arm in a rhythmic arc to and fro, to and fro, then sat back on her haunches, satisfaction in the very set of her thick body.

Jenny wandered back into the kitchen, biting her lip. 'I suppose it could be hours before he gets here,' she told the cat, who rolled an eye politely in her direction. 'I know Charlie usually docks at dawn, though I couldn't say why.' Her tone was absent, as she deliberated on the vagaries of a seaman's way of life. 'It could be teatime even. 'Appen an officer has other things to do besides just pick up his ditty bag and jump ashore.'

Her heart lurched and she felt sick with the idea of waiting like this for the rest of the day. She sighed deeply.

For the next two hours she walked backwards and forwards from the kitchen to the bedroom, each time twitching aside the bedroom curtains to stare sightlessly past the row of closed doors and netted windows to the end of the street.

Figures came and went. Housewives off to the market. The rag and bone man, calling and rattling an old saucepan, crying his unintelligible message to those who might not have seen him. The postman made his slow, patient journey up one side of the street and down the other, and a cart piled high with the contents of someone's home, jolted its way towards Scotland Road.

At twelve o'clock, in a flurry of positive decision, Jenny put on her hat, and at five past, took it off again. She had been determined to go down to the Pier Head and meet Nils' ship. She would dearly love to see it sail up the river towards her, if it had not already done

144

so, but how was she to recognise it, she asked herself, and suppose, whilst she was out, Nils should come? It was quite possible that their paths would cross. For a crazy moment she had a mental picture of herself and Nils, on trams going in opposite directions, staring at each other across the tramlines. Should she go, or should she stay, or should she sit here and go quietly mad? She laughed to herself and sank back in her chair, twisting her hat in nervous fingers.

Jenny rocked backwards and forwards as the clock ticked the minutes away. Slowly, slowly. She started to count the times she rose from her chair to go and look from the bedroom window, but when she reached ninety-three she gave up. She washed her face and put on some more lipstick and a touch of rouge for by this time her cheeks had lost the rosy flush of morning. She thought she would take off her dress and iron it, then changed her mind. What if Nils should come and find her in her cami-knickers? She tittered, a hint of the hysteria she was beginning to feel, sounding in her voice.

She sat down for the hundredth time in the rocking chair and began to rock, back and forth, back and forth.

Kate found her still rocking, in the dark cold kitchen when she returned at eleven o'clock after an evening at the pictures with Lily.

She had been waiting for fifteen hours.

With fumbling fingers, scattering matches about the rug like confetti at a wedding, Kate re-lit the fire. Her heart knocked frantically against her ribcage, and her legs shook so beneath her, she almost toppled against the empty grate. She turned her head constantly, further slowing her progress, and her eyes were wide and frightened in her round young face.

At last the papers which she had stuffed between the bars of the grate, began to catch and carefully she placed small pieces of coal about them, swearing rudely for a moment as the yellow flame licked her finger. When the blaze was leaping to her satisfaction she turned and knelt before the still figure of the girl in the chair, and looked up into her face. The light from the flames played about the sunken cheeks, the slack skin, the blank eyes which sat in the purple eyesockets, and for a brief and merciful moment, Kate could have sworn that a mistake had been made, and that Jenny was dancing in the arms of her love at the Mecca and some other poor soul sat in despair in her chair. But she wore her sister's dress, and her hair fell and shone like Jenny's and the arch of her brow . . .

With gentle, hesitant hands Kate reached for those which rested

145

in the stranger's lap. With some fancy in her head that it was dangerous to awaken a sleepwalker abruptly, and did not the seated figure appear to be in that state, Kate began to stroke the rigid clasped fingers with feather-like touch, whispering her name.

'Jenny, Jenny love, it's me, Kate.'

She rubbed the ice-cold hands, and still talking, drew her chair nearer to her sister's until they sat knee to knee. The fire took a firm hold and the space around it warmed imperceptibly. The glow reflected in the blank eyes of the expressionless face before her, and Kate's terror grew.

She'd lost her reason. Their Jenny had lost her reason. She looked like one of those poor folk she'd seen being led by the hand when she and her brothers and sisters had gone on an outing to New Brighton. Daft they were. Looneys. Grown up but looking like kids with empty eyes and impassive faces, taken for the day from the institution in which they lived, to sit upon the sand and stare, unknowingly at the sea and the ships. What was Jenny doing, sitting here like a . . . like . . . if she weren't . . . and where was that sod . . . ?

Her thoughts scampered about like mice in a pantry.

'Jenny,' she whispered, stroking her face softly. 'Come on luv, talk to me. Tell me what's happened.' As if I didn't know, she said to herself. He's not come. It were all pie in the sky. Promises, empty words to get Jenny to lie down for him. He'd just taken off, forgotten Jenny the minute she were out of sight, and on t' next one for him. God, she could murder him, she could. She'd swing for him if she ever saw him again, not that there was much likelihood of that, the lousy bastard.

Tenderly her hands held Jenny's. 'Come nearer to t'fire, my lovely, and get warm. Yer that cold, yer 'ands are like ice. Come on, I'll put kettle on, and we'll 'ave a cup of tea.'

Kate gazed anxiously into the blank white face but there was no response. She rose hurriedly and went into the scullery, her head constantly turning to look back at Jenny, unwilling to leave her, even for a minute or two. Her hands automatically performed the familiar task of making the tea. She poured the strong brew into a large mug, and returning to the kitchen, wrapped Jenny's unresisting hands about it, praying wildly that the warmth, or the sweetness, or the strength of it, might bring her back from the shock which held her fast. She lifted the mug and the hands which held it, to Jenny's lips, crooning words of comfort and reassurance.

'There, there, lovely, drink it up, good girl, good girl.'

Jenny sipped obediently and, scarcely noticeable at first, the greyness began to slip from her face, and a glimmer of awareness, moved in the flat brown eyes. She continued to drink until the mug was empty, holding it to her as though it were a link, a rope of security bringing her from the drowning sea to the safety of the shore. When it was finished and it seemed she was standing firmly on dry land, she placed it carefully on the fender. Her head turned stiffly in the way of one that has not been moved for many hours and her eyes looked directly into Kate's.

Kate caught her breath and her heart wept compassionate tears as she saw the naked agony in her sister's eyes. Her voice faltered as she repeated the foolish question she had put to Jenny, minutes ago.

'What is it, chuck. What's happened?'

'He didn't come Kate, he didn't come, he didn't come.'

Jenny uttered the words over and over again. Her voice was high and distraught and her eyes, those dead eyes which had held nothing but empty space, were so filled with pain, with such a tearing scream of anguish, that Kate bowed her head and was unable to speak.

'What am I to do, Kate. He didn't come. He didn't come.' It was as though the words were trapped within her head, moving round in a circle to spit from her mouth in a rhythmic chant, before taking another turn. The agony she suffered was beyond the tranquillising relief of Kate's sympathy. It was as though she offered a kind word of consolation to one who was already in the coffin.

Kate's spirit, always so brave, faltered. What must she do? What could she say? The man was obviously all that Kate had feared from the first moment Jenny, her face hallowed with love, had told her of him. It had been too much. Too soon. His supposed adoration of Jenny had come too quickly. And now, now, the seed which had been delicately planted a month ago, so hopefully, so full of trust that it would flower and be the loveliest bloom in the garden, had become a weed, bitter-tasting, ugly. She prayed as she knelt on the rug, her hands held before her as though in church, for the right words, for the wisdom to choose the phrases which would free her sister from the pain which held her. But it was hard. Was she to speak of delays, of breakdowns, of engine trouble which might have held back the Norwegian vessel? Should she say there was still time, that a seaman could travel only as fast as the ship on which he sailed, or should she cut the hope, that last pale sigh of hope from Jenny, along with her heart, by repeating the words and the warnings of a month ago?

Afraid, putting off the evil moment of truth with a contemptuous sneer for her own cowardly heart, Kate managed a tremulous laugh whilst a silent prayer winged its way to a God who appeared to be looking the other way this night.

'Jenny love, don't be daft. You know as well as me what can 'appen to a man at sea. Yer should do,' she said derisively. 'Yer've lived in a sea port all yer life, and 'ow often 'as Charlie bin late? Go on, yer daft 'apporth. 'Ow many times . . .' Which was true and in Kate's own heart a small flicker of hope raised itself from the ashes of her despair. She almost began to believe her own words.

'The weather can 'old them up, or a late cargo, or a dozen things. 'E's not just gone over the water to Wallasey, yer know. Now come on, our kid, pull yerself together. He'll be 'ere tomorrow, just you see if 'e's not.'

The incredible happened. The breathtaking transformation began. The lifeless face became alive. As the words sank slowly into her anguished mind, hope, the life giver; belief, faith, all took root and became a wondrous certainty. What Kate was saying was the truth, of course it was. Tomorrow he would be here. There had been a storm, a hurricane even and he was only now steaming up the Mersey, his dear, loving eyes on the shore, looking for her, searching the crowds on the dock for a sight of her.

Jenny's face became alive, beautiful with hope and joy. Ravaged sorrow disappeared and her eyes flowered like golden pansies after a rainstorm.

'Oh, our Kate, you're right, you're right.' Relief made her incoherent and her tongue tripped, thick and stumbling, over the words which poured from her. 'Of course he'll be here first thing, perhaps tonight.' She turned her head like a bird, all a twitter and a tremble. 'When's the last tram, d'you think. I've never been down there this late. Eeh.' She smiled brilliantly, 'I must have bin potty to think . . .' The feverish babble flowed on as she convinced herself that he would be here soon.

It was all she had to hang on to.

She sprang from the rocking chair making it lurch frantically, its rockers wildly dashing the floor like that of a wooden horse on whose back sat a vigorous child.

'I must get down t'Pier Head.' She began to run from the room, her crumpled pretty dress a rag about her knees. 'Eeh, he'll be looking for me, wondering where the 'ell I've got to. I best get me face washed, and look at me dress,' she wailed, her voice trailing behind her up the narrow passage.

Kate's heart died a thousand deaths in that moment and the feeling of dread almost swamped her. Oh, God, what had she done? In her eagerness to bring Jenny back from whichever private hell her sorrow had flung her, she had probably done more damage than if she had told the truth. Kate was certain, though she didn't knov' ·•hy, that they would neveı see Nils Jorgensen again. That probably at this very moment, he was sweet-talking some foreign innocent into believing the lies he had told Jenny, and now look what she had done. The very words she had spoken had got their kid into a whirl of hopeful anticipation and she was off to meet the sod. Kate had just postponed the inevitable; put off for twenty-four hours the consequences which must surely derive from the mischief done today. The shameful way in which this man had treated her sister, perhaps of small consequence to some who would say it was the way of the world and must be borne, would break her heart. It would put her in torment for she truly loved him. Foolishly it had turned out, but it was a strong and deep love, not given lightly and not cast out easily. Was false hope to be her only comfort?

Kate's head drooped and her eyes swam with tears. Eeh, she thought, I want me Mam. I want me Mam. But her Mam wasn't here. Only her. If only Charlie . . . she thought, or even their Elly . . .

Jenny's voice could still be heard as she crashed about the bedroom pulling drawers out, opening cupboards, flinging wide the wardrobe to find a suitable dress to wear. The violet on which she had sewed industriously for weeks, would have to be ironed and she had no time . . .

Kate crept wearily to her feet and began to make her way towards the bedroom to stop Jenny from dashing from the house this very minute to hurry to the Pier Head to meet her lover.

She felt so tired, but she must dredge the words from somewhere to convince their Jenny that it would be foolhardy to go down to the docks tonight. Dear God, what should she say, what should she say?

Four days later, as the darkness fell, the unmoving young girl sat in her rocking chair looking with dead eyes into the empty grate. She was numb, filled with an icy calm that deadened all pain, leaving her raw exposed nerve ends bandaged with kind insensibility. Kate sat opposite her, staring, her eyes wide, her youthful face white and afraid. She could scarcely bear to look into the days ahead. She knew the depth of the love Jenny had for Nils and though she was calm now, the day would come when she would be brought to the full realisation that he would never return. Oh,

149

she'd get over it, she had to, but God, it was goin' to break the poor kid's heart when it really struck her.

Kate felt the tears brim and watched by the unblinking eyes of the girl in the rocking chair, she put her head in her hands and wept.

Chapter Fourteen

The woman walked slowly away from the grey waters of the river towards the open gateway of the dockyard. She was only a girl really, but the expression of utter sadness on her young face gave it a maturity far beyond her years. It was the end of November and she was just eighteen years old. Her hands were pushed deep in the pockets of her long tweed coat and around her neck was wound a vivid red, hand-knitted scarf. A tam o'shanter of the same colour was pulled well down over the smooth polished wings of her dark brown hair, and her soft face, barely formed into the beauty that was to be hers, was pink with the cold.

A sharp wind slashed at her back, shaping the folds of her coat against the contours of her body and into the mind of the young woman came the thought that it was pushing her directly away from the past; telling her that she must now stop looking over her shoulder for what might have been, and go forward to what would be. Her steps slowed even further until she was almost at a standstill and she felt her heart contract in pain, pumping its message of despair into every part of her body. She had not known that such agony could exist. In her youthful, expectant naïvety she had imagined that only the old suffered, and that when her turn came for the desolation of loss which now held her in its vicelike grip, she would have developed the equanimity to accept it, and the memory of long happy years to sustain her, but it was not so.

From the river behind her came the long drawn out melodic stridor of a ship's siren. It was a liner edging its way into the middle of the channel, escorted by half a dozen tug boats, their own highpitched shrieks synchronising with the solo of the huge ship, like an orchestra accompanying a singer. Sounds of human voices drifted over the cold waters from the berth where the ship had lain, and the cries of 'Good-bye . . . good luck . . . nice holiday,' could be clearly heard as those left behind cheered on the lucky ones who went to seek the sun in other parts of the world.

The girl turned and looked back for the last time. She watched

151

the liner inch its way towards the mouth of the river and wondered apathetically where it went on its pleasure-bent cruise.

Ships. Her life seemed to be bound up with ships, she thought. Enchantment had been given her, an ecstasy that had changed her life, but the ship which had brought that joy had taken it away again, leaving her only despair. She stood for almost half an hour, still as a young tree which is rooted in the earth, only her eyes moving as she looked at the familiar scene.

A group of men walked towards her. As they noticed her still figure they seemed to hesitate, then moved on, passing her in an unusual show of haste. As she turned to look, they touched their caps, and one or two muttered, 'Good evening, Miss.' They were clearly uneasy. They knew her well, these men whose lives centred about the dockyard, and she was aware, though they had been polite and tried to be helpful that they thought it unseemly that a decent woman should hang about their world of rough, out-spoken, often rudely swearing men. The sailors, too, the dozens she had questioned, timidly at first, then with more bravery as her desperation grew, had been awkward in her company. They did not immediately understand what it was she wanted of them. They knew what they would like from her as she stood to meet them as they swarmed down gangplanks, but something, some shining innocence, some feeling of strangeness which surrounded her, made them hesitate, and, filled with a feeling of disquiet they had left her to rush away to find the bright lights and cheerful, uncomplicated company to be had in the city. The strange girl who had enquired of a Norwegian sailor was forgotten before they had passed through the dockyard gates.

It was dark now, but the world about the quiet figure of the girl was filled with lights. Above her they swung in the stiff wind, the wires to which they were attached jumping like skipping ropes, and from every porthole of all the ships which stood against the quayside, they shone like tiny searchlights. From across the river they glowed, casting a reflection in the dark, silvered surface of the water, and behind her beams shone from a million windows and flickered from a thousand street lights.

The gatekeeper's hut was encircled by a glow from a fire and the outline of the old man who kept his vigil there could be seen hunched over a blazing brazier of heaped coals, his hands held out to the heat. The cold bit deep into the flesh in this exposed part of the river and those forced to be out hurried in their eager ness to be home with feet to fender. The sky was a dense purple-blue scattered with stars, and the sorrowing young face turned to look upwards, and the brown eyes searched the darkness.

The girl cast her mind back to the very first time she had come here. She had dreamed her young dreams and imagined the tall figure of a bright haired man coming towards her, his arms outstretched hungrily in anticipation of the feel of her body. Her own had ached with longing for his and still did, but he had not come.

A low cry, soft and agonised, caught the back of her throat and the girl turned and began to hurry in the direction of the gateway. Her mind was overflowing with bright, lovely and unbearable memories and it must be stilled. It must be made to put away the thoughts that only tore her composure to shreds and made life impossible to be lived. It must be forced to dwell on the one tiny life-raft to which her sanity clung. The future. Tomorrow. Next week. Yesterday was gone, but she had tomorrow and soon when she . . . when she. Her vulnerable mouth quivered and lifted in the faint trembling of a smile.

One day, when the wound had healed a little and a scar had formed that would not break open at each tender thought, she would take out her bright memories and look at them and remember. She would share them with another and re-live those lovely days and they would be hers forever.

She reached the gate and the old man, his eyes almost closed in the smouldering heat which enveloped him, jerked awake at the sound of her footsteps. He was alarmed for a moment, forgetting she was still about, then seeing her, recognising her, he relaxed. He touched a finger to his cap.

'Goodnight, Miss,' he said.

'Goodbye,' the girl answered.

Kate would not have believed it had she not seen it with her own eyes.

Joy. Quiet and clear and as shining as the gleam of sunshine on water. It shone in the golden brown eyes. A sweet and joyful look that cut Kate's heart, but at the same time filled her with an elation she had not felt for weeks.

Jenny stood in the centre of the kitchen turning and turning the bright red tam o'shanter which she had just snatched from her head. Her face was rosy and her whole body seemed to be overflowing with some gentle emotion which she could scarcely contain.

Kate began to smile, the simple action of muscle moving on

muscle in her face the most wonderful thing that had ever happened to her, or so it seemed. It was weeks since she had enjoyed anything so much, so she kept on doing it. She could scarcely believe it was true. Could their Jenny be standing there with what was almost laughter coming from her in soft, delicate ripples. After all those weeks of sorrow, of agonised weeping in the depths of the night; of distraught beseeching to be told that Nils *would* come back to her one day, had she finally accepted, become resigned? Was the tide to turn for her?

Kate felt her cheeks begin to crease into a huge grin, as big as the Cheshire cat in the story their Mam used to read to them when they were kids, and though she didn't know the reason for it, she began to laugh.

'Wharris it, our kid?' The reaction to the weeks of strain just gone was so great, she almost giggled.

'What the 'ell are we laughin' at, yer daft 'apporth?' she asked affectionately not caring what it was so long as it took that haunted expression from Jenny's face. 'Yer look as though yer lost a tanner and found a quid.' She got up from her chair and reached for the poker, ready to give the fire a stir and heap on some more coal, for Jenny had brought in the wintry chill of the night.

'An' where yer bin, chuck? I was gerrin' worried about yer. I knew yer finished work at five burrit's gone seven now. Did Waggy keep yer? 'E's a bugger that one. Cute as a cartload o' monkeys. Yer shouldn't lerrim put on yer. 'E knows yer soft so you're the one 'e always picks on. 'E never asks me, I can tell yer. Now sit yerself down luv, by t'fire an' I'll get yer a cup of tea. Kettle's boilin' so it won't take long to get us a brew.'

Kate bustled about, taking Jenny's coat, plumping up the cushions on the rocking chair, stirring the somnolent cat with her toe to make room for her sister, happy to be about the business of some ordinary, everyday activity which did not involve the effort of trying to comfort Jenny. For so long she had worried and fretted, careful of what she said, anxious to avoid another crying scene, overcome with the burden of concocting half-truths that might put off the dreadful realisation that must surely come to Jenny, that Nils would never return. All the doubts that Kate had quietly kept to herself regarding the handsome stranger who had come into Jenny's life, had proved to be true, but how could she say so to Jenny?

But Jenny still stood, twiddling with the hat, smiling shyly, ducking her head like that of some child who is about to perform her party piece but is overcome at the last moment.

'What is it chuck?' Kate smiled, the steaming kettle in her hand, the other reaching for the brown teapot which was warming on top of the range.

'I got summat to tell yer, our kid.'

The words were filled with pleasure but at the same time a degree of uncertainty had crept in. It was as though the news she had to impart was joyful to her, but would it be to Kate, or so her expression seemed to say?

'Well, then,' Kate prompted smiling, unprepared for the blow which was about to fall on her. Afterwards she was amazed that she had not guessed, but then hindsight is easy, and she was so happy to see Jenny smiling, her guard was down and the sword struck her before she had time to brace herself.

'I'm goin' to 'ave a baby, our Kate.'

Jenny's eyes were luminous with tenderness for the tiny bud which grew within her, the seed planted by the man she had loved from the first and would until the last, and in her trust and simplicity she had given little thought to her sister. Since early morning when her startled mind had become aware that twice now she had missed her 'monthlies', her heart could only beat to one rhythm, the enchanted thought that she carried in her womb the child of the man she loved. Now, with a sudden understanding it came to her that what to her was a gift, a tangible remembrance of her love and therefore to be treasured, would not seem that way to Kate. She had not thought it through. She had given no mind to the months ahead, to the struggle they would have, to the distress her pregnancy would cause others, the hardships and yes, the shame it would bring to her family. Her heart had only cherished the feeling of joy that she was to have some part of Nils remain with her, and all day she had worked, and then walked the docks with a quiet serenity building up inside her, that was as sweet to her as honey after the bitter despair of the last two months.

No one, not even Kate, could comprehend the pain which Jenny had suffered. For weeks after Nils had gone she had lain in the night, still and rigid as stone. The flesh had fallen from her and her face had fined to bone, with the misery she knew. Her eyes died and her mouth was silent. Her head had bowed with the weight of her loss. The ache within her was a wound which would not heal, and day after day, the dull throbbing agony of it had almost driven her to ease herself gently into the murky waters of the river which had taken her man from her. Only hope had kept her sane. Later, as the weeks passed it was as if not only hope, but life itself drained slowly from her and she became empty. A hollow figure who went about her day, a vacuum, not only within, but existing in one. The weeping which had at first overcome her whenever she was alone, stopped, and her eyes which had shone constantly with tears, became dull, as though a film had grown across them, and she looked unseeing, uncaring on the world in which she lived.

Only at the docks did she become alive.

Now, in one day, her soul breathed again, given new life by the one which Nils had left with her. She would have his child. A child with golden hair and shining blue eyes which would look at her from Nils' face. Her joy could scarcely be contained, and in her childish innocence she had rushed home to tell Kate that she, Jenny, was whole again, would be herself again. That she could face whatever life had in store for her because of . . . because of . . .

Kate's face seemed to slip, the flesh slackening in waxen pallor and her mouth opened. No sound came from it, though. Her shoulders drooped, and the hand which held the kettle fell and for an awful moment Jenny thought she would let it slip from her fingers, spraying the boiling water onto the cat who still lay protesting loudly at being disturbed, at Kate's feet. Slowly, Kate began to move her head from side to side in denial. Her eyes, which had dulled as Jenny's words sank painfully into her consciousness stared and stared and she seemed unable to move from the awful frozen rigidity into which the words had put her. Only her head moved in rejection, as if to say she wouldn't have it. Oh, no, not this, it seemed to say. Not this after all we have come through. Weeks of it and her seeming to accept it, and now this. She could not stand it. She had been forbearing with her sister, though she had not understood how any girl could let a chap bring her to the state Jenny was in, but now, her mind said, she wasn't having it. She'd had enough.

Still she stood like a rock her head rolling on her neck, her face like putty, only her hair seeming to have life in it. Her mouth opened and closed but she could not find the words in which to convey the deep, deep hurt she felt. Not that Jenny had got herself into trouble, that could happen to any girl, especially one as innocent as their kid (or simple depending on how you looked at it, she thought bitterly) but that Jenny seemed pleased about it. She stood there, a silly simpering smile on her face as if she'd done summat clever. You'd think she'd won the pools or summat. Pleased she was. Bloody pleased.

'Haven't yer got anything to say, our Kate?' Jenny's face was anxious and her voice trembled. She knew she shouldn't have expected Kate to feel the thankfulness that she did, but after all, she was Kate's sister and if it . . .

Kate came to life. Putting the kettle down carefully on the hob, as if to make sure she had both hands free for whatever purpose they were needed, she turned to Jenny.

'Anything to say,' her voice was menacingly quiet. 'Yes, I've got summat to say. I got this to say. You must 'ave your 'ead screwed on wrong, our Jenny. That's what I got to say. I never seen a girl get in such a bloody mess as you're in and be so pleased about it. That's what I got to say. First yer meet some two-timing sod straight off a boat and before 'e 'as time to gerris 'at off, yer let 'im in yer pants.'

Jenny's face went as white as the tablecloth which Kate had just laid for their supper and her hand pressed against her mouth to keep in her cry of horror. She backed away from this virago she had never seen before.

'Yer fall in love with 'im.' Kate's face sneered and her eyes flashed venom. 'In love if yer please, and now yer've the gall to stand there smilin'.' Her voice cracked. 'Smilin', and tell me yer in t'family way. I give up, our Jenny, I give up.' She lifted her hands and let them fall to her side in a gesture of complete mystification. 'I bin patient with yer. I tried to 'elp yer, to understand. You said he were comin' back and was goin' to marry yer.' She laughed shrilly. 'Oh I knew then, what 'e was after, and apparently, he gorrit. Oh aye, he gorrit it all right. Well 'e 'ad 'is birra fun, and you 'ad yours, but I'm damned if I'm gonna pay for it. Yer gerrin shut d'y hear. It's the old Pennyroyal for yer, me girl, and right now before it's too late.'

Kate began to untie her apron strings with fingers which trembled with madness, throwing it onto the chair. She sat down and took off her slippers, reaching for her shoes which she had taken off when she came in from work. Her face was set, her mouth a thin line of determination, but in the depths of her eyes was already a look of uncertainty, of fear, and a deep sadness. Though her anger still burned in her breast, even now she was regretting the harsh words she had spoken in her first moments of terrible rage. Her quick temper, got from her father, had spoken for her and the frightening knowledge that she and Jenny were alone in all this. But she must go on. Jenny couldn't have this child. It would ruin her life. No one would want her if they knew. Even if she had it adopted everyone would know. Oh God, why do you have to put so much on me? Me mam's gone and me dad doesn't give a damn. Oh Lord. Kate began to cry. Her hands which had been busy with her shoelaces, hung loosely down and her head was bowed between her knees.

'Oh Jenny, oh Jenny, luv, what are we to do?'

Jenny had been petrified, like a child whose favourite character, the good fairy, had suddenly changed into a monster before her eyes. Her face was rigid and her eyes stared at the ogre who had been her loving Kate. The things she had said had cut her, a knife that slashed and slashed, but suddenly, with the new awareness which was emerging in the timid girl who had been Jenny Fowler, she understood that Kate had spoken in sheer blind panic. Stampeded by the terror into which Jenny's words had driven her, she had struck out in that first moment of shock, at the one who had caused it.

Jenny walked slowly across the room and sat down in the chair opposite Kate. Pulling a clean tea towel from the line above the fireplace she handed it to her. Kate put it to her face and sobbed inconsolably, her shoulders shaking. Putting her hand out, Jenny stroked Kate's head, then patted her shoulder, waiting patiently until the storm had passed. As Kate quieted, Jenny rose from her chair and went peacefully about the business of making the tea, her step sure, her hands steady, her eyes clear.

When they were both seated with their mugs, she began to speak. Kate stared into the fire with swollen, slitted eyes.

'I know yer didn't mean what yer said, our Kate, about me an' Nils, cos I know yer and yer heart's as big as the moon. I've bin with yer all me life and I know yer wouldn't talk ter me like that if yer weren't . . . upset, and yer know me well enough by now ter know I wouldn't let the first chap I fancied into . . . me pants.'

Kate looked up, startled, but Jenny was smiling.

'I loved Nils, Kate and I know . . . I know as sure as I'm sittin' here that he loved me and that he meant every word of what he said to me. Now, I don't know why 'e 'asn't come back an' maybe I'll never know, but he meant to, of that I'm sure. P'raps 'e 'ad an accident.' Her face crumpled and a tear trickled slowly from the corner of her eye. 'But he loved me, Kate. He did. An' I'll tell yer this, our kid. Nothing you or anybody else can say will make me change my mind. I'm not killin' his child. Never. It's all I've got left of 'im.' Her eyes stared off into the corner of the room and became misty. 'I sometimes think . . . p'raps it's just . . . well I dunno . . . that one day 'e'll come back . . .' She looked up at Kate, '. . . but whether 'e does or not, I gorra get on with me life and the life of 'is child. 'Ow would I feel if 'e came and I 'ad to tell 'im I killed 'is . . . Don't ask me to do it, our Kate, or you an' me'll fall out.'

Kate's breath shuddered from her lungs in a long, painful sigh. For several minutes there was silence. They sipped their tea and anyone entering the room would have been struck by the peaceful domesticity of the scene. Two pretty young girls sitting companionably by the glowing fire, the sleeping cat curled between them. No remnants of the hurtful words remained and the atmosphere was cosy, homelike and told of safety and peace.

Listlessly, Kate spoke. 'We'll 'ave to make some plans, our kid,' she said, but her heart was heavy with dread.

Chapter Fifteen

Elly was the first to be told. Kate did it whilst Jenny was at work. For the past week she and Jenny had been on different shifts at the café, so it was easy for Kate to get up to Elly's without Jenny knowing. She felt she would rather tell her older sister on her own. She knew Elly's reaction would be the same as hers had been and it was no good putting the poor kid through the same experience twice.

Kate was still numbed from the scene the day before and she let Elly's words flow over her like a current of seawater passing over a drowning man. Somehow, just at the moment, it didn't seem to matter. Since yesterday she had found that if she put her mind outside the confines of her present misery and made it as empty as a slate upon which nothing had been written, the hours could somehow be got through. She allowed no thoughts to slip into her silent head, no fear for the future, no recriminations for the past. A blank and vacant mind feels no sorrow. She knew that tomorrow, or the next day it would all be there waiting for her and by then she would cope with it, but just for today, let Elly take it from her.

She sat at Elly's kitchen table whilst Elly slipped out the back for 'something'. She could hear the sound of Pat's hammer in the shop and the occasional 'ting' of the bell as customers came and went, but she just sat sipping her tea, staring at the brown wall, not even wondering where Elly had gone.

Ten minutes later Elly came back. She carried a small package wrapped about in newspaper, which she placed carefully and with a great air of melodrama on the table.

'Yer troubles are over, our kid,' she beamed.

Kate looked indifferently from Elly's face to the package.

'Warris it?'

'Listen.' Elly looked about her, glancing at the door which led into the shop as if afraid Pat might hear. Not that he even cared, but should he know and drop a careless word to a customer, it'd be up and down the street in an hour. 'I bin to see this woman who lives at the back o' me and we got talkin' about . . . yer know . . . well,

160

she's 'ad a lot of experience with this sort of thing. Not 'erself, mind, but folks about 'ere who got caught. Lots o' girls gerrin this pickle Kate, and she's well known. The minute yer said, I thought of 'er.' Elly sighed and her eyes became unfocused as she thought about her own brood, '. . . only wish I'd known about 'er when . . . well any road,' she turned back to Kate, 'she made me up this bottle, cost ten bob, is that all right, only you'll 'ave to give it us, before yer take it, cos I give 'er me last, but she said give our Jenny three tablespoons right away and then another dose in three hours . . . oh . . .' as an afterthought, '. . . an' she's to sit in a cold bath, as cold as she can stand.'

Elly began to count on her fingers. 'Mind you, she's in her third month now so it might not work, this woman said, but if it doesn't, you're to bring her over 'ere tomorrow, an' she'll see to 'er.'

She looked at Kate, an expression of pleased self-congratulation on her face, waiting for Kate's reaction. She watched for the look of reprieve, of thanks, of appreciation for what she, Elly, had done for her. This was the end of Kate and Jenny's troubles, hardly before they'd begun really, but Elly had found the answer and by heck they would be pleased.

She waited for Kate to show some sign that she was pleased. None came.

Kate turned her head and it was as if for the first time the full appreciation of what Elly was talking about and what she herself had been considering, had sunk fully into her tired mind. The expression of hopelessness began to shift slightly, moving across her face, and those impassive eyes which had stared at the wall came to life. Slowly, they became aflame, a furnace, and as though the furnace had melted the cold heart of her, her whole being exploded in shame as she leapt to her feet with a force that had Elly falling backwards from the chair which she had drawn clandestinely close.

Picking up the packet, Kate flung it with all the strength she could muster, against the wall, where it fell apart in a shower of paper and smashed glass. The liquid within it dripped down Elly's wallpaper, joining the other stains, and forming a puddle against the skirting board.

Elly cried out and began to hurry across the room as if to catch the precious brew for which she had just paid her last ten shillings.

'Aye up, our kid. What the bloody 'ell d'yer think yer playin' at?' she screeched and her hair, so like Kate's, bristled like that of a bitch about to get in a scrap with another.

But Kate's dander was up. It was not just Elly with whom she was enraged, but herself. How could she . . . how could she . . . ? Her thoughts flew through her head and came from her in a flow of self-disgust. Her voice stormed about her sister's small room.

'Never mind that, our Elly, yer'll get yer ten bob, never fear, but don't let me 'ear yer talk like this to our kid, or I'll land yer one.' Elly's mouth dropped open in amazement. Kate's voice lowered and she continued in a calmer manner.

'This is our sister you're talkin' about, Elly. Yer sister an' mine. Not some slut from the backstreets with a load to drop. Yer want to kill 'er? Is that what yer want. Is it? Sit 'er in a cold bath. A cold bath in this weather. Oh, I admit it were my first thought an' all. Get shut I said to 'er, but I'd cut off me right arm before I'd do it to 'er.' Kate was incensed. 'Feed 'er some muck made up of snails and rat's pee an' if that don't kill 'er, send her along, and we'll shove a needle up inside 'er and do it that way.'

Kate was weeping now and the great heaving sobs tore her frame and shook the flesh of her face and the wetness slid in waves across her cheeks. As the violence swept from within her, she felt her insides melt and ease. The apathy which had gripped her was cleared away with the tears, and her heart began to beat with a steady determined thump. It was not Kate's nature to go under and for twenty-four hours she had. She was a scrapper, a stayer, a survivor and would be all her life and as her numbed mind returned to its usual sharpness, she knew she and Jenny would come through.

'She's not doin' it, Elly. She's 'avin this baby. She wants it, an' if she wants it, that's good enough fer me.'

Charlie came home the following week and before he was over the doorstep Kate was about him.

Since Jenny had told her of the coming child her mind had been working in the precise and efficient manner of a piece of well-oiled and carefully tended machinery, and her plans were made and ready to be put into action. It only needed Charlie's sanction to set them in motion and Kate knew that where Charlie was concerned she could do no wrong. It would be like taking sweeties from a baby.

The flustered and delighted man was treated to a loving welcome which had his head spinning, his body throbbing, and his hands reaching for areas of Kate which were still off-limits to him even as her fiancé. Kate was not a woman for nothing, and she knew the softening up process was most important. Her kisses were fondly languishing and her arms clinging. Poor Charlie was transported, but before his yearning could be turned into something more substantial, Kate slipped away to make him a cup of tea, beseeching him to 'Sit yerself down, Charlie and take the weight off yer feet.' Charlie would have been happy to sit with his Kate upon his lap, but having shown him what could be his for the taking, Kate now wanted to get to the crux of the matter before his ardour cooled, and his head was in command again.

Whilst they drank their tea Kate told him what had happened. It did not take long. Charlie had heard the tale of Jenny's 'feller' until he felt he could cheerfully do away with the bloke, but this was different. His face, still rosy with the bedazzlement Kate had aroused in him, became grave and he listened without speaking.

Charlie loved Kate more than any other person in the world. He loved her with the love of the steady, decent ordinary bloke that he was, but he was no fool and he knew Kate was leading up to something, and he waited patiently for her to get to it. It was part of Kate's enchantment for him, this belief on her part that she led him by the nose, and he did nothing to disillusion her, but he had a mind of his own, did Charlie, and could be stubborn when he was in disagreement with anything in which he did not believe. Thus far, Kate had done nothing which did not delight him. All the years he had known her, she had charmed him with her bright cheerfulness, her outspoken vigour and liveliness, and he had had no occasion in which to dispute anything which she had said or done.

Because of this Kate thought she had him wound around her finger.

'. . . and she won't get rid, Charlie. Not that I want her to, mind. Not now. I did at first luv, I was desperate, but when Elly talked about . . . well . . .' Kate was embarrassed. You did not speak of such things even to the man you were about to marry. 'Well, I realised it weren't right. And she's a different girl. Not like she used to be, I don't think she'll ever be that,' she said wistfully, 'but she's made up with the baby comin'. It's given 'er summat to live for, she says.' Kate's face became stony for a moment. 'Eeh, I could kill that bastard for what 'e's done to 'er. Still . . . that won't put the eggs back in the shells, will it?' Her face cleared and she smiled brightly as she came to the bit where Charlie was to be brought into her scheme of things.

'Well it's like this, luv.' She stroked the sleeve of his coat and lowered her lashes. Charlie smiled to himself. – Here it comes, he thought.

'Well I thought . . . that is if you . . . well yer know you an' me are goin' to be wed in . . . well as soon as we could, you said.' She stopped and looked up into his steady grey eyes and was suddenly at ease. Charlie knew and she wondered why she'd thought it necessary to go through this performance when all it needed was the truth. She felt ashamed and at the same time, proud that it was her that he loved.

'Can we get wed right away, Charlie, can we move away from 'ere to a new house and take Jenny with us? I'll keep on workin' and so will she as long as she can. I'm gonner pretend she's a widow, in the new place. I mean so no one there'll know and then when the baby comes she can go back to work an' I'll see to it, cos by then I'll probably be in the family . . .'

She stopped abruptly. Charlie's eyes were gleaming and his face was twitching. Spasms ran across his cheeks and his mouth quivered, and suddenly with a gasp like a rush of air from a pair of bellows he began to laugh. Great choking guffaws rang to the ceiling of the room, echoing about in a way which had not been heard for a long time, and for a second Kate was affronted. Then her face began to smile and in a moment Charlie's laughter caught at her and the two of them were shaking, hanging on to each other as they exploded with mirth.

At last Charlie was able to speak.

'Eeh, Kate, you're a cracker, yer really are. 'Aven't I bin begging yer to marry me for months, but no it didn't suit you said. Not yet. An' I always knew, chuck, that if I took you, I took your Jenny. Don't I know what she means to yer? I always thought she'd be company for yer while I was at sea until she was wed herself, and then I always fancied she'd settle somewhere near you. You've bin close, you two, more than usual with you practically bringing 'er up. And I know, it'd mither yer without 'er near. No queen, I knew Jenny'd always be part of our life, but I must admit I 'adn't bargained on bairn an all . . .'

His face split into a grin and his eyes became filled with a pretended leer, '. . . but if it's in t' family way yer gonner be, I reckon I can 'elp you out there.'

For half an hour Jenny, Nils and all that was past was forgotten as Kate and Charlie loved each other. Soft kisses, warm arms, loving hearts. They whispered endearments and tenderly touched cheek and brow and hand for Kate and Charlie were at one, and in their minds was the fixed and certain conviction that what they wanted so ardently was to be saved for their wedding night. They did not need the instant gratification of their physical love, though Charlie was sorely tempted, for Kate's gratitude made her less restrained than usual.

'Christmas then, chuck,' he said huskily as they rose hurriedly at the sound of Jenny's key in the door.

'Christmas, Charlie,' she whispered. She smoothed her ruffled hair, and they both turned to smile at Jenny as she came into the kitchen.

On the same day that Charlie's ship docked, and as the last huge, wet slapping hawser was placed about the bollard that held fast the bow, Jenny was sitting on the slatted seat of the tramcar which was taking her to work. It was still dark and the streetlights passed in a string of blurred blobs, dipping in the cold wind which blew straight off the river. The tram was full and hands clutched the backs of seats and the straps which hung from its roof as it swayed down Scotland Road. It clicked over the points, hissing out small jets of steam in the cold air at every stop.

The other passengers were cheerful; chattering of last night's picture, the latest dance, or the football results from Saturday's match. Jenny was quiet, seeing her own reflection hazing in the window against the darkened buildings as the tramcar turned into Victoria Street. Her mind was preoccupied with the coming day and she was barely conscious of the people who pressed about her, or of the blithe conductor who asked her three times for her fare. She felt as though a lifetime had passed since that evening on which she had embarked so happily with Lily. It had changed the course of her life with such swift urgency she could scarcely remember what had gone before, but now, on this very day she was beginning the first day of the future for herself and her child.

Jenny got off the tram in Victoria Street and walked through North John Street into Dale Street. In one of those quirks of coincidence which now and then occur, there was a sudden lull in the city sounds of tram and motorcar and hurrying feet and voices, and clear on the cold air, as the sky lightened and the day began, could be heard the awakening twitter of sparrows and the soft 'whoo-whoo' of pigeons which nested on the high ledges of the old buildings. She stood for a moment on the pavement and shivered. It was not the cold which shrivelled her skin, but for a strange moment, she felt the hairs lift on her arms and across her skull. She fancied some awareness was, from far off, trying to penetrate her mind, as though a voice had spoken her name. A voice she could not hear.

Lifting her head and squaring her shoulders Jenny passed through the doorway of the café, closing the door behind her. It was already full. The breakfast trade was under way and the warmth, the delicious smell of bacon cooking, the clatter of cutlery, the goodhumoured voices which enveloped her gave her a sense of optimism, of good things to come and her chill of a moment ago was forgotten.

Jenny worked hard until noon. She ignored the nausea which arose in her as she served bacon, eggs, sausage, fried tomatoes, mushrooms, bowls of thick porridge, thick wedges of toasted bread; and later hot buttered teacakes, cream and jam and scones, dainty cakes and endless pots of tea. Her back ached where her spine met her buttocks, and her legs trembled as she climbed the stairs. Her ankles swelled, but when her break came, she did not sit thankfully down as did the other girls with whom she usually had her meal.

Jenny climbed the stairs to the top floor to Mr Wagstaffe's office and knocked on his door.

'Come in, come in,' an irritable voice told her.

She opened the door and went inside. The room was small and seemed at first glance to be drowning under a sea of papers. They were everywhere. On top of bureaux, filing cabinets, on chairs; under chairs, piled on the windowsill and stacked against the wall, two feet high. They floated about willy-nilly and there seemed to be a distinct possibility that before long, the rest of the room could sink without trace beneath their weight.

Behind a huge desk which also appeared to be in danger of going under, sat Percival Wagstaffe, a pencil behind each ear, his spectacles on the end of his nose, and his crisp, iron grey hair curling in profusion about his large head. He looked up as she entered, his full lower lip protruding belligerently, his vivid blue eyes blinking in the dim light of the midday shadow which fell across the desk from the small window high up on the wall. For a second he peered vaguely then in an instant, through sheer force of habit and nothing else, he began to shout.

'What the 'ell are yer doin' up 'ere, lady. Yer know this is our busiest time of the day. If yer must see me about summat, can't yer come when we're quiet. Not that we ever are,' he mumbled, a gleam of satisfaction in his eye, 'burr I'm sure there's a better time than this. I dunno, you girls, yer think I've nowt else to do but sit chewin' the cud with anyone who wants to pop in. Look at this lot, all to be got through by tonight . . .'

He waved his arms about, the draught caused by the movement lifting a dozen papers. They drifted lazily into the dustfilled air, before settling once more on the littered desk.

Jenny stood impassively as the tumult raged about her. It was

166

always this way with Mr Wagstaffe. Before a body had time to utter a word he was about them, afraid they might take advantage of the softness which lay beneath the exterior of his outrage. He made it known he held no truck with slackness or timewasters, and his lack of feeling for girls who suffered when they had the 'curse' was well known.

'Come on, girl, come on, out wi' it. I 'aven't gorrall bloody day. Yer can see what I gorra do,' then in mid-sentence, without stopping for breath, his voice changed and he said gently, 'What's wrong, lass?'

Jenny looked at him sharply, bewildered and for the first time saw beyond the maliciously twinkling blue eyes which flashed beacons of wrath at any member of his staff who, in his opinion, had stepped out of line. There was kindliness there, warmth and sympathy. For a moment she was confused. She had expected the explosion of irritability with which she had first been greeted and had been prepared to put up with it. This was Waggy's standard behaviour with any request, from the begging of a day off to bury a grandmother, to the simple entreaty for a new apron when the old one was virtually in tatters. She had been determined not to cry. What she was about to put to Mr Wagstaffe was business. A plan which would ensure her own future security and at the same time give the old man a viable proposition which she hoped he could not refuse. His unexpected kindness undid her.

Bending forward she placed both her hands, palm downwards on the cluttered desk. Bowing her head, she wept.

Standing up, the plump and untidy figure of the man she barely knew except as a loudmouth and a thundering voice, lumbered round the desk. He pulled a chair from beneath the mountain of papers, carelessly allowing them to tumble in a heap on to the floor, flapping the seat impatiently with the clean white handkerchief which his Mam had tucked into his top pocket that morning, and with tender concern, pressed Jenny into it.

'Sit yerself down an' tell me all about it.'

Percival didn't smile as many men would at the tale of a silly girl losing her head, and her virginity, to a chap she scarcely knew. He didn't show surprise or scepticism when Jenny told him simply, and with the clear truth of it shining in her eyes, of her love for Nils Jorgensen, and of her hope which would not completely die, that he might return to her. It took a long time of telling for she found herself sparing no detail. The words flowed from her with a simple directness which touched the man's heart, and he didn't interrupt. He lit one cigarette after another, filling the already smoke

167

shrouded room with whirling patterns of milky haze which dipped and bobbed, searching for some means of escape from the tightly closed office. He gave no sign of scandalised shock when Jenny spoke the final words, for he felt none.

'I'm going to have a baby, Mr Wagstaffe.'

Composed, Jenny looked into Percival Wagstaffe's eyes which shone from beneath a growth of eyebrow bristling like two small furry animals. Her mind was sharp now that it was done, the first part, and she prepared herself for the second. As she marshalled her thoughts, she marvelled absently at her own lack of perception in the past in not seeing the understanding which lurked in the depths of those merry eyes which searched hers. She saw the red, fleshy, pendulous face and wondered at her own blindness, for it was there for anyone to see. The big heart of the man.

'There's summat else, isn't there, Jenny?'

'Aye, Mr Wagstaffe, there is.'

'Go on then, lass, I'm all ears.'

Jenny looked down at her hands which were folded in her lap. She was not afraid any more. Not of anything. She lifted her head and smiled.

'I want to be your secretary, Mr Wagstaffe.' Encouraged by Percival's seeming disinclination to show sign of amazement or tendency to laugh, she continued. 'I'm not goin' to be able to work in the café after I begin . . . to show, an' I've gorra 'ave work. You see, I'm gonner 'ave a child to care for, Mr Wagstaffe. I've no one to . . . support me while I'm carryin', or afterwards. Oh, I know our Kate'll 'elp me and me brothers for a while, but Kate's gerrin wed, and me brothers 'ave got their own families. So yer see Mr Wagstaffe, it's all down to me.'

She leaned forward and her young face round and rosy, with the curves of girlhood still in her cheeks, became businesslike.

'What I want to do is go to business school. I want to learn to type and do shorthand and filing and . . .' she waved her hand vaguely in the direction of the upheaval of papers which surrounded them. 'I could sort this out for yer, Mr Wagstaffe. I could help yer to run the office while yer did more important things. Eeh, Mr Wagstaffe, with your business head and a good chef, you could open another café in . . . well, I saw a place in the Corn Exchange the other day . . .'

Mr Wagstaffe held up his hand. He leaned further back in his chair and with the air of a man who has just done ten rounds with 'Gorgeous Georges Carpentier' he shut his eyes and let out his

168

breath slowly. Jenny sat silently and her heart pounded. She waited for the old man to speak.

Waggy took a deep breath and put his hands squarely on the desk top, then with an air of purposefulness he picked up some sheets of paper, straightening and squaring them up into a semblance of neatness. Though Jenny was not aware of it, he had never enjoyed a moment such as this for a long time, and he made it last as long as possible.

'Well, luv,' he said at last, an expression on his face which was impossible to fathom. 'It's a question of experience y'see and time, and of course there's the money to be found for the business course . . .'

'Oh I've thought of that, Mr Wagstaffe,' Jenny interrupted eagerly. 'I've gorra little bit put by and me an' Kate live very economically. Yer know what they say about two living cheaply as one, an' I thought, if yer could . . . well, help me . . . lend me . . . I'd pay yer back out of me wages. Every penny, Mr Wagstaffe.'

Waggy's face was sombre and Jenny's heart plummeted. He wasn't going to do it. He thought she was daft, off her head and a cheeky, impertinent little madam into the bargain. What a nerve she had, coming to him with such a scheme. She must have been mad.

Jenny had forgotten Percival Wagstaffe's love of what he considered was a good joke. He was impressed and amazed that little Jenny Fowler, a pretty mouse of a girl, had so much spunk. And not only that, she seemed to have a good sense of what business was all about. She hadn't been the only one to realise the potential of the empty shop in the Corn Exchange. And with all she had on her plate an' all. He was confounded that she could even think up such a scheme, let alone come to him with it. He admired her for it, by God, he did, and she was right. He did need some help in the office, it was getting beyond a joke. He'd half a mind to start her right away. He could easily get another waitress, but a girl with a head on her shoulders was another thing, especially one with the incentive this one had. By God, he'd do it.

But he still couldn't resist that last bit of teasing.

'Well, lass, I dunno,' shaking his head, as though in doubt.

Jenny's heart rose again, like that of a swallow soaring into the sky. He wasn't saying 'no'.

'Please Mr Wagstaffe, yer'll never regret it. I'll work me fingers to the bone, I will. Our Kate'll be wed by the time . . . when the child comes, and she'll see to it for me, while I'm at work, an' I'll not let yer down. Every hour God sends I'll work . . .'

Waggy bellowed with laughter so loud and so long, folks in the café below stopped eating and glanced upwards, forks halfway to open mouths. He couldn't stop, holding his sides and shaking his head with delight.

At last he had himself under control. 'Eeh lass, yer'll go far, yer will. I never 'eard such damn cheek in me life, but yer on. Shake on it.'

He held out his hand, grasping Jenny's warmly. Jenny tried to speak, her heart overflowing; to stammer her thanks, but he would have none of it.

'Save yer breath to cool yer porridge, kid. You'll owe me no favours, time I've finished with yer. Now let's see what we can work out . . .'

Chapter Sixteen

It was almost like the old days, Kate thought, as she and Jenny drowsed in their bed the following Sunday morning. The early days when they had first moved into number thirty-six and had been full of themselves and their own daring. How certain they had been in those first months that life was sweet and would be, always. Nothing of what was to come had even entered the minds of the two teenagers who had giggled and danced and dreamed of their own bright futures.

Now, even before the year was out, the life they had envisaged – had clutched at with such glee was to be changed again. But for the better, Kate thought as she pulled the eiderdown up over her shoulder. Please God the bad days were over now, and they could have a bit of peace. She smiled in the dimness of the room, for though it was daylight outside, the curtains were still drawn as she and Jenny had a 'lie-in'. Their Jenny was fixed up, thank God, her future secure, and that of the child's, and she and Charlie were to be married on his next trip. Three weeks and she'd be Kate Walker.

Her mind wandered in a contented, half awake, half dreaming state, as she contemplated the miracle that had happened, or rather, their Jenny had made happen. Who would have thought she had it in her, or that Waggy would have gone for it? Jenny was a constant amazement to Kate now, and to everyone who knew her, with her newfound strength, and it had only come about when she had discovered she was pregnant. It must be something to do with the maternal instinct, Kate mused. The instinct that all mothers have, to defend, to look out for their young. Nobody had ever needed their Jenny before. No one had leaned on her, so she had seemed, well, soft, vulnerable, easily hurt, but now with the baby coming, a small creature who would totally depend upon her, she was like a rock, so confident that she would do this thing she'd set her mind on.

A secretary, their Jenny a secretary.

''Ow about a cup of tea, kid?'

171

Jenny's voice was muffled by the sheets which she had pulled up to her nose.

'I wouldn't mind.'

'You or me?'

'I did it last week.'

'Aye, but I'm in an interesting condition, and should rest.'

Kate laughed, still bewitched by Jenny's ability to joke about her pregnancy.

'Yer a cheeky devil, but I suppose I'll 'ave to humour yer, only think on, it's your turn next . . .'

The words were shattered by a violent pounding as a fist thudded against the front door, and it seemed in imminent danger of being knocked from its frame as the echoes of the blows filled the room. The two girls shrank together in the bed, clutching at each other as though they were both about to fall over its edge. Kate's face was comical in its consternation, and her hair seemed to stand on end.

'Who the devil . . . ?'

Again the hammering shook the house.

'Dear God, who the hell's that?' Kate pulled the bedclothes to her chin and turned to stare into Jenny's enormous eyes. The two young girls lay like puppets whose strings had been cut, the very savagery of the attack on the door freezing them to stillness. They were afraid to get up to see who it was. It seemed that subconsciously they knew who had come to destroy their peace of mind.

Bang, bang, bang. The fist smashed against the door. A voice thundered like the firing of a cannon, and their worst fears were verified.

'Open this door, or I'll break it down. I know yer in there, so there's no use yer 'idin' away.' *Bang, bang, bang.* The door shook and a man's voice from further up the street could plainly be heard in complaint, though the words were indistinct. Kate and Jenny lay petrified, enthralled in a paroxysm of fear so great it took the speech from their lips and movement from their limbs.

'Open this door, you . . . you whores of Babylon. No daughters of mine are livin' in a brothel, for that's what this place is. A brothel . . . a sink of iniquity, and if it's the last thing I do, I'm 'avin' an end to it.'

At last Kate spoke. Just two words.

'Me Dad.'

The very sound of Henry's voice was enough to send Jenny back into that mindless fear which had captured her as a child. The hundreds of times she had heard that fury rage about some hapless

172

head; Elizabeth's, Kate's, one of the boys, Elly – poor terrified Ah-ah, and on occasion, her own, and now, like a nightmare which she had thought over, he was filling the street with his murderous rage.

Other voices joined the first, and footsteps could be heard running in hobnailed boots towards their own door.

'What the 'ell d'yer think yer doin' at this time of day on a Sunday? Wake the dead, yer will . . .'

''E must be off 'is 'ead, silly old bugger.'

'. . . only bloody day I gerra lie-in, an' . . .'

Kate lay like one felled by a blow, as the storm outside gathered force. She could hear her father squaring up to whoever was protesting, and she felt her heart shrivel in shame. He'd let the whole street know why he was here if she didn't let him in, in fact they probably knew already, what with words like 'brothel', and 'whores' being flung about.

Jenny was moaning, her head under the covers. There was no thought in her head but the ghastly revelation that her dad had come for her. All her plans for her future, for hers, and her unborn child, would come to nothing if he dragged her back to the chip shop. She knew why he had come. He had come for her. She had been a naughty girl and must be punished, just like he had punished them all when they had gone against him. So great was her fear she regressed in thirty seconds from a girl just emerging to adulthood, to the child she had been, and she began to suck her thumb as she had done then.

Kate pulled back the sheet and looked at her. With all the explosive force which only she and Elly had inherited from Henry, her rage broke her fear. The sight of her sister cowering like a terrified child in the middle of the bed set Kate free and before the next blow fell on the sagging door, she was out of the bed, up the hall and had it open. She grasped her father's arm, and so great was her anger, her strength was doubled and she had him inside and backed up against the wall, before he had time to recover his balance. Kate had a snap impression of a dozen intrigued neighbours grouped about her doorstep, before she flung the door shut in their faces.

It was as though the two protagonists were continuing the same battle that had separated them almost twelve months before. The atmosphere crackled and the faint light in the passage, illuminated only by the glimmer from the fanlight above the door, seemed to glow with the flames of fury which spewed from father and daughter. Henry had recovered from his surprise but his passion

173

was such that he could barely speak. His eyes were the bright, blood-engorged red of a beast that had been tormented beyond endurance and the loose skin of his face seemed to fill and stretch until the flesh beneath was in danger of bursting through. His lips were drawn venomously back from his teeth; a lion about to snarl before it leapt to tear its victim limb from limb. Spittle flecked each corner of his mouth and flew in droplets about Kate's head.

Pushing her face close to his, unafraid, Kate shrieked, 'What the 'ell d'yer think yer doin'? Yer'll 'ave the door off its hinges, the way you're goin' on, and who the 'ell gave you the right to come shoutin' round 'ere like summat not right? I told yer when me Mam died we wanted no more to do wi' yer. 'Ow dare yer come shoutin' the odds, showin' us up in front o' t'neighbours? We done nowt to be ashamed of, me an' Jenny, an' even if we had, it's nowt to do wi' you. We finished wi' yer, see. *Finished*. D'yer gerrit? We want no more to do wi' yer. Come blusterin' into our front door like a bloody bull in a china shop. I'll 'ave the law on yer. In fact I'm gonner send for a Bobby right now. 'E'll deal wi' yer, yer great lumbering sod. Leave us alone, see. We can manage our own lives now an' we don't want no interference . . .'

Henry raised his thick arm and with a roar that silenced the twittering voices outside the door, he knocked Kate to the floor. Her head bounced from the wall, and her senses reeled, and she lay across the hall, her mind slipping away into a mist.

'Where is she?' He was almost out of his mind, so fierce was his wrath. 'Where's that slut who's blackened my name with 'er goings on. Where is she?' He looked about the unfamiliar surroundings and stepping over the floundering girl on the floor, forced his way into the kitchen, pushing the door against the wall with a savagery that cracked a panel of wood.

'Yer thought yer could do as yer pleased, didn't yer, once yer left my house. Carry on like a couple of tarts. Well yer got paid back didn't yer, but by God it's nowt to what yer gonner pay now. Yer'll be sorry lady, you'll see. Where are yer, our Jenny?'

His barbarous rage carried him into the scullery where, on finding no one but the cat, he kicked it from his path, before turning back to search for his quarry.

Kate was trying to get to her feet as Henry returned to the hallway. Her face was swelling visibly and blood streamed from a cut high on her cheek where the ring on his hand had opened it to the bone. She tried to speak. She put out her hand, but her father brushed past her, towering, rampant, his face so implacably cruel, Kate began to fear for their lives. She had never in all her days at the

174

chip shop seen him so enraged. Dear God, if he should get to their Jenny, what might he do to her? He'd kill her, he would. He'd drag her from the bed and throw her from one end of the room to the other. Someone must have told him about the baby and in his black rage . . . Already he was feeling for the buckle on the belt which held up his trousers.

Without hesitation Kate flung herself to the front door. Her nightdress was streaked with blood and her hair fell about her face, but she no longer cared about her neighbours' opinions. Her only concern now was for Jenny.

A thin scream, like that of a hare caught in the jaws of a stout, came from the bedroom and words, obscene, filthy, roared from Henry's mouth.

Throwing open the door, clinging to the frame, Kate looked at the ring of fascinated faces that crowded the pavement. Most were women, but one or two men loitered on the edge of the group, as enthralled as their wives but trying not to appear so.

'Please,' Kate whispered, then more loudly, 'please will some-one . . . he's goin' mad and our Jenny's . . .' She began to slip towards the step and one woman, more compassionate than the rest, stepped across the pavement, grabbing her arm before she fell.

'Oh dear God, won't one of you men stop him,' Kate cried.

The kindly woman spoke, 'Eeh luv, us'n can't interfere in a family matter. If yer dad's givin' your kid a beltin' it's up to 'im.'

'But 'e'll kill 'er, 'e will . . . oh please.'

From the end of the street, now filled with dozens of captivated spectators, dragged from their beds and from kitchens where Sunday morning breakfasts were being cooked, the piercing shrill of a whistle made all heads turn. A police constable was running in the wake of a young boy. His highly polished black boots pounded the flagstones and in between whistles he was heard to shout, 'Out of me way there. Move along now.'

He clutched the strap of his helmet, which had slipped to the back of his head as he ran, even in the midst of this drama, aware of his own dignity and that of the law. It would not do for a police constable to be seen with his helmet dangling from his neck like a girl's bonnet.

Kate turned from the sympathetic arm which held her and on faltering feet which seemed to be a mile away from her head, tried to run towards the bedroom. Holding the wall she reached the open doorway. Jenny lay face down on the bed.

Henry was standing, arm raised, with the belt which he had just

175

removed from his trousers in his hand. The buckle end dangled, the vicious prong of the fastening gleaming in the dim light as he gathered his strength to bring it down with every scrap of force he could gather on to Jenny's cringing flesh. Kate leapt forward. Fear and hot-blooded rage gave swiftness to the feet which moments before had dragged her along the passage. She grasped Henry's arm and as he let it fly towards the bed, he took her with it as though she were no more than a moth which had alighted on him.

'You as well, ay,' he chuckled, 'well that suits me madam. You're as bad as 'er, I've no doubt, so you can 'ave a taste 'an all. I've strapped yer before, both of yer, burrit were nothing to what yer gonner get now. The 'idin' of yer life, that's what.'

He licked his lips in anticipation. To his credit, though he had struck them both before, he had always known what he was about, and had tempered his punishments to fit the nature of their girlhood. Now, in his outrage that his good name had been besmirched by one of his daughters, and fury at what he considered was Kate's deliberate interference as she tried to defend her sister, he no longer knew what he was doing. He had completely lost control of the vicious temper that was his.

The belt whistled through the air, but he hadn't got his eye in yet and the buckle struck the bedpost. The two girls lay on the bed, Kate half covering Jenny's quivering form, in a heap of white exposed limbs, crumpled nightgowns, and the bedcovers which Henry had pulled back.

He raised his arm again. He'd get it right now. Just there where Jenny's silken thigh gleamed in the misted light of the curtained room.

But the blow never fell. Bolstered by the arrival of the Bobby; upheld by the law, men filled the room, eager to be heroes, not wanting to miss any of the drama which could not be seen from the pavement. Henry, bellowing, struggling, kicking, thrashing, was dragged from the room and thrown unceremoniously into the street. Women tittered and children stared, hypnotised by the thickness of the belt and the size of the buckle which was still grasped in his hand.

The young boy from next door, Wally was his name, stood at the back of the room and looked with pity at the sobbing, distraught girls who lay in disarray on the bed. It was he who had had the sense, and sympathy, to run for the policeman.

He had always admired the two cheerful, pretty girls who had moved into the house next to his. Jenny had smiled at him in that shining way she had; she had talked to him as though he were a man and him only twelve, and once, when he had been playing 'footy' in the street, she had stood and watched as he scored a goal and clapped her hands to show her admiration. He had been her adoring slave from that day on, dreaming his boy's dreams of becoming old enough to take her dancing. His Mam said vindictively to all who would listen that Kate and Jenny were no better than they should be, living alone with no man in the house, but he didn't believe it. His Mam could not abide Kate, not since the time when their Peggy had gone missing, and his Mam had accused Kate of hiding the hen in their privy and of stealing the eggs she lay. Kate's volatile temper had run away with her, and she and his Mam had had a right ding-dong, and all along the missing Peggy had been roosting, out of sight, on the privy roof. His Mam would not say she was sorry to Kate. Oh no, not her, and since that day, she hadn't a good word for the sisters.

But Wally's youthful love cared nothing for that. He could not bear to think of that old devil strapping that lovely pale skin, or blacking those golden eyes. Despite his Mam's objections he had run as swiftly as his would-be footballer's legs could carry him to the corner of the street and miraculously, the police constable who usually walked Wavertree Street was standing at the kerb.

Later, when the policeman had gone, disappointed that the young women did not intend to prefer charges, Wally sat in his own backyard, leaning against the hen coop, watching Peggy scratch the mouldy bricks on the path. He ate his bread and dripping and tried to shut out the harsh voice of his mother who was expressing regret that Henry had not been allowed to continue his thrashing, and that she had not been there to see it.

The hen strutted delicately about the cluttered yard, cocking a red winking eye at the boy, unaware that in a way that would have been ludicrous had it not been so tragic, she was to be the instrument that would alter the lives of many people.

Chapter Seventeen

Charlie and Kate were married on 21 December 1922, at the Church of All Saints, Netherfield.

The day was cold and bright and beautiful. As they stepped from the dimness of the church porch into the sunshine, the stirring notes of the *Wedding March* followed them, quivering on the crisp air, floating upwards into the bare branches of the beech trees which lined the pathway. As if disturbed by the lovely music, a few copper leaves which had clung on tenaciously through the autumn and winter months, fell like fragile butterflies and drifted to the feet of the young couple. As Kate and Charlie took a hesitant step forward, not quite sure what to do with their newly-married state, the dry leaves crunched beneath Kate's feet and she turned and smiled at Charlie, delight shining in her eyes.

The solemnity of the past half hour was gone with that smile and Charlie bent to kiss his bride, unmindful of the smiling crowd of onlookers who always gather on such occasions, whether the bride and groom are known to them or not. There was an appreciative round of applause and some cries of 'Good luck', and then the couple were surrounded by the congregation who streamed behind them from the church to form a phalanx of affectionate comradeship on the worn stone step. There were embraces, kisses, handshakes and the radiance of the bride, her face not at all marred by the tiny scar high on her cheekbone, seemed to kindle an answering brightness in the expressions of those who crowded about her. The soft laughter spread, the sun shone, though there was no warmth in it and the house martins who nested in the eaves above the porch winged upwards and outwards, agitated by the noise of the wedding party.

In groups of two or three, the guests slowly made their way along the gravel path, smiling and nodding at the sightseers, passing the gravestones which leaned towards each other as though in discussion of the appearance of the bride. Along the grass verge they wandered to the gateway where a charabanc, hired for the occasion, waited to take them to Waggy's for the

178

wedding breakfast. There were trills of feminine laughter as Lily's high heel caught in the hem of her bright, signal-red skirt when she climbed the steps of the vehicle, and Chris Thompson, a mate of Charlie's and his best man, helped her gallantly aboard, but not before she had given him more than a good look at her slim and shapely leg.

Mrs Walker wanted to sit at the front of the vehicle because, she insisted, she always felt sick at the back, and why their Charlie couldn't have had two or three taxi cabs, or even landaus, she didn't know. Kate and Charlie became so engrossed with one another, the charabanc almost went without them, and Waggy, whose wedding present to them was to be the party he was giving, tried to pat the skinny behind of Charlie's sister, Annie, now fully recovered and Kate's second bridesmaid, and received a not-so-friendly clout for his pains.

But first they must go to Gales, to have a photograph taken. Charlie and Kate standing, Kate's arm shyly through his, Charlie's usually merry face as serious as the moment demanded. His mouth was set sternly, for like most men he detested having himself pose like a simpering fool just to provide an image of his own face to stand upon the piano. Kate smiled enough for two, her eyes misted like dewed bluebells with the rapture of it all.

Then Charlie and Kate were placed side by side on two chairs. Annie was required to sit beside Kate with Jenny next to Charlie, and behind them, like two roosting hens, perched Chris Thompson and Mrs Walker. Charlie's mother wore a maroon woollen frock which looked remarkably like a man's dressing gown, complete with tassled cord and on her head, jammed to her eyebrows was a black hat of enormous proportions.

The bridesmaids were delectable in softest peach, but there was no doubt, and as it should be, that Kate outshone even Jenny on this day. She was beautiful in her homemade dress and no one but Charlie knew that their outfits had been sewn, every stitch by Jenny.

Kate was in white, of course. Satin, draped with misty lace that fell to the hem of her dress. The waist was low, gathered on her hips and round her neck she wore, at Jenny's insistence, a simple row of pearls. She wore elbow-length white gloves. Her hat, white also, high crowned and wide-brimmed was swathed in osprey feathers, snowy and soft, and on her feet she wore white satin shoes with a pearl buttoned strap. She carried a drape of dainty pink carnations, embraced in a froth of ivy which fell almost to the floor.

179

The rest of the party chatted and laughed at the back of the photographer, and it was only when the man was about to go under the sheet which covered himself and the camera, that it was discovered that Charlie had left his hat in the church. Consternation reigned, for what groom on his wedding day could be photographed without his wedding hat? It was too late to go back for it, and so, long after he had gone to his Maker, Waggy was fondly remembered whenever Kate looked at her wedding photograph, for clutched to Charlie's breast was the old man's Homburg.

Kate and Jenny chose the neat new house in which Kate and Charlie were to spend their years together. The two girls took the tram from the corner of Scotland Road, along Walton Road and on until they reached St Mary's church at the beginning of Rice Lane. They had left behind the sprawling mass of back-to-back houses, the near slum in which they had lived for almost a year. Gone were the row upon regimented row of flat-faced, blank-eyed boxes which served the millions of working class people in the city. Here, in a rural area on which the growth of building had scarcely begun, were tidy, identical lines of semi-detached houses, still small, but with their own little garden, front and rear, bay windows with lead lighting, neat paths and the first planting of young trees to join the ancient ones which had been left undisturbed. Women walked with smart perambulators and dogs on leashes and none wore a shawl or clogs.

Delighted with the fresh crisp smell of the countryside; with the space, and the sight of green fields at the end of each quiet avenue, the two girls had ventured hesitantly in the direction of the area of land which was now being covered by curving rows of streets full of new 'villas'. These were to be had for rent by those who were moving, with their families, into the brighter world of suburbia. The smell of varnished wood and paint hung about, and the pleasant fragrance which assaults the senses when buildings are new and unlived in. Men hammered lustily on half-erected skeletons of what would be a home, and there were appreciative whistles as the girls skipped aside to avoid potholes full of water, piles of bricks and lengths of timber, for the road was not yet made up.

A bowler-hatted gentleman in overalls, who told them when timidly asked, that he was the foreman and 'Yes, from the end there, where that 'un's just finished to way up yonder' – pointing to the end of the crescent – 'were all h'available for rent.'

180

It seemed so easy. They paid a week's money in advance; five and ninepence, filled in a form and were given a key, and Kate and Charlie became the tenants of a brand spanking new cube of a house in Crescent Road, Fazackerly. It smelt of timber and whitewash and looked out at the back on fields of waving grass and meadow rue, and beyond that to a wood that seemed to stretch for ever, and to be filled, even on that cold December day, with birdsong.

Bobby and Jimmy walked the same handcart borrowed in January from Mick Tulley, taking the accumulation of their sisters' possessions from Seacomb Street to Crescent Road. Balanced on the top was the sagging old armchair and Jenny's rocker. Kate and Jenny moved into the new house two days before Charlie came home.

On that day, they stood, the sisters, for the last time in the empty kitchen of Seacomb Street, silent now, but filled with the ghostly sounds of laughter, of agonised weeping, of crackling cheerful fires and the echo of the cuckoo clock which was now perched on the wall of Kate's shining new kitchen in Fazackerly. Words, spoken in jest, in anger; words of love and longing and passion, whispered in the corners of the room. It was dismal now without the trappings of its departing occupants, and against the window the net curtain, torn and discarded, stirred as though moved by an unseen hand. Jenny closed the door gently, but just before she did so, she saw in her mind's eye a beautiful man and girl, bronzed in fire-glow, embrace lovingly, their lips moving in wonder upon each other. She shivered and felt something slip within her, as if her heart had come loose. She held a cardboard box to her chest clutching it fiercely, and almost ran up the passage to the front door.

Kate and Jenny put the key in the lock for the last time, then stood back on the pavement, looking at the soot-stained greyness of the house front; at the windows which Jenny had polished dementedly as a salvation against thought, and at the paint-scarred door which still bore the wounds of Henry's assault upon it, and into the minds of both girls came the thought of the joy and sorrow which had passed between this sagging frame.

Then, without a word, they turned, smiled at each other, and began to run towards the end of the street to catch the tram to their new life. From behind a curtain, filthy as a floorcloth, a face peered and a sneer turned down the corners of Wally's Mam's mouth. 'Good riddance to bad rubbish,' she muttered as she watched them go, then turned to berate whichever luckless child happened to be under her feet.

But Kate's thoughts were not on her new home as she sat, the arm of her new husband possessively about her, at the damask-covered table upon which the most beautiful wedding cake she had ever seen soared in delicate glory. The absent Mrs Wagstaffe; – 'too old to venture far these days' – had made it for her, none of the skill with which she had delighted Royalty, deserting her.

Charlie made a speech, likening Kate to a peach, for she was as sweet that day, with skin that glowed and was soft to the touch of his tender finger. Privately he was wishing it were all over and he could take a bite from her in the seclusion of the nuptial bed, and he blushed as he spoke, his hot thoughts tripping his tongue, so that the company laughed, thinking he was tipsy. But he wasn't. Only with love.

Annie, whose skinny frame and flat bosom hid a strong contralto voice, sang *Because*, and the company hushed to listen, and many a female eye shed a tiny tear. After all it was a wedding.

The platform at Lime Street Station was a noise-filled, laughter-swept arena of people who had come to throw rice and confetti and cheer on the blushing couple. Passersby smiled at the goodnatured raillery and the knowing winks as the red-faced bride and groom were escorted with due ceremony along the waiting train and into a third-class compartment. They were to honeymoon in Blackpool for three days and the jokes were saucy, making Kate go hot under the wool of her 'going-away' outfit, and caused Charlie to grit his teeth.

For three days, almost on the eve of Christmas, and with the town empty of holidaymakers, Charlie and Kate bound themselves to one another with bonds which were never to break. It was the start, the lovely bright start to which all lovers are entitled before the mundane, peaceful days of marriage begin.

They had a large sunny room on the first floor of a boarding house which overlooked the sands. They walked the firm and rippling beach arm in arm, jumping like children the shallow pools left by the receding tide, searching for seashrimps and cockle shells. They stood and laughed at the strutting seagulls as the birds tippy-toed jerkily, followed the tiny lapping waves in and out. Charlie told Kate that when a chief stoker died, his soul did not go to heaven, but came back in the shape of a gull, and each morning Kate laughingly greeted the day, and the multitude of lovely floating birds with a bright, 'Good-morning, chief stoker.' The salty tang of the sea breeze filled their lungs and had them running on the empty promenade, and they danced each evening at the Tower Ballroom, moving round the floor in each other's arms to the gentle rhythm of *Whispering*, and *Let the Rest of the World Go By*.

But the nights in the soft double bed more than made up for the hundreds of long lonely hours they had spent apart. Charlie was not an experienced lover. It was not an age when young men had easy access to the bodies of young women, unless they were paid for, and in consequence the majority of working class newlyweds came together having known no other. Charlie was a seaman and had been to foreign parts. He had visited certain places with his shipmates, but they were not to his taste.

So Charlie and Kate learned the delights of love together. Slowly, shyly, tenderly, they discovered each other's body, watching, touching, giving and taking pleasure until their joy was complete. They became bolder at each successful encounter, and were eager each night, to turn out the light and come lovingly together, afterwards sleeping peacefully, bodies close, comfortable as though they had been married for years.

On their last night they walked the promenade, the quiet sea a silvery, almost invisible moving carpet on their left, the fretwork of the Tower like black lace against the navy blue sky. Pale stars glimmered and above their heads, as the night deepened, fragile and graceful as a kite on a string, rode a solitary seagull on a shifting wind.

'Goodnight, chief stoker,' murmured Kate.

Charlie smiled in the dark and held her arm more tightly to him.

'It's bin grand lass, grand.' A whisper in the night.

'Ay, it 'as that.'

They stood for a moment, arms about each other, one shape against the black and silver sky and sea, looking out towards the future which was unfolding its bright beckoning wings. They were sustained by their love for each other and their hope, nourished by the days and nights they had spent strengthening that love, and maintained by the faith that had set itself to grow and flower in their hearts. Like a weed it grew, strong and tenacious. No matter how often it was to be torn up by despair and misery, it would come again and thrive and flourish, for that was its nature.

They hummed as they walked back to their room,

With some one like you,
A pal good and true,
. . . and let the rest of the world go by.

It was on Christmas Eve that the man was first seen in Seacomb Street, though he was to become a familiar sight for several weeks after that. One irritable husband was to remark to his simpering and captivated wife who had just been cross-examined for the third time by the stranger, that if he came round again, he'd smash his face in.

The man was tall and so handsome he set female hearts a-twitter up and down the street. He was thin, almost emaciated, but the gauntness, the pale drawn look about him, gave him an air of vulnerability that had mothers of ten, and even grandmothers, longing to draw him into their comforting embrace. His eyes were a brilliant sapphire-blue, the only living feature in his anguished face, and his hair, cut so short it was almost as if it had been shaved from his skull, was a bright golden yellow.

He spoke English with a faint attractive accent.

But no one knew where the girl he asked for had gone. Speculation was rife as he went from door to door. The sisters had worked in the city, they told the man, as waitresses at a café, but which one no one knew. They'd only just flitted, they said, the coincidence, like fate amazing them. Flitted? That meant removed, they explained to him. Gone to live elsewhere. But someone must know where they had gone, implored the seaman, for it was obvious from his clothes, and even the way he walked, that he was from the sea.

'Somewhere up Sefton Park Way,' one ruminated,

'Nay, it was Wavertree,' said another.

But the one who knew said nothing. Her spite was vengeful. She'd not forgotten what that Kate had called her, and to this day she'd swear she'd pinched their Peggy's eggs. And that Jenny, stuck-up little cow. Thought she was better than anyone in the street, she did, with her high falutin' ways. Well, she'd get her own back. And so she surmised with the rest, on the whereabouts of Kate and Jenny until that last time when he knocked on her door.

'Ee luv,' she sighed sympathetically, 'I wish I could 'elp yer, I really do.' Her face lightened for a moment, as if a thought had just struck her. 'One thing I do remember.' The man's face shone with sudden eagerness, hope spilling from his bright blue eyes. 'Don't know whether it'll 'elp. There was gonner be a wedding. The young one, I think it were.'

She watched the light drain from the man's eyes and her own gleamed with satisfaction. That'd teach 'er, stuck up little madam.

The man was never seen again in Seacomb Street.

Chapter Eighteen

Henry Fowler reclined comfortably in the armchair placed to one side of his kitchen fire. He had a large mug of strong tea in his left hand, from which he sipped appreciatively, smacking his lips after each taste, and in the other he held last night's *Liverpool Echo*.

The day was bitter. He could hear the wind whistle in the chimney and the flames in the grate danced as each gust fanned the coals to roaring red heat, like bellows at a furnace. Henry's feet were placed upon the fender and his toes moved sensuously inside his socks. The top button of his trousers was undone to allow for the maximum of comfort and he had not yet put on his collar and tie. Henry had put on some flesh in the past twelve months, and his clothes did not fit him with quite the ease they once had, though he would not have admitted the fact. His face was fleshy and highly coloured, due no doubt to his growing fondness for a 'walk' down to the pub each evening. His thighs strained like tree trunks within the confines of his trousers.

The widow from Agnes Street and her children had taken over the work once done by Kate and Jenny, and increasingly Henry left her to 'see to things' as he sauntered forth to partake of a pint or two at the Old Swan. She had moved into the house several weeks after his daughters had deserted him, ostensibly as his housekeeper, and as yet, liking the feeling of power it gave him over her, he had made no more mention of marriage. It had been implied at the beginning; he had needed some lever to get her into the shop and what better way than to suggest that she was working in what would one day be her own business, but there was no hurry, he told himself. His eye had been drawn temporarily to the barmaid at the Swan, since the widow had moved into the chippy, and he was enjoying a mild dalliance with the enthusiasm he had once known for the widow. The barmaid was younger, pert and pretty and not averse to a hand on her seductive bottom, or down her lowcut blouse to cup her large breast. He was a good tipper, old Henry Fowler, and a bit of slap and tickle in the snug after 'time' often doubled her nightly takings.

Yes, Henry was satisfied with the way in which his life had changed since the death of his wife. His appetites were adequately taken care of by the widow each night, and she and her daughters had proved a worthwhile investment. The only aggravation on the serene plane of Henry's life was his own daughters. He would never forget the mortification he had suffered on the day he had gone to their home to give them a piece of his mind – his phrase – on the evil of their ways. His chagrin, the bitter sense of ridicule he had known as he had been put out into the street, was something his mind mulled over again and again, and the blame had been laid squarely at Kate and Jenny's door. One day, he had sworn he would make them pay for that humiliation. A father was derelict in his duty if he did not chastise his children for their wrongdoing, and that was what he had been about. Their Jenny had sinned in the worst possible way a girl could sin, and she must be made to pay for it. One day, he told himself. The time would surely come, one day.

Ah-ah Gertie crept about the kitchen like a soft-footed and ancient dog, her eyes turning regularly to her master, rolling in their sockets in a flicker of apprehension. She could think of nothing she had done wrong, but who was to know with Henry? A finger placed wrongly upon a fork could send him into a paroxysm of rage, and a far greater heresy might go unnoticed. You never knew which way he would jump, so unpredictable were his moods. Quietly, she placed the breakfast dishes in the kitchen sink, no mean feat when you were washing pots and pans which had been dirtied in the preparation and eating of a meal by seven people, but years of practice made her adept. The water swished gently as she wiped the cloth around an egg-coated plate, but apart from that, the crackle of the fire and the slurps made by Henry as he drank his tea, the room was silent.

A sudden sharp intake of breath from the man in the chair made Ah-ah turn her head instinctively. Fearing a tirade of abuse, she clenched her thin shoulders and shrank against the draining board, but Henry was reading something in the newspaper, taking no notice of her, and she relaxed again.

Henry sat upright in his chair and peered in disbelief at the advertisement in the *Echo*. His own name stared out at him and for a second he was confused. What was his name doing in the Personal Column? There it was in black and white, plain as the nose on your face. He had only been flicking through on his way to the sports page at the back and might never have seen it, for it was not his habit to read the sentimental slush that appeared on this page. Births, marriages and deaths had no interest for him, nor the problems which seemed to beset half of Liverpool, but there it was right at the top of the column. *Fowler*, as bold as you please. He read the message beneath, his lips moving as though to give more sense to the written word, and as he did so, his cheeks above his white beard became suffused with fury.

Though no name had been printed; no clue given as to who had inserted the advertisement, Henry knew who had put it in the paper. Who else, but that bastard would do such a thing? How dare he? How dare that . . . that . . . fling his good name about for all to see? Hadn't he done enough to this family, shaming them with that hussy, without bleating about it in the bloody paper?

Ah-ah watched in fascination as Henry, muttering imprecations, smashed his half-empty cup to the table and brought his feet to the floor with a resounding crash. She turned away grimacing to herself. Summat 'ad upset the old bugger, this time. Summat in t'paper by the look of it, but it were nowt to do wi' 'er, and she'd learned early the advisability of keeping her nose out of other folks' business. The less yer knew, the least likely yer were to be 'urt.

'By God, the cheek of 'im,' Henry thundered, unable to keep quiet any longer. 'The cheek of 'im, the bloody nerve.' He read it again and as he did so an idea, sweet and perfect, began to form in his mind. This was it. This was the day he had waited for. The chance to get his own back. He'd known it would come all along if he waited long enough, and here it was.

'*Fowler*,' it said, 'Would anyone who knows the whereabouts of Jenny Fowler late of Seacomb Street, please contact Box No. . . .'

With an air of smug self-satisfaction, Henry sat back in his chair and smiled. At last, at last it had come. With careful fingers he tore the small message from the paper and placed it on the table. Turning, he shouted to Ah-ah, 'Get me the writin' paper, woman and a pen and ink, quickly. Come on, look sharp.'

Flying across the kitchen, drying her hands upon the piece of sacking which served as an apron, Ah-ah pulled open a drawer and withdrew a notepad and from a cupboard beneath, a bottle of ink and a pen. She placed them on the table in front of Henry. He looked up at her and she recoiled at the venom which glowed in his eyes.

'Thank you Gertie,' he said smilingly. 'I have a letter to write and then I shall be goin' out.'

He was the picture of the well turned-out gentleman of means as he stood on Kate's doorstep on that cold February morning. His

Homburg had been brushed lovingly and his overcoat sat snugly on his broad shoulders. His spats, pale grey, covered the tops of his well-polished boots and his gloved hands rested comfortably on the gold top of his walking stick.

He had chosen his time well. He had seen Kate leave the house only minutes before, hiding his face from her in a pretence of interest in a shop window, for he wanted to have Jenny to himself. He had watched Kate run for the tramcar at the end of Rice Lane, before proceeding in a leisurely manner to Crescent Road. He had savoured every step of the way.

He was delighted by his reception.

His daughter stood as if turned to stone, her hand instinctively moving as though in protection to the gentle mound of her belly. It was Saturday, and neither she nor Kate was working, but Kate had gone to do some shopping in town as she did most weekends.

Henry had done his homework well. He had watched and waited and artfully questioned his sons and daughter until he felt he knew the movements of the 'sluts' as he called them privately, as well as he knew his own. It would not have been the same with Kate present. Her turn would come one day: Today it was this one's go.

''Ello, our Jenny,' he said genially.

Jenny's face was like a sheet. It had the colour of bleached bone and the flesh was stretched, tight as a drum, across her nose and cheeks. Her eyes were like pools of dead brown water in which no ripple moves nor life infiltrates. She was so mortally afraid she could feel the muscles of her bladder relax and some part of her mind was busy with the horrid thought that she was about to wet her knickers.

'Aren't yer goin' to ask me in, chuck?'

Henry smiled, looking for all the world like Father Christmas in mufti, but his eyes were bright with malice. 'I've only come to see 'ow yer are,' he went on. 'I 'eard as 'ow you were . . .,' he coughed delicately, '. . . in the family way, an' I come to convey my condolences.' He showed his teeth and Jenny was reminded of the many times he had baited her mother with just such a smiling mouth and snapping, vindictive eyes.

He's mad, she thought, quite, quite mad. It was only a few months since he had forced his way into the flat at Seacomb Street, and if the Bobby hadn't come she was sure he would have killed her. His temper was like an explosion, rocking all about him in a blast of destruction. Violent, unpredictable it shook the very foundations on which life was built. It terrified. It created a fear so

188

great it turned flesh to shaking jelly and made limbs rigid. But this, this benevolent amiability seemed, in its departure from the wildness with which Henry usually showed his displeasure, a hundred times worse.

His cruelty hung about him like a miasma.

Stepping over the threshold Henry closed the door behind him and gently propelled the mindless girl before him up the hall. When they reached the cosy kitchen, he looked about him with interest. 'Hmm, our Kate 'as done well for 'erself, 'asn't she?' he remarked in a friendly fashion. 'That sailor of 'ers must be doin' a bit of knockin' off. Yer don't gerra place like this on a seaman's wage.'

Jenny had not yet uttered a word. 'Well, 'ow about a cup of tea for yer old Dad then?'

Henry sat down in the armchair. Like a clockwork doll which has just been wound up Jenny put the kettle on, placed the tea in the teapot, filled it with hot water and poured the tea into the cups just as though she and her father were accustomed to taking morning tea together every day of the week. She sat down in the rocking chair and waited.

'Well now,' Henry said, 'tell us all about it.'

The silence was heavy and he sighed patiently. 'Come on, lass, I only want ter know the name of the lucky lad who put my daughter in t'club.'

Jenny's face twitched as agony struck her and she made a small sound in her throat. The cup she held in her hand slopped tea onto her dress as her hand became palsied. 'What's up lass? Don't yer want to tell yer Dad all about it?'

Henry's voice was soft with malevolence. 'Go on chuck, tell us what 'appened. Tell us 'ow 'e gorrin' to yer knickers. Did 'e promise to wed yer? Was tharrit?' He laughed gaily. 'Times I've done that. More times than you've 'ad 'ot dinners, I can tell yer. It always works. What was 'e? A sailor? Our Elly tells me 'e were Norwegian. Big chaps some of 'em and good-lookin'. Charm the birds off the trees, they would, or the knickers off any willing . . .'

'Don't . . . please God don't . . .' Jenny sprang to her feet and the rocker crashed backwards against the dresser. Anguish peaked her voice to a cry of aching appeal for mercy, but the man paid no heed. He hadn't enjoyed himself so much for years. Yer didn't need to use the belt. She was fair game, but then she always 'ad bin, just like 'er mother. His lip curled in contempt.

'Well yer seen the last of that 'un, I can tell yer. 'E'll be . . .' Here he used a word so vile, Jenny turned fainting against the table, clutching the chenille cloth for support, '. . . some other brainless slut out of 'er skull. No, yer seen the last of 'im. Still, I bet yer glad really, aren't yer? Any bloke that'd purra decent girl in t'family way and then run out on 'er is not worth the shit of a dog. No lass, I wouldn't piss on him if 'e were on fire.'

Jenny had slumped to her knees, her hands gripping the cloth, her arms stretched across the table, and for a second Henry regretted the fact that he had not his belt handy, for her back presented the perfect target. He sat sipping his tea, glancing about him with the air of a welcome visitor who waits for his hostess to bring on the cakes.

'An' when's the 'appy event then?' he continued brightly. He expected no answer and waited for none. His mind was wallowing in the joy of the pain he was inflicting on the girl before him, and as he did so the words he had written to the man who had advertised for her so pitifully returned to him.

'. . . and so my daughter has asked me to inform you that as she is now married she would be obliged if you did not bandy her good name about in the local newspaper. She is most . . .'

Jenny moaned, sinking slowly to the floor. Her fragile hold on life, on her own sanity; fought for with every fibre of her being since the night at the Pier Head when she had known of her pregnancy, was slipping away on a sea of such intense pain, she could scarcely hear her father's words any more. She could distinguish his voice as he slowly stripped her of her last vestige of strength, of dignity, of everything that was sweet and cherished, and she felt the agony tear her heart and she cried out.

'No . . . no . . . no . . . dear God . . . have pity . . . please . . . no more . . .'

Henry mused on, impervious to the cries of the girl.

'I don't know how you women can be taken in by the sweet talk of a man. Say pretty please and you'll do 'owt, and look what a mess it gets yer in. I bet 'e's laughin' up 'is sleeve, the sod, thinkin' of you layin' down for 'im. Yer should a' known better our kid. Sailors are the same the world over. I bet that chap of our Kate's 'is stickin' 'is thing in everythin' that moves.' His coarseness was appalling. It was as if he must do, or say, anything which might degrade the daughter he held in such contempt. His tongue lingered on the filth which poured from it.

'An' yer don't know what they leave behind, besides a bun in t'oven, I mean. They consort wi' t'dregs. I wouldn't 'ave bin surprised to 'ear you'd bin left with a dose of . . .'

'Stop it, for God's sake, stop it.' Jenny's scream echoed about the small room. 'He wasn't like that.' Her breath caught in her throat as her heart brought back for an instant the clean masculine smell, the engaging grin, the lively, loving eyes, the warm arms and the sweet whisper of adoration which Nils' memory evoked. 'He wasn't like that,' she repeated. Her eyes were blind with tears as she turned to face her father, and he was disconcerted to see the pure, glowing clarity of belief which swam in them. She seemed to emanate the goodness of her trust in the man she loved and Henry could see she would fight to the end to preserve that belief, that trust.

'Don't tell me 'e took yer in?' he protested laughingly. 'Yer mean to say, yer still think 'e's comin' back to yer. Don't be daft, girl, 'e's gone, gone, I tell yer, and yer'll see neither hair nor hide of 'im again.' He snorted derisively. Somehow his pleasure in what he had done seemed to be slipping away. He'd told the sod who'd caused all this that their Jenny was married, and if that didn't get shut of 'im he didn't know what would. He'd had a good go at 'er an' all. All his taunts had hit home, he could see that, but still she seemed to be . . . well he didn't know how to describe it. She was stickin' up for 'im for a start, an' she didn't seem to care what he, Henry, said. She didn't . . . she didn't . . . believe him. He felt the sour bitterness well up in him as he watched her face light with some inner sureness. She looked like she'd bin given a sign which told her that what she believed was true and that he, her father, spoke nothing but a pack of lies. He'd love to tell her. Tell her what he'd done. What he'd said to the matelot but that would mean she'd know the bloke still searched for her and she'd be down at the dock, or even the offices of the *Echo* lookin' for 'im. No, he must keep his trap shut. Just think, in the years to come, he, Henry Fowler, would have the satisfaction of knowing he'd kept them apart. He'd paid her back for what she, and that bitch of her sister, had done to him. With knobs on. If he hadn't seen the bit in the *Echo* he might never have had the gratification of knowing that the man still looked for her, and she didn't know. A thought struck him, and for an instant he felt a thrill of apprehension. What if one of his sons should see the advert? They'd be down here like bloody greyhounds, spilling the beans. But they'd never see it. His brow cleared. There was only their John took a paper now and again and then it was only the 'Pink' to read the sports news. They weren't a reading family, his lot, in fact he doubted if that layabout husband of Elly's, *could* read. He was safe. No one would know.

Jenny was standing straight now, and her eyes, though filled with the agony he had inflicted on her, were clear.

191

'I don't know why you came here, Dad, but it's done no good. The man who . . .' she faltered, but her voice was steady, 'he loved me. He wanted to marry me and would have, only something stopped him from coming back. We were . . .'

'Don't talk such bloody rubbish. 'E were no good, and you know it . . .'

'No . . . no . . . that's a lie, we loved each other. You don't think I'm the sort of girl who would . . .'

'Oh I know what sort of a girl you are, madam.' Henry's lip curled in a sneer, and he got to his feet. 'Oh yes, I know. You're the sort who . . .'

'Stoppit, stoppit. I won't listen to any more . . .'

'Oh won't yer? Well, we'll see about that . . .'

He was interrupted by a sound in the hallway. A door banged and footsteps could be heard clattering across the lino-covered floor, and before the man could register surprise, Kate stood in the doorway. Her face went slack with shock and her eyes blinked rapidly. She held a large shopping bag and her hair had escaped from her knitted beret to stand in dishevelment about her head. The wind had put a banner of scarlet in her cheeks. Her eyes were filled with a cold look of still hatred.

'What the 'ell do you want?'

'Kate, oh Kate, please send him away. He says . . .'

Kate ignored Jenny. She began to walk purposefully towards her father and again, despite himself, as he had done on that last day in the shop he stepped back. Her face was livid and reaching out she took the heavy, brass-knobbed poker from the grate. Holding it above her head like a man about to throw a spear she cried, 'If you're norrout of this house in five seconds, I'll brain yer. I don't care if I swing for yer, I'll do yer in.'

Henry laughed. Who did she think she was threatening him? He'd knock 'er for six, soon as look at 'er.

'Give over, lady. What d'yer think . . .'

'Get out of this house now,' Kate hissed, 'or I'm sending Jenny for t'police. She can run up the road t'phone box and they'll be 'ere in five minutes. Oh yes, I know yer can kill me before they'd come, but by God, yer face'll never be the same again, time I've 'ad a go at it wi' this poker. Now, are yer goin' or not?'

The heavy weapon stirred the air menacingly. She held it with two hands now, like a baseball bat, and the hate and fury made her into an Amazon.

Henry turned. What the 'ell. 'E'd done what 'e came to do, and there was always another time.

'Well I must say, fine welcome to a man who 'asn't seen 'is daughters since . . .'

'Don't say it Dad. Just clear off!'

Henry walked towards the door which led into the hallway. His face was petulant. Somehow it hadn't worked out quite how he had planned. He had relished the notion of their Jenny on her knees before him. He had wanted to see her beaten, defeated, grovelling and at the mercy of his vituperative tongue, but it hadn't happened. She had flinched at first, true, but then bewilderingly, she had stood up to him. Defended the man who had deserted her. Well never mind. He shrugged his shoulders and smiled secretively. She didn't know what he knew. Hugging the knowledge to him gleefully, he banged the front door behind him and strutted down the road towards the tramstop.

Chapter Nineteen

There was always a leaping fire of welcome in the hearth. The kettle would be balanced in its glowing centre, singing like a lark, its lid clattering as the steam lifted it. The teapot would be warming; three teaspoons of tea, one each and one for the pot, and nestling succulently within the oven would be a bubbling hot-pot, or a pan of stew. The lovely aroma would meet Kate at the door as she turned the key and Jenny would be there, a rosy hue about her rounding cheeks, her eyes glad with greeting. There would be a line of freshly-ironed clothes airing on the pulley. A 'fatty-cake' keeping warm in the oven, ready to be buttered and spread with syrup, and across the table would lie a flurry of fine flannelette, scissors, patterns, a bodkin of pins, as some fresh and dainty article of baby's clothing was cut and stitched. Delicately embroidered nightgowns, no bigger it seemed than a man's hand; lacy matinée coats, knitted so soft and fine, like spun sugar, and bootees laced in white satin ribbon. Angora bonnets made from odd balls of wool bought by Kate at St John's Market, as were the remnants, ends of rolls of material, all going for next to nothing, that Jenny stitched upon.

'This'll be the best dressed kid since the Prince of Wales,' Kate remarked, smiling, but her eyes were soft with gladness at the sight of Jenny's contentment.

Mrs Wagstaffe sent over skeins of embroidery silks in shades of pastel pink and blue, saying she had no need of them now, having completed the piece of work for which they were intended, and asked, through Percival, if this length of broderie anglais could be made use of, and towelling, thick and white and fluffy, destined for the 'Sally-Ann' perhaps might be cut up and used as nappies.

Jenny sewed and rocked in the absorbed world of the mother-to-be, and if tears should well and trickle to her chin, they did so without appearing to shatter her expression of dreaming composure. She would brush them away before they had time to fall and spoil the fineness of the fabric upon which she worked, and though her mind did not allow her to forget, her memories were

194

softened by the thoughts of what was soon to come. She had firmly opposed Kate's scheme to pretend herself a widow, saying that the father of a child whose mother was a widow, must be dead, and Nils was *not* dead. She did not say he would return. She had stopped saying that months ago, but hope lived hidden in her heart.

It was April now and Jenny no longer went to the café and the office where she and Percival Wagstaffe had worked side by side for almost five months. It had been a picture of neatness when she left and she had known where to lay her hands on every invoice, every receipt, every letter and scrap of paper which came into the office, though it was doubtful that Waggy did. She knew that within a week it would be as chaotic as it had been when she had started, but after her child was born she was to return, and then, when the new term started in September she would go to the Moorfields Business College to learn to be a proper secretary.

In the period following her promotion to Waggy's office she had worked in the cloister of his protective concern, learning the difference between an invoice and a receipt, fending off the curiosity of the girls with whom she had previously worked, but as the weeks passed and her figure thickened, their speculative conjectures as to why she was so favoured were answered, and the obvious choice for the father, was, of course, Waggy himself, else why should he show such an interest? She seemed to do as she pleased an' 'im fawnin' an' smarmin' like the randy old goat he was. Girls stood in corners and wondered in the morbid way of those who delight in another's troubles, eyeing Jenny when she was about, and asking innocently misleading questions of the old man.

He stood it for a while, hoping it would be, as they say, a nine day wonder, but as the gossip blossomed and grew, wherever he went, it seemed eyes watched him and Jenny together. At last he turned on them, and roaring like a wounded buffalo plagued by a swarm of flies told the lot of them to 'mind their own bloody business an' if they didn't shurrup and gerron with their work, he'd sack the lorrof 'em.' After that, with nothing further to feed on, the whole affair became yesterday's news and their interest turned to fresher fields of scandal. The girls in the café became used to seeing Jenny in the role of office girl and her situation was left alone. Things unique are quickly accepted as commonplace with usage and time, and so did Jenny's relationship with Mr Wagstaffe, and the day came when the waitresses could scarcely remember when she had been one of themselves.

Jenny moved through the days serenely. So unaware was she of what was happening outside the confines of the office and her friendship with the old man, it might have been a stranger over whom the girls licked their lips. She seemed invulnerable now, and had been from her fifth month of pregnancy.

She had been dreaming, remembering, soaking her body in the depths of the shining new bath tub in the small bathroom which Kate's new home boasted, when her baby had moved for the first time. For a moment her heart had plunged as the memory of the sweet thrilling butterfly which had fluttered within her at the closeness of Nils, had cut through her mind and she almost cried out for she had thought it the same. Then it happened again, a delicate ripple of feeling just beneath the stretched skin of her belly, moving gently across the small mound, up, up until it lodged within her heart. It had warmed her and her whole body flushed and seemed to tingle with the delight of it and for the first time she smiled with the wholehearted joy which she had thought gone forever. She placed her soapy hands against her stomach and her fingers pulsed and as if in loving answer, the tiny rosebud of her unborn child moved again and the link was forged, a strong loving chain between mother and child.

Jenny's body had slipped further beneath the warm water, relaxed, like a cat in the sun, and another small degree of pain had left her for she knew Nils' child lived.

Kate was working only half a shift now, in the morning, and again there was muttering over the consideration given to the Fowler sisters, for that was how they were still known. Once more Waggy was forced to quell the small rebellion with a thundering oration on the ease with which he would acquire new staff if the necessity arose.

Charlie came and went, pressing Kate for a date when she would give up her job and let him support her as a husband should, but something in Kate's strong and independent nature could not concede. The future for Jenny was, to all appearances certain, but in Kate's mind the fates had a way of turning things about until what was one day an unshakeable fact, could the next, become as precarious as walking on water. She wanted to put a bit by for she knew not what contingency. Like throwing salt over your shoulder, or knocking on wood, it seemed to her that every little asset helped, and if she had a small nest egg to call upon, it would be like a goodluck charm. An insurance against misfortune.

Besides, as she told Charlie in their deep and tumbled bed, there was nothing for her to do at home until Jenny's child was born.

196

'Two women together all day in one kitchen doesn't make for peace, love, and the money'll come in handy for us later,' and she told him, with satisfied, loving arms about him, that by Christmas there would be two babies in the house. Charlie, mollified by the knowledge that his masculine pride would be restored to him, and full of his own prowess at what was practically the easiest result in the world to achieve, hardly had time to have misgivings at the idea of a house filled, it seemed, before he had time to draw breath, with babies, when he was drawn again into the soft flesh and loving spirit of his wife, and by morning had accepted with equanimity the prospect of his fatherhood.

Kate had doubts at times when she saw Jenny's drawn face at breakfast and knew that it had been a bad night. One of those in which Jenny had wept in the darkness for her love. On days such as these she would swear she was giving up her job and staying at home, stating that Jenny should not be left alone all day.

'But I'm not on me own, our Kate,' Jenny had answered softly, and she looked down at the jutting swell of her stomach, placing protective hands about it, as though to cradle the child within. Her eyes had smiled then with that lovely candid appeal which had stolen the heart of a sailor, and deep in their depths shone something sure and strong. It was to be seen in the eyes of all creatures, animal or human, which give birth to, and protect their young; in the eyes of a mother who defends her child and is the realisation that, to no one in the world is the progeny more important, more earth-shatteringly beloved than to the one who gives it life. The emotion was as old as time itself. It made the weak strong and the indifferent, caring. It gave endurance where once had been fear. Jenny Fowler had found it in her love for her unborn child. It had given her a purpose, a goal to strive for. Because of it she was strong again. Though her heart would break in the night, she knew now the road she was taking.

In May, as Jenny floundered like a landed fish in the last weeks of her pregnancy, splay-footed, huge and awkward, she and Kate were washing up after their simple evening meal. The days were beginning to draw out and the pastel spring sky, apricot tinted, arched above the stand of dark trees across the fields. The sun had gone, sliding quickly beyond the horizon, and the land was dark, but the last delicate touch of its light shone into the kitchen, touching the girls' cheeks with gold. The room was filled with shadows, but the firelight flickered lovingly about, gliding over shining surfaces, glowing against the pretty red curtains, painting the white walls with orange, and the peace drenched the two girls

197

as they pottered about. Kate took cups and plates from Jenny's hand, reaching to put them into the cupboard on the wall, dreamily folding the teacloth across the line above the fire, almost in a trance, so hypnotised by tranquillity had they become.

It was broken by a knock at the door. Looking at Jenny questioningly, as though to say, 'Who on earth can that be at this time of night?' Kate walked down the hall to the front door. When she opened it she found herself looking into the blue and whimsical eyes of Percival Wagstaffe. He stood, half bowing, his black bowler hat which he had whipped off his head as the door opened, held to his chest in what he considered to be the acme of courtliness, and his rough, lumpy face split into a rogueish grin. Behind him, drawn up to Kate's front gate was a brand new Austin seven motor car, gleaming, black and shiny. The paintwork was as slick as though it was wet and the chrome flashed in the last rays of the daylight. An inquisitive group of children stood in a semi-circle about it.

Kate was too astonished to speak. Her mouth opened but no sound emerged, though she could feel the breath move in her throat. She smoothed her apron with the automatic gesture of women found unprepared for visitors and ran her fingers through her uncombed hair. Her hand was still on the door but she made no attempt to open it wider. Waggy told her later he expected her to say, 'What the 'ell do *you* want?' But now he winked and waited for her to recover her composure. Kate's eyes flickered from him, looking at the car, and up and down the road as though seeking some explanation for Waggy's appearance on the doorstep – after all, she had only seen him that morning in the café.

Waggy watched the play of expression on her face, delighted with the effect of his surprise visit. Putting his hat back on his head, but retaining the half-bowing position, he turned, waving with his left hand towards his new car and said cheekily, 'Care for a spin, lady?'

Kate came to life. 'Eeh, Mr Wagstaffe.' She was flustered and her feet shuffled on the linoleum as though she was unsure whether to close the door in his face, or open it wider to allow him inside. A few months ago she had known no more of this man than the greeting she received from him each morning, usually irritable; the bellowed good night, and the interminable bickering he kept up with his staff in between. He had been kind to Jenny, more than kind, with his agreement to help her after the birth of the baby. He had put up with a deal of petty jealousy and grumbling amongst the girls who worked for him, by his leniency in allowing Kate to work as she did, but apart from that his attitude towards her had not altered. She was a waitress, a girl who worked for him and that was it. It was his business and she worked for him.

Now he was here, away from his own territory. He was her boss and he was on hers. This was her home and he stood on her doorstep, asking her to go for a ride in his motor car. She who had never been in a motor car in her life.

The newness of the situation threw her into a most un-Katelike dither. She was completely overcome.

'Eeh, Mr Wagstaffe,' she said again and blushed to the roots of her hair.

Waggy glanced round at the staring faces of the children. The woman who lived opposite had found some absorbing task which had suddenly to be done in her front garden, and here and there curtains moved.

'Ask me in Kate,' he beseeched. 'The neighbours are gettin' a real eyefull, and I'm beginnin' to take root.'

Still, as she put it, all of a 'doo-dah' Kate ushered him into the newly painted hallway. His feet resounded on the polished linoleum, echoing up the staircase. It was obvious that the house was empty of all but the bare essentials, but it was bright and clean and apparent to the old man's eye, Kate's pride and joy. Just before he shut the door behind him he turned and shouted to the gape-mouthed children, 'If any o' you little buggers so much as lays a finger on that motor car, I'll knock yer bloody noses off.' They scattered like petals in the wind. Kate was mortified. This wasn't Seacomb Street where language like that was common-place. This was Fazackerly and she doubted whether any of the children who played in the new street had ever heard such words before. Sighing, knowing there was nothing she could do about it for who would ever change Waggy, she led the way to the kitchen.

As she opened the door, the light spilled out, shining on the large untidy bulk of the old man. Jenny was about to lower herself into the rocking chair, but when she saw who it was she gave a small cry of pleasure. Heaving herself from the fireside and with the grace of a gambolling hippo, she moved across the strip of rug to Waggy. Before the bewildered stare of her sister, Jenny put her arms about his shoulders and impulsively kissed him on the cheek. Percival Wagstaffe was enchanted. His arms rose and grasped her and like two elephantine figures, stomach to bulging stomach, they hugged each other. Kate was amazed. So were Jenny and Waggy. Standing back, surprised both of them at the spontaneous

199

affection which had drawn them together in a reflex of goodwill, they smiled at each other.

'Eeh, lass, yer look grand.' Waggy was the first to recover. 'Yer like a little puddin'. Almost as fat as me.' Far from being embarrassed at the mention of her size, Jenny began to laugh, putting her hands to her stomach. Blue eyes looked into brown with clear understanding of how it was to be between them. Kate felt as though she had become invisible as the pair of them sat, Waggy solicitously lowering Jenny to her chair before taking the one opposite. They chatted like old friends catching up on the news and gossip of weeks, about the café and the girls who worked there; about the office and the 'dreadful state' it was becoming without Jenny's guidance, about invoices, receipts and finally, with a suddenness which took both the girls by surprise, about doctors.

'. . . So what does he say, queen? Is everything all right with the little one?'

Jenny and Kate looked at each other. The Fowlers had always been in good health and Kate could not recall any member of the family ever having had need of medical attention, excepting for poor Elizabeth. It was the custom of most working class mothers to have their children in their own beds at home, and if they were lucky, to be helped by the local midwife, but even in these enlightened times, many a poor woman would deliver her child with only a friendly neighbour on hand. The sisters had discussed it. They had said that next week, soon, before long, they would go to see the doctor. Perhaps the clinic in Rice Lane, or the midwife whose name was on a plate outside her house in Lochinvar Street but the dreaded anticipation of telling someone, of admitting that Jenny was not married had held Kate back. Jenny was fit, healthy, eating well – enough for two – and there had seemed no reason, not yet, to consult a doctor. Nearer the time, she said to herself, for the era had not yet come when women went as their right to be cared for from the first weeks of pregnancy by experts, and so, as most did in their walk of life, they waited until the last to seek medical advice.

Waggy looked from one sheepish face to the other.

'Don't tell me yer've not seen a doctor, our Jenny.' The possessive 'our' went unnoticed. That welcoming kiss had changed their relationship in some way, and with almost the irritated concern of a father, Waggy's eyes flashed beneath eyebrows which moved up and down like two dancing furry caterpillars.

'Yer've bin to see a doctor, 'aven't yer?'

200

'Well not yet, yer see . . .'

'Not yet. Yer daft 'apporth. 'Ere's you nearly at yer time and yer've not bin to see a doctor. Eeh lass,' softly 'don't yer think yer should go and 'ave some sort of check-up. I know nowt much about it, but yer ought to go. Me Mam said . . .' He stopped suddenly, 'Tell me I'm an interferin' old bugger but promise me yer'll go.'

Later that evening with the indolence brought about by pregnancy and the approach of birth, Jenny eased her way about the kitchen doing last minute jobs which might have been left until morning.

She smiled as she emptied the contents of a big paper bag which Waggy had left on the table.

'Me Mam sent these,' he had remarked offhandedly as he shoved the bag awkwardly in her direction before leaving. A heap of soft knitted toys fell in a pile on to the table, 'Just made from odds and ends, me Mam said,' as if in apology for the kindness, 'she's nowt else to do.'

A bright sweet joy lit Jenny's face, and she picked up and cradled a miniature pink rabbit. Her hands fondled it as though already her child was there to share her quiet pleasure.

During the last weeks it became an accepted thing every Sunday afternoon to hear the rat-a-tat on the front door and to find Waggy winking and beaming, and each time he came the bond of affection between the old man and the young girl, grew. He brought her spring flowers, or a bar of chocolate. He would take the girls for what he called a 'spin' in his new motor car, proud to the point of insufferability of it, and of the two pretty women he escorted.

And at the end of May, Jenny was taken by him and Kate, one cool, sunny afternoon to the clinic in Rice Lane and she was examined by the young doctor who was in attendance that day.

His name was John Clancy.

Chapter Twenty

Kate was fond of saying in the first half of that bright new year that she felt as though she had died and gone to heaven, so great was her joy in her new home.

No dark paint and small windows. No outside lavvy or poky rooms. No cockroaches, or mice or old paraffin lamps or uneven floorboards. No smells of the city or smoke and dirt and grime. Lightness and brightness, new white paintwork and pretty flowered wallpaper. A parlour, a scullery, a neat modern kitchen. A bedroom for each of them and one over, and an indoor bathroom and toilet. She had a small backyard and over the wall she could see fields of sorrel and rock rose, clover and buttercup, and smell the tangy aroma of cattle, horses, the sweetness of hay, and hear no sound but the sigh of the wind in the grass and the high, lilting call of the thrush. At the front of the house was an even smaller garden leading from the newly tarmacadamed road. Across from her own house and on either side, stretched an identical row of houses, neat, new, and housing pleasant, warily friendly young families with whom she was on nodding acquaintance.

She was three months pregnant now and had at last given in to Charlie's insistent demands – and those of Waggy who could not stand to think of Jenny alone – to stay at home. She polished and cleaned and cleaned and polished and could not get enough of the sweet shining loveliness of it all. Jenny had let go of what she had considered *her* kitchen for the past few months and sat back in her chair to rock and wait. She had that look of stolid patience that comes in the last few days of pregnancy. Her face was placid, almost withdrawn, but her eyes seemed to shine with a lustre of anticipation. Her fingers still stitched on some small garment, this time for Kate, for she could not bear to sit with hands folded, and her own chest of drawers in her bedroom was already jammed with wisps of garments for her child.

On the night of 14 June the sisters went to bed later than usual. It had been a cold drizzling day, more like November than June, and they had kept the fire in and the curtains half drawn to shut out the sight of the ceaselessly dripping water from the roof and the grey clouds whipping across the sodden fields.

Dr Clancy had called at breakfast time, tired and grey-faced after a nightlong vigil at the bedside of a child dying of consumption. He was quiet and kind as usual as he examined Jenny, but his thoughts were still in the cheerless room of the emaciated, flush-faced boy, and he sensed no coming disaster in the serenity and warmth of Kate's kitchen.

Jenny sewed a little, but she seemed restless. She repeatedly levered herself from the rocker to wander back and forth from kitchen to scullery, touching this and that, as if only half aware of what she was doing. She clucked to the cat, but for once the rapport she shared with the animal was missing. It capered and played the fool, dashing sideways to avoid her outstretched hand as she bent awkwardly to fondle it, and she heaved herself upright, one hand on the table, saying breathlessly, 'Please yerself then, yer daft beggar. See if I care.'

She moved back to the rocking chair, carrying her burden cumbersomely, supporting her distended belly with protective hands, and sat down heavily.

The day had passed peacefully enough. Kate did some ironing after their simple midday meal, and at about half past four made a pot of tea and some ham sandwiches for their tea. They ate almost in silence. After they had eaten, Kate picked up a book and as Jenny dozed, began to read the first page. Within half an hour she was deeply involved in the heartrending love story, and was surprised when the cuckoo told her it was nine o'clock. She washed their few tea dishes and stood for a moment smoothing the teacloth over the line above the fire. The kitchen was stuffy, and as the room darkened, she opened the window to let in a little fresh air. The rain had stopped and the thin clouds parted against the violet sky to allow a sprinkle of stars to shine fitfully. The night smelled of rain on soil and the last small sounds of sleepy birds trilled across the yard. She stood for a few minutes enjoying the feel of the cool air on her face. In the far distance, across the wet leaves of the wood, a delicate, fast disappearing streak of rose followed the sun which had sailed behind the rain clouds over the lip of the horizon.

'It's gonner be a nice day tomorrer, our kid,' she said, 'red sky at night . . .'

They pottered aimlessly for another hour, reluctant it seemed to go to their beds, but as the cuckoo called eleven o'clock, they

203

slowly climbed up the stairs. Kate helped Jenny out of her voluminous dress and into her equally voluminous nightie. She supported her as she climbed clumsily onto her narrow bed, holding her shoulders as she turned, as graceless as an elephant in mud. Her legs were apart, sticking out before her and she rested on her elbows panting with the exertion. A thin slick of perspiration clung to her face.

'Phew, I'm hot tonight,' she murmured.

Kate looked at her sharply for the air in the bedroom was cool but though her cheeks were flushed, she was calm, her eyes clear and placid. Jenny shifted awkwardly, trying to get on to her side, but gave it up resignedly.

Later from the bathroom, as she washed her face and put on her own nightdress, Kate heard her sigh. In the double bed she shared with Charlie, Kate smoothed her own stomach pensively, thinking about the day when she would look like Jenny and her last thought, as usual, was about Charlie and what he would say when she was . . .

She slept. A troubled sleep. Dreaming, dreaming. It was their Jenny. She was running, falling. She couldn't reach her and Jenny was that scared. She was calling Kate's name over and over again, pulling her down, down, into the big black pit, a pit with high sides, slippery with some oozing horror that she could not hold on to. She tried to shake off the hand but it was no use. Jenny had her by the arm tightly, still calling her name.

She came awake on a wave of panic, her heart thudding, her eyes staring, piercing the darkness. Jenny was clutching her arm in a vice-like grip, saying her name over and over again.

'Kate, Kate, for God's sake, our Kate, will yer wake up. Me water's broke. Oh Kate, wake up will yer. I'm in an awful mess.'

In the dim light which filtered from Jenny's room, Kate could see the bulky figure of her sister beside the bed. In an instant, like a mother alert to a child's cry in the night, she was awake. Cool, steady, calming Jenny with a quiet word, she reached across to the bedside lamp which had been a wedding present from their Elly, and switched it on.

'Eeh our Jenny, don't get so mithered, luv. It's yer baby at last. The day we've all bin waitin' for.'

Jenny sagged onto the bed and her shoulders relaxed and panic left her. The corners of her mouth lifted in a tentative smile, and her eyes cleared. 'Just think, queen,' Kate went on, 'in a few hours you'll 'ave yer own baby in yer arms.' She shook her head smilingly. 'Ow about that then?' She eased herself from the bed. She

204

shivered in the cool night air and moving quickly, pulled off her nightdress and huddled into the clothes which she had discarded only three hours before. Still murmuring soothingly, as much to alleviate her own nervousness as Jenny's, she helped her from the bed and began to lead her towards the bedroom door.

'It'll all be over soon, chuck, and then yer'll be luvly and thin again. Won't that be grand? Yer'll be able to wear all yer nice frocks. That one yer made just before . . .'

For a moment Kate was mortified as she recognised what she had been about to say, but Jenny was absorbed in getting her cumbersome form through the doorway, and it went unnoticed. 'Now, 'ang on to me luv, an' we'll get yer changed and comfy,' she continued, relieved that the bitten-off sentence had not been heard by Jenny. They had enough to contend with, without memories of what might have been. She threw a quick, backward glance at the clock which ticked importantly on the dresser and saw that it was nearly two o'clock. She'd have to get Jenny settled and then run down the street to the telephone box at the corner of Willowdale Road and ring Dr Clancy. Any time of night or day, he'd said, and he'd be there. Comforted, for that was the feeling the young doctor gave to his patients, she steered Jenny down the stairs and into the still warm kitchen. Its peaceful familiarity welcomed them, and the two shuffling figures felt its tranquillity fall about them gratefully. It was as though the coming event could be dealt with safely in this, their own harbourage. Surrounded by warmth, and holding the possessions they had gathered and treasured, no harm could come to them here.

'There chuck, stand by t'fire while I get yer things sorted out.'

Pulling a clean, freshly-aired nightdress from the line above the fire, Kate fussed about her sister, removing her wet garment and easing the clean one over her head and down her thickened body.

'Tell yer what, our kid,' she chuckled, 'it's a good job this kid's on its way.'

She stretched the tent-like nightdress over Jenny's stomach, '. . . 'cos I reckon yer'd not get this nightie on in a week or two. Now sit yerself down an' I'll put kettle on, and whilst tea's brewin' I'll run t'corner and ring the doctor.'

The tea made and mashing; leaving Jenny staring placidly into the flames of the fire which she had just stirred with the poker, Kate ran down the dark road towards the corner. There was not a light on anywhere. Ragged clouds lazed along in the direction of the river, and a star or two gave a faint light to guide Kate's hurrying feet.

She read out the number to the operator from the piece of paper on which John Clancy had written it; the piece of paper which had stood for the past three weeks on the mantelpiece in readiness for this moment.

A sleepy, irritable voice answered and as Kate's tongue tripped and stumbled over the words in her haste to get at Dr Clancy and be away back to Jenny, the irritable voice became even more so as it repeated: 'He's not in, Mrs Walker. He has been called away to . . . but as soon as he returns I will give him your message.'

Kate couldn't take it in at first. 'Not in,' but he *must* be in. Their Jenny was in labour and needed him. He said he'd come right away. '. . . But what shall I do?' she entreated the cool voice at the other end of the line. 'Me sister's started with 'er pains an' I don't know what to do . . .'

'Is it her first baby?' the voice interrupted.

'Yes.'

'Well, don't worry dear. With a first child it always takes a while. I'm sure the doctor will be there long before . . . Now just give me the address again . . . now go home and wait. If the doctor is not back directly I will get a message to him. Don't worry.'

The phone went dead. Slowly Kate returned it to its hook. Now what? Their Jenny in labour and Dr Clancy out on a call. The thought had never once occurred to her that the doctor might be out, that he would not instantly be round at their house in the little old car which carried him, somehow, from patient to patient. Well it couldn't be helped. It'd be hours yet before the baby came. She knew nowt about it really, but from what she'd heard the first always took hours. The woman had said so, and their Elly was always going on about it. She'd had ten so she should know.

For a moment Kate contemplated running down to Saint Domingo Road to fetch her elder sister. She'd feel better with someone with her, and Elly'd be just the one with all her experience. She looked towards her own house and saw the light streaming from the front window. She'd left it on to guide herself back. Jenny was there alone, and it'd take a good half hour to get to Elly's. She didn't like the idea of leaving Jenny alone for so long. An hour with the walk back. For a moment Kate dithered, then began to run back up the road in the direction of her own home.

In the gentle warmth of the kitchen Kate and Jenny sipped their tea and smiled at one another. They were safe, sheltered, and they felt quite pleased with themselves as they counted the minutes between Jenny's faint contractions as Dr Clancy had instructed them. They were managing very nicely, they told each other.

206

The cuckoo came out to greet them cheerfully, then returned to its pretty house. Once again it came, four times this time, blithe as a . . . cuckoo.

The minutes between the sharp stabs became fewer, and Jenny's pains mounted and multiplied, coming with increasing frequency, until she doubled up in her chair grasping her bent knees in shock.

Kate made another cup of tea but Jenny couldn't drink it. Kate helped her to climb the stairs to the bathroom and while she was there, slipped to the front bedroom window to peer anxiously along the black tunnel of the road, straining her eyes and ears for the sight or sound of Dr Clancy's car.

Jenny stumbled about the room now, gasping, hanging on to the table and Kate's arm, her eyes wide and frightened, the sweat pouring from her, dampening and darkening the clean nightdress which she had put on earlier. Her hair was limp about her face and she bit her lip until it bled, clenching her teeth to stop herself from screaming.

'Oh Kate, oh Kate, oh Kate,' she moaned.

Kate's heart clenched in terror. She tried to speak reassuringly to the agony-racked girl who faltered and clung to her, but she was only a girl herself, inexperienced, frightened, facing an event, the mechanics of which she knew nothing. Oh God, where was Dr Clancy? It was over two hours since she had rung him. For the first time she felt the lack of the nosey, but friendly intimacy of her own working class background, where, a sudden death, an accident, or a birth as now, would bring a dozen willing neighbours to help. But how could she knock on the door of any house in this street, where, as yet, she knew no one, and when half of them looked as though the sight of a drop of blood might make them faint. Coolly polite, they were, when they passed by. 'Good morning, lovely day,' but no more. She would have to go and telephone again. Things were moving too quickly, even she, unknowledgeable as she was, could see that. If he didn't get here soon, the baby would come without him.

'Look luv,' she said placatingly to the staggering figure who seemed hardly to be conscious of her presence, 'I'll 'ave ter go and give Dr Clancy another ring. 'Appen that woman's forgotten to tell 'im. I won't be long. Only a . . .'

Jenny's swollen sweating face worked in panic and she turned, falling against the table in her fear. 'Don't leave me, Kate, please don't leave me.'

'I'll only be gone a tick, honest. I'll 'ave ter ring . . .'

'I'll come with yer.'

'Nay luv, yer can't come down the road like . . .'

'I'm not bein' left, our Kate, even for a minute.'

Kate's head was in a whirl. She didn't know what to do for the best. She just wanted the doctor to come and then she'd sit down and have a damn good cry. She would, honest. Was it right keeping their Jenny on her feet, or should she lie down? She didn't know. She felt as though they were on a nightmarish merry-go-round as they stumbled round and round the kitchen table. They couldn't just go on like this. Up and down, round and round and Jenny's cries became shriller.

'I'll 'ave ter gerrof me feet, our Kate,' she moaned. 'I can't stand much more of this.'

Kate managed to half carry, half push the struggling straining figure up the stairs, for Jenny was fighting now, hysterical in her fear and pain. The sisters staggered about the tiny bedroom. Every few minutes Jenny collapsed upon the tumbled bed, begging to be allowed to sit down, to sleep, to be relieved of this burden she carried, then in a moment, she would be up again as the pain tore her. Each time she did so Kate ran to the front bedroom window to peer dementedly for the sight of the doctor's car. It was like a bad dream from which she would never awaken. Dear God, *where was he*?

Those last screams sounded like an animal, one which has been tormented beyond endurance. Kate's face became set and her mouth clamped firmly over her teeth. Taking Jenny's hands, she held on and on as her sister thrashed like a soul in torment.

'Help me, dear God help me.'

'Give over our Jenny,' Kate hissed through tight lips. 'Yer've got me. I'm 'ere, an' we'll manage, like always.'

An hour later Dr Clancy's car turned the corner into Crescent Road and hurtled along it with a force which far exceeded the speed at which it was meant to travel. Everything rattled in protest, from the lid of the bonnet to the handle on the boot.

Stopping with a squeal of brakes he flung open the door, leaving it swinging on its hinges. His feet skidded in the puddles of rainwater as he ran up the path and hammered on the door. He waited impatiently for the door to be opened and when it did so, pushed it inwards flinging Kate against the wall.

She stood immobile where he had thrust her, her skin the colour of a dirty floorcloth. She was streaked with blood from her neck to her knees and it dripped from her finger ends to the linoleum. There were smears on the wall where she had touched it and on her face and hair where her fingers had trembled. She did not speak. She was not able, so great was the shock which enfolded her.

John Clancy took one look at her; at her stunned face and empty eyes and raced up the stairs and into the bedroom. He stopped, aghast, and the colour drained from his face, leaving it as ashen as Kate's.

Jenny lay on her back on the battlefield of the bed, her arms stretched out on either side of her grasping the edge of the mattress. Her eyes stared, black pools in which no reflection glimmered, straight at the ceiling, unseeing, dead. Her knees were drawn up, her heels digging into the bed which had been covered with newspapers. Lying between her thighs, flung this way and that from Kate's frantic ministrations, was the small bloody body of a child. The umbilical cord, coiled like a piece of rope, was knotted firmly about its tiny throat. Jenny's blood pumped vigorously in bright waves over its dead face.

Kate moved slowly, her body stiff, like that of an old, old woman. She paused in the doorway behind the doctor. The bright red of Jenny's blood was almost too colourful to be borne. For an instant the hideous tableau was still, then, with a hoarse cry, the young doctor sprang to life.

Barely stopping to douse his hands in the disinfectant he took from his bag, he thrust one hand into Jenny's body, the other feverishly massaging her lower abdomen. By stimulating the uterus to contract, he endeavoured to stop the flow of blood.

Gradually, second by second, the pressure he applied began to work and the flow became a trickle, and then stopped. For the space of five heartbeats he was still, the only sound his laboured breathing, then turned, and took a wad of clean towelling – the baby's napkins supplied so kindly by Waggy's Mam – which he packed tightly between Jenny's thighs. With a sigh which shuddered from the bottom of his lungs, he turned hopelessly to the child.

He worked feverishly and Kate moaned deeply in her throat at the rough manner with which he treated the tiny limp form. Grunts forced themselves from his mouth and his face became florid and sweaty. For ten minutes he worked, then was still. He stared, defeated at the small body. Trembling with exhaustion, he gently wrapped it in a towel and handed it to Kate.

Later, as Jenny slept deeply in the strong sedative given her by John Clancy, the young doctor sipped black tea from a mug and watched as Kate washed the lovely golden child, Nils and Jenny's daughter, for the first and last time. She cried no tears. She had none left.

The tall slim figure of the seaman walked slowly passed the row of shops which stood between North John Street and Temple Lane. The rain swept from the east and though it was June now, it was cold on his face. His eyes darted like brilliant beacons in the grey murk of the day, searching, searching. Shop after shop was passed over as his gaze swept both sides of the busy street. His face was brown, lean, still drawn, but the hollows were gone from beneath his eyes. His hair was a bright cap of gold curling about his head, the drops of rainwater gathering to hang like tiny dewdrops before slipping to fall on to his wet collar. His eyes were intent on the buildings which lined both sides of the road. A tram clanged past, its wheels clicking over the points, its top deck empty, for no one wished to sit in the deluge which poured unceasingly from the leaden skies.

Suddenly the expression on his face changed from one of focused concentration to hopeful interest. His eyes rested on the café and the sign which was painted above it. Wagstaffe's. His eyes became hazy as his mind reached back into the memories which lay there. Wagstaffe's. Was that the one? Did the name mean anything to him? He tried to force his brain to centre on the name, but it brought nothing back. Crossing the street, barely aware of the traffic which came from both directions, he stopped outside the café and looked over the checked ruffled curtains to the scene within. Every table was taken. The windows were misted with condensation and as the door opened to receive yet another customer, a delicious smell drifted across the man's nostrils and a rush of saliva filled his mouth. But it was not for food that he had come.

Pushing open the door he went inside. There was a smart waitress at the till, taking money from a man who was paying his bill, and as she turned away, ready to move back to her station, the tall sailor spoke to her. He had a soft, very slight accent.

'Miss, Miss, may I . . . could you spare a moment?'

The girl turned and the pupils of her eyes dilated in the automatic sign of a woman attracted to a man.

'Yes,' she murmured, her hand going to her hair.

'I wonder if you could help me?'

'I'll try,' she smiled, pleased. He was very handsome.

'I'm looking for someone, a girl,' the man went on, moving closer to the till. Disappointment clouded the young girl's face.

'Oh yes?'

'Her name is Jenny Fowler. She's a waitress in a café in Liverpool, but the trouble is I don't know which one. I had . . . an accident, and my memory . . .'

Instantly, the girl was all solicitude and her eyes wandered eagerly across his face. They were soft with romance and a longing to help.

'Well, I don't know . . . there's no one 'ere of that name.'

She called across to another young waitress who carried a loaded tray in the direction of the kitchen. 'Flo, d'yer know a . . .' She turned back to the seaman.

'Jenny Fowler . . . er she may have changed it . . . married.' The muscles in his cheek spasmed in pain as he said the last word.

'. . . a Jenny Fowler?'

Flo considered for a moment, harassed and not a bit pleased to have to stop with the heavy tray about to break her arms.

'No . . . never 'eard of 'er, but I've not bin 'ere long. P'raps Mr Wagstaffe'll know.'

''E's not 'ere. A friend of 'is is poorly.' The waitress turned back to the tall young man. 'Sorry chuck, there's no one 'ere of that name. Try Johnson's round the corner, they may know.'

Thanking the girl politely the man turned away. The girl's eyes followed him as he walked towards the door, her girlish heart sad. He was so downcast. She wished she could have helped him. Better yet, taken the place of the girl he looked for. Wouldn't that have bin grand? A new job and a new boyfriend all in one week. She sighed and returned to her station.

'What's up wi' you?' Another voice, lilting and full of cheek enquired as a third girl came from a door at the back of the café.

'Nowt really, just some chap I fancied.'

'Hey, who doesn't kid? Never mind, come wi' me to the Mecca some time an' you an' me'll click wi' a couple o' likely lads. You'll see.'

The girls laughed together, the lively one with the bright red hair and thrusting breasts, winking suggestively. A voice called, 'Lily yer tray's ready,' and the two girls ran up the stairs together.

The man who had left the café began to walk towards the corner and the tenth place he had been in that day.

It was the fifteenth day of June, 1923.

211

Chapter Twenty-One

Later, as they became accustomed to Jenny's state they would sit, a family gathering, at ease together, laughing, talking, drinking tea and eating Kate's homemade cakes, as though the figure in the rocking chair was a pretty clockwork doll who someone had for the moment, forgotten to wind up. The men would stand on the rug and warm their bums to the fire and a stranger might have thought them callous for their careless disregard of the everlastingly rocking girl at its side. They would lean across her to knock the dottle from their pipes against the grate, and sometimes push her chair further into the corner to make room for another, and on one occasion, young Jimmy, on finding himself alone with their Eddy, told him in pleased and explicit detail, exactly how far he had got with a judy he had taken out the previous night, before he remembered that their Jenny sat by his side.

But not that first week, or for many weeks to come.

Elly was there before the night had lightened to dawn. John Clancy brought her, driving his car almost beyond its limited capabilities along Rice Lane, County Road, Walton Road and into Saint Domingo Road to the cobbler's shop. He had been afraid to leave the tranced creature that Kate had become, but she must have help and the only name and mumbled address he could force from her punchdrunk brain was that of her sister. He was almost in a state of anaesthesia himself when he left Elly with her, Elly crying her grief and horror, but sensible with it, and already taking the stony figure of her sister in hand, putting her into her bed and shushing her as she would have one of her own.

Jenny lay where John Clancy had left her, looking as if she were already laid out, though death had not come for her. Since the agonised scream which had erupted from her throat; from the very core of her soul when she had been told her child was dead, she had uttered not a sound, nor did she hear any voice that spoke to her.

They all came that day, the brothers crowding into the kitchen which seemed to shrink in size as five restive men stood about.

212

They cleared their throats and spoke softly to Elly, telling her the shocking words their father had spoken when Pat had come to fetch them, and Elly cried again and cursed the man who could say such dreadful things about his own daughter.

'Shall we go an' . . . d'ya reckon she'd be berra off left . . . ?'

They were eager to help, filled with pity for the poor wretched creature who lay like one dead in her bed, but hesitant in their masculine horror of illness, birth or death, to see what it might have done to Jenny. Glad to come, glad to leave though, for the atmosphere of suffering which hung about the house was a weight on the spirit and almost too much for them to bear.

Only Bobby, Kate's twin and nearest in age to Jenny, slipped quietly up the stairs to look in on his younger sister, and what he saw upset him so greatly, he left the house without a word, walking the streets for hours, consumed by his anger for the fates which had wrested this last remnant of joy from Jenny's life.

Waggy. Pitiful in his distress, his great red face soggy with tears, his eyes bleared and veined. Grown old and slow in his movements as if the sorrow he felt had been caused by some family loss, as indeed it had, it seemed to him, for he had come to love Jenny as a father would love a daughter. He could not speak, even to Kate, but sat and noisily slurped the tea from the mug which Elly had put into his hand, the tears dripping to join the ash which fell onto his waistcoat from the cigarettes he smoked, one after the other. The flowers he had dropped onto the table seemed indecent somehow, too cheerful and bright to be brought into this house of sadness, but the buying of them had comforted him a little for he knew how Jenny loved them. He did not go to see her. Elly would not have it, and in his grief he was glad, for he knew what he saw would torment him beyond endurance.

'There's nowt yer can do for 'er, luv,' Elly said kindly, 'an' it'd only upset yer. She . . . she don't know anyone yer see. Give 'er a few days . . .'

Kate's remembrance of the next few days was mercifully hazed. She was reminded of the time when she and Charlie had gone to the pictures and due to some fault in the projection room, the film had run at less than its usual speed. The figures in the scene had wavered and faltered through a slow moving mist, taking an age to perform some simple task. Now the people around her appeared to move like the actors in the picture. They were unreal, speaking with hollow voices, moving in and out of her vision like swimmers in a restless sea of currents. Outwardly she was calm. As day followed day she was fixed in a feeling of apathy almost amounting

213

to indifference, or so it seemed, though the quiet doctor who came each day sensed the detached repression of feelings which hid the turbulence beneath, and he waited for it to break through the casing of shock which held her. She answered when spoken to and cared tenderly for the inert figure of her sister, washing her, changing the frequently soiled bed for Jenny had become incontinent, leading her time and time again to the bathroom. She murmured soft words of encouragement as she placed her in her clean bed, and patiently spooned food into the obediently opened mouth. She would allow no one, not even Elly to help her with Jenny, but when Jenny lay in her bed, Kate sat like one turned to stone in the chair by the fire, uncaring of her own appearance, or the needs of her home.

Kate was defeated at last. The hope which had returned to her months ago as Jenny had accepted her first loss and had improved with the joy of the coming child, was dashed to pieces on the stony ground of her heart and she was bitter and beaten.

Dr Clancy explained to her that the baby had strangled on her own lifeline, the unusual length of the umbilical cord becoming entangled around her neck just minutes before her actual birth. He had used a word which Kate had never heard before. *Catatonic.* He said that Jenny's mind had vanished behind the door which was firmly shut upon the event which it could not endure, and that until it healed, until she could cope with the reality of the loss of her child, it would stay hidden. He told her sadly that even had he been there it was unlikely that he could have saved the baby, but nevertheless, as he spoke, his own feeling of guilt and remorse enveloped him. Though he knew with the logic, and his own experience as a doctor, that he was blameless, his saddened heart would not listen to his mind, and his concern, not just for Jenny, but for Kate, grew with each day.

He had learned during the past three weeks, something of the hard life these two young girls had suffered. Words dropped as he had sipped a welcome cup of tea in their kitchen, many of them spoken with a smile, but the pathos was there, nevertheless. A mother dying painfully in 1921. A hard and tyrannical father. The younger sister Jenny had no husband, though no mystery could be attached to a girl who was to become the mother of an illegitimate child. It was a story as old as time, but she seemed to him to have risen above whatever tragedy had struck her and to have been calm and unafraid of what was to come. The lot of an unmarried mother was not to be envied, and most would have welcomed what had happened and the release from that particular complication. But

214

not this young woman. It was as though the structure of her hope for the future had been knocked from beneath her and she had fled into the blankness of her own mind for safety.

And now her sister, Kate, pregnant herself and in that particularly nervous state that can beset a woman in the first months, was as shellshocked and uncaring as a man just come from a battlefield.

It was the dying boy with consumption who had caused his delay. Called by the frantic parents he had gone to try and ease the child's passing, and the slight figure he had held in his arms had died at almost the same moment as Jenny's daughter. When he had left, the tears of the dead boy's mother were still wet on his cheeks.

Kate listened in stony silence, neither interested nor even caring, it seemed. Her eyes were shuttered and unreadable and looking at her, Dr Clancy knew that if he did not quickly break her from her grief-burdened prison, she would remain behind its bars and he would have more than one patient in this family. Thank God the husband would be home soon, though what the poor chap had in store for him was enough to bring the strongest man to his knees.

It was several days since that horrendous night and he and Kate were alone in the kitchen. Each time he had called, the small house had harboured some visitor and not once had he been able to see Kate on her own. The sister, the older one they called Elly, had gone on some errand to do with her own family, and for the first time Dr Clancy could take the opportunity to put into action the plan he had formulated in his mind. He was sure it was strictly unconventional by medical standards, but then John Clancy was not a conventional man, nor doctor. He read in each face the strength, or weakness of the man or woman he treated, and in a sense let himself be led by what he supposed was his own intuition. Hunches, he called them, that sixth sense which is the gift of a good doctor. And his sixth sense told him that what Kate Walker needed was something to crack the icy exterior which had encased her since the death of Jenny's child. Though he scarcely knew the woman who drooped on the other side of the table, something told him that beneath that ice was a strong and steadfast heart that, once it was pumping with life again, would be horrified at what it had become at this moment.

He watched her now, assessing how far he should go. Her despondency weighted her shoulders and bowed her head. Should his device be too savage it could drive her further into her refuge of silence; too gentle and it would pass over her rumpled head without stirring a hair upon it.

215

His strong young face was resolute as he looked at her. Her hands clasped a mug of tea which she lifted rhythmically to her lips, taking two sips before returning it to the table before her. Her eyes stared over his shoulder at the wall behind him. Strain had drawn fine etched lines from her nostrils to the corners of her mouth. There was no sound anywhere in the house, except for the cheerful noises of the road drifting up the hallway and through the opened kitchen door, left ajar in the unlikely event that Jenny might call down. The soft crackle of the coals in the fire sounded comfortable and homely and the cat added to the feeling of well-being as it wound itself around the table leg. It was still raining as it had done all week.

He sipped the strong tea, gathering his thoughts before he spoke.

'Your man will be home soon, Mrs Walker?' he said.

Kate tore her gaze from the wallpaper, startled, as if she had forgotten he was there and with a visible effort clutched her torn thoughts about her.

'Er . . . yes.'

'Charlie, did you say his name was?'

Again she blinked, dragging herself back into this world, back from the one of misty nightmares and clouded thoughts.

'Yes.'

'Has he been a seaman for long?' he enquired politely as if making conversation at the vicarage tea party. She set her mind in motion with an effort.

'Er . . . ten years.'

'A long time. Will he keep to the sea now that you are pregnant?'

Her eyes came slowly back to his again as if the question had begun to dig beneath the hard surface of despair which encased her.

'Pregnant?' she said, her voice cracking.

'You are to have a child, are you not, Kate?' he said agreeably, using her Christian name for the first time. She hesitated, her tired mind considering the question as if it had been spoken in a foreign language.

He continued, saving the last question to use as a detonator to explode the mass of hopelessness in which Kate was floundering. He must take a gamble, a gamble on his belief in Kate's love for her sister, her loyalty and her ferocious sense of the rightness of what she should do.

'When would you like me to arrange for Jenny to go?' he said.

Kate turned her eyes slowly, shifting her gaze from the wall

216

where it had resumed its contemplation when Dr Clancy had stopped speaking.

'Go?' she said, a pinprick of light piercing the darkness of her eyes. 'Go where?'

He drew a deep breath. 'To the hospital, the mental home, where she will be looked after. With a child coming you can hardly be expected to look after Jenny. It might be months before she is herself again. They have doctors there, and treatments which might help her. The staff are trained . . .'

He got no further. Like an animal rearing up to defend its young, she rose from her chair, her face purpling in its rage. Her eyes were blazing now and her hair sprang up and about her head in a violent surge as if her anger was spreading. The mug in her hand crashed to the table, even the thick flock of the tablecloth not deflecting the blow, and it smashed into twenty pieces. The cat fled in terror, disappearing beneath the dresser where it huddled against the skirting board, its fur bristling and lively as Kate's hair.

John Clancy was exultant. He let the storm rage round him, prepared almost for physical abuse so incensed was the woman. She had responded as he had hoped she would and the battle was in full swing.

'My sister's goin' to no looney bin!' she hissed through her clenched teeth, saliva spraying across the table with the vehemence of her words. Her fists clenched and unclenched as if she would like nothing better than to land one on his jaw. The congestion drained from her face as quickly as it had come leaving it white and demented.

'If you think I'm purrin 'er away with a lot of crackpots, you've got another think comin',' she screeched. 'Over my dead body, see, over my dead body!'

She made an aggressive move towards him as though to defend Jenny against a hostile army and he rose from his chair and backed away from her. She thrust her face towards his until only inches separated them. 'She's not goin', d'yer hear? She's stoppin' 'ere wi' me. I can see to 'er. There's nowt they can do for 'er that I can't, is there?'

A note of uncertainty crept into her voice, and she stood away, a look of dread on her waxen face.

'*Can* they, Doctor? There's nothing they can do, is there, that I can't do? I can look after her.'

The clarion call of battle was dying now and all that was left was a vulnerable young woman pleading for her sister, for the right to care for her as she knew she must. The dreaded word 'asylum', though it had not been spoken, crept between them, and Kate shuddered at the very thought. With trembling hands, she found the back of her chair, pulling it away from the table. She sat down heavily. Her face was becoming calm now, determined, alive, aggressive even in its new resolution, but calm.

'I'm sorry, Doctor, I went a bit mad there, p'raps it's me should be in t' . . .' she couldn't say the word, so abhorrent was it to her. She tried a smile, but it slipped somewhat and Dr Clancy felt his heart move at her gallantry. As he sat down opposite her, she put out both her hands and clasped his on the table between them.

'Let me look after 'er, Doctor. She'd be better 'ere wi' us. I've got friends, me brothers and sister, yer know that. They'll all 'elp me and p'raps it won't be for long. 'Appen she'll be better soon, with rest and the like. Get 'er mind back proper. Don't take 'er away. I'll see to 'er for as long as she needs me. We've bin together through thick and thin, me an' 'er.'

Her voice rose and cracked on the last word. Kate wept now, the fat wet drops sliding gently down her ravaged face. Pulling her hands from his, she lifted her apron and flung it up over her face and head and gave way at last. Great sobs shook her frame as the healing tears came to mend her. With the apron pressed to her eyes soaking up the moisture which streamed from them and dripped from her nose, she sat and rocked and was comforted.

John Clancy left the house knowing that the first hurdle was satisfactorily jumped.

Charlie was whistling cheerfully as he walked along Crescent Road. His thoughts were on his last homecoming and the glorious welcome he had received then, and his face split into a grin of anticipation. His arms flexed in eager expectation and his footsteps quickened, preceding him in a lively tattoo on the pavement. With a blithe heart surging in his chest, he turned the key in the door, dropping his seabag to the floor as he stepped into the hall. Nothing must impede his yearning arms as they lifted to enfold his Kate. His eyes shone and the skin about them crinkled, and his lips moved as if they could not wait to present themselves in that first delicious kiss.

'Kate,' he called. 'Ka.a.a.ty, I 'ope yer 'usband's out, cos it's yer fancy man come to see yer. Where are yer, girl?'

The kitchen door opened and his smile dissolved slowly, melting from his face like butter from a hot knife. Two eyes set in a pale face peered into the gloom. For a moment, Charlie was hard pressed to attach a name to the face which looked out on him, but with a thrill of dread he realised that the mournful countenance was that of the irrepressible Elly.

Even so he was not yet certain.

'Elly?' he questioned, his heart beginning to beat a rhythm of fear. The figure in the doorway put her hand to her mouth and the deepset eyes widened in surprise. It was as though Charlie was the last person in the world she expected to find in his own hallway, and for a second even as the fear began to chill him, a ripple of amusement touched him at the comically bewildered expression on Elly's face.

'Elly?' he repeated. He smiled tentatively, picking up his bag and carrying it in the direction of the kitchen door. What the 'ell was up wi' the woman – she looked as though she'd seen a bloody ghost. He was expected home today, wasn't he? Well then.

The face before him crumpled and tears welled into the corners of the staring eyes.

'Eeh, Charlie . . . eeh lad,' she began, then shook her head as though she could scarcely believe some dreadful event of which Charlie was ignorant. A great fearfulness began to grow in Charlie's bewildered mind, swamping the heady prospect of moments ago. Elly's head continued to shake from side to side as she opened the kitchen door an inch or two wider, but Charlie in his now frantic haste to get inside to Kate, swept it and Elly to one side. Kate. That was the only name his panicstricken mind could conjure. Kate and the baby. There must be summat up wi' Kate or why would their Elly be standin' like a great lummox, shakin' 'er daft 'ead and weepin' like a kid. He could scarcely breathe and the trembling in his legs made him lurch against the door frame. The shaking reached his head, filling his ears with a buzzing noise and he did not hear Elly as she spoke Jenny's name. His racing feet propelled him into the kitchen and he was only halted from continuing into the scullery by the figure of a woman who rose from the table as he entered. She was awkward and slow. She took a hesitant step towards him and he stopped, brought up short by a dreadful familiarity in the woman's stance. Her face was slack and grey, her eyes tired, swollen with the hours of weeping, and her hair hung in dead strands about her shoulders.

Charlie gaped in horror. It was Kate. It was his lovely Kate. He couldn't take his eyes from the travesty of the rosy face which had smiled a loving farewell to him only a few weeks since. Twenty years old and looking fifty.

'What's 'appened, for Christ's sake?' he croaked.

'Charlie, oh Charlie,' Kate faltered, her newfound resolve, so new and unmanageable, hard to cling to. For three days, with Dr Clancy's encouragement, she had thrown off the despair which had engulfed her, but now, with Charlie's love and sympathy and horror at what had been done to her, enveloping her like a familiar and warmly comforting blanket, she let it all go. All she really wanted was for someone to take away the heavy weight which had been placed upon her. She had carried it from that first day. The day when Jenny had told her, liltingly, of her love for Nils Jorgensen, and it was becoming too unwieldy. It had nearly taken her down a time or two. She wanted strong arms to hold her, and a firm and tender voice to tell her what she must do. A voice to tell her not to worry for all would be well. She longed to put down her burden and let another take it up. In her heart she knew that this would not happen. Her own self, the one which was buried beneath the fear and uncertainty of the present, knew she was Jenny's sheet anchor and that she was the one to whom Jenny would cling when she began to recover, and she must be ready, but just for that one exquisite moment, when Charlie stood there, strong and brown and manly, she allowed herself to give way for the last time.

'Charlie, oh Charlie,' she repeated, taking another step towards him. 'It's our Jenny. She's lost 'er baby and she's not right . . . in 'er 'ead. She's got *cata* . . . *cata* . . . something, the doctor said.' Her eyes swam with great bright blue tears and she sniffed, desolation pouring from her. ''E said 'er mind's hurt. Like when yer gorra broken leg or summat, only it's 'er mind that's broken. 'E says it'll mend one day just like a broken leg would, but I'm that . . .' Her voice trailed away, distorted by the sobs which shook her, and she pushed her hand in a familiar, frenzied sweep through her hair. Her poor sad face looked at him hopelessly, hopefully, as if begging him to take away the hurt but unsure whether he was able. Then, in the way of women, she suddenly became aware of her own appearance. Charlie's heart squeezed with love for her as she began to smooth her apron and pat her limp hair into place. She bit her lips and wiped her hands across her wet cheeks. He stood, mesmerised, his eyes aching with unshed tears for her, and as he froze there, not moving, it was as if his immobility was the last light whip across Kate's bloodied back.

Like a naughty child she cried, hanging her head in shame. Her tears dripped silently onto her breast.

With a hoarse cry of loving pity, Charlie was across the room and she was in his arms. He held her shaking body against his and kissed her wet face and lips, smoothing back her lank hair with tender hands. He whispered to her as he drew her down onto his knee in the armchair, and cradled her to him, and as he did so, her fear began to leave her. Charlie was home. She was safe and sheltered in his strong arms. He was a harbour for her tired, dispirited mind and body. Charlie was home.

Elly slipped away upstairs.

That night in their bed he loved her. It was the last restorative Kate needed to lift her completely from the blackness into which she had slipped. From that moment she began to recover the spirit which had been knocked from her by Jenny's senseless state. Charlie was here and he loved her. Later they drowsed together, and as she floated in that pleasurable state which comes between the act of love and the gentle sleep which follows, she heard him say, his voice low but strong, 'I promise you this, our Kate. As I love you, and I do, you know that wherever you and I go, until she's able to look after herself, Jenny goes too. We'll see to 'er you an' me. Don't fret lass. You an' me, we'll see to 'er.'

Kate's eyes filled with tears but no longer anguished and she raised herself on her elbow. In the hazy dark she looked at his face on the white pillow. She kissed him reverently, murmuring his name against his lips. Putting her head on his shoulder and bringing his arms about her, they lay quietly, the pledge drawing their souls and the goodness of them together. Their hearts carried their compassion to the broken girl who lay in the next room and Kate felt the peace move gently in the house and hope rested beside it.

Chapter Twenty-Two

Jenny knew no one. Her own brothers who had tossed her in the air when she was a baby, who had guarded their little dear, their golden-eyed, tumble-legged, little pet, for she was still an infant when they were almost grown, were strangers to her, as were Kate and Elly.

Kate and Elly never left her alone. Whenever Kate went out, whether it was with Charlie when he was home, or just to town to do a bit of shopping, Elly would come and sit with Jenny, and when Charlie was at sea, Kate had taken to bringing the silent girl into their bed, though she didn't tell Charlie. It was as though she was afraid to take her eyes from her. Someone must watch her for fear she would slip away from them completely, Kate thought, and even when Charlie came whistling into the house and took her to the deep warm bed, when he slept she would slip along the landing and bend in the dark across the sleeping form of her sister. When she had satisfied herself that the breathing which whispered in the tiny bedroom was deep and natural, she would creep back to the warmth and security of Charlie's back and fall into the light sleep which nowadays was hers.

Kate was in her seventh month of pregnancy and the tiredness weighed heavily upon her. Elly came as often as she could, sometimes for a couple of days, banging the cobbler's shop door in her protesting Pat's face. He was fed up with it, he told her, and could see no reason why their Jenny couldn't go in the asylum like the other 'looneys', but he only said it once. Elly hit him with the frying pan that time, and his breakfast still in it.

Without her, Kate would have gone under. Elly, with her cheerful challenging, careless outlook on life was the tonic Kate needed when the pleasing, pretty, blank face of the doll who sat opposite her from morning till night, began to get her down. Elly would 'cock a snook' at anything, and though she had cried when Kate had shown her the pale and lovely form of her sister's dead child, she did not dwell upon it, nor on Jenny's illness. Elly was at odds with the world, with life, as well as with her husband.

Anything she could find to laugh at, or fight with, in the dreary round of her days, she welcomed. Not that she welcomed her sister's despair, either of them, but the challenge of bringing a 'right good laugh', or a flare of temper to at least one of them, proved that life was still there, and as she was fond of saying, 'If yer didn't laugh yer'd only bloody cry.'

In the beginning, when she did not turn her head as they entered the room, nor answer when they greeted her, Jenny had frightened her visitors. The men stood around looking in compassionate bewilderment at the silent, unknowing girl in the chair. The creak of the rocker, like a metronome; the strict tempo-ed tick of the clock, the whisper of the fire, the hushed silence, alarmed them. They were used to noise and laughter, arguments and shouts – in the pub, at work, in their own homes. Here they were out of their depths.

But Elly stopped all that and at heart, though she had for a while felt like a mourner laughing at a funeral, Kate was glad. At least they could be normal, or as normal as was allowed with Jenny sitting like a spectre at the feast. After a few weeks even that thought ceased to enter her mind. As Charlie said in his sensible way, 'life must go on chuck', and it did. A routine was established and life went on.

During the shortening autumn days Jenny and Kate wandered daily across the fields towards the woods at the back of the house. Jenny had begun to put on weight. Too much, said Dr Clancy, and she must have exercise. Kate held her hand, like a mother taking a child for a 'tata' in the park, leading her through the backyard gate and into the fields. The sunshine tinted Jenny's pale skin with a wash of gold. Her figure became slim and supple again, though her cheeks were rounded, pink and smooth. Her still, perfect loveliness took the breath away. Kate sometimes packed a picnic, and often with Elly, they would wander the fields and woods and sit in the mild sunshine, shoulder deep in the grass. Kate and Elly gathered lengths of wood, broken from the branches of the old trees, to be thrown to the back of the crackling fire of an evening. There were blackberries growing in profusion. Big, black, lustrous, their heady scent brought out by the warmth of the sun. The grass was as springy as a mattress and the chestnut trees, which in the spring had made an umbrella of pink blossom, spread a roof of green above their heads. The sun filtered through the leaves, playing on the quiet face of the young girl, and her sisters, used to her silence, scarcely glanced in her direction. As they gossiped idly, drugged by the peace, they did not see the tiny light pierce

223

Jenny's eye, nor notice the movement of her hand. Her fingers trembled in her lap as her gaze rested dispassionately on the golden yellow of a buttercup, as though they would touch it if they knew how.

The party was Charlie's idea.

'It's yer birthday, sweetheart,' he said fondly, 'and we never 'ad an' 'ousewarmin' did we? Yer don't get much fun, what with your Jenny an' me away all the time. What d'yer say, shall we 'ave a do?'

He looked at her eagerly. How could she say 'no', though a 'do' was the last thing she wanted. With a belly out to here and their Jenny as she was, it was as much as she could do to get through the day, so tired did she become. But Charlie was so patient, so good and understanding. Not many chaps'd put up with what he did, so she agreed.

October now, and the evenings drawing in. On this special night they lit a fire in the front room for the first time, and the smoke curled up the chimney, sweet and straight into the dark blue autumn night, drifting in a pearly haze towards the woods. The branches of the bare trees were silhouetted against the night sky, like bony arms upstretched to the pale stars. The house blazed with lights from every window, falling across the empty yard and garden. But inside the warmth was welcoming and the laughter and song merry.

In an overwhelming tidal wave of love for his bonny wife, and without a thought as to who would play it, for Kate and Jenny could scarcely pick out a tune despite the lessons they had had as children, Charlie had bought Kate a secondhand upright piano for her birthday. It was in perfect condition, obviously lovingly cared for by its previous owner, polished until it shone, and in perfect tune. It stood in splendour in the front room, locked, for Kate had allowed no one to touch its keys since Charlie and Bobby had carried it there a week ago. A plush runner protected its top, and upon that stood the two sepia-tinted, framed wedding photographs of herself and Charlie. Kate doted on it and dusted the glowing rosewood with a soft cloth which she kept especially for the purpose. She would have bolted up the door of the room if she had been allowed, so afraid was she that some greasy finger might be laid upon it, or even, God forbid, a wet-bottomed glass. She fought to have a sheet thrown over its shining beauty at least, on the night of the party, but Charlie put his foot down.

'Give over our Kate. I'm not 'avin' a bloody sheet on it like some ghost sittin' in t'corner. I'm proud of it, and so should you be. I want to show it off, any road, there might be someone comin' who 'as a way wi' t'ivories.'

Tommy Johnson. He did have a 'way with the ivories' and the party was assured of success from the moment he sat down at the piano, flexed his fingers and said, 'Right, what'll it be?'

With a show of reluctance Kate had produced the key and unlocked the lid. Charlie had given in and let her put a folded flanelette sheet along its top to protect it from careless hands and with that she had to be content. She hovered anxiously for a while, entreating the guests who stood about Tommy's shoulder to 'go careful with yer glasses lads', but as the effect of several ports, a chorus of *Nelly Dean* and the conviviality of the atmosphere took over, she mellowed and grew careless, singing as lustily as the rest.

John Clancy was there, his arm about a young lass, a Scot like himself, and bonny as the plaid she wore across her shoulder. Lily, luscious as a ripe melon, and as round. Her pink satin dress was so tight, the seams pulled beneath her arms and the fabric stretched across her ample breasts, threatening to spill them into her plate of trifle and cream. Her hair, red as fire, lit the room like a beacon and her eyes sparkled for every man present. Bobby and Jimmy, a 'Judy' apiece (a new one every week, Kate said) did the Black Bottom, the Charleston and disappeared, it seemed with blatant regularity for a breath of 'fresh air' into the backyard, accompanied by the young ladies of their choice.

They all came, old friends and new, and in their midst sat the gentle figure of Jenny. She rocked in her chair, the violet-blue dress she had worn for Nils draped charmingly about her slender form. Her hair had been washed and brushed and hung about her face in a shining curtain. The party flowed around her, the voices and music washing like the tide upon an empty beach.

Waggy, more himself now and used, as were they all, to Jenny's silence, waiting for the day when she would speak again, held her hand as he sat beside her, smoothing the heel of her thumb with loving fingers. He talked to her, telling her about the café and the doings in the office, hoping in his concern, that the words might penetrate the barrier of her wounded mind.

Tommy's hands flashed across the keys, moving unhesitatingly from one tune to the next. He was an instinctive pianist, never having had a lesson in his life, and could read not a note of music, but he made the piano come alive. *Dreamy Melody*, *Who's Baby are You?*, *It ain't Gonna Rain No more, No more*, *Kitten on the Keys* and *My Honey's Lovin' Arms*.

Waggy felt the flaccid hand he held, tense. The fingers parted and then clenched and for a moment Jenny's hand gripped his. He turned, his eyes bright with hope, to look into hers.

'What is it, chuck? What's up? Jenny luv, it's Waggy, what . . .' but her hand had relaxed and her eyes stared placidly, brown and deep, like burnt syrup, into the heart of the fire.

Waggy slumped back in his seat and sighed. It were nowt. Just a reflex. Looking at Jenny, he wondered how long this was to go on. He could hardly remember the sweet laughing girl he had first seen nearly two years ago. Her great brown eyes had stared into his, solemn, childlike, and then something he had said had made her laugh. He remembered his own surprise at the brilliance of it, the light which had shone there, and now look at her.

'Imagine she is resting,' Dr Clancy had said, 'after a serious illness. As the body needs peace and quiet when it has been afflicted, so does the mind, and that is what nature is doing with Jenny. Protecting her, resting her, giving her time to heal.'

Waggy turned away sighing, watching the seething mass of people who moved from the kitchen where he sat to the front room and back again. His eyes rested appreciatively on Lily's gyrating bottom as she shimmied with Charlie, and he laughed. Jenny's hand still nestled in his. The lovely melody drifted hauntingly across the smokeladen room, and as the last rippling notes died away, a tear slipped down her cheek. Tiny, translucent, as though it had a life of its own apart from the girl from whose eye it had welled, it moved slowly across her cheek to drop silently on to the wool of her dress.

The room was warm and in a moment the silvery track it left was dried. When Waggy turned back to her, she was as she had been minutes ago.

Chapter Twenty-Three

Kate's baby was due to arrive on Christmas Day.

Charlie's last trip home before the birth of the child fell in the middle of November, so Kate's mind was at rest knowing that all being well, he would be home for Christmas and the baby's birth. To ensure that Kate would not be alone in the event of the child arriving before Charlie, Elly was to come in each morning just for half an hour. Charlie had slipped a few bob into her hand for her tram fare on his last trip. On his way home, a circuitous route, but nevertheless willingly taken for it also gave him a chance to see Jenny, Waggy stopped by each evening, so as Kate put it, 'Comin' or goin', I've gorrit licked.'

When Charlie came home in November the sky was hung with clouds looking like empty wet sacks. Each line was edged with silver and the rain poured inflexibly from the dull grey sky. It was so low it seemed to touch the treetops of the distant wood. The sound of the rain was like a waterfall as it dripped from gutter to windowsill to ground. The windows were patterned as drops of moisture met and parted and met again in their journey down the glass.

In sharp contrast the kitchen was rosy with the flush of warm, welcoming firelight, the crimson of the tablecloth and the soft hued gleam of the dresser on which stood a row of copper pans. It seemed to wrap around the man and woman like a cloak, protective and comforting; the safe harbour about which a traveller dreams as he sails a foreign sea. Charlie drew a deep sigh of satisfaction.

Jenny had been bundled off to bed, and though he and Kate could no longer, at least for the moment, enjoy what he called his 'conjugals' they had spent a satisfactory hour in the armchair.

'Come 'ere girl, I'm starvin' for you,' he said, barely stopping to drop his seabag to the floor. Drawing Kate onto his knees they kissed and cuddled, Charlie's hand reaching into her dress to uncover her bounteous breasts. They talked with delightful pauses for Charlie's lips to taste her sweet nipples, recounting the every-

227

day events which had gone since they had parted. Flushed with longing, both of them, impatient, and on Charlie's part, careful of Kate's enormous fecund body, they snuggled together lovingly. He nuzzled his unshaven chin into the soft skin where her chin and neck were joined mumbling tender words of love.

'Mmm Mmm lovely,' he murmured thickly, 'soft as a little mouse . . . soft.' His hand cupped her breast, thumb and forefinger rolling the erect nipple. He groaned as his erection grew, for that part of his body cared nothing for Kate's pregnancy.

'Ooh, Kate, *Kate.*' His face pressed between her white breasts and she held him fiercely with eager hands. 'I love you, Charlie,' she whispered. They were aware of no one but each other.

A sound like the click of a door opening made them lift their heads, alarmed, for they had thought themselves alone. Who . . . ? Charlie half-turned in the chair his eyes going towards the kitchen door. Kate was awkward in his arms, and she tried to stand, clutching her dress to her exposed breasts which tumbled ripely against Charlie's cheek. She almost fell in her haste to rise, her bulk holding her in his lap.

It was Jenny. She stood in the doorway, her white nightdress, which was wet with a yellowing stain, clinging soddenly about her legs.

Kate slumped back against Charlie and groaned.

'Oh Lord, I thought she'd be asleep by now. An' look at 'er, she's wet 'erself again. I suppose it's my fault. I forgot to take 'er to t'lavvy.' She sighed deeply. 'Give us a push love, will yer, and I'll gerrer cleaned up and back to 'er bed. Sorry chuck, on yer first night an' all, but I won't be long.'

Struggling like a felled ox; with a mighty shove from Charlie, Kate finally got to her feet.

Charlie sat quite still, but the tension within him revved like the engine of a racing car. His sexual longings had been fully aroused by Kate's sweet flesh and the necessity to damp them down made him edgy, but that was only a small part of what caused Charlie Walker to change from his usual unruffled and easygoing self into a man run berserk.

Though he said nothing to his wife, the sight of her each time he came home fussing round Jenny like a woman with a 'mardy' child, had gradually strained his patience to its limits. He had watched her cajole her sister to open her mouth so that she might pop another spoonful of boiled egg inside it; he had seen her take the girl each hour to the bathroom, up the stairs and down, up the stairs and down, dress her, undress her, bath her, and kneel at her feet to take the very shoes from her feet. He had stood by whilst Kate pushed and pulled and entreated, her own ever-increasing size making her puff and pant at each strenuous encounter.

'Come on, lovey,' Kate was saying patiently. 'Let's get yer cleaned up an' back to yer bed.' She had Jenny by the arm, trying to turn her in the direction of the hall, but the girl was like a block of stone, immovable, her dead eyes seemingly fixed on the cuckoo clock, which, five minutes since, had jumped cheerfully from its nest, sounding eight o'clock.

Kate took Jenny's other arm, pulling her awkwardly, but Jenny would not be budged. 'Come on chuck,' Kate appealed tiredly.

Charlie felt the frustrated anger rising from within him, filling the hollows of his body as though it was being poured into him from a jug. When he was full it would overflow. His mouth thinned until his lips were barely discernable and his jaw clenched with the effort of keeping himself under control. He stood up abruptly, intending only to help Kate, but the sight of her weary face, the sound of her careful voice, as if she too were straining for control, broke his.

'Oh for God's sake, give over,' he thundered. 'I'll see to 'er. It's too much for you in your condition. She's like a bloody puppet standin' there waitin' for someone to pull t'strings. Stop it Kate. Leave off.'

Pushing Kate to one side, he roughly pulled Jenny from the doorway and started to drag her towards the stairs. She followed like a stuffed doll towed by a careless child, her feet tripping over one another in her haste to keep up with him.

Kate screamed his name.

As the sound bounced from one wall to the other, it stopped Charlie where he stood. The momentum with which he had pulled Jenny stopped abruptly and she crashed into him, standing at his shoulder as though she searched his ear for some small lost item. Charlie was rigid at the bottom of the staircase. With the action of a man at the end of his tether he banged his forehead savagely against the newel post at its foot. The hollow sound filled the hall and the silence that followed was as thick and heavy as a water-soaked blanket. Kate stood in the kitchen doorway, clinging to its frame with both hands. Her face was pillarbox red, violent in her fury and voice trembling so, she could barely make herself understood.

'You touch 'er like that again, Charlie Walker, an' I'll kill yer. I will. Leave 'er. Leave 'er alone. Take yer hands off 'er. Go on.'

Charlie let go of Jenny's arm. Leaving her standing at the bottom of the staircase he began to walk like an old man towards his wife. His face was grey but for a bright scarlet trickle of blood which ran from the raw skin above his eyebrow where he had gashed it on the wood. He shook all over, like a tree in a violent storm. Pushing Kate into the kitchen, speaking quietly he said, 'This can't go on. We can't take much more, Kate, it's too much for yer with the baby coming, and I can't bear to see yer . . .' His face softened and he put out a conciliatory hand, but Kate stepped back. Charlie's face was anguished now. He knew he had gone too far.

'Can't yer see, lovey, what it's doin' to yer. Go an' look in the mirror if yer don't believe me. Please Kate, give it up, lerrer go.'

Charlie had loved Kate since she was fifteen years old. They had been together as man and wife for almost a year, but still he did not know her completely. The fierce, loving loyalty which she felt towards Jenny had been ingrained in her from that first day when her mother had put the pretty baby into her three year old care. She was a duty, a responsibility which had been entrusted to her. The sense of what she believed to be right would make her stick through fire and water, to those who depended upon her, and her Mam had given her Jenny all those years ago, and told her to see to her. It was as simple as that. Charlie did not intentionally mean to hurt her, nor would he allow a hair of her head to be harmed, but where emotion is concerned, judgment often goes out of the window, and Charlie threw his out with both hands.

'She'll 'ave to go now, love. With this baby nearly 'ere, it's all yer can do to keep yerself goin', never mind 'er. When the baby's born what then? She's like a child 'erself, isn't she, but not small and easily managed like a kid. Yer can't pick 'er up an' carry 'er up to bed, if she's naughty, can yer now? What d'yer say we 'ave a word wi' Doc Clancy, eh? 'E'll purrus right, find the proper place an' then . . .'

He stopped and a horrid dread trickled down his back like icy water. His anger and frustration had flowed away and the commonsense of what he was saying filled the empty places the feelings had left behind. But the expression on Kate's face left him in no doubt of what he had just done. No matter that his words made sense. To Kate they were obscene.

Charlie's heart pounded and he took a step back.

The colour in Kate's face had drained away. The lovely glow and sparkle at his homecoming, the vermilion of rage which had replaced it, had faded and died leaving it the hue of a field mushroom, beige, muddy and speckled. She began to weep. Her belly held protectively with clasped hands, she paced about the

230

room, as though her sorrows would not let her be still. As she paced, she shook and the words began to tremble and become clear, louder and louder.

'It's only six months ago,' she chanted, as though she spoke to some unseen being. 'Just six short months ago and already 'e's forgotten.' She shrugged her shoulders, the perfidy of man beyond belief. 'The words 'e spoke to me then 'ave bin chucked on t'back of fire. 'E might as well 'ave spoken 'em to that clock on t'wall for all the meanin' there was in 'em.' She clasped her arms about herself.

'Them words 'e spoke . . .' Kate turned on Charlie like a tiger and he recoiled, backing up against the fireguard. 'Them words you spoke, Charlie Walker, on our love, on our love, you said.' She was beside herself with rage. 'D' yer remember? 'Course yer don't, 'cos it doesn't suit any more, does it Charlie? Well I remember, oh yes I remember. They went like this, Charlie.'

She advanced another step towards him and so great was her contemptuous anger, Charlie put up a placatory hand, as though to defend himself.

'Wherever we went Jenny was to go too. That was what you said. "Wherever we go Jenny goes too until she can look after herself." Now you want to be shut of 'er. That girl, that poor kid out there . . .' she pointed to Jenny who stood like an actor in a piece, waiting for her cue '. . . she's bin through . . . all she's been through . . .' Kate was becoming incoherent, as her distress increased '. . . after all she's 'ad to purrup with, you want to shut 'er up in a . . . oh Charlie, 'ow could yer, 'ow could yer.'

Her face was a mask of tears, and sobs shook her so violently Charlie began to fear for the child. He put out his hand, like someone attempting to pat a rearing maddened horse, but she slapped it aside, turning away to lean on the table. For a moment there was no sound but the harsh, snuffling sounds made by a woman as she attempts to control her tears. Then, turning, she looked him directly in the eyes and said, 'Let me tell you this Charlie. If you send our Jenny away, it'll be over between you an' me.'

Charlie gasped and took a step towards her.

'Aah chuck, don't . . . don't . . .'

She interrupted him.

'If she goes, I go an' I'll tell yer why, Charlie. Even though I love yer more . . . more than . . . her voice shivered and nearly broke and Charlie felt his heart wrench – 'she needs me, Charlie an' you don't. It's as simple as that. An' as long as she needs me I'll be with 'er, even if it's fer a lifetime.'

She turned, cumbersome as a whale out of water, and as she made her way to the door, Charlie sprang across the room barring her way. His face was the colour of cement and as stiff.

'Kate, listen to me please.' He took her arm but she shook off his hand and reached for the door handle.

'Please Kate, oh my lovely, I didn't mean . . . It's just with the child comin' an' seein' you pullin' 'er about from pillar to post . . . I was only thinkin' of you, please Kate.'

She turned a little, caught by the entreaty in his voice and he seized his opportunity eagerly. He put his hands on her shoulders and gazed into her cold eyes.

'I meant what I said six months ago, believe me, but surely to God this makes a difference. I never thought it'd be so long. It were . . . well Jenny wasn't ill . . . but this . . . this . . . and a child comin' . . . our child. How will it be with a child in the 'ouse and 'er rockin' like a zombie . . .'

As he said the last word he realised he had taken his last step to damnation. With a cry of rage she tore herself from his grasp and was out of the room and up the hall as though she were sixteen years old again and weighed eight stone instead of twelve. She grasped Jenny's arm and began to urge her in the direction of the stairs. Jenny went unresisting. After a moment a door banged and then there was silence.

Charlie stood for several minutes, shifting his weight from foot to foot. His gaze, as he turned it upwards, gave the appearance of trying to pierce the wood and plaster which hid Kate from him, and his breath came in gasps.

Then he turned slowly and made his way back to the fire. He sat down heavily in the rocking chair and in a manner strangely reminiscent of Jenny, he stared into its blazing heart and began to rock back and forth.

He sat for half an hour until he heard her footsteps on the stair. She came into the room and her face was grotesque, swamped and wet with the tears she had shed. He stood up and without a word she moved into his arms. They did not speak, but rocked each other silently, seeking and giving forgiveness with their arms and bodies.

Kate's heart eased. Charlie. Oh Charlie. 'E's not to blame for what 'e said. 'E'd been so patient. For twelve months now, 'e never said 'no' to anything. 'E'd given Jenny a home where many a chap would've stuck 'er in an asylum. 'E put up wi' 'er about the 'ouse whenever 'e was 'ome. 'E'd bin the best, the very best. But 'e must see she couldn't let the kid go. Not now. She'd manage, she wouldn't be beaten, she wouldn't. It would be as though she 'ad two children, but if she could just get through the next few weeks she'd be all right.

Kate strained Charlie to her, pressing him to the mound of her stomach, her heart aching with love for him. The tears had subsided and she raised her face to his.

'Charlie love, I'm sorry. I know she gets on yer nerves, she does on mine an' all. Eeh sometimes I could knock 'er block off, but we'll be all right, honest. I'm tired an' she's bin . . . a bit funny lately . . . stubborn somehow . . . as if she were settin' out to resist me. I don't know why . . . she normally goes up when I tell 'er . . . I don't 'ave to pull 'er. . .'

Charlie stared over her head. His face was set, the skin above his eyebrow still seeping blood. His eyes, usually so merry and twinkling with good humour, were flinty. He sometimes felt he hated the girl who was tied so firmly about his neck like an albatross. Would she never leave him and Kate alone to get on with their lives? Was she always to be lurking in the shadows, like a Peeping Tom?

Kate looked anxiously up at him, and with a visible effort he smiled.

'I'm sorry too lass, but sometimes it's more than I can bear seeing yer 'eave her about, especially now. Yer shouldn't be doin' it. You could hurt yerself, or the child, but I suppose there's nowt to be done about it. I know how yer feel about 'er.' He sighed deeply. 'Neither of us is ourselves at the moment, what with the baby comin' and me off all the time. I 'ate leaving yer on yer own queen, it worries me sick.'

He rested his cheek on her springy hair and clutched her to him, feeling the child kicking strongly between them.

'What yer said about me not needin' yer, it's not true. I couldn't manage wi'out yer. I'd go outta me mind if 'owt 'appened to you, our Kate,' he whispered, and his voice broke on her name.

The first tear in the fabric of their marriage was carefully mended with loving words, and Kate and Charlie were zealous during the next few days in their efforts not to put too much strain on the weak spot.

In the room upstairs, the quiet figure of the girl who sat on the bed where she had been placed, turned her head as the sound of the cuckoo clock rose from the room below. A small frown appeared on her smooth empty face as if she strained to hear some far-off unidentifiable words, then it was still.

Chapter Twenty-Four

The December day was like a crystal, sharp and clear, the wintry sun spilling facets of sparkling light, reflecting them from every surface it touched. During the night a hoar frost had lain a fine skin over the land and painted every roof in luminescent spun sugar. The dazzle hurt the eyes, but the beauty caught the throat. The sky was a pale silver blue, and it was cold.

Kate was restless.

She moved about the kitchen, heaving her enormous bulk from one unnecessary task to the next, conscious only that she must be doing something. Her back ached slightly and her ankles were swollen, but some impulse drove her to rearrange the copper pans upon the dresser shelf, to change the position of the tea caddy which had stood for twelve months in the same spot upon the mantelpiece, and to polish energetically the three silver spoons which she had bought at St John's market for her bottom drawer. She took a duster and went to wipe an imaginary film of dust from the rocking chair, but with Jenny in it, rocking placidly in her own blank world it was difficult, and with a 'tcch' of annoyance Kate gave up.

'I wish yer'd give over fer a minute, our Jenny,' she complained irritably. 'I only want to dust it, but yer will keep on and on. Can yer not stop while I . . . oh never mind.'

Again she bent clumsily, this time lifting the rag rug which lay before the fire, carelessly throwing Jenny's feet to one side. Jenny was still for a moment then she moved them back, placing them neatly side by side, her eyes focused on the brightly glowing coal. Kate appeared not to notice.

'This damn mat. It does nowt but gather dust. I don't know why I give it 'ouse room.' She dragged the offending article across the kitchen, and opening the back door, shook it vigorously, scattering a fine dust and several clots of cat's fur into the snapping cold air.

'Just look at that lot. I'm getting shut o' that damn moggy an' all, she just makes work.'

She flung the rug on to the floor before the fireplace, heedlessly

234

covering Jenny's feet. Jenny moved them again and as Kate smoothed the mat into place, put them once more into a tidy position on the brightly coloured fabric. Again the action went unnoticed.

Kate sighed and moved to stand by the window, staring out into the brilliance which lay before her. Her body seemed to be full of little nerves which would not allow her to remain still. Even Elly, who had just left, had remarked upon her nervous energy.

'It's nearly yer time, our kid.' Her gaze had assessed Kate with the expertise of one who had given birth many times. 'I've 'ad it meself, yer feel as though yer wanna be on't go all day long, an that's not like me,' Elly laughed impishly, 'as yer well know.' Elly hung over the fire with her hands cupped about a strong mug of tea.

She enjoyed the visits she paid to Kate's. She had her tram fare, though sometimes, if the weather was fine, she walked it, and treated herself to five 'Craven A', and the half hour often stretched to an hour or even two. With her knees up the chimney, innumerable cups of tea, and now and again a 'borrow' of a couple of bob off their Kate, who knew nothing of Elly's arrangements with Charlie, Elly was 'made up'. And Kate was always so pathetically pleased to see her. Her gratitude would overflow and encompass her older sister, who had never had such a fuss made of her since her Mam died. Kate would not admit, even to Elly, but she got to screaming pitch sometimes, with only their Jenny to talk to, and her never saying a word back. It was enough to drive yer mad, in fact sometimes she could cheerfully have strangled her. When she stood and would not be moved, as often happened these days, Kate had the violent urge to land her a fourpenny one, yelling, 'For God's sake, pull yerself together and snap out of it.' It was hard not to imagine that if Jenny would only make a bit of effort she could throw off this trance she was in, and be herself again.

Moving back to the armchair Kate fell heavily into it, her feet kicking into the air with the force of her weight. Taking some needles and a ball of bright yellow wool from behind the cushion – Kate's taste in colours, even for her child, had not altered – she began laboriously to knit. Her tongue protruded from between her lips and she whispered to herself as her fingers moved.

'Knit one, purl one, knit one, purl one.'

For ten minutes she worked, her fingers twisting and turning the wool, her face creased in a scowl of concentration. Then in a spasm of nervous frustration she flung the knitting from her.

'It's no good, our kid, I can't settle to it.'

235

Her glance fell about the shining kitchen as though looking for some further activity with which to occupy herself, then wandered to the window. A shaft of pale sunshine had crept beyond the sill and fell like silvered butter across the draining board. Kate could see a square of blue sky, cut in two by her washing line which stretched from the house to the yard wall. Swinging blithely upon it was a robin, its bright red chest feathers ruffled as it dipped up and down. The loveliness of the day suddenly called to the restless woman.

'Let's go for a walk, shall we,' she said eagerly to the silent girl opposite. 'Not far, just across t'field. Just ten minutes, shall we?' she begged, as though Jenny's permission must be sought before they could go. 'Come on. Get yer 'at on, our kid, we're goin' fer a tata.'

Excited now, at the prospect of an outing, even a short walk, Kate gripped the arms of the chair and, red in the face, strained to lift herself from its depths. It was a question of inclining her bottom forward until she had enough leverage in her arms to push herself upwards. At last she was on her feet. Still gaily chiding her sister to 'get yer skates on' she waddled to the bottom of the stairs and almost on her hands and knees, laboured her way to the top, panting slightly with the effort of lifting her own bulk upwards. Her feet could be heard moving about as she gathered stout shoes, hats, coats and scarves ready for their outing.

In five minutes she was back.

'I've been to t'lavvy,' she said confidentially to Jenny. 'I don't know I seem to be forever wantin' to wee. It must be this baby.'

The incongruity of her unacknowledged monologue did not occur to Kate. It was as though, in the way of those who live alone she spoke to a dog or a cat, expecting no answer. The sound of her own voice broke the silence and gave her comfort.

'Come on chuck, up yer get.' She took Jenny's hand and with no hesitation the girl rose from her chair, almost as though Kate's words had some meaning for her. She stood whilst Kate put her into her coat, and pulled her bright red tam o'shanter about her ears. But when Kate floundered to her knees, tapping Jenny's left foot with her hand and said, 'This one first, flower, that's a good girl,' Jenny's head moved fractionally and her eyes looked down at the bent head of her sister. A tiny light glowed for a fraction of a second, and a look of surprise passed across her face.

'T'other one now, that's right.'

Jenny hesitated, then the light went out and obediently she lifted her right foot.

The cold was exhilarating. Kate felt it pinch her cheeks, flying flags of crimson there, and her eyes watered as the sun glittered on the whiteness all about them. The fence was black, the top brushed with frost, and the back lane was rutted in brown and silver and white, each hollow filled with tiny pools of frozen water. It crunched deliciously beneath Kate's heavy shoes. She felt the weight of restless oppression lift from her as she took Jenny's hand and began to walk in the direction of the gate. Their breath hung about their bright heads as they walked rising into the pale washed blue of the sky. Jenny's step was light, springing, and it seemed she would go on ahead of her sister, but Kate held her back as one would hold a child, clinging to her hand, like a liner tied to a skimming yacht.

The wood was a flow of black lace on the other side of the field, the sunlight blurring and washing through the branches of the trees. It gave the appearance of being appliquéd against the sky, like delicate embroidery, black on silver white.

'Eeh, this is grand, grand,' breathed Kate. The blood coursed through her veins and her whole body was warm and wonderfully alive beneath the layers of clothing she wore. The baby stirred and for a moment Kate was surprised, realising that she had felt scarcely a movement for several days. She turned and looked back and the sunlight caught the window of Jenny's bedroom reflecting a beam of welcoming light. Kate's heart turned with gladness. It was her home and she was safe. Soon, perhaps tomorrow, Charlie would be here, and when he came, she would have her baby.

Kate and Jenny reached the wood. The ball of the sun just touched the fingers of the top branches of the trees, outlining them with scarlet and gold and Kate stopped, overcome for a moment with the stark beauty. Jenny's hand slipped from hers and she moved on slowly, walking with hesitant steps between the trunks of the huge oak trees. She stepped delicately across spreading roots, placing her feet with the grace of a fawn.

'Just a minute chuck, wait for me.' Kate followed in the path of her sister, a faint twinge of alarm settling itself in the pit of her stomach.

'Don't go so fast, our kid,' she said fretfully, for Jenny had begun to hurry. Her head was cocked to one side as though she listened to something which was beyond the hearing of others, and her feet skipped, light as air, across the frozen vegetation beneath the trees.

'Jenny, Jenny, come back. I can't keep up wi' yer.' Kate's alarm was turning into fear. 'Where are yer goin', come back, there's a good girl.'

But Jenny took no notice. Her red hat bobbed, like the signal light at the rear of a train, moving further and further away into the depths of the wood. Although there was no foliage on the trees, the trunks stood close together here, and as the weak afternoon sun sank in its winter's path towards the earth, it was becoming dark and forbidding.

'Jenny, Jenny, come back at once, yer a naughty girl. Come 'ere when I say.' Kate's voice trembled as the apprehension grew inside her. What was up wi' 'er? She'd never acted like this before. Every time they came up 'ere, an' they'd been a lot in the autumn, she stood or sat, when told, and never moved an inch without some-one's hand 'olding 'ers. She could barely see 'er now, she'd gone so far. The little madam, she'd give 'er what for when she gorrer back.

No presentiment of what was to come shaded Kate's mind. She was afraid, not for herself, but for Jenny. She knew that beyond the wood lay the railway line to Cheshire and meeting that at the top of the triangle of the fields and wood was the line to the north. If their Jenny should . . .

The rabbit hole was not very large. Kate's foot fitted very neatly into it; so neatly it might have been made for her. It brought her down like the woodman's axe brings down an oak. The sky and the trees, the lowering sun, all tipped crazily as she fell and her voice peaked into a scream which lifted a flock of crows from their nests almost half a mile away.

Jenny stopped. Her head moved slowly on her neck, and her nostrils twitched, like those of an animal as it scents danger. Her eyes blinked rapidly and her breath quickened. The muscles of her throat rippled as though some sound had just passed through it, then with a fluid movement, as graceful and as poignant as the death glide of a shot deer, her neck arched and she sank slowly to her knees.

She heard her own scream bounce from one wall to the other, echoing backwards and forwards as it ricocheted. It rose to the ceiling, trying to escape from the small room. Her hands clung to those of Dr Clancy and the words of denial erupted from her lips.

'Noo . . . o . . o, Noo . . . o . . o, No . o . o, No . o . o.' He looked at her, his pain twisting his face and his eyes misted. Throwing off his hands, she beat at him with angry fists. He was lying to her . . . lying to her. '*Please*,' she entreated him, '*please . . . please . . .*' He shook his head, his own compassion for her suffering tearing the words from him.

'I'm sorry Jenny, I'm sorry.'

The girl in the wood rocked to and fro, her head sunk on her

238

breast, her arms wrapped tightly about herself. The warmth of her knees where they touched the ground melted the white frost, but the biting cold froze it again, welding the girl and the hard ground on which she knelt, together. For half an hour her agonised grieving filled the air, and not a bird, nor an animal stirred. She wept for her child and for the man she loved, and as she wept another sound, one that had been obliterated by the noise she was making, gradually forced itself into her consciousness. For several minutes, though she heard it, she took no notice, her sorrow drowning her, making her oblivious to anything but herself. But the sounds persisted. They went on and on until she could no longer ignore them.

Jenny Fowler lifted her head slowly. Someone was calling her name. The voice was peaked with terror and she did not know it.

'Jenny . . . Jenny . . . oh God, where are you . . .' Anguished sobbing as if the sufferer were in torment, echoed about the trees, distorted beyond recognition. 'Jenny, please Jenny . . . come back . . . oh Lord . . . make her come back, Jenny, Jenny . . . Jenny.'

Jenny's eyes moved in her face, looking about her in bewilderment. They widened, a bright golden brown, and the thick black lashes framed them in arcs of dread. Where was she? Her heart thundered sickeningly in her breast and the ache in her knees sent shafts of pain up her legs. She tried to stand but the frost gripped her and she fell forward awkwardly on to her hands, the feeling gone from her feet. There was that voice again. 'Jenny . . . Jenny . . .' Jesus, sweet Jesus where was she? How had she come into this nightmare? Just a moment ago she had been in her bed and Dr Clancy had told her that her . . . that the baby . . . She shook her head, clamping her jaw together to stop the sound of agony from escaping, then looked about her wildly. She was in a wood. There were black trees all about her. Oh God. Oh God she must be dead – and in hell. She had died with . . . her baby, and for her sins she had been sent to hell.

Standing up Jenny turned from side to side, her face working in horror. It was cold in hell and she thought it would be hot. She had always been told that hellfire . . .

'Jenny . . . Jenny . . .'

This time the voice pierced the shell of fear which had Jenny trapped within its case. She stood still and listened. She was like a fox standing with one foot poised ready to spring away from the sound of the hounds. Her eyes still darted jerkily about her, warily, attempting to make sense of what they saw, but her heart had stopped its lurching, and her mind recognised that this earth beneath her feet was rock hard, but real; that the trees were trees and nothing more, and though she was still ignorant of how she came to be here, there was no immediate danger. But the voice . . . it sounded . . . it sounded so frightened . . . and in pain . . .

'Oh God our Jenny, where the bloody 'ell are you?' The words brought recognition and at last she knew – it was Kate. Kate. It was Kate. Jenny's eyes filled with glad tears. Oh Kate, lovely Kate, where are you? She began to run in the direction from which the plaintive voice came.

'Kate, Kate, I'm coming. I'm coming. Where are you, I can't see you?'

'Ere, over 'ere, I've got me foot stuck in the bloody hole an' now I can't gerrup, an' me bum's frozen to t'ground, an' me water's gone. I'll ring that bloody robin's neck if it comes swingin' on my line again, 'onest our kid . . .'

Jenny leaped across a low stand of winter fern, brown and dead-looking, and there she was, a small mountain of quivering flesh. Kate's face was streaked with soil and tears, and her eyes floated, blue and frightened between swollen lids. She sprawled awkwardly on her side, her elbow beneath her. Her coat, which had fallen open in her efforts to regain her feet, revealed her dress, wet through with her own waters.

'Oh Jenny, oh love, I'm that glad to see yer. I thought yer'd gone. I thought the baby'd come an' me 'ere all on me own.'

She appeared not to notice Jenny's alert expression, nor the smile of joy which lit her eyes. Until two arms came round her and held her, until a cold cheek pressed against hers and a soft voice spoke.

'Give over our Kate, we'll 'ave yer in yer bed in two ticks, stop witterin' on, so.'

Kate's heart which had been fluttering and circling in panic, for one time-stopping minute, stood stock still then gave a pure leaping throb of joy. She turned and looked incredulously into her sister's eyes, bright, alive, glowing, living, and her shout of happiness lifted the same flock of crows which had just settled itself after the last.

Now two voices cried together, the soft, silly tears with which women show their joy, streaming across two sets of cold red cheeks. The sounds poured from two mouths but not a word was heard by either girl. Their eyes spoke though, blazing into each other as though each could not get enough of the sight of the other. The wood was darkening quickly, but neither of them noticed, until, with a spasm which shook her, Kate's first contraction came.

240

'Bloody 'ell, our kid, we'd berrer gerrer move on. We don't want Charlie's son born in t'wood, do we?'

And it was a son. They named him Frank Percival Walker, Frankie to those who loved him. He grew strong and bonny, and in his young mind he was always to some degree unsure which of the two women who filled his baby days, was his mother. He knew of course, later, that his Mam was his Mam, but his Auntie Jenny loved him just as much, and he loved her. She was so beautiful, and was always laughing. Sometimes it seemed to him that she was the most laughing person he had ever known. Her brown eyes gleamed and when the light caught them, he distinctly saw a star appear, right in the centre of each one. Her mouth stretched in soft, pink arcs about her white teeth and when he was a baby she would kiss his warm neck, snuggling her mouth against him, nibbling his fingers as he grabbed her hair. He would sit on one lap and then another, leaning his downy curls against a bosom, one full and swelling, the other smaller, but just as cosy, and his infant heart could find no difference.

His Aunty Jenny was not always there after a while, and he missed her, though he was too young to say so.

A man came and went. It was said he was Frankie's Dad. He was kind to Frankie, but he slept in the place that Frankie considered his own, beside the comfortable body of his Mam and when he did so Frankie was made to sleep in his cot.

When he grew old enough, he would climb from its protective bars and slip in with Aunty Jenny, so he didn't mind after that.

His Dad got to be good fun, especially after the girl came. Her name was Dorry and everyone hung about her. The women argued who was to hold her, but his Dad took him out into the field and showed him how to play cricket, so he felt better. He loved his Dad more and more after that, and could not understand why he had considered him not as good as Mam and Aunty Jenny.

He sat on the rag rug before the fire, protected from its flames by the brightly polished guard, and played with his cars and the conversation passed over his wiry mop of brown curls, so like his mother's, but he didn't understand what was said.

In May 1926 he was only in his third year, and the late arrival of his father's ship meant nothing to him. He was unaware that all the great ports were silent and empty, that the milk which he drank had that morning been delivered by a student, helped by a handsome, well-spoken lady of society, and that for eight days the country had ground to a halt as sympathy for the miners brought out every worker in the land.

241

The baby grew into a young boy and the worst day of his life came, the day he was torn from his Mam's arms, her tears dripping on his new cap, and made to sit at a desk in a dreadful place called school.

But the boy became accustomed to being away from his mother and his dependancy upon her and his Aunty Jenny began to dissipate. He was allowed to 'play out' with other children up the road, and to go messages for his Mam to the shop. Oh, he was a big boy now. One day he sat at the table, eating his bread and jam which his Mam gave him for his tea and gazed longingly at the evening sunshine, listening to the shouts of Jimmy Townsend and Alfie Baker in the fields, and the words his Dad spoke to his Aunty Jenny (his Mam didn't seem much interested) went in one of his mucky ears and out of the other.

What did he know, or care, of the growing, accelerating numbers of unemployed? From a million at the beginning of the decade it was increasing and swelling the dole queues, and as the Twenties drew towards their ending it had doubled. He heard his father use a word which was to become as familiar as his own name – Depression – and in October 1929 when he was almost six years old, he thought his father was going to cry and his young heart was frightened. He'd never seen his Dad look so bad. He had put his head on the table and his Mam stroked his Dad's hair and Frankie was bewildered. Grownups didn't do such things. His small world tottered and was about to crash when Aunty Jenny smiled at him, gave him a halfpenny, rumpled his hair, kissed and hugged him and sent him on his way, relieved, to the sweet shop.

When he got back his Dad and Mam were his Dad and Mam again, and his world was secure.

He was a child, safe in his family's love and was not to know, as his family was not to know, of the days that were to come.

Chapter Twenty-Five

The young woman was lovely.

Every male eye in the room turned to watch her as she moved slowly between the tables, stopping occasionally to speak to a customer. Some peeped surreptitiously, aware of the presence of their female companions, but others eyed her openly, letting their glance linger and caress.

One such was Bill Robinson.

He was twenty-four years old when he fell in love with Jenny Fowler. He could not have told you how it happened, or even why. Jenny was pretty, with a sweetly curving figure, but so were a number of other young women of his acquaintance, and he loved none of them. He had loved no one, no woman, apart from a certain affection for his Ma, in his life. His one aim was to persuade as many attractive young women as he was able, to allow him as many liberties as he could cajole, and he was supremely successful.

He was a strong, well made, good looking young man who had never had the slightest difficulty in getting people to like him. He had a way with him, part cheek – his eyes twinkled with it – and part sheer determination. What he wanted, he got, one way or another.

People took to him despite themselves. He might irritate, exasperate, goad and infuriate, but his sunny appreciation of his own worth had his contemporaries shaking their heads, and smiling at the sheer impudence of him.

He enjoyed life immensely. It had never let him down. He was the consummate egotist, selfish and spoiled all his life by his doting mother. She had placed within him from an early age the belief that his good looks and charm entitled him to the devotion which she gave to him, and which consequently he expected from every woman he met. She saw to his every material need, from cooking his favourite tripe and onions every week, despite the fact that she, her husband and her younger son detested it, to laying out each morning his clean shirt and a pair of socks to match the suit of his choice.

243

She ruined him completely for any other woman.

Bill had no intention of marrying until he was at least twenty-eight or thirty. It was a good age to settle down, in his opinion, not too old to enjoy a young family nor too young to miss the delights of bachelorhood. This was his reasoning. Logical and concise; his life mapped out as if it were, in straight paths of time, and then, in the tick of a moment, from being heartwhole and fancy free with nothing on his mind but making sure that his cash balanced at the end of the day, for Bill was a bank clerk, he was in love.

Nothing had prepared him for it. In the brief space of time it took him to glance through his window, across the counter, and into Jenny Fowler's bright and beautiful eyes, he fell in love.

He was poleaxed. His heart tripped and bruised itself against his ribs, and his mouth became dry and grainy. His tongue felt several sizes too large for his mouth and he could not find the spit to speak in his normally engaging manner.

He had taken the paying-in book and the cash bag she handed him, but his fingers did not seem able to open the drawstring and when they eventually did so, he could not get his hand into the necessary position to count the notes and coins inside it. He dropped several halfcrowns and a threepenny bit upon the floor, muttering apologetically, whilst the man who had stood behind the smiling young woman, tutted irritably.

When she had gone and the minutes passed; when his heartbeat slowed to a reasonable rate and he was able to swallow, he convinced himself that it was all in his imagination. A thing merely of the flesh. He was smitten, that was all, and the obvious cure was to take that delicious bit of crumpet out once or twice; have her fall into his manly embrace, as they all did, and he would be over it. Probably be bored out of his mind in a week, once he had what he wanted.

Bill Robinson's lips curled, and his merry eyes crinkled at the corners. His thoughts flashed as quickly through his brain as did the money through his counting fingers. He would take her out, flatter her, make her laugh – that always gottem – and before you could say 'knickers' she would be his.

He looked again at the paying-in slip which the young woman had given him. *The Corn Dolly* it said, signed by J. Fowler. The Corn Dolly – that was the restaurant next to the Corn Exchange in Brunswick Street. He had been there once himself when a young lady he was hotly pursuing had proved temporarily obdurate and he had needed a touch of sweet persuasion. It had worked too. She had been so impressed she had fallen into his hands as swiftly as he could undo the buttons of her blouse.

He was not one to let the grass grow under his feet. With a single minded purpose and some considerable expense – it was costly to eat at The Corn Dolly and a bank clerk's wages were not high – he had made himself known to her. He smiled impishly, was his most charming self; coaxed, flattered and generally tried to insinuate himself into her favour. To his chagrin, none of it worked. Jenny smiled, she laughed, she joked, but she did not become his. Nothing that he did, or said, seemed to matter to her. Of course, she was most polite. He was a customer and was treated to the courteous warmth which Jenny accorded to all her customers, but that was all.

He stayed away for several weeks, trying new tactics. They said that absence made the heart grow fonder, but when he returned, she greeted him as though she had seen him only the day before, and appeared not to have missed him at all.

He grew desperate and began to plead, something he had never done in his life. Jenny, conscious that he was a customer, and therefore to be treated politely, nevertheless began to show coolness when he appeared, and complained to Charlie and Kate that if he didn't leave her alone, she would ask Waggie to give him one of his 'blasts'.

On this night Bill watched her as she bent her head to speak to a middleaged couple who sat at a table in the centre of the tastefully appointed room. The lights were soft, gleaming on the shining cutlery, snowy damask; reflecting from the dark polished wood of the walls. The carpet, rich and darkly red, softened the sounds of the restaurant to a pleasant hum.

It had been opened originally to cater to the businessmen who worked in the Corn Exchange and its attendant offices, but it had become so well regarded, for the food was exceptionally good and the decor and service superb, that it had grown from what had been meant to be purely a daytime trade into one of the most popular eating places in the evening.

Jenny moved on to another table. She smiled. The peach glow from the table lamp touched her cheekbone, highlighting the porcelain delicacy of her skin, making her golden eyes darken to amber. She was smartly dressed in the very latest fashion. Her dress was soft, feminine, the colour of honey. The bodice crossed just at the soft hollow between her breasts, and was tied with a floppy bow at the hip. At the front the hem fluted about her knee, showing her slender, shapely legs, but at the back it almost reached her ankle. Her high-heeled shoes were the same colour, in suede. Her nut brown hair was polished with a sheen which glowed, dipping until it touched her shoulder.

Bill was mesmerised. His eyes followed her movements as she went from table to table, and the girl who sat beside him was forgotten. She did not matter. She had been invited solely in an attempt to make Jenny jealous. She was the kind of girl to whom he was usually attracted – pretty, vacuous, and willing, and intoxicated to be brought to this 'posh' place. She'd have laid it out for Bill Robinson for the price of a fish and chip supper, and so in her simple way thought she had him hooked, else why would he spend his money bringing her here?

She watched where his eyes focused, and knew. Her face became petulant.

'Bill, you 'aven't said whether yer like me new frock.'

'Very nice, it suits yer.'

His heart beat faster as Jenny neared their table.

'Yer never even looked.'

'Yes I did. Yer look grand.'

'An' what about me 'air? I 'ad it done special.'

'Very nice.'

The girl was becoming more fretful by the minute. Still Bill watched Jenny, waiting patiently until she got to his table. It was her custom to have a word with all the diners, a pleasant touch, appreciated by the men and women who ate there regularly, making them feel that she cared about their comfort, and enjoyment of the food they ate.

At last Jenny turned and saw him, and for a second he could have sworn an expression of dismay clouded her eyes, then she looked at his companion and relief made her smile.

'Bill,' she said 'how nice to see you and . . .' she turned politely to the girl with him, waiting for the expected introduction. The girl gawped for she was out of her depth in the smart simplicity of her surroundings and awed by Jenny's friendly charm.

But Bill was delighted. Just what he wanted, he exulted. Indeed the very reason he had come. If Jenny Fowler could be made to see that she was not the only pebble on the beach; that she'd have to look sharp and make up her mind, or Bill Robinson would be snapped up, then this expensive evening would not be wasted. He was still, even yet, convinced that it only needed the right tactics to have her eating out of his hand. He hadn't found them yet, but he would. Hadn't he always? It never once entered his mind that Jenny did not find him as irresistible as he found her.

246

Introductions were made, and small talk, then Jenny moved on, unaware of the seething emotions which flowed beneath the bland and smiling countenance of Bill Robinson, only glad that he appeared to have found another girl on which he could lavish his particular brand of charm.

Bill watched as she moved away. He had stared intently into her eyes as she talked to his companion, watching for some reaction. There had been none. Her eyes, clear and direct, unconcerned, had looked into those of the girl's and she had smiled pleasantly. He knew then that she didn't give a damn.

The girl was speaking.

'Well she was right nice, wasn't she. I thought at first she'd 'ave been a stuck up cow, but . . .'

'Oh shut up, yer soft bitch,' he said venomously.

'Well I must say . . .'

'Oh shut up and eat yer damn shrimp cocktail.'

Jenny walked along the tiled passage which led from the restaurant to the kitchen. She kept to the right hand side, avoiding the girls who hurried, loaded trays of food balanced on steady hands, in the opposite direction on the left. She was still smiling when she entered the kitchen.

It was immaculate, looking as though it had never had a meal cooked in it since its inception eighteen months ago. The lights gleamed on bright shining stainless steel and white counter tops and tiles. The huge pine table in the centre of the room had been scrubbed until it was white as hoar frost, and the red tiled floor had a polish on it that boded ill for the unwary foot. Despite this virginal cleanliness, there were plates and containers of food everywhere, on tables and shelves and serving trolleys; on heated trays and cooker tops, and in every corner there lingered an appetising smell succulent enough to please the most demanding of gourmets. A saddle of lamb, its fat crisp and juicy, its centre a delicate pink, leaked gravy onto an oval platter as a young man in a white coat and chef's hat cut generous slices from its side. A roast of beef was kept hot under a cover on top of the oven, and a girl, also in white, stirred a huge pan of gravy made from its liquor. Fillet steaks almost raw, garnished with water cress, were placed on a silver platter and a smart waitress, white gloved, bore it away, smiling at Jenny as she did so.

Charlie was decorating a strawberry soufflé, squeezing a forcing bag filled with cream, placing sliced strawberries on each rosette about the edge of the dish. His eyes were slitted as he concentrated on the delicate positioning of each perfect fruit, and he seemed

247

scarcely to breathe as he worked. Taking a fine sieve from the table beside him he dredged caster sugar over his creation.

Jenny watched him, awed, admiring his skill, and wondered for the hundredth time where he had gained the artistry he showed. He had had no formal training except that which he had picked up as a galley chef aboard the merchant vessels on which he had served and the seamen for whom he cooked did not demand a high standard of epicurean genius. He had cooked plain, but good, nothing fancy. That is until Waggy's Mam took him in hand. The old lady was now well into her nineties, but Charlie went to her and she had given him her secrets. But that was not all. He was that marvel of marvels, an imaginative cook who could, like Waggy's Mam, from almost nothing produce a meal of such excellence, and such beauty to the eye, that even before the first mouthful is taken, the mouth waters, and the hands itch to be about it with a knife and fork.

Jenny waited until he had finished before she spoke. Charlie looked up and grinned and as the tension dispersed, his breath sighed from between pursed lips.

'That's the last an' let's 'ope it's enough, 'cos we've finished the cream.' He looked around him, his eyes darting in a professional manner about the busy scene. Though it appeared to have no order, with each person intent only on whatever concerned himself, it all hung together and interacted like a well made plan. A plan of action, for that was what it was, put into operation by Charlie Walker and Jenny Fowler.

And all begun over six years before by Jenny when she had begged Percival Wagstaffe to give her, and her coming child, a chance to start a new life.

He had never forgotten that day nor the impression young Jenny, just eighteen, had made upon him, and when she had recovered from her illness and her sister's first child was born, he had called her to him and they had continued with the idea which had been formulated that day. He loved Jenny, as most did, for her own grief had given her a rare sweetness, a tolerance, an understanding that let her see into the hearts of others. And she saw into Waggy's and knew him for what he was, and loved him for it. She was bright and beautiful and strong now, Jenny Fowler, shaped by pain and tragedy, forged by it, like steel on fire, and she took up the challenge which life had flung in her face, and though she had almost lost it once, when it came again, she grasped it with both hands.

She was happy that night as she watched her brother-in-law

finish the delicate creation which he had put together with an artist's skill.

Charlie too had put the past behind him, swearing that he couldn't take his eyes from his wife's person for more than five minutes at a time without she put a 'bloody foot in a rabbit 'ole', or some such tomfoolery. Besides, she wanted him with her as her family grew and so when her second child was born he had accepted Waggy's offer of employment at his shortly to be opened new venture beside the Corn Exchange.

It was Jenny who named it, and Jenny who ran it.

In 1924, just after Easter Jenny Fowler took the first step towards her new life. Waggy had watched her from the first floor window of the café as she stepped out along Dale Street and his heart had swelled with pride. She had a head on her shoulders that one, he thought smugly, as if he had put it there. It was a Monday afternoon. Spring. Cool and sunny, and the blossom of rose in Jenny's cheek caused a few heads to turn as she crossed the threshold of 'The Moorfields Business School for Young Men and Women'. Her heart was thundering in her chest and she held her books tightly to her to hide the rapid rise and fall of her breast, convinced that the crowd of confident young people who streamed about her, would notice and stare.

They were a new breed, these serious young men and women who sought a better way of life than the one which had been available to their largely working class parents. They were ambitious, no longer satisfied to follow the trades which had been the prerogative of a mother who was in service, or a father born to be a navvy, a dockie or a brickie. They were climbing out of the mould in which they had been set for generations, elbowing their way into banking, accountancy, the law and teaching. The war which had decimated a complete generation had changed the set pattern of class distinction for ever, especially that of women. Some of them had the vote now, and the rest would follow soon, and they had proved that they could work in a man's world. Their pride in themselves and in what they had achieved was unbounded and they were not prepared to return meekly to the employment which had been theirs before the war. They wanted equality; they wanted to stay in the world which had been exclusively male-dominated for so long. They wanted better jobs, jobs that were fulfilling and demanding, and they knew that the only way to achieve this miracle was by education.

Floating on this rising sea of defiant, under-privileged society, determined on bettering itself, was a sprinkling of what had once been known as the gentry. The idle, mainly female offspring of the wealthy who before the war had been content, because they knew no better, to sit at home and embroider or paint or play the piano. From 1915 onwards they had driven ambulances in France, become nurses, worked in factories and canteens and done jobs which previously had been performed by men, and they had lived, and died, some of them, proving that they were not the brainless breeding machines which men had made them. They came together, these two groups, like sugar and salt, but the resulting mixture was the forerunner of what one day would be taken for granted. Equal opportunities for men – and women.

Jenny's class consisted of twenty such women. They aspired to be no more than secretaries, lady typewriters or even a clerk in some office, but it was a step up from shop assistant or factory worker, and better than sitting at home drinking tea with the vicar's wife. Their education, at one end of the class scale, or the other, excluded them from banking, the law, or medicine – that was still to come for their younger sisters, though a few were determined enough to succeed, had they been given the chance – but, with enthusiastic resolve, they battled to gain for themselves a foothold in their exciting new world, to break away from what had always been considered the lot of women, and to compete with their brothers in their brothers' world.

Jenny spent three hours each afternoon at the college. With a cloth thrown over her hands and the keyboard, she learned to touch type, bending over the typewriter until her head and back ached. She pored over the complexities of double entry book-keeping. She was taught the first strokes of shorthand, and to compile a simple, but efficient system of filing. The last she found easy. Hadn't she already put Waggy's files into such a degree of smooth-running neatness that even he was able to lay his hands on the very piece of paper for which he searched, and at the first time of looking!

The instructor in all these wondrous and bewildering accomplishments was an indomitable grey haired, stern-faced spinster called Miss Wilkinson, who had all the gentleness of a steel tank and the tolerance of a brick wall when met by one. She had the distinction of being one of the first lady typewriters in the country. She was a perfectionist and asked nothing less in her pupils. She asked, no demanded, that they gave their best to what she taught them, and if their best was not considered enough, her tongue was like a whip, slicing the flesh from their bones, and felling the unfortunate to kneeling supplication. It was a common occurrence at least once a day, to see some young lady hurriedly leave the room, handkerchief to face, but it was to her credit that they always returned, and that, at the end of the course, the twenty young women who had started, finished it, many with distinction. She was tall and thin and straight without a curve anywhere about her person. She wore grey always.

The college was one of the best of its kind in the north and the competition for places was keen. The fees were high; at least half of the pupils worked mornings, evenings and at the weekends, doing any menial task to earn the money to support themselves while they studied and to pay the fees.

There were classes in every branch of the business world. Banking, insurance, accountancy, all types of secretarial work, mathematics, economics, catering to a small but expanding need. There were classes in English, foreign languages, art and literature. These all provided the basis for a higher education, to better oneself in a competitive world that was just emerging as the Twenties crept towards the Thirties and unemployment was king.

Jenny moved about in their world, these enterprising ones, careless of the appreciative glances which followed her as she stepped lightly along the corridors. The young men watched her and nudged each other. She was exceptionally lovely now, with an appeal that was innocently sexual and which called to the men with a sweet signal that found an answering chord in their masculinity. There were other pretty girls, lively and not unwilling to be friendly but something in Jenny delighted them and turned their heads as she passed.

She noticed none of them, so absorbed was she in the world which was opening itself up to her like an oyster slowly revealing the precious pearl within. She answered their greetings politely, flashing her shy smile in a way which caused weak knees, sweaty palms and flushed necks. Had she known of it, it would have filled her with dismay. But she was unheeding. She worked hard and long, studying into the night, practising shorthand from passages in a book which Kate read to her and typing, typing, typing at the brand new machine which Waggy had bought for her.

She had one goal.

That goal was the precious Diploma which was awarded to each student at the end of the course if they attained the high peak of perfection which was set by the demanding Miss Wilkinson and the rest of the tutors. This was Jenny's purpose in life and all else was profitless. She wanted to justify Waggy's faith in her, she wanted to make up to Kate by repaying her, not in cash but in the

251

gift of her own independence, for all the years she had spent in her loving care. She wanted, above all, to prove to herself that she was Jenny Fowler again, the Jenny of the happy nature and singing heart who had lived before Nils.

Five years later, she had succeeded far beyond even her own hopes and expectations. She ran both of the businesses now, The Corn Dolly *and* Wagstaffes taking on the demanding work which had been Waggy's, leaving the old man to potter about in the belief that he was still top man. Waggy, sharp as a tack, let her think so. He watched over her lovingly, saying little, doing less, and if she should err sometimes; less and less often as the years went on, he quietly put it right.

On the birth of her second child, a daughter, in 1926, Kate had become fretful complaining that Charlie was missing every time he was needed; that she wanted him to be home for his children's births as well as their conception. Oh, he was good at that, she said, but what about the rest. Four years they had been wed and only once had he been home for Christmas.

In 1927, when The Corn Dolly was opened, Charlie too began his new career, and though he sometimes missed the easy-going camaraderie of his sea-going days, the feel of the ship beneath his feet, the smell and sound of the sea, he was more than recompensed by his wife's sweet amiability, the joy of his children, and the grand feeling of security, of manly pride in his ability to provide, not only the material things of life for his family but the occasional luxury. He was even considering a small car! In 1928 their third child, another boy was born. Their family was growing with their prosperity.

Now he wiped his hands on a clean cloth, then took the utensils he had used to decorate the soufflé to the huge sink. With a sharp look at the young boy who did the washing up, Charlie indicated that there was work to be done before turning back to Jenny.

''Ow's it goin' chuck?'

'Full up Charlie, an' guess who's out there?'

'Who?' Charlie's expression showed scant interest.

'Bill.' Now he looked more alert. It was the chap who was after their Jenny, and anyone, anyone, who would take their Jenny off his hands, was of interest to Charlie. Though he held her in high regard and affection, he would very firmly shake the hand of the chap who wed Jenny. With knobs on!

'Well I never,' Charlie said affably. 'Who's 'e with, 'is Mam?' Smiling, not expecting the answer he got.

'No, he's got a girl with him,' Jenny answered absently.

252

'A girl!' Charlie's mouth fell open and Jenny laughed.

'Yes. Why shouldn't he?'

'I thought he was sweet on you.' Jenny frowned, her silky brows dipping, then one raised, questioningly, coolly, she said, 'I don't know where you got that idea, Charlie.'

'Yer told me, yer said 'e . . .'

'I said 'e'd asked me to go out with him, but that doesn't mean anything. Anyway I said no.'

'Why?'

Jenny searched Charlie's face for some reason for his interrogation, but she knew; deep down she knew the reason, and she didn't blame him, not one bit. He wanted his home to himself. It was that simple. He wanted Kate and his children and his home, all to himself. She had known for a long time that Charlie would be glad to see the back of her. He was fond of her, she knew, but since he left the sea, eighteen months ago, the strain of living in a small house; three adults and three children, was beginning to tell. Even Kate was aware of it despite the newfound happiness of having Charlie beside her each night. And Charlie and Jenny worked together as well. Not all of the time, of course; she divided her time between the two cafés, but the tension was tightening.

At last she answered him.

'I don't want to go out with 'im, Charlie.'

'Why not? 'E seems a nice enough chap.'

'Give over, Charlie.'

'What's wrong wi' sayin' that. It's time you were . . .'

'*What*, Charlie?' Jenny's voice was cold, her eyes hot.

But Charlie backed down. He wasn't ready for that yet. Kate'd 'ave his guts for garters if he upset the loving relationship which she shared with Jenny.

'Well I dunno, our kid,' he grinned engagingly. 'Tell yer what – why don't yer bring 'im to tea on Sunday. Lerrour Kate 'ave a look at 'im.'

Jenny laughed and shook her head and the dangerous moment was gone, but she knew it would return and she knew something must be done.

'Charlie, you're incorrigible.'

'If you say so, chuck.'

Chapter Twenty-Six

'As one door closes another opens.' So said Kate when she was told the news. She said a lot more besides, blaming Charlie, in a way. She had known how he felt though she had kept it to herself. Like Jenny, she did not censure him, for what man doesn't want the undivided attention of his wife and his home uncluttered by visitors, family or not. Jenny was no visitor either. She had been a permanent fixture in Charlie's home for seven years.

The day started like any other. Charlie had gone, clattering off up the road his heavy boots ringing as he ran for his tram. It was December and the clouds, filled with sleet, hung motionless above the city, as though undecided whether to dump the lot on Merseyside or pass on to the Irish sea and heave it into the deep waters there. Soon it would be Christmas and young Frankie's sixth birthday and Charlie had promised Kate he would make him a cake.

'With a football field on it?' Kate wheedled.

'Yer what?'

'A football field and some players, and in Everton colours, don't forget.'

'Yer must think I'm a bloody magician. A football field?'

'Well yer know how he loves football.'

A warm kiss, a hug – for Kate and Charlie had lost none of their love for one another in the seven years of their marriage – and he was gone.

Dorothy, nearly three years old, trundled her miniature pram across the kitchen murmuring a string of words which meant nothing except to herself and to the doll within, her bright cap of ruler straight hair, brown like her mother's, glowing in the light from the fire's flames. She took her baby from the pram, sat down on the rag rug, and holding the toy tenderly in her plump little girl arms, crooned a song of sweet tunelessness, soothing herself almost immediately to sleep. The cat crept stealthily across the kitchen, her tail swirling, her eyes cutting towards the figure of the woman who stood by the sink. Seeing she was unnoticed, the animal sidled up to the sleeping child, curling against her in the warmth.

Kate absently stirred the washing up water with her dishcloth, her eyes staring blindly into the distance. Her hands did their job automatically, wiping, placing the clean pots on the draining board, reaching for the next. Her thoughts were vague and meaningless. She was in that half focused state of semi-awareness which allows us to do a job, and when it is finished, to wonder how it came to be done, for we have no remembrance of it. The field and the distant wood were scarcely visible in the grey overcast which hung almost to the ground. The tall grasses were flattened by the weight of the moisture which clung to every blade, and the trees seemed to float halfway between harsh ground and dirty sky. Kate dreamed on, the warmth of the kitchen, the monotony of her task, lulling her, like the child.

A sound from upstairs brought her to alertness, and briskly now, she finished the washing up, wiping her hands on her apron.

'Coming,' she called, and the noise, that of a child crying, turned into a contented gurgling.

Kate was twenty-six now, and, as women do when they have babies had put on weight. Her breasts were firm and generous and her hips curved from her waist in a gentle womanly sweep. She was a lovely armful, Charlie told her in the privacy of their marriage bed as he buried his face in the softness of her and he was right. She was not, and never had been, the fashionable sticklike woman of the Twenties. She was bonny. Her cheeks were round and rosy like two polished red apples and her eyes were as clear and blue and untroubled as a summer's sky. Her hair still stood about her head like a dandelion clock, brown and wiry and though it was now the fashion to wear it long, she kept it cut short. Her smile was as warm as her heart. Her temper, quick to erupt and just as quick to subside, kept Charlie on the hop, but she was still as steady in her loyalties and devotion to her family. The salt of the earth. She had a strength of character, tried and proven, and a practical good sense that had carried her through the bad days and though, as Charlie said, she was like a kid sometimes in her enthusiasms, she had a good head on her shoulders.

She ran up the stairs, and the gurgling became a full throated laugh of joy as the child, another boy, named Leslie after Kate's idol, Leslie Howard, stretched out his arms to his mother.

'Ssh – ssh,' Kate whispered. 'Yer'll wake Aunty Jenny, she's 'avin' a lie-in.' But the baby, just twelve months old, cared not for

Aunty Jenny, and bounced up and down in his cot, grasping the sides with fat hands.

'Be quiet, our Leslie.' But Kate's face was warm and loving. How could she be vexed with him. She adored him.

Swinging him into her arms, kissing his hands as he placed them to her lips, she took him down the stairs and into the bright kitchen. She murmured into his chubby neck, imploring him not to waken Aunty Jenny, or Dorry, 'there asleep by the fire, see' but the child giggled and so did Kate.

Only when she sat down in the same old overstuffed armchair that had come with them from Seacombe Street, and opened her dress, did the child quieten. He fastened his rosy pursed lips to her nipple and mother and child became one again and there was peace.

The ringing of the doorbell awakened Kate from the light doze into which she had fallen. The boy still clung like a small pink leech to her erect nipple, a trickle of milk smearing his chin, but his eyes were shut tight, his long fair lashes, like spider's legs upon his flushed cheek. Laying him on the rug where he curled like a puppy against the cat and his sister's back, Kate hastily buttoned her dress and made her way along the hall to the front door.

She was unprepared for the sight which met her eyes as she opened the door.

Waggy stood in the middle of the path. He had evidently taken a step back from the doorstep after ringing the bell, and he gave the impression of having been placed upon the path by some unknown person who had then run away and left him. He looked exactly like a child lost in a department store; as though his Mam had turned a corner and he could no longer see her. On his face was the bewildered frightened expression which comes to that of a boy left alone amongst strangers and tears poured from his old, blue eyes. His clothes appeared to hang about him, as though they had suddenly grown too big, or he had shrunk.

He just stood and looked at Kate.

Kate's heart ceased to beat and she thought she would faint. She felt the lovely bright colour drain from her face and a shiver ran through her.

'Waggy . . . my God . . . what is it . . . is it Charlie?'

Waggy did not move. Great sobs tore his chest and he began to cough as he tried to get his breath.

'Whorrisit, Waggy . . . what . . . for God's sake.'

Kate faltered down the step and onto the path, putting her hand on his arm. She tried to lead him into the house, feeling she would rather have bad news inside . . . but something, some inner sense told her that this was Waggy's trouble, not hers. This man, though he would not be unfeeling would not cry like this for Charlie.

'Come inside, chuck, come on.'

Waggy allowed himself to be drawn into the hall and Kate closed the door behind him. As she did so, Jenny came down the stairs, fastening the cord of her dressing gown about her.

'I heard the door. I . . .' her breath exploded from her mouth in a gasp of horror when she saw the old man, and for a second, a fleeting second only, the old look of despair touched her eyes, then it was gone and she ran down the stairs.

'Waggy . . . Waggy, love. What is it?'

At last Waggy spoke.

'It's me Mam,' he moaned.

Tears dripped unceasingly from his eyes and the end of his nose.

'She's dead. Me Mam's dead an' . . . I don't know what I'm gonner do wi'out 'er.'

It might have been ludicrous had it not been so heart-rending. Percival Wagstaffe was sixty-nine years old and his mother ninety-four, and he cried for her like a child, but she had been the lynchpin of his life, his teacher, companion, guiding light in all he did, and he had needed no other.

The funeral took place three days later.

Jenny stayed with Waggy, and sat beside him as the carriage in which the two of them drove, followed the horsedrawn hearse to the cemetery. They put her away in style, Waggy's Mam. She'd not have wanted to be taken to her last resting place towed by an engine which made a dreadful noise and smelt worse. Horses. She'd been brought up in a gracious era of stately charm and though she had lived it as only a servant, on the fringes, so to speak, she had loved the beautiful house, the well-tended gardens, the stables, the horses which had belonged to the man she served. She had never been in Waggy's motor car and she'd have thought nowt a' pound going on her last journey in one. No, she'd 'ave wanted 'orses, Waggy told Jenny, and so she had them.

Waggy was calm as he threw the handful of earth on to his mother's coffin, though sad tears coursed down his cheek. His other hand was in Jenny's and he was comforted. His Mam had had a good innings and he knew she would have been pleased with the turn out.

It never occurred to him that scarcely one of the dozens of mourners who stood about the grave had ever seen his Mam.

It was after the funeral party that Jenny broke the news to Kate.

257

Most of the people had gone. Waggy sat in his Mam's dark drawing room, his old knees to the fire. Charlie sat beside him and on the other side, legs halfway up the chimney was Elly. It had been a right good do, and Elly's stomach was distended with the wonderful food she had eaten. Her Pat was tearfully helping himself to another drink, consoling himself, for funerals upset him. He had never met Waggy, let alone his Mam, but he had cried at the graveside as though it was *his* mother who was being laid to rest.

Jenny and Kate stood in the huge, old-fashioned kitchen, wiping the last of the pots. Trees surrounded the house, elbowing up to the walls like guards encircling a prisoner. One tapped at the kitchen window and Kate shivered.

'God, I could no more live 'ere, than fly t'moon. It's like a mausoleum. Give yer the creeps it would. All that dark furniture and heavy curtains at every window. Wouldn't yer think, with all the money they got, well 'im, they'd 'ave 'ad a bit o' decent net. Let in a birrer light.'

She folded the teacloth and placed it neatly over the rail above the stove. Jenny was putting cups and saucers in the cupboard of the Welsh dresser which stood against the wall.

She seemed to be considering something and her expression was far away as her hands caressed the lovely polished wood.

'Oh, I don't know . . .' Her fingers ran along the top looking for dust. Mrs Wagstaffe had been dead three days and a light film dirtied Jenny's hand.

'What d'yer mean?' Kate said sharply. 'Don't tell me this lot's to your taste, 'cos I know better. 'Ow many times 'ave yer said to me, "light an' bright an' white", our Jenny?'

'I know that Kate, but with a bit of . . . careful elimination.'

'What d'yer mean?' Kate repeated. Their Jenny used some big words sometimes, and it got on her nerves.

'There's some lovely pieces 'ere, our Kate,' Jenny said dreamily. 'If yer threw some o' the . . . well it's not rubbish . . . but if yer kept the best and 'ad light curtains, pale colours . . . yer could . . .'

Kate felt the onset of what might be called alarm, though she could not have said why. She should have known, God knows, what with Charlie, and his long face, and then Waggy's Mam dying and the old man as he was about their Jenny, but it came like a bolt from the blue.

'I'm stoppin' wi' Waggy, our Kate,' Jenny said softly.

The silence in the kitchen was complete. Outside the branches of the trees moaned as the wind tore through them. Dead leaves hurled themselves into the air outside the window, as though they would see what was going on inside. They whirled and twisted, higher than the rooftops, before lurching down to the hard winter ground.

Kate was stunned speechless.

For the space of a minute only though.

'Yer coddin' me.'

Both women wore black but the contrast between the two was sharp. The family likeness was apparent in their round, high cheek boned faces, the shape of their eyes, and in the firm delicately moulded jawline. In the case of the older sister, a faint blurring could be seen in the tautness of the flesh and in the soft and generous curves which proclaimed motherhood. Kate looked a wife. She was decently dressed, but had not the keen fashion sense that was inherent in Jenny. Her dress, though new for the funeral was too long, and her hat made her seem older than her years. It was deep, helmet-shaped, hiding the ebullience of the hair which was essentially Kate, making her look doleful. Jenny could have stepped from the pages of the latest French fashion magazine. Her dress was exquisitely simple. The waist was where a waist should be and the skirt flared very slightly to her kneecap. The sleeves were full, the cuff tight, fastened with a tiny button. Her hat was close-fitting but one side was lower than the other, slipping over her left eyebrow and ear. Her black stockings were sheer with a hint of a design of lace, and her black suede shoes had high heels and pointed toes. She was the epitome of elegance.

The air was electric, but Jenny did not answer. She knew that Kate would have her say, choose how, and there was no way she could be stopped. It made no difference. Jenny had made up her mind. 'It was an ill wind' had been almost her first thought when Waggy had told her of his mother's death, and though she did not speak of it until later, the simplicity and the rightness of the idea, was clear to both her and to Waggy. It solved her problem and gave Waggy something to which he could cling in the shocked aftermath of his mother's going. His fear had been appalling to him. His fear of the loneliness, the emptiness of the ugly house which he had shared with his Mam for so long. His gratitude was pathetic, and his eagerness to install Jenny in 'any room, anyone yer want, chuck'—pitiful. 'Do what yer want, queen, 'ave new furniture, paint it, me Mam wouldn't mind.' He could not, even yet, rid himself of the need to mention his Mam. It was her house still. Tears again, but of relief, and the matter was settled before Mrs Wagstaffe was barely cold in her coffin.

'Yer can't stop 'ere on yer own with a man who's not related,' Kate continued sternly. 'I'll not 'ave it. It's not proper.'

Jenny laughed out loud, the expression of righteous indignation on Kate's face more than she could stand.

'Oh give over our Kate. Waggy's old enough to be me Grandad, never mind me Dad.' She turned away, her shoulders shaking with laughter. Kate's face became stony.

'D'yer mean to say yer goin' to live in this . . .' she looked about her, '. . . this museum . . . an' nobody but an old man fer company. Eeh our Jenny. It's not right.' Her eyes clouded with dismay. 'Lovey, yer only twenty-four. Yer can't spend yer life between t'café an' . . . an' . . . 'ere. It's like shuttin' yerself off from . . . why, yer'll never meet anyone yer own age . . . hanging about wi' Waggy.'

'Well if that's all that's worrying you, tell me how I'll meet "Mr Right"' – Jenny's face contorted whimsically – '. . . at your house . . . 'cos that's the only difference there'll be. They don't come knocking on the door there, do they? Anyway,' her face closed up and a fleeting expression of sadness obscured her eyes '. . . I'd not be interested if they did. I like the way I live. I like the job I do. There's not many that could do what I do, Kate, an' I'm proud of it. I love it, I've made 'The Corn Dolly'. It's mine.'

'I know, I know that, but it's time you were thinkin' of gettin' married, our kid.' Kate was becoming agitated, the unease which had niggled at the back of her mind for a long time, spilling over. 'Don't yer want a family?'

The horror of what she had just said suddenly hit her and her hand flew to her mouth as though to press back the words. She was stricken. Jenny had turned away, wounded, unable to answer.

'Oh God, Jenny, I'm sorry, my bloody big mouth again. I'm sorry, I'm sorry, love.'

Kate hurried across the kitchen. Putting her hands on her sister's slumped shoulders, she leaned her forehead against the back of Jenny's head.

'It's just I still worry about yer. I know what yer've done since . . . since . . . well, it's marvellous an' I'm proud of you. But to me there's nowt like a home of yer own, a husband, kids. I'm that content, I want you to be, as well. Yer never go anywhere. Even that young chap Charlie told me about, yer won't go out wi' 'im. Charlie said 'e's a bank clerk an' all. If yer'd just go out wi' someone yer own age, I wouldn't mind. I know yer thought the world of . . .' she felt Jenny's shoulders stiffen beneath her fingers, and she hurried on '. . . but yer life's in front of yer. Give it a chance, our kid.'

Jenny turned around and her face had lost its look of blanched sorrow. She smiled and hugged the plump form of her sister to her, then stood back.

'Just listen to me first, Kate an' tell me I'm not right, will yer?' She shook Kate gently. 'Will yer?'

Kate nodded, her face serious.

'Yer've got three children now, our Kate, and a 'usband who comes 'ome each night. Yer've a lovely 'ome, but it's got three bedrooms, and I'm in one of them. Yer need that room, Kate and, more important, yer need yer 'ome to yerselves. Just you and Charlie and the kids. Charlie's never said a word. 'E's the best bloke in the world an' I only wish there was two of 'im,' she laughed, 'but 'e wants to be . . .' she paused, choosing her words carefully '. . . 'e wants 'is family to 'imself. Every time 'e turns round, 'e finds me. For seven years Kate, nobody could've bin better to me. I love 'im dearly, and you, but I've got to get out of yer . . . lives. Don't say anything our Kate . . .' as Kate would have objected '. . . I've made me mind up and it's all arranged.'

Kate's face crumpled, and her eyes filled with tears.

'And before yer start blubbering, if it'll make yer happy, I'll go out with Bill Robinson. Just once mind, and if I'm bored to tears I'll blame you.'

Chapter Twenty-Seven

But Jenny wasn't bored to tears. She was surprised to discover that she found Bill Robinson's company quite pleasant. Pleasing. He pleased her. She was not to know he did so deliberately, that he set out with that one aim, to please, and therefore seduce.

They made a striking couple and heads turned to look at them wherever they went. The women's glances warmed to Bill Robinson's dark good looks and the devilish green of his eyes, and the men found they could not look away from Jenny's sweet beauty. She was so soft, so feminine. In a world which was recovering from the shingle, the shimmy and the sound of jazz, Jenny's loveliness was somehow of an era more elegant. More womanly. Bill was her perfect foil. Strong, manly, almost earthy. His hair curled about his head in attractive disorder, and needed frequent trips to the barber to curb its unruliness, and his skin always looked as if he had just returned from a holiday in the sun. His lips smiled confidently, the grin rippling across his face until it reached his eyes. His teeth were big, white and even, and he had a dimple in his left cheek which he made the most of. He was a very personable young man and he knew it.

He had never had to strive for anything in his life. He had been indulged by doting parents and had been brought up in a pleasant bay-windowed house in Old Swan. He was clever. His position in the National and Northern Bank in Castle Street was moderately well paid and he was expected to go far. He was the same age as Jenny, earning three pounds twelve and six per week, and would have been mortified to know Jenny earned two pounds more. That was his usual attitude towards women. Not quite as good as a man. Slightly inferior where brains were concerned, their talents lying (no pun intended) in other directions. He rated them in varying degrees on their availability and performance.

But he fell in love with Jenny. She was an enigma to him and he was bewitched.

Wisely, made cautious by his love for her, he did not rush her. For the first time in his selfish life he was conscious of the needs of

262

another, and his instinct told him he must go slowly with this one. She was different. This was no nine days wonder, like the rest. To his own amazement he admitted to himself that this could be a church do! So he let time slip by pleasantly while he wooed her.

Jenny was not aware of his hopes. To her, he seemed a pleasant companion. In her innocence, that which had been awakened once, and now lay dormant, she enjoyed the stimulus of male friendship. She liked the way he made her laugh, and the excitement of the quick-witted, lighthearted banter which was Bill's way of conversing. He was never serious, and in the beginning she found it had a tonic effect on her. He seemed to be always at the top of a high peak of energy, always on the move, ready to be off somewhere on a whim.

She did not see his love for her as it grew. He was hopelessly lost in it and anyone more experienced in its ways would have known. It shone from his eyes as he looked at her when her glance was elsewhere, and moved with him as he touched her arm to guide her across a busy street. It walked between them as they sauntered the crowded streets of Liverpool on a Saturday afternoon and caressed her retreating back as she left him to catch her tram.

He waited for her, one wet March afternoon, studying the printed menu which was pasted in the window of the café. The wind blew the rain in a diagonal sheet between the tall buildings, searching with cruel fingers into the doorway where he sheltered. He could have gone inside and up the stairs to the office which she shared part-time with Waggy, but Bill did not like Waggy and Waggy did not like Bill. It was as though the old man sensed the shallowness of Bill's nature, knowing it was not what he wanted for his girl. And Bill did not care for the thought of Jenny living under the same roof as Waggy. He knew there was nothing but the affection a daughter and father might share between Jenny and the old man, but nevertheless, he had been shocked when Jenny had moved in last December. Bill, despite his experiences with many women, was a prude, and to him it was not seemly for a young woman to share a home with an old man not her father. He did not say so to Jenny.

The streets, as usual, were crowded, people flowing in the curtain of rain, like shadows in a mist. The day was grey and dark, and though it was only mid-afternoon, the lights were turned on in the shop.

Jenny came down the stairs, stopping to speak for a moment to the cashier at the till. The light above her turned her brown hair to chestnut, throwing the shadow of her long lashes onto her pink

263

cheek. She laughed at something the girl said, and her head turned showing off the lovely white line of her throat. She had not yet put on her coat and the sweater she wore clung to her breasts. Bill's eyes devoured her. He knew she had not yet seen him and he was safe in letting the yearning lust wander across his face. God, she was a beauty. He ached for her, the pit of his belly and his loins pained him, hot like a flame.

She came out of the café, pushing her arms into the sleeves of her coat, her breast lifting as she pulled it about her. Bill put out his hand to help her. She looked at him and for the first time saw the look in his eyes and was suddenly aware of him sexually. Her heart began to race and a lovely colour spilled across her cheeks, and she felt a thrill of dread run through her.

It was the beginning of knowing for her.

He took her arm and they ran across the drenched street, dodging its oil-streaked puddles, and the wet slicked cars as they whirled past. The rain fell in ice cold needles, soaking them through and running like water from a tap off the brim of Bill's trilby.

Waggy watched from the window of the office and his face was grim. He held his left arm with his right hand, kneading the ache which grew there, then belched loudly. Aah, that was better. He turned away as Bill and Jenny disappeared in the misted rain.

Waggy was not happy. If there was one thing he wanted more than anything in the world, it was to see his lovely girl walk up the aisle on the arm of a good chap. Oh – he knew she was happy with her job, and damn well she did it an' all, but every woman should have a bloke. And that wasn't Bill Robinson, not by a long chalk. Waggy was a fair judge of character and he'd taken a dislike to Bill Robinson right from t' start. Nice looking fella he was, true, with a good job and it was plain as the nose on your face he idolised their Jenny, though she didn't seem to know it poor lass, but he was too . . . fly. Too bloody clever by half. No, what she needed was someone like Charlie to look after her an' give her a good home. That reminded him. He dropped down heavily in his chair behind his desk. He must get down to see the solicitor. He'd been meaning to do it for weeks now, ever since Jenny moved in with him, but what with being busy at Christmas, he never seemed to get the time. Tomorrow he'd go. He must make sure that Jenny was taken care of.

The sound of the traffic became fainter. Waggy's eyes closed and with the ease that belongs to only the young and old, dropped off into a light doze.

Jenny and Bill sat in the damp, warm intimacy of the cinema. She had wanted to see Jeanette McDonald and Maurice Chevalier in *The Love Parade* and Bill was happy to indulge her. Anything she asked for tonight was to be hers, anything. Tonight Bill intended to make the first move in the seduction of Jenny Fowler.

It might have been a re-run of that night almost eight years ago, when the young Kate had sat with her Charlie, laughing at the funniest man in the world. His name was Charlie too. Then, Kate had stared entranced at the screen and Charlie Walker had been entranced by her. But on that night, when Charlie had diffidently put out his rough sailor's hand to hold hers, she had let it stay there and her heart had thumped with pleasure.

Jenny did not at first realise what Bill was doing. She felt a touch on her arm, the one that rested on the wood between the seats. Just a light pressure of Bill's elbow against hers. When she turned to look, Bill was staring raptly at the flickering images on the screen. Jeanette's beautiful voice filled the cinema, and Jenny, enraptured by its vibrant sweetness returned her attention to the screen. But the pressure of Bill's arm against hers grew. Her hands rested in her lap and they gripped each other fiercely but it was no use. It was as though she had known what would happen; had tried to avoid it by keeping each hand occupied with the other. Bill's fingers probed hers, gently forcing them apart, pushing her left hand to one side, holding the right. Tenderly his thumb rubbed the heel of hers, and then crept into her palm, circling it, caressingly.

Jenny sat rigid, her hand flaccid in Bill's. Every inch of skin that covered the bones of her fingers, her palm and wrist, shrank from his touch. He seemed not to notice, but kept on rubbing and rubbing, not looking at her. The film rolled on; the characters capered, laughed, talked and sang, but to Jenny it was as if she sat in a silent empty world with no contact except that of her hand in Bill's. Her heart shuddered in her breast and she could feel the trembling from her chest move to her shoulder and along the length of her arm to her hand.

Suddenly with an almost audible cry of relief, she became aware that the film was over. People were standing, the National Anthem was being played and Bill had let go of her hand. She found herself rubbing her palm down the side of her skirt as she stood, and she could not look up at the man who was beside her.

They emerged from the cinema. Bill was laughing, his eyes bright, full of his own sense of success. Jenny could see it now. The proprietary air; the confident mien of a man who is ready to take the next step in a relationship of which he is sure of the outcome.

He fell into step beside her and took her arm, smiling down into her face. She felt sick, and a fool. Her mind was stunned by her own foolishness. Had she thought that Bill Robinson, so obviously a favourite with the opposite sex and so eager to let her see it, would be satisfied forever with a non-physical relationship? Had she even considered it? She had enjoyed their outings together and had not thought about the future. That was the truth of it. He had held her hand in the cinema, that's all. But it was the beginning. For three months he had held back, why she didn't know, but now he had let her know that the next move was about to take place.

Jenny hurried along the dark and windy pavement, her feet flying over the flagstones in her eagerness to be home. She thought of Waggy. He would be waiting for her, the fire like a furnace to warm his old bones, the soft reading lamps which she had introduced in her first hesitant step towards 'doing over' the house, making the dark room cosy, homelike. Bill's hand through her arm was like an anchor, stopping her, holding her back from the safety, the familiarity she craved.

'Whoa, whoa, what's the hurry?' His hand held her firmly and she resisted the temptation to shake it off and cry to him to 'Let go!'

'What's all the rush? I thought we'd go and have a drink. The pub next to the Corn Exchange is nice and cosy.' Unconsciously his eyes gleamed and Jenny stared into them, hypnotised. The second step was about to be put into action. – He's going to try to get me drunk, she thought and she edged away.

'No, Bill, thanks, but if I don't get me tram, I'll 'ave to walk.' She tried to laugh. 'It's a long walk to Aigburth.'

'Who said anything about walking?'

'What d' yer mean?'

Bill tapped his nose and grinned.

'It's a special night tonight, kid. We're doin' it in style.'

Jenny blinked and stepped further away from him, but each time she did so, he moved forward. She smiled nervously, her lip twitching. She tried to stop it by putting her hand to her mouth, but it seemed to have a life of its own.

'No really Bill, I must get home. Waggy will . . . an' I've got to be up early tomorrow.'

'On a Sunday?'

'Well I said I'd go to our Kate's. Frankie . . . Frankie . . . I'd said I'd take 'im to . . .'

'Now come on, Jenny. A little drink won't hurt, and then . . . and then . . .' Jenny's insides felt as though someone was twisting them, wringing them out like a wet cloth.

266

'. . . and then,' Bill laughed in delight, '. . . we're going to take a taxi back to your place. Now what d'yer think of that? Never mind about a tram. Bill Robinson's doing it right tonight for the sweetest girl in all the world.'

He's drunk already, Jenny thought wildly, but he gave her no time to refuse this time. Slipping his arm firmly through hers, he began to walk in the direction of Brunswick Street. Jenny's feet scurried beside his long steps. She was afraid that if she didn't keep up with him, she would fall to the ground and be dragged along. He quickened his stride, so that she was almost running. One or two people turned to watch as they crossed Fenwick Street, curious, but not alarmed at the sight of the man half dragging a woman along by the arm. Bill laughed merrily, and they turned away. It was just a couple having a bit of fun.

And that's all it is.

As the thought entered her mind, Jenny relaxed wondering at her own stupid fears. This was Bill she was with, not Jack the Ripper. Just because he had held her hand in the pictures, then asked her to go for a drink, didn't mean that he was going to rape her, for God's sake. It was the suddenness that had startled her, that's all, and her own reaction. No one had touched her, no man since . . . since Nils, and she wanted no one to . . . well, the man had not yet been born who could . . . There was no one that . . .

Her thoughts were confused as she tripped along beside Bill. He had never stopped talking, joking, since they left the cinema, but Bill didn't need an answer a lot of the time, so he didn't notice her silence. It gave her a chance to think.

She'd have a drink with him, let him take her home in the taxi. She could come to no harm. What she meant was, there would be no more chances for Bill to put his hands on her. The pub would be crowded, it was Saturday night. The taxi driver would restrain any ideas Bill might have on the drive home, and he would have to keep the taxi to take him back to Old Swan. In an hour or so she would be home, safe with Waggy. This would be the last time for her. He was . . . well he just wasn't for her. No one was really, she thought sadly. No one. Not after Nils.

It took her a while to respond to the laughter and lighthearted banter which Bill kept up, but the infectious good humour of a pub crowd in Liverpool on a Saturday night was more than anyone could withstand, and within half an hour, Jenny was answering Bill's repartee with a wit which matched his own.

Bill was excited. It was working. She was smiling impishly up at him with that certain look in her eyes which told him she was

267

interested. Her cheeks were flushed and her eyes snapped. Her right hand held the shandy she had ordered, and though he tried to extricate it, her left was pushed firmly in her coat pocket. She laughed coquettishly though, as she pushed him away, or so Bill would have it.

The taxi journey through Princes Park and on into Sefton Park seemed to take forever. Bill put his arm round Jenny's shoulders, trying to draw her head down to his shoulder but she edged away from him, mouthing laughing remonstrances and indicating the driver with a nod of her head.

'Bill, please,' she whispered. 'Stop it, not here.' Which further signified to the besotted man that if not here then it would happen elsewhere.

The taxi pulled up smoothly in Ashfield Road. The lights were on in almost every room of the detached house, and Jenny smiled to herself. She could just imagine the old man going from room to room, murmuring in the way he had, turning on a light here and a light there, forgetting as he left to turn them off again. He was seventy now and still bright as a button, but so careless where money was concerned, so generous and eager that she be comfortable in her new home, he kept the rooms as warm and well-lit as a hothouse.

Jenny turned to Bill, her left hand on the door handle, already depressing it, ready to spring from the car as it stopped, but before she could speak, the opposite door was open, Bill was out of the car, and the driver paid.

'Bill – don't let the taxi go!' she called frantically, as she scrambled from the car, turning her ankle as she did so on the kerb.

But it was too late. Triumphantly Bill smiled at her as he stood in the road, and the taxi's rear light vanished round the bend.

'Oh Bill, yer shouldn't 'ave done that.'

'And why not? Surely you were going to ask me in for a . . . cup of cocoa?'

'But 'ow will you get 'ome?'

'I shall 'ave another taxi.'

'How will yer get one at this time o' night?'

'Who said anything about this . . .' Bill looked archly at her as he walked slowly towards the kerb, but something told him he had gone too far and he quickly changed the sentence to '. . . strappin' young chap 'aving a taxi anyway. What's wrong wi' shanks' pony?' He stopped in front of her and the street light fell about his head. His eyes shone in the shadow of his face. Time leaped backwards and another face looked down at her; and other eyes shone, but with such love, such tenderness, sweet, gentle . . . oh God, oh dear God.

With a cry Jenny stepped back, wrenching herself away from the hands which reached for her.

Harshly she said, 'Yer can come in if yer like Bill, and 'ave a cup of cocoa, but that's all. I'm sorry you took it upon yerself to let the taxi go, but that's your fault.'

She turned and began to walk across to the lighted front door, taking a key from her bag as she did so.

'Waggy will still be up. 'E always is when I come back. 'E's very protective.'

She laughed over her shoulder and Bill Robinson knew he had lost. The first round anyway.

Chapter Twenty-Eight

Bill asked her to marry him in July.

She said 'No.'

Kate thought she was crackers, and said so frequently during the three months in which Bill pursued Jenny until she thought she'd go mad. No matter what she said, or did, he would just not give up. When she knew he was working, she moved confidently between the two cafés, running along Dale Street, and cutting through to Brunswick Street, knowing she was safe from his attentions, but if she worked in the evening, which she often did, she would send one of the girls out before her to scan the streets, and the shop doorways, to make sure he was not lurking there.

He no longer alarmed her. In fact he made her laugh with his infectious grin and his persistent good humour. A head would appear, bodiless, from a doorway in front of her, or a disembodied arm would wave. A voice would call her name from she knew not where, and there he would be, charming, innocent-looking, begging forgiveness, attention, a smile, anything she was prepared to give him. He sent her flowers, daffodils laced with gypsy grass, a pot of hyacinth, and one single red rose.

He would not let her be. Bill Robinson knew he had made a mistake in March. The result, Jenny's repudiation of him had made him doubly aware of how much he loved her, wanted her, must have her, but he had that night gone about it the wrong way, he knew that now.

So he changed his tactics. He did not stop to think about Jenny's reaction to his advances, nor did he consider for a minute letting go. It did not occur to him that she might not eventually give in. That was how he put it to himself – she must be made to 'give in', surrender. Her love, or lack of it for himself, did not appear to concern him. She would love him in the end, they always did.

'Go out wi' t'lad, Jenny,' Charlie said plaintively, sorry for Bill. 'That's all 'e wants, fer yer to give 'im a chance.'

'A chance for what, Charlie?'

'I dunno, but there'd be no harm in goin' t'pictures wi' 'im would there?'

'Charlie, will you let me alone! What with you an' Kate, I don't know whether to go mad or emigrate.'

But she smiled. Despite herself she was flattered. What woman would not be. A handsome, personable, well-set up young man who adored her, whose amusing tricks and love-lorn eyes were meant to soften her heart in his favour, and quite often did. But only in the way one would feel affectionate amusement for the antics of a pet, or the showing off of a precocious child.

She had not been out with him since March. She had been content in the life she led, knowing in her heart that there would never be again for her, what she had had with Nils. That kind of rapturous love came only once in a lifetime, and sometimes never. There could never again be that joyousness she had once known. Though the years had gone by and Nils had become a sweet memory, that memory still had the power to move her to tears in the loneliness of her bed. It could make her smile as she lived again the laughter; it filled her body with a passionate aching longing, and in the darkness it seemed that his hands touched her, his mouth kissed her lips, and she would wake with tears on her cheeks. Those lovely days, like the delicate tracery of the finest lace, lay over her life, holding her with the tenderest bonds to the past. She had never seen her child. Her mind had gone spinning into the shadows before her heart could ask to look upon her baby's face, and often, as she wandered back into her dreams, when she was alone, she would imagine how her and Nils' daughter would have been. In fantasy she held the warm, soft flesh of her child and traced the roundness of the tiny face; the rosebud of her mouth and looked with maternal love into the eyes which would be the same colour as Nils'.

She admitted to herself that she wanted a child. She longed for a child of her own. Though she was at peace, fulfilled in her work, happy to bask in the protective love with which Waggy surrounded her, she had an empty space within her which could only be filled by the warmth of a child's love. Children.

And so she came back to Bill Robinson. The answer to her secret yearning.

For three months Jenny Fowler swung like the pendulum of the Grandmother clock which stood in the hall of Waggy's house. For three months, as Bill played out the charade in which even he believed, that of a decent young chap, self-sacrificing, modest, kind, perfect husband material, Jenny viewed the future and reviewed the past, almost as though she compared one with the other. Which in a way she did. Though she knew Nils was gone forever, and with him her love, the days ahead spun out like the markers in a race. Who would be the winner?

'A penny for 'em, our kid,' Kate said to Jenny.

They were sitting dreaming, one on each side of the glowing, embered fire, each with a child upon her lap. The rain hissed and spat against the window pane, and though it was midsummer the high, whining note of the wind fluted down the chimney, the draught moving the tiny, flower-like flames of the fire. The baby, as he was still called though he was eighteen months old, moved in his sleep and made soft plopping sounds with his pale pink lips as if he still nuzzled Kate's full breast, though she had weaned him, reluctantly three months ago. His mother held him close, touching the pale brown hair on his head with a gentle finger tip.

Charlie and Frankie, with the eternal optimism of the sport loving male, had gone to Sefton Park to watch the cricket, though the rain poured and the wind howled, and the clouds swept like a herd of racing horses across the sky.

'It'll clear up, chuck,' Charlie said cheerfully, winking at Frankie, as he kissed his wife goodbye.

Jenny's cheek rested pensively on the head of the little girl, and she stared into the fire, a frown creasing the fine skin of her forehead. She chewed her lower lip, and her eyes were clouded as though a mist obscured them.

The cat stretched on the rug between them and yawned delicately, her pretty pointed ears twitching in the heat.

Kate's words fell softly on Jenny's ears and she looked up, startled, then she smiled.

'They're worth more than a penny, our Kate.'

'Go on then, don't keep me in suspenders.'

Jenny sighed deeply.

'It's Bill.'

'I thought it might be.'

'He's asked me to marry him.'

'And are you going to?' Kate held her breath.

'I said I wouldn't.' She let it out.

'What d'yer want me to say then our Jenny. If you've made yer mind up, there's nowt I can do that will alter it, is there?'

The last word had a slight inflection to it, questioning.

'No, I suppose not,' Jenny answered slowly.

'What's yer problem then, love?'

272

'No problem, not really.'

Kate shifted restlessly, and the baby murmured again, this time as though irritated by his mother's fidgets.

'Come on love, this is me, Kate. There's nowt you an' I 'aven't shared, all our lives. We don't live in t'same 'ouse any more, but I still know yer better than most. That's not an end to it, is it?'

'No.'

Kate's face was soft and compassion shone in her eyes. She leaned across the fireplace, taking Jenny's hand in hers. Jenny turned to look at her, and a tear slid across her cheek.

'Nay love, there's nowt to cry about. A chap's asked yer to marry 'im. Where's the tears in that? 'E loves yer, does Bill. 'E's only bin 'ere a time or two, but it shines from 'im, whenever he looks at yer. Don't yer like 'im?'

'Yes well, I suppose so . . .'

'But not enough to marry 'im.'

'I don't know . . .'

Kate's face was serious, troubled, and it was apparent she was about to say something which might not find favour with Jenny, but Kate liked to have everything on the table, so to speak, and if there were words to be spoken which might clear the air, or to help straighten out a problem, she would say them.

'I 'ope I can say this, without upsettin' yer,' she said. 'I know 'ow yer felt . . . how much yer cared about . . . but . . . well it's been a long time.' She looked down at her sleeping son, collecting her thoughts.

Without raising her eyes, she continued, 'It's the other one, isn't it . . . the Norwegian chap?'

Jenny's heart quivered with a sharp pain, and her eyes closed for a second as the picture of a smiling golden-haired man imprinted itself against her eyelids.

'The Norwegian chap.'

He dwelt in a corner of her soul, carefully locked away from curious eyes, not even spoken about now.

The hurt slashed her.

'The Norwegian chap'. That was all he was to Kate.

Turning her head Jenny looked into the fire.

'He's still here, Kate,' she touched her breast 'and he always will be, no one will ever take his place. What we had will never come to me again, never.'

She turned and smiled at her sister, the tears gone, dried on her face, but the sorrow shadowed her eyes.

'But that doesn't mean I can never love anyone else, does it Kate? In a different way. I like Bill, but I don't know whether I could . . . love him. We have a good time together, but I'm not . . . I'll have to think about it.' She paused. 'Bill's . . . good fun, kind.' For a second a shiver touched her, and the hair on the back of her neck rose. A shiver of a memory, a thought; something to do with the way Bill looked at her, stirred a subconscious unease. She shook it off. Touching Kate's hand, whispering she said,

'We'll see, Kate. We'll see. It's just . . . well,' she hesitated, 'I want a child, babies like yours.' She ducked her head almost shyly, and Kate was reminded of the vulnerable young girl who had innocently given herself to a sailor.

Jenny stood up, lifting the sleepy child.

'I'll put her down for a nap, shall I?' she said, and carried her across the room.

Kate remained still for several minutes, listening to Jenny moving about upstairs.

'Dear God,' she prayed silently, 'don't let this chap hurt her. Let him be good to her. Let her find peace and the happiness I know with Charlie.'

She bowed her head over the soft breathing child and felt hope flow in her.

'This time,' she murmured. 'This time.'

So Jenny resumed her relationship with Bill. She allowed him to take her out.

He was patient and sweet and funny and he made no attempt to touch her. That would come later, he thought. Slowly, slowly, keeping a leisurely pace so as not to alarm her, he made himself into the perfect companion. As they alighted from a tram, or crossed the road, he might put a protective hand to her elbow, but it never lingered. His manners were pleasant, courteous, and the relaxed easygoing way he had put her at ease. He let her take her time in the development of their relationship. He knew he had been given a second chance and that something had been added. He didn't know what it was, but there was a change in Jenny. So he was cautious with her. Restrained. Some inner feeling made him hesitate to push onward, to take the next logical step in the sequence of courtship. Give her time, he said to himself, give her time.

It was in September that Waggy decided that they must have a party. His crumbling old face was creased into a beam that would have illuminated a Christmas tree, and he almost hopped from foot to foot, like a child planning a prank, as he told her. He had been out of the office several times that week, hauling his increasing weight down the stairs, murmuring of an errand or two to be done. Once Jenny found him poring over a large document; parchment with beautiful copperplate handwriting upon it, but he had hurriedly folded it away as she entered the office. He had been a trifle flustered but his eyes had twinkled and he was obviously not displeased. He had the air of one who has a secret and is dying to tell, but is not yet ready. He loved to be mysterious.

'What's it in aid of, then?'

'What?'

'The party, of course.'

'That'd be telling.' He winked and grinned and tapped his nose and she had laughed. He'd never change. He'd be like a big, overgrown lad till the day he died, with his secrets and his love of a good joke, particularly if it was a bit smutty. But he was the most lovable, generous, bighearted man she had known, and where she would have been without him, she didn't care to think.

'Come here,' she laughed. Putting her arms about him she hugged his ponderous bulk to her, kissing his cheek.

'What's that for?' he beamed, pretending to back away, but then his arms came up to encircle her. They clung together, moving about the room until they were almost waltzing.

They stopped, still touching; they gazed deeply, seriously into each other's face for a moment, saying nothing more, but their eyes spoke of their fondness, then laughing again, they whirled clumsily about, Waggy's flat feet stumbling in an effort to keep up with Jenny's.

'Eeh Waggy, I wish you were ten years younger, I'd marry you tomorrow.'

'Give over, yer daft 'apporth,' but he was pleased and touched. 'An' I'd 'ave yer an' all,' he said, then he collapsed, laughing, mopping his face exaggeratedly with his hankerchief.

Kate left her babies, though Frankie protested they needed no one, in the care of Elly's eldest girl, a quiet responsible young lady of nineteen, as different from her mother as meat from fish.

Though it was Saturday night, Waggy had insisted on closing both of the restaurants. A neat printed notice was placed in each window to the effect that 'Due to a family matter . . . closed for the day'. Jenny had been horrified and said so. Saturday at The Corn Dolly was the busiest night of the week and her cool business head had calculated what it could cost them. But Waggy had been adamant. It was a special occasion. He was celebrating an event that . . . well, he was saying nowt else, but she'd know soon enough.

They all came. It was like old times, Charlie thought, as he watched his wife, her arm draped across Lily's shoulder, a port and lemon in her hand. She was giggling as she used to years ago. She was sixteen again, and she and Lily fell about in paroxysms of laughter, swopping memories of their days together in the café.

'. . . An' wha' about that chap who ordered steak and kidney pudding an' you brought him golden sponge an' asked him if he wanted extra gravy . . .'

Shrieks of laughter as they collapsed against each other.

'. . . An' wha' about that day that posh lot from the town 'all in those daft 'ats came in an' we . . .'

Elly and Pat, quarrelling as usual, but with a mellow amiability which twenty years of marriage to one another had given them.

All the brothers, all with their wives, except Bobby who had never married, and Dr Clancy.

John Clancy, older, with grey in his hair and tired lines about his kindly eyes, with the pretty Scots lass who was now his wife. Their romance had started years ago, in the parlour of Kate's house at another party. Now they had a son and another on the way. They danced together in the drawing room of Waggy's house which had been cleared of all its furniture, their unborn child between them, and she smiled shyly at anyone who spoke to her, still somewhat in awe of this outspoken and ebullient family, so different from her own quiet spoken and dour folk.

They danced and sang, they ate and drank and the room became so hot and airless the front door was propped open to allow some of the fug to drift away into the cool September air.

A couple of constables on their beat slowed their footsteps at the gate, then made their way round to the back of the house. They disappeared for several minutes and when they left again, their eyes sparkled with good humour, and their ruddy north country faces were split from ear to ear in a grin that breathed the rum they had imbibed.

At the stroke of midnight as the revellers climbed to a loftier peak of inebriation, a strange sound was heard in the distant reaches of the garden. It was faint, ethereal as thistledown, and could scarcely be heard over the sound of the gramophone. Those who first heard it, stood as though turned to stone, and feathers of apprehension ran up the skin of their arms and lifted the hairs on their necks. The sound came closer and closer, and women edged nearer the protection of their men. All but one, Janet Clancy, and she had grown up with the noise of it in her ears. It seemed to waft, soft as air about the ceiling, coming from the very walls.

Suddenly, as the wailing rose like an approaching eldritch being, two hairy legs appeared, neatly stockinged and above swung the swirling blues and greens of the tartan which gave the plaid its name. John Clancy's eyes stood out like marbles on stalks and his cheeks blew red and swollen as his lips gripped the chanter of the pipes.

From wary caution and arm-gripping apprehension, the crowd became shrill with laughing relief and breath which had been held in with nervous expectation, exploded.

They danced the *Eightsome reel*, *The Gay Gordons* and *The Dashing White Sergeant* until John Clancy begged for mercy, but they wouldn't have it.

It was almost two o'clock and the doctor, sweat streaking the front of his frilled shirt, was firm. Just one more, just one, and then he must be allowed to waltz with his wife. '*Strip the Willow*' he shouted, and began to play. Waggy, his face like a fire engine, his shirt unbuttoned, and his tie under his ear, held Jenny's hand, pulling her from Bill's possessive grasp.

'Come on lass, last one,' he bellowed. 'This'll melt yer stays.' As he spoke his eyes were looking into hers and his love for her poured from them. He seemed to hesitate as she put her hand in his. A surprised expression twisted his features. Then, with a thump which shook the floorboards, he fell flat on his face.

Chapter Twenty-Nine

It was a lovely, mild autumn afternoon and the daisies and stray buttercups which sewed stitches of pale colour in the grass verges, stood to attention in the sunshine as though at the passing of an important personage.

There was no shortage of volunteers to bear the coffin. Charlie was one and Bobby, but the rest were strangers, images from Percival Wagstaffe's past before he knew the Fowlers. There had been no decision made, no instructions given. When the gleaming walnut box was taken from the hearse, it simply fell to the men nearest to lift it reverently to their shoulders. It seemed for a second that there might be some slight disagreement; the crowd of men was thick, but those not nimble enough merely fell back, then moved quietly into step behind the two women. Kate and Jenny walked arm in arm behind, two silently grieving figures in the black they had worn to his Mam's funeral, only nine months before. They were followed by a long, untidy river of people, which flowed gently along the gravel path to the church, as though haste might show disrespect. A light breeze flicked golden brown leaves from the branches of the trees. They fell in a drift of beauty, spreading a carpet for the mourners to step on, falling onto the coffin around the simple spray of flowers which lay in its centre. There was a card tucked behind the tapestry of lovely cream rosebuds. It said simply 'Jenny'.

The church was completely filled and the size of the crowd of sorrowing people amazed even Charlie who had been aware of the extent of Waggy's generosity. A patient, silent mass of men and women gathered in the churchyard, many so far from the site of the grave, not a word of the service was heard by them. From above the scene was like a large mosaic, fragmented groups of darkly clad men and women, linked together by row upon row of gravestones, set in a pattern of glowing autumn trees.

Waggy was laid beside his beloved mother. The minister intoned the words and for Jenny the moment became a blur. The faces, the trees, the church behind her, all faded into a mist of memories and

Waggy stood beside her. She heard his voice clearly as she lifted her head and tilted it, as though to listen.

'By God, girl, you'll 'ave nowt to thank me for, time I've finished with yer . . .'

'Yer've gorra 'ead on yer shoulders – use it . . .'

'. . . Course yer can do it, woman . . .'

Those far-off days, was it only six years ago? When she had struggled, not only to learn the mysteries of Waggy's business, but to start again a life shattered by grief and loss. It had seemed an almost impossible task for a girl brought up as she had been. A girl with the shyness of a doe, and the inclination to step down when confronted with unpleasantness. The first time she had encountered the hostile disdain with which many men treated a woman in business, she had been near to tears, near to giving up and retreating to the safety of what they considered her place in life; to putting back on the dainty cap and apron they deemed appropriate, but Waggy had shouted rudely, had told her to stand up to t'buggers and she had. Waggy had known that she could do it; had made her do it. This loving encouragement, so often hidden beneath words which seemed derisive and hurtful, had been the spur, along with her own determination, to keep her on the path towards her goal. She had started on that road with the idea of making a life for her child, but the gods had decreed otherwise and she had been made to go alone. But she had not been alone. Waggy had stood beside her, walked beside her, and he had given her back her life, her sanity, and filled her with a sense of her own esteem.

'Try it, yer scone 'ead, go on, see if yer can do it, but don't come cryin' to me if yer can't.'

'Tell old what's 'is name to take a running jump. You're the boss . . .'

And she had learned. Learned to be herself, to know that her judgment was sound, that her ideas were good, that though she was a woman, and young at that, she could do all that a man could do. She was intelligent. Waggy had shown her how to use her brain, her own good sense and she had known that the people with whom she worked respected her.

'That's it, kiddo . . . you can do it.' Waggy's voice spoke softly in her ear and in her heart she answered him. She could do it.

Kate was leaning forward, her arm still through Jenny's, and as she bent down, Jenny went with her. She grasped a handful of soil, still smelling of summer and Jenny did the same. Together the two women threw the handfuls of earth into the grave. The minister's voice was soft and serene, he was very old himself, and seemed immune to the thought of death.

'*Ashes to ashes, dust . . .*'

The crowds dispersed slowly. Those who had been at the edge of the cemetery made their way through the press of people, to stand for a moment beside the grave. They nodded kindly to the two young women, then made way for others.

Kate sobbed noisily and Charlie came to take her arm, drawing her away, his arm comfortingly about her shoulders.

For a moment Jenny stood completely alone. For the last time she heard Waggy's voice, bellowing good humour.

'Give over, do, our Jenny. Yer make a bloody mountain out of a molehill.'

Then Charlie looked over his shoulder and called her name and she turned her back on the grave and walked to where he and Kate waited for her.

The two grave diggers whistled cheerfully as the first spadeful of earth fell on the coffin.

A week ago they had filled the house with foot-stamping, hand-clapping music. Laughter had bugled in every corner. People had grouped in the hall and drawing room, and in pairs upon the staircase, gathered in the kitchen and had even erupted into the clear, cool September garden. In the midst of it all moved the man who had been the essence of life, the teller of jokes, the instigator of many a prank, and the giver of benevolence. Now he was gone and those who had laughed and sung and danced with him that night, sat in his chairs and mourned him.

In the kitchen, where only nine months before, Jenny had stood with Kate and dreamed of turning the forbidding grandeur of Waggy's house into a bright and comfy home for herself and the old man, she and Charlie gazed from the window onto the garden and the last fading glow of summer. Chrysanthemums stood in slowly nodding rows; yellow, white and bronze, and the roses, once a sea of shimmering colour, held up a solitary spot of red or pink here and there against the browning leaves.

The high wall was almost covered by an ivy, shining a pale milky green against the red of the brick. Rowan trees crowded against the boundary, their orange berries caught like flames in the sunlight. The lawn was a carpet of copper leaves, wet and shiny from the rain that had fallen the night before, and the beech trees waved delicate, almost naked branches to the pale sky. A clock ticked on the kitchen wall, and the crackle of flames from the fire made a pleasing background to the hiss of steam from the kettle. A young woman entered the kitchen, one of the waitresses from the café. All of his present team of girls were at Waggy's funeral. Though he had chased them, pinched their bums and called them every name he could lay his tongue to, they came to weep at his grave. In the final analysis, Waggy had fooled no one but himself. The girl held a teapot in her hand. She looked from Jenny to Charlie, then said hesitantly.

'Can I 'ave some 'ot water fer t'teapot please, Miss Fowler.'

Jenny turned, startled, her thoughts a mile away, dwelling on the happy months she had known in this house. For a second she scarcely seemed to know where she was, or who had spoken to her, then lifting her chin she moved towards the girl.

'Of course,' smiling. 'Pass me the pot, Nora.'

The girl stood respectfully, eyeing Charlie's back then, suddenly, as though she had been drawing her courage about her, she said, 'When will we be goin' back to work, Miss Fowler?'

There was a silence and in it Jenny felt, rather than heard, Charlie's sigh. She knew why he sighed. Her heart sank.

'I don't know yet, Nora. Mr Wagstaffe's solicitor is . . . will let us know. You see . . .' She handed the full teapot to the girl who stood, waiting.

'You see,' she continued '. . . with Mr Wagstaffe's death . . . circumstances have changed.' The girl did not understand. She knew that respect must be shown and until the deceased was disposed of, the café must remain closed, but surely now . . .

Jenny's voice cracked slightly as she said, 'We'll let you know Nora, and the others.'

'Righto Miss Fowler.' The girl took the teapot, 'Thank you.' As she walked towards the door she hesitated, then turned slightly, 'Only . . .'

'Yes, Nora.'

'Well, it's been a week now . . . and some of us, well, we're a bit short like, with no wages . . .'

'I'm sorry Nora, but you see the solicitor . . . as soon as . . . Mr Walker and I . . . We will see to it right away and let you know.'

After the girl had gone Charlie said, 'Yer know what'll happen, don't yer, our Jenny.'

'Yes.' She sighed deeply.

'It's all over!'

'I know.'

'Who's 'is next of kin?' Charlie spoke almost indifferently. He knew it made no difference to him.

'I've no idea, Charlie. I think . . . I seem to remember him saying his mother had a cousin.'

'What we gonna do, Jenny?'

'I don't know, Charlie, honest. I suppose the solicitors . . .' It was quiet again, then Charlie spoke harshly.

'Where am I gonna gerrer a job now, and me with a wife an' three kids. I should never 'ave left the sea.' His shoulders sagged beneath the good black stuff of his jacket. His hands gripped the sink tightly, the knuckles gleaming white in the dim light of the darkened kitchen. His face was still turned to the window and as if in ridicule, a blackbird hopped onto the path and began to sing. Its cheerfulness mocked them.

Jenny's face was pale and her eyes were sombre. She sat down in the chair before the fire and stared into its depths. Her heart was heavy. The old man had gone. He had given so much, to her and to Charlie, and now it seemed they grieved not for him, but for what his death would do to them. Charlie could think of nothing but his job and who could blame him? As he said, he had a wife and three young children. He had been well paid. For over two years he had lived in relative luxury, but like Kate, he had had no thought for the future. It would go on forever this good fortune, or so they thought. His wages had been spent every week. On clothes for Kate and the children, on things for the house. They had spent as they lived, eagerly, generously, and with no concern for the rainy day which might come.

And here it was.

Kate walked briskly into the kitchen. Already the sadness of the funeral was passing from her. A realist, Kate did not dwell on the past. She had been fond of Waggy and deeply grateful for what he had done for her family, for Jenny and Charlie but he was gone now, and life must go on. Not for a moment had it occurred to her that with Waggy's passing, so had the jobs of both Jenny and Charlie.

'Come on, you two. It's no good moping in t'dark. Yer know Waggy wouldn't 'ave wanted it.' Jenny knew it was true. If he was here, that's just what he would have said. The incongruity of the thought amused her and she smiled. Kate saw the smile and was relieved. Somewhere in the back of her mind had always lurked a tiny pool of fear and for the rest of her life she would never quite be able to dispel the dreadful feeling that some tragedy, some sorrow might send their Jenny back into the void. It would always haunt the edges of her consciousness. She took Charlie's hand.

'Come on, love, Bobby's gotta bottle of whisky. It's outa Waggy's

282

cabinet. Is that all right Jenny?' In Kate's head, the house and all its contents now belonged to her sister, and it was polite to wait to be asked. Still their Jenny wouldn't mind, and neither would Waggy.

Charlie and Jenny exchanged a look of understanding over Kate's head. It said, 'Let her have another couple of days, it does no harm' but the blow, when it fell, and the escalating consequence nearly finished her.

'He left a will, Miss Fowler, but it was not signed.'

'Not signed.' Jenny looked uncomprehendingly at the solicitor, then at Charlie, who cleared his throat awkwardly. Charlie was out of his depth in the dim and almost holy atmosphere of the solicitor's office. The elderly gentleman was courteous, but the words he spoke and the way in which he said them, were not of Charlie's world and he was dismayed. He looked at Jenny, almost shrugging, and his goodnatured face was awash with embarrassment.

The solicitor, Mr Worthington, was speaking.

'Mr Wagstaffe and I have been in consultation for many months now. He wanted his will to be set out in a certain way . . . I think he was afraid that it might be . . . contested . . . so he wanted it drawn up . . . he has a cousin . . . no . . . a second cousin who would inherit . . .'

'Why wasn't it signed, Mr Worthington?' Jenny's voice was soft but firm.

'It would have been, had he lived two more days. He was to have come into my office last Monday.'

'I see.'

'I don't think you do, Miss Fowler. If the will had been signed . . . you would have been sole beneficiary.'

The silence was complete.

Charlie broke it and his voice was strangled in his throat. 'Beneficiary,' he said, as though the word was foreign to him and he wished the solicitor to translate it into English.

'Yes, Mr Walker. Your sister-in-law would have inherited everything that Mr Wagstaffe owned. Everything.'

'And now . . .'

'Now it will . . .' Mr Worthington checked the paper in front of him '. . . now it will all be sold, everything, and the proceeds will go to his next of kin. That is what he wishes. The businesses are of no interest to him. He lives in Brighton,' as though that explained everything.

The silence struck again and Mr Worthington cleared his throat.

At last Charlie spoke.

'Who . . . what about our jobs . . . the girls . . .'

'I'm sorry, Mr Walker.'

Mr Worthington lifted his hands expressively as though to say he understood, but was powerless to help.

Jenny's voice was so low, it could scarcely be heard.

'Could we . . . my brother-in-law . . . and I . . . could we buy it?'

Charlie gasped and his mouth fell open. He turned to stare at Jenny as though she had gone mad. The solicitor was forgotten as amazement brought back the confidence which had deserted him as he entered the room.

'What the 'ell are you talking about, our Jenny?' He put out a hand to her in bewilderment. 'Where the 'ell are we to get the cash for . . .'

Jenny ignored him.

'What is the asking price, Mr Worthington?'

The solicitor named a sum of money and Jenny's body seemed to sag in the chair, as though it would slip off and collapse onto the carpet.

'. . . A loan . . . ?' she managed to gasp.

'Have you collateral, Miss Fowler?'

Jenny shook her head, anguish jerking the muscles of her face.

The solicitor looked at her kindly. His face was full of admiration, and his voice was soft.

'It is you who have made the restaurant what it is today. Mr Wagstaffe told me so repeatedly and believe me, if there was something I could do, I would gladly do it. I know you are a good businessman,' he smiled at his own joke, 'but unless you have something which can be put against a loan . . . ?'

He turned suddenly to Charlie, hopefully.

'Do you own the house in which you live, Mr Walker?'

Grey-faced, Charlie answered, 'I own nowt, Mr Worthington, not even a job.'

Mr Worthington stared down at his desk. There was nothing more to say.

Jenny stood up.

'Well then . . .' she said.

She moved towards the door and Charlie followed her. Turning at the door she smiled, her eyes dead, her teeth gleaming between her pink lips.

'We won't take up any more of your time, Mr Worthington.'

'I wish I could . . .'

'I know, you have been most kind.'

284

Jenny ran down the steps from the solicitor's office and out into the sunshine of Victoria Street. Charlie followed.

They sat, the three of them, round the dying fire. It was almost dark and the children had been put to bed. Three pairs of eyes stared at the tiny glowing heart of the flickering embers, hypnotised, dazed by the enormity of what had happened. Their whole world had collapsed, falling about their ears with the suddenness of a house of cards in a high wind. There seemed nothing left to say. Charlie got up to put more coal on the fire, but Kate stopped him. He looked at her, not understanding. She shook her head, holding his arm as he reached for the coal tongs.

'What's up lass?' he said quietly.

'Don't put any more on, Charlie.'

'It's goin' cold, chuck.'

'Don't love, we'll be goin' to bed soon.'

At last he realised what she was saying. Angrily he shook off her hand.

'Give over, woman. I'm 'avin' a bit a coal on me own fire when I want to.'

Defiantly he picked up the coal scuttle and with a look like that of a child who is determined to best his mother he threw on half a dozen large pieces of coal. The fire caught and the blaze crept cheerfully up the chimney. The flames danced, flickering across the faces of the man and his wife, emphasising the misery and despair which was there. Jenny watched them, and her heart felt like a stone in the middle of her chest.

Charlie was afraid. There were nearly two million unemployed in the country and the worst hit was the industrial north. Where was he to find a job? How was he to pay the rent of this place on twenty-nine shillings a week which was all the dole money he would get. He and Jenny had been to sign on that day, joining the queue which stretched from one end of Leece Street to the other, but there were no jobs to be had. Jenny had been prepared to work again as a waitress, anything, but there was nothing. No one wanted a waitress, or a highly qualified and competent secretary. For every job which now fell vacant in Liverpool there were seventeen applicants.

The boom had ended in October 1929 when the whole of Wall Street stockmarket collapsed. Hundreds and thousands of Americans had been ruined and the ripples, ever increasing, had washed ashore on the beaches of Great Britain. Depression in trade was world wide. Industrial production had slumped; the demand for raw materials fell away and every kind of national economy was involved.

'I'll get summat, chuck,' Charlie said desperately. 'It's early days yet. It's only bin a couple a weeks.' He turned to Kate and took her hand. They seemed impervious to Jenny's presence, as though she were not there, and with all her heart she wished it was true.

'We'll be all right, chuck.'

Kate began to cry.

Charlie held her in his arms and kissed her cheek.

Jenny stood up and left the room, walking slowly up the stairs to her bedroom, the bedroom which had been Frankie's. The walls were still covered by pictures of his idols, Dixie Dean and Ted Sager, and his books were placed neatly on the dressing table. Jenny's cases were stacked against the wall and a cardboard box, full of the few pretty things she had bought for her bedroom at Waggy's was pressed behind the door so that it would barely open.

There was no room to put them in the tiny room. There was nowhere to put anything. Frankie was sleeping 'top and tail' with Dorry. His high piping boy's voice had protested vigorously at the indignity of sleeping with his sister, and Kate, pushed to the edge of tolerance, had smacked his head. He had cried, brokenheartedly, clasped to his Mam's breast, and so had Kate when she had left him. 'Tears, all tears, and where would it all end,' she had demanded to know. No one had the answer.

Jenny sat on the edge of the bed and looked sadly into the days to come. The thoughts which had knocked timidly on the door of her consciousness, began to hammer more determinedly. She tried to shut her ears, to close out the ideas which grew there, but it was no use.

Lying back in the darkness, she allowed herself the relief of tears, sorrowing tears, tears of farewell for a golden-haired, bright eyed man who had walked beside her for seven years. Then, her face still and calm in the dark night, she opened the door of her mind and ushered in the thoughts of what she must do.

Chapter Thirty

They were married in January 1931. Bill wouldn't wait any longer. He was just twenty-five, three years short of his target for marriage.

The church was so empty the echoes rose into the high rafters as the parson intoned the wedding service and their quiet responses whispered like floating leaves to the back of the old building, dissipating amongst the cobwebs which festooned the dark corners.

The parson's gaze faltered over the congregation. A man and a woman who sat in the front pew. They were ill at ease in the vast, open space of the body of the church, and huddled shoulder to shoulder, as if for comfort. The man held the woman's hand protectively. They were obviously husband and wife, with that look of togetherness which falls over a happy union. The man had given the bride away.

They stood to sing. *O Perfect Love* wafted gently upwards. Four voices, thin, reedy, nervous, reinforced by the minister's robust baritone. – Oh God, thought the woman in the pew, this was a mistake, and tried to put a bit of strength into her slightly off-key rendition, but it did no good. The man beside her glanced at her, his eyebrows raised.

The parson was asking the handsome groom whether he was willing to take the lovely woman who stood beside him for his lawful wedded wife, to which the groom replied fervently, that he was. The bride was willing too, she said, though her eyes looked strangely haunted, and the rose in her cheeks had faded to pearl. They kissed, the bride lifting her soft mouth to the groom's eager lips. They stood, unsure of what they should do next and the smiling minister indicated with his hand, that they might proceed towards the vestry to sign the register.

Afterwards they walked slowly up the aisle, the groom proud, his bride's hand in the crook of his arm. Her gaze looked directly in front of her. It turned neither to left nor right. The couple who had

witnessed the ceremony followed, their faces reflecting the unusual blankness of the bride's eyes.

As they stepped out of the dark, arched porch into the cold
wintry sunshine, a robin, perched on a headstone nearby, hopped
swiftly down almost to the feet of the new bride, head cocked,
unafraid, cheeky eye searching for crumbs.

The bride smiled for the first time, her golden brown eyes
relieved at the moment's merriment. The bridegroom turned to
draw the attention of the second couple and for an instant the four
were encircled by a shared pleasure. The two men shook hands,
smiling to hide masculine embarrassment, and the women held
each other, and kissed. Then each man kissed each woman and the
rituals were complete.

One pair behind the other, they began to move along the path
between the grey, pitted headstones; angels and cherubs, plain
crosses and ornate monuments slumbering peacefully in the crisp,
diamond-sharp air. Snowdrops were massed in a multitude of
white beauty, lancing the spiky winter grass. The gravel crunched
beneath their feet as they moved in step towards the gate where a
small crowd gathered.

Kate and Charlie smiled at each other, and simultaneously into
their separate minds came the same thought.

At last it was done. Their Jenny was wed, and yet, though it was
a day for which, albeit for different reasons, they had both waited,
there seemed no joy in it. The sun shone; the day was fine and glad
with that lovely snap to it which sometimes comes in the middle of
winter. The bride was beautiful, like a slim and delicate lily of the
valley, pale, breathtaking in her fragile loveliness. The groom was
manly, so obviously doting on his new wife, handsome, his eyes
bright and merry, so what was it that put a feather of disquiet in the
soul of Kate Walker? For eight years nearly, she had prayed to
some indefinable God to look kindly over her young sister. Always, for as long as she could remember, Charlie had been at her
own side, hovering nearby waiting, and the strength of his devotion had given her an anchor to hold her steady. He was like . . .
like one of those magnificent Shire horses; strong, dependable,
trustworthy, and always, always just an arm's length away
whenever his quiet endurance was needed. He was the rock on
which she had built her life.

And she wanted the same for Jenny. Innocent, vulnerable Jenny,
whose life had shattered and whose heart had broken. If only, Kate
had prayed, Jenny could find a man like Charlie. To watch over
her, keep her from harm, give her a home, warmth, love, compan-

ionship and the children she longed for. Now she had all of this, now she had a man of her own, she was settled. Her future was secure, even sunny, for Bill had a wonderful job and was well thought of in the bank.

Then why did she feel uneasy? Perhaps it was their Jenny, she was quiet . . . almost withdrawn, as if she wasn't all there. As though some part of her was somewhere else. Kate's hand pressed Charlie's, and he turned to look at her as they stepped along the path. Kate's eyes burned into his. She knew him well, this man of hers, and what she felt, showed in the pale grey depths of his eyes.

The crowd at the gate clapped with all the enthusiasm which seems to take over at the wedding of perfect strangers. A photographer stepped from behind a large lady, imploring her to clear a space in front of the camera and the two couples posed awkwardly.

An onlooker might have been excused for thinking that not a care or worry had ever troubled the lives of this handsome quartet, and of one it would have been true, but not of the other three. On closer scrutiny, the deepening grooves at each side of Charlie's smiling mouth would have become apparent and the dusting of grey in the brown at his temples. Wonder might have been shown at the gash of pure white which cut Kate's halo of hair, and she so young, and at the tension which tightened her lips. Always it stood between them now, the spectre of the poverty which stalked them relentlessly. The sweet content had gone, the ironic twist of fate which could casually flick a life from one road to another, was a reality to them. They lived with their defeat as did millions of others, their pride in themselves and in their children eroded by the ignominy of being on the dole. There was a look about them. It was in the downcast eyes and droop of Kate's mouth, and the almost guilty cast of Charlie's once cheerful face.

But strangely, the years which had gone by since she had left her father's home had brushed lightly, if at all, on Jenny. She might have been frozen in time, her girlish loveliness almost as it was then. She was as slim as she had been at seventeen, and though twenty-five, her face might have been that of a young girl. She had a hesitancy about her, a childlike caution, as though she were cast amongst adults in a world which she did not quite understand. Gone it seemed, was the confidence that had given her the purpose to move in a world of business; to speak and act with the positive sureness that comes with experience. Gone was the decisive manner of one who must take an action that affects the lives of others.

Jenny and Bill stopped under the porch of the lychgate and at the instigation of the photographer, Bill bent his head, lifting Jenny's chin with his forefinger, and they exchanged their second kiss as man and wife. The proprietary and careless fashion of Bill's embrace brought the colour flooding to Jenny's face and she ducked her head in embarrassment. The pretty scene fetched a shout from a black faced man who drove a coalcart pulled by a huge horse; his wide grin removing any offence his words might give.

'Go to it, mate, an' I'm next.'

Several ladies with shopping baskets stopped to smile and remark on the bride's outfit and from the back of the small group an old lady dressed in the fashion of thirty years ago, edged her way forward leading a small dog of indeterminate breed, on a bright red leash. She smiled genially when she saw Jenny and spoke in a soft Irish brogue to the dog.

'Will yer look at the sweet colleen, Patsy. Isn't she as fair as the hills of Killarney!'

Her eyes bright, she produced a packet from her handbag and opening it, threw its contents over Jenny and Bill. As the delicate scraps of confetti drifted like snowflakes about their heads, the woman turned, clucked to the dog and ambled away.

'Eeh, yer in luck, queen,' shouted a merry voice from the crowd. 'That were daft Molly what chucked that confetti. She brings good fortune to a marriage, she does.'

The heart of the bride, frozen fast in her breast, moved in its casing of ice, and a tiny thread of hope filtered her numb brain.

'Please God, let it be so. Let me learn to love this man.' Her lovely face, serene as a madonna's, trembled in a faint smile, but her eyes remained clouded.

Bill grinned from ear to ear, placing his brown trilby, which he had carried from the church, on the back of the dark tumble of his hair. He was well pleased with the omen of good luck which had been given to them, and he hugged his bride of twenty minutes to his side. He glanced down at her, then back at the crowd, his attention centred on himself, the interest and admiration of the circle of well wishers, giving him a grand sense of his own importance. It was a wonderful feeling he enjoyed; that of having achieved all he had set out to do. She was his now. Jenny belonged to him, and the envy and approval he saw mirrored in the eyes of other men, somehow rebounded on him, for they were recognising the worth of his possession. He did not observe his wife's self-containment, nor would he have been unduly concerned had he done so, for his self-indulgent conceit would have put it down to pre-marital nerves. What woman isn't a trifle timid when she is about to go to her husband's bed for the first time?

Jenny held herself together with tight control. A tiny tremor ran through her and for an instant she strained away from her husband's encircling arm, but it was a strong, firm, demanding arm and would not let her go.

'Just one more,' shouted the harassed photographer, hemmed in by the goodhumoured gathering, 'An' will the bride smile this time. Come on dear, cheer up. It's a wedding not a funeral.'

Bill laughed, enormously amused, but the soul of Jenny, Jenny Robinson, died a little. Kate watched her, and wondered, on this day of days, this happy occasion for which she had longed, why should she feel so bloody miserable.

It had been a bitter disappointment to Bill Robinson when he discovered on the first day he took his 'fiancée' to meet his parents, that his mother didn't like Jenny. He was amazed when she was distantly polite, no more. It was beyond his understanding that she did not immediately fall beneath Jenny's spell, as he had done, though it gratified his ego to see his brother Douglas, two years younger than himself, and even his father, eyeing the beauty of his beloved with obvious appreciation. The two men made Jenny cautiously welcome, but Mrs Robinson ruled her menfolk with a well hidden rod of iron, and their attitude depended upon hers. She fielded all Bill's efforts to soften her position, and refused to reveal why she acted as she did. Or even to acknowledge she acted in any way other than normal.

Bill was mystified. He did not see the situation with his mother's eyes, however, and the ways of a woman where her sons are involved, are curious indeed. Ellen Robinson had borne him, raised him, loved and scolded him, nursed and spoilt him and for the past twenty five years, though he had dallied with many girls, he had been hers. Just hers. She had watched complacently the efforts of the young ladies he had brought home as they fell over themselves in an attempt to shine for him, to win his approval, to show him – and her – what unspoilt, sweet-natured good-humoured, hardworking wives they would make, and she had smiled. His mother adored his good looks, proud that she and Mr Robinson, both homely, had produced such a handsome offspring – they didn't do as well with their Douglas – and his cleverness was something about which she constantly, but modestly boasted at the Church Women's Guild.

She resolutely refused to believe that he was going to marry this one.

'She's only been brought up in a fish an' chip shop, Albert,' she fretted to her husband as he hid behind the *Echo*. 'It's not as if she's had the education our Bill's had, either. Oh I know she's got this certificate thing an' no doubt she's a head on her shoulders to run that business, but that's not like a School Certificate or Matriculation. I mean, she hasn't even got a job. On the dole,' she sniffed. 'I think our Bill's just fallen for that pretty face of hers, if you ask me.' She threaded her needle with a length of embroidery silk, squinting into the light as she did so, '. . . an' I think he'll come to his senses before long.' Hopefully she glanced at Albert as if seeking reassurance. 'She knows when she's on to a good thing. Not 'alf she doesn't. I mean, look at our Bill. Good job, nice looking.' She lifted her head proudly. 'He's a real good catch is our Bill, an' what's she? I ask you? Comes from Scotland Road or as near as makes no difference. I said to Mrs Merryweather last week, I said, he's too young, I said . . .'

But it did no good. Bill continued to bring Jenny for Sunday tea. Jenny did her best, but she was shy and awkward in a situation which was new to her. She wanted to make a success of her coming marriage; she wanted Bill's family to like and accept her, but she knew there was something lacking in her own approach to the Robinson family, and she knew why it was. She did not feel for Bill what a woman who is about to marry should feel for the man of her choice, and she realised that, though it might be only an instinctive maternal intuition that put Mrs Robinson on the defensive, Bill's mother sensed it. Jenny tried to do all, and be all, the things which a woman must do and be, to impress the parents of her intended, but at the same time, she began to feel a sense of resentment against this woman who really meant nothing to her and who rebuffed all her attempts to make a friend of her. Ellen Robinson's manner implied, as the weeks went by, that it was not *she* who was being difficult.

'She's jealous, our Jenny,' said Kate. 'You're the first serious lass in Bill's life. A threat to her, I suppose, though I don't know why. She's gorra let go some time, but yer know what Mams are like about their sons. 'Alf in love with 'em, some of 'em. Gawd, I 'ope I'm not like that about our Frankie when the time comes. I'll more than likely be glad to see the back of 'im.'

She eyed her seven year old offspring fondly and her look belied her words.

And so it came about that when the wedding day dawned, Mr

and Mrs Robinson and their Douglas, on Mrs Robinson's command, did not attend their son's nuptials.

On that last morning, the fields at the back of Kate's house were veneered with white; hung about with a curtain of mist through which a late star glimmered. Jenny leaned her head against the window frame and her flesh prickled, trembling in the cold. Frost glazed the window and she breathed on it, rubbing it absently with a clenched fist to clear a spot through which she could see. It was a lovely morning, not yet fully light, and the sky was pearly in the dawn. The trees were blurred in a formless frieze against the horizon, and as she looked, a small scrawny object ran from them, skittering across the pale field towards the fence. It was a brown rabbit. It stopped and lifted its head, still, silent, as if sensing danger, then flashed under the fence and was gone.

Free.

Jenny had known, though she had not acknowledged it, from the moment she had looked upon Waggy's dead face, that she was trapped in the fate which was mapped out for her. It had been inevitable. She had struggled. She had haunted the labour exchange, willing to take any employment which might be offered to her. She had gone each day with a hundred others to the library, queueing patiently for her turn to scan the newspapers for jobs advertised. She had walked the streets of the city, going from shop to shop, café to café, even into the offices of solicitors and accountants asking the same question, but it had always been the same answer.

'Sorry chuck, there's nowt at the moment.'

'I'm sorry, Miss, but we have no jobs just now.'

Bill had lurked, like some enduring ghost at the edge of her vision, as though trying to catch her eye. She felt each time they were together, that he was waiting, waiting; the question on his lips forming inexorably into, *'Are you ready yet?'*

She had been trapped. Kate and Charlie said nothing but their eyes, their increasingly haunted expression, spoke for them. They existed on the meagre pittance allowed them from the dole, and there were rumours that even that was to be subject to a means test. The three of them moved uneasily about the small house, trying constantly to avoid colliding with each other or one of the three children. Nerves were strained, stretched to breaking point, and tears were shed in the privacy of bedrooms.

One night, after listening to Charlie and Kate quarrelling, and trying to do so quietly, in the dark of the night, Jenny knew that the time had come. She could fight no longer. Bill offered them a way

293

out. Marriage to him meant security, not just for her, but to a certain degree for Kate, the children, and though he would not know of it, for Charlie. She would be able to repay Kate for all that had been done for her in the past, and Kate and Charlie would have their home once more. They would have the room to row in privacy, if they so wished and to comfort each other in any way they chose without fear of interruption. It was the only answer. For all of them.

A tear ran, as silently as the rabbit, across Jenny's cheek. It splashed on to the windowsill and another formed. The scene of wood and field ran together, wavering, blurring as though under water, and the years that had gone, the years of pain, of love, stood for a moment, in the woman's heart. How it might have been, she breathed, making no sound as she wept. This day, this day, how it might have been. A tall man, his eyes brilliant, filled with an aching tenderness smiled at her, and she clutched the curtain for support.

Nils, Nils, my love.

Chapter Thirty-One

It was only one hour in each twenty-four, she told herself, only one hour and sometimes not even that, and surely the outcome would be worth it. If what he did to her; if what she was forced to undergo night after night brought about the result she longed for, then she must find the strength to endure it, though her flesh shrank and her inner sense of her own self died a little at each meeting.

Bill was proud of his lovely wife. He wore her like a medal, flaunting her wherever they went like a boy who has won an award. He was pleased with his continuous access to her body, and if Jenny seemed less enthusiastic than he in their lovemaking, he did not take it amiss for he belonged to the era which believed that women were made for the pleasure of man and to be otherwise would be indelicate. A woman who came a virgin to her husband, a woman as innocent and inexperienced as was his Jenny should be reticent, submissive to her husband's wishes, and providing she made no demur to his nightly onslaughts upon her white flesh, he was, in those first weeks, perfectly content.

Jenny learned to lie apart from the moving figures on the bed. She watched dispassionately as the man removed the woman's nightdress. He liked to leave the light on. It was as though he could not get enough of the sight of her slim white body. For months, years, he had longed for it above all else and now it was his, his alone. He would slowly draw back the bedclothes, letting her lie quietly for ten or fifteen minutes whilst he anticipated the coming moments. His hand would slide inside the bodice of her nightgown, caressing her breast. He would uncover it lingeringly; fasten his avid lips upon her nipple, suckling like an infant, then regretfully leave, modestly covering that part where he had been. He would step back to consider which portion of her he would savour next and with a rapt expression, almost as though he were alone, he would draw up her nightdress to reveal, inch by inch, the long slim stems of her legs, her thighs and the dark 'V' of her pubic hair.

Only when he had fulfilled a part of himself that gloated over her delicate loveliness; that lusted to take what was his, did he remove

295

his own clothes. When he was naked, he would proceed with the second part of the ceremony, the ritualistic procedure which never varied.

He began to hurt her. He was rough, chanting words which were coarse as his lust grew and he attempted to stir her from the passive submission he had at first insisted upon. It was not enough for him now that she lay under him, available, acquiescent. He wanted more but what it was eluded him and his body punished hers for withholding it. Like a pile driver hammering home a beam into the soft bed of a river, he pounded upon her. His eyes would glaze as he came to climax and his voice would spiral to the ceiling in his subjugation of the being into whom he spilled his seed.

It was for this that Jenny waited. Her arms clasped him. Her hips moved with his, and her womb waited, open, ready, longing for the child.

They were married in January and by the end of February she knew she was pregnant. That day, before she told him, before she told Kate, she held the knowledge to herself as tenderly as though it was the child. She treasured it in her heart. No one knew but herself and John Clancy. For a few precious hours she hoarded it alone, exulting in the awareness that within her grew the fulfilment of the last dream she had. With Nils and the death of her daughter had gone the bright golden hope that a woman in love cherishes. She had married Bill for security and for a child and for nothing else and already she knew that Bill sensed her apathy towards him, and his failure to make her love him. He did not admit it, not even to himself. That would throw doubts on his own prowess, as a man and as a lover, but it was in his eyes as they fastened on her shrinking flesh.

It was March. Jenny walked from the clinic where she had just seen Dr Clancy and as she turned the corner into Walton Road, the wind caught her, tugging her along the pavement, whipping her hair about her head like a flag. She clutched her beret to her head with one hand, holding her coat about her with the other, and her face creased into a smile. Her eyes were luminous with love and hope and she felt she wanted to run with the wind. Her feet almost skipped, like a small girl playing hopscotch but she remembered John Clancy's words, and soberly she restrained herself. She slowed her steps to a sedate walk and wrapped her arms protectively about her stomach. Nothing, nothing must harm this child.

'Sit down, Jenny,' he had said as she finished dressing after he had examined her. He fiddled with his pen, jotting a note or two upon his pad as he sought for words to put her mind at ease. He knew more than anyone, except Kate, how much she wanted this child and how dreadfully she feared a repetition of what had happened to her first baby.

'For every thousand babies born in this country at the present moment, eighteen die. Eight years ago your daughter was one of them.' He took her hand as she flinched. 'I'm sorry, Jenny, but I wanted to shock you a little to make you realise that you must be prepared to rest, rest and more rest. No rushing to town, or helping Kate with her brood. Just take it easy. At the same time,' he paused and looked intently into her frightened eyes, '. . . there is absolutely no reason why there should be . . . why this child . . . your baby will be fine, lass. I'll see to that. I want to see you every month for now and if there should be anything, anything at all, dinna be afraid to come and see me.' His eyes were warm with affection and concern. 'There's just one thing Jenny. I hope you won't be offended if I . . .'

'What is it please, Dr Clancy?'

'Have you told Bill about . . . ?'

Jenny flushed but her eyes were clear and steady as she answered simply,

'No.'

'Right, then I . . .'

'Thank you, I would be grateful . . .' Dr Clancy pressed her hand and they exchanged understanding glances.

'Now promise me you'll do as you're told. Go home, tell the family what I've said and then put your feet up for six months.' He laughed at the expression on her face. 'Och lass, I've women on my panel who'd give a gold clock to be able to do just that. No,' he sobered for a moment. 'You must take a reasonable amount of exercise but slow down. Right.'

She left the surgery and as she began to run the tram to Fazackerly rattled past the end of the road. On an impulse she turned to look in the direction of the surgery. Two twinkling grey eyes peered at her over the top half of the green painted window. It was Dr Clancy. He shook an admonishing finger. With a laugh she slowed down, sauntering a few paces before turning once more. He was still there. She waved, and her heart felt light as a bird and her anxiety disappeared as he returned her salute.

The March wind blew at her back. The clouds lashed across the sky, torn white streaks against the blue. Women polished their windows and shook mats out of open front doors, and the ring and clang of the trams made an excited clamour in her head.

Oh, she longed for this baby, yearned to have a child of her own.

She loved Kate's children, especially Frankie, for it was as if he had been her own. She had been there, coming from the spell which had held her, as he was born. The happiness ran in her veins like honey and her mind suddenly remembered. This was how she had felt before. When she had been pregnant with Nils' child. Nils' daughter.

'She would have been nearly eight . . .' She cut the thread of thought like scissors snipping cotton.

'We're having a celebration.'

To Bill it was confirmation, in the eyes of those who knew him, of his manhood. His wife, Jenny, was pregnant. She was with child. *His* child. He had made her his own in the sight of God when he had married her, but now, the evidence of his virility was there for all to see. What he had done to Jenny; what he did to her night after night in their marriage bed, to the envy of all the men who knew him, or so he imagined, was verified. It was important to him that they should know. Now it was proved. He boasted of her pregnancy as if what he had done had made him into a man to be admired.

'We'll take Kate and Charlie, have a meal somewhere, make a night of it. I know, we'll go to The Corn Dolly and see what the new owners have made of it. What d'ya say?'

Jenny managed to talk him out of that. Sometimes she wondered at the unthinking heedlessness of this man she had married. He was generous, and, though subject to abrupt changes of mood, goodtempered providing he had his own way, but he seemed to see no further than the end of his nose. The inner self of the people he knew was a mystery to him. In fact, not even that. He would have been surprised to hear that those around him *had* an inner self. He was insensitive to the point of stupidity. He genuinely thought that Jenny and Charlie would enjoy the experience of seeing how the restaurant which had been their brain child, their creation, had progressed since they had left. The idea that they might be reluctant to be reminded of happier days just did not occur to him.

They left the three children, two already tucked up and Frankie 'reading' with his Aunty Phyllis. Even before they left home the glow of the evening was generated by a 'wee dram' supplied by Bill in honour of his own prowess. Charlie was quiet at first, standing before his hearth, thinner, strained; but a couple of tots of whiskey relaxed the tight muscles of his face and before they left to catch the tram to town, he was laughing, his arms about Kate's shoulders.

Kate was glad to see him, her old Charlie, and grateful to Bill for giving them these few hours of relief from the grinding worry that lay eternally about their lives. Charlie had been reluctant. She had had to persuade him. He wanted no charity, he said, even from his brother-in-law, but with careful words of how much this meant to their Jenny and a reference to her past misfortune, Charlie had given in.

They queued for, and were enraptured by Chaplin in his latest film *City Lights*, and after the show, arm in arm, the two couples made their way to the restaurant—not The Corn Dolly – and were shown to a table in the corner of the room. It was pleasantly comfortable, though not, Jenny privately thought, as smart as The Corn Dolly, but the tables sparkled with gleaming white cloths, glittering cutlery and crystal glasses which were soon filled. Bill must have wine. Wine to toast his wife's bright eyes, his baby, his King, Charlie, who he was sure would soon have a job, the health of the occupants of the room in general, and his bonny sister-in-law.

He was captivated with himself, and though he would not admit to it, delighted to be able to play the 'big fellow' distributing largesse to relatives not in such fortuitous circumstances as himself. His laugh rang out and his bright, winning smile encompassed the other diners, and as usual, they could not resist him. Glasses were raised in his direction as the word got about that the handsome young couple were celebrating the expected arrival of their first child.

He was at his best. Jenny smiled, and could not be cross with him, though her embarrassment knew no bounds. She shook her head as she clinked her glass against his for the sixth time. She looked at Kate and Charlie. They were flushed with the unaccustomed wine they drank, and their eyes sparkled. Her heart softened with gratitude towards her husband and she leaned forward to touch his hand. Her eyes smiled into his and his elation at the success of the evening showed in the tilt of his head and the set of his shoulders.

A young man with a supercilious, fresh-faced girl watched the merriment which flowed about the foursome who were seated at the table in the corner. At the sight of Bill and Jenny his face had lit up and he half rose from his seat, then, as if noticing for the first time the other couple, sat down again. The girl glanced at him enquiringly as she delicately spooned pink icecream into her pursed, ladylike mouth.

'What is it, dear?' she said, arching her eyebrows.

The young man was about to speak just as Bill, a forkful of succulent pork halfway to his open mouth, met his glance. Bill stared, then, his face alight with pleasure, dropped his fork with a clatter, sprang up, and made his way towards him through the group of tables.

'Doug, you old fool,' he bellowed. 'Where the 'ell 'ave *you* been. Why 'aven't you been to see us? It's good to see you, boy.'

Douglas Robinson stood up, clutching his napkin to him, his face awash with shy pleasure. Bill slapped him on the back, gratified beyond measure that his brother should be here to see the party he was throwing. It seemed to give the evening an added thrill to know that it was witnessed by a member of his family, and that his accomplishments, as a husband and father-to-be, would be reported back to his parents. This would show his mother.

Suddenly, as if he had just remembered her, Douglas turned hurriedly towards his companion who was drumming her fingers in a vexed way upon the table. Her prim mouth was set in a line of annoyance. She obviously did not like to be ignored.

'Oh Bill,' Douglas held his hand out to the girl, 'This is Mary. Mary Whitaker. We have just become engaged.' He smirked selfconsciously. 'Mary, this is my brother Bill.'

Bill smiled at the girl, his engaging charm turned on to the full, and she preened. She held out a limp hand, her wrist flaccid in what she considered to be genteel manner.

'Pleased to meet you,' she simpered.

'And I you,' Bill smiled. Turning to Douglas he nudged him with his elbow. 'You dark horse, you. Why didn't you say you 'ad a lovely young lady. You could 'ave brought her round to see us. Jenny and I would 'ave been delighted.'

The girl smirked, sending a languishing look in Douglas' direction, pleased with the attention, then her gaze fell on Jenny who was smiling towards them and nodding at Douglas.

'Why don't you join us?' Bill exclaimed jubilantly. 'We're having a celebration.' He leaned forward confidentially, at the same time giving the impression that he was standing ten feet tall and proudly puffing out his chest.

'Jenny's pregnant,' he whispered, 'so we're wetting the baby's head, so to speak. A bit early, but then, it's not every day that . . . well.' Realising that what he was about to say might be considered a trifle forward in the presence of a lady, he did not finish.

'Come on,' he continued. 'We're 'aving a great time and you'll like Kate and Charlie.'

Douglas looked at Mary and Bill could see the mould of Douglas'

300

future setting already. She wore the trousers – that was plain. With another glance at Jenny, Mary set her prim mouth. Though Bill's wife looked nice enough she did not think she cared to be seen in the company of someone as common-looking as the woman in red who was with her. And that laugh! You could tell she was no lady.

'That's very kind of you . . . er Bill, but Douglas and I are having a celebration too. This is for our engagement, as Douglas said, and we promised ourselves just a quiet affair, dinner à deux,' she smiled archly. 'You will forgive us if we decline, won't you? Convey our regrets to your . . . friends.'

Bill's expression hardened. He did not like to have his generosity refused. He was deeply offended.

'Of course. I quite understand,' he said politely, looking with obvious pity, an expression which did not go unnoticed by the girl, at his brother. 'Perhaps some other time.'

He turned to Douglas. 'Tell Ma she's to be a grandmother, will you, and don't *you* be a stranger, you know where we live.'

Pointedly he nodded in the direction of the mortified girl, then returned to his own table. It had been spoiled for him now. Like a child who is showing off and has been firmly squashed by its elders, the evening was ruined.

There was silence as he sat down, Jenny's face registering the questions which hung in the air.

'Our Douglas and his ladidah fiancée. They're 'aving a meal to celebrate their engagement and don't want to be disturbed,' he said bitterly.

'Well, it's understandable . . .' Jenny began, but Bill interrupted her.

'No, it's not. This is the first baby in the family and if that's not important, I don't know what is.'

Kate looked surreptitiously at Charlie. His face was a blank. The wine had worn off, and she could see that this storm in a teacup, this childish behaviour of Bill's had dispelled the gaiety which had for the moment allowed Charlie to forget his troubles.

Jenny had taken Bill's hand propitiatingly.

'Bill, they have just got engaged and they are entitled to be alone, after all . . .'

He threw her off petulantly. 'Surely to God they could just 'ave 'ad a drink with us. That's all I ask. Is that too much to ask?' he turned to Charlie and Kate, but they looked down at the table.

'Bill, please, don't let's . . .'

'Oh for God's sake, Jenny . . .'

Charlie stood up suddenly. His face was set and his eyes were

301

like grey flint. 'It's been a grand evening, Bill, but me an' Kate 'ad best be off.'

Bill turned to look at him in amazement. 'Oh, come on Charlie, don't be like that. The night's young yet. Come on lad, 'ave another glass of wine.'

It was as though Charlie had suddenly become aware that he was being bought. With the offer of a few drinks and a meal he had allowed himself to be cajoled into coming on this jaunt when it was against his very nature to go even into a pub if he couldn't pay his whack. If he couldn't say, 'This is my shout' Charlie Walker felt he was less than a man. And he couldn't. Not now. It was beyond his small allowance to buy his brother-in-law even a pint of beer. It was more than he could stand. And now this. Bill was behaving like some kid whose party was going wrong because some small guest refused to play the game *he* wanted.

They parted at the door of the restaurant. Douglas had waved a shamefaced hand at Bill, but it was Jenny who had returned his farewell.

It was not until he and Jenny were inside their own front door, did Bill allow his own true temperament to show. She stood, appalled, frightened at the viciousness of his fury. At Douglas who had allowed 'that cow . . . that *bitch* to tell 'im what 'e could, or could not do. Catch him letting a woman dictate to him' – and at Charlie, who'd 'taken the hump over nothing'.

It was the first indication to Jenny of what her life with Bill was to become.

Chapter Thirty-Two

Bewildered, Jenny stared at the woman who stood, one arm still uplifted after ringing the bell, on the mat outside the front door of the flat in Rice Lane. For several seconds, although subconsciously she recognised her, she couldn't for the life of her remember who she was.

She realised later that it was the hat. She gasped. It was Bill's mother. They stared at each other, neither knowing what to do next, each waiting for the other to make the first move.

Jenny spoke at last. 'Bill's not in,' she said coolly.

'I know. I came to see you.'

'What for?'

'I wanted to talk to you.'

'What about?' still holding the door half shut.

'Can I come in, Jenny, please?'

With reluctance Jenny slowly opened the door to allow her mother-in-law to pass through. She closed it with a sharp click, and led her down the narrow hallway and into the bright living room.

It was almost three months since the unhappy meeting with Douglas and his fiancée, and Bill, with the resilience of one who is emotionally unable to care deeply about another, had forgotten the episode. Basically, Douglas meant nothing to Bill. It was the slight which had infuriated him, and so, as the days passed, and his body was fulfilled night after night by Jenny's, it went from him and became nothing. He bore no grudge and should Douglas and Mary have come to his home, he would probably have welcomed them, eager for them to see how well he did with his pretty wife, his good job, and the prosperity which had come to him. His shallow nature did not allow for the seeds of resentment to take root for long.

March had blown itself out into a mild and perfect English April. May was cold but now it was June, and the weather had turned again, and the day was warm and sunny.

The room shone with the loving care which Jenny polished into it each day, and the fragrance of a huge spray of lilac which she had picked from the wood behind Kate's house the previous Sunday, drifted from the vase standing in the empty, mushroom-coloured, tiled fireplace. A fringed rug was placed symmetrically before the hearth and a large square of carpet covered the floor. The linoleum which edged the room where the carpet did not reach had a high gloss upon it. A standard lamp stood behind the deep armchair to one side of the fireplace, and against the big bay window was placed a dining table with four chairs to match in limed oak. Everything was brand new. The walls had been distempered in magnolia and the floor-length curtains had been made by Jenny in a soft velvet to match the damson coloured carpet.

Mrs Robinson looked about her in admiration and her mother's eyes gleamed in satisfaction. They proclaimed the pride she had in her son's achievements, and even now, in the awkwardness which the situation, and her own previous behaviour had wrought, she could not help the expression of self-esteem which crossed her face.

Jenny stood by the door, watching as Mrs Robinson's gaze wandered about the room. Bill's desk stood against the wall opposite the fireplace. On its gleaming top was the framed photograph which had been taken on their wedding day. It was a lovely picture. It showed Jenny's dark beauty against the frosted background of the trees. Bill was looking down at her worshipfully, for once the arrogance which was inherent in him, missing. He looked vulnerable, his eyes seemed to plead for something and it was for this reason that Jenny had chosen it from the others. She knew her husband needed her, more than she had ever needed him. He wanted the constant reassurance that he was lovable, worth something. Outwardly confident, the yearning in him to shine in her eyes was always there, and the essence of him had been caught by the photographer. When Bill had what she privately was beginning to call a 'tantrum', she would look at the photograph and pity him for though he was a grown man, he was still only a child.

His mother crossed the room eagerly. She picked up the photograph and taking it to the window, scrutinised it avidly.

'Oh Jenny, it's lovely, lovely.' She touched Bill's face tenderly and a look of such yearning came to her stern face, Jenny felt her heart move with compassion.

'Sit down, Mrs Robinson,' she said softly. 'What can I do for you?'

Her mother-in-law regretfully returned the photograph to the desk, and sat down in the chair opposite Jenny. Jenny looked at her expectantly, and for the first time noticed that she had deep brown, warmly shining eyes behind her spectacles. She wondered how she could have missed the gentleness in them at their previous meetings. It melted her reserve, and she said, more agreeably, 'Why have you come Mrs Robinson?'

There was silence as Ellen Robinson marshalled her thoughts. She was a proud woman who considered she had married beneath her when she had wed Albert Robinson twenty-eight years ago. But no one else had come knocking at her door, and she did not want to be left on the shelf, so she took him. He had been a bricklayer. Hard-working, conscientious. He was not an educated man but his perseverance had gained him the position of gang foreman. He was working at the moment on the new Mersey Tunnel which reached from one side of the river to the other, and was consequently assured, in this day of mass unemployment, of work for many years to come. There had never been any shortage of money in the Robinson household. They were both careful, and their combined endeavours, his financially, hers domestically, had provided them and their family with what was known as a 'nice home'.

Ellen was a Yorkshire woman and stiff-necked with it. She wanted the best for her sons, and quite honestly did not consider the daughter of a fish and chip shop proprietor good enough for her boy, pretty and sweet though she was. The news that Bill was to be a father – not Jenny a mother – had softened her views and the generous, but well-hidden side of her nature had triumphed. And naturally, the thought that her grandchild might be born and she have no hand in its raising was a contributing factor that could not be ignored.

'I want us to be friends,' she said with difficulty, her high cheekbones colouring with the effort of making such an admission. 'I'm sorry I did not make you as welcome as I might, but . . .' she floundered on '. . . William is my son. You were the first girl he had brought home who seemed . . . I thought . . . well, I didn't know he was serious about you,' she lied, and her voice meandered on, her eyes begging Jenny's understanding of a mother's jealousy. She could not say so in words but it was there in the expression of regret on her face. She looked down at her gloved hands, smoothing the fingers one by one, asking with her bent head, for forgiveness.

Jenny looked at the top of the neat brown hat. It looked like an upsidedown coal scuttle. It was pulled down firmly covering the greying hair, touching the straight eyebrows. It was that which had disguised her mother-in-law when Jenny had first seen her at the door. She almost smiled. It was such a ridiculous hat.

305

Suddenly she felt lighthearted. How could she refuse this poor woman whose only happiness lay in her children? She wanted a small part of her grandchildren too. Didn't every grandmother?

Jenny rose to her feet. 'Let's have a cup of tea, shall we?'

'You could've knocked me down with a feather, our Kate, honest. I was flabbergasted. There she stood on the mat with t'daftest hat you ever saw on 'er 'ead. I didn't know 'er at first and if you could've seen Bill's face when 'e came in, well 'e was made up. Of course, 'e wanted to swank . . .' She bit off the rest of the sentence quickly, but it did not go unnoticed by Kate. She understood too. That was what Bill Robinson loved to do. Swank. He was like a big soft kid at times. He had to tell you the price of everything he bought as well, which drove Charlie mad, with things as they were, but it could be worse. Jenny seemed content enough, especially now with the baby coming.

Jenny was making her daily visit to Kate's, her promise to Dr Clancy to rest and rest, not yet having been implemented. She looked so well and bonny and felt it too, and some inner feeling, some instinct told her that all was as it should be this time. She was nearly five months pregnant now, and her trim figure was thickening, her breasts ripening, and the serenity sat well on her.

Kate was open-mouthed with astonishment at the mental picture painted by Jenny of her high and mighty mother-in-law asking to be forgiven. 'It's the baby, kid. That's what brought 'er round. Like as not that their Mary 'll never do owt as undignified as makin' love by the sound of 'er, an' Ma Robinson knows it, so you're 'er only chance for a grandchild.'

The two sisters fell about laughing, the earthy Kate making further bawdy remarks regarding the habits of Douglas and Mary in their marriage bed, until they both had tears streaming down their faces.

'Eeh, a good laugh does me the world of good, our Jenny,' she gasped, a fresh giggle escaping from her, and they started all over again.

At last they had themselves under control and Kate managed to wheeze, 'Put kettle on, love, before I wet me knickers.'

The guarded relationship which developed between Jenny and her mother-in-law, brought a growing degree of pleasure to them both. The initial overtures made by Ellen Robinson were viewed warily by Jenny who felt that it was not on her account that they had been made, but she was willing to overlook that and try to bring about the family affection which she wanted for her child. It would have no other grandparents.

Nothing had been heard from Henry Fowler since that dreadful day seven years ago, when he had come to gloat over what he considered the downfall of his youngest daughter. Bobby and Jimmy called to see Jenny, mainly during the day when they were on the nightshift at the dock, and they knew Bill would not be there, and they brought news of the old man from time to time. He had not wed the widow from Agnes Street but she was still there in the chip shop, her hope of a wedding ring long gone along with the chance of another life which Henry's attentions had denied her. Jimmy was married now and had moved to Netherfield, but Bobby was still up in the attic bedroom which he now had to himself. The widow's daughters, both in their late teens, had stepped into Kate and Jenny's shoes and worked fourteen hours a day in the shop and the yard at the back. But business had declined with the recession which was crippling the country. The unemployed did not buy fish and chips. Where once the evening was not complete without a bag of chips to follow their beer, it was only those who had a job who could afford to eat what they had not cooked themselves. Chips from the chippy were a luxury now.

The first few visits made by Jenny and Bill to the house in Old Swan for Sunday tea, were tense and formal, not helped by the presence of Mary, bride-to-be of Douglas. She insisted on regarding herself as a cut above the others, mainly one supposed because her father was an insurance agent and therefore middle-class as opposed to their working-class. He was a white collar worker. He didn't get his hands dirty as did Albert, and certainly he was a step up from a man who owned a fish and chip shop. She held her nose so high it might have been assumed that she could smell the frying from here.

Jenny developed a fondness for the old man, her father-in-law, whose simple pleasure at the news of the coming child, and his growing affection, surreptitiously shown, for Jenny brought forth similar feelings from herself. He was an innocuous little man, overshadowed by his strong-willed wife, happy to come home from work, put on his slippers, and read the *Echo* until it was time for bed. Ellen did all the talking, whilst he nodded in agreement, his eyes partially glazed as the words passed over him, but when Jenny came, the paper was put away, and when he was able he would pat her hand, and enquire after her health and his eyes would twinkle.

'A little girl, d'ya think, Jenny?' he would say hopefully, and his

307

calloused hands would curl inwards as though he imagined small female fingers twined in his.

Ma, as she had been bidden to call Mrs Robinson, was not as easy to like. Not at first. She was a good woman, a regular churchgoer, and generous to a fault with those she loved, but her affections, though strong when aroused, were buried deep within her, and she found it almost impossible to display them. She hid behind a stiff exterior, and was embarrassed, though, if she were truthful, secretly pleased, when given a kiss by Jenny. She was a keen needlewoman and her embroidery was exquisite. She spent hours doing the fine sewing, to the detriment of her eyesight, and her shortsightedness gave her the excuse to hide any expression which might show in her eyes, behind thick pebbled spectacles. Despite this, it was obvious to Jenny that Ellen regretted their inauspicious beginnings and was, in her own way, doing her best to make amends.

Jenny was now in her sixth month of pregnancy, and was following Dr Clancy's instructions to the letter. Her day took on a routine which became a habit and helped by her sister and eager mother-in-law she rested for the best part of each day. She was blooming and beautiful, with that special glow only given to pregnant women, and her heart was light with the sure inner knowledge that told her that everything was going well. She felt the baby kick vigorously within her and rejoiced in its lusty activity. She would lie beside the sleeping form of her husband, her hands on her belly, and it was as though the child was aware of her past fears and was eager to reassure her.

'See,' it seemed to say, and Jenny would feel a tiny foot push against her hand, 'look, here I am, we shall be together soon. I won't be long. Here, here is my hand.' And there, almost visible though the fine skin of her swollen abdomen was the shape of her child's hand. No, this baby would not suffer the fate of her first.

There was also the wonderful release from Bill's nightly attentions. He seemed not to mind the curtailment of his 'rights', going out several evenings a week on what he called 'a bit of business' for the bank, though his breath often smelled of alcohol when he came home.

The weeks passed placidly by. She visited Crescent Road, and the Robinsons each weekend when Bill, who was on his best behaviour it seemed as her time drew near, could find the time to take her. The mellow autumn weather turned colder. The trees in Rice Lane became stark and bare, against the grey washed skies and the fallen leaves were wet and sodden underfoot making a squelching carpet of green, copper and brown. Winter was approaching and as it came, so did Jenny's time.

Bill sighed and puffed, struggling to ignore the persistent hand which shook his shoulder. He snuggled deeper under the eiderdown, grumbling wordlessly, holding onto the comfort of sleep, resenting the hand which tried to drag him from it.

'Bill, Bill. Will you wake up, or shall I fetch the doctor myself!'

Still no response. Jenny sighed with exasperation. She knew from nine months' experience that it took more than a gentle shake to part her husband from his slumbers. She whacked him with the flat of her hand across his back which he had turned towards her, and putting her mouth close to his ear, she shouted in ringing tones, 'Bill Robinson, your child is about to be born and if you don't look lively you'll be delivering it yourself.'

With a surge of bedclothes, rising like a fish from a white-crested sea, Bill sat up looking wildly about him, his eyes still misted with sleep.

'Wha . . . what,' he mumbled, peevishly.

'Oh come on Bill, for 'eaven's sake man. I'm 'aving regular contractions and I want Dr Clancy and our Kate 'ere, and right now Bill.'

Shaking his head, clutching the sheet to him as though it were a lifeline to the dreaming state from which he had been dragged, Bill stumbled from the bed. He stared about him, then, in the best comic tradition of the father-to-be, tried to put on his trousers back to front, over his pyjamas.

'Eeh Bill, yer as good as Charlie Chaplin,' Jenny gasped, 'but I'm not in the mood. Pull yerself together and fetch the doctor, there's a good bloke.'

Another tremor caught her, starting in the small of her back and growing each second, moving inexorably until it knifed her in the pit of her belly. It grasped her in a grip of agony and she strained backwards towards the bedpost.

'Hurry up Bill, please hurry up.'

At last Bill was in full command of himself. 'I'm going, I'm going,' he shouted. He pulled the pillow from his side of the bed and placed it awkwardly in the small of her back. He had not the slightest notion which position she might find most comfortable, but with the remembrance of his mother having a bad back years ago, he had the idea that a bit of support might be acceptable. Clutching his trousers, he ran from the room, his expression as he went, one of great relief to be away.

It was at 5.30 in the morning of 30 October that Jenny's daughter made her appearance, plump and pretty like her mother, mewling like a kitten. Kate took her from Dr Clancy's hands, her own arms going hungrily about the lovely child. They looked at each other, she and John Clancy over the baby's angry face and their eyes smiled and their expressions were soft, relaxed. The good doctor had delivered hundreds of babies since the day he had first met Jenny so many years ago. Some had not survived, like Jenny's firstborn, but as he knelt by her side that night, gazing into her tired face on the pillow, his heart was too full for the words he wanted to speak.

Jenny understood. Touching his cheek gently, she spoke so that he alone could hear. 'We did it Dr Clancy, we did it.'

He put his cheek against hers for an instant, a gesture of affection between friends, then as her eyes closed in sleep he rose to his feet and crossing the room, softly kissed the cheek of Jenny's child as she lay in Kate's arms.

Jenny awoke to the muted, but excited sound of voices coming through the half-open door of the bedroom. She could distinguish those of Ellen Robinson and Kate, and within her grew the urgent, almost desperate need to see her sister. She wanted to see Kate, the round, high-coloured smiling face that had always been there at every sorrow, every joy. She could not remember a day when Kate's smile, and Kate's hand had not been immediately available, reassuring and durable and . . . just Kate. Before anyone she must have a moment with Kate. She lifted her head, her eyes resting on the cradle which stood in the corner of the bedroom. It had been there for the past two months, brought from Kate's house, re-lined with white organdie and painted a delicate yellow. She had dreamed over it, for hours on end, waiting with scant patience for the moment when the baby would be laid within its pretty depths. Jenny strained her eyes in the semi-dark.

It was empty.

Her voice rose shrilly as she called.

'Kate, Kate, where's the baby, where . . . oh please Kate . . .'

There was silence, then the sounds of footsteps coming along the hall. The door was flung open, light poured in and Kate stood there, a warmly wrapped bundle in her arms. An expression of joy lit her face and her blue eyes glowed like jewels. Tears of deep emotion flowed across her cheeks. She, of them all, remembered most clearly that other night when another child, just born, had died.

She knelt carefully by the bed still cradling the baby in her arms, and said gently, 'Here she is, my lovely, here's your daughter. She's all there an' every bit's perfect.'

A look of loving understanding passed between the two sisters.

Chapter Thirty-Three

London. It was the greatest money market in the world and was considered the safest banking place above all others. In August 1931, due to pressures from abroad, a serious run on the Bank of England began. The Bank had not enough gold to stand the strain. To ease the situation it was suggested that the huge unemployment dole should be cut as it was draining the country of her financial resources. In September, Britain abandoned the gold standard, and the Chancellor of the Exchequer introduced an Emergency Budget. The pound slumped heavily; its value dropped to only thirteen or fourteen shillings, and in October the 'means test' for all those who were unemployed was introduced.

Charlie was at the head of the queue that morning, and he was filled with trembling hope when the clerk asked him to go to the cubicle at the end of the counter. The large room was filled with men, and a few women, who stood patiently in one queue or another, or sat where they were put, or like himself, made their humble way to the cubicles which were set aside for interviews. The room was cold, and yet, at the same time humid, as a hundred people breathed out their despairing aspirations.

It was raining outside, a straight, needle-sharp, vertical wall of water that wet through those who could not yet get inside the doors, and the dampness of the clothing of those who had, made the fug less than cosy. Every man wore a dark cap. Some possessed a threadbare overcoat, most did not. Their faces might have come from the same mould. Muscles were slack in pasty faces and eyes stared at nothing. No man looked another in the face. The pattern of their lives had gone, as month after month went by without work. It showed in the pathetic humility, as though in each man the purposelessness of his existence, the feeling of being unwanted, had taken away the sense of being in any way able to decide his own course of action. To be dependent upon a government 'hand-out' and to be permanently at the beck and call of officials, removes most effectively from men the capacity to stand straight and answer bravely, like a man should.

Old men acted like children in school, doing obediently the bidding of youths young enough to be their grandchildren.

Charlie sat down, putting his cap on his knee, staring at the neat white parting in the hair of the man at the desk. – Dear God, let it be a job. I don't care if it's sweepin' bloody streets, let it be a job. I'll do owt, mister, owt, he said silently to the clerk, who, as yet, had not lifted his head as he wrote busily on a form.

At last the man raised his head and his eyes looked fractionally to the left of Charlie's face. His pen was poised over the form and he cleared his throat.

'Mr Walker?' He wet his lips with a narrow pointed tongue.

'That's me.' Charlie's face was falsely cheerful, conciliatory.

'Charles Walker?'

'Right.' Charlie nodded his head.

'Sixteen Crescent Road?'

'That's it mate. 'Ave yer gorra job . . . ?'

'No, no, Mr Walker. I'm afraid not. That's not why you're here.'

Charlie's insides contracted with disappointment and he felt the apathy close in on him again. It was getting worse, this feeling that he no longer cared, one way or the other. As each week passed and the humiliations multiplied, a man learned to withdraw to some part of himself that insisted that it no longer mattered. It was the only way to survive, and so the indifference became a habit. The worry and strain was more than he could bear at times so he taught himself the knack of detachment.

They all did, and as time passed, that detachment became real. The reading rooms at William Brown Street Library were always full of men who came to read the free newspapers. The warmth was free too. The crowds of men were silent and all had that slow, wandering look of those in whom a poor diet had produced the capacity for daydreaming. It was a kind of self-hypnosis and it became the one true friend of the hopeless, poverty-stricken, out-of-work men who came there to get out of the cold. In the summer it was the street corner. In the winter, the library.

The man was speaking.

'Now Mr Walker, I am from the Public Assistance Committee and it is my job to interview each recipient of unemployment benefit. You will probably have heard of the 'means test' which the new government has introduced. Well . . . I'm here to . . .' the man looked uneasy and his eyes shone compassionately at Charlie. 'You see Mr Walker, I'm afraid I must ask you . . . ?'

'Yes?'

313

'I'm afraid I must ask you if you have any private means . . . money . . . something?'

'I'm not with yer . . .'

'Have you any money besides that which you collect each week from the dole?'

Charlie was bewildered. What the 'ell did the bloke mean? Other money? What money? Would 'e be 'ere with his 'and out if 'e 'ad something tucked away? Anything? He thought of his children and the state of his home and he wanted to break down and cry.

'I don't know what you mean,' he whispered.

The man looked down at the form on which, so far, was written only Charlie's name and address. He put his cap on his pen, then took it off again.

'Mr Walker, I'm sorry, but your dole money is to be cut by ten per cent. If you should have any . . . any assets at all; if your wife has anything, if your children should be given money, you must declare it, by law, and your benefit will be cut further.'

The silence was appalling. Outside the cubicle, which was backless, a tiny ripple of sound hummed around the room as men learned what was happening. Up and down the counters they were sitting like Charlie in stunned disbelief. Only they knew the wretchedness their wives and children had suffered over the past decade, and this, this would be the last straw. They barely existed now, and to have what little they were given reduced even further, was more than a man could stand.

Poverty brings with it the necessity for rigid economies. Charlie thought of the distances Kate trudged to find the shop which sold the cheapest food. She would leave it until late on a Saturday night, just before the butcher closed, to buy bits and pieces of meat which would not keep until Monday and which therefore, were to be had for sixpence a pound cheaper. She struggled to the market after the children were in bed to buy leftovers from the vegetable stalls. Her shoes were lined with newspaper for they had not the money to have them resoled. They used oil lamps, for gas and electricity were beyond their means and Kate cooked all their meals on the fire. They went to bed at the same time as the children to avoid burning lights and using coal, and got up late so that a cup of tea would do for breakfast. He could have wept when Kate counted out each halfpenny, trying to make it do the work of a penny. She cooked and mended – Kate sewing, who couldn't put a button on a shirt – she washed and cleaned and the children, so far, were adequately fed. She had unbelievable courage, had Kate, but the struggle was it seemed, to be useless.

314

Twenty-nine shillings and three pence was to be cut by ten per cent. It was the difference between just managing and deprivation.

The official spoke softly for several minutes but the words which flowed from his mouth drifted about the numb figure of the man who sat opposite him. Occasionally a word caught Charlie's vagrant attention. *'Occupational Centres . . . trades can be learned . . . clubs . . . training . . . creative use of enforced leisure . . . resettlement on the land . . . emigration . . .'*

It was this last which remained subconsciously in Charlie's mind. As he began the long walk back to Fazackerly it seemed to keep step with him though he was not really aware of it. His jacket was heavy about his shoulders with the weight of the rainwater and as he turned into Scotland Road he felt the squelch as his paper-lined boots allowed in the first tide of water from the puddle-streaked pavement. He stopped when he got to Walton Station, and on impulse turned right, taking the footpath across the fields which lay at the back of his house. The grass was knee-high and his trousers were soon sodden about his legs. When he reached the railway line which he must cross to get to his home, he stood, his head bare, and he wept into his cap. There was no one to see his despair, nor the light finally leave his grey eyes.

Jenny pushed the pram up Rice Lane in the direction of Kate's, the cold wind biting at her flesh even through the good, thick wool of her winter coat. She stamped her feet as she stepped out and her face lifted to the pale blue-white of the December sky. Clouds, like tufts of windblown wool, scudded across the winter sun, chasing shadows of grey along the road in front of her. Her mind was peaceful and relaxed as her gaze wandered from the sleeping child in the pram to the high, cloud-streaked sky. A tram whistled past going in the direction of the city and the guard who hung on to the rail on the platform gave her a friendly wave.

Reaching the corner of Crescent Road, she crossed over and pushed the pram down the jigger until she arrived at the rutted backstreet which ran at the back of Kate's house. Bumping along it to the gate she pushed it open and backing through it, pulled the pram behind her into the yard. She put the pram against the back wall of the house, making sure the hood was securely up and that her sleeping daughter was well tucked in. For several moments she gloated wonderingly over the apple-cheeked beauty of her child, lightly putting a tender forefinger to the pale brown curl which escaped the baby's bonnet, then, without knocking, entered the kitchen.

Kate sat before the fireplace. Her arms looked strangely empty, as though a child should be there, for it was seldom that Kate sat down without one or another of her children on her knee. The fire sputtered lifelessly, and the room was barely warm. The usual crackle and glow was missing. The dancing flames which lit up this room, this hub which was the centre of the small home, did not dance today, and Jenny shivered as she banged the door behind her.

Kate did not even look up.

Alarm brushed a feather up Jenny's spine and she felt her heart trip.

'Kate?' she said questioningly.

Kate turned to look at her and the utter dejection which overlay her face, bottled up Jenny's throat and sent a trickle of apprehension over her body. Kate's eyes were bleak and as Jenny stared in horror, silent tears welled and flowed across her cheeks, dripping unheeded off the edge of her chin. She looked worn, faded, and with a pang of dread, Jenny noticed for the first time how thin she had become. As a part of her mind assimilated this, wondering why she had not seen it before another part cringed with guilt, and pity, and the sudden frightening knowledge that some unendurable event was about to take place in their lives.

Kate put her head back on the chair, and a deep drowning moan sounded in her throat. Jenny's skin prickled. Kate shook her head from side to side as though she were in agony and the curtain of her tangled hair swept her dripping face.

'Dear God, when's it goin' to end?' she beseeched, 'when, when? I can't take much more. We get over one thing and another starts. My God, 'aven't I 'ad enough, 'aven't I? I'm twenty-eight years old and I've 'ad more to purrup with than a woman of fifty.'

Jenny raced across the kitchen, the numbness which had frozen her in shock, draining from her at Kate's distress.

'Kate, what the . . . what's up? Dear Lord, I've never seen yer like . . . tell me . . . what is it . . . tell me chuck?'

She knelt before her sister, trying to capture the demented figure in her arms, but Kate was distraught and as easy to get hold of as an eel.

'Kate, will you tell me what's wrong? Stop it, now stop it, or I'll crack you one.'

Kate continued to roll from side to side as if Jenny wasn't there. Her hands flew to her face and she bent into them, crouching forward. Jenny pulled at them, crying over and over again, 'Kate, will yer look at me. Tell me what the . . . *stop it now*, stop it.'

316

'Jenny, oh Jenny, Jenny . . .'

At last Kate began to quieten, her hands falling to her lap. Her head sank on her chest in a fashion so childlike, so filled with misery, Jenny felt her heart move with loving pity.

'What is it, love?' she whispered. 'Tell me.'

At first she could understand nothing that Kate said. She mumbled and sobbed, a word here and there distinguishable, but as fresh hopelessness struck her with the telling she wept again. But at last it came.

'It's the house, Jenny. We've gorra leave the 'ouse. We can't afford it anymore, y'see, the rent I mean. D'yer know what we've bin livin' on since Waggy died? Twenty-nine and threepence a week. Twenty-nine and bloody threepence a week, our kid. Try an' feed a man an' three kids on that, and clothe 'em and pay the rent. I didn't lerron like, cos you were . . . well you 'ad yer own life to see to . . . and any road, Charlie wouldn't 'ave liked me to . . . well, now they're puttin' it down another three bob. Oh God,' her voice rose again. 'Where will we end up?'

The rocking chair thumped the kitchen floor, faster and faster, as the demented woman lost control once more, her chest rasping with the force of her weeping.

Jenny rose from her kneeling position and reached blindly for the tea caddy which stood on the mantlepiece. There was nothing in it. Her eyes misted over with tears and they spilled across her cheek. Her sister's pain filled her body. She should have known, should have realised. In her sad, self-absorption with her own marriage and the dreaming state which pregnancy had wrought in her, she had been blind to the ever-increasing austerity in her sister's life. The cheap cuts of meat, the lack of new clothes for the children, Charlie's polite refusal to go for a 'bevvy' with Bill, and the 'fender-ale' always in evidence in most Northern homes; she hadn't seen Charlie offer Bill a drink in months.

How could she have been so stupid? So thoughtless? So careless? She had been on the dole herself. She knew the miniscule amounts on which whole families were expected to survive, she had stood in the queues, she had known, she had known, but she had not seen. She walked slowly towards the kitchen door, through the doorway and into the hall. Pushing open the door of the parlour which was firmly closed, she entered the room which was Kate's pride and joy.

It was empty. No three-piece suite, no piano, no nothing. Still holding the tea caddy to her breast, she went up the stairs and looked into the bedrooms. In each stood a bed. Nothing else. They were clean, the beds made up, but apart from a cupboard which was built into the wall of the front bedroom, over the staircase, and which contained what clothes they had left, there was nothing besides the beds and the curtains at the windows.

Jenny retraced her slow steps to the kitchen. Kate was sitting quietly now, her head hanging down, her hands limp on the arms of the chair, the storm which had raged within her, burnt out. She looked up as Jenny entered the room. The knowledge that the bitter facts were shared; that the façade was no longer needed, gave her a small measure of peace and she smiled damply, a faint glimmer of her fighting spirit crossing her face.

'Come on our kid, run up road for a packet of tea.'

Charlie and Kate moved from Crescent Road on Christmas Eve, to a two-roomed tenement in Green Street, just off Scotland Road, and with the move, Kate's spirit went out of her. She had loved the snug little house which had been her home for nearly eight years, and the feeling of pride which she and Charlie had shared when they had moved to Fazackerly, the sense of bettering themselves, was sorrowfully left behind as they followed their last remaining possessions to their new home.

Bill, to his credit, tried to raise the subject of a loan to Charlie, but at the look of bitter resentment on Charlie's face, had hastily dropped the idea, but the sisters were not so proud. Many a ten bob note found its way from Jenny's purse to Kate's, and the relief of seeing the look of tension ease from her sister's face, even for only a day or two, was repayment enough for her.

'I'll pay yer back our kid.' Kate pushed her hand through the ever increasing greyness of her hair and put the money into her apron pocket.

'I know, lovey, when you've got it, I know you will. In fact I'll remind you,' and the small joke helped to bring a glimmer of humour into Kate's dull eyes. Her heart was breaking as she and Jenny stood in the dirt-encrusted 'living room' of her new home. Living room, kitchen, scullery, parlour. One room did the work of all four, and upstairs was an area hardly bigger than Kate's bedroom in Crescent Road, split into two with a flimsy partition through which the light streamed where jagged holes had been made by a previous tenant. The 'lavvy' was at the back of the row of houses, shared by four families. Jenny's pram, with the daintily dressed baby inside, stood in the middle of the filthy room, and, shamed by the thought, Jenny prayed she would find no extra passengers aboard when she got home.

318

Together the sisters worked, arms to the elbows in lye soap and water. They scrubbed until their hands were raw and the place stank of disinfectant, but even then Kate was not satisfied. She sent Jenny for whitewash and after several coats had been applied, and the hanging of the curtains to the windows completed, she had to make do.

Charlie was nowhere to be seen, but the landlord of the pub at the corner of the mean street was heard to remark to his wife that he hoped the chap at the end of the bar wasn't going to ask for 'tick'. Charlie, for the first time in his life was doing what thousands were doing in their despair; spending his dole money on beer.

The children, as children will, played in the street, until they were called, but it was Frankie, seven years old, born and brought up in the suburbia of Fazackerly and used to having the company of children who wore shoes, rode bikes and never played 'saggie' from school, who summed it up in language he had picked up within the last hour.

'I don't like this place, Mam,' he said. 'There's more shit 'ere than up me arse'ole.'

But he carried home far worse from school. Head lice, which he generously shared with Dorothy and Leslie. Fleas, impetigo, ringworm and the rebellious attitude brought about by the drastic change in his young and hitherto sheltered life. He could not understand, and frequently and irritatingly said so, why they should have to leave home and live in this horrible place. He liked neither the house, the area, his new school, the boys with whom he was forced to mix, the food he ate – 'why couldn't they have Kate and Sidney pie, any more?' – and the dreffle clothes his Mam made him wear, 'this was your coat Mam and boys don't wear sissy colours like these'. His boyish heart cracked a dozen times a day. No football, no sweeties and why didn't Father Christmas bring him what he asked for? was the last accusing question which drove the final stake through Kate's heart.

Charity. That was what they had come to. Bloody charity. If it hadn't been for the few bits and pieces Charlie had allowed Jenny to buy for the children at Christmas they would have had nowt but the 'Goodfellows' parcel. It had contained a bit of stewing steak, some margarine, sugar, tea, an orange or two, and some sweets for the children. Kate had picked it up on Christmas Eve at Cooper's Department Store along with hundreds of other wives of unemployed men, and had it not been for the children she would rather have starved. Wasn't it enough that she had a constant battle with the cockroaches and mice which invaded her home; the damp walls to which no plaster would adhere, the leaking roof and worst of all, Charlie's increasing indifference to what was happening to them and which was cracking the foundation of their once happy family life.

It seemed that Charlie's spirit and heart were broken by the humiliation which crippled all men of pride who were unable to support their family. The torment of the long, humbling wait in the dole queue to receive the pittance on which he was expected to feed, clothe and house his family, was turning the once cheerful, open face to a sullen mask.

Jenny was at her wits' end. She and Bill were prospering and ready to move to a smart, new semi-detached house in Walton, but how could she flaunt their good fortune in the faces of Kate and Charlie; how could she even visit their mean little house in Bill's new Morris Eight motor car. It was two years old, to be sure, but it had cost Bill ninety pounds when he bought it from a friend of Douglas, and was a further symbol of Bill's success and Charlie's failure. How could she help the suffering pair without taking away the one thing of value they had left? Their pride.

Chapter Thirty-Four

Laura was three months old when it happened the first time and though Jenny did not have in her heart the love that a woman recently married holds for her husband, nor ever would, the event shocked her deeply. During the past year she had forced herself to accept her commitment to this strange inconsistent man who shared her life; to compromise in her relationship with him, though often his manner confused and frightened her. He loved her, she knew. She clung to that fact, and he had given her the blessedness of her baby daughter, but on that night, understanding was beyond her. She had thought her marriage a tolerable success, at least for Bill. She had imagined herself to be giving to him all that he needed. Though he was often out of temper, his eyes followed her about and his lovemaking was once again a nightly occurrence.

That day she had walked to Kate's, pushing the pram along roads which were painted in a silvery white hoar frost. The trees were stripped of foliage, severe against the pale sky and the cold drove an ache into her lungs as she breathed and brought bright poppies to her cheeks. Her eyes were as bright as golden stars and she marched along briskly, feeling that her world was good; that the New Year would surely bring some luck to Kate and Charlie; that perhaps with the child she and Bill would become closer, and lastly that her daughter was beautiful. What a lovely, lovely day it was. A good day to be alive. She hummed a tune under her breath as she stepped out.

Kate was ironing, thumping the flat iron up and down the kitchen table with relentless vigour as though some energy within her was trying to escape. Leslie played before the fire, bundled up in two jumpers and wearing a pair of Frankie's old trousers, taken in at the waist with a stitch or two, the legs which had fitted to his brother's knees, just reaching the young boy's ankle bone. His socks were pulled up and the trouser legs tucked inside them. The fire was low, just kept in by a couple of lumps of coal and some slack, on which the spare flat iron was being reheated. The room was only just warm. There was no sign of Charlie.

'Hello, love. You've got the best job there. Just the day to be doing a bit of ironing. It's 'taters out.' Jenny manoeuvred the pram into the kitchen, absorbed by the rosy, sleeping face of her child. 'I'll put 'er over 'ere. It's too cold to leave 'er outside. Mind, I put a hot water bottle in the bottom of the pram wrapped up in flannel. Ma says if their feet are warm, so's the rest of them. She's full of little tips like that.' Jenny gazed lovingly beneath the hood of the pram, then turned to Kate.

'Shall I put the kettle on, our Kate?'

Kate sighed and banged the iron across one of Charlie's shirts, her mind subconsciously noting the frayed cuffs and the thin state of the material beneath the arms. Where would the money come from for a new one, she thought idly. She turned to Jenny, 'Aye, if yer like, love. I was just gonner 'ave one meself.' A lie, but appearances must be kept up, if only for the sake of Charlie's pride.

'Charlie out?' Jenny filled the kettle and put it on the stove. She reached down for the teapot and caddy noting that the latter was nearly empty, and put two heaped teaspoonsful of tea into the pot. Kate's sidelong look at the last of the tea went unnoticed.

'Aye, 'e's gone down to t'labour.'

'Anything doing?'

'No, burr 'e'll find summat soon, you see.'

'Of course 'e will, love, then we'll 'ave a real night out, all on you an' Charlie, of course.'

Kate smiled and her face took on a wistful expression.

'Eeh our Jenny, a real night out. That'd be grand, an' with Charlie payin'.' She shook her head reminiscently. 'D'yer remember 'ow 'e used to treat us in the old days?' Her hands were stilled as she looked back to the time when money was there for the spending and who cared what tomorrow brought. ''E was a good lad, generous, and now look . . .'

Jenny put her arm around her sister's shoulders. ''E will again, love. Just you wait. Tell yer what, how about you and me 'aving a night out. Let's go to the pictures. I know Charlie'll never agree to . . . well not after the last . . .' They looked at each other, both remembering the evening when Charlie had been persuaded to allow Bill to take them out for a meal; the night when Bill had met his brother in the restaurant last year. What a mistake that had turned out to be. Charlie's pride had taken a hammering that night and Jenny knew there would be no repeat performance, but she and Kate could go. If she could coax her.

322

'Come on love, say yes. Gracie Fields is on at the Rialto. *Sally in our Alley*. It'll be a good laugh.'

'No Jenny, no love. Thanks all the same but I wouldn't feel right . . .'

'Oh come on Kate. It's only a couple of bob and you've treated me a dozen . . .'

'No, our Jenny, I said no. I can't leave Charlie . . .'

As she spoke his name Charlie's key could be heard turning in the lock. The front door opened, and Charlie, his face mottled with the cold appeared in the doorway. He looked dragged down, weary, but when he saw Jenny the corners of his mouth lifted in a smile. It did not quite reach his grey eyes.

'Hello chuck,' he said, artificially cheerful. 'Is that tea in the pot? I'll 'ave a cup if there's one goin'.'

Kate's eyes questioned him silently but his gaze avoided hers and she knew he had had no luck.

'Now then Charlie.' Jenny poured him a cup of thick, strong tea and he felt his mouth fill with saliva. It was a long time since he had drunk a cup of tea like that in his own house, but there, Jenny wasn't to know.

'What love?' he asked.

'I'm trying to persuade our Kate to come to the pictures with me tonight but she won't. You 'ave a go at her will yer. Bill's going out. I'd 'ave to bring our Laura 'ere, but you'd not mind would yer, and it would do Kate the world of good. Go on Charlie, make 'er say yes.'

'I'm not goin' our Jenny, I've told yer.'

'Give over, our Kate, Jenny's right. A night out'd do yer good an' if she's no one to go with yer'd be doin' 'er a favour.'

Put like that, with the two of them against her, Kate could not refuse.

And she did enjoy it. It really took her out of herself. Gracie Fields was a treat and what a lovely voice. Yes, she did enjoy it, they both did, until they saw Bill.

It was cold again that night and already a thick frost coated the pavement. They stamped their feet as they waited for the tram, arm in arm, laughing at the unforgettable moments of the film and the superlative talents of Lancashire's own lass.

It was Kate who saw him first and her sudden silence stopped Jenny's laughter in her throat. She stared for a moment at Kate's stricken face, then her eyes followed the direction of her sister's gaze.

He was there, across the road, walking unsteadily along the

pavement, his feet stepping in that particular way of those who have had too much to drink, as though not quite convinced that the ground on which he was about to place his feet would be there. His trilby hat was pushed to the back of his curly head and he laughed foolishly. On his arm, clinging, as drunk as he, was a young girl. She was no more than fifteen or sixteen. Her hair was a mass of pretty blonde curls on which a diminutive blue beret hung and her youthful face, smooth and childlike, was thick with make-up. As Kate and Jenny stared, openmouthed, Bill and the girl fell into the narrow doorway of a shop, and he kissed her hungrily, one arm holding her tightly. His other hand disappeared inside the front of her coat.

Though people passed by, laughing, talking; though footsteps rang on the pavement and trams banged and rattled across points; though cars hooted and the noise of the busy street rang in her head, Jenny heard nothing. All her senses were concentrated on the fascinating horror of the scene which was being enacted across the street. Passersby were looking in contempt at the couple who clung together in the doorway and in the distance, coming from the corner of North John Street was a police constable. If he should reach the doorway and find a drunken couple . . .

Kate pulled on her arm.

'Jenny, Jenny.' Her voice was low, filled with compassion and Jenny came from her trance.

'Come on love, 'ere's the tram, leave it . . . just leave them . . .'

'No Kate, no . . . the policeman . . . if 'e should see . . . Bill would lose 'is job if . . .'

'Serve 'im right. Leave the bastard . . . 'e's not worth it . . .'

'Kate, oh dear God Kate, what shall I do?' Jenny began to cry, the tears blurring the scene which had etched itself on her mind so that she still saw it clearly.

Kate's attention was focused on the constable. 'Look, the bobbie's crossing over. 'E 'asn't seen 'em. Come on chuck, gerron the tram, leave 'im to it. Come 'ome, come on love, come 'ome.'

Bill and the girl had come from the doorway of the shop, still laughing animatedly, their eyes unfocused. They stepped to the kerb, their intention to cross the road. Jenny began to tremble. She didn't want them to see her. Oh God, she didn't want them to see her. It was as though she had been caught in some dreadful act, not they, and must not be seen. But it was too late. As Bill stumbled onto the pavement, not five yards from where she and Kate stood motionless, his eyes for a moment became unglazed, and he saw her. His face went white with shock, and something else. As Kate dragged her towards the tram which had just stopped before them, Jenny saw that it was anger.

That was the first time he hit her. In front of Kate and Charlie he hit her. He was still drunk when he arrived at Green Street, and abusive in his rage at, as he put it, being spied upon.

'I was only seeing the poor kid 'ome, wasn't I? She was . . . well . . . we got to talkin', yer know how it is. I'd been to the meeting at the bank. You knew I was going, and when it finished I thought I'd 'ave a quick bevvy in the Royal and this . . . well she was with a friend . . . and we got to talkin'. I've done nothing wrong. What's wrong wi' talkin'?' His tone was aggrieved. He turned to Charlie appealingly. 'Come on Charlie. Don't tell me you've never talked to a judy in a pub?'

Charlie stared at him in disgust, saying nothing. Kate began to speak, her quick temper brewing, spilling over, but Charlie stopped her.

'It's nowt ter do wi' us, lass,' he said quietly.

'Give over, Charlie Walker. Yer weren't even there. I saw 'im maulin' that bit of a kid fer all the world . . .'

'Stop it, our Kate.'

'Yes, just shut yer mouth Kate,' Bill hissed, 'it's got nothing to do with you. It's between me an' Jenny. Jenny knows I've done nothing wrong, don't you love?' He looked innocently into Jenny's huge, horror filled eyes; confident, reckless, full of himself and his own ability to smooth things over. He put his hand on her arm placatingly. 'Come on sweetheart, let's go 'ome and then I can explain to you what happened without these . . .' He stared contemptuously at Kate and Charlie, his green eyes cold with venom.

'Take your hand off me.'

Bill whirled in surprise. Jenny's face was livid with rage and scorn. 'Don't touch me, Bill Robinson. D'yer honestly think yer can act in the way I saw – yes I saw – yer act tonight and have me go on as before. The only reason nothing happened with that . . . that child, was because yer 'ad no opportunity. If Kate and I 'adn't seen you with 'er, no doubt at this very moment, you and she would 'ave been . . . Yer make me sick, sick . . . yer always 'ave . . .' Her voice began to rise hysterically, all the pent-up revulsion of the past year forcing her to lose her hard-won composure. 'Make love to 'er, go on, go back and make love to 'er. I don't care. P'raps yer'll leave me alone then.'

He hit her, the sound of flesh on flesh resounding loudly off the four walls. Charlie had him then and he collapsed, crying over and over that he was sorry, he was drunk, he loved her and she must forgive him. She didn't mean it, did she, did she? He hadn't meant to hurt her. He loved her. Oh God, he loved her, and anyway, he cried, it was her fault as well. What could you expect, he said, his eyes beginning to tear with the look of one who couldn't be blamed for his own actions, what could you expect if you had a wife who . . .

He turned to Charlie, who still held his arm.

'What's your Kate like, Charlie?' he enquired confidentially, as though he and Charlie discussed Kate's merits as a pastry cook, or needlewoman. Charlie didn't understand at first. 'Does she like it,' Bill went on artlessly. 'Jenny doesn't. She lies there like a block of wood. Never says no, mind, but she doesn't like it. Frigid, that's what she is. I wondered if it ran in the family. Well, I mean . . . who can blame me for wantin' a bit . . .'

Charlie lifted his clenched fist and his eyes slitted in rage. He would have hit Bill, drunk as he was, but Kate was in like a whippet between them, screaming shrilly, holding Charlie's arm, whilst Jenny stood like someone turned to stone.

She forgave him. She had no choice. Forgave him! If she were truthful; if she searched her mind and faced the fact which she had refused to recognise, she would admit that deep, deep down she really didn't care. She had been shocked. She had convinced herself that marriage to Bill; that her lovely child, all made up for the unhappiness she had known in the past, but now, after what had happened, she knew it did not.

But life must go on. Her marriage must go on. She had a child who needed the stability and security of a calm, peaceful home and how was she to get it if she and Bill were fighting. Besides, a corner of her mind told her, Bill had violent, dangerously excessive tempers. She could no longer call them 'tantrums'. He was ugly if he were crossed, this night had taught her that, so she 'forgave' him. She let him make love to her again. She let him into her life and her body, and to Bill it was as if the incident had never occurred. She knew he hadn't been unfaithful, not physically, at least that time, remembering the other evenings he had been away from home on 'bank business', so she closed her eyes and, like countless others in the misery of a loveless marriage which must be borne, she bore it.

But things had been said, and done, that night by both, and they would never be forgotten.

Chapter Thirty-Five

It was March and the anniversary of Waggy's birthday. The churchyard at St Andrews, Aigburth was bright with spring sunshine. The trees were gauzed with the first timid emergence of new tender greenery, each branch studded along its length with unfurling baby buds. The early grass was a fresh, juicy green, speared with a spreading harvest of daffodils, and scattered between each grave, primroses lifted delicate faces to the blue of the sky. The sun floated, a pale lemon disc, just above the roofline of the church, and its rays touched the bent heads of two women who stood beside a headstone, which as yet, was unmarred by the grey moss which crept across its neighbours. On it was written,

Percival Wagstaffe. 1860–1930. Waggy, a dear friend

The women were silent. One was smartly dressed in a warm, belted coat, the colour of pewter, and around her neck she had a tiny fur collar to match the hat which tipped over her right eye. She wore ankle-length boots and her hands were gloved in the same fur as her hat and collar. The biting March wind had whipped a rose into her cheeks and a tendril of brown, shining hair flicked across her eyebrows. She raised a hand to smooth it back behind her ear and as she did so her gaze turned to her companion.

Jenny's eyes burned with compassion as she looked at Kate. She saw her sister's shoulders move in a spasm of cold and watched as she stamped her feet against the ground. It was still hard with the leftover winter frost and the thin shoes she wore could scarcely have kept out the chill. Kate's hands were stuffed as far as they would go into the shallow pockets of her old coat, and on her head was an ancient woollen beret she had worn when she and Jenny had worked at Waggy's. Jenny wondered where she had kept it all these years, and why? It was pulled well down over her ears, hiding the once splendid profusion of her vigorous hair. As Jenny watched, a long shuddering sigh of utter despair shook Kate's frame. She slowly lifted her head and her eyes moved apathetically until they met Jenny's. She smiled, the effort barely lifting the corners of her mouth.

'Well, our Jenny, I wonder what 'e would 'ave made of all this?'

'All what love?' Jenny murmured softly.

'This bloody mess me an' Charlie's in.'

Jenny put her arm about Kate's shoulders and hugged her. 'If Waggy was 'ere you wouldn't be in a mess, chuck.'

Kate sighed again. 'No, yer right queen.'

There was a pause before Jenny spoke again. 'I wish yer'd let me . . .'

'Don't say it, our kid, yer've done enough.'

'Just a few bob, Kate, buy yourself some new shoes.'

'Give over, our Jenny.'

'Please Kate, I can't bear to see you . . .'

'No Jenny . . . anyway . . . it won't be for long . . .'

'What do you mean, it won't be for long?'

Kate turned away from the grave and began to walk slowly towards the gravel path. She stared at the ground as she moved her feet instinctively side-stepping to avoid the dainty clumps of primrose on the grassed path. Two men were digging a grave on the far side of the churchyard. One whistled cheerfully and his spade made a chomping noise as it bit into the hard ground. His companion stuck his spade firmly into the soil which was beginning to form a mound beside the hole, and leaning upon it, took a packet of Woodbines from his pocket. Putting a cigarette in his mouth he cupped his hands about it to shield the flame of the match from the wind as he lit it. With the cigarette between his lips, he took up his spade and resumed his digging.

A woman, a young girl beside her walked briskly along the gravel path. The girl held a small posy of flowers in her gloved hand, and her voice lifted merrily and carried on the wind across the rows of headstones. The woman shushed her and as they reached the grave they sought they fell silent as the child placed the flowers carefully upon the last resting place of a loved one.

'What d'yer mean, Kate?' Jenny repeated sharply as she followed her along the path.

Kate stopped, then turned slowly until she was looking directly into Jenny's eyes. Her next words were flat, unemotional.

'We're goin' to Australia, Jenny.'

She might have been announcing their intention to take a ferry ride across the Mersey to New Brighton. Jenny stared into Kate's dull blue eyes uncomprehendingly.

'Australia?'

Kate lifted her bare hand and rubbed her forehead above her left eyebrow tiredly. 'We're emigratin'. Charlie's 'ad it, our kid. If 'e doesn't work soon, it'll be the finish of 'im. We're sellin' up.' She laughed humourlessly, 'sellin' up, that's a good 'un.' She seemed unaware of Jenny's frozen-faced shock. 'There's work over there, a good life. 'E's bin thinkin' about it since before Christmas, but 'e asked me to say nowt. 'E wanted to make a few enquiries about the life and the fare and that. What sort of jobs there were. It seems there's a good chance for us. There's thousands goin' our Jenny, thousands like us any road. The fare's thirty-seven pound but with us bein' . . . ,' her voice cracked and the veneer of indifference began to chip away,'. . . with us bein' destitute, we go for nothin'.'

Jenny's eyes were fixed on Kate's face unblinkingly. She watched her mouth move as the words came out and she heard them as they fell on her ear, but they made not the slightest sense to her. Her mouth hung open and it was as though a bolt of lightning had come from above and welded her to the ground. Even her brain was fused to stillness.

Kate regarded her sister impassively, but at the back of her flat, blue eyes a shimmer stirred, like the signal of pain which comes to flesh when a nerve is exposed.

'Don't look like that, love. Yer know me an' Charlie can't go on like this. 'E's become a different man, less than a man since 'e was out of work. 'E doesn't come near me any more. Afraid of failure, even there.'

'Kate, oh love, don't . . . please don't . . .' Jenny's voice was like the cry of a child and Kate was reminded of her own Leslie. He whimpered like that when his dreams were bad and his baby heart was frightened.

'It's no good sayin' don't our kid. I gorra go where Charlie goes. It's bin nearly two years since 'e 'ad a job. Yer've seen 'im, you know what 'e's like.'

A movement of her cheek muscles pulled her face into an expression which was almost a smile. For a second, she was back in Seacomb Street and she and Charlie walked arm in arm, youthful feet in step. The street lights glowed about Charlie's head and shone on his brown, laughing face. His eyes flashed like crystal. Love, life, optimism. The years stretched ahead before them, filled with promise, as he kissed her. Charlie, so young, hopeful, proud. A man.

'D'yer remember 'im, Jenny?' Kate said softly, and her eyes were alive for the first time in months. 'D'yer remember how 'e used to stand so straight. Frightened o' nothin' and no one was my Charlie, and laugh! Nowt gorrim down. 'E looked after me, an' you an' all. 'E's bin everythin' to me. 'E'd give 'is right arm if 'e could, to

329

get us back where we used to be, but nobody wants 'is right arm, or any part of 'im. Only me. 'E needs this, luv, this bit of 'ope, an' 'e needs me.'

She looked sorrowfully into Jenny's face which had become anguished. She watched it crease and crumple with the force of her emotion but no words seemed able to get past Jenny's strangled vocal chords since that first despairing cry of denial.

'Don't say owt, not yet, luv,' Kate went on. 'Yer'll get used to the idea of us leavin', everybody will . . .' She was close to breaking point. 'Yer don't need me . . . any more. Yer've got Bill, yer own family. Laura. Bill's Mam and Dad . . . Elly'll still . . . yer don't need me . . . yer strong . . . Charlie's not . . . 'e needs me an' 'e needs ter work.'

She put her arms about herself and raised her face to the pale spring sky and began to rock backwards and forwards. 'I've gorra give Charlie his chance, you know I 'ave, but to go so far away, to know I'll never see any of yer again . . . oh God, Jenny, it's breakin' my 'eart.'

'Don't, oh don't Kate . . . I can't . . . I don't know what to do . . . to say . . . I can't bear the thought of yer . . . What will I do? Yer know I don't love . . . not like I loved Nils . . . There's only you and Laura . . .'

Jenny clutched at Kate's arm desperately, and she shook as though she had been stripped naked in the bitter March wind. Her hands gripped the cloth of Kate's coat and her face was awash with frightened tears, the merciless pain more than she could bear.

Kate, scarcely aware of what she did, stepped away, slapping Jenny's hands away from her angrily.

'Christ, Jenny, dear Christ, stop it. Don't . . . touch me. It's bad enough.' She felt as though she were made of brittle glass and the slightest touch could shatter her into a million glittering pieces on the ground. And the way things were, she didn't care. It would be a relief to be trampled into the black soil and never know another thing. But it was Charlie. Charlie. She clung to the sound of his name in her head, and turned a bitter waxen face to Jenny.

'You can't stand it. *You* can't stand it. What about me, our Jenny? It's me that's goin' thousands of bloody miles away. It's me that's leavin' everyone I love, all the places I've grown up in, to go to a country I know nowt about. I'll be livin' with strangers, not a soul I know. No one to . . . Christ Jenny, don't talk to me about not bein' able to stand it.'

She squared her shoulders and stared stonily into her sister's eyes.

330

'Stand up Jenny, stand up and grow up. Yer a big girl now and yer family need yer, just like mine need me.'

She turned away and began to make her way towards the gate.

The first distraught shock was over, but the strain of keeping up the pretence of normality was almost too much for the sisters to contend with. The following Sunday, the flat in Rice Lane was seething with the excitement which flowed from Charlie like an erupting spring of fresh, life-giving water. He was effervescent with it, and, catching the quicksilver intoxication from his brother-in-law, Bill was as eager as he to discuss the adventure on which the Walker family was setting out.

The rift of 2 months ago had been clumsily patched up. Kate and Jenny would have it no other way and Bill, in his feckless, superficial fashion had forgotten it before a week had gone by. So, in the euphoria of the moment had Charlie.

Always forced to walk the tightrope of Charlie's stubborn pride, Jenny had got into the habit of inviting them to Sunday tea as often as she was able without arousing the suspicion in his mind that she was offering charity. She put up a huge meal, big enough if he had thought of it, to make Charlie suspect immediately that she was making sure that they had at least one decent meal in a week, but in the pleasure of seeing his children spooning cream trifle into their eager, and sweet-starved mouths, it did not seem to occur to him. The meal was over. The table which had groaned with cold meats, pork pies, cheese, celery, pickles, plates of brown and white bread and butter, fruit, trifle and chocolate cake, was almost empty and while Kate and Jenny silently cleared the table and washed up the dishes, Bill and Charlie, each with a child upon his lap, sat before the leaping fire and eulogised over the prospects to be had in the far-off continent to which Charlie and his family were going.

'It started wi' the Empire Settlements Act, Bill, 1922 it was. Summat to do wi' the development of Empire Production and trade. They need folk in the dominions. Settlers, they call 'em and the bloke at the office said there would be plenty of jobs goin' for a chef in lots of the 'otels there. It's an up and comin' place, is Sydney. Hotels goin' up, staff wanted.' Charlie leaned forward and his daughter looked up at him as his enthusiasm flushed his thin face and put a sparkle in his eyes.

'. . . An' the weather, Bill. It's like summer nearly all the year round. Sunshine and norra lot o' rain, an' the schools. Well, I 'eard tell where the kids sit outside to do their lessons. Can you credit it?'

331

He turned his head in the direction of the kitchen. 'No more botherin' about gerrin yer washin' dry, eh our Kate?'

The silence from the kitchen appeared to go unnoticed.

'What sort o' wages do they pay, Charlie?' Bill asked. 'Do they get as much as 'ere?'

'Well, I'm not too sure about that mate,' Charlie answered cautiously, 'but it'll be a damn sight better than t'dole. Eeh Bill lad, what it'll be like to be workin' again.' His elation was a visible, wonderful thing. He was the old Charlie again. Merry, excited, filled with the joy of living and the blessed relief of actually doing something, planning a future for himself and his family.

Frankie and Leslie scrambled about the floor, arranging the miniature cars they had brought with them in a line across the carpet in readiness for a race between Henry Segrave and Malcolm Campbell. As the voice of their father rose in rapturous gladness, Frankie looked up, caught, young as he was by his exaltation.

'Will I be able to play soccer, Dad?' he piped, his eyes serious. If they didn't have soccer, he didn't want to go.

Charlie turned eagerly to his son. 'Course you will, son, and cricket, and yer'll be able to swim in the sea every day of the year, and . . .'

'Every day, even at Christmas?'

'Aye, and on Christmas Day yer'll eat your turkey with yer cossie on, it'll be that hot.'

This was more than the boy could absorb. Christmas Day with yer cossie on. Sounded a bit daft to him. Going back to his toys, he was soon lost in the thrills of his speedking heroes, and the rest of Charlie's words passed over his head.

'. . . We'll 'ave to stay in a sort of camp to begin with, but as soon as I start earnin' we'll be able to move into our own place. I fancy summat lookin' out over the harbour,' he said optimistically. ''Ave yer seen the picture of the 'arbour. It's a sight for sore eyes, Bill, and another thing,' Charlie warmed to his theme, '. . . there's this bridge they're buildin', there'll be work on that, that's if I can't get into catering right away,' he added hastily. 'Any road, they give yer trainin' in new trades if yer want, an' give yer an allowance while yer learnin'.'

'How long did they say it would be Charlie, before yer go?'

'Not long, the bloke said. P'raps a few months, but I don't care, it's summat to look forward to, Bill. I can take this . . . well, I can purrup wi' dole queue an' . . . everythin' now I know there's summat to look forward to.'

332

'An' what about you Kate?' Bill shouted, 'are you excited?'

Jenny held the plate she was wiping in her still hands and watched her sister as she bent her head until her chin touched her chest. Her tears ran silently down her face and dripped into the washing up water. As Bill's words floated from the other room, Kate turned in anguished appeal to Jenny, and she shook her head unable to speak. Her eyes begged for help. Her heart was like a lump of cold metal in her breast, but how could she break Charlie's dream?

'Course she is,' Jenny answered. 'Who wouldn't like all that sunshine?'

Kate's weeping eyes thanked her. Her hands automatically cleaned a plate and put it on the draining board, then reached for another, but with a soft moan, heard only by Jenny, she ran silently from the kitchen, along the tiny hallway and into the bathroom. Closing the door behind her and locking it, she began to run the cold water. She filled the basin and dipping her face in it, let the coolness lave her hot, swollen eyelids.

Jenny finished the job in the kitchen, half hearing the animated conversation which was still taking place in the sitting room.

Couldn't Charlie see what it was doing to Kate? Was he so blind to everything but his own deliverance he could not see the torment his wife suffered at the prospect of separation from all she held most dear? No one could deny the pain and humiliation Charlie himself had known for the past two years. The anticipation of work and a bright future for his family had imbued him with a vigorous hope. The relief was plain in his enthusiasm and eagerness, but did he need to be quite so . . . buoyant? Kate's silence must speak worlds. She was going only for his sake, but surely he knew that? Couldn't he, at least for the next few weeks, until she was more accustomed to the idea, be a little more understanding of her feelings?

But Jenny knew in her heart that Charlie was not to blame for what he did. His spirit had been dragged to the lowest level it could go, and here, as if in answer to his prayers, was a way out for them all. A man must work. He must have respect for himself or he will not function. She was aware that Charlie, deep in the core of the goodness which made him as he was, knew of Kate's suffering, but with the hopeful optimism of men when their women's tears scourge them, he believed it would blow over. She was upset, he knew that, but she'd get over it. Just let her see that paradise which waited for her on the other side of the world. That sunshine, the great beautiful open spaces, the golden beaches and the blue endless sea; the magnificent flowers and trees and the wonderful healthy life which awaited her children. She'd change her mind then. He was certain of it.

Chapter Thirty-Six

They were to sail in two weeks' time on 10 June. Kate, thinner than
Jenny now; gaunt, looking ten years older than her twenty-nine
years, sat quietly in her armchair beside the grease-spotted range
in the kitchen of her room in Green Street. She could hear Jenny's
voice from upstairs as she read to the children before they went to
sleep and from the dainty, frilled cot which was placed across two
chairs in the corner of the room, Jenny's daughter burbled con-
tentedly. Kate could see two fat hands clutch and grab at each other
above the side of the cot and the pretty pink quilted cover which lay
across the child, lifted as two strong little legs suddenly kicked it
onto the floor. Their Jenny wouldn't like that, Kate thought idly. To
see her child's lovely clean cover on Kate's damp and mouldy brick
floor wouldn't go down too well with their kid. Jenny imagined she
was being diplomatic, but Kate knew she dreaded bringing her
beautiful adored daughter to this dump. And who could blame
her, she thought dispiritedly? Jenny fancied Kate didn't notice
these things, but she wasn't daft. Half out of her head with misery,
but not daft. She'd seen the way baby Laura was always made to
wear a bonnet, even indoors. That was so she wouldn't catch the
nits, and Jenny kept her in her cot as much as she could and never
let the cot touch the floor so that the cockroaches, the mice, the
fleas and the silverfish wouldn't contaminate her precious child.

Oh God, will yer listen to me? Kate's face spasmed in anguish. –
Talkin' about me own sister as if she was some high falutin' snotty
lady mucky muck, when all she wants to do is protect 'er child.
Wouldn't I be the same? Wasn't I the same once? My kids were
clean, well-fed, cared for, loved, petted and pampered, just like
Jenny's. They're still loved, but how can you keep a child clean in
this? How can you pamper them when you're on the poverty line?
You get that you don't much care after a while. Well, she'd be soon
out of it. In the land of eternal bloody sunshine, eatin' fruit till it
came out of 'er ears and rollin' in 'er cossie on the golden beach.

Kate was in a state of perpetual, spirit-sapping depression now.
She never wept, or gave much heed to the words which poured

from Charlie in an ever-increasing self-reassuring torrent. Jenny cried. Whenever they were together Jenny cried, and Kate knew it caused trouble between her and Bill, but she couldn't seem to get up much concern. Jenny and Bill must sort out their own lives now. Jenny'd have to manage without her from now on, but could she manage without Jenny?

A ripple crossed Kate's face. It was funny really. All these years she had seen herself in the role of protector. She was the strong rock upon whom their Jenny had leaned. Kate had looked after her, nursed her when she was ill, but in a strange way, she had, though she had not been aware of it, depended upon their Jenny. She had Charlie. She had her children, but where she was going she would have no one else. A woman needed another woman. Perhaps it was only to indulge in the gossip, in the grumbling which is a part of the female nature. A wife was loyal to her husband, but it was lovely now and again to have a little grouch about his awkward ways, and who else to grumble to but one's own sister. Kate and Jenny had no close women friends. They had not needed them. Even as children they had played together and as they grew, their confidences, secrets, had been shared only with one another, now there would . . .

Her reverie was broken by the sound of Jenny's feet clumping on the bare boards as she came down the stairs. She went immediately to her baby. Picking up the cot cover, she turned surreptitiously to look at Kate, then gave it a good shake, inspecting it minutely before she put it back in the cot. She leaned over the baby, the strong maternal love pouring from her as she smiled at the round laughing face on the pillow. The baby's eyes were a clear pale green like Bill's, but the rest of her face was a duplicate of Jenny's. Her fists lifted to her mother, and Jenny held them to her lips, biting the fingers gently. She was lost in that wonderment of fulfilment the sight of her child gave her and for a moment Kate was forgotten.

'Where've they gone?'

Kate's voice broke the spell. Jenny turned and walked towards the dead range. Though there was no fire, the chairs were still placed on each side as if to find the most advantageous position in the squalid room. Jenny sighed.

'I don't know chuck. They've gone in the car, so I hope Bill doesn't drink too much, but I don't know which pub.'

'I dunno what they want to go for.'

'Well, I suppose it's . . . like a . . . farewell . . .'

'Shurrup Jenny.'

It was quiet except for the slap of the rockers on the floor as Jenny set the chair in motion. A child's voice could be heard from upstairs and another answered sleepily. The infant in the crib made sucking noises as she fell into her baby sleep then there was silence. Kate stared at the wall, her mind a blank. A picture or two flitted across her vision, vagrant thoughts of nothing much, and she might have been alone for all the notice she took of Jenny.

They began the silent vigil which had taken place each day since Kate had told Jenny that they were emigrating.

Bill and Charlie stood elbow to elbow at the bar of the Dog and Partridge on the corner of Green Street and Stanley Road. Bill had wanted to take Charlie to the old pub in Fazackerly where they had once done their drinking, but Charlie had demurred. He did not say so to Bill but he was reluctant to stand amongst the men for whom he had once bought a drink. His suit was shabby now; the one in which he had been married, and though he wore a tie for the occasion, he would have felt out of place. He had pawned a pair of cufflinks his Mam had given him for his twenty-first birthday and which he had been saving for when he and Kate were really desperate, but now, with only a fortnight to go before they sailed for their new life, he felt he might spend the few shillings he had on a bevvy. He could keep up his end tonight, even at tenpence a pint.

The word got round. The chap at the end of the bar was off to Australia. By 'eck, that took a birra doin'. Draggin' up roots which were buried deep in the 'Pool an' transferin' 'em to the new soil of Australia. A finger was raised here and there to indicate a drink was to be sent over for the voyager. His spirit was admired. The men hereabouts knew the plight of those who had no work, and understood Charlie's desperate flight across the world to find a job, and a new life which would ensure that this which he had suffered would not happen to his children.

The evening became merry, and those who passed the Dog and Partridge speculated on the unusual sounds of jocularity which erupted from the boozer, and it only a Thursday night. Charlie was the life and soul of the party. It was as though he had been transported back to those carefree days when he was a young sailor, and he had been encircled by the special camaraderie of those who live hard, as the sea demands, and play hard when they are ashore. He appeared not to realise that he still had his few bob in his pocket, and had he done so, would have been perplexed as to how he had become so drunk, without parting with any of it.

They sang all the old songs, banging their glasses on table top and bar. The landlord and his wife couldn't keep up with them and the landlord's grin was stretched from one side of his face to the other. He hadn't had such a good night since the Coronation.

They were on the last chorus of *Keep the Home Fires Burning*. Most of the men were veterans of the war and it had been a particular favourite in the trenches. Though fourteen years had passed, it didn't take much to bring it to their lips, and they ranged from the cheerful to the maudlin and back again, as men will when they have a few pints inside them and the missus is not present.

Charlie's eyes were full of tears as the last faltering male voice quavered to a halt. He was having a lovely time. He hadn't enjoyed himself so much since . . . since . . . he couldn't remember when. Bill swayed beside him, clinging for dear life to his glass as though it were the only thing which kept him on his feet. They stood, the pair of them, laughing at nothing, each telling jokes to which neither listened, gesticulating with flaccid hand to drive home an opinion to which there was no point anyway, and tottering on feet which, for some reason, seemed to wander about with a will of their own.

Charlie sagged gently as a hand rested on his shoulder.

'Come on, me old luv,' said a friendly voice behind him. 'Can yer manage one more with an old shipmate?'

Charlie turned jerkily, almost knocking the man who had spoken to him off his feet.

'Steady on, Charlie. It looks as though I'm too late. I think yer've already 'ad enough.'

It was Tommy Johnson.

Charlie tried to focus his eyes on the smiling face which wavered in front of his own but it was too late. He sat down abruptly on a handy chair, and putting his head down on the beer-soaked table, passed out. Bill shook Charlie's shoulder fretfully, then sat carefully beside him, and in the fashion of those in the penultimate stage of inebriation, remained perfectly still as though any sudden movement might be dangerous.

The landlord looked at the stranger and smiled wryly.

'Sorry about that, pal, but as you can see, they've 'ad one too many. That 'un's' – indicating the snoring Charlie – 'off to Australia an' I think 'e an' 'is friend were doin' a bit of celebratin'.'

'Australia?' Tommy looked surprised. 'Last time I saw 'im was in . . . eeh I dunno . . . a few years back. 'E was a seaman then.'

The landlord breathed on a glass and wiped it lethargically with a cloth.

'Well, I dunno about that but 'e's off to find 'is fortune on t'other side o' t'world, in a fortnight's time, an' from what 'e said to-night 'e'll be berrer off an' all. Two years since 'e 'ad a job, poor sod.'

Bill jerked in his seat wincing at the sudden movement and gazed blankly round him, evidently in some dilemma as to where he was.

'God, my head's like Birkenhead.' He stirred gingerly, rising to his feet with the minimum of movement.

'I'm not surprised.' The landlord grinned in a friendly fashion, 'but I think yer'd berrer get yer mate 'ome.'

Tommy put his hand under Charlie's arm. 'Come on, me old lad, let's get yer home or that bonny wife of yours'll 'ave yer neck in a sling.'

Bill, who had not drunk the amount Charlie had, tottered delicately on his other side, and between them he and Tommy angled Charlie to his feet. His eyes were like slate in his slack face, but somehow he managed to walk between them. The car was left outside the pub and the three men, arms about each other – a familiar sight at this time of night – made their way along the length of Green Street.

Charlie had begun to sing again, appropriately, *'There's a long, long trail a-winding . . .'.* The look of surprise was very evident on Tommy's face when they halted outside Charlie's squalid house. You could see he thought it was a far cry from Crescent Road. They knocked on the door for they were unable to keep Charlie upright long enough to find his key. He was by this time what was known as 'falling down drunk', but genial with it. His babbling laughter was the first thing which Kate heard as she opened the door.

'Katie, chuck . . . yer look . . . booti . . . booti . . . luvly. Eeh, yer a bonny lass, that you are . . . now what d'yer say to a big kish . . . a kish for yer old Charlie.'

He missed the step and landed at her feet, laughing helplessly. Kate stared down at him as though someone had placed a complete stranger on her doorstep. Jenny crowded behind her, the expression on her face as astounded as that of her sister.

Tommy grinned engagingly. ''Ello Kate, d'yer remember me?'

Kate took her eyes from the foolish capering antics of her husband and looked at Tommy.

'Don't yer remember?' he said. 'I came to yer 'ousewarmin' an' yer wouldn't let me off bloody piano.'

Kate had no interest in parties nor pianos. Her gaze returned to Charlie.

'What the 'ell's up wi' 'im,' she croaked, 'as if I didn't know, an' where the 'ell did 'e get the money to get like it?' She turned accusingly to Bill. 'Is it you, did you gerrim bevvied?'

'No, it wasn't me Kate.' Bill was fractious. His head ached and his stomach felt as though it were about to heave up all that it contained. 'It got round Charlie was off to Australia and one or two of the chaps stood him a pint.'

'One or two,' Kate screeched. 'One or two dozen more likely. Well, fetch 'im in, but I'm not gerrin 'im to bed.'

Charlie was lifted from his supine position on the front doorstep and, thanks mainly to Tommy Johnson, dumped unceremoniously on his bed upstairs.

Tommy came down the stairs. He stood in the kitchen and looked about him awkwardly. Kate had resumed her seat beside the range. Jenny had put on her coat and was fussing with the sleeping child and Bill had gone back to the Dog and Partridge to pick up the car.

'Well Missus, I'll be off then.' Kate did not turn. The scene with Charlie might never have happened. Jenny looked at the discomfited man and smiled tentatively. She turned to Kate, but still Kate stared at nothing in particular. She was back in the nightmare which had contained her for the past six months.

'Yes . . . well . . . thanks Tommy. It was good of you . . .' Jenny said hesitantly.

'Don't mention it, queen. Anything for an old mate.'

'You were at sea with Charlie?'

'Oh aye like. We were on the old *Franconia* together when she was torpedoed. Good mates we were. Many's the game of "Crown and Anchor" we 'ad in the galley, the two of us, like. Made a few bob, we did, but 'is always went first port we called in. Them was good days, them was.'

Jenny waited to see if Kate would speak. Poor chap. He'd done them a good turn and Kate was treating him as though he were a leper. But Kate took no notice, not of Tommy, nor of what was being said.

'They're off to Australia then?'

Jenny's face spasmed and she hung her head so that Tommy would not see the quick tears.

'Yes.' Her voice was thick with emotion.

'What's to do? Can't 'e get a job over 'ere?'

Jenny cleared her throat wishing Bill would hurry up. The effort of making polite conversation with this complete stranger – she had no recollection of him from the party – was more than she

340

could manage, especially if he insisted on discussing the trip to Australia.

'Er, no. It's been nearly two years but . . .'

''As 'e tried gerrin back on the boats?'

'The boats?'

'Aye, Merchant Navy.'

'Well, I . . .'

'They're wantin' a roast cook on the ship I've just bin on.'

'Roast cook?'

Tommy remembered Jenny from the party at Kate and Charlie's. She'd been elevenpence halfpenny in the shilling then and from the look of her, she still was. He began to explain patiently. His voice was deliberate, as though he was speaking to a child. It went on and on, rambling in the way of those who like the sound of their own voice, and relish the telling of a tale. Especially when you have a listener who is attentive as this one. Even the one in the chair had turned to look at him. Tommy warmed to his theme, going into great details of the roast cook who had picked up a bad case of Malta dog . . . er . . . dysentery, in a Middle East port, and who had been left behind; of a new chap being signed on the next day but of the necessity for those interested to look sharp, because once word got around, it'd be every man for himself. The ship was to sail on Saturday night, just to New York this time, thank God. The last trip had been bad enough, too long it was, and the missus didn't like him being away for . . .

The voice from the chair startled him. It sounded like the caw of a crow and it took him several seconds to realise that Charlie's old woman was speaking to him, or to understand what she said.

'Roast cook?'

'Yer what luv?'

'Did yer say . . . *roast cook*?'

At last he got the gist of what she meant and away he went again.

Kate was on her feet by now, moving slowly, like an old woman whose rheumatism troubled her. She reached Jenny's side and they stood stiffly like two old soldiers who had been brought sharply to attention. Tommy was charmed with his engrossed audience, and whilst wondering at the intense look on the face of Charlie's missus proceeded to discourse cheerfully on the joys of being at sea, the freedom of a sailors's life, and the boredom of being a landlubber.

'Mind you, like as not Charlie'll settle down to a job at 'ome. Not that Australia's 'ome, but yer know what I mean. After all, 'e's been away from t'sea for a number o' years, that young chap told

341

me. Well, I've bin on the boats since I left school and I couldn't see meself doin' owt else. Now this trip to America, it just suits me. Just long enough for my missus to be glad to see me back but not long enough . . .' He rambled on in an agreeable manner until slowly it became clear to him that the two women were strangely silent and the atmosphere electric.

'Did I say summat?' he said at last, gazing from one to the other, perplexed.

'Tommy, for God's sake, did yer say . . . did yer say there could be . . . a job?' Kate's voice cracked and she clutched at Jenny, never taking her eyes from the man's face. 'D'yer mean there might be one goin'?'

Tommy looked surprised. 'That's what I've bin sayin'.'

'Would . . . would Charlie stand a chance?' Kate's eagerness was pitiful. She swayed as she spoke and would have fallen if Jenny had not held her steady.

'Burr I thought 'e were off to Australia?'

'Bugger Australia.'

Tommy's face was comical in its amazement.

'But I was told that . . .'

'Never mind what you were told.' Kate was steadier now as hope pumped its way into limbs that had long since atrophied. She took a step towards the bewildered man and in her face a miracle was at work. The colour flooded, and her eyes began to snap. In the midst of his confusion Tommy had time to ponder idly that Charlie's wife was a damn goodlooking woman, now she 'ad a bit of life in 'er.

'If Charlie went down tomorrow, 'as he gorra chance?' she repeated intensely.

Tommy scratched his head. 'Well, I don't see why not. 'E's worked for the line before. They know 'im, so I don't see why they shouldn't take 'im on.'

Kate clasped her hands together and closed her eyes in ecstasy. Her face turned towards the ceiling and it was as though she winged a prayer of thanksgiving heavenwards. She stood for several moments and the two who were with her were struck dumb by the sheer, unadulterated waves of joy which seemed to flow from her. Jenny felt herself begin to tremble and a tiny flicker of something which was indescribable touched her heart. She felt it move and glow and spread until the most perfect sense of happiness filled her and lit up her whole being.

Kate opened her eyes and turned to Jenny, then with the speed and grace of a gazelle she raced towards the bottom of the staircase.

'What are you going to do, our Kate?' Jenny's voice trembled and

342

the man looked from one woman to the other, on his face an expression of wonderment which asked – how on earth he had got into this?

'To get Charlie sober, what else.'

She didn't think she would ever forget that night as long as she lived. Tommy Johnson had been a Godsend. The minute he had it sorted out in his mind what Kate was up to, he had set to with a will, even making up some remedy which was guaranteed to get a man sober quicker than it took to get a woman . . . well, he didn't finish the sentence, ladies being present, but it were bloody good stuff.

Bill, still nursing his thick head and a queasy stomach, sat in the armchair – the rocker was too much for him in his present condition – and watched as the feebly protesting Charlie was brought down the stairs and walked up and down the tiny room until Kate was satisfied he was in possession of his senses.

He had been horrified.

'But the passage is booked and everything.'

'I don't care. If there's a chance of a job, summat to keep us 'ere, we're takin' it.'

'But I might not get on t'boat. Yer know I've tried before.'

'Well we'll go to Australia then.'

'We can't just turn round and . . .'

'Why not? Someone else can 'ave our tickets.'

'But yer don't like me goin' to sea.'

'I'd rather 'ave it than live so far away.'

Charlie's face creased into a pitifully hurt expression and, aware of it but uncaring of the silent spectators, Kate took him in her arms and held him. Her words were low in his ear. Her cheek was pressed to his, and the tears of desperation wet them both. They rocked together, all the caring need which had dried up during the past months, flooding over them. Charlie relaxed in the warmth of his wife's love.

He was at the shipping office the next morning. The news had not yet got around that the SS Samaria needed a roast cook and before ten minutes had gone by Charlie had signed up and would sail on the evening tide the next day for New York.

In his quiet way, Charlie was disappointed not to have gone to Australia. It had seemed to him that the life, and work, which was offered to those prepared to put their minds to it, would have been a wonderful opportunity, not just for himself, but for his children. It was a new country compared to old England, but that was what

343

had excited him. He was used to being away from home. He had pulled up his roots at the age of thirteen and though recently he had been settled to the domesticity of family life and the everyday routine of a working man, his heart had sometimes yearned to be away, and his eyes to see new sights. To feel the warmth of the sun upon his face as he had known it on the West Indies run; to see the blue sea and the crashing rollers and to move in a space so vast and empty, the like of which the denizens of the cramped city had never imagined, let alone seen.

But he loved his Kate, and he knew her well by now. He had realised in the depths of his mind that she had agreed to Australia only for his sake. He had known her terror at the thought of being away from familiar faces and places, and though he had recognised that eventually she would have overcome it, his heart had quailed at the knowledge of her unhappiness.

On his first trip home in July, eager to depart from Green Street as soon as possible, he and Kate began their search for a new home. They combed the suburbs to find a house which would compare with the one they had left in Crescent Road over six months ago, but it was as though Kate's heart had been left in the home she had loved so well, and nothing would do.

It was by chance that she met someone in the market whose face, familiar, but for the moment unplaced, took her back to the day when Waggy had come in his new car to her house, just before Jenny's first child was born. The scene flashed in front of her as she picked over the apples on the fruit stall and the woman smiled.

'You don't remember me, do you, Mrs Walker?' she said.

It was the woman who had lived in the house directly opposite her own in Crescent Road. Kate remembered it as though it were yesterday. Her embarrassment as Waggy postured proudly and in a voice loud enough to wake the dead, threatened the group of children who had gathered to admire his new car.

To her delight the woman told her that their old house was still vacant, which was not really surprising in these hard times; houses to rent were ten a penny, and before the week was out, Kate was back there and the 'scrubbing brush brigade' as Bill sourly called his wife and Kate, were scouring the house from the roof down. With a coat or two of white paint, the house was as pristine and shining as it had always been. The joy which Kate felt as she stood in the still empty parlour, listening to the sounds of the familiar creaks which the house made, and sniffing the clean smell of carbolic and new paint, was made the more poignant by the realisation of how nearly she had lost it. She could hear the excited

344

voices of her children. Frankie, delirious at being home with his old friends and the prospect of the good games that would be renewed in the woods, followed closely by Dorry and Leslie, was pointing out to his young brother and sister the place where he and Alfie had built a den and telling them from the lofty pinnacle of his eight years of all the wonders that would be theirs, as though he were the only one who had ever experienced them.

It would be many months, even years, before Kate and Charlie would be able to furnish their home as it had once been, but they had a bed, camp beds for the children, a table and four chairs in the kitchen, culled from the secondhand shop, the old armchair, still going strong after all these years, the rocking chair, and a good glowing fire in the grate. With nourishing food in their bellies and love in their bed at night, what more did they need, remarked Charlie fatuously, as he held her again in his eager arms. The loving was back, her man was returned to her, and life was good.

Bill and Jenny were on the move as well. It was really only Kate and Charlie who had held them back. Bill had hankered after a semi in Walton since the day Laura was born and in the heedless way he had, could think of no good reason why they shouldn't move immediately. What if Charlie *was* on the dole? It was no fault of his, and why it should affect himself and Jenny was beyond him. Was the fact that Charlie was down on his luck going to hold them back forever? Just because Charlie and Kate couldn't afford to live in a good neighbourhood, did that mean *he* was forced to stay in a pokey flat forever? It was a pokey flat now, the neat home of which he had been so proud, and it took all Jenny's charm and wits to keep him, for the time being, from flaunting his success in the faces of Kate and Charlie.

But now it didn't matter and she let him have his head. They moved into a brand new 'villa' in Walton Park, Walton in October 1932. It was expensive. Ten shillings and threepence each week but Bill was earning three pounds and fifteen shillings now and they could afford it. They had a small garden at the front, and a long narrow plot of ground at the rear. The houses had been built on an orchard and the builder had had the foresight to leave, where possible, the fruit trees. The grass was rough but the walls around the garden were high and Jenny sighed with pleasure as she looked to the days to come when she and Kate would sit beneath the trees and watch the four children play.

It never once crossed her mind to imagine herself and Bill lazing harmoniously in the privacy of their first garden.

Chapter Thirty-Seven

Helen Robinson and Kathleen Walker, Kathy for short, were born within a few days of one another in June 1933, and from the day that one became aware of the other, they were Kate and Jenny over again. So close, so beloved of one another did they become it was a battle at the end of each encounter to part them. They were so alike. Dark chestnut, fat and shiny curls. Eyes so brown as to be almost black, like gypsies, moist red lips and cheeks to match and skin the colour of honey and as sweet to taste. They were taken for twins, and their devotion to, and dependence upon one another was touching to see. Their love for each other brought their mothers even closer, if that was possible, as if they shared their two lovely girls, Kathy belonging to Jenny and Helen to Kate.

It was Elly who shattered Jenny's fragile marriage beyond repair.

The babies were two months old. The joint christening took place at St Mary's Church, Walton, on a warm August day in which everything seemed to be hazed with the golden glow of late summer. The leaves on the trees drooped delicately, a pattern of crochet work against the fine cornflower sky. The lawns about the graves had been mown the day before and the fresh smell of cut grass made a sweet summery fragrance in the air. The short grass was a bright vivid green, latticed with wild pansies, and the children, forced to stand quietly during the ceremony, raced in their new shoes about the headstones, letting off steam.

The group posed for photographs. 'Lady Mary', married now to Douglas, and pregnant herself, was Godmother to Helen. Whether marriage, or pregnancy, had mellowed her it was hard to tell, but she had become fond of Jenny and adored the lovely child Laura, and her face was proud as she held her new niece in her arms. Kate had asked Janet Clancy to stand for Kathy, and the two women, Mary pleased even in a tenuous way, to be associated with the wife of a doctor, stood in the sunshine, the two beautiful children held in their arms.

Next it was the turn of the parents. The grandparents were added, and finally the whole family. The children fidgeted. Frankie

346

was embarrassed in his new suit. The trousers reached to his knees, and though it was a warm day, his mother had insisted he must put on his new fair isle pullover. His cap jammed to his eyebrows, he glowered into the camera. Dorothy, like all small girls, was speechless with joy to pose in her fetching new dress and hat, but Leslie, like his brother, could only stand with all the patience an almost five year old could muster, his head filled with the thoughts of the sumptuous feast set out in Aunty Jenny's front room. Laura clung to Jenny's hand, her infant face mystified and ready to crumple into the ready tears which had assailed her since the arrival of the new babies. Jenny lifted her up into the safe cradle of her arms, kissing her cheek, and the two faces, so alike in their beauty, smiled into the camera.

The photographer emerged from under his cloth and began to fold away the tripod, packing his camera into a case. The party broke up into small groups of two or three, or four, standing about in the sunlight which filtered through the leaves of the trees. They laughed and chatted, sometimes with slight strain for Mary found it hard going to converse pleasantly with Pat O'Reilly, and Elly was none too happy with Douglas, but on the whole they agreed that it was a happy occasion which had so fortuituously brought together the two families.

Jenny wandered away in the direction of the grass verge. Laura skipped ahead of her, bending to prod with clumsy baby fingers at the delicate bloom of a pansy. She turned to look at her mother, her bright eyes laughing, inquisitive, and babbled some words most of which only Jenny understood.

'Yes, sweetheart, it's a pansy. Say "pansy" for mummy.'

'Panthy,' the child lisped.

Jenny crouched beside her and Laura leaned against her knee and the two dark heads bent together over the clump of flowers. Golden eyes stared solemnly into green, and the pretty scene had the photographer wishing he had not packed away his camera.

Bill sauntered slowly down the path towards Jenny and Laura. His face was pleased and smiling. He was proud of his elegant and lovely wife and of his two pretty children. Taking Jenny's hand, he lifted her to her feet, then picked up his daughter and held her high to see a thrush which cocked its beady eye in their direction. He posed grandly, overbearing in his self-conceit.

Ellen Robinson glanced at her son and daughter-in-law, and her mother's heart filled with joy. What a lovely picture they made, she thought. He'd done well for himself after all with Jenny. She'd made him a real good wife. They had a lovely home and those babies, they were a credit to her. Ellen preened, as though it were all her doing, then returned to her chat with the vicar. She had never been so happy in her life.

They crowded into Jenny's front room, drinking the cheap champagne Bill had insisted upon, though Charlie was heard to remark plaintively he'd rather have had a pint, and eating rich Christening cake. They sat or stood, even the vicar, and wandered about admiring Jenny's neat new house and the children raced around the garden until Laura cried the easy tears of babyhood and Frankie got a clip across the ear for teasing Dorry.

It had been a splendid day everyone agreed, but the children were cross and bored, and Pat O'Reilly had had as much as he could stand of Jenny's 'posh' relatives. Bobby and Jimmy had got into an argument, of all things, about football and Kathy Walker was sick all over her delicate lace Christening dress. Bill, as if determined to show his guests how used he had become to drinking champagne was on the way to being irritably tipsy, and held his new daughter in a tight grip of possessive love which Jenny knew presaged a maudlin protestation of his parental feelings. She shook her head and winked at Kate who smiled back at her. They all knew Bill by now.

It was the last peaceful moment Jenny was to know.

The guests began to leave, wending their way through crying children, laughing women, relieved men and the remains of the feast which Kate and Jenny had prepared the day before. Kate and Charlie were almost the last to go, trailing rumpled children at the handle of the pram in which the smelly baby slept.

Pat and Elly were the only ones left. Elly, smart in a cream crêpe de chine dress she had purchased only last week in St John's Market, moved across to Bill where he stood with his baby daughter in his arms. Elly scarcely came to Jenny's house any more. It had been made clear to her by her brother-in-law that the wife of a cobbler was not to be compared in any way to the status he had attained. To be honest, Jenny's family offended him with what his brother's wife would have termed their 'commonness'. Even Kate and Charlie saw little of him now. Whilst Charlie was away Bill could see no reason to accompany Jenny on her visits to Kate's, and, in fact, in the past six months he had become so involved with the friends he had made at the Golf Club he had joined out Netherton way, that even when Charlie was at home, he barely had the time (or inclination if he were honest) to go for a bevvy with him.

'Can I 'old 'er for a minute, Bill?' Elly said diffidently, her arms going out to the child. Though she had nursed her at Kate's house where the three sisters met and were comfortable together, the sight of the tiny girl, so lovely in her long white dress and dainty frilled bonnet, brought a strange yearning to Elly's heart. Her own were all grown up. There would be no more. She was forty now, the stuffing knocked out of her by the life she had led. Pat was forty-five and though they had settled into an uneasy, semi-peaceful existence within their marriage, he did not come to her as he once had.

Bill smiled stiffly.

Elly took the child from him, looking down into the lovely formless smile the baby directed at her. The dark brown eyes seemed to stare in a friendly fashion into her own. Her hair escaped in tiny tendrils from beneath her bonnet, and she smelt sweet as though she had just come from her bath. Elly kissed her cheek and moved away from Bill to where Jenny sat in the chair beside the sun-filled window, her eldest daughter upon her lap. The window had been opened wide to let in a breath of air and the smell of apples warming in the sunshine on the laden branches of the trees, drifted into the room.

Elly looked from one baby face to the other. Laura's skin was pale and delicate like Jenny's, the cheekbone touched with rose and her enormous pale green eyes, fringed with thick black lashes looked curiously into Elly's. The child in her arms raised a fat hand and in that moment Elly remembered vividly the golden loveliness of another baby.

She didn't think. Before she knew what she was about the words came, softly, gently, compassionate with sad memories, from her lips.

'They're neither of 'em like yer first, are they Jenny?'

Jenny could feel the warmth of the fabric on the arm of the chair where her hand rested. Her body, against which the child lay, was conscious of her weight and the fragrance of the soft hair, touching her cheek, and strangely, though it was many miles away, she thought she heard the sound of a ship's siren. She was conscious of Bill's tight strung figure beside the fireplace, stiff and unyielding, rigid with shock, but, as she stared into the appalled eyes of her sister, she was aware, as clearly as she was aware of the child on her lap, of the tanned laughing presence of the man she loved. He was there in her heart as he had always been, and now, though she could not have said why, his memory gave her the strength to turn and look at her husband.

349

Bill's face was blanched, like suet, except for two thick veins which beat at each side of his temple. They stood out, blood-red. His eyes were bewildered, lost, anguished, all at the same time, and Jenny was overwhelmed with sorrow. But in them, as she watched, there began to burn a tiny flame.

Elly stood between them, turned to stone. She stared at Jenny as if pleading to be struck down where she stood, for surely, her expression said, there would be no atonement for this day's work. She knew, for who could not be aware, of Bill's attitude, of his possessiveness, his intense pride in his beautiful wife and children, and in that first agony of despair, she realised that she had destroyed with a few unthinking words, the basis on which Jenny's marriage was built. Bill's whole world, his image of who he was and what Jenny meant to him, was formed on the premise of his possession of her. She was his. The two and a half years of marriage had blunted his obsession to a small degree. His access to her body was taken for granted but she belonged wholly to him, and no one, no one, had ever possessed what was his.

Elly began to babble.

'Sweet Jesus . . . what 'ave I . . . I didn't mean to . . . it was just that I remembered 'er, and it just came . . .' She turned to Bill, her smile a travesty, and put out her hand to him. 'Don't take any notice o' me, chuck . . . me big mouth 'll . . .'

But she knew it did no good. Bill did not even look at her, and she doubted whether he had heard what she said.

Jenny moved. She stood up and carefully placed the drowsy toddler in the chair. Taking her baby from Elly's arms, she tried to smile reassuringly.

'Ssh, Elly, it's not your fault,' she said gently. 'I'm to blame. I should have . . .' She nodded in the direction of the window. Pat could be seen waiting impatiently by the gate. His red face was slicked with sweat and he had loosened his collar and tie.

'See, Pat's waiting for you. Go on, it'll be all right.'

Elly looked sadly from Bill to Jenny and knew it would not be all right. Never again. Her eyes stared, deeply anguished into those of her younger sister. – What next, our kid, they said. What bloody next, an' it's all my fault.

Without looking at Bill again she turned and walked slowly through the doorway. At the gate she took Pat's arm. Tears streamed across her white face and through the open window Jenny heard Pat's bewildered voice as they walked away up the road.

'*What did she mean?*'

Bill's voice cracked, tormented by what he knew was to come. 'What did she mean, your first?'

'Let me get the children to bed, and then . . .'

'I want to know what she meant.'

'Bill, please Bill, let me . . .'

'If you don't explain what that . . . that . . . cow meant I'll knock your teeth down your throat.'

Bill's face was stiff, like a plaster cast of his own death mask. His eyes had turned as cold and as merciless as flint and he spoke through lips that moved as though they had been stitched together. He began to move purposefully towards her. Gripping her arm above the elbow in fingers of steel he pulled her to him roughly. The little girl in the chair began to whimper. Jenny tried to turn in her direction, but she was off balance as Bill grabbed her away from the window.

'Please, Bill, Laura is . . .' but Bill was beyond thought for anyone, even his child. The dread and anguished fear grew in him.

'What the bloody 'ell's goin' on?' he hissed. His grasp upon her arm was like a vice. His face was pushed against hers, his eyes were inches from her own, and the colour pounded in waves across the taut muscles of his skin.

'Bill, please . . . if yer'd just let me . . . please.' Fear ran through Jenny like quicksilver. Any thought of a rational explanation, a plea for forgiveness, understanding, perhaps sympathy, had long since left her. She had thought with the children present, Bill might, for their sakes, have been held in check, but he was out of his mind, unaware, wild with jealous rage.

'Never mind bloody please. I want to know what your sister meant by the remark she just made.' His words were slow, spaced out, deliberate. 'She just said that our daughters were not like your first. Your first what, Jenny? *Your first what?*'

He began to shake her and the baby flopped about in her arms like a bundle of washing. She began to wail.

'What did she mean Jenny?' Bill's shallow control was completely gone. His eyes were suffused with red as though he had been crying. He knew, in the deepest recess of his heart, exactly what Elly had meant. She had been talking about babies, hadn't she? Babies! Babies! She had said to Jenny, 'They're nothing like yer first.' Baby! Baby! Jenny had had a baby . . . her first . . . first . . . first . . . Before she met him she had had a baby . . . her first . . . her first. It beat through his head like a hammer and he felt he would sink to his knees with the pain of it. Oh how he wanted . . . longed . . . agonised to be told he was wrong, that Elly had meant something else, something . . . anything . . . oh God.

'Bill, for God's sake let me go. The baby . . . I'm . . . at least let me put her down.' Both children were crying, the sound carrying through the open window, and the woman next door turned to look as she pruned the dead heads from her roses. It was not like Mrs Robinson to let her children scream like that. She was such a good mother, and what was all that shouting? She stared for a moment, then turned and went indoors. It was none of her business, but still it was strange about the children.

Jenny tore herself from Bill's vicious grasp. Great red marks were forming on the white skin of her arm where his fingers had been, but as yet she felt no pain. Her only concern was for her children. Laying the baby upon the settee, she turned, intending to plead for a moment in which to speak, to beg that she might put the babies safely in their cots before baring the agony of her innermost soul, but Bill was past reason.

Gripping her by both arms, he dragged her to the living room wall. Standing her rigidly against it, he placed both hands upon her shoulders, forcing her back until she could not move.

'Now then, Madam. We'll 'ave the whole story.' He stared dangerously, his eyes hot and demented. 'Did you have a child before you met me? No lying, no evasions. I want the truth, and I want to know every bloody detail. Right.'

Raising one hand he slapped her deliberately across the face. Her head snapped to the left and she cried out.

'Right, that's for starters!'

'Bill, let's sit down.' Tears streamed down Jenny's face. 'I won't lie to yer. I'll tell yer the truth, but there's no need for this. Yer don't 'ave to hit me to hear the truth. I should've told you before . . . before we were married . . . but I thought . . .'

'I just want you to say, yes I 'ad a child, or no, I did not 'ave a child, that's all. Now answer me or I'll kill you.'

'Yes, I 'ad a child.'

Bill's face became as still and as cold as that of a dead man. Only his eyes had life. They burned with a terrible, livid hate, with a deep and dreadful pain and with a hopelessness, that more than anything cut Jenny to the core. She knew that she had just taken from her husband something that was the substance of his life. The fundamental bedrock on which he existed was, though he did not know it himself, his complete and absolute belief that Jenny was the princess in the fairy story. The fairy princess he had won for himself, by himself, and that, to the last eyelash and toenail she belonged only to him. Without this fantasy he was nothing, a nonentity, null and void. She was innocent and untouched. His hands and lips were the first she had known. To learn that she had been 'despoiled' by another lent a madness to him and he gave way.

He lifted his hand and with all the force he could muster he hit her again. As she fell, half stunned, he gripped her hair, dragging her upwards. Again and again he struck her. He punched her breasts and stomach and as he did so, words, filth, spewed from his mouth. Her blood spattered his knuckles and splotched his clean white shirt. The child in the chair hiccoughed quietly, her eyes glazed with terror, and deep in the cushions of the settee, the baby squirmed to escape their smothering grasp. She cried pitifully, her tiny face turning instinctively away as she tried to draw breath. Her legs kicked as she struggled for life, and her cries grew weaker. Her mother did not hear her. Bill sobbed harshly in his throat as he looked down at the smashed face of his wife. Then, picking up his jacket, he left the room. The front door banged behind him and a moment later, the engine of his car sprang to life.

They found her, Kate and Charlie and Elly, crumpled behind her living room door, before the blood had time to dry on her battered face, and Kate cried like the child in the chair as they lifted her to her bed. The baby in her struggles had almost buried herself beneath the cushions of the settee, but her cries now were more of anger than fear. Laura, nearly two years old and in all her short life knowing nothing but love was rigid with terror, but with the resilience of a child and the comforting depths of Aunty Kate's breasts to burrow against, she became calm.

John Clancy worked for more than an hour, helped by Elly, over the poor shattered face and body of the semiconscious woman on the bed. A stitch was needed at the corner of Jenny's mouth, but the rest were bruises, livid against her white flesh, and they would disappear with time. Both her eyes were closed to slits, puffed and angry and her face was swollen, the skin taut across her cheekbones. Her body was a red and livid mass of bruises which would turn black within the hour but no bones were broken, though the doctor suspected a cracked rib.

They sat in the kitchen and drank the tea which Kate had made. The children were asleep and so was Jenny. Elly cried silently, and Charlie and John Clancy stared into their teacups in the way of men who do not know what to say to comfort. What was there to say? They all knew the reason, and in his heart Charlie felt he understood, though it was beyond him how any man could do to a woman what had been done to Jenny. But how could he judge? How could he say what he himself might have done had he been in the same position? A man was a strange and unpredictable creature when he loved a woman.

The sound of Bill's car returning brought them to their feet.

Chapter Thirty-Eight

He never did to her again what he did to her that night. She threatened him bleakly with the police, and exposure to the bank of his violence. She was on her guard now. He sometimes managed to catch her a backhander when he was drunk but not often. His aim was wild and weak when he had had a few, and she became adept at side stepping. He was drunk a lot of the time. The bruises he had inflicted upon her faded, her rib healed, and the neat stitch which Dr Clancy had put into the corner of her mouth had the appearance of a dimple. When she smiled it deepened, giving her an engaging mischievous look.

It was his words which hurt her most. He tried to destroy her with them as she had destroyed him. He would not let her alone. He probed her past like a dentist drilling a decayed tooth and the agony was the same. Night after night he was at her with his persistent, cruel interrogation.

'What was his name, this great lover of yours?'

'Was he young, handsome and strong?'

'And did he love you to distraction then?'

'Why didn't he marry you?'

'He soon got fed up, didn't he?'

His voice sneered. His face twisted derisively. His eyes glowed like devils in the light from the bedside lamp. It was a long time since he had had the fancy to make love to her with the light on, but now he did it again. It was as though he wanted to see the pain on her face, the appeal in her eyes as he derided the love she treasured still. But worst of all were his demands to be told that the love-making of her lost lover could not be compared to his own prowess.

'Did he do this? and this? Did this excite you, did it? Did it? And look at this, go on – take a good look. I bet his wasn't as big?'

She endured it all. But that was later.

In the beginning she tried to answer. To speak truthfully of those days so long ago. To tell him about her feelings, her agony at the loss of her child. She hoped to mend the damage done by being

355

honest. To repair, by atonement the great rent which had torn apart the fragile fabric of their marriage. For her children she wanted a safe, love-filled home in which they would be secure; she hoped that with communication would come understanding, perhaps sympathy, and the working out of a relationship which would allow if not happiness, at least a semblance of normality. She was willing to forget the terrible beating she had taken, for knowing Bill, she was aware of what she had done to him. He had been provoked beyond reason and she knew now that she was partly to blame for not having told him the truth before their marriage. That would have been the fair, and honest action to have taken and she knew she had, from the first, disappointed him in her apathy towards his lovemaking. She tried to make amends. She tried.

It did no good. He used her body when he felt like it, humiliating her with his sullen violence and bitter, obscene language, but beyond that, he ignored her. And he was unfaithful to her. He did little to hide his indiscretions, leaving handkerchiefs smeared with lipstick for her to wash and smelling of perfume and the whiskey he drank each night. His life was lived between his Golf Club, the bank and the evenings he spent God knows where with the women who were only too pleased to consort with a handsome free-spending gentleman.

Even his love for his children, self-admiring as it had been – for were they not an extension of himself? – seemed diminished as if the capacity for affection had been taken from him with his pride.

Life moved on, and gradually, as things have a way of doing, what had once seemed unbearable, impossible to endure, became commonplace and in the love of her children and the affection and trust of her own, and Bill's family, Jenny learned a different contentment.

Her relationship with her mother-in-law had now settled down into a deep and loyal friendship which she could not have believed possible in the early days of her marriage.

Each Thursday she and 'Ma' spent the day in town, window shopping, taking lunch at the Kardomah, buying cakes at Lunts to take home for tea with the girls, and drifting from counter to counter in Owen Owens where Ellen had an account. Jenny had to be careful not to admire too enthusiastically a dress, a pair of shoes or her mother-in-law would have her in a cubicle, trying something on before she could say 'knife'. Ellen's gratitude for the love, the new life which Jenny gave her, and for what she thought was

356

Jenny's successful marriage to her son, made her overwhelming in her generosity.

Ellen and Albert, of course, knew nothing of the abyss which yawned between her son and his wife. Bill, ashamed, stripped of self-esteem and pride, could endure it only if no one else knew. Jenny's family saw nothing of him. He went no more to Kate and Charlie's. Kate had never forgiven him for what he had done to her sister and would not have allowed him over the doorstep, but almost every Sunday he took his family to his parents' home in Old Swan and played out the charade which kept his vanity intact. Along with Mary and Douglas and their baby son, he and Jenny acted out their roles of players in the perfect family gathering. If Bill seemed restless it went unnoticed. The love that Ellen and Albert felt for their two beautiful granddaughters and to a lesser degree for their grandson bordered on adulation, and, as Jenny remarked wryly to Kate, if Bill had stripped naked and done the Charleston, the doting grandparents would scarcely have noticed. They adored them, the two lovely girls of Bill and Jenny and sometimes as Jenny watched, like a member of an audience or a play, her heart would grow sad at what might have been.

That year, a name which was to become synonymous with everything that was evil, was heard for the first time by the people of Great Britain. A name that was to grow and fill the very world with horror. They turned on their wireless sets to listen to the news, but it barely registered in their minds as they waited for *In Town Tonight* or the music of 'Ambrose'.

A year later in 1934, that same name was mentioned again. Adolf Hitler became Führer of Germany, but still the rest of the world – bar those who were becoming involved, mostly Jews – was not particularly interested. To the man in the street he was just a name, like Franklin Roosevelt or Neville Chamberlain and they went about their lives, unaware of the fury which was to be unleashed.

Jenny and Kate went to see *The Barretts of Wimpole Street* and sang *Smoke Gets in Your Eyes*.

In 1935 to celebrate the silver jubilee of King George V and Queen Mary, Kate had her fifth and last child, a son whom she named Harry. In her eyes he was the best of the lot. He was plump, fair, grey eyed like his father, and rosy cheeked. His ears were soft and sweet and his gurgling laughter filled his home, and his mother's heart with sunshine. He walked at eleven months and his sunny, affectionate nature endeared him to all who knew him. He was loved wherever he went and as he grew, Kate never knew where to find him. If he wasn't giving Alec, Kate's next-door neighbour a hand in the erection of some shelves, he was across the road with his head under the hood of the pram, sweet-talking Mrs Turner's six month old Lucy. He gave away his toys to any child who took a liking to them and his warm heart induced him to share his bags of sweeties amongst his friends until there were none left for himself.

Kate adored him.

Jenny conceived no more children. It was though her womb had closed up in abhorrence of Bill's seed, rejecting the prospect of bearing a child to the man who spilled it without love.

In the years since he had gone back to sea, Charlie had been to many parts of the world, leaving Kate alone for months on end. When she became lonely she would cast her mind back to 1932 and the days when they had been waiting to sail for Australia, and her heart would swell with relief and joy, and she would walk round the little house which she and Charlie had gradually restored to what it once had been.

Even to the piano.

In January 1936, the nation mourned the death of George V, and his eldest son Edward became King.

In March, Adolf Hitler's troops re-occupied 'The Rhineland' but the people of Great Britain were too enthralled with a drama closer to home.

The Prince of Wales had been perhaps one of the most well-known and admired members of the Royal Family. The common man loved him for he came amongst them. But his indifference to official ceremony; to the eligible princesses presented for his approval, and all the trappings of the life style expected of a prince of the realm, was well known. One name, amongst those with which his was linked began to be heard more and more as the year went on. Mrs Wallis Simpson. The common people were perplexed. What did he see in her, they asked?

In that same year she obtained a divorce from her husband and Edward made it plain that he intended to marry her. The nation was appalled when in December King Edward VIII, as yet uncrowned, made a solemn broadcast announcing his abdication, and in May 1937, his younger brother was crowned King George VI, in Westminster Abbey. The Duke of Windsor, as their beloved Prince of Wales had become, left his country, and married this woman for whom he had given up his birthright.

In 1938, Adolf Hitler, well known now throughout the continent of Europe and beyond, went ahead with his plans to unify all

358

German-speaking peoples into a glorious Reich, and in March 1939, the Germans marched into Czechoslovakia.

ARP duties were imposed upon local authorities. Kate hardly heard Frankie's voice as he explained to her that it meant 'Air Raid Precautions', for her mind was concerned with what to have for Sunday dinner, and the possibility of whether Morag, Alec's wife, might come and look after the kids whilst she and Jenny went to see Deanna Durban in *Three Smart Girls* at the Rialto.

She was bewildered when some chap knocked on her door several weeks later to tell her she was to be presented with an Anderson Shelter. She sent him packing saying she had never heard such rubbish in her life. An air raid shelter, indeed.

In August she and Jenny were alarmed when a trial blackout took place in Liverpool. They had been to see *The Citadel* starring Robert Donat and Ralph Richardson, and when they came out of the cinema it was to a city so dark, it was impossible to see a hand in front of a face. They had stumbled along Dale Street, their fright turning to laughter as people bumped into one another, and as she said later to Charlie, 'It was a right good night out', the blackout lending a humorous note to the occasion.

But on the first of September the merriment died away as the blackout became permanent, and on the second of that fateful month, the last day of peace died in a violent thunderstorm that swept the country like a warning of impending doom.

'Since eleven o'clock this morning, Great Britain has been at war with Germany . . . In this grave hour, perhaps the most fateful in our history, I send to every household of my peoples . . . We have tried to find a peaceful way out of our difficulties . . . For the second time in the lives of most of us, we are at war . . . Stand calm, firm and united . . . with God's help we will prevail . . . May He bless and keep us all.'

The three grave-faced adults sat motionless around the kitchen table as the voice of their King died away, and the dignified notes of the National Anthem filled the room. Without thought, over-whelmed by the solemnity of the moment, they stood instinctively to attention. Their eyes flickered and met, and looked away again as the women's searched the man's for some expression of reassurance.

But Charlie could give none. He was too stunned by the words he had just heard. He, more than Kate and Jenny, had been aware of the unease which had crept insidiously from across the Channel, but like millions of others, had not believed that it would come to this. The months of almost stealthy preparations for war, should it come, had not gone unnoticed, but it had been with an air of disbelief that most men had viewed these activities. – War. Don't be daft. The last one was enough. It'll never happen again. Never.

He tried to put on an air of cheerful determination; to comfort the women with his hopeful demeanour. But it did no good. Later would come the trite phrases, when he had recovered his composure, but not yet. He should have realised he told himself numbly, the inevitability of the horror which was about to descend upon them, and the events of the past six years should have made more impression upon him but he had been too busy putting his life, and that of his family back together again. But he was not alone in his thoughts.

Who, amongst the nation's people had taken any interest in 1933 when the man called Hitler had become Chancellor of Germany? Who had heard the tramping of the booted feet of the brown-shirted troops? Who had heard the cheering crowds, the blaring loudspeakers, and seen the swastikas hanging on the streets of his New Germany? It was all so far away, and what was it to do with them anyway? Who had been aware of his imperceptible steps towards re-armament, the withdrawal of Germany from the League of Nations, and the insistent demands of the new Führer to have returned to Germany, the colonies taken from her at the end of the last war.

Certainly not the ashen-faced figures round the kitchen table, nor the millions like them up and down the country.

They had heard, vaguely, of the Munich Agreement, and seen Mr Chamberlain – a fuzzy figure on a newsreel – clutching a piece of paper and smilingly assuring them of 'Peace In Our Time'. Even then, the majority of them had not been quite sure what all the fuss was about.

And now it seemed that at last the roar of the beast was heard by every ear, in every home, in every corner of the bewildered country.

Poland had been attacked at dawn on Friday the first of September 1939. An ultimatum had been delivered to Adolf Hitler stating, as guaranteed by Great Britain to Poland in March of that year, that unless the attack was called off by eleven o'clock on the third of September and German troops withdrew, a state of war would exist between Great Britain and Germany.

The ultimatum had been ignored.

It was war.

'God, I wish I'd taken that bloody air raid shelter now,' Kate wept.

Chapter Thirty-Nine

In the bright kitchen in Crescent Road, the dust motes danced in the shaft of sunshine which streamed through the open back door. The peace and quiet seemed improbable in the light of the words which had been hesitantly spoken there, through the medium of the wireless, and the two people who stood in the doorway, staring across the fields with blank, shadowed eyes could scarcely comprehend what was taking place, what would take place in their lives.

Seven children streamed across the poppy-strewn field as the couple watched.

The first was Frankie. He was nearly sixteen now. Stocky, like Charlie, with his father's shock of brown unruly hair. He whistled tunelessly as he walked, slashing at the grass with a long, whippy branch he had found in the spinney.

After him came Harry, four years old. His hair was thick and blond and straight. He sang as he leaped and skipped, and his childish voice could be heard clearly on the hot summer air.

'I'll be seeing you, on every lovely summer's day, on every . . .'

The words were incongruous in one so young and his mother felt tears spring to her eyes. A great one for popular songs was her Harry, and he knew most of the words an' all.

Another boy followed. Leslie, ten years old and a replica of his older brother. He was firing an imaginary machine gun. *'Ha – ha – ha – ha – ha . . .'* his voice stuttered and Harry fell down, laughing, in the long grass. The man's flesh prickled as he watched, as though some ripple of apprehension, some glimpse of the future touched him, but the boy sprang up and ran on.

Two young girls of five or six, alike as twins, did cartwheels, showing their white knickers, their slim legs flashing in the clear air. They were dark and lovely, their burnished curls glinting as the sun touched them. Kathy Walker and Helen Robinson watched each other critically, then satisfied with their performance, their arms linked, continued in their private world towards the fence at the edge of the field.

Lastly came Dorry, she was thirteen. A child-woman. She held

361

the hand of Laura who was eight, and her dark head was bent towards her confidentially, as she told her some secret. These were the treasures, the beloved children of the couple in the doorway, and with their cousins, the daughters of Jenny and Bill Robinson, they wandered in happy ignorance towards the destruction which was to engulf their world.

Kate and Charlie stood motionless, quiet. Their arms were linked tightly as they watched the youngsters make their way across the field. Their minds were numb with the knowledge of the grim news which had been broadcast the day before, confirmed in a way which gave it credence by their King, and the fear which they each felt showed plainly in their faces.

They turned and looked at each other and sighed simultaneously. Putting his arms about her, Charlie rested his cheek against Kate's tumbled brown hair. The sun caught the white streak which was an inheritance from long ago sorrows, and Charlie kissed it, remembering.

The children were gathered at the fence now. They stopped in a circle, laughing and falling about at something Leslie said, and like healthy, unthinking young animals, their eyes were bright and unclouded, and their voices confident as they cried out to each other. Frankie pulled Leslie to the ground, wrestling, his arms behind his back, showing off to the girls. Kathy and Helen sat on the top rail of the fence, apart, as if unaware of the others, their heads close together, and Harry began to gather some poppies for his Mam.

Kate and Charlie drew apart, looking steadfastly into each other's eyes, the love of nearly twenty years still shining between them.

'What's to be done then, Charlie?' Kate asked.

'Eeh love, I don't know.' Charlie shook his head in sorrowful bewilderment. 'I can't believe it. At war again. I was in the last one, an' I never thought I'd make it then. Remember when I was torpedoed on the old *Franconia*? An' now it's 'ere again. It'll not be like the last one though, a different kind of warfare altogether, I'm thinking.'

Realising that what he said might frighten her more than she already was, he stopped speaking, absently stroking her hair off her forehead. His eyes were pensive. He had known last month that things were looking serious when he had heard that the Admiralty had been authorised to adopt control of the movements of the merchant shipping, and there had even been a rumour of cargo vessels being armed. Like the rest of his shipmates though, he had thought, hoped, that it would all come to nothing.

As millions of others had done, he had put his trust in Mr Chamberlain and his piece of paper.

Becoming brisk, he put Kate from him and began to move towards the door that led into the hall.

'Now come on, lass, let's gerron wi' t'packing. I'll 'ave to be gerrin down to t'docks an' I want the lot o' yer on the train before I go.'

Kate went on staring out of the back kitchen door, scanning the sky and fields as if fully expecting to see hordes of German bombers, or soldiers, advancing towards her. When none appeared, she turned hopefully, speaking to Charlie's back.

'Oh Charlie, need we go yet, love? Surely we're safe enough 'ere. I can't think why you want us to go, I really can't.'

Her voice was fretful with worry. Charlie was supposed to be sailing to Newfoundland the day after tomorrow, and she didn't know how she was going to cope with a war all on her own, and with five kids to see to.

Charlie was patient as he turned back to her. He knew when this lot really got going, Liverpool would be a prime target for the fury of the German bombers, like all the other big ports, and he wanted his family out of it. Especially with him away. God knows where he would end up, or for how long, and with Kate and the kids safely evacuated, he could get on with whatever was expected of him with an easy mind.

Of course she wouldn't go without their Jenny. That was taken for granted.

'Now Kate, we've been through it a dozen times and we've decided, me an' Bill.' Kate sniffed. If 'Clever Dick' had 'owt to do with it, it'd bound to be wrong, but still Charlie seemed to think it best, and anyway, it'd be a nice change. She hadn't had a holiday for as long as she could remember.

Charlie went on. 'Bill and Jenny will be back soon an' I want you all settled in St Annes by tonight. Mrs Spencer said she'd expect us by six an' we've a lot to do. Now me an' Frankie an' our Leslie will go on the tram to the station an' you an' Jenny an' the other kids can go in the car wi' Bill, then tomorrow, me an' Bill will bring the rest of yer doings. 'Appen it'll all be over by Christmas an' yer'll be back 'ere trimmin' the tree. Now don't cry, lovely,' as the tears rolled down Kate's cheeks. 'Yer not worried about me, are yer? I'll be allright where I'm goin'. There's no war in Canada yer know.' He winked in a effort to coax a smile from her but the tear gates were unlocked and Kate was suddenly overwhelmed as the realisation washed over her that she was to be in the middle of some dreadful experience with no Charlie to stand by her.

'Oh Charlie, oh Charlie,' was all she could say. 'Oh Charlie.'

He hugged her to him lovingly, kissing her streaming eyes and cheeks. His thoughts left the familiar comfort of his own kitchen and mingled with those of the millions of men and women who were enacting this same scene in which he now played a part. Separations. Heartache. The upheaval of family life. Children and young mothers, bewildered, frightened, leaving the security of their own homes for unknown and strange surroundings. Forced by something they scarcely understood to leave the big cities for the safety they were told lay elsewhere. They didn't want to go but *they* said they should. Bombing was expected and their children were in danger. It was almost incomprehensible to most.

'Go on, queen. I'll be up in a minute to help yer, I just want a word with our Frankie.'

He pushed Kate, still sobbing quietly, but in control now, towards the door, and turning on his heel, stepped into the shaft of sunlight which streamed through the open doorway to the yard.

He was surprised when a young figure rose from the upturned bucket on which he had been sitting. It was Frankie.

He spoke eagerly, the words tripping over his tongue in an effort to impress his father with the importance of what he was saying.

'I don't 'ave ter go, do I Dad? To St Annes I mean, with the women. Dorry can help with the kids. Let me stay 'ere Dad. I can look after meself. I don't want to miss 'owt stuck up in St Annes and they might be starting summat like the "Hitler Youth" thing.'

Someone, at least, had been aware of some of what was happening in Germany.

'I'd like to join if they do, Dad. I'd like to get in on it Dad . . .'

His voice trailed away as he saw the expression on his father's face change from one of worry, to horror, and he recoiled as Charlie raised his arm as though he were about to strike him.

What had he said?

Charlie's eyes were anguished, as he looked into Frankie's. Oh the young, the young men. Will it be like the last time? Will we lose a complete generation as we did then? Would Frankie have to go? The thought lanced through him as he laid a gentle hand on his son's shoulder. He was sixteen, but if it lasted he could easily become engaged in the storm that was coming. It must be stopped. It must.

'Listen, son. I know you're sixteen and damn near a man, but at the moment I need yer t'stay with the women.' He smiled to himself at the word, women. His Mam'd have a fit if she heard him. 'Yer mam and Auntie Jenny can't manage on their own. They need

364

a man with them. You're in charge of the other kids an' all. I know it's a lot to put on young shoulders, and I hate to ask yer, but I've no one else to turn to.'

Frankie's young chest puffed up.

'I rely on you, our Frankie, to see to them. Look after them like, while I'm away. All right son?'

This was exactly the right note to strike, and the half-boy, half-man responded as his father had hoped.

At first Jenny and Kate and the children enjoyed the novelty of a seaside holiday so late in the year, and the weather was glorious. As if to put hope in the hearts of people frightened by the events of the past few weeks, the sun shone from cloudless blue skies, day after day. Kate and Jenny hired a beach chalet and sat in a state of false euphoria on the pebbled beach while the children ran about in their knickers and underpants – they had forgotten to pack their 'cossies' – or went tumbling down the soft, honey-coloured sand of the dunes.

The days passed and the weather broke. Kate and Jenny took the children to Blackpool, riding along the promenade on the tram to the Pleasure Beach. They rode on the Big Dipper, the rain soaking them through to their skins, then wandered aimlessly up the almost deserted Golden Mile, the stalls which had been hastily re-opened at the influx of the evacuees, closed once more. They ate battered cod, chips and peas out of newspaper, the rain dripping from the brim of the children's sou'westers, and driven by the persistent downpour, went to the pictures three times in four days.

As their money slipped away, they were forced to sit in the boarding house bedroom, playing rummy in turn with the irritable children.

They nearly went mad with boredom and homesickness.

Three weeks after war was declared and Liverpool was still unbombed, the two women and seven children boarded the train for home, and the evacuation was at an end.

The children went back to school, along with thousands of others who had fled the city and returned, and life settled down to the usual domestic routine which had prevailed before September the third.

Conscription was the word which was on every woman's lips. Will my husband have to go? At first it had just been the young ones, the unmarried, but now men between the ages of eighteen and forty-one were to be called, married or not.

Bill Robinson volunteered.

Chapter Forty

Bill left at the end of October for an army training camp 'somewhere in England' and for the first time in nearly nine years, Jenny knew peace of mind. The pleasure of having her children, her family, her home in a state of tranquillity without fear of the havoc he could produce with his uncertain temper, was like sailing into sunshine after a fierce storm.

It was ironic, Jenny thought, that it took a war, to bring her peace. She did not realise until after he had gone, what disruption her husband had caused. Though he had never struck her children, his raised voice could send them running from his path to the safety of their room, and Jenny had been reminded of two other young girls who had fled from the path of a short-tempered bully. Bill's sharp-edged tongue, critical, especially of Laura, who was so like her mother, (and her grandmother Elizabeth) caused the child to become reserved and silent in his presence.

She flowered like a blossom in the warm summer rain when he left. Helen, more confident than her sister, less easily hurt, had not been as much affected by Bill's undermining sarcasm and besides, she had Kathy. The quiet evenings which Jenny and her small daughters enjoyed together, listening to *ITMA* and *Band Wagon* made her feel guilty at times. The war, or what was purported to be the war, hadn't even started yet, or so it seemed. The 'phoney war' they were calling it, but all Jenny could think of was how good life was without Bill.

As did Kate. She could nip round to their Jenny's whenever the fancy took her now. She and Jenny spent most of their time together. Just like the old days, Kate said, squeezing Jenny's arm, but saying no more, for after all, Bill was Jenny's husband and had gone to defend his country, but by God it was grand without him glowering from behind his *Echo* or making snide remarks about something or other.

She and Jenny bought blackout material from the market at fourpence a yard, sewing it into large squares and fixing it across each window with curtain rings on hooks, putting a towel rail in the hem to hold it taut. Each morning they were rolled up neatly like blinds.

Jokes about the blackout abounded.

'I can see a chink in your window, Missus.'

Answer: 'Don't you know the Japanese Ambassador when you see him.' Harry loved that one and told it everyone a dozen times a day before his Mam told him to 'shurrup or she'd land him one'. It was bad enough having to be out in it, she said, 'without 'earin' daft jokes about it mornin' noon an' night.' She'd collided with twenty complete strangers on the short walk from her house to Jenny's, stubbing her toe on the kerbstone, and apologising profusely to a lamp post. Women were in tears through sheer panic, and men swore at her, she complained, and her face was white with fright and temper by the time she arrived.

They all carried gas masks, and the two sisters were enormously relieved that their children were old enough not to have to be placed in the ghastly constricting contraptions devised for young babies and which must be hand-pumped in order that they might breathe.

In January, rationing began. Ration books were introduced for butter, sugar, bacon and ham, but food was still plentiful and the restrictions were scarcely noticed.

Charlie came and went, as he had done for years, and Kate's mind was undisturbed, imagining that it wasn't so bad after all, this war. Nothing seemed to be happening that was out of the ordinary. She saw more of Jenny, her children continued to be well fed and grow; Charlie was cheerful and optimistic when he was home, and all in all, it was better than she expected.

But Charlie kept from her the danger he was in each time he left the safety of the Mersey.

In February, the ship he was on left in a convoy, the first time it had done so. Ships had to steam at the speed of the slowest straggler, but those which could, went ahead, confident that they were safer alone. Charlie was on one of these. A gale blew up, and those merchantmen who had gone on, lost their formation. By the time daylight came, many ships were missing. Rough seas concealed the lurking submarines, and the men on watch did not see the periscope, nor the torpedo as it streaked through the heaving water.

A dull explosion woke Charlie as he lay in his bunk, and his next few hours were a haze and blur of smoke and debris, of wounded men and cold seawater. Seventy-seven of the crew of Charlie's ship and others who had suffered the same fate, were picked up by other vessels, Charlie included, but eight men were never found.

He never told Kate but from that day he knew he would get through the war. His number had come up twice now, this one earlier than he had expected, but he had not been called either time, and some conviction told him he never would.

Kate and Jenny both had Anderson Shelters in their gardens. Kate was disdainful in those early days. She didn't want that ugly thing in her backyard. It spoiled her view over the fields, and besides there were no air raids. It was as peaceful as the graveyard and she was seriously beginning to think the expectation of danger was greatly exaggerated. The workmen arrived to erect the corrugated curving metal walls, which were bolted to steel rails and sunk three feet into the ground, then covered with eighteen inches of earth. She drove the men to distraction with pleas to have it put deeper so that she might still admire the fields and woods.

'Look Missus, this 'ere shelter will protect you against anythin' except a direct hit, an' there is no bleedin' reason for it to be any deeper. Now we've not got all day to be messin' about wi' you. We've got the rest of the street to do by Friday.'

On top of this ignominy, she was obliged to pay him for the thing as well. Six pounds fourteen bob it cost her because Charlie earned more than five pounds per week. Robbery she called it, downright robbery, an' she never wanted the bloody thing in the first place.

In April her smug sense of well-being ended with the last days of the 'phoney war'.

German tanks crossed the Danish frontier and German troops entered Oslo, and in the streets of Liverpool, military uniforms began to be seen everywhere. The pride of women knew no bounds as they walked with husband, sweetheart or son, and no serviceman was allowed to wear 'civvies' when he was home on leave.

On Friday 10 May at six pm, Winston Churchill became Prime Minister, and a Coalition Government was formed.

The country had a leader at last. And what a leader!

'*I have nothing to offer you but blood, toil, tears and sweat,*' he said.

It is with these words that the ordinary, bewildered civilian became not merely willing, but eager to take part in the fight. The effect on the people was magical. Morale soared and any defeatism which might have lingered, disappeared.

But now, one crushing blow followed another.

In that same month, Germany invaded the Low Countries and Holland and Belgium collapsed. The campaign in North Africa began, but events much nearer home caught the hearts and imagination of the people as hundreds of little boats formed an armada to bring back the British Expeditionary Force which had been stranded at Dunkirk. It was a colossal military defeat, but the grim good humour which was to sustain the British people through six years of war, turned it into a victory.

'We shall fight on the beaches, in the fields and streets. We shall fight in the hills. We shall never surrender,' he said.

Over 338,000 men came home during those two days and nights of continuous and merciless dive-bombing attacks, and the Luftwaffe waited patiently for their next prey on airfields across the Channel.

In June, the British evacuated their troops from Norway, and with them came thousands of Norwegians, eager to continue the fight on foreign soil. One such was forty-six years old now, but his eyes were still as blue as sapphires and as clear, and his arms as strong as when they had held his love twenty years ago.

With Bill away and the children at school, Jenny decided she would do her bit for the war effort and find a job. She didn't need the money, far from it, for Bill had his wages made up by the Bank. When he volunteered for the army he had been earning seven pounds fifteen shillings per week.

The wife of a private in the army with two children was allowed twenty-five shillings per week plus seven shillings from her husband's army pay. For leaving his home and risking his life, an ordinary soldier was paid two shillings per day of which he must give his wife half. Bill's family was one of the lucky ones.

Jenny was a qualified shorthand typist. She had done book-keeping, even run a successful business and with men enlisting or being conscripted, she could have found a demanding, well-paid job in any of the hundreds of businesses in the city, but somehow, though she knew it was foolish, to do so did not seem to be helping win the war. She wanted to be connected with some industry which was directly involved with the defence of her country.

As the war gathered swift momentum, depressed areas where unemployment had been rife began to work day and night to produce ships, tanks, planes and munitions. Liverpool was no exception.

In July, Jenny began work in a factory on Hood Street, off Whitechapel, making barrage balloons. She worked a twelve hour shift, four days on and two days off. In the two and a half years she was to be there, her body never really adjusted to the irregular rhythm.

Ellen was made up. Her son had gone to fight the foe and she thought her heart would break, but now, in recompense, her two darling grand-daughters practically lived with her. All in all, till now, the war seemed not to have disturbed the even tempo of the lives of the Robinsons and Walkers. Jenny was enjoying her freedom from Bill's malicious tormenting which had scarcely let up for nine years. To be without the constant cloud of his presence was heaven, and when he was home on leave she was ashamed at the relief she felt when he spent most of his time at the Golf Club. He rarely came to her in the night and she knew that his sexual needs were taken care of elsewhere. She found she no longer cared, about that, or the failure of her marriage.

By August rationing was beginning to pinch. Each person was allowed eight ounces of sugar, eight ounces of fat, and one and twopence worth of meat each week, and for five minutes every day, after the eight am news, *Kitchen Front* explained to the patient womenfolk how to make 'War and Peace Pudding' ready for Christmas, 'Carrot Croquettes' and soup, scones without fat and 'Chestnut Stew'!

In the blue skies above Kent and Sussex, fighter pilots, young, brave and alone, became the symbol of Britain herself as they fought the battle which was to hold back the might of Germany – 'The Battle of Britain' it was to be called and remembered by generations to come. Thousands of spectators watched in terror and excitement as the dog fights were fought in the battlefields, above them.

'Never has so much been owed by so many to so few,' he said.

Even before that battle was over, another started, one in which, for the first time, others beside servicemen lost their lives. London. Coventry. Birmingham. Victims of the blitz found a new unity as the Luftwaffe bombed them for fifty-seven consecutive nights and in the daytime as well. Between September 1940 and January 1941 over thirteen thousand men, women and children were killed and more than seventeen thousand were injured.

In October, Bill Robinson came home for the last time on embarkation leave before he sailed for North Africa. Every night he was home he brutally assaulted the soft, white flesh of his wife's body. She wept tears of humiliation as he raped her, and his words seared her mind as his penis speared her body.

'Right lady. If it's the last thing I do before I go, I'm going to make damn sure no bloody sailor fancies you while I'm away. You'll not lay down for some randy sod if I can help it. Before I get on that boat I'm going to shove a bun in the oven. Savvy? You'll be in the pudding club or my name's not Bill Robinson. And I shall quite enjoy doing it too. Now get those knickers off and lay down. Spread 'em, go on spread 'em, and no noise. We wouldn't want to wake the children, would we?'

But Jenny's womb rejected the unwanted sperm which Bill forced into her in those last few days, and her heart rejoiced when the sign came that she was not pregnant. Another child would not have been unwelcome, but not one which was conceived as the result of this vile coupling. It seemed to her that she would forever look upon the face of a child of this union and remember how it had been. She had not loved Bill Robinson, ever, but her daughters had been born when she and Bill had still seemed, at least outwardly, a happily married couple, and hope had not yet died within her.

In November Jenny had her thirty-sixth birthday. From a delicately lovely girl, innocent and fresh and vulnerable, she had grown into an incredibly beautiful woman. She was still slim, but motherhood had given a fullness to her breasts and hips, and she had the rounded figure of a woman now. Her waist was neat, and her ankle, and she walked tall and straight, confidence in her step. Her hair, the style of which she had scarcely altered in ten years, fell in a soft burnished swing to her shoulders, framing the bright radiance of her face. Her skin was fine, pale, with the fair flush of poppy on her cheekbones and her eyes were soft as golden velvet. Men turned to look at her wherever she went, and, had she been so inclined, she might have spent every evening in the company of a handsome serviceman.

But Jenny's heart still slept and would not awaken until the touch of love returned.

Chapter Forty-One

The sirens sounded just before eleven o'clock and for the space of five seconds Jenny didn't know what to make of it. She had heard it before, of course, in June last year, but nothing had happened, though in July some bombs had been dropped. In August there were sporadic raids and in November landmines had floated down to earth, carried gently below pretty green parachutes. They had demolished a school in Durning Road in which three hundred people were sheltering and many were killed. But mostly they had been nuisance raids, sent to keep folk awake, and doing little damage. The Luftwaffe wandered so wildly, bombs meant for Liverpool often found targets in other towns.

It was Saturday the first of May 1941 and Jenny had just completed her fourth day of twelve-hour shifts. She was bone weary. Her whole body ached and she felt half inclined to ignore the wailing which rose and fell for the space of two minutes, and just go to her bed. She had let the fire go out after it had heated the water for her bath and now all she wanted to do was sink into oblivion.

She cocked her head to listen. There was nothing. She stood in the dark hallway. The lights were all out so she risked a peep through the blacked out windows. All she could see was the vague outline of her own reflection in the glass. Still there was nothing. She hesitated, her foot on the bottom step of the staircase, clutching her dressing gown about her, wishing suddenly that she had left the children with Ma. If it wasn't for them she'd be up the stairs and into her bed and the sirens could wail till the cows came home for all she cared.

From far away, sounding like the sleepy drone of bumblebees on a hot summer's afternoon came a noise which she could not at first identify. It hummed gently against her ear, and as she listened, though as yet she was only half aware of what it could be, the primeval instinct that had warned her ancestors of danger, pricked her skin and the back of her neck and lifted the hairs on her arms and legs.

It grew louder and louder, nearer and nearer until it was upon her. A mighty roaring which filled her head and shook her body. The house trembled, and the china ornaments which lined the shelf above the picture rail began to shiver and move in little dancing glides. Over her head it thundered, wave after wave after wave, and the terror gripped her. Frozen, her heart thudding in her chest, she stood at the foot of the stairs and knew at last what it was.

Planes. Bombers. They had come. It was the turn of Liverpool, and she was all alone. Between the machines which had come to rain death and destruction out of the skies, there stood only herself to keep her babies safe. She was alone. She didn't think she could do it. Not on her own. She knew she couldn't. She wanted to sit down and curl up on the stairs and hide her head and call for her Mam. Why wasn't there someone here to help her as there always had been? Whenever there had been fear, or trouble or sorrow, there had been someone to stand beside her and hold her hand. Her Mam when she was a child. Kate, Waggy, even Elly. Now there was no one.

She cowered against the bannister. The tinkle of breaking glass could be heard, and from everywhere came the sounds of dogs howling terror into the dark skies. Even they were afraid, and they didn't know what it was that put fear in their hearts. Everyone was filled with the same dread, the panic and sheer blind terror which she felt. Kate. Kate was alone. She had only herself to care for her five children. Every woman with children to protect and no man to help, must feel as she felt now. The thought gave her a feeling of comfort, as though all those countless thousands who were suffering as she was, alone and afraid, had come into her house to reassure her.

'Mummy, mummy, mummy.'

The sound of Laura's voice brought her back from the senseless nightmare into which the sound of the bombers had plunged her. For a brief span she had retreated into the abject fear which only children are allowed, but with the terror of her own child, calm cloaked her.

'I'm coming. It's all right, sweetheart, I'm here.' Running swiftly up the stairs, she went into the children's bedroom and drew Laura, who was sitting up in bed, into the comforting warmth of her arms. The child sobbed and her small frame shook, but as her mother's tranquillity fell over her, she became quiet. Jenny stroked her hair and kissed her wet cheeks, at the same time, without seeming to be concerned or in any hurry, lifted the child from her bed and began to pull her dressing gown about her.

'Now I want you to be a good girl and do everything that I tell you. I'm going to wake Helen, and then we shall get our blankets, and our picnic, and go into the shelter. Remember how we practised we would do it?'

Laura nodded doubtfully, her enormous eyes, spiked with wet eyelashes, looking upwards to where the ceiling light swayed with the tremor caused by the planes roaring overhead. She was not convinced despite her mother's calm, that she was going to like this, and her little face quivered. Fresh tears threatened to spill and she clung to Jenny's dressing gown, determined no matter what, not to let her out of her sight for a second.

From away towards the river a new noise could be heard. It sounded as though someone was throwing large clumps of earth against a brick wall, and once again Jenny was mystified by the sound.

'Crump . . . Crump . . . Crump'. It was hollow, reverberating like rhythmic, distant thunder, or a drum beaten in a procession.

'Come on now.' Jenny turned briskly to her younger daughter who was, amazingly, still asleep. Kate always said it needed a bomb to wake their Helen. Well she was wrong. Jenny shook her shoulder with swift urgency, ready to grab her the moment she woke. The little girl was bewildered, and, as she became aware of the noise of the planes, and the explosions from the distant dockyards, her face crumpled and she began to cry, clinging in terror to Jenny.

'Helen darling, it's all right, it's all right. Mummy's here and Laura and we're going to go into the shelter and have a picnic. Don't cry sweetheart, don't be frightened. Mummy's got you. Now get up, baby, and put on your dressing gown.'

There was a loud crash from somewhere nearby, and Jenny could hear a clatter, like tiles falling from a roof, and she knew that already incendiaries were dropping on houses and falling into the streets.

With a growing need for haste, she hurried the two children down the stairs, through the dark kitchen and out into the back garden. It was not cold, but the darkness was intense and frightening. She had never been out alone at this time of night before and it seemed filled with the unknown as though she had inadvertently strayed into alien territory, and not her own familiar garden of shrubs and flowers, planted by her own hands.

An incendiary bomb exploded in the next street, lighting up the backs of the houses which ran parallel with her own and for a moment it seemed like bonfire night so bright was it.

'Mummy, let's go back, please,' Laura sobbed and pulled on her mother's hand. 'I don't like it out here. Please, Mummy, please.'

'We can't, darling. We'll be much safer in the shelter and when we . . .'

'Safer from what, Mummy?' Helen cried.

Dear God. How to tell a small girl that the planes which had just passed over were dropping bombs onto defenceless men, women and little girls like herself. How to explain that their home, which seemed so safe and secure now that they had left it, might be blown to pieces, and them with it.

'Laura,' she said firmly. 'Take this torch and shine it on the shelter door. Now I don't want to hear another word. Come along Helen. Keep hold of Laura's hand and we shall soon be snug and warm.'

It did not take long to soothe the frightened children. The novelty of being wrapped up warmly in the big blankets which Jenny had placed there for a night such as this; of lying in the funny little bunks and drinking hot milk and eating biscuits; the cosy glow cast by the paraffin lamp, and the dreadful noises shut out by the strong door at the entrance, made the drama into an adventure. Jenny read them a story and watched them relax; their bright, apprehensive eyes grow heavy with sleep, and safe in the calm assurance of their mother's strength, they were quiet.

Elizabeth Fowler's shy little daughter had taken the final step into maturity that night. From the timid, unsure girl who had left her father's house, nineteen years ago, she had become the steadfast support of her family. The fixed, unchangeable safeguard which was denied by her own mother. Though she had shown fear, longing to be gone from it, the strength of her character, built brick by brick over the years, had remained steady, and she knew herself now. She would survive.

The thump, thump of high explosives seemed to come from the direction of Wallasey, and once, putting out the paraffin lamp for a moment, Jenny peeped out and was appalled at the lurid brightness of the sky towards the city. The earth still trembled, but just before twelve-thirty it became quiet and at one o'clock the All Clear sounded. It sang the joyful tidings that the skies were clear, and the citizens of Liverpool were safe to come from the holes in which they were forced to hide.

They came fearfully, anguished at the devastation which had

overcome their city, grieving the dead and wounded. Homeless, many of them, but glad to be alive.

They did not know that this was to be the first of eight nights of hell.

Jenny walked slowly along Castle Street in the direction of the Town Hall. She had no idea where she was going, or why. Tears poured unchecked down her blackened face, making shiny, silver runnels across her cheeks. They dripped unheeded onto her coat which was caked with grit and dust and cut in many places by splinters of glass. Her bare hands were torn and bloody, the nail from one thumb gone completely. Her hair hung about her head in damp and filthy curls. One of her shoes was missing, and she lurched lopsidedly, like a child who walks with one foot in the gutter.

It was the fourth of May and Jenny was on her way to work.

She had left Walton at six o'clock that morning. Even so far away from the docks, many buildings had been flattened, and a large number were burning brightly in the soft spring morning. The Parish Church had been destroyed by high explosives and the police station was severely damaged. The front wall had gone and inside a police constable stood at the high counter, conducting business with the phlegmatic air of one who was used daily to many such emergencies.

The tram had gone as far as it was able but Scotland Road had been badly hit and street after street was flattened. Twisted tram-rails curved like some gigantic roller coaster and the tram was forced to give up. Jenny, along with the rest of the passengers, began to walk towards the city, but they did not get far.

Infected by the frantic urgency of the men and women of the Civil Defence; by the firemen, air raid wardens, policemen, and indeed everyone who could give a hand, some who had toiled unceasingly for three days and nights, she found herself scrabbling alongside half a dozen others in the rubble of what had once been someone's home.

Everywhere men and women worked side by side to rescue those who had been buried. Excavators and diggers, with lorries, were moving along Scotland Road, brought in to remove rubble which hampered operations.

A fire raged on the next corner as Jenny tried to go on, but a sharp voice urged her to give a hand and a hose snaked across her path. From a group of frantically digging people a voice was raised shrilly.

'Hush, hush, for Christ's sake, be quiet.'

The words were passed from mouth to mouth and a curious silence fell about the still figures as they poised upon a smoking tumble of masonry.

Jenny heard a noise, like that of a kitten. The weary workers rested on their shovels. It came again, that tiny thread of sound. Frantically she helped the men to tear at the rubbish and as her thumbnail caught on a jagged brick, it was torn from her flesh in a gout of blood. All the men about her had hands that were burned and bleeding, for they dare not use picks. They found the baby, a boy, only a few months old, held in the protective arms of his dead mother, and for a moment Jenny held him as he was passed along the line to safety. She tenderly wiped the dirt and dust and blood from his tiny face and kissed his cheek and rejoiced that he was alive.

Hour after hour she worked. Time had no meaning, and the tiredness and pain might have belonged to another. The sights she saw wrenched her heart from her breast and her eyes became slits in the swollen flesh of her face as she wept, but she did not stop.

She helped to lift a cot, its broken occupant barely recognisable as a child from beneath tons of rubble, and her head was held for a second or two by a kindly woman, as she vomited into the gutter, but she did not stop. Her brain became mercifully numb with the horrors she witnessed, but she continued to work like the robot she had become. She watched a young soldier, just come on leave, working dementedly shifting piles of rubbish with his bare hands in the wreckage of his home where his wife lay.

She was half choked by dust and the fumes from smouldering woodwork. A cup of tea was pressed into her hand and she drank it without seeing the face of the person who placed it there.

The smell was indescribable. Sewage from broken pipes belched forth the obscene fetor of excrement, and a fractured gas main spewed foul-smelling fumes dangerously into the air. Over all lay the acrid odour of explosives.

A woman sat alone in the gutter watching indifferently as bright blood pumped from an artery in her injured leg, washed away by water flowing from a broken pipe. The ends of white bone protruded from her torn flesh. Jenny moved towards her, but a nurse, filthy as herself, knelt down, a bandage in her hand.

A row of stunned victims sat on the kerbstone like birds on a washing line. The men had their caps pulled firmly down about their eyebrows, properly dressed, even in the midst of destruction, and the women nursed strangely silent children. Behind them lay a heap of smoking, tortured rubble, here and there dotted with a recognisable object such as a chair or a saucepan. A man in pyjamas, deep in shock, industriously moved about what had once been his home, collecting assiduously bits of brick and wood and putting them in a sack, ignoring that which might be useful. No one took any notice.

Men cried, a young girl laughed hysterically. A woman fed her cat from a saucer whilst her baby screamed beside her, and a dog, its fur bristling, its teeth gleaming viciously, stood guard over a doorway beyond which there was no house. It growled fiercely as a warden tried to approach.

The city had suffered the most devastating raid yet, and Liverpool quivered and groaned like a wounded animal as it attempted to regain its feet. The bombers had come in the night, wave after wave after wave. Besides the thousands who had lost their homes, the area bounded by Lord Street, Paradise Street, and Canning Place had been devastated. Lewis's had gone and Black-lers Store. The William Brown Library had taken a five hundred pounder and all the books, gathered into a vast store of knowledge over many decades, had been lost in minutes. Cinemas, the Head Post Office, offices and shops were shattered, razed to the ground. The Docks had been pulverised, hour after hour. Ships had been blown out of the water and the SS Malakand, loaded with ammunition, had been set on fire and exploded, taking a whole dock with it.

Jenny wandered now, scarcely aware of the hurrying, moving, frantically digging ghosts who moved on the periphery of her vision. A school had been hit and she had helped to pick up articles which blew about the yard. She found a small pink purse which was passed to the warden in charge. The mother of the child to whom it had belonged held out her hand, her face so anguished, it was frightful to behold. She took it and was led away wordlessly.

It was this last which had sent Jenny's mind spinning away into the mazed state in which she walked. For an instant she had seen her own little ones lying shattered beneath fallen masonry and burning woodwork and she had begun to run, but the shock had her fast and she forgot why she ran.

She stumbled and almost fell against a mass of soot-covered bricks and her bare foot squelched in the muddied water from the fireman's hose. Piles of rubble reared on each side of the street, blocking her way and clouds of steam swirled about her. Miscellaneous debris had been flung into the air, and a tree, it's trunk stripped of bark, its leaves gone, was draped with stockings, clothing, and at the end of one branch hung a man's hat.

She leaned against it and began to shiver. Her strength, that which she had held about her children on the first night when the need was there had gone and she was lost again, afraid and alone. She didn't know how to get home.

A man walked towards her from the white, cloaking mists. He wore the uniform of a naval officer, but the smooth dark blue of his overcoat was as streaked and torn as her own. It was obvious that he had spent the last few hours as she had done, though he came from a different direction. His face was strained with pain and compassion for what he must have witnessed. He was tall, broad-shouldered, and though he moved tiredly he had the suppleness and hidden strength of an athlete. His mouth which was wide and generous, did not smile, but his eyes, a curious mixture of brilliant blue and green had the fine lines about them which spoke of laughter. His cap was gone, swept from him in the confusion. Soot had fallen about his head and shoulders as he worked with the rescue teams by the docks and his hair was streaked with it, but under the dirt the gleam of gold shone.

He saw the woman crumpled against the blackened tree, and stopped.

She was covered in muck, smoke and blood and as she sagged there he thought she was injured, but still he was unable to move.

She stared at him unblinkingly.

Like creatures frozen into immovability by the existence of the impossible, they both stood as though turned to stone. Each felt time slip and the horrors they had both witnessed whirled and vanished and they were transported to a quiet plane of vast, unmoving silence. The years between fell away like veils drifting, one by one, into memories of the past. The great, groaning sounds of the wounded city died away, and hushed quietude enfolded the two still figures.

Jenny's heart began to hammer and shake inside her and she felt her senses tilt and reel. Her head seemed to drain of all thought and she clung to the tree, afraid she would fall. The ground canted beneath her feet and the buildings tottered. She put out her hand to the dream figure, the lovely, bright vision which a million times her breaking heart had evoked, but this time it did not go away.

The man took a hesitant step forward, softly, as though he walked on quicksand, and his hand rose to hers. His face became ashen under the coating of soot and blood, and an expression of disbelief and wonder rippled across it. His lips formed her name

379

but no sound emerged. Again he moved, but he seemed afraid. It was as though that last step might prove her to be a figment of his imagination and he was reluctant to take it.

Jenny clung to the tree and something inside her wept great tearing sobs of joy. Her eyes were incandescent with recognition and love. She felt the world move as their glances met and held fast, but in that last ecstatic moment she became lost and frightened. Dear God, it could not be . . . It was a trick, a cruel, cruel trick which the smoke and steam and all that she had witnessed was playing on her eyes. Her mind had absorbed so much, more than it could take that day and in her anguish and need, her heart had conjured up the ghost of her . . .

The man's eyes blazed and his voice was hoarse as he shouted her name. He lifted his arms and the sorrow and loneliness of the years between left her, and she moved into them.

Without a word they clung together, and he held her as if she were the most precious thing in the world.

Chapter Forty-Two

Nils, Nils, Nils.

She touched his cheek with her fingertip and he grasped her hand roughly, pressing it to his lips with a desperation born of years of longing for this moment. Their eyes locked, looking deep, deep into each heart and they knew that it was the same as it had been. As it had been, as it would always be. The look stripped away the years, bringing back the seventeen year old girl who had loved for the first time, and the young man who had loved her.

Twenty years and it was still the same.

Somehow they had got home, to Jenny's house, though later she was to wonder how, for she remembered nothing. She was aware only of the hand that held hers, the arms that went round her protectively, as she would have fallen, and the blaze of remembered love in his eyes.

And that moment when as they closed the front door behind them, he put his arms about her and they kissed. In the back of her mind there was only room for a tiny thought of gladness that the girls were with Ellen Robinson, then she poured herself into the unbelievable joy of her love.

At first they could do nothing, say nothing, but touch and stare and murmur incoherently, whispering each other's name. For half an hour they stood just inside the door and clung to each other afraid, even now, that this magical moment would vanish. Their bodies pressed together, and his arms held her to him, and she wept as he rained kisses on her eyes, her cheeks, her lips. Her fingers grasped the thick golden hair at the back of his head, and stroked the smooth skin of his neck, and she strained against him, knowing if she stepped back she would fall.

It was almost dark when at last they could bear to part for a moment. She leaned back in the circle of his arms and looked into his beloved face, and smiled, her eyes shining in gladness.

'I knew you would come,' she said, as though it had been yesterday.

'I have looked for you every time.'

They moved, hands still clasped, into the sitting room, and she allowed him to leave her for a moment to light the fire which she had laid aeons ago, that morning. As he put a match to the kindling, she moved to the window, rolling down the blackout blinds, and drawing the velvet curtains. The wood caught and lit the coals, and the flames danced merrily on the wall and ceiling and they were transported back to that other time, that other place.

'I'm so dirty,' she grimaced, as he stroked her cheek, 'and so are you.'

Their eyes met and they drowned in the look of wonderment which passed between them.

'I can't believe it,' he said. He shook his head and the sweet, loving expression which had lived in her memory, crossed his face and he put his lips to her cheek.

The fire began to roar, the flames leaping up the chimney and they sat on the rug before it, holding each other, not speaking. All the words would come later. The explanation, the sorrows and longings, the words of what had happened and why, but not now. Their hands were enough; and lips touching, and eyes looking and loving.

The boiler behind the fire began to hum as the water heated and Jenny stood up, pulling Nils to his feet. She smiled. There was no shyness, no restraint, no false modesty. This was her man. She was a woman now. The innocent girl had gone ten years ago when Bill Robinson took her. Here she was with the man she loved; who loved her in return, and by the same measure, and she was sure in her need, and his.

They went up the stairs, stopping to put up the blackout curtains as they went. They turned on no lights, the glow from the cheerful fire in the sitting room illuminating their way. In the bathroom the last blind was hung and Jenny turned on the light.

Nils stood bemused, drugged with love, watching as she turned on the taps and began to fill the bath with hot, steamy water. She threw in a handful of tangy pine bath salts, and as the water inched up the sides of the bath, she began to remove her clothes. Like a starving man placed before a feast, his eyes poured their message of longing over her. Beneath the filth and matted clothing her body was white, glowing with love, and her breasts drew his hands. Her nipples stood proud and pink and he felt himself throb and become erect.

'Come, my love, a bath first, then we will . . .' She did not finish. She had no need. They lay in the water together, her back against his chest and she felt the thrust of his penis against her buttocks and knew she could hold him back no longer. They had soaped and sponged each other lovingly, every curve and valley. They had laughed a little, splashing, waiting. They had been children again for a while, physical longings damped down by the loveliness of their joy in each other.

But now it was time.

He would not love her in the bedroom. Though no words had been spoken, he knew that she had shared a bed in this house with another man, and he was unwilling to ask which one.

He carried her, still wet and smooth, like silk, down the stairs, and laid her tenderly before the fire, as the last time. And loved her, and loved her, again and again, in the night. Their bodies dried in the warmth of the fire and became wet again with perspiration, in the strength of their loving.

Over their heads the sky was a moving phalanx of German bombers who had come for the fifth night running to pound the inhabitants of the city to submission, but the couple dreaming and loving and remembering, by the fire, paid no heed. The noise drowned her cries of rapturous joy, and the sound of the man's deep throated roar of triumph as he took her.

They slept, awaking only to throw more coal on the fire keeping the room warm and glowing. As dawn broke they kissed lingeringly. He licked the delicate rim of her ear with his warm tongue and his hand traced the outline of her cheek, the sweet roundness of her jaw and the velvet smoothness of her throat. He sat up and his eyes travelled the length of her lovely body, his own strong, lithe, masculine and proud. She touched the hard muscles of his arm and shoulder and as he lay down beside her she slid down his body, kissing every rib, the hollow of his navel, the inside of his thigh, the strength of his long slim legs and the softness of the arch of his foot. Her warm mouth travelled upwards until it reached the magnificence of his erect penis, and it began again. The loving.

It was daylight when they rose from their bed before the fire. They bathed again together, and he watched her as she dressed, his eyes touching her with such love, she wondered how she had lived these twenty years without it. In the few short hours since they had met he had become a part of her again and she of him, and she knew she would never give him up.

They talked as they breakfasted before the fire. Not of the past, nor of the future, but of themselves, their feelings, their love. They could not stop touching each other.

The sound of the doorbell ringing awoke them from their dream. Jenny lifted her head to listen, as though the sound had come from some far-off, unfamiliar and unknown world. A startled expression lit her eyes, then she smiled.

'It will be Kate,' she said, gently pushing Nils back into his chair.

As Jenny opened the door Kate burst over the step like an explosion. The worry and strain of the previous two days made her voice strident and harsh.

'Oh God, our kid, am I glad to see you. I tried ringin' yer at work yesterday but they said the factory had taken a direct hit. The telephone operator tried all ways to get through but there was so many lines down or summat, they 'adn't a chance. I was round 'ere 'alf a dozen times but yer weren't 'ere. Where the 'ell were ya all day?' Without waiting for a reply she went on, distractedly running her fingers through her hair. 'I sent our Frankie over to Ma Robinson's on his bike and 'e said it were awful. Roads blocked and everything, but the kids are OK. Mrs Robinson wouldn't let 'em go to school and I don't blame 'er. I kept ours in, except Frankie of course an' nowt'll keep 'im at 'ome.' She sighed resignedly as she began to move along the hallway towards the living room. 'Thank God yer all right anyway.'

'Eeh, I could murder a cup a' tea, love,' she continued, 'then I'll 'ave to be gerrin back to the kids. Frankie's with 'em now, but I'll 'ave to go in a minute.' She stopped and turned to Jenny. ''Ow much more can we take, our kid.' Her eyes filled with tears and her face quivered. 'I'm that frightened, bein' on me own. Why don't yer come round tonight? Now that the factory's gone yer'll not be working for a bit, not until they find somewhere else, and the kids are safe at Old Swan. Yer know Mrs Robinson'll guard 'em with 'er life.' She gave a wan smile. 'Just let a bomb try and drop on 'er precious grandchildren and she'd 'ave a word or two to say.'

As the words poured from her, and the strain of worry eased away, she looked more closely at her sister, noticing for the first time the luminous glow in her dark eyes and the flush of exquisite beauty on her face. She stared and took a step backwards as though to get her into focus.

'What's the matter wi' you,' she said anxiously. 'Yer all right aren't yer? Yer've not been hurt, 'ave yer? Yer look very flushed.' She searched Jenny's face suspiciously, stepping back further into the living room. Taking Jenny's hand she drew her with her, turning her to the light so that she might see her better. As she did so she became aware of the figure of the man who sat quietly in the armchair. He stood up as she turned to him.

Perhaps it was that which brought the memory so immediately

384

back to her, for it had been his 'lovely' manners which had impressed her nearly twenty years ago.

The silence was unbearable. Jenny wanted to say something but it all happened so quickly; it was all so new and unbelievably beautiful, she could find no words. Her body was alive with nerves which tingled with happiness, but her tongue had lost its fluency and her mind its quickness. She wanted to stand and look and look at the beloved face and see the love which glowed there, and wonder at the miracle which had brought him back. She knew she must make some explanation, but what? She had none herself, and found no need for one. He was there and that was enough and eventually, when they were ready, they would speak of it, but Kate . . . something must be said to Kate.

'It's Nils, Kate,' she said, almost shyly.

'I can see it's bloody Nils,' Kate hissed. Her words were like a curse in the quiet room. It was as though someone had sworn in church. Her fingers curled into claws and she took a step towards the bewildered man.

'Oh yes, I can see it's Nils.' Her voice was sarcastic. 'An' where 'ave *you* been for the last twenty years, may I ask?'

'Kate, please, don't . . . Nils has . . .' Jenny grasped Kate's arm and tried to draw her away, but Kate shook her off. Her fury was devastating and her eyes flashed with loathing. She was re-membering, and the pictures which wormed their way into her brain made her want to lash out at the handsome face before her.

'Yer sod,' she whispered. 'Yer rotten sod. 'Ow you 'ave the bloody nerve to show yer face to this family again, I don't know. Come fer another go, 'ave yer. A few days in port so why not look up the judy who was so willin' before. Is that it?'

'Kate, stop it!' Jenny screamed her pain, grasping Kate's arm; pulling her roughly across the room. Nils moved towards the struggling women. 'Jenny, don't. Leave her, she doesn't under-stand. Neither of you do. *You* are prepared to trust me because you . . . but Kate – she doesn't know . . .'

'Oh, don't I? Well let me tell you I know exactly what you are and if my sister is fool enough to be taken in again, she's no need to come cryin' to me when yer piss off.'

'Kate – *fer God's sake Kate!*'

'Where were you when she was ill, eh? Where were you when she nearly died 'avin' your . . .?'

'*Kate!*' Jenny's voice was like a whiplash, curling about her sister's back, and the sound of it cut off Kate's words like a knife. Her shoulders drooped, her head bowed and she began to cry.

385

The man indicated the chair in which he had been sitting. Taking Kate by the hand he led her gently to it. She tried to resist, but with a quiet strength which demanded obedience, he placed her in it. Turning to Jenny, his face alight with his love for her, he pointed to the chair on the opposite side of the fireplace.

'Sit,' he said softly. When both women were seated he turned and walked to the window, staring out at the garden. The trees were budding in pale and lovely green, and the grass, beginning to grow with the re-awakening of spring, was bright with daisies. For several minutes he stared into the delicate lacy sky then he turned to the women who waited for him to speak. Kate still glared at him, but his actions were not those of a man who had a guilty conscience and she was intrigued, dispite herself.

Nils sat down at the table and began to speak.

'Many years ago, in 1922, a young seaman came to this city. He fell in love. The girl he loved was sweet and beautiful and the man never loved another. He never will.' Jenny's face was rapt, like a worshipper at an altar, and her eyes glowed with a love that was almost mystical. Nils smiled tenderly, and Kate felt her heart move in her breast.

'The young man had to go away but before he left he told his love that he would return and they would be married.' Jenny nodded her head. 'But he had an accident.' She gasped and her hand went to her mouth. 'Whilst he was in New York harbour, he was injured and spent many weeks in hospital. He scarcely knew who he was, or why he was there, and then, as memory crept back, and he would have written, the name of the road where she lived eluded him.' Kate's eyes became blue pools, and she bent her head as she imagined his despair. 'When he recovered he returned to find the girl he loved, but she had gone, and no one could tell him where. For months he looked for her, in every café, in every street, but she was not to be found. Desperate, the sailor put an advertisement in the paper, and in answer, he received this.'

Reaching inside his jacket, Nils pulled out his wallet and from it produced a yellowed, dog-eared piece of paper. The writing on it was faded, but readable.

Passing it to Jenny he waited as she unfolded it with trembling fingers and began to read. Tears flowed from her eyes in a stream of terrible anguish and in her heart grew a great agonising sorrow for what had been done to them. Without lifting her head or speaking she passed to Kate the letter which Henry Fowler had written to Nils Jorgensen in February 1923.

Kate had gone. Before she went she embraced the tall figure of the man who loved her sister, and though she said nothing, her eyes shone with sorrow, and begged for his forgiveness.

They talked then for many hours, Nils and Jenny. Nils had married an American girl in 1932, he told her, but she had died four years later in an influenza epidemic. They had no children. On the death of his wife he had returned to the home of his birth and had gained command of his own ship the following year. When Norway fell to the Germans in 1940, he had not returned there with his cargo of raw cotton from America, but had taken his ship to England. He had volunteered for the Royal Navy and was given the rank of navigation officer aboard a flower class corvette. It was this ship which was now in port, and from which he had forty-eight hours leave.

He told his tale simply, never taking his eyes from her face.

When he had finished there was silence but for the sound of the embers falling in the fire. Jenny moved absently, picking up several lumps of coal from the scuttle with the tongs and placing them in the heart of the glow.

Nils watched her, marvelling at her beauty. Her skin was as flawless and smooth as it had been at seventeen and her mouth was like a full-blossomed pink flower. He felt the thrill of wanting her, touch him again like a fire. He caught his breath as it spread within him, but now he held back. He knew nothing of her, nothing of her life. She loved him still, of that he was certain, but what of the years which had gone since they parted?

'And you, Jenny, what of you. You are married?' There was infinite sadness in his voice as he spoke for he guessed the answer.

Jenny knelt on the rug in front of the fire.

'Yes.'

'You have . . . children?'

'Two daughters.'

He didn't know what to say next. He had found her too late. His heart was like a rock in his chest and he felt the constriction grip him, reaching for his throat.

'You are – happy?'

Jenny turned and looked into his eyes. Her voice was high with naked emotion.

'Oh God, Nils. How can you ask it?' Her face spasmed in despair and he felt the core of his heart split with the pain of his love for her. 'I haven't known happiness with a man since you left. Don't you know? Can't you see? I loved you then, as a young girl, with a young girl's mind and heart, but as I became a woman, I loved you as a woman. There has been no one else, ever. I married Bill ten years ago. I wanted a child, and for other reasons, but there was never, has *never* . . . I love you, Nils. Dear God I love you.'

She fell against him and his arms claimed her, and their tears of joy and love and pain for what they had lost, mingled and ran until they tasted the salt of them on their searching lips. He strained her to him and it might have been the two young lovers of years ago as they kissed again hungrily. The love they had for one another poured about them like a tidal wave, drowning the sadness, lifting them buoyantly towards the rapture which neither had known when they were apart. The past was forgotten, the future not yet born, uncertain and obscure. It was here that mattered, here and now. She looked at him. The sweet longing in her eyes lanced him. She took his hand and lifted it to her lips, repeating her innocently sensual action of twenty years ago.

The enemy bombers filled the sky in a circling fleet again that night, the sixth night they had come, but the sounds of the explosives scarcely rippled the surface of the lovers' consciousness. He loved her splendid woman's body, gilded by the flames of the fire. Delicate gold, amber shadows, rosy-tipped peaks. Her hair tangled in a riot of curls, fell about her radiant face, urchin-like, and he smiled, enchanted.

His mouth murmured against hers.

'My nutbrown maiden,' he said softly, running his hands across her hair and down the sides of her face. His hands cupped the soft weight of her breasts.

They came together again with a fervency that took away time and reason. On and on it went, again and again until they both cried out with deep and ringing sounds which might have been grief or joy. Emotions joined together so closely they were indivisible.

They lay, beautiful in the aftermath of their loving, the dying fire bathing their bodies with gold. They murmured soft words, speaking of the past and at last Jenny told him of his daughter. She held him against her breast as he wept and as his tears flowed, the last anguish left her, and they shared the sorrow of the loss of their child.

It was four-thirty when the All Clear sounded and he knew he must leave her soon. He held her in his arms and his mind returned to their last farewell. He had gone from her then with a young man's optimistic belief that nothing would keep him from his dreams. His step had been light, though it had been hard to leave her, and his hopes had been sure, certain that within the month he would return to claim her. Bleakly he remembered and he knew that he could not bear to lose her again.

Quietly, as she drowsed against him, he spoke.

'What will we do now, my darling.'

Instantly she was awake. Without hesitating she answered, 'We shall be together for the rest of our lives.'

Nils' heart soared.

'But your husband. You will . . .' For a moment his spirit quavered. A man had gone to war, to defend his family and his country from an enemy who threatened, and while he was away, another had come to steal what was rightfully his. Sweet Jesus, how could he do it? How could he take her though she came willingly? The man was vulnerable, far away from his home, his wife defenceless . . .

Jenny's voice was cold, bitter, and her words took his breath away.

'My husband and I have nothing. I cannot tell you of the things that have been done to me. I can only say this. My marriage ended years ago, when my younger child was born. Since then –' She hesitated and her arms clung to him and he felt her tremble.

'I shall never be a wife to him again,' she whispered.

He left her just as the light turned the sky in the east to pearl. By the river the night was a great red scar as the city burned on the sixth night of the terror.

Chapter Forty-Three

For a terrible, heart-stopping moment Jenny thought the police-man had come to tell her that Nils was dead, and the breath sighed from her in terror. Later she was to wonder, and to be ashamed that her first consideration had not been for her children or even Bill, but the constable asked for Mrs Walker and the relief she felt made her tremble and almost smile. How could she be so foolish, she thought? Nils had only been gone two days and would be scarcely out of the Channel yet. Besides, they would not send news to Kate's house, would they? Nils had said he would inform the Admiralty that Jenny was to be named as his next of kin, just in case. He had tried to smile, holding her tightly in his arms, the conception of death and parting so soon after they had found each other, almost more than they could bear.

But as the deliverance flooded her, knowing it was not Nils, a tiny thrill of apprehension ran through her veins. The children – dear God, not her children, or Charlie, let it not be Charlie. Please, oh please, Kate would – it would kill her if it was Charlie.

Kate came to the kitchen door, her hands floured with the 'fatless' scones she was making.

'What is it, chuck?' she called cheerfully, her hands held out before her. Catching sight of the blue uniform, she leaned sud-denly against the doorframe, and the colour drained slowly from her face. The constable, used by now, during these past few days to the look of dread which his presence brought, spoke kindly, questioningly.

'Mrs Walker?'

Jenny looked over her shoulder to Kate, where she sagged in the doorway.

'This is Mrs Walker.'

Kate began to whimper in her throat.

'It's not my . . . please . . . no not Charlie.'

'Can I come in, love.' The constable removed his helmet respect-fully and it was this gesture more than anything which told Jenny that within the next few moments their lives were once again to be seared with grief.

For two days she had remained alone, not wanting the company of her children, not even Kate. She had telephoned a neighbour of her mother-in-law, leaving a message for Ellen to keep the children for a day or two, knowing she would be more than willing, then, closing the front door on the world, she had retreated into the dream which Nils had brought back to her. The bombers had come again in the night, but she lay serenely in her bed, unafraid. Eating when she was hungry, sleeping a little, needing none, she let herself drift, her mind peaceful, her love gathered round her, and lived again the two nights she had spent with Nils. She knew, though her spirit denied it, that the man she had loved for twenty years, sailed into danger and might not return again. The future might not come for them as they dared hope, but, though she prayed it would, the tranquillity of her mind, assuaged at last by the knowledge that Nils had not deserted her all those years ago, gave her a happiness she had not believed possible. The words he had spoken to herself and Kate had removed the scar forever. It had healed with the years, but now it was gone. She did not know what was to happen. What of Bill and her daughters? He meant nothing to her. She would leave him and live with Nils, that she knew, but she would not desert her children. But now, on this day, she wanted nothing but to sit in the stillness and silence and wrap her newfound love and joy about her.

Kate, sensitive to her needs, kept away. Her own fears, for her children in the horrors of the air raids, for Charlie far away in the dangers which lurked at sea, she kept to herself, giving her sister the privacy she knew she needed at this time. Jenny would come when she was ready.

Strangely, on the next day, as if to remind Jenny that the problems which were to come were not far away, an airgraph came from Bill, the second in the seven months since he had gone overseas. There was not a lot in it, nearly half had been censored and she wondered idly what he had said to make the censor slash his words so violently. But Bill was a million miles away to her now. He had gone from her life and thoughts as though he were dead, and for a fraction of a guilty second she wished he were.

He sent his love to his children and, in words which only she would understand referred lewdly to their last night together. Her flesh crawled and she felt dirty. Even so far away, he tried to humiliate her. Though the man who censored Bill's letter had no knowledge of that night, Jenny felt debased as though her husband had disclosed to a stranger, the shameful events. She tore the letter up, throwing it on the fire, and as it burned, the flames consumed cleanly the revulsion of feeling it had aroused in her.

At peace, she walked round to Kate's.

They had embraced. Kate smiled into her eyes, saying nothing, but her expression was glad as if to say she knew and understood.

Now, closing the door behind the constable, Jenny followed him as he moved slowly along the hallway and into the lovely smell of baking which filled the kitchen. The children were all at school. They could not be kept at home forever, though mothers saw them off in fear, not knowing if they would return.

The kitchen table was littered with the ingredients with which Kate had been baking the scones, and a fine haze of flour misted the air.

The policeman stood almost at attention. Kate and Jenny sat down, never taking their eyes from his face. Though he had performed this task many times during the last week, it was obvious he did not know where to start.

'Mrs Walker?'

'Yes, yes, for God's sake –'

'I'm sorry, lass . . .'

Jenny's voice cracked in anguish.

'Please, *please*, what is it . . . who . . . ?'

'A house in Saint Domingo Road. The whole row.'

The sisters' minds cringing from thoughts of husbands, lovers, children, could not for the moment understand the words the man had spoken.

'Saint Domingo Road?'

'Aye, lass.' His voice was heavy and said. 'A woman who . . . who survived gave us yer name.'

The silence settled in the room filling the hearts of the women, like lead.

'Elly, dear God, not Elly!' It was Jenny who cried out.

'Aye, lass, and . . .' The constable hesitated.

Kate looked up, anguished, her face distorted with grief.

'Not – not Pat – not . . .'

'There were six bodies, six of them . . . I'm sorry.'

'All of them – *all of them*?' Kate began to rock herself as the tears poured from her closed eyes. 'Not all of them. What was Phyllis doin' there. She's lived in Dingle since she was wed. Oh God, what about 'er 'usband, 'e's in – Oh Lord, Oh Lord, not our Elly, not . . .'

As if drawn together by their need, as they had always been, the two women stood up, clinging together for support. They could not take it in. Elly's children were all grown up now, the eldest three married. Jack and Tommy were in the navy and Edna, the youngest worked on munitions. What were they all doing at home together? It was as if the mystery of it obsessed their minds, diverting them from the real tragedy.

The policeman cleared his throat.

'I'm sorry ladies, but I've gotta ask you –'

Two white faces, blotched and gaunt with grief, turned towards him. What more could their sorrowing hearts be asked? What other burden would he place on them?

Kate sobbed helplessly, hardly aware of what was being said.

'I'm afraid someone, one of you, must identify the bodies.'

'No, oh please no!' The sisters voiced their horror in unison. They began to gabble incoherently.

'My brothers – surely –'

'It's me Dad's responsibility!'

'Please don't ask us –'

The policeman, compassion shining in his troubled blue eyes, eyes which had seen more suffering during this last week than in a lifetime on the beat, was firm.

'Apparently your elder brothers cannot be reached and, of course, the others are away, and your father is, well his doctor said . . .'

'His doctor?'

'I believe he's poorly.'

'Poorly?'

'I'm sorry missus, I know no more than that. Now if you'll get yer coats, I'll take yer to the . . . to the mortuary.'

Kate cried helplessly, clinging to Jenny as once Jenny had clung to her. It had seemed to hit her harder than Jenny, and she fumbled about the kitchen like an old woman. She turned as they left the house.

'My children, I can't . . .'

'The lady next door will see to 'em, I've already 'ad a word with 'er.'

That day, would it ever be erased from Jenny's mind? Would the nightmare of it ever leave her? Would peace of mind, the lovely serene joy with which the day had started, ever return? As the bright sun slid gracefully behind the stand of trees at the back of Kate's house that evening, and her sister lay in a drugged sleep upstairs, put there by John Clancy, she had the idea that she would never know happiness again. In one day it had been poured upon

393

her, as lovely as a river in full spate, then, within hours, that river had dried up, leaving desolation, drought, despair.

The mortuary had been like some fantasy from the blackest vision which comes to haunt us in the night. The large room was covered from wall to wall with sheeted bodies. In one corner was a door through which men brought shapeless, covered bundles on stretchers. As they were placed on the floor, the covers were removed and hoses played across the pitiful blackened, cruelly injured bodies, so that they might be recognised by harrowed relatives. The stench was sickening. Many of those here had been buried beneath the rubble of their homes for several days.

As Kate and Jenny entered by another door a woman in a rubber apron hurried across to them. Her face was stiff, expressionless. She was only young, a VAD and though Kate and Jenny did not know it, had been given the job because she had studied anatomy and could piece together the jigsaw puzzle of limbs, torsos and bodies ready for identification and burial.

'Which street?' she said brusquely.

'What?' Jenny stared at her bewildered.

'Which street did your relatives live in?' she said more kindly.

'Saint Domingo Road,' Jenny whispered.

For the last time they looked on Elly's face. She had a bruise upon her cheekbone, but her expression was almost smiling. Beside her lay Pat and the young woman lifted a corner of the sheet so that Kate and Jenny might see that in death they had clasped hands.

'We didn't want to separate them,' she said compassionately. Phyllis; Jack still in uniform; Tommy, most of his face covered, for his injuries had been mutilating, and Edna, her face so like her mother's, cheeky even in death.

Kate and Jenny kneeled beside their dead sister and remembered. She had been a pain in the neck at times, they had told each other smilingly, but how staunch had been her loyalty. Her help, often misguided, had always been freely given as had been her cockeyed advice, but always, she had been there.

Weeping silently, arms about each other, Kate and Jenny walked slowly from the building surrounded by dozens on the same sad errand as themselves.

'Oh our Jenny, 'ow could it 'appen? 'Ow could it. Six of 'em in one go. 'Ow can we stick it.'

They boarded the tram for home, still shedding tears, watched pityingly by their fellow passengers. The conductor put his hand on Kate's shoulder, saying nothing, conveying with his gesture, the sympathy felt by the inhabitants of the stricken city, one for the other.

The small boy wandered across the sunlit field, his eyes searching the newly growing grass for a splash of colour which might indicate a flower. There wasn't much to be had at this time of the year, only dandelions, and he wanted his Mam to have a nice bunch of flowers to put in her glass vase when she came home. Aunty Morag had told them sadly at dinner that Aunty Elly had died, and Uncle Pat, and his Mam would be unhappy and he wanted to cheer her up. His childish heart was bewildered. The bombs dropped and killed people and it frightened him sometimes, but today the world about him was as it had always been. The field was part of his life and the woods and he felt comforted. He would pick some flowers before he went back to school and put them where his Mam would see them when she came home.

His footsteps took him closer to the wood and as he drew near he could see the lovely colour which carpeted the ground. The trees seemed to float in it and his heart lifted excitedly. The woods swam in a sea of bluebells.

Eagerly he began to pick them, clutching the juicy green stalks in his plump boy's hand. He bent and moved on rhythmically until his eye was caught by what looked like a large butterfly. It was white, but delicate and pretty and his inquisitive mind was intrigued.

Reaching forward he grasped it, the bluebells for his Mam still held lovingly in his hand. The small explosion was scarcely noticed. A woman hanging out her washing in Crescent Road heard a sharp crack and looked towards the wood. A drifting haze of smoke and debris and a handful of leaves lifted gently above the trees. The woman's hands faltered and the pegs she held fell to the ground. Her husband's shirt drooped on the line. She hesitated, a feeling of alarm running through her, then still looking over her shoulder to where the mist of grey smoke was disappearing she went inside to fetch her husband. His cry of anguished horror was heard by every inhabitant of the road, and as he ran from the peaceful spinney, he vomited. He could not speak of what he had seen – then, or ever.

The screams of the two women lifted high in the air and they both beat angrily in denial at the constable who told them. The kitchen seemed filled with people. A young policewoman, her face wet with tears, a soldier from the bomb squad, a police constable,

Morag half-fainting in the armchair, and later John Clancy. The street was alive with terrified women, most of them weeping, clutching their children about them and dozens of soldiers searching the gardens and surrounding fields.

It had been a butterfly bomb and there might be more.

There seemed no one to turn to now. In her desolation, for who could not help but love the sweetnatured child who had died, Jenny was alone in her role of comforter. Charlie, Elly, Waggy . . . all those who had supported her were gone or far away, and Kate had slipped into the darkness of shock and grief beyond bearing.

It was only herself she had now. Kate's children clung desperately to her. Nils was gone and she was alone.

A week later on 14 May 1941 Jenny and Charlie stood with the hundreds of others and mourned their dead in Anfield Cemetery. They were buried in a common grave. The communal tomb prepared for them – a tunnel of red brick – was left open at certain points along its length so that coffins could be seen and wreaths laid upon them. Old men and women, young mothers with babies, children, servicemen and members of the Civil Defence laid flowers, singly and in bunches, along its length. Each coffin was covered by a Union Jack.

Charlie wept harshly as he laid his flowers on his son's coffin. He had wanted the boy to be with his own, and the seven coffins rested side by side, the small one in the centre as though in death, his family grouped protectively about its youngest member. His heart broke for the lovely child who had gone. He swayed, clinging to Jenny and John Clancy held him or he would have fallen.

The service was short and simple and the words compassionate.

'One day, no doubt, this will be marked by a monument cherishing the memory of the men, women and children of Liverpool who fell in a fight . . . The enemy has broken their bodies and may break ours, but they will never break our spirits.'

Two days later, Henry Fowler died of a second, massive coronary. He was buried at the same cemetery but no one followed his coffin to its last resting place, not even the widow from Agnes Street. He had never married her, and though she stayed with him till the end, she never forgave him. When she left the chip shop which she had run for twenty years, she had in her suitcase every penny Henry had hoarded away in a secret hiding place. She deserved it.

Chapter Forty-Four

Nils came back in July, but Jenny was still with Kate, and could spend no time with him.

They sat in Kate's kitchen, surrounded by children, staring and curious, and held a stilted conversation, but their eyes spoke and Nils' heart bled for the sorrow he saw in hers. Whilst he had been away her world had been torn apart by grief, and though the blitz was over, the fear was not.

Kate's mourning for her son would not leave her. Charlie had returned to sea after two weeks' compassionate leave, hollow-eyed, a shadow of himself but, Jenny suspected, glad to go. For the first time in their marriage, Charlie and Kate were of no use to each other. In the depth of their separate grief they could not reach each other, and Jenny stood in the middle, a strong rock to which both clung. Her own daughters had to share her with the bewildered, frightened children of whom their own mother scarcely seemed aware. Kate moved in a quiet ghost-filled world where no one must intrude. She lived on memories of her baby, the one she had loved the most, and in the depth of her frozen heart, refused to believe that he was really dead. She went to church every day, desperately clinging to God. If God existed, then there must be a heaven, her broken heart told her. If there was a heaven, then her Harry was in it, and that meant that she would see him again, if she was good. It was all she had to hold on to, for how could she bear it if she were never to see him again.

The year ground on, remorseless in its misery, and Jenny thought she would live like this forever. Nils came and went, where she never knew, but he was gaunt, thin, always tired, and the small time they had together seemed like a dream. When would it become real, she thought, as she watched her sister drift about the house like a spectre, disinterested, uncaring. Kate's children, with the bouncing ball resilience of children, turned more and more to Jenny, as though she were their mother and Jenny knew she could not leave now. They squashed together in Kate's small house, and when Charlie was home, refusing to allow Jenny to leave the double bed she shared with Kate, he slept on the settee in the parlour.

In December another grief fell about the shoulders of Kate and Charlie. Their eldest son, dearer than ever to them now, was eighteen years old, and on his birthday, he followed his father to the sea. The Royal Navy. He looked like a child in his smart new uniform, but he walked away from his Mam with the straight back and proud set head of a man.

That same month, the Japanese attacked Pearl Harbour and Great Britain and America declared war upon that nation.

Charlie was jubilant when he was home, just before Christmas. He had three day's leave, and somehow, as though the news that America had entered the battle and the tide would now turn, it seemed to drive the agony of the death of his son from his heart, and give him acceptance, and his old self began to reappear.

It was on Christmas Eve that Kate came back.

Charlie had gone to the wood that afternoon. He went whenever he was home, as one would visit the grave of a loved one. The spot had been covered over, and during the summer, grass and plants, shy violets and pansies, had grown over the spot where Harry had died. When Charlie came back, his cheeks red with the cold, he had brought a lovely young pine tree with him. It was small, smelling deliciously of pine needles.

'It was growing just where – where he died, Jenny,' he said simply. 'I brought it home as a present from him to the others.'

With tears in her eyes, Jenny embraced her brother-in-law. A sound from the doorway made them both turn.

Standing there, her face wet with tears was Kate. Her hair, white now, as it had gone at the shock of her boy's death, stood around her head and her face worked with grief, but strangely, there was a healed look about it.

'Kate,' Charlie said softly, his eyes warm with love.

'Did you say it was a present from – Harry.' Her voice trembled as she spoke her son's name for the first time.

'Yes, love, I thought with it bein' so close – it was meant . . .'

Kate walked slowly across the room. She had grown thin and her dress, thrown on carelessly, hung about her.

'Yes,' she murmured. 'Yes, I like that.'

She took a handkerchief from her pocket and wiped her face. She blew her nose vigorously and smiled.

'Run an' get the decorations, our Dorry,' she said, 'an' we'll get the Christmas tree done up.'

Jenny went home in January, taking her children with her, and a week later Nils came.

It was the beginning for them. The day in May when they had met again seemed so long ago. So much had happened, so many heartaches, it was like the first sweet memory of twenty years ago, unreal. But now, with Kate starting to be herself again, her marriage renewed, her strength returning, Jenny was free at last.

Her daughters loved him. Like women everywhere, whatever their age, they could not resist his handsome face, nor the kind and friendly manner with which he treated them. He was never cross, like Daddy; his patience with their endless questions was inexhaustible, and his stories of his childhood in Norway a delight to them. They thought his name was funny and giggled when he insisted that they call him by it. They had never addressed an adult by a Christian name without aunty or uncle before it, and they felt very grown up. It was Nils, Nils, Nils, all day long, as it was in Jenny's heart, and she longed for the day when they could be together, the four of them. A family. Under the patient warmth of Nils' growing affection, Laura lost her hesitant shyness and began to blossom with a sweet and merry confidence which filled Jenny with thanksgiving. The little girl's face became lively, and her spirit, so often deflated by her father's caustic remarks, grew brave and unafraid. She loved Nils with all the trusting belief a child gives to a father. Helen, extrovert, with friends from the gang of men who emptied the dustbins, to the teachers at her school – from dozens of small girls who invaded the house at the weekend, and of course her beloved Kathy, was more casual in her affection for the handsome officer who came and went so regularly, but she gave him her trust and her sunny friendship, and approved of his uniformed appearance when he took her on outings.

Incredibly, Ellen and Albert had conceived the idea that Nils was a seaman friend of Charlie's. Though his name must constantly have been on the lips of the children, who in their innocence, talked of him to their grandparents, the couple did not connect his visits with their daughter-in-law. Jenny surmised that the girls' chatter – of Nils, of Aunty Kate and Uncle Charlie, of Leslie and Dorry, of Frankie's homecoming, of Kathy, and friends and neighbours, must, in their grandparents' fond hearts, be so involved in the children's lives that the name was just one amongst many. They would know one day. They must, but not yet, not until the time was right. Her heart quailed, and her sorrow for what they would suffer brought her to tears, but one day it must be so. She and Nils had waited for so long and had endured so much.

The nation groaned and faltered under the heavy yoke of war which had been placed upon it, but with the humour which was inherent in the British character and the spirit which flowered in adversity, they gallantly rose up each day, intent on survival, smiling as they licked their wounds.

The shortage of food and household goods became acute. Prices rocketed and black marketeers made fortunes, and the ever-lengthening queues told of hardship and scarcity. A new word was added to the English language. Utility.

Food rationing became more severe. A pound of jam, margarine and syrup must be made to last a month, and cheese, enough to make one sandwich, a week. Eggs were virtually non-existent. Clothes rationing began with a system of points, and the same with sweets. Strangely, half the people who in 1939 had suffered some degree of malnutrition became, due to a balanced diet caused by rationing and a fair distribution, healthier than they had ever been.

Beer was rationed and men's faces became gloomy. The news cast them down as the rest of their many inconveniences could not do. Coal was rationed and Kate was horrified to be told that her kitchen fire, which was the hub of her home and never allowed to go out, was to be given only a ton a month to feed its voracious appetite.

The newspapers lifted the morale of the weary civilians with stories of retaliatory terror bombing of Germany. 'They've had a go at us, now it's our turn,' and the people of Coventry, of Merseyside, Clydebank and those who were going through what had been likened to 'the second Great Fire of London', cheered the news, listening with one ear cocked for the heart-stopping wail of the siren.

Posters exhorted them to:

Carry your gas mask always
Keep your children in the country
Do not waste food
Be like Dad, keep Mum
Eat wholemeal bread
Dig for Victory

Each week seemed to bring worsening news from war fronts. Words were used. Retreat. Siege. Evacuation. Never *Victory*.

Singapore fell to the Japanese, and in April that gallant little island, Malta, bombed to the limits of her existence was awarded the George Cross.

Jenny and Nils waited, loving each other joyously when the girls were with their grandparents. They waited for the day to come which they knew must be theirs. Their hearts had yearned for twenty years, and surely they would not be denied.

Jenny went about her day to day activities, outwardly the same, her face serene, her children loved and cared for as usual. She worked at the factory, which had moved to Edge Hall Lane when the old building had been bombed, making parachutes now.

She saw Kate almost every day. She visited Ellen and Albert, reassuring them of Bill's safety, even though reassurance was not hers to give. She scarcely heard from him, though Ellen and the children wrote regularly. Her love and need for the man who had re-entered her life grew every day and the weeks when he was away with the convoys, passed at a snail's pace, filled with the terror that he might never come back. She was held to the routine of her home and work, and although her every instinct pleaded with her to haunt the docks area, she forced herself to keep to her well-regulated domestic tasks. She knew he would come to her when he was in port, but the days and nights of waiting began to tell on her. For the sake of Bill's parents and her children, she must pretend a calm she did not feel; show a strength which was gradually slipping away from her, and the strain of it tearing her to shreds.

He was there the next day. Standing quietly against the building on the opposite side of the street. His eyes searched the doorway from which she would come. Crowds of people streamed past, shifts coming on: going off: those who had finished hurrying home as quickly as possible before the blackout.

She paused, her heart thudding, her throat thickening with emotion. Without looking to left or right, he ran across Edge Hall Lane, dodging the traffic, until they faced one another.

He murmured her name, saying something in his own language, his face haggard with longing and utter, utter weariness. His arms rose, and as if they were alone, they clung to one another, their mouths pressed together, their kiss a desperate appeal for comfort. Unaware of the rushing mass of humanity, which was equally oblivious to them, they stood together, their love for each other swamping them.

They drew slowly apart and with eyes sad and loving, each looked deeply for a long moment into the other's.

'Come,' Jenny said, taking his hand. 'Let's go home.'

Dodging the scurrying wet crowds and lethal umbrellas, they caught the tram to Walton.

Nils lit the fire and removing their wet coats they sat down on the settee, arms about each other. His eyes drank in her damp flushed face; the droplets of rain caught in her hair, and the small lines of tension about her mouth.

She returned his look, her concern for him growing. It was as if he had not slept for weeks. His eyes were bloodshot, sunk in purple hollows, and the strain of the battle he had come through gave him a pallor that was almost grey.

'You must have some rest, my love,' she said and reached up to smooth the blanched cheek tenderly. 'Where will you stay?'

'I don't know, anywhere I can be with you.' A tired smile lifted the corners of his mouth. 'I have a week. The ship is being re-fitted. She was damaged in –' He did not finish, but his face was bleak.

Jenny felt her heart lurch with fear for him, but she asked no questions.

'You need sleep.'

'I need you.'

'I know.'

He took her hand, the love in his eyes causing the butterfly of love to flutter within her as it had done so many years ago.

He was speaking. 'I know an inn, just outside Chester. I have been several times when I was on leave before we met. If I go there, can you follow me tomorrow?'

He gripped her hand fiercely. His fingers clung so tightly it was as though he was afraid he would spin away if he let go.

'I'll make arrangements for the children. Kate will have them. Give me the name of the hotel.'

Chapter Forty-Five

It was October, 1942 and the German-Italian Army had been defeated at El Alamein. The 'desert rats', named after the tiny kangaroo-like creature called a jerboa, which could survive in almost impossible conditions, had fought in North Africa since August 1940. Burned almost black by the sun; tormented by thousands of flies which swarmed in ears and nostrils, in eyes, on arms and behind knees; frozen by the biting cold at night, the British Eighth Army units fought their way over hundreds of miles of sand, grit, rock, flint and hardbaked mud, the only vegetation a shrub called camelthorn which survived off the dew from the Mediterranean Sea in the north.

The soldiers were allowed a gallon of water a day in which to wash, cook and to drink. They were given fifty cigarettes free each week. They scarcely knew what day it was, for the dreadful routine was broken only by horrific battles during which infantry men crouched in pits, packed with others, heads down as shells screamed overhead. Helmets were crushed onto heads by the impact. Bodies lay heaped, black with flies, and then it would be over for another day.

That day, as the victorious army moved into the city, a stray German tank fired its last shell, and in the sudden loud noise and the flash of blinding light, a group of cheering, marching British Tommies were flung like toys into the air.

One of these was Bill Robinson.

Jenny was not thinking of her husband as she took the bus through the meandering streets of Birkenhead, past Bebbington, Ellesmere Port, Whitby and on through the wet curtain of rain which had fallen for two days and gave no sign of easing, until she came to the outskirts of Chester.

As she rubbed it with her gloved hand, the steamed-up window revealed a view of dripping trees, shiny wet roads, almost deserted, neat suburban houses, and standing in the downpour, scorning the comparative dryness of the bus shelter was Nils, his top coat sodden, the rainwater running off the peak of his cap.

His face was still drawn, anxious, until he saw her, then, as if the sun had glinted on a golden field of corn, the ripple of his smile lifted his mobile lips, crinkling and lighting his eyes, revealing his white, even teeth.

Ah, Nils, my love, my love. Her heart raced and she thought she would burst with the love which flowered inside her. Everything, everyone was forgotten. Her children, Kate, the war, the life she had known, as the beloved figure moved eagerly towards the bus.

She stepped down through the deluge and into his arms.

He held her tightly to him, the water from his cap running onto her shining hair and she could feel the tension, desperate and at breaking point within him.

The room he had booked for them at the ancient inn had no heating, only a huge fireplace which was filled with logs to be lit at the occupants' convenience. With the crackling, spitting fire, smelling of autumn, of English woods, and all the lovely fragrance that thrills the senses with its evocative memories, Jenny watched Nils sleep. He had undressed her, worshipping her with his eyes, but as they lay together in the huge feather bed, his had closed and his exhausted mind and body had fallen into the abyss of sleep which only men who have gone through the hell of war can understand. Men in the blitz, who night after night battled the fires, rescued the bombed and defended the weak and helpless, could, without warning, lose consciousness and fall to the ground through sheer exhaustion of mind and body. They knew, these men under constant shellfire. They knew. Jenny lay beside him in the night as the fire died, holding him against her, savouring for the first time the joy of having him there, asleep, secure in her bed. She slept a little, waking instantly when he moved, lost in the wonder of knowing that when she woke again, he would still be there.

As dawn broke and the pale, golden light of the morning sun touched the room, they woke together and, passion instantly flaring, reached for each other. He took her swiftly, urgently, as though afraid she would slip away in a dream he had imagined, but she clung to him, and would not let him go. Her soft woman's body demanded the hardness of his, and he thrilled to her sensuality. Her body was on fire and trembling with the response he had aroused in her. The physical contact as she submerged herself in him was so sweet, so filled with ecstasy his head spun. Wanton excitement washed over her, and she groaned, pleading for more.

404

With a cry of joy, he plunged himself into her again and again, then fell back shuddering in orgasm, empty, fulfilled, complete. Words, incomprehensible, murmured from his lips against her shoulder.

Afterwards, as they lay tumbled together in the plethora of love which follows, his fingers tangled in her hair, his lips still drinking at her nipples, she asked him what he had said in that final exquisite moment.

He raised himself on his elbow smiling at her lovely flushed and languid face.

'It was a cry to you, my love. A cry from my heart to yours to tell you how much I love you.' His eyes caressed her body, and Jenny revelled in it. This was the look of a man who loved a woman. Loved her, cared for her, held her above all others in the protection of his masculinity. A look that said no harm would come to her; that with his body he would love her, and keep her safe, for the rest of his life.

Later he slept again. It seemed there were two things he could not get enough of, sleep and her body. Each time he woke, she was there beside him, waiting, loving, healing. They did not leave the room until noon the following day. The willing wife of the landlord brought up food on a tray, leaving it outside the door, used to – and well paid by – the transient customers who occupied her rooms. Servicemen, mostly, with ladies who did not wish to be seen, and she was discreet.

They spent their days upon the lovely vastness of the Cheshire Moor, walking, walking, until the strain left Nils' eyes and the colour of the soft sunshine tinted his skin. An Indian summer blessed them as if their union was smiled upon by the gods. And in the night he loved her, filling her, giving her all the adoration which she had craved as a girl, needed as a woman and had never had.

He was a mature man now, no longer the golden haired laughing god-like young man he had been. The idealised romantic love, strong and passionate though it had been, had become resolute, overwhelming, unyielding and he knew he would never let her go.

And he knew they must talk now. It was time.

The warm breeze blew in their faces as they tramped the last few hundred yards of the hillside that sloped towards the water. They had taken a bus from Chester to Flint, alighting at the Castle and walking westwards. They clasped hands, swinging their arms, laughing like children and Jenny's heart was soft with gladness at the carefree expression on Nils' face. He was so incredibly beautiful, she thought. It seemed so strange to say that of a man, but it was true. His goodness, the true spirit of him, shone from his laughing eyes. The skin of his face and neck was as firm, as smooth as on the day she met him, and his hand, as he pointed to something was that of a young man. The sun danced on the small, gently swelling waves of the sea as they walked on, an occasional white cap breaking the surface, the pure, strong smell of ozone assailing her nostrils.

Dropping their knapsacks, they sank to the soft springy ground, moving instinctively to each other until their shoulders touched. They watched a faint line of smudges on the horizon, a convoy heading towards the Atlantic, and for a second, a shadow touched each face. The sun shone from a cloudless blue sky, beautiful in its vast and perfect emptiness. The faint whisper of the trill of a bird was the only sound to break the silence.

Jenny lay back, shading her eyes from the bright golden disc of the sun, and waited for him to speak. With that strange telepathy which comes to those who love, to those who are close in mind and body, she knew it would be now.

'Why did you stay with him?' he asked diffidently. His face was still as he spoke. 'You have told me a little of the way he was, the things he did.' His face tensed as he imagined those things, and his hands clenched with anger, but he went on, 'You said he was unfaithful, yet you stayed all these years. Why?'

Keeping her hand across her eyes, she said, 'I don't know. I was . . . I wanted to leave many times. But I had the children. It is not easy for a woman, Nils, if she has children.'

'You . . . you loved him?'

'No . . . oh no . . . never.' She sat up, taking his face in her hands turning it to look into hers. 'Look at me, Nils. I never loved him, loved him, never. There was a certain affection at first, gratitude for the security he gave me, but he . . . he killed it.' Her head drooped and her voice was sad. 'It might have been different, I don't know, but he found out . . . about you, and our child.'

Nils cried out in horror. 'No . . . oh God Jenny. No. Who . . . ?'

'It was a mistake . . . my sister, the one who died. She did not mean it. I should have told him, but I didn't.' She shrugged her shoulders. 'Maybe it would have been the same even if I had. Bill was . . . is . . . a . . .' She did not know how to continue. How to tell the man who loved you, that the man who was your husband was a selfish, egotistical sadist. That he hurt his own children with his indifferent uncaring ways. How to put into words the beating he had given her and his rape, for that was what it had been. Bitterness had eroded the mind of Bill Robinson until it had become cruel and obsessed with its own desires. How could she explain this to the gentle man beside her? It could not be said.

'I cannot speak of it, my darling. It is over. When he returns I will tell him and you and I . . .'

'When he returns?' Nils' face was white now, and his eyes flashed angrily. 'When he returns. Do you mean when this war is over, Jenny, or are you expecting him to come home on leave from wherever he is? Do you intend us to continue as we are doing now? Hiding our feelings, pretending to be only friends, dodging in the backstreets not to be seen by your friends and family?' His eyes were brilliant, blue-green as the sea as his anger grew. 'I want you for my own. In *our* home, not Bill's. How do you think I feel when I make love to you in the house which is his? I know we do not use his bed.' His face spasmed in pain, 'But even the rug before the fire belongs to him, and, in the eyes of the world, so do you. I know we cannot marry.' He spoke more quietly, drawing her hands into his, 'but we can have a home together, and when Bill comes back, you can get a divorce.'

Jenny's eyes looked into Nils'. She had never seen him angry before, and the depth of his pain broke her heart. His words hung in the still air above them as he waited for her to speak. She was aware of his self-guilt. Though he knew her marriage to Bill was a sham and that he stole nothing from him, it seemed, in these days of war and separation and desperate patriotism, the worst thing a man could do to another was to take his wife, and not only his wife, but his children, for he knew no matter how much she loved him, Jenny would not go without them.

'Well, my darling?' His voice was soft with love and longing, his quick anger gone. 'Will you come to me? Make a home for me. A home with you and Laura and Helen in it. Waiting for me when I come back. You know I love them, your daughters . . . and . . . I want children of my own. Your children, Jenny.' His voice died away on a whisper. 'Let me buy you a house, somewhere away from Liverpool and its bad memories, but not too far from Kate.' He laughed wryly. 'I know how much she means to you, and the girls' grandparents . . .' his voice faltered, '. . . they will want . . . I would not wish to stop them from seeing their grandchildren.'

His look was steady, firm and his eyes steadfast. This was their chance, they said, and they must take it. There would be no other.

Jenny's mind was in turmoil. It seemed the 'decent' thing to do to wait until Bill came home before making a new life with Nils, but why? What did she owe him, besides her beautiful daughters? And the girls. How happy they were in the constant affection which

Nils gave them. It never varied. He did not send them away when he was tired, nor grow impatient with their constant demands for his attention. And she wanted another child. A son. Nils' son.

He was waiting, the dread of refusal swamping his eyes.

'I want to be with you, live with you, be your wife.' Jenny touched his face lovingly, then leaned forward to brush his lips with hers. 'You know that, don't you?'

He nodded, relaxing a little.

'But it just seems so . . . so underhand to . . to just walk out, leave the house empty . . . take his daughters. Ellen and Pop will be devastated.' Her eyes were clouded with pain. 'It will kill them, Nils. To them, Bill is perfect. Our marriage is . . . successful and they adore the girls. This will tear their world apart.'

'I know, I know.' Nils turned from her, staring across the sparkling ripples of water with eyes which had become dull. A gull soared, free as air, a white blur of beauty on the wing, and he watched it as it skimmed away towards the River Dee. 'We have waited so long, Jenny. All these years we have given to other people. Through no fault of our own we have been denied a happy marriage, children.' He groaned, resting his forehead on his arms which grasped his bent knees. She could barely hear him as he whispered, 'Don't leave me, my love, don't leave me.'

'Oh my darling, how can I leave you. I will never leave you. Never.'

Nils lifted his head and turned to look at her. The sun turned her brown hair to copper, and the soft gold of her eyes was limpid with love.

'I said to you, on that night when you came back to me that we would spend the rest of our lives together. I answered your question unthinkingly, emotionally, with my heart, but I meant it. We will, my darling.'

Putting her arms about him, she drew his head to her breast, feeling the tension run from him, holding him securely in her loving grasp. 'I promise you, Nils, that we will, but give me time, my dearest. I will tell Ellen and Pop. I must prepare them . . . and Kate, though she will be easier. But . . . I must . . . we must . . .' She lifted his face to hers and looked into his eyes. 'We must find some way to tell Bill. I don't know how . . . but soon, very soon, you shall have your home, and your children.'

That night Nils' and Jenny's son was conceived. She had fallen asleep in his arms, loved, safe, sure in her heart of the rightness of what had been planned that day. She woke in the night and for an instant could not orientate herself to the sounds which filled the room and the movement of the bed beneath her. She felt Nils' body against her own, shaking in long convulsive shudders and his voice groaned and shouted and words of horror and fear rose, like birds of prey to the ceiling. His teeth chattered and his head thrashed from side to side on the pillow, and as she moved, he threw her from him in a gesture of revulsion.

He was asleep and in a nightmare of remembrance. She heard his words rasping in his throat and knew he re-lived some dreadful event which had happened to him in the weeks he was away. Holding his threshing body close to her own, she showered his twitching face with kisses, drawing her hands delicately about his body, caressing his as he slept, driving away the demons which plagued him, in the only way she knew how. She felt his penis rise eagerly and as it did so, he came awake and, the nightmare gone, reached for her delightedly.

Afterwards he talked as she drowsed. 'I long for this war to finish, my Jenny, for an end to this madness. I want a home, a life, a child. I cannot see a world in which you are not with me. Now I know it will come. I shall have the dream I have dreamed . . . you are my life, my world, my love.'

Jenny heard his voice, soft, and she fell asleep as he whispered of his dreams for the future.

They spent those days, each one more beautiful than the last, as though they alone existed in their world of love. They were alive, they lived, and he took her every night with a loving fierceness which she matched.

The weather continued glorious, day after day of warm, sun-filled hours, the wild beauty of the paths they trod an anthem to their happiness.

They packed their knapsacks each morning with whatever their friend the landlady could produce, and always hand in hand, they walked northwest to Ness, Burton Point and the Saltings. They stood and listened to the sea breezes singing in the coarse grass and rushes and, hardly speaking turned south along the coast. They stumbled by chance on an old sandstone quayside, a mile or two below Neston, on the old shoreline, and sat basking like a pair of seals in the sunshine, avidly eating their 'carrying-out' as Jenny laughingly called it.

They roamed the ancient city of Chester, strolling along Eastgate Street, marvelling together over the road plan of the city centre which had been laid by the Romans two thousand years ago, and ventured out of the noonday sun into the museum to pore over the

Roman remains. Nils was enchanted with the medieval galleries, Jenny with the Cathedral, and the peace which descended upon her as she entered the great door. And in the insane world which was clamouring about them, they found an acre of sanity in the world of the animals at the zoo.

It came to an end with a suddenness which was like a door slammed in an unsuspecting face. They had been under a spell for seven days, and the emergence from paradise to reality took them by surprise, so engrossed had they become in each other and the small, tranquil world through which they had drifted for a week.

They said goodbye at the Pier Head, in the company of scores of others, the heartache, the grief of parting multiplied by weeping women, silent men. A line of American soldiers, usually so full of cheek and humour, was silent as it marched from a troop ship just docked, memories of their own farewell to a loved one still fresh, the sad scenes about them taking the brashness from them.

Jenny did not cry. They stood, not touching, amidst the hustle and bustle of the quayside, an invisible cord fastening them together, a lifeline between them along which passed the softness of their love, the strength of their devotion, and the words of farewell and comfort they did not speak.

He touched his hand to his cap in salute, and turning walked away into the crowd. A dockie somewhere was whistling *Lili Marlene*.

Chapter Forty-Six

The telegram boy stood on the doorstep, his finger pressed firmly on the bell, the yellow envelope in his hand held slightly away from his body, as though he were afraid it might contaminate him. His face was sombre, for his job was onerous. He waited impatiently for the door to open, at the same time dreading it, already flinching from the expression of terror which would greet him.

Jenny saw him at her door as she came round the corner from Moss Lane into Walton Park Road. The suitcase in her hand grew heavy, feeling as though someone had just packed it with lead weights. She stopped, her heart beginning to pound, the blood pulsing in her veins seeming to fill her ears like a drumbeat. The unbearable ache of the parting with Nils was still twisting inside her, and she wanted to turn and run, to hide and cry the tears which gathered, to scream, 'No more, no more!'

Picking up the case which she had placed on the ground, she forced her reluctant steps forward, calling to the boy as he came through the gate and retrieved his bicycle from the hedge.

'I think that's for me,' she said flatly.

'Robinson?' he asked.

'Yes.'

'Shall I wait? There . . . er . . . might be an answer.'

He knew that what he said was foolish in this time of death. What answer was needed from a family who had been told that their son, father, husband was gone for ever?

Jenny looked at him sadly, and he backed away, climbing hastily on to his bicycle, unwilling to witness the scene which had occurred so many times in his young life. She watched him go, feeling sorry for him. To be the bringer of bad news must haunt the poor lad's dreams and colour his days with death, she thought.

Going up the path, she opened her front door and without entering the house, put her suitcase in the hall, then banged the door behind her and began to walk in the direction of Kate's.

She knew the telegram was about Bill. It must be. A confusion of

411

feelings filled her head with pain. Wicked thoughts, which she was unable to block, crept insidiously closer and closer and she began to weep – Dear God, please help me. I want him dead, I want Bill to be dead. But how can I let such evil into my mind? I don't really, God, she said, not really in my heart, but it would solve all my problems. It would make it so easy for Nils and me, dear Lord. I daren't open this envelope for fear it will tell me Bill is dead, and I can't open it in case he is not – Tears flowed like rain across her face. The pain of saying goodbye to Nils was mixed up with the fear of reading what the telegram would say. Passersby looked covertly at her as she began to run along Willowdale Road, one or two recognising her as the sister of poor Mrs Walker, who had lost so many members of her family, and wondered what other tragedy could have struck.

Kate was scrubbing her kitchen floor. The autumn sun streamed through the window, falling across her rhythmically moving body as she pushed the stiff brush backwards and forwards. The sweat stood out on her face, and she wiped the back of her soapy hand across her forehead, never stopping the tempo of swish, swish, swish. The humdrum routine of the mindless job soothed her and her thoughts were placid as she sat back on her heels to admire the clean shine and fresh smell of the floor.

She almost toppled over as Jenny burst through the back door, her coat streaming behind her like two wings. She had lost her headscarf in her frantic dash across the shortcut of the fields. Her face was pinched and white and her eyes were like pools drowning under the weight of her tears.

Kate reared up, her scrubbing brush at the ready. 'What the . . . ay up, our Jenny. I just scrubbed that floor. Look at yer mucky feet all over it, and what . . .?'

'Kate, oh dear God Kate . . .' Jenny held out the yellow envelope and at the sight of it Kate's face drained of colour and her eyes became glassy. It was the most hated, feared sight in the world, that envelope, its arrival heralding sorrow, and Kate could not bring herself to take it.

'It's for me, Kate,' Jenny whispered.

'Sweet Jesus, our Jenny.' Kate's face was as white as her sister's.

'Will . . . will you open it, our kid?'

Kate was bewildered by the pathetic appeal in Jenny's voice. For years now she had known their Jenny had thought nowt a pound of Bill Robinson, as she herself did. She had never forgiven him for what he had done to Jenny, nor for the way he had treated her and his children, since the day of the christening. She was also aware, though not a lot had been said between them, of her sister's love for Nils Jorgensen. The couple had spent the last week together, and she held Jenny in no blame. If the kid could find a bit of happiness, well good luck to her. It was hard to come by these days. So why was she in such a state over this telegram? It must be about Bill. Who else did Jenny know?

Kate took the envelope from Jenny's hand and turned it over, as though searching for a clue to its contents, then opened it, tearing its edges roughly. She read it quickly then looked up, no expression on her face.

'Bill's been wounded. He'll be home in the next few weeks.'

Jenny's mouth opened and her eyes widened. She looked as though she had been struck savagely, and in the back of her throat a great cry began.

'Oh no, oh no. Dear God, no. I can't bear it, I just can't bear it any more. Kate, Kate. Don't ask me to . . . please Kate . . . I can't . . . we'd just decided . . . planned . . . we were going to buy a house, be together . . . and now . . .'

Sitting down at the table, she put her head in her arms and wept as though her heart would break. Kate stood beside her, stroking her hair and her eyes looked far away into the past, and into the future. So that was it. They had made up their minds, her sister and the man who meant so much to her. They had made their plans and now Bill Robinson was coming home to spoil them. Her heart full of compassion, Kate murmured useless words of comfort to her sister, and dread fell about her. Would it never end?

Ellen Robinson fainted when Jenny told her wooden-faced, that her wounded son was coming home, and Laura cried, her memory in fear of the man who had once lived with them, and was to do so again.

'Will it mean Nils won't come again, Mummy?'

Jenny looked at her daughter. She was eleven years old and becoming aware, in an innocent way, as all women do, earlier or later, of the feelings which are part of growing up. Unconsciously she had absorbed the love which was always present when her mother and Nils were together. The happiness which emanated from her mother's eyes; the involuntary expression of tenderness with which Nils' look followed Jenny as she moved about a room; the warm feeling of security which the couple had unwittingly built around her, had shaped, for the past two years, the happy, untroubled child she had become. It was a constant joy to her mother to see the devotion which had sprung up between Laura and Nils, and she was afraid as she thought of Bill's return. Would he be the same? Would the war have changed him? And his wound, whatever it was, for the telegram gave no indication, how would it affect him, and them?

'I don't know, sweetheart.' She took her daughter's unhappy face between her hands. 'Nils has been such a good friend to us all, but . . . perhaps with Daddy home . . . and not well . . . Nils might have to stay away . . . for a while. We shall have to see how Daddy is, won't we?'

'But Nils loves us, Mummy. I know he does.' Jenny's heart felt as though a knife were turning in it, 'and where will he go when he is on leave? He'll miss us dreadfully.'

'I know, darling, but let's wait and see, shall we?'

She lay in the dark that night and tried to think. Her brain seemed to have become frozen, unable to comprehend the enormity of the disaster which had loomed up, like a thundercloud on a day of blue skies and sunshine. What of the plans she and Nils had made in the soft nest of the feather bed in the inn at Chester? Wonderful plans for the future. For when the war was ended and the peace that everybody longed for had come. Bill had not needed her for years. He had gone his own way. He had his golf, his club, his women and she had existed in his life as someone to wash his shirts and cook his meals, and providing no stones were cast into the pool of their lives causing no ripples, it had been relatively peaceful. Occasionally, she had been subjected to his sexual demands, to his verbal abuse, but she had made a life for herself, content with her children and in the affection and love she received from the rest of her family. But what of now?

Throwing back the bedclothes, she got up and crossed to the bedroom window. There was not a light to be seen anywhere, but a pale sickle of a moon hung in the sky above the river and black outlines of houses and trees could be seen against the dark velvet sky. She heard the footsteps of the warden as he walked quietly along the road, and somewhere, far off, a dog barked. Though the city was quiet, still, invisible, she knew that beneath the pall of blackness it hummed with activity. Munitions factories worked night and day; the docks would be alive with dockworkers, fitters, ships being repaired, unloaded, sailors embarking and disembarking and soldiers. Some would be leaving for far-off places, the names of which were foreign, unknown, never before heard by the majority of the British people. El Agheila, Tripoli, and Kasserine, Tunisia, Sicily. Liverpool was in the front line. The second biggest port in the country, and Britain's gateway to North America and

Canada. It was the main base for the North Atlantic convoys and for the embarkation of troops. It never slept.

Jenny rested her forehead against the cool glass of the window and her breath misted it. Where was Nils? How far had he gone on one of those convoys? Was he still here in port, or had the line of ships already slipped silently from the mouth of the river into the waiting peril of the U-boats? Lord, keep him safe, she breathed silently, and as if in answer she saw etched against the dark glass the beloved face. He smiled, the corners of his mouth tilting in the humorous engaging way he had, and his eyes were bright with love.

– Nils, oh Nils, what is to happen to us now? You have sailed away with the trust in your heart that when you come back we will be together for always. She remembered his eager, excited face as they pored over a map of Cheshire. His faintly accented tongue had curled caressingly about names, towns, villages in which they would look for a house, and his face had been strong, serene in the sureness of their love and of the life they planned together.

She climbed slowly back into the bed. Tears ran from the corners of her eyes, wetting her hair and the pillow, and desolation filled her heart.

The ambulance drew up outside the house and a blue uniformed attendant leaped nimbly from the seat at the front. Running round to the back of the vehicle he opened the rear door, and, his voice cheerful, he called out to those inside.

'Righto lads, who rang the bell? Who's for this stop? Come on then, me old son. Next stop the Pier Head.'

The driver, who had alighted with him took a folding wheel-chair, snapping it sharply until it stood ready for its occupant. Gently, with the patient cheerfulness with which all ambulance attendants seem to be endowed, they lifted the thin figure of a man dressed in hospital blue from the vehicle and, joking, laughing, telling him not to be in such a hurry, they placed him in the chair, wrapping him warmly in a bright red blanket.

'Shan't be a minute lads,' they informed the remainder of their pitiful passengers, and began to wheel the man up the path, towards the door. It was open. A woman and two young girls stood there, and behind them, an older woman and a man. They all looked frightened. The two children hung back, their eyes wide as they stared at the man in the chair, and the elderly woman moaned and covered her eyes with her hand. The man put his arm about her, murmuring soothingly.

'Well missus, 'ere 'e is. The conquering 'ero, aren't yer mate?'
The driver gently punched the shoulder of the man in the chair, his
eyes filled with compassion for him and his stricken family. The
times he had done this, and he never got used to it. The men lifted
the chair over the steps and wheeled it up the hall.

'In 'ere, chuck?' they enquired cheerfully, indicating the living
room in which a bright fire crackled. The elderly couple stepped
aside without a word, as though they were uninvolved witnesses
to someone else's tragedy, and the wheelchair was trundled past
them and placed before the fire.

'Yer'll be comfy 'ere, lad,' one said. 'Only wish we'd time to stop
for a cuppa and a fag with yer, but we gorra get the other lads 'ome.
Good luck mate.'

They left, taking their breezy good humour with them, but
just before the door was closed upon them, one stopped and
turned.

'Oh me blanket, luv. It's 'ospital property.' Returning to the
room he removed the cover from the silent, inanimate man before
the fire, and ran after his partner.

Jenny, Laura, Helen and Bill's parents stood and looked at the
man who had been brought home to them.

He had only one leg.

No one spoke. It was as though they had all been preserved, like
so many images of themselves, in wax. Each waited for the other to
break the awful silence, to make some move towards the man in
the chair.

It was he who spoke.

He turned and looked at them. His face was a dirty brown, the
cheeks hollowed out below dead, sunken eyes. The fine tan he had
sported for two years had turned the colour of pale mud whilst he
had been in hospital, and his dark hair, so luxuriously and untidily
curly, was streaked with grey, and hung like hanks of wire wool
about his forehead.

'Have none of you seen a one-legged man before?' he said
bitterly. Still no one could find the voice to speak.

Laura began to cry, hiding her face against her mother's
shoulder.

'Still the same old crybaby, I see.'

Jenny felt the pity and the awful dragging fear and dread
dissolve. She moved towards her husband. 'Welcome home, Bill,'
she said calmly. 'I'm sorry we were strange . . . but . . . it was a
shock, you see. No one told us how you were injured . . . or to
what extent, but now you are here . . .' She turned to Laura and

Helen, smiling brightly. 'Kiss your father, girls, and say hello to him.'

But the children hung back, reluctant to go near this gaunt, sharp-spoken stranger, who had not even glanced in their direction. They stared in horrid fascination at his empty trouser leg, pinned neatly above where his knee had been.

'Ma, Pop, aren't you going to give Bill a kiss?'

Ellen took a step towards her son. She was bewildered, fearful, shaken to the core of her mother's heart by the sight of the sullen, broken man who had once been her son. Fine he had been when he went to war. Handsome, straight, laughing as he kissed her goodbye, promising to bring her back a camel. Who was this stranger who had returned?

'Bill,' she breathed, her eyes anguished. 'Son, how are you?'

He turned on her, staring at her with eyes that had come to life suddenly. They gleamed with anger, with vicious hatred for what had been done to him, and his voice grated hoarsely.

'How am I? How am I? Oh I'm fine, Ma, fine. I'm off dancing tonight and tomorrow I think I'll 'ave a round of golf with our Douglas. I'm in the pink, Ma. This is Scotch Mist, this is.' He slapped his thigh above the stump of his leg and laughed. 'Never been better, Ma, as you can see. I'm just sitting in this chair for the 'ell of it.'

Fiercely he turned from them, his hands on the wheel of his chair, until he faced the window.

'Nay, son.' Albert took a faltering step towards him. 'Nay lad, that's no way to talk to yer mother. We're sorry, eeh Bill we're sorry.' Tears came to his eyes and suddenly he looked ten years older, 'But your mother . . . she's upset.'

'She's upset, how do you think I feel?'

Jenny's shoulders sagged. Turning, she left the room and walked up the hall towards the kitchen. Automatically her hands performed the task of putting on the kettle for a cup of tea. Her eyes were blank and her heart bucked in her chest like a tethered animal which strains to be free.

Free. Would she ever be free now?

Angry words echoed from the living room, and she heard her children run up the stairs, their frightened weeping soft and wretched. Ellen's voice wailed and there was a crash as though something had been thrown.

Jenny bent her head and looked into the emptiness of the days ahead.

It was the first week in November.

Chapter Forty-Seven

The still figure stood rigidly, eyes turned to the line of ships making its slow laborious way up the river to its anchorage. Wisps of fog, torn, like spiders' webs when they are brushed aside, blew this way and that, revealing the battering most of the ships had received in their desperate run across the Atlantic.

The convoy had sailed from Halifax, Nova Scotia. Many ships had deck cargo of crated bombers, and the freighters, protected by destroyers, sloops and corvettes, were low in the water with the weight of their load. There had been thirty-eight ships when they set out; two had been torpedoed and had sunk almost immediately but the rest limped home, wounded, bleeding like animals to their lair. Some listed to one side, others were low at the bows, crippled by torpedoes. Empty davits swung where boats had been lost, funnels were holed and decks, and on several, damage to the bridge testified to the ferocity of the air attack they had suffered as they neared home.

The day was bleak, grey, the clouds low and merging with the mist, dripping flurries of ice-cold rain onto the busy scene below. The dock was alive with hurrying figures. Men on bicycles pedalled furiously from the guarded gate to the docks where they worked. Seamen, wrapped up against the cold, dufflebags across their shoulders, walked slowly, joining ships about to sail, turning to wave to tearful faces, whilst others sprinted joyously into the loving arms which welcomed them home. Hammers clanged and voices shouted, and over the mass of noise the cheerful sound of someone whistling, *I'm dreaming of a White Christmas* rang merrily.

Jenny had waited each day for Nils' ship to come in for almost a week now. She knew how long he was usually away, and providing he had done the same trip she could gauge when he would be home. He was late, and her heart was afraid, but nothing showed in the blank emptiness of her face. She stood like a statue, her woollen hat pulled low over her eyes and ears, a scarf wrapped tightly about her neck. Her hands were pushed deep in her pockets and she stared sightlessly at the grey waters of the river. She was unaware of the curious eyes which passed over her, and scarcely heard the hopeful friendly greetings of those who came ashore looking for comfort and forgetfulness from what they had just been through.

She continued to wait, hour after hour, as each ship docked in turn, waiting for the tall, fair-haired officer who would come eventually. Her mind was as blank as her face, the torment she suffered too deep for thought.

She saw him in the distance, his usually upright figure sagging with exhaustion. His head was bent wearily and his feet dragged, as did those of the men who walked with him. He rubbed a hand tiredly across his eyes, unaware that she watched.

He saw her and stopped and miraculously, his face became alive. His shoulders lifted and his stooping figure straightened. His eyes lit up and the love and gladness shone from him like a bright glowing light in the dark. He opened his mouth to form her name and his arms lifted to her, and as they did so, the wonder and joy changed and slowly doubt and fear took their place. She had never met him before. She had never known when he would return. Always before he had made his way to Walton Park Road, or Edge Hall Lane, and she had been there, waiting for him.

Now she was here, on the dock, and his stricken heart knew that something dreadful had happened. Swiftly, like a runaway horse, his mind accelerated, leaping ahead to the words she was going to say, and his heart began to die a slow death.

She looked appalling and yet more beautiful than he had ever seen her. The flesh had dropped from her bones, leaving a fragile vulnerability that tore him to shreds, and he wanted to draw her into the protection of his arms and hold her there for ever. Something beyond words had happened to her whilst he had been away, and her eyes and face were haunted by it.

They stood a few paces from each other, not touching.

'What is it?' Nils' words were a whisper in the clangour of the dockyard but she heard them.

Her voice cracked as she spoke.

'Bill is home.'

Nils' face lit up, and for a dazzling moment he thought she had come to tell him that he knew about them; that she had left her husband and was coming to him, but her eyes, the very way she stood, told him it was not so.

'What . . . what has happened?'

'He's been wounded.'

He flinched as though she had struck him. Of course. Why

hadn't they thought of this? As he drowned in a sea of pain, he heard the gods laugh. In their hopeful dreams of the future he and Jenny had not imagined that when Bill came home there *still* might be some reason to keep Jenny tied to him. After all, she was Jenny. Loyal, devoted, true, staunch, and being as she was, she would never leave a man who was injured and could not fend for himself. Unless . . . unless it was some injury that would mend. Perhaps . . .

Hope flared again, then was stamped cruelly underfoot.

'He has lost a leg.'

'A leg . . . he has . . .' Nils' voice broke and he could not go on.

The stone which was Jenny Robinson's heart moved in her breast as she watched the despair pulling him apart. She clung desperately to her fast-disappearing composure, knowing if she let go she would be lost and unable to do what she had come to do.

'We must say goodbye, Nils.'

'Oh dear God, no.' His voice was hoarse, anguished.

'Yes, my dear love, yes . . . and you must help me.'

'Jenny . . . oh please, my Jenny . . .'

'I cannot do it alone Nils . . . help me.'

'The world will be empty . . . my life . . .'

'I must stay with him . . . he is helpless.'

'Please . . .'

'Nils, I must go, whilst I am still able . . . forgive me.'

He stood looking at her, his face grey, dead, hopeless. Without once touching him, she turned and started to run. He stood, a lifeless rock, around which crowds of seamen parted and flowed. He whispered her name as he watched her disappear in the mass of people making for the Pier Head. He stood, alone, until the dock was almost deserted, then turning stiffly, began to make his way back to his ship.

She was blind and deaf as she walked. The Liver Birds stared dispassionately across the river, their hearts no less stony than hers as she stumbled past the Cunard building. Along Dale Street. Curious passersby eyed the stiff, sightless figure as she blundered from corner to corner, and eyebrows were raised. A man, yes, but it was not often one saw a woman as drunk as she, they said to one another, and all alone too. She reached Scotland Road, and instinctively turned left, like a homing pigeon making for its nest. But she had no nest, no home now. The place where she lived with Bill was not her home. The man who sat in his chair and tormented her and the children beyond reason had turned her home into a place of misery and hopelessness from which her daughters fled to the safety of Auntie Kate's. She had told herself that he would improve; that his injury, the trauma of adjusting to the loss of his leg, would get better with acceptance. He would become softer, more patient. His children would surely bring him some peace, if she could not , but he frightened them and they kept out of his way.

He was helpless. John Clancy, and then the district nurse, came each day to attend to the stump of his leg, but it was she who must help him to dress and undress, to leave his chair for his bed and back again, to wash, and worst of all, to bathe the emaciated body of which once he had been so proud. His eyes had watched her balefully, sensing her distress, and his lips had sneered as she carefully sponged his nakedness. Her revulsion was complete as she saw his flaccid penis become stiff.

'Come on girl, get it up,' he had taunted her. 'I didn't get one off on you before I left, but I'm willing to have a go now, that's if you'll do the work.'

Why, why did he despise her so? Years ago she had hurt him, but she had tried to make it up to him. She had done her best then to be the wife he wanted, and even now, because of what she had done – because of what had been done to him, and with her feelings of guilt and pity, she still tried.

Mile after mile, she walked. Walton Road, County Road, Rice Lane. She hesitated, her numb mind flickering, her face for an instant showing indecision. It was here she would turn to Kate's house, and with all her heart she longed to go there. To be held warmly in Kate's loving arms; to pour out the hopelessness, to know kindness, and to be in the sane world of Kate's kitchen, just for an hour, but she knew if she went to Kate's she would never leave.

As she crossed the bridge which spanned the railway line, she was conscious of the rattle and clack of a train passing beneath her feet. She hesitated, and dreamlike, walked to the shoulder-high wall and stared down in the gloom to the flickering motion of the train below. She watched it until it was out of sight, the gleaming lines it left behind seeming to fascinate her.

A woman hurried by, a small child clutching her hand, the sound of their feet clipping the wet ground sharply. The child's voice was high and excited, falling on the ears of the silent figure standing so close to the wall.

Turning away from the bridge, she walked on in the rain.

Week followed week, and Bill grew no better. Even his own mother

421

chided him for his sharpness to Laura, daring his wrath in defence of the crying child.

'She's always bloody crying, Ma,' he answered sullenly. 'I've only got to raise my voice and she's away.'

'But she's frightened, love. She's always . . .'

'Frightened of what? There's nothing I can do to her, sitting in this bloody thing.'

'I know, I know,' soothed Ellen, 'but it's just . . . well, she's not used to . . .'

'Not used to a cripple . . . is that it?'

'Oh Bill, don't, love, don't say that word.'

'Well, that's what I am, isn't it?'

'No . . . I won't have you . . .'

'Oh give over Ma!'

Ellen would cry the sad tears of the old, and from the kitchen window Jenny stared out into the bleak barrenness of the winter garden and she cried too, for she knew now she carried Nils' child.

Chapter Forty-Eight

Kate held her in arms strong with compassion and wept with her. Their cheeks wet, one against the other, the sisters' quiet grief was made more poignant by the sounds of merriment which came from the other room. She felt Jenny begin to shiver and heard the sound begin in the back of her throat, like that of an animal wounded beyond description, and was afraid. Jenny clung to her, arms gripping, hands locked behind Kate's back, and she knew that her sister was being driven to the state of desperation which had had her once before. She had lost him then, and she was losing him again, and this time she would never recover.

'Come on, chuck, come on,' she whispered against Jenny's tumbled hair. 'Come on, sit down an' blow yer nose.' – Blow yer nose, she thought. That was a good 'un. Who was the daft 'apporth who made that one up. If it was only so easy. 'Yer don't want anyone to see yer so upset. 'Ere, sit by t'fire an' I'll make us a cup o' tea.'

Kate led the distraught woman to the rocker by the kitchen fire and placed her carefully within it. Jenny hardly seemed aware of where she was. Her silent racking sobs whispered about the warm room, raising ghosts of memories, sweet and sad and Kate felt her heart twist in her breast as she looked at the dimmed light which was flickering out in her sister's eyes.

Jenny was a pale shadow of the golden-skinned, vibrant woman who had walked hand in hand across the rolling moorland with the man she loved; who had slept in his arms and healed his war-weary, anguished mind with her body only a few short weeks ago. In the six weeks that Bill had been home he had whittled the flesh from her as thoroughly as if he had taken a razor and shaved it off, layer by layer. Her face was gaunt, hollow, the cheekbones jutting from beneath eyes dull and lifeless with lost hope, and her hands trembled with tiredness and something which Kate was afraid to name. It showed in the furtive way, even now, though her husband was in the next room, she glanced continually over her shoulder, listening for the hiss of the chair's wheels, and in her expression, like that of a child who has been whipped and whipped and can take no more. It sat strangely on her woman's face.

It was Christmas Day. They were all here. All except Charlie and Frankie. And Nils. There wasn't a lot to prepare. No turkey, nor Christmas cake. No mince pies, but Kate had made a War and Peace pudding in place of Christmas pudding and by pooling their meat coupons, the family had managed a nice leg of lamb. John and Janet Clancy had brought their two sons, some sausages, and a bottle of sherry and Ellen had managed a few sprouts from Albert's allotment. They had made Christmas presents for each other and for the children, and with another small pine tree from the wood where Harry had died, they had managed to make the day a good one for the children.

Dorry was sixteen now. She looked like Elizabeth had at her age, pretty, fragile and shy as a violet in her adolescence. Kate often wondered where the bit that was herself had gone into her eldest daughter for she had none of her own vigour, but there, Charlie had been shy as a lad, and she had her Dad's kind heart and his lovely crystal grey eyes.

Leslie, robust, the man of the house at fourteen now that his father and brother were away, Kathy, Laura, Helen. All growing up into the sweetness of young adulthood, but excited and noisy with the fun of children at Christmastime.

Ellen and Albert had brought their sad hearts and sorrowing eyes which scarcely left the embittered face of their eldest son, for even yet it seemed they would not believe that soon, tomorrow, next week he would turn back into the charming, lovable boy who had gone to war with a joke on his lips. Boy! To his mother he was still a boy. He would never be a man.

Bill sat morosely by the fireside in Kate's front parlour staring scornfully about the brightly decorated room. His expression seemed to say he was beyond understanding the need to celebrate. What did he have to celebrate, it said, what did any of them? Christmas should be dispensed with in these times. What was the point of it all, anyway? What was the point of anything?

He was cushioned in the most comfortable chair, his remaining leg placed on a stool, a rug thrown over his knees for he felt the cold intensely. His eyes watched his younger daughter as she tried to blow up a balloon, her round young cheeks red and distended with her efforts. Kathy egged her on, shouting and laughing in a high pitched voice, jumping up and down and slapping her hands and arms against her sides.

424

'Here, give it to me,' he said irritably. 'Talk about a fuss. Can't you do a simple thing like blow up a balloon.'

Silence fell and the abashed child handed the balloon to her father. Kathy sidled away to lean against John Clancy's shoulder where he sat in the opposite chair. He put his arm about her soothingly.

'Well, I must say, I'm hopeless at blowing up balloons. I never seem to have enough puff.' He laughed and the tension eased. 'Anyway, how about a tune, Mr Robinson?' He turned to Albert. 'I've heard tell you're the best exponent of *The bells of St Marys* this side of West Derby. How about it?'

The gentle sound of the piano drifted down the hall and through the closed door to the kitchen. Jenny heard it and lifted her head. She looked into Kate's eyes and hers became hard and bitter.

'Why didn't it kill him, Kate,' she whispered. 'Why does God hate me so? It wouldn't have taken much to have blown him up. Blown him off the face of the earth. Instead it takes his bloody leg and sends the rest back to me.' She laughed harshly. 'It doesn't make sense. All the fine chaps who are gone. Men loved by their families. Women grieving for . . . and I get him back. God forgive me, our Kate, I hate his guts. He's driving the kids into frightened little shadows, scared of opening their mouths, and you've seen what he's done to Ma and Pop. They've gone like two old sticks since he came home. The injury nearly drove Ma mad, but the way he is with her, it's worse than the loss of his leg. He's breaking her heart.'

She bent her head and the tears dripped silently on to her clutching, moving hands.

'Kate, Kate.' Her voice was broken.

'What, love.' Kate bent forward, gently touching the agitated, wrenching fingers, her face soft with pity.

'Kate, oh dear God, Kate, what shall I do? I've told Nils . . . I told him I had to stay with Bill, that he and I couldn't be . . . be together.' Her voice split in agony, 'but I . . . I can't do it. I can't live without him. It's cutting me to ribbons. I'm coming apart, Kate, I'm dying.'

Oh Lord, let me help her. Kate's heart moved painfully inside her and she felt the helplessness, the hopelessness wash over her. There was nothing she could do. Nothing. Except be there. Be there beside her. Hold her hand. Give her love, sympathy, support, and it wasn't enough. But what else could she do? What could any of them do but grin and bear it, and by God they'd had enough practice at that. It seemed to be one bloody thing on top of another.

If only she hadn't met Nils again, perhaps she would have had the strength to hold up against Bill's injury, and worse, his vindictive bitterness. She would have fought him tooth and nail. Stood up for her children against him, but her spirit had gone with the man she loved. To find him and lose him again had taken from her the resolution to go on. It was too much. Jenny was right. God did not seem to look kindly on her.

'Kate.' Jenny was speaking again. 'Kate . . . d'you think . . .'

'What, love?' Kate breathed.

Jenny's face was like bleached bone, but another expression had taken the place of the despair which had drawn lines of pain about the soft mouth. Kate was suddenly reminded of Elizabeth.

'I wondered . . . I heard of someone who . . .'

'Yes, chuck, what . . . ?' Kate prompted.

'A . . . a divorce. D'you think I could get a divorce?'

Kate drew in a sharp breath. A divorce. Bloody 'ell. She'd never even considered it. She'd never even known anyone who'd got a divorce. People in their station got married and stayed married. You made your bed and no matter how prickly it was, you bloody laid on it. She didn't know what to say. Jenny's eyes pierced hers, holding her gaze fiercely, and way down in their depths Kate saw a tiny gleam of hope. Oh God, what should she say? She could see all the pitfalls which lay ahead and she knew her sister. She talked of leaving him. She spoke of her hatred and contempt and yes, her fear of the man who was killing the life she had longed for, but she was a woman of great compassion. She had a strong sense of responsibility towards those who depended upon her. And there was no question that just now, Bill needed her desperately. Perhaps later, when he had adjusted to the shock of losing his leg; when he could walk again; could take up the job which still waited for him; when he was no longer dependant on the care Jenny gave to him, then she could go. Nils would wait. He would wait for her forever. He loved her. He would wait. Besides what . . . what was the word . . . what *grounds* did Jenny have? What grounds were needed?

Kate spoke quietly. 'Eeh, I don't know, lovey. I know nowt about it. Yer'd 'ave ter go an' see a solicitor. That Mr Worthington'd 'elp yer.'

'He's dead.'

'Well, there'd be someone.'

Jenny's tearstained face had dried in the warmth from the fire, but she still trembled in the aftermath of the storm of sorrow which had engulfed her. She could still see Nils' face when she had left him. She would see it till the day she died. It was this day; this day which was special and on which families drew together and celebrated that first Christian family. It was the agony of knowing that Nils was alone on this day; would always be alone. Would never hold his child, the child she carried; his family, for that was who she and the tiny embryo in her womb were. Nils' family. All he had. It was this which had sent her like a being possessed from the Christmas table to the kitchen.

Now she spoke of her secret dream, the vision she had carried since Nils had come back into her life. She looked at Kate imploringly as though it were in her sister's hands to grant her this boon, but Kate shook her head. Divorce or not, the impediment which kept Jenny from her goal was Bill. What she considered her obligation to a man who was helpless. What did she want Kate to say?

'Who would look after Bill?' Kate's words were quiet, solemn, and she watched as the words which her sister dreaded ripped her apart. They were out. It was this which kept her tied to him. Not marriage or the vows she had pledged as a bride. If he were whole she wouldn't hesitate. If she could even talk to him with any hope of understanding. If he were normal; if his mind was not filled with the pus of his inflamed bitterness, perhaps she could have . . .

Jenny's voice was shrill.

'There are people, Kate, medical people, hospitals.' The words poured out frantically, helplessly, pitifully. 'He could be looked after, taught to walk, to look after . . . he would meet someone else . . . someone to love him, to look after him. Not me, Kate, not me. It's always me. All my life I've lost . . . people I've loved . . . I'm thirty-seven, Kate and I've never . . . I can't, I can't . . .' The tears spilled again and the words flowed, hopeless with fear and the longing to be free. 'Not me, Kate, let me go, let me go to Nils.'

'I'm not stoppin' yer, queen, Bill is. If there was anything I could . . . Yer know, don't yer. I'd cut off me right 'and if it'd . . .' Kate's voice was filled with pain. Words. Useless words but all she had to give. They were not the ones Jenny wanted to hear but what else was there to say. 'But Jenny, if yer think it'll . . . I mean if yer want to make enquiries, go an' see a solicitor, yer know me an' Charlie are behind yer all the way. It's just with Bill being . . . so . . . He's not able to see to himself and it's not as if he was cruel to the girls . . .'

Jenny reared up. 'Cruel, you haven't seen him when he shouts . . .'

427

'All men shout at their kids, Jenny, yer know that. Yer've seen Charlie clip our Leslie round the . . .'

'It's not the same, Kate. Your kids know Charlie loves them. They're not frightened of him. Bill's bad, our Kate, bad, bad . . .'

Kate bowed her head, looking away from the anguished face before her. There was nothing she would like more than to see their Jenny set up with Nils. A kinder, lovelier chap you couldn't wish to meet. He reminded her of Charlie, but what would be said of a woman who walked away from a man who had been crippled in the defence of his country. Poor sod. Bad as he had been to their Jenny, you couldn't help but be sorry for him. He'd been so handsome, so full of himself and now look at him.

Her thoughts were sent scurrying away as Laura burst into the room, her face, which for two years had been merry and carefree, beginning to lose already the lovely innocent trust which is the prerogative of a child.

'Uncle John says to tell you the King's on in a minute.'

Kate smiled at her.

'Righto chuck. Yer Mam an' me will be there in a jiffy.'

The child disappeared and Kate turned to Jenny.

'Come on, love, put yer face on. We'll sort summat out. We always 'ave.'

Jenny got slowly to her feet. Arms touching, the sisters made their way to the front room. As she did so Jenny wondered why she hadn't told Kate of the baby.

The first week in January she made an appointment to see Mr Carstairs. Kate went with her.

The office was the one in which she and Charlie had sat over twelve years ago just after Waggy's death. She had thought the end of her world had come then. She had thought nothing worse could happen to her. She had lost her love. She had lost her child and that day she had lost the bright place she had made for herself out of the dark shell of her past. Waggy had done it for her. He had given her back her life, her self esteem, the confidence and spirit which had made her what she was. She had fought a hard fight to become Jenny again, and on that day it had been whipped from her with the speed of a hawk on the wing.

But again she had struggled back. Again she had made a tiny niche for herself; a space in which to grow and bring up her children who were the centre of her world. It had not been the way she had hoped it would be. Bill had not given her what she had,

428

unrealistically she knew now, longed for, but she had found love again.

Now it was shattered. With Bill's injury had come the raging torment, the sour decaying rot of his acrimony and she knew it would not be repaired by her devoted care. The burden was onerous but she carried it. With teeth-gritting resolution she carried it, and was given back nothing but contempt and a neverending flow of complaints which sapped her life like a slashed vein.

Kate looked like Charlie had on that long ago day. Overwhelmed by the hallowed quiet of the solicitors' office; by the shelves of books, the sombre pictures of men in funny wigs which hung on the walls, the rich furnishings and the atmosphere of hushed and dignified calm that was unnerving. Kate had never spoken to a solicitor in her life. She put him somewhere between a doctor and God.

Mr Carstairs had been a young partner of Mr Worthington twelve years ago, enthusiastic, full of vigorous spirit to help put right the injustices to which the law gave him access, but now, his zeal somewhat dimmed at the age of fifty, he waited dispassionately for Jenny to begin. His masculine eye noted the fragile beauty of her face and, strangely, for he had seen a lot of suffering in his career, his heart was stirred by the despairing sadness which haunted her.

Jenny stumbled through it. Her words were jumbled together, out of sequence, incoherent and hard to follow. The days when she could confidently discourse with a man of business, when she could and did gain their respect for her sharp wit and quick brain, were gone. Gone with Bill's shattered leg and mind, and the hell he had put her through over the past decade. But she tried and Mr Carstairs listened.

'On what grounds do you wish to sue, Mrs Robinson?' he asked when she had finished.

Jenny looked blank and Kate sighed.

'I just want a divorce, please, Mr Carstairs,' Jenny said, like a child asking for a pennyworth of sweeties.

Mr Carstairs shook his head patiently.

'I know, Mrs Robinson, but you must have some grounds. I must know for what reason. You say your husband has been unfaithful so that could presume adultery.' Jenny's face lit up and her eyes glowed, '. . . but that was years ago. Before the start of the war. Have you evidence? Proof, and even if you had you have lived with him . . . ahem . . . co-habited with him since then, have you not?'

Jenny flushed as she took his meaning, then the rose drained from her face and she hung her head as though in shame.

'So you see that supposes forgiveness. It cancels it out so to speak. Has your husband been unfaithful since he returned from the war?' Jenny stared mutely, then shook her head, unable to speak. 'I'm sorry.' The man's voice was pitying, 'but I must ask these questions.' His manner became brisk. 'Now to cruelty. It's hard to prove. Very hard, but possible. Has your husband struck you, or done anything . . . er . . . some act that could be described as . . . well . . . obscene, or of a sadistic nature.'

The two women opposite him looked blank and he sighed.

'He has never hit you . . . ?'

Jenny's face brightened and Kate leaned forward eagerly.

'Oh yes, Mr Carstairs, 'e 'as,' she said. 'I've seen 'im fetch 'er a real back'ander.'

Mr Carstairs smiled in gratification and Kate sat back in her chair, pleased with her own contribution. At last they were getting somewhere.

'Yes, now that's what we want.' Mr Carstairs picked up his pen. 'When was this?'

'Just after Laura was born.'

'And Laura is . . . how old?'

'She's eleven.'

Mr Carstairs sighed and looked down at the paper on which as yet, he had written nothing. It seemed the blankness of it spoke for itself.

'That again took place a long time ago. Mrs Robinson is considered to have forgiven him if she has continued to live with him since the event took place.'

The two women looked at him, waiting. He glanced up and lifted his hands, shrugging his shoulders in a fashion which spoke more than words.

'Has he done anything, anything at all which might be considered dangerous, cruel, a threat to your life or those of your children, since he came home?'

'He shouts at the children . . . and . . . and he says horrible, vile things to me . . . and . . . well . . .' Jenny looked down at her hands.

'Has he abused the children?'

'They're frightened of him, but you see he can't reach them . . . they run away . . .' Her voice trailed away forlornly. She looked at the man on the other side of the desk and her heart died a little more. It was no use. There was nothing he could do for her. The cruelty which was in Bill's mind couldn't be seen and so it could not be proved. Not until someone . . . someone was actually a victim of that cruelty . . . Mr Carstairs was doing his best but without proof, evidence, it was hopeless. Unless he could come and live with them, see how Bill was day after day, see how afraid they all were, he could never know.

She stood up suddenly, and the old Jenny was there. Proud and defiant. Brave.

'Thank you Mr Carstairs, you have been most kind. If . . . if something . . . if there should be . . . I will keep in touch with you.'

She held out her hand with dignity and the solicitor took it.

'I'm sorry, Mrs Robinson. Bring me something concrete and I will . . . I'm sorry.'

Chapter Forty-Nine

'. . . Ramsbottom and Enoch and me.'

Bill and Jenny sat, one on each side of the merrily blazing fire, the picture of contented domestic bliss. The opening strains of the start of *Happidrome* filled the warm room, and Bill laughed at something that was said. His wheelchair had been folded in the corner of the room and he lounged in the deep armchair, the crutches he was supposed to use lying beside him.

Jenny turned the sock she was darning into the light. Her face was still and expressionless, but her brain whirled like the mainspring of a clock. Her slim fingers moved swiftly, the needle flashing in the wool as she tried to compose her mind to logical thought. She was three months pregnant now. She had not seen Nils for nearly two months and the words she had spoken to him rang in her silent head like a bell. She glanced up at Bill, and he laughed again, the flesh which was building up on his face quivering. He was putting on weight. Though Doctor Clancy had warned him that he must do the exercises the hospital gave him, he was lazy, indifferent to how he looked. He was taken several times a week by ambulance to the infirmary, and was being prepared for the artificial limb which when fitted would enable him to walk again, but he seemed to care for nothing. He listened to the wireless all day long and refused all offers to be taken for a walk in his chair.

'I'm not 'aving the bloody world and 'is wife staring at me,' he announced, and after a while, Albert, Douglas, Jenny and even young Leslie who had volunteered to take him to Sefton Park, had given up asking.

Jenny bent her head over her darning. Almost three months he has been home and I can't take any more. The time has come. No matter what I do it will never change. His mind is set in a pattern of self-pity and bitterness for those who try to help him. His children, his own mother are afraid of him. I must get the girls away before he destroys them. I must find a way. Find a way. Find a way. The words beat a rhythm in her head, ticking in tempo with the thud of her heart. A way. A way. *Lord, help me for I am afraid.* Her face was set and still and her eyes were bleak, but her mind was calm. She knew there was only one way, and she must take it. Proof. That was what Mr Carstairs had said. Unless she could prove to a Court of Law that Bill was a man now capable of an act of cruelty which would be a danger to herself or the children; that he was, though crippled and fastened, seemingly, to his chair, violent, there was no likelihood of a divorce.

She lifted her head courageously and a quiver of fear ran across her thin face. By God, she'd give him proof. The risk she must take was enormous, to herself and the child, but she must do it. She had to.

Jenny didn't realise she had been staring at her husband until his voice cut into her thoughts.

'What's up with you, lady? Has my face turned green or something?'

Jenny stood up. It was no good arguing, or even answering.

'Would you like a cup of tea?' She was sure he would hear the nervous tension in her voice.

'Why not?'

'I'll put the kettle on then.'

She turned deliberately, reaching up to the shelf to return her sewing box to its place. She had removed the long woollen cardigan she wore to conceal her figure and the soft folds of her dress clung to her hips and belly. Outlined against the light of the reading lamp was the gentle but unmistakeable swell of her stomach. It was only slight, but her breasts had become full as her pregnancy progressed and there was no mistaking her condition.

She meant there to be no mistake.

The flesh of Bill's face, which still had a smile upon it, slipped downwards like a candle on which the wax melts, and his mouth dropped open. His eyes ran over her and the colour flooded his face. His eyes became slits and the breath sighed out of him. He sat up in the chair, balancing himself on arms which had become strong as his leg weakened.

'What's this then?' he breathed. 'What the bloody 'ell is this?' From the expression on his face he might have been pleased, and suddenly in her heart, Jenny knew that he was. She had given him a reason, a perfect excuse to do what he had done years ago and he licked his lips as though in anticipation of what was to come. Her eyes darted towards the closed door, but with surprising agility Bill was up, balancing perfectly on one leg. He reached down for his crutches, never taking his eyes from her face. She was afraid,

433

mortally afraid, but she had made that first step towards freedom and she had no choice now. She must go on. *Dear God, help me, please help me.*

'Don't do anything you'll regret, Bill.' Even now trying to keep his violence under control.

'Oh, I won't regret it Jenny. Whatever I do I won't regret it. You see, no one will blame me if I give my wayward little wife a good hiding, will they? Wounded hero returns to find his missus with a bun in the oven. They'll think you deserve it, and you do.'

His eyes were as cold as green flint and he began to breathe heavily as though he were going to make love to her. He twitched his crutch under his arm, moving closer to where she stood in the corner.

Jenny knew she was fighting for the life of her child. For her children. For their future and her own. There was no one to defend her. There was no one to do for her what she must now do. She was alone. The girls were at Ellen's where they went with increasing frequency and there was no one to hear her if she screamed. Bill would hurt her. He wouldn't kill her. His mind was still stable enough to realise the limits to which he could go, but he would kill Nils' child. It was in his eyes.

'Who was it this time, eh? Which lucky chap got to dip his wick this time? By God, you can't do without it can you? But you will get carried away, won't you?'

Where had she heard it before? Her terrified mind cast about and suddenly the man before her was replaced by another. He had said these words to her and laughed derisively as Bill was doing. A man. An older man with a neat white beard and eyes as cruelly pleased as were Bill's. Her father. He had taunted her and through him she had lost Nils. Lost him for twenty years, but she wouldn't again. This time she would win.

Bill was chuckling as though a good joke had just been told him. 'Another little mistake, just like the last one and this one's going the same way. You'll not carry it. I'll have no one pointing the finger of derision at me, by God.'

His face was a mask of loathing. Without warning he thrust his second crutch forward, driving it with all the force he could gather at her stomach. She had only time to lurch sideways before he hit her, just below her right shoulder. She fell, crashing to the floor and before she could protect herself, he hit her a second blow, this time with the tip of the crutch. She felt the bone in her cheek crack and something wet and warm flooded her eye and dripped to the carpet. She couldn't see. Her senses slipped and the room

434

was growing blurred and dim. *Oh Nils, my love, your child, your son.*

Her vision cleared for a second and before her eye, the one which was not blinded with blood, the end of Bill's crutch appeared, the one on which he leaned. She heard him laugh hoarsely and knew he was mad. Mad with longing for vengeance. Vengeance against the world which had cheated him of the recognition which should be his; against a fate which had taken his fair manliness when it robbed him of his leg, and against her for giving to another what was rightfully his.

In the background the wireless babbled on.

Raising her hand weakly, her strength almost gone, she grasped the crutch. She pulled it towards her, feeling the weight of it as it slipped along the rug. As it moved, his balance gone, Bill crashed to the floor, cursing, struggling, crying her name over and over again.

Jenny began to crawl towards the door of the living room, her hand pressed to her face. She reached the door, hanging on to the last thread of her consciousness. Pulling herself up, she opened it and stumbled along the hallway. The front door. If she could reach the front door. Blood poured from her split cheek, and her fast swelling eyes could barely see. The door, the front door . . . the light would pour out into the black world beyond . . . the light . . . the blackout . . . the warden . . . the air raid warden would see . . .

He was just turning the corner from Moss Lane. He could hardly believe his eyes. It was like a bloody beacon, streaming across the road and if 'Jerry' came tonight it would light his way like a torch.

'Put out that light,' he bellowed as he ran, his hobnail boots striking sparks on the pavement, but nobody took any notice. By God, 'e'd 'ave 'em in court for this, 'e would.

His face was white as he looked down on the still figure of the woman who lay across the step. Her face was a mask of blood. A man was shouting obscenities from somewhere within the house.

The warden began to blow his whistle.

Chapter Fifty

They held hands, not caring who saw them. Charlie stared, then looked away embarrassed. He caught Kate's glance, and she frowned, as though to say – 'and why shouldn't they?' and he grinned. If it was OK with Kate, it was OK with him. And after all, it was he who had brought the chap here anyway. What a day that had been.

Jenny's face was still bandaged when Charlie came home, and his eyes had hardened when he saw the injuries that bastard had inflicted upon her. The swelling had nearly gone, but she would wear the thin scar above her eyebrow and across the smooth skin of her cheek till the end of her days. The house had been filled with people, and in his weariness and confusion he had thought for a moment he had come to the wrong address. What was Ellen Robinson doing sitting in his kitchen sipping tea with Kate as though they had been close friends for years? And in the fields, there was Albert helping Leslie with a kite as big as a bloody 'spitfire'. The sun shone, cold and brilliant, as eagerly as though it couldn't wait for spring, and there had been a feeling of joy, a hopeful bustle, which suddenly made Charlie glad to be alive, even if he was bewildered by it all.

Later that night, when Ellen and Albert had gone and Jenny and the children were asleep, Kate told him what had happened.

'He's gone into hospital now. A special place somewhere. I don't know what we would have done without John Clancy, love. That man's been a good friend to us. When I think . . .' Kate's eyes took on a musing expression as she looked back, then sensing her husband's impatience, she continued.

'You should have seen her, Charlie. Her poor face. God, I could kill that bugger, I really could, an' what with the baby . . .'

'What baby?'

'Oh, I forgot, Jenny's pregnant,' she said matter of factly.

'D'yer mean to say Bill's . . . ?'

'Oh, it's not Bill's.'

'Not . . .'

436

'No, it's Nils'.'

Charlie sat up in bed and switched on the light. His face was incredulous and he cast his eyes heavenwards as though to say, Lord give me patience.

'What the bloody 'ell's bin goin' on while I've bin away. I feel as though I've missed about three episodes of *Pearl White*, or summat.'

'Oh Charlie, you are a laugh.'

'Laugh. I'll give yer laugh,' and for half an hour, tired as he was he did more than make his Kate laugh.

Afterwards, arms comfortably about each other, they continued.

'Yer don't mean the Nils that . . . ?'

'Yes.'

'But where did he come from?'

'From Norway.'

'I know that, but what's 'e . . . Oh for God's sake our Kate tell us what's bin goin' on.'

Charlie was a straightforward, no-nonsense sort of a bloke. He loved his wife devotedly, with a deep emotion which would stand for ever. He was not one for pretty speeches, especially as he grew older, but he would never forget to his dying day that moment on the dock, nor the tired face of the Norwegian officer when Charlie diffidently told him Jenny was asking for him.

'Honest to God Kate, I thought he was gonner kiss me. It was like . . . like seeing the sun come out from behind a cloud.' Kate was enraptured. What a lovely turn of phrase Charlie had when he got going.

'What did he say, Charlie?'

'Nowt, absolutely nowt, but I could 'ardly keep up wi' 'im as we ran for t'tram. Well, I thought we were running for t'tram, but 'e was into a taxi before you could say, "Everton". God, 'e was like a bloke demented.'

'I know, I know. I only 'ad time to say "she's upstairs in the back", an' 'e were up the dancers like the devil was after 'im.'

'What a bloody mix up. I dunno, some folks seem to 'ave the most topsy-turvy lives, and your Jenny's one of 'em. 'Eeh luv, I'm glad we're us. We've 'ad our ups and downs.' Their faces were sad in the darkness, 'but we've always 'ad each other.'

'Yes, Charlie.'

Nils stayed in a hotel; there was no room for him at Kate's but he spent his days with Jenny. Their happiness was like a flower garden, giving pleasure to everyone who walked in it, and Kate

437

found herself singing all the time, as though it was she, and not Jenny, who had come from the darkness into the light. The joy, the worshipping love which shone from Nils' eyes as he watched Jenny, made her want to cry for the sheer loveliness of it, and she longed to kiss him for the serenity which he had given to her sister. He could not take his eyes from her, and Kate found herself knocking on her own kitchen door before she entered for fear she would find them in each other's arms, or Nils with his hand on Jenny's stomach as though to be in contact with his child.

The girls were enraptured to see their beloved friend again and Laura clung to him desperately, her little face resolute in her determination not to let him go.

But, as Jenny had expected, the worst casualty was Ellen Robinson.

When she and Albert received the message, delivered by Leslie that they were to come to Kate's, bringing the children, she had walked along Kate's hallway and into her kitchen as though she were being led into a chamber of the inquisition. Her elderly, sad face had been afraid. What was to come next, her expression said.

When she saw Jenny, and John Clancy told them compassionately what their son had become, Ellen didn't believe it. Not her boy. It wasn't in him to hit a woman. There had been a mistake. Her head had turned desperately, looking from Jenny, to Albert, to Dr Clancy, imploring them to tell her that it was all a terrible mistake. It couldn't be their Bill. Why, he was going to be the manager of the bank, one day.

She was going to see him, she said firmly. She was going to hear the story from his own lips. He'd tell her it wasn't true. Why would he hit Jenny like that? It wasn't in him to strike a defenceless woman, was it Albert? He was a good boy, a good boy. He wouldn't hurt a fly let alone his own wife. Only a man who was driven to the edges . . . only a man who had . . . It would take a . . . Her face became resolute in defence of the child she loved, the child she would always love. She appeared to have lost sight of the man he had become. A man didn't hit his wife for no reason. She must have . . . she must have goaded him. There must be some provocation for a man to . . .

Jenny told her the truth.

Ellen listened in silence, and Albert with her.

The silence stretched for what seemed hours when Jenny had finished though it was no more than seconds.

Ellen began to rock backwards and forwards in her chair. Her face contorted with grief and unutterable contempt. – So that was it, her expression said. While my boy was away this little mouse played and look what she's done. Look what she's done to my son. Driven him to commit an act which never in his right mind would he dream of doing. It's her fault, her fault. She drove him to it.

She stood up violently, the heart of the mother which beat strongly inside her demanding retribution.

'You slut,' she hissed. 'I've heard tell of women like you. Knocking about with other men while their husbands were away. Whores, all of them. You should be tarred and feathered. My lad, my poor lad.' She began to cry loudly, her thin frame wracked like a tree in a storm. 'You can't blame him. I've a good mind to give you a good hiding myself.' She made a threatening gesture towards Jenny but Albert stood between them suddenly, his face wise and sad.

'Stop it, Ellen, stop it.'

'Stop it. Stop it,' she screeched. 'Whose side are you on, Albert Robinson? Your own son is married to a . . . a . . . and you're telling me to . . . Well I'm not stopping in the same house with her.' She turned blindly, reaching for her coat which she had placed carefully across the chair, and began to fumble her way into it.

Jenny put out her hand. 'Ma . . . don't . . . let me tell you . . .' But it did no good. Ellen was through the kitchen door, dragging her Albert with her, but surprisingly Albert would not go. For the first time in his life Albert Robinson stood up to Ellen.

He had taken her into Kate's front room and there were no sounds bar the soft hiss of his voice and the harsh grate of her weeping. For over an hour they were there. No one knew what Albert said to Ellen. No one ever did, but when Ellen came from the room she walked into the kitchen and put her arms round Jenny and the two women wept tears of grief for the man one of them loved.

Albert watched. He had known for many years what his eldest son was becoming. It had started at his mother's knee when she had indulged him for the joy he gave her and had grown from a tiny seed of self-approbation into the destroying belief that the world and all that was in it, owed him a living. That he was something special. His mother had never seen it. But Albert had and on that November day when his son had come back from the war he had been appalled, but not surprised by the look of venom in his son's eyes. He had known that their boy had gone, along with his leg, and that a bitter, twisted stranger sat in his place. He had heard him speak cruelly to Albert's precious grandchild and

439

seen her cry in fear. He and Ellen had themselves borne the brunt of Bill's wicked words, and he had secretly been afraid. Not for himself, but for Jenny and her children. Now it had happened that which he had feared and in the great breach which was coming a choice must be made. And Albert loved Jenny and the children she had borne his son more than he could ever express in words. He was not going to lose them, ever.

Ellen went to see Bill, where they had taken him. She was his mother after all, but he told her airily that he wanted nothing more to do with her, nor Pa. The only one who had any spunk was Helen, he said, and he fancied he'd keep her with him when he left this place. She was a chipper little devil and good company. A bit like him really.

Ellen's heart had frozen in her breast at the very thought of her sweet granddaughter alone with this man, and with that thought had come recognition. He was no longer her son but 'this man'.

Mr Carstairs was optimistic, but cautious.

'It might be we will have a fight on our hands, Mrs Robinson, despite the evidence of your doctor who saw you after the attack. You see, your husband's solicitor informs me that your husband states categorically that he does not want a divorce. He is going to contest the action. Of course we will petition on the grounds of cruelty, and on the evidence you have here . . .' he shuffled through the papers on the desk in front of him '. . . it seems you have a good case, but . . .' He raised his eyebrows delicately. 'I must be blunt. In your condition it will be difficult . . . a man comes home from battle, wounded, to find his wife has been unfaithful. He will have the sympathy of the Judge. Provocation, you see, particularly as he states he wishes a reconciliation. He wishes to make a fresh start. He will forgive you and take you back into the marital home. He will bring up the . . . child . . . as his own. He loves his children and cannot part with them, so you see . . . it may take a while. I know you are hoping to . . . to marry the . . . father of your child before . . . ahem.'

Mr Carstairs cleared his throat embarrassedly.

Jenny bent her head, feeling the strength flow from her. – Dear God, how could he? The bastard. The low down rotten sod. And she had thought it all cut and dried. Plain sailing. Down hill all the way. Why? Why? He didn't want her, not really. Only to taunt and humiliate. Why wouldn't he let her go? She had been so certain that now, after all that had happened, he would agree to a divorce. How could she have been so naïve? She should have known, and there was the underlying threat in his words about the girls. Suppose he was awarded custody, should the divorce be granted. Dear Lord, never, never.

She raised her head. Jenny Robinson spoke with the authority she had not used for years.

'Mr Carstairs, for the past ten years my husband has treated my children and myself with a degree of inhumanity that surely is grounds for divorce. Do you see these scars?' Jenny raised her lovely face, gazing with limpid eyes into those of Mr Carstairs. 'He inflicted them. My children fear him. Even his own mother. He came back from North Africa wounded. He lost a leg. In defence of his country he lost a leg and I'm sure that many people will regard him as a hero and feel pity for him. I did myself, Mr Carstairs. I was prepared to stay with him. To devote my life to caring for him. With some understanding . . . and . . . adjustments on . . . if he had given me just a little . . . I would have stayed with him. He was to be . . . pitied . . . but even so that does not give him the right to beat me as he did. This child is not his as you know. I love another man, but I would have remained with my husband and tried to make a new life . . . but he was . . .' Jenny shook her head wildly and her soft hair flew like a veil of silk about her head. 'Look at me, Mr Carstairs, do I deserve this? Does what has happened to Bill give him the right to treat me as he has?'

Jenny began to cry, her impassioned plea dissolving her composure.

Mr Carstairs was gentle as he spoke.

'Mrs Robinson, we will go ahead, of course, but it will take many months if it is defended, and even then it might be thrown out. I'm sorry, but the circumstances, you see. The fact that you have done nothing before. For ten years he has abused you but you did nothing, so, in the eyes of the law you condoned it. In other words you forgave him and continued to live with him. Now . . .' Mr Carstairs shrugged, '. . . now, when it suits your purpose, or so it will seem to the court, you wish to be rid of him.'

'I want him to divorce me, Mr Carstairs. To divorce me. He will come out of it smelling like a rose. His banking career will continue. His character will be unblemished, whilst I, I will be the scarlet woman. The slut who betrayed her brave husband whilst he was away, but I don't care. I know what I am, what he is, as do my family and that is all that concerns me. I am willing to do anything to marry the man I love. I will tell the world that the child I carry is his. He is willing, eager to be named as co-respondent. This is his child and he wants it to have his name. We want to be married

441

before July when the child . . . I know there is little time, only six months, but that is enough. If I could persuade Bill not to contest . . . we could do it. Oh, please Mr Carstairs, tell me what to do, I beg you. There must be something.'

She lifted her wet eyes and tears spangled her eyelashes.

The solicitor looked at her and his logical, legal mind knew that this lovely, tragic woman could make the Judge believe that the moon was made of green cheese if she so pleased, but still . . .

He leaned forward and began to speak.

The confrontation with Bill nearly annihilated her. She went alone. He sat in his wheelchair in the small room which had been allowed them for half an hour, and he listened.

It took only ten minutes to say the things she had come to say.

'. . . And if you do not agree to divorce me on the grounds of my adultery with Nils Jorgensen, I will tell the world what you have done to me and your children over the past ten years. The newspapers will have a hey-day. The bank . . . well . . . you can imagine how they will feel when they know the true character of the hero they are waiting to welcome back with open arms. Perhaps at the moment you don't care. Perhaps all you want is revenge, but you won't get it, Bill, because whatever you do, Nils and I will be together. If we never marry, we shall be together, and the girls. Do you think any judge will allow you to have them when John Clancy has had his say, and your own father? Divorce me, Bill. Get your own back that way. See my name reviled by the rest of the world as the woman who carried on with other men whilst her husband was away fighting for his country. Make me out to be a woman who will lie down and open my legs for any Tom, Dick or Harry who wants it. You couldn't do it, so anyone would do. That's what they'll say, Bill. Poor sod, he couldn't get it up so . . .'

She stood with her back to the closed door, her hand upon the door knob, ready. She watched his eyes suffuse with rage and his face jerked. She saw his hands tense on the arms of his chair, and she was ready.

As he sprang towards her, his roar of outrage echoed off the walls and ceiling, and as she opened the door, stepping lightly into the hospital corridor, figures stopped, heads turned, and two nurses began to run in her direction.

It took them, and a doctor, to hold him from her. She looked at him as he shouted obscenities, and saw in his face the knowledge come to him of what she had done, of what she had goaded him to.

442

Fresh witnesses, with medical expertise, had heard him threaten her life, and he knew she had won. He knew she could call them to court, show him up for what he was. His life, his career, everyone would know what he had done. She would bring it all out in the open, and all the people who had admired him for a fine fellow would know. She didn't care . . . she was strong, invincible. She had won.

His words, disgusting and coarse, followed her down the corridor, and she walked into the cold clean winter day with them ringing in her ears.

She never saw him again.

They were married on 29 July 1943, the day after the decree became absolute.

Mr Carstairs, sympathetic to her condition and the urgency it commanded, and caught in her spell of sweet beauty and wistful charm as were most, had used his influence to put her case to the top of the divorce lists.

Jenny clung to her husband's uniformed arm as they came from the registry office, and Kate edged protectively beside her, for Jenny was huge and awkward in the last days of her pregnancy.

Charlie had to smile as he watched the faces of the people who passed by, imagining the thoughts that went through their minds.

'Only just made it', was the kindest.

They had no photographers. Well they couldn't, could they, Kate said, eyeing her sister's bulk, but later, when the baby came, would they go and get one done? She wanted it for her piano, to put next to her and Charlie. She was made up, was Kate. They went to her place for a bit of tea afterwards and the joyousness strained at the seams of the small house, pouring out into her sunlit backyard, and over the fields to the memory-filled wood.

For a moment the two sisters stood, looking into the setting sun, and they both saw them.

There was Elizabeth, radiant and lovely, a golden-haired baby in her arms. Waggy, grinning, seeming as usual to be about to say something rude. Elly. Was she winking? And Harry, holding her hand. About them stood the others, Pat, his face beaming and Elly's children.

Spellbound, Kate and Jenny watched. The sun was in their eyes and the dazzle outlined the group, and then it disappeared behind the summer trees, and they were gone.

Kate took Jenny's hand, and amidst the happiness of this day and all it contained, a small sadness caught them. A sadness for those who were not there to share it.

'D'yer think they know, chuck?' Kate breathed, her eyes soft and cloudy. 'All the dear faces that are gone?'

Jenny smiled and nodded, and holding Kate's hand drew her back into the kitchen.